LEAP

TAMING DESTINY

BOOK ONE: LEAP

S. L. Winter

Podium

Cover design by Tommypocket Illustrator and Pius Bak

ISBN: 978-1-0394-8237-1

Published in 2025 by Podium Publishing
podiumentertainment.com

Podium

LEAP

CHAPTER ONE

Shadow of the Man I Used to Be

I'm sorry, what?" I can barely believe my ears as I stare at the woman sitting in front of me.

Helen sighs, as if destroying what little is left of my life is simply something she'd dearly like to tick off a list. But then, what else should I expect from a woman who met my request for bereavement leave with the question, "Can't you take it another week?"

How she ever started working in HR, I have no idea.

"I said, we regret to inform you that you are fired, Markus." She says the words with such a lack of emotion that it's not surprising I need to hear it twice. Then again, she's not called the "Ice Queen" for nothing. "You are to remove all personal effects from your desk immediately. Jones will walk with you to ensure that everything is cleared correctly."

More like to ensure that I don't decide to do something stupid for revenge like delete or steal employee details, I say bitterly to myself.

According to them, my conduct over the past three weeks has not been appropriate for my role and is worthy of dismissal. "As a member of human resources, you should be demonstrating the epitome of good conduct," Helen had said.

Apparently, being late three times in that time period along with missing two deadlines by a day is sufficient justification for summarily firing me. Never mind the fact that I'd never been late before. Also completely ignoring my past history of religiously meeting every deadline, even when it meant I had to stay until almost midnight on some evenings. Apparently, the fact that my father was dying meant nothing to them. That, and the fact that the deadlines fell on the day of his funeral, which I had officially been given leave for, albeit grudgingly.

I'm numb as I'm escorted out of my manager's—former manager's—office by Jones, the security guard who I've nodded to on the way in and out of the office every day for the last five years. My pink slip—not actually pink, but white—is clutched in one hand. I barely notice the looks of my colleagues as I am marched through the familiar corridors.

Then I'm at my desk, though I don't really remember getting here. Jones hands me a cardboard box, and I stare at it for a moment unseeingly.

"You need to put all your stuff in there," he says gruffly, but not unkindly. I look up and meet his eyes. There's pity there, and I quickly look away, unable to bear it.

Reaching out, I take my picture of Lucy from the desk. Recently it's been turned to the wall, but I haven't been able to get rid of it completely. Even now I can't leave it, but I don't look at it either. Next is the pen my father gave me when I graduated from uni. Then my penholder—nothing special, just something I bought myself when I got irritated with my pens lying all over the place. Item by item, the remnants of my presence in this shared office are removed. And as each object is taken and packed in that small cardboard box, I find the numbness fading and being replaced by anger. How dare they treat me this way? After everything I've given up for them? Glancing around the half-walls of the cubicle, I see the three colleagues who share—shared—this office watching me. My team. Or they were an hour ago, anyway. I see the same pity in their eyes that I saw in those of Jones. Pity and judgement. They think I've earned this somehow. That I've earned being treated like a criminal.

You'll be next, I think without saying it, scowling at my cubicle walls instead. Now that my brain is working a little better, I know what's happening here. At least, I think I do. Outsourcing has been bandied about a good number of times; more recently, it's been a process of replacing less-key members with AI. Thinking about my recent task list, I can see that it would be ripe to be taken over almost entirely by software.

I don't know when it happened. At some point I got shunted out of a more face-to-face role dealing with people and into more administrative tasks. Was it after Lucy left me? Or when my father first got diagnosed with stage four cancer? I don't know. Either way, I can't remember the last time I conducted the interview of a candidate or did an actual performance review with an employee. I've still been preparing them—finding the data about the employee, writing the job post description and the key requirements. But someone else has actually been doing the meetings. I bet that this dismissal is just so they can buy a much cheaper technological solution.

Actually, when was the last time I was invited to a meeting with more than just my team? Maybe that should have been a red flag. I shake my head. *I've been completely off the ball recently*, I mourn to myself. But facing the loss of my father brought back all the trauma of losing my mother so many years ago. I just . . . couldn't focus on anything. But couldn't they have given me a break? I've given them five years of my life. Five years where I've been a model employee. Haven't I earned three weeks of slight leeway? Especially when I did actually do everything they asked me to.

Apparently not. But then, if my theory is right, it really wouldn't have mattered what I did—they would have found fault and a reason to fire me eventually. It looks like replacing Helen as HR director isn't going to happen now. Perhaps I was a fool to ever believe that it could.

"Done?" Jones's question jolts me out of my thoughts. I realize that I am and have just been standing there, staring into space, for who knows how long. "Yes," I croak through a dry throat. I'm done. Done with this company. Done with this job.

As I am escorted out of the office, more eyes follow my walk of shame, I feel the recent events on my shoulders like a mountain of regret. By the time I'm standing on the pavement outside the office, my cardboard box in my hands, a few meaningless words of sympathy from Jones thrown at me like change at a beggar, I wonder something else.

With everything I've lost, what else do I have left?

Although I uncomfortably dismissed the question when it was first posed by my subconscious outside the office building, it comes back to me later. And then again when I'm halfway through a bottle of whisky. It's not my habit to drink my troubles away. But this afternoon, after getting home at least three hours before I normally would and with nothing else to do, I realize the emptiness of my life. I couldn't resist trying to find solace in the bottle. Honestly, though, all I've found there has been the same question I asked myself earlier: what do I have left? And its natural brother: what do I have to live for?

My mother is dead, and my father has now gone to join her. I have no other family I'm on speaking terms with. Especially not after my father's funeral and the way my aunt behaved at it. I drove my girlfriend away weeks ago with my dedication to the company that has just fired me. I have no friends, my connections with schoolmates disappearing with age and distance, and my busy job didn't offer me much time to socialize. Apart from with work colleagues, of course, but the thought of trying to continue those relationships after what just happened . . . ? No. Just . . . no. And so I drink. At some point I find myself on the edge of my roof, staring down at the street below. Do I dare take another step? End it here and now?

The playful wind pulls and pushes, as fickle as a woman promising to always be there one moment and then disappearing the next. A gust pushes me back hard enough that my drunken limbs fail to keep me balanced, and I fall flat on my ass, barking a humorless laugh. Is that a message from God? Or the Devil? If either exists, which I doubt. Either way, I find that I cannot summon the courage to step up to the edge again. Unsteadily, I make my way back into my apartment, collapse back into my overstuffed armchair, and raise my bottle to my lips once more. Time passes.

Drink by drink, I make my way steadily through my alcohol cabinet starting with wine, then moving onto spirits to keep the buzz going and keep the impact of my memories at bay.

It's a catch-22. Being drunk adds a layer of fuzziness between me and the memories, covering the glass shards with a soft blanket. But at the same time it stops me being able to think about anything else.

I wallow in thoughts of the past, of happier times. And of not-so-happy times, which at the very least were better than the present if only because of the people sharing them with me. My mother—dead. My father—dead. My girlfriend—gone. My friends—vanished like the morning dew. For a moment I almost stand outside my own body, looking at this hopeless loser sprawled on the sofa. And then I'm back in my body, alcohol sloshing over my face as I tip it too far backwards. *I'm a dead man walking; Hell's at my door; I'm a shadow of the man I was before.* I find the song running through my mind and smile bitterly. If Lucy had still been here, she'd have been ragging me to pull myself together, telling me that losing my job isn't the end of the world. And it's not. I know that. In my head. But everything together . . . It's too much. I pulled myself together after my mother died. Then again after Lucy left me. Then after my father died. How many times do I have to get up and try again? How many more times do I *want* to?

I'm tempted to take myself up to the roof once more, but when I finally push myself to my feet, I'm distracted.

Something's happening just next to my overstuffed bookshelf. It takes my sozzled brain a good few seconds to register what I'm looking at. Then, in the very eloquent way all drunks have, I question reality.

"Whas'a?" Stumbling forwards, I wave my hand vaguely in the air underneath the apparition, then through it.

"Stop that," the ghost says, a mite crossly. "This is difficult enough without you interrupting the projection."

"Wha? It speaksh?" I murmur, my words slurring together as I stare at the approximately thirty-centimeter-tall pearly-white figure floating a few centimeters off my table.

It looks like a man, neatly dressed in what I muzzily recognize as a vaguely medieval doublet and hose. A bit like what my male coworkers and I wore at an Elizabethan-inspired Christmas party, though with less-poofy trousers and a more normal-height collar—we'd almost poked our own eyes out with the cardboard points of our costumes.

As for the face of the ghost, it looks rather like a stereotypical villain with a pointy beard, moustache, and a dark look that grows even darker as I prod it again.

"Stop that, I said!" the figure barks at me. "Are you . . . drunk?" it— he—then asks. I shrug languidly.

"Maaaybe," I drawl. Looking around, I can't see the whiskey. If I can question whether I'm drunk or not, I clearly haven't had enough. "Where's z'whiksy?"

"From the looks of it, you've had more than enough," the ghost tells me disapprovingly. "This is the only hope for my legacy?" he mutters under his breath. "Gods help me." Sighing, he speaks louder. "I don't have much time. Drunk or not, listen to me now." I hold up one finger that turns into two as my eyes lose focus.

"Whiksy firsht," I tell him as firmly as I can make it. The man sighs again, clear annoyance in the sound.

"Next to you, on the floor." I lean over the arm of the chair quickly, almost tipping over it as my center of gravity shifts a bit too far. I see the bottle on the floor and grab it, sloshing its contents as I lean back. Already down by more than half, the liquid doesn't actually spill out of the bottle despite the abrupt movements.

I tip it back, almost missing my mouth again. Taking gulps of the liquid, I barely feel the burn, but the alcohol content soon gets to me as the world starts spinning even more. I tip my head back to stare at the ceiling, marveling at the way the cracks are moving round and round and round . . .

"Now will you listen?" the apparition asks with frustration in his voice. I wave one hand vaguely in the air, almost hitting myself in the face. "I hope you remember at least some of this when you sober up," he mutters to himself before once more speaking loudly and clearly.

"I come with an offer. I need to bestow a powerful inheritance on a successor, and the Oracle has indicated that you are my only option if I do not wish my legacy to be destroyed within the next generation." He continues speaking, but I have lost the ability to focus, staring at the ceiling vacantly as his voice becomes background sound, the odd word filtering in but not making much sense. It's almost soothing—too much so for my drunken state to endure, and my eyes slip closed without me even noticing.

My hands shaking a little, my head and throat still killing me even after the paracetamol I took, I once more smooth out the piece of parchment. I've already read it at least three times since finding it, but I read it once more now, still disbelieving it could be real.

Greetings,

I will briefly reintroduce myself, as due to your . . . inebriated state during my visit, and the fact that you seemed to fall asleep halfway through, I doubt you took in much of what I had to say. I must be brief. To send the transportation emblem is effort enough; a message is a further expenditure and is greater the longer the message. It is also an expenditure that I had not anticipated needing after already having paid the cost to project a semblance of myself to explain in person and to answer all the questions of the candidate. Nevertheless, I shall present myself again: I am Lord Nicholas of Azaarde. I offer you a new life and the potential of power and influence beyond what you ever thought you could achieve, beyond what you ever thought possible: the inheritance that I and my family have built over the last few centuries. A powerful Class, Skill set, wealth, and further benefits I will inform you of in person await you. I have no heirs of my own and so I must choose one suitable. I have been informed that you are the only hope of my family's legacy surviving to the next generation, but you will have to prove yourself worthy of it. I would rather it dies with me than that it is destroyed by a drunkard. I say this so you know I do not make this offer lightly. You have the opportunity now of deciding the rest of your life. You can walk away and forget this ever happened. Imagine it was a dream. Or you can take your destiny in your hands and decide who you will be now and in the future. Should you decide to gamble everything on the chance that you show yourself deserving of what I can bestow on you, hold the transportation emblem accompanying this letter and acknowledge aloud your acceptance. I will warn you: the magic of the emblem will draw you across worlds and universes and there is NO way to return. Any unfinished business will, therefore, remain unfinished. You have twenty-four of your hours to decide; after this, the emblem will return to me, and I will know I must attempt to look elsewhere for a worthy heir. I am aware that it would take an unusual type of person to accept such an uncertain offer of potential power in exchange for everything you currently possess. For the sake of my legacy, I can only hope that you might be such an unusual character and, moreover, that you might overcome the trials ahead and prove yourself more than unusual—that you may prove yourself worthy.

My sincerest and most cordial sentiments,
Lord Nicholas Titanbend of Azaarde

My fingers are numb, my heavily hungover brain still unable to fully understand what I'm looking at here. After waking up and worshipping the porcelain god a few times, I'd found this missive folded below an odd-looking emblem. It's thick and heavy, about three times the size of a coaster, and has an intricate golden design inlaid in a black background. It's a coat of arms with three sections: a fox in a side profile; a hammer crossed with a sword; and, filling the lower section, a fine spiderweb.

The object isn't anything I've seen before and definitely not something I put there. The parchment is odd too, much heavier and thicker than normal paper, the words written in fountain pen or something. What the hell is the letter talking about, anyway? An inheritance? And why are Class and Skills capitalized? I have a feeling he's not talking about going back to school. But there's one line my eyes are drawn back to again and again. "You can take your destiny in your hands and decide who you will be now and in the future." If it's somehow real . . .

Cutting through the depression that I have been mired in for far too long is confusion, incredulity, and one more emotion. Like the light at the end of a long, dark tunnel, I feel the faintest glimmering of hope.

Take my destiny into my own hands . . . ? It's a siren call, but my doubting mind quickly pulls me back down to earth. Magic doesn't exist. Does it? Though there have always been peddlers of miracles, I've never truly believed that any of them were genuinely capable. But then, what created that spirit-like apparition last night? I remember it, recall waving my hand around and through it. I recall it speaking to me, and the letter here proves that it wasn't just a figment of my imagination. Unless

I'm being set up, of course—technology nowadays is probably able to produce that effect. But who would bother trying to trick a loser like me? I'm already weighing whether stepping off my apartment roof would be the best option. Trying anything on me now would be kicking a man already prone on the ground.

So, really, what do I have to lose? If it works, great—with magic in the picture, maybe I might even be able to turn my life around for good. And if it doesn't? If it turns out that this is just one of those reality TV shows where they're going to leap out from behind the curtain to film my reaction? At least I might be able to offer someone a good laugh. I'm tempted just to accept right away, my hand moving towards the emblem to say the activation phrase and get it over with . . . but then I hesitate. I'm filthy, covered in alcohol that I sloshed over myself and still in my work clothes from yesterday. Is this really the self I want to take to my new life?

Do I have time, though? Twenty-four hours, he said . . . It was dark when the apparition came; I remember that much. And the letter must have come after he appeared because he's referenced my . . . drunkenness. I eye the window in my bedroom. The light is already falling—between my tiredness from alcohol and my genuine exhaustion, I've slept almost the whole day away. I should have time to have a shower, though.

My eyes fall on a picture on my night table, the last taken before she was killed. Maybe I even have enough time to pack a few important keepsakes. If I'm leaving this world for good, I don't want to leave anything behind that I'll sorely miss.

Decided, I pull a suitcase from under my bed and start moving around my bedroom and kitchen like a whirlwind.

Wait. I hesitate, pausing in the middle of the room. Can I even take anything with me? It's a good point. I rush back to the letter and read it again. There's no indication either way, but surely I wouldn't just be teleported in the nude? So, I should at least be able to bring whatever I'm wearing. Surely it's not too far-fetched to imagine I might also be able to bring anything I'm holding? Though, I should probably be able to lift whatever it is off the ground, just to increase the odds.

But, again, what do I have to lose? If I don't pack the things, they're lost anyway. If I do pack them, I have a chance at taking them with me. *Though, I'd better not take too long about it—I don't want to accidentally miss my window of time.*

It turns out that fitting a life into a few bags is actually pretty difficult. It's like packing for a holiday in a country I've never been to, where I have no idea what awaits me.

In the end, I've filled most of the two bags with half my wardrobe and a few pairs of shoes. I've got my Kindle and phone and their chargers, but I'll probably have to rewire the plugs since I don't know if my universal adaptor is *actually* universal. Or trans-universal. I've taken a cross-head screwdriver anyway. I've got my favorite books alongside my Kindle, so at least I should have something to read even if the plugs don't work.

My bathroom still looks a bit like a bomb hit it. When the alcohol turned my stomach earlier, I wasn't always quick enough to get to the toilet. Or well-coordinated enough. I've settled for just grabbing the items on the basin—my toothbrush and shaving kit. I should be able to buy shampoo and that sort of thing later, I guess. Either way, I'm not walking through vomit and broken shower glass to get them.

Otherwise, I've made sure I have my wallet and a few family pictures. I hesitated over including the couple with Lucy I had turned towards the wall after she left, but in the end, I decided to take them. It's a one-way trip, after all. I even remembered to grab my swimsuit and a pack of condoms, just in case. I pick up a few little nick-nacks that I figure might not be in Nicholas's world and with that, I'm ready. About to grab the emblem, I pause, a final thought occurring.

Nipping into the kitchen, I wrinkle my nose at the smell and carefully avoid the puddle of broken glass and alcohol lying on the floor to access my pots. Maybe it seems a bit weird, but it took me *years* to find a wok that cooked food to my satisfaction; I'm not going to leave it behind now.

After finding a spot in my bag to stuff the wok into, I finally grab the round disk of the emblem, hoping that it won't suddenly disappear out of my fingers, a minute too late to accept the offer. It's heavy in my hands, both with its physical weight and the weight of this decision. I hesitate, even though it feels like precious seconds are trickling out of my fingers. Do I really want to do this? Go into something completely unknown? Even assuming that the presence of "magic"—or technology sufficiently advanced to be called such—is real and I'm about to be teleported somewhere else, there's still a lot that could go wrong. What if this is actually some sort of scam for human traffickers or something? What if by "accepting the offer," I end up becoming some sort of alien slave? I have no guarantee that this Nicholas guy is telling the truth about his motivations. And is my life really that bad? Maybe this dark emptiness won't always be all I have to look forward to; maybe one day I could pull myself up, maybe make something big of myself . . .

I bite my lip and then my grip tightens on the emblem. No, I've made my decision. *Here's* my big chance to make something of myself, to turn my desire to end my life into a desire to transform it. If I don't at least try this, I might as well just throw myself out of my window and hope I don't hurt anyone by landing on them. This is my decision, for better or for worse. "Hold the transportation emblem accompanying this letter and acknowledge aloud your acceptance," said the letter. I'm about to do so when it occurs to me again that I might be better off lifting my suitcases off the ground rather than just holding their handles. It takes a bit of juggling to succeed in holding both suitcases as well as the emblem; the effort it takes to lift what has to be forty-plus kilos reminds me that, as well as everything else, I've been neglecting the gym. Still, I succeed eventually and even as my fingers strain and my face reddens from the effort, I gasp out the activation phrase.

"I accept."

CHAPTER TWO

Proof of Worthiness

For several long moments, nothing happens. I open my eyes, realizing I've screwed them shut, only to see my familiar apartment. Did I do something wrong? Or is it a prank after all? No one's jumped out from behind the door to laugh in my face and film my reaction, but maybe it hasn't been long enough yet.

Then, as if it just needed a bit of time to get going, I feel the emblem heat up, almost burning my palm. The world lurches sickeningly around me, and I feel my stomach crawl into my mouth as I hear the rushing of a great wind. I close my eyes again in a desperate attempt to quell my motion sickness and only open them again when the rushing wind calms down. What meets my gaze is completely different from anything I was expecting. My mouth hangs open, and I lose the battle with my stomach and, unimpressively, empty it all over the surface on which I stand.

When my stomach is finally empty and beginning to feel settled again, I look around, hoping that my initial impressions were wrong. Unfortunately, it doesn't appear to be that way; if anything, it's worse. I don't know why, but when I imagined where I would be taken, I'd always envisioned a city, or a manor house, or even a palace. The "lord" in the letter must have been what gave me that idea, I realize. This . . . It's not a city. It's not even a village, let alone anything more palatial. Instead, it looks like there are no signs of civilization in sight.

I'm standing on the upper slopes of a mountain, a rocky area covered only in a thin layer of hardy grass. Above me on one side towers a great snow-covered peak; on the other side lies a vast valley full of trees. It's cradled between mountain peaks and disappears into the distance; my eyes are unable to even make out the mountains at its end. The humid mistiness to the air above the trees doesn't help in that respect. Otherwise, as far as my eye can see, there is a sea of other mountain peaks stretching out from the mountain on which I stand. They, too, are obscured by mist when my gaze travels too far. I've never been anywhere with such untouched nature; there's not a human construction in sight. It's intimidating and yet, at the same time, almost exhilarating. To think that I might be the first person to see this view . . .

The temperature itself is actually rather pleasant, perhaps on the slightly chilly side when the wind blows. The air is crisp and fresh. Too fresh. There's not a hint of the polluting smells of human presence—not fire, nor petrol. It truly appears to be a paradise for the intrepid backpacker.

Unfortunately, I've never been into the whole backpacking thing, and I don't think anyone would label me as "intrepid." Heck, I don't even go on camping trips! I hated them as a child, and then there were no more childhood holidays after . . . the incident. As an adult, holidays to me meant relaxing in whatever luxury I could afford. I always chose to stay at a hotel, either picking a warm place for a sojourn to the beach or a cold place for skiing. A nice convenient location, some fun or relaxing activities during the day, good food cooked by someone else in the evening . . . That's what I call enjoyable.

The only reason I own the massive backpack I'm currently wearing is that I was convinced to take part in a "team building" exercise soon after being hired by a previous employer. Instead of being some fun, well-organized time for us to get to know each other and improve our working relationships, it was a week's camping trip in the wilds of the Brecon Beacons. Apparently, going hungry, cold, wet, and miserable for a week with a whole load of co-workers who barely knew each other was supposed to help team spirit. And the reason I'd bought a whole new fancy backpack was because I was trying to impress my new colleagues.

Spoiler alert: it didn't work. Perhaps it would have if my sturdy, practical backpack had been accompanied by a sturdy, practical man, but, as I've already established, camping isn't *my thing*. Which is why I'm currently desperately hoping that this is some sort of a joke and Lord Nicholas is about to jump out from behind a rock or something. Or that there might be some well-hidden palace just around the corner.

As I think that, the emblem in my hand warms up again. Hope and nerves both rise inside of me again. What if, despite what the letter said, I'm actually about to be transported back? Honestly, I don't really know how to feel about that. As it happens, I don't have the time to do any deep soul-searching, as that apparently isn't the reason for the emblem's reaction. Instead, it crumbles into glowing motes of dust, which easily fall out of my hand.

The motes drift down, but instead of coating the ground as normal, they take shape in the air. Under my disbelieving gaze, a wooden table comes into existence, rather incongruously placed in this completely natural landscape. It's a good solid-looking piece of furniture, though the slightly rough ground means that it doesn't look completely stable.

I rub my eyes, I'll admit it. My mouth might also be hanging open. I touch the table tentatively, wondering if it will just shatter into dust again before my fingertips can come into contact. It doesn't, of course, and I just spend a few moments marveling at my first experience with *magic*. To create something solid from nothing? Amazing!

Once I manage to get past my amazement at *how* the table appeared, I start to explore what is actually *on* it. At least, I try to, but the gloves I'm wearing rather impede my ability to pick things up. Cursing softly, I strip them off and shrug off about three extra layers of clothes while I'm at it—I'm hot!

Now more comfortable, I turn back to the table. There are a number of items.

Some of them are recognizable, if a little alarming in what they imply; others just look like strangely glowing stones of different shades and sizes. Right in the center is another piece of paper; however, it's a scroll rather than a folded piece of parchment. It's rolled up with a blue ribbon and sealed with black wax, indented with the same heraldry that had been on the emblem. Picking up the scroll, I crack the wax reluctantly, briefly admiring the way it looks like something out of the medieval era.

Greetings,

You have taken the first step. You are an unusual person indeed to have dared the unknown in search of a fleeting greatness. However, greatness requires a proof of worthiness, and the price for transporting you from your world to mine is not small. Thus, for the purpose of efficiency, the task for the two aims shall be one and the same. Your objectives in this task are twofold. First, survival: you must survive in your current world for a year. However, you must do more than just survive to achieve your second objective: collecting enough Energy to pay for your passage to my world. I am sure that you will be confused about this last point, so let me explain.

I stop reading at that, taking a deep breath and then starting at the top again. No, I *had* understood what it was saying. I have to survive here. For a *year*. Anger rises within me, but I'm self-aware enough to recognize the fear that curdles my stomach underneath it. All my self-awareness doesn't stop me from feeling this, though, and my thoughts are quickly overtaken by emotion.

As the wave of heat rises within me, my hand clenches and the rustle of paper crunching sounds loudly in the still air. A small part of my mind notes how much more effort I have to use to crush the paper than I would expect, but most of my awareness is concentrating on my thoughts about what I've just read.

This is completely ridiculous! What kind of "opportunity" or "new life" is this? Setting aside my worst-case scenarios of some alien version of human trafficking, if this guy Nicholas was on the level, I would expect him to at least welcome me in person! Not dump me in some deserted area and tell me to "survive"—for a *year*. The fear curdling in my stomach quickly turns into panic. What do I know about survival? A week in the Brecon Beacons hardly counts! I've never even watched those reality TV survival shows!

I curse and kick the leg of the table making the items on it wobble alarmingly, one of the colorful stones almost rolling off completely. How the hell is this supposed to show my worthiness? By failing miserably to even set up a tent? No, that's *not* referring back to an incident during my previous ill-fated expedition in the "wilds." Really!

I swear again and storm away from the table. My behavior can be best described as a tantrum as I shout, stamp, wave my arms in anger, and kick the ground. In reality, it's about more than just this particular problem; I realize after a while that I'm venting all the pent-up anger and frustration and, yes, grief that has been brewing in me over the last few days. Hell, *weeks*. I'm crying and I don't even realize it until my eyes blur enough that I can't see clearly.

This ends my tirade as I kick a hidden rock in a tussock of grass. Sharp pain shoots up my foot. Of course, when I say my tirade comes to an end, that's only once I've turned the air blue while hopping on one leg. I decide to pretend that the tears are from the pain and let myself go a bit. It's not like anyone is here to see me, after all. Slowly the pain ebbs and with it goes all the intensity of emotion that had been moving me. In its place

I feel calmer, emptier, and ever-so-slightly more settled, like perhaps not now, and not anytime soon, but one day I might feel better. About myself. About my life. Of course, if I really have to survive in an untouched jungle by myself for a year, my life isn't likely to last very long, but then, I'm the stupid one who decided to accept magical transportation without reading the small print. Or even having the small print *to* read, as a matter of fact. Maybe that should have been my first warning. Honestly, when I think about it, I'm not angry at Nicholas. Not really. I'm angry at myself. Of course it was going to turn out to be too good to be true; it always is. Anytime I've let myself get sucked into something that seems fantastic on the surface, it's always turned out to be a smelly, putrid bog underneath. This is no different. And although I know I didn't actually expect magic—or highly advanced technology capable of teleportation and materializing objects out of nothing—to be real, that's not really an excuse. Nor is the fact that I made the decision under a sense of time pressure and while hungover. I'm better than that. Or I should be, at least.

Contracts are kind of my day job, after all. Were. I sigh, my shoulders slumping, feeling exhausted all of a sudden. Well, I made the decision, and now I'm trapped somewhere with no way to go home, completely at the mercy of nature and whatever these items are. I suppose I'd better make sure I know everything I can about the situation in which I find myself, even if it feels a bit like locking the door after the horse has bolted. Still, I might find out that it's not quite as bad as I think—maybe the letter will say that there's a city beyond this valley that I need to get to or something.

After picking up the crumpled piece of paper from where I had thrown it in my tantrum, I smooth it out once more and continue to read.

> *Energy is found in all things, even on your original world. On your world, however, there was such a minimal density of it that you could not even detect its presence. On my world, Energy is an essential part of life. Relevant to you at this moment are Classes and magic. It is why the stones I have sent you are so useful: the Class stone gives you the Tamer Class and all the advantages that come with this;*

the knowledge stones allow you to instantly absorb knowledge of a subject, up to a certain limit; the Skill stone instantly gives you access to a Skill outside your Class set, which you can then use immediately. All of this is only possible because of our ability to use Energy. As, of course, is my ability to contact you and pull you part of the way towards my world.

Why only part of the way?

For one simple reason: the amount of Energy to pull you all the way is significant. Frankly, I would need to know that you were worth neglecting all my other responsibilities for the task. As I said at the beginning, it is far more efficient to combine a test of your worthiness with the practicality of paying for your journey.

To be completely blunt, you need to collect sufficient Energy before the year is up. If you do not, the spell will take its due regardless. Given the distances involved, this would most likely cost you your life. As the anchor and initiator of the spell, I would be held partially accountable for your debt should you arrive in my world without having fully paid it, so you can see that it is also in my interest that you gain in strength.

I stop reading for a moment, staring sightlessly over the top of the letter. *Great. From bad to worse,* I say to myself bitterly. Not only do I need to survive here for a year, but I can't even plan on just finding a hiding spot and becoming a hermit. No, I actually have to *do* something to gather "Energy" or I'll be signing my death warrant anyway. Feeling sick again, I look back at the letter. Better get it over and done with so at least I know what I'm dealing with.

CHAPTER THREE

A Treasure Trove

Scanning the letter to find the point where I'd left off before, I feel my anger rekindle at the cavalier approach Nicholas seems to be taking to my life. Sure, maybe *he* might have some consequences too if I fail, but it seems very much that the risk is all on my side of things. I continue reading.

> *At this point, I imagine you are wondering how to collect Energy to pay the debt of your passage. In short, by killing beasts. When a creature is killed, part of its Energy goes to the one who kills it. Believe it or not, the same was true on your previous world; it was just such an Energy-starved place that it would take longer than you have to live currently for you to even start making noticeable progress to pay for your passage. Indeed, that is why I made the choice to pull you to your current world: it may not be populated by civilized beings, but it is well suffused with Energy. A treasure trove, of sorts, if you would only reach out to harvest it.*

I feel my heart sink. "Not populated by civilized beings" is the fatal blow to my last, clearly futile, hopes of there being a city beyond the valley that I could travel to. Apparently, I'm being abandoned to the wilderness. What was that term Nicholas used? I check the letter again. A "treasure trove," he considers it. Somehow, I doubt there are chests full of goodies anywhere near me . . . And even if there were, where would I spend gold or jewels without any cities? I read on to find out what exactly has been given to me in order to even hope to survive in this unpopulated "treasure trove" of a world.

> *I have provided the following resources for you:*
>
> - *A Tamer Class stone (Epic—orange)*
> - *A System lore stone (Novice—light blue)*
> - *A woodcraft knowledge stone (Novice—light green)*
> - *A hunting knowledge stone (Novice—light brown)*
> - *A tracking skill stone (Initiate—brown)*
> - *A Lay-on-Hands Skill stone (Beginner—aquamarine)*

*- A survival pack including a knife, a water flask, 2 days'
  rations, and some other essential items*
- 2 minor health potions

*These resources should be sufficient to allow you to start the
path to power. Because your world seems to be one of technological
advancements rather than individual survival, I have included several knowledge stones on this topic.*

*It is kill or be killed, traveler. Harvest the Energy of others or be
yourself harvested. I hope to see you on the other side.*

My most cordial and hopeful sentiments,
Lord Nicholas Titanbend of Azaarde

*P.S. I suggest that you use the Class stone first and then the Skill
stone. Once you have received your Class, you will gain access to
your status screen. Check your Intelligence stat before deciding
how to use the knowledge and Skill stones; unless you have an
Intelligence stat of ten or more, I would suggest not using more
than one knowledge stone per day, as you will be unable to absorb
the majority of the second. You would need an Intelligence stat of
more than twenty to absorb more than two stones in one day with
reasonable efficacy.*

I stare at the letter, feeling numb. Then I snort; I suppose I *have* been given
what I asked for. If my guess is correct, the things this Nicholas guy has given
me *are* awesome. I just wish I didn't have to be in the wilderness for a year to get
them. Sighing, I lower the piece of paper down and regard the items on the desk
thoughtfully. Nicholas suggested using the Class stone first—that's apparently the
orange one. Easily spotting it among the other colors, I pick it up and turn it over
in my hand.

The stone is warmer than I would have imagined, almost like someone else has
just been holding it. There's also some slight . . . buzz or static electricity—the way
a rubbed balloon attracts hair except the other way around? Something like that.
Either way, I don't think it's my imagination to say that I feel something I shouldn't
from a simple stone, never mind the fact that it's *glowing*. I figure that I should
probably follow Nicholas's advice; he's the one who sent me these items, after all.
Sure, since arriving in this uninhabited place—instead of wherever he is, to receive
the inheritance promised—I'm taking his words with a bit more salt. Even so, I can't
really see why he would give me *bad* advice—thinking otherwise is just letting my
paranoia take over. If he'd wanted me to die immediately, he could have just not
sent me anything.

Taking a deep breath, I activate the stone. Well, that's what I try to do. Turns out, staring intently at the stone is *not* how to activate it. "Activate?" I say hesitantly. Nothing happens. "Gain Class?" Still nada. "Start? Infuse? Osmosis? Damn you, do *something!*" I shout at it, squeezing and glaring.

My eyes go wide as a crunching sounds and a crack appears on its surface. My stomach drops as the crack spreads and fractures further until the whole stone falls into a million pieces no bigger than finely grained sand. Fear claws at my belly— have I just broken my only chance to survive the next year?

The dust glows and suddenly starts melting into my skin. For a moment, it's like the world has paused, and then the next thing I know, pain is shooting through every atom of my body. It isn't excruciating, but it's *everywhere*. Like pins and needles but not just in one limb. Plus, after a breath, it's not just at the surface but under as well.

I'm struck with the thought that I could almost map my entire body out, organs included, if I could build a picture based on the prickling sensation. While not terribly painful, it's enough to make me want to tear my skin off as my mind interprets the prickling as insanely itchy. Then, a few moments later, the pain vanishes as if it was never there. Everything feels . . . off. Just . . . wrong, somehow. Like the feeling when you walk into a familiar place where something has changed, but you can't immediately spot whether it's the furniture that's moved or the wall that's been painted a slightly different shade.

The feeling of wrongness intensifies as a screen suddenly appears in front of me. The screen is made of whitish mist formed in a boxlike shape. The main part of the box is almost opaque, but it fades abruptly around the edges until I can see normally with my peripheral vision. I can just about see through the box enough to tell if I'm about to walk into something, but it would definitely be a better idea to stay still while using it, I think.

Black words in a clear font style are printed on the densest section of the misty space. At the top are two separate words; they look almost like tabs. One says "Status" and the other says "Messages." From the looks of it, I'm in the "Messages" section.

Congratulations! You have absorbed a Class: Tamer.
You consequently have access to your status. To see this, think or say "status."
You have 0 status points to assign.
You have 3 new messages.

Next message? Y / N

I think "yes" and the words dissolve away and are replaced swiftly with another message.

Congratulations! You have new Class Skills (2).

Tame: activate this Skill on a being and it will offer the being the option of becoming bound to you. Warning: beings may choose to reject the Bond or require actions from you in exchange for accepting the Bond.

Dominate: activate this Skill on a being to enter into a Battle of Wills, success in which binds the being to you as a Bound. Certain previous actions may increase your likelihood of winning the battle, even with a lower Willpower than your opponent. This includes, but is not limited to, having already defeated the being physically, having trapped the being so that they are unable to move, and having terrified the being. Warning: if you lose the Battle of Wills, you will be rendered vulnerable for ten seconds as you recover. Recommended Willpower before attempting a Battle of Wills: 10–30 for a Stage 1 beast.

Next message? Y / N

Once more, I think "yes" even while my thoughts whirl.

Congratulations on achieving a Class.
You have gained access to an Inventory and a Map.

Your Inventory can hold up to 10 item slots per Class level, starting with five additional spaces per Class-rarity rank above Uncommon. Identical items can stack; the number of items per stack is determined according to the item. Live items cannot be stored. Please note that the storage and withdrawal of items consumes Energy and will not function until you have gained some. You can access your Inventory by thinking or saying "Inventory."

Your Map keeps track of your environment. This is a passive ability, which you can toggle on or off. This ability consumes a small amount of Energy and will not function until you have gained some. You can access your Map by thinking or saying "Map."

Next message? Y / N

Congratulations! You are now able to absorb Skill stones. 1 Skill stone detected in range. Do you wish to absorb this Skill stone now? Please note: you can choose to absorb this Skill stone later by holding it and thinking or saying "absorb Skill stone."

Y / N

I hesitate but think "no" for now. I have enough to consider right now without adding an extra dimension to it. A new message forms in front of me.

> Close interface / Return to message panel / View status summary

Nicholas said something about looking at my status screen or something, didn't he? I think to myself.

"View status summary," I say. The screen dissolves and reforms, but I don't have time to register anything it's showing me. A flash of light scrambles my view and pain explodes in my head.

CHAPTER FOUR

Zest for Life

Wha—?" I mumble blearily, my eyes crossing. I can see white and black in front of me, but the shapes aren't resolving themselves into anything recognizable. *What happened?* Light, pain . . .

A screen. A status screen. That's right. There's the sound of something thudding next to me, and a strong musky smell meets my nose, which wrinkles in response.

I can't see. I *need* to see. What was the thing I needed to say again? Oh yes. "Close screen." The blurry figures disappear, and I find myself staring at a rock. A rock that is covered in blood. My blood. *I got hit by a rock? Is it raining rocks now?*

I can only blame the almost certain concussion for the glacial progress of my thoughts. Honestly, I'm surprised my skull didn't explode like a watermelon—it must have only been a glancing blow. If it's raining rocks, I need to get to shelter *yesterday.*

Abruptly, I hear a rustle of feathers. Turning towards it, I'm just in time to see a sharp beak coming at my face. I flinch back, my head protesting fervently at the movement. It's enough to avoid getting my eyes pecked out. Instead, the sharp beak latches onto my nose.

"Gerrof!" I shout, squinting through tears of pain. I flail my arms in front of me and, more by luck than design, manage to hit it in the neck.

"*Wark!*" I hear, and the bird lets go. The relief is temporary—now it's released my nose, it has full access to the rest of my body.

I curl up, trying to avoid the painful bites as much as possible. Meanwhile, my stomach is trying to exit my body and my head is aching fit to burst. My nose would also like to register its discontent, but I have no time for that. This is not working. The bloody bird is going to win at this rate. The rock it must have dropped on my head has done half of the job for it already. *The rock!*

Bit by bit, I shift back towards the rock and cover it with my body. I grip it with my hand, preparing even as the bird starts drawing blood through my clothes. Summoning up all my strength, I explode into movement.

Well, I stagger to a half-kneeling position, at least, and scrabble with one hand to grab the bird anywhere I can—its neck, it turns out—and flail with the rock. Once more, luck seems to be with me. I've actually grabbed it at a good point to drag its head down to the ground, where I can start beating at it with the rock.

I start swearing with each blow, taking out all my anger and fear at the situation

I've found myself in on the now-helpless bird. Eventually, it stills and its body collapses. Its wings go limp from where they had been battering at my body, and it becomes a dead weight against me. I stop myself when the head is just bloody mush and lean back to sit on my heels, staring blankly ahead of me.

Emotions course through me, unfamiliar both in their type and intensity. Recently, all I've experienced this strongly are fear and grief. And, of course, the leaden dragging of hopelessness and depression that has almost consumed me more than once in the last week. This . . . There's fear, to be sure: the lingering twisting, curdling sense of terror. But how ironic for someone who stood on the edge of a building so recently, only a bare few centimeters away from tumbling to my death, that the fear is of dying.

The perfect opportunity to solve all my problems by just letting the bird do its thing appears and I suddenly discover that I *don't want to die.*

I laugh suddenly, feeling like a weight has been lifted from my chest. It's illogical, and ridiculous, but so many of my thoughts over the past while have been consumed with questioning whether I even wanted to continue living. To suddenly be confronted with an unmistakable desire for survival is . . . a relief. A decision, finally.

Having acknowledged that, I now realize what the other emotion running riot through me is. Triumph. This bird attacked me, tried to kill me, and it failed because I succeeded in killing it first. It's been so long since I have felt the triumph of *winning* that I almost don't recognize the sensation. Of course, then I realize I've "won" by killing another living creature, and I feel a moment of guilt and not a little nervousness at this new side of myself. I'll admit it—I'm a soft office worker. I don't even kill spiders I find in my bathtub! Never in a million years would I have imagined I would brutally beat in the head of some bird.

I console myself that I didn't go seeking this fight; the bird is the one who dropped a rock on my head. That, of course, reminds me of the pain in my head, my nose, and innumerable other places in my body, which are no doubt becoming dark bruises as I sit here and think. Plus, if another of those creatures attacks me with my head the way it is—both my state of mind and my actual physical state—I'll be done for. Actually . . . wasn't there something about healing in the list Nicholas wrote?

I check the table and see that either the bird's flailing around or mine has knocked everything off its surface. I curse and my stomach drops. Now that I've rediscovered a zest for life, I feel like I'm scrabbling for every possible advantage I can get. I need to find those stones!

Setting the table back on its legs from where it had been knocked onto its side, I search around the area for Nicholas's gifts. The letter is an obvious pale spot, and I grab it. It's slightly smudged by blood but still legible, thankfully. I use the list of items to find everything and put them back on the table. Then, with a wary glance up at the sky, I grab the items instead and tuck myself under the table—just in case another avian decides to try to drop a stone on my head.

Feeling a little bit more secure under cover, my stomach only settles once I'm sure I haven't lost anything. With how disadvantaged I am already, I really can't afford to lose even one of these lifelines.

The last few minutes have proven just how quickly things can turn into a fight for life or death. I take in a deep breath and try to pull myself together a bit. I may still have a stomach that feels like a pile of quivering jelly and probably a concussed head, but that doesn't mean I can't think. Still, sorting out my physical discomfort would probably help.

I knock back one of the health potions. In just a few seconds, my head is significantly clearer—and painless. My eyes widen as the implications sink in, then my stomach sinks again as I realize that I might have made a mistake. If it cleared my cracked skull and other bumps and bruises so easily, how would it do with more significant life-threatening problems? I have no idea what is facing me; what if tomorrow I end up with a broken bone or something, and no potion?

Come on, Markus, I tell myself sternly. *Pull yourself together. Think logically. You can't change the past, but you* can *change the future. All right, try to think through this logically, like it's just another problem at the office.* Though, maybe that's a bad idea as I *was* recently fired, probably to be replaced by some ticketing system based in India . . . *No, don't think about that*, I reprimand myself. I have no desire to once more sink into dark depression. I'm stuck far from home in a completely unfamiliar environment. That's the problem.

However, I do have resources available to me. I have a lot of things in my bags—though, whether they'll prove useful for survival in the wilderness remains to be seen—and I have the items Nicholas gave me. Surely I can find a solution to my issue about survival among all of those? I review the item list in the letter again. Which items are essential for my survival now and which will be more important later? I've already absorbed the Class stone, and Nicholas suggested absorbing the Lay-on-Hands Skill stone after the Class stone. I don't know what it's supposed to be for, but I've already decided that I need to trust his advice. Maybe it's some sort of crafting Skill, enabling me to magically make the things I need for survival by touching the right materials? That would be pretty useful. Absorbing the stone seems like the natural next step.

After that, there are four more stones: two knowledge stones, a lore stone, and a skill stone. I don't know if there's any difference between the capital *S* for the Lay-on-Hands Skill stone and the small *s* for the tracking skill stone, or if that's just a writing error. From what I understand of the implications in Nicholas's letter, I can absorb a "Skill" stone and knowledge stone without a problem, but can I do the same with a "skill" stone and knowledge stone? Do I want to take the risk? Probably not, as the consequences would be that I lose a large part of the information from the stone, making it worthless. All of these seem far too important to my survival to do that. In fact, that's the problem: I can't really decide which one stone is the most important now. They're *all* important!

Though Nicholas didn't put a description of the stones into the letter, I have to guess that the tracking skill stone and hunting knowledge stone are what they say on the tin. The problem is that both of those are going to be absolutely essential for me once the rations Nicholas has given me run out—hunting to provide the meat and tracking to find the animals in the first place. As for the other two, the System lore stone will probably tell me more about the Class system, which will be important as I progress.

Of all of them, this is the only one I can put in the "important later" category, as it doesn't seem quite so essential to my immediate survival. The final one, on the other hand, is a good candidate for the first stone I use after the Skill stone, if it does what I think it might. Woodcraft *could* mean carpentry—literally crafting with wood—but I have to guess from what Nicholas said that it's more likely to mean the other sense of the word: being able to survive in the wood. While that might not help me much with the mountain I'm currently on, it will no doubt be invaluable in the forest that fills the vast majority of the valley I'm more likely to spend time in.

Of course, before I can decide on the order, I need to check out my Intelligence level. Nicholas was clear: unless I have an Intelligence stat over ten, I can't absorb more than one knowledge stone a day. That said, I would imagine my Intelligence is over ten unless I start at zero because I've just gained my Class. After all, I always did pretty well at school, and I left uni with a First Class degree. Plus, I've worked most of the time since leaving uni, and my employers have generally been satisfied with my performance. Until the last one—cost-cutting misers. "Status screen," I say, then reflexively flinch sideways. The last time I did this, a rock landed on my head. I don't *think* the two are linked, but better safe than sorry.

When nothing comes flying at me or lands on the table above my head, I focus on the screen itself.

CHAPTER FIVE

Lack of Wisdom

Name: Markus Wolfe		Race: Human	Class: Tamer
Level: 0	Energy to next level: 2%	Energy absorption rate: 5u/hr	Energy towards debt: 0%
Intelligence	6	Mana: 60/60	
Wisdom	3	Mana regeneration rate: 75u/hr	
Willpower	4	Health regeneration rate: 4u/hr	
Constitution	4	Health: 40/40	
Strength	5	Stamina: 20/20	
Dexterity	3	Stamina regeneration rate: 30u/hr	
Class Skills: Dominate – Beginner 1 Tame – Beginner 1		Non-Class Skills: Lay-on-Hands – Beginner 9	

Six," I splutter indignantly, ignoring everything else. "*Six?!*" How could I only have a six for Intelligence? And how could that be my *highest* stat? I mean, the fact that it's my highest stat isn't in itself a surprise. I've always been more than half-decent at academia. It's the fact that it's so low, along with all my other stats, that shocks me. Did all the days at the gym mean nothing? Or maybe they did help since Strength is only one point behind my Intelligence stat . . .

I smile wryly as I note my Wisdom stat—not inaccurate, I suppose. I have made some rather stupid decisions, and not just today. Perhaps I ought to think about increasing that at some point, though probably not immediately, as I can't really see its benefit in the immediate future. Though, maybe that's my lack of Wisdom talking . . .

Sighing, I close the screen. I need to spend some time thinking about it and trying to work out how all the different elements function. But not right now. For now, I know that I definitely can't absorb more than one knowledge stone a day. So, which knowledge stone? I look over the stones again thoughtfully. Hunting, tracking, and woodcraft are all essential for me at the moment, and I'm grateful Nicholas sent them; though, not so grateful that it outweighs my resentment at him sending me here in the first place. I wrench my thoughts back from that dark place again and reconcentrate on the subject at hand. Based on what I surmise is the function of each of the stones, I reckon that woodcraft is my first priority, and I'll have to hope that it *doesn't* mean carpentry. After that . . . Well, I'll have to decide later whether I'm going to need to know how to hunt before learning how to track or vice versa. If the bird was an exception and most creatures here avoid me, I'll need to be able to find them; therefore, tracking. If today is *not* an exception, then probably the animals will find me, so hunting becomes more of a priority. Either way, it's not a decision I can make now.

Looking back at the letter, I identify the two stones to absorb and triple-check that it should be fine to absorb both of them. "I suggest that you use the Class stone first and then the Skill stone. Once you have received your Class, you will gain access to your status screen. Check your Intelligence stat before deciding how to use the knowledge and Skill stones; unless you have an Intelligence stat of ten or more, I would suggest not using more than one knowledge stone per day," I read to myself, glancing around every so often just to make sure that nothing is sneaking up on me.

"So, that means that the Skill stone, the"—I check the letter—"aquamarine one doesn't depend on my Intelligence stat while the . . . light green one does." I'm not *completely* sure, but I'm sure enough. *Now, which one is "aquamarine" and which is "light green"? Because there are three stones that all look similar to me!* Arranging them so they go from blue to green, I pick up the middle stone. "Here's hoping my color identification is the same as Nicholas's," I say to myself grimly. Thanks to the previous instructive message, I focus on the object and think, *absorb Skill stone.*

It takes a moment, but then it's almost like the stone turns to gel, slumping into a pool in my hand. The semi-liquid is quickly absorbed, leaving a faint glow in the palm of my hand that just as quickly disappears.

Unlike the previous time, there's no pain. Instead, a sort of ecstasy envelops me, an energy running through every cell in my body and making it feel completely fresh. It feels like something is going through my body, searching for problems to solve and injuries to heal. *I don't think this is a crafting Skill,* I think to myself muzzily, my eyes rolling into the back of my head at the bliss.

And the next moment, I groan and collapse forwards over my crossed legs as someone drives a railroad spike through my head—fortunately, not a real one; though, honestly, it might be better if it was. Then at least it would be over quickly. In reality, it's memories, or perhaps impressions would be a better word, which are being forced into my head.

I suddenly realize that I know all about Lay-on-Hands and how to use it. I curse out loud as I suddenly regret taking the health potion. Lay-on-Hands most definitely isn't a crafting Skill—it's a *healing* Skill. Sure, it might not have healed my cracked skull in a single cast—I can't tell what level it's at without looking at my status, nor how much mana I have—but I could have used it multiple times until I was healed. I only have—had—two health potions; now I only have one. What if I'm severely injured and out of mana at some point in the future?

Gritting my teeth, there's not much I can do about the new wave of chagrin that washes through me. All I can do is try to do better in the future. That last health potion is going to be kept for a real emergency. Then I realize that I should be grateful that it *is* a healing Skill at all. This way, I have on-going access to medical treatment—something that's going to be very important in a world without hospitals or doctors. Heck, I might even be better off than I would have been in the UK, considering the state of the NHS. I'd probably still be sitting in the waiting room if I'd even gotten to the emergency room.

When the pain finally fades, I breathe a sigh of relief. Though tempted to try to use it, I don't actually have anything to heal right now and don't want to waste the mana. Besides, it feels like the memories haven't quite "settled," like I've just learned something new but need to sleep on it to let the connections form fully. I hesitate as I pick up the light green stone. Should I risk taking it? It felt like an awful lot of information was shoved in my brain just now. What if Nicholas was expecting me to have a higher Intelligence level when he gave me the advice? I look at the letter again, trying to parse through the wording. At the same time, I'm starting to get a bit jittery. My skin is itching from the drying blood, there's a bird carcass in front of me that is starting to attract flies, and who knows when something bigger will come to investigate. Even *I* know that blood attracts predators. That's why the expression "blood in the water" exists, right?

"It's got to be okay," I decide finally, my voice sounding uncertain even in my own ears. In the letter, he talks about "knowledge" stones being the issue and recommends taking the Skill stone before even checking my status. Deciding that just sitting here and agonizing is probably worse than the other options, I pick up the light green stone and absorb it as I did the Skill stone. It's not a railroad spike this time—it's worse. More like the *train* being driven into my head, all lights and horns blazing. I reel, lose my balance drunkenly, and fall. The added pain of hitting the floor is a sidenote to what's happening with my head.

Why am I in so much pain? I ask myself blearily through the sensation. *Has something gone wrong?*

Fortunately for me, nothing has gone wrong. It simply turns out that shoving years' worth of knowledge about surviving in the wild into my head all in one go is just a little more impactful than the vague sense of how to use a skill that I'd received before. Worse, I can sense that some of it is slipping away. Maybe I shouldn't have absorbed it so close to the Skill stone, or maybe it would have happened anyway. I'm just too unfamiliar with even the basics of what is being shoved into my mind; some of it just isn't sticking. Maybe it's even because of my recent concussion. Even though it's healed, what if it's left some sort of lingering difficulty in absorption?

Fortunately for me, it's only a small portion that's lost, as absorbing this stone *is* within my capabilities—just. That said, I have to admit that I only draw these conclusions *after* the pain starts to subside. "Ow," I groan, daring to open my eyes;

they had slid shut. The sunlight dazzles me for a moment and sends a bolt of pain spearing once more through my brain.

I slam them shut again, waiting for the spinning to subside a bit more, but make a new attempt as soon as I feel remotely ready. As soon as I think about what to do next, my new wilderness survival knowledge screams at me that lying out in the open with closed eyes is *not* the best way to see the next day. Or even the next hour. And it *is* wilderness survival, thankfully. More than just surviving in the forest, this stone has given me the knowledge of how to survive in a range of environments—all of them, of course, far from any inhabited area.

Newly armed with knowledge, I find my hesitancy about the path forward clearing up a bit. I quickly crawl out from under the table and put the remaining stones into the pocket that wasn't torn up by the bird's attack. I shrug on the extra clothes that I had pushed off at the start and then sling the pack with the other survival supplies over my shoulder, where it joins the other backpack I brought with me.

My most important items now stored, I gaze at my bright orange and green suitcases wondering how I'm going to carry them. Then I remember something else important.

"Inventory," I say quietly. The message said that I could either say it or think it; for this test, I decided to say it. For the next, I'll try thinking it. Twenty empty squares appear before my eyes, only a faint mistiness making them stand out from the area in front of me.

I decide to test with something I don't care about and pick a stone up off the ground. I first try to put the stone in one of the boxes in front of me, but my hand just waves in the air, and the stone remains stubbornly held within it. Something's missing. *Hmm.*

"Put stone in my Inventory?" I ask uncertainly. Nothing happens. I think back to my previous interactions with this System. Most of them have required verbal or mental instructions. Verbal isn't working, so what about thinking them?

Put the stone in my Inventory, I think, concentrating on the stone being in one of the boxes in front of me. Suddenly, the weight of it is missing from my hand. I raise my eyebrows. *That worked?* Leaning down to pick up another stone from the ground without closing the Inventory, I heft it in my hand thoughtfully. Was it the clear thought that was missing originally? Or the intention?

This time I don't put words to my thoughts and just imagine the stone being in the same slot as the other one.

A moment later, it's gone from my hand and there are two stones in the same slot. "Good to know," I murmur to myself. *Close Inventory,* I think, and the boxes disappear from my vision. "All right, time to test opening it again." Hopefully, the stones will still be there. This time I don't say the command out loud; instead, I make the thought as firm as I can. The boxes reappear. The two stones are still there.

Right, now to get them out. As it turns out, removing the items from the boxes is simply the reverse of putting them in—instead of focusing on putting them in the box, I have to focus on them being in my hand. It's good to work out the exact method, but I do find it a little cumbersome. *Not useful for an emergency situation,* I note, resolving to keep my health potion and knife on my person. I swiftly drop them unceremoniously on the floor—common pebbles, after all, are not what I wish to store. Instead, I hold onto the handle of my bright orange suitcase and focus on putting it into one of the boxes. Nothing happens.

Is it because it's a bag full of items? Does it not count as a single item and that's why it's not working? Are there are too many items within it to fit in the twenty boxes? Dismay fills me at the thought. In neither design nor color is either of my suitcases adapted to my new environment, but I'd rather not have to just ditch everything either.

I sigh. If I'm going to have to ditch everything I can't carry, I'd better first work out how many slots I'll be able to fill. Releasing the handle of my bag, I go over to the carcass of the bird I've just killed. My new wilderness survival memories are screaming at me that this is a useful food source but also that butchery and blood are a perfect way to lure predators. Right now, that's the last thing I want to do. Plus, there's no water source nearby to enable me to clean up the mess. As much as I want to prioritize the photographs of my family, I cannot. Food is going to be far more important. So, reaching down with a heavy heart, I touch the body of the bird and focus on putting it in my Inventory. Nothing happens. I frown. *This can't be because there are too many items. It's a single item. If the body of a creature is counted according to its organs or feathers or whatever, then what* is *considered a single item? Beyond stones, of course.* No, there must be another explanation. I think back to when I put the stones in. *What's the difference between this and that? They were smaller, for sure, and I held them in my hand rather than leaving them resting on the ground. Is that the difference?*

Returning to my suitcase, I lift it off the ground and then once more focus on it being placed in one of the empty slots. This time, to my delight, I feel the weight disappear from my hand, and a picture of my bag appears in the slot.

A grin splits my face. I'm more relieved than I thought I'd be at realizing that it wasn't the nature of a bag full of items that was the problem. I quickly place my lime green bag right next to my orange one; a weight lifts off my chest when they are both stowed safely away.

For a moment I wonder at the nature of the Inventory. It had no issue with taking the two suitcases and can apparently hold a lot of items. I don't feel any extra weight on me, so it's not like an invisible backpack. Is it some sort of non-physical space? What are its limits? Looking at the dead bird, I have to hope that at the very least it will hide the smell of blood. It would be immensely helpful if the Inventory space held the items within it in stasis; if not, I may find that the meat has spoiled before I manage to finish butchering it. Assuming I can get it inside my Inventory, of course.

The bird is big and dead—it's a literal deadweight—but by carefully arranging its limbs and heaving with all my might, I get it off the ground. Though it's only been raised by a centimeter or so, I'm impressed with myself . . . and also in pain. Before I drop it, I quickly activate my Inventory and imagine putting the bird in it. To my relief, the whole carcass suddenly vanishes.

I stagger, thrown off-balance by the abrupt disappearance of the weight I was pressing against. So, the theory is proven thrice over: I need to hold whatever I wish to put in my Inventory off the ground. No putting an airplane in my Inventory— if I found one, that is. And I don't know if there's any size limit per item slot. Another thought has me pulling the precious knowledge stones out of my pocket and putting them into three of the seventeen slots that remain. No way do I want to lose those! About to set out once more, I have another thought. *I wonder . . .*

Shrugging my backpack off again, I try to put that in my Inventory. I grin as it also succeeds. Even better, it only takes up one slot. *This Inventory is awesome! Maybe I should do the same with my new survival pack?* I try it, but this time it doesn't work. I frown. Why did the suitcases and backpack work and the last bag didn't? A loud cry rings out and I jump, reminded of where I am. No time to continue testing out theories—not sitting out in the open as I am. Frankly, I'm lucky I haven't been attacked while playing around with my Inventory in such a vulnerable position. I quickly fill up a few more spaces in my Inventory with the bulky coats I'm wearing, giving me more range of movement. I now know that the difference of speed between wearing them and not could save my life—or end it. As I'm about to leave, my gaze is caught by the single item remaining, which is sticking out from the mountainside like a sore thumb. The table.

That could be useful, I think to myself. As a table, as a barrier, as material for weapons, or simply as firewood, there are many uses for this piece of furniture. Lifting it is as cumbersome as the bird was, but I manage to get it off the ground. However, the moment I try to enter it into my Inventory, it crumbles to golden dust, which then disappears with the breeze. I'm left staring at my empty hands, the single slot intended for it left bare. *Well,* I think to myself, a little dismayed, *at least that didn't happen to anything else.*

CHAPTER SIX

Wealth of Information

I cut down towards the forest line in a meandering route. Wanting to block the view of myself from the sky as much as possible, I take advantage of the many outcroppings of rock dotted about the mountainside. Fortunately, no other rock-bearing bird—or anything else—comes along to test the soundness of my choices.

When I reach the tree line I start walking along it, at right angles to the way I had been walking before. Why? My reasoning is that I need to find fresh water as a priority, and this is most likely to come from the mountain. With any luck, I'll come across a stream bubbling into the forest. If that doesn't work, I've got a few more ideas to try, but this is the easiest one.

As I walk, I try to plan a bit for the future while doing my best to keep a wary eye out for rocks about to drop on my head. Or anything else, really. Who knows what other dangerous creatures could be lurking in this forest? Better to keep my eyes peeled as I walk.

There are lots of things that need doing, that's for sure. More than I would have ever thought of before absorbing the wilderness survival knowledge stone. Nicholas gave me a knife, which, when I consider what I would have had to use otherwise, is a godsend. A knife is an essential tool, as well as a useful weapon for all its lack of reach, and having a metal one will make a *lot* of difference. The one Nicholas has given me is practical: a single-sided straight blade about twenty centimeters long with a slightly curved tip, quite similar to a bowie knife. It even has a serrated section on the part of its spine closest to the handle, which will come in handy for sawing through smaller pieces of wood and tough flesh. Fortunately, it also comes with a protective sheath; otherwise, I'd probably have stabbed myself with it already.

Still, I'm going to need a good number of other tools too, and those I'm going to have to make. Not having either blacksmithing equipment or expertise, I'm going to have to go right back to basics and make them from flint. If I can find any, that is. That's another reason to find a stream. If I'm lucky, there's flint below this mountain or forest and a stream will have cut deep enough into the layers of sediment to have unearthed some nodules for me. If not . . . Well, at least I still have my knife. I can use other rock types to make blunt instruments, but flint is truly the best— according to my newly absorbed wilderness survival knowledge, anyway.

So, I need to make tools. I also need to sort out my food supply a bit. I have the dead bird in my Inventory, which is a start, as long as it's being kept in stasis.

While it's possible that the bird will be inedible for me—I am in a different world, after all—my newly gained memories say that it will most likely be fine. Generally, animal flesh is safe to eat, though it should really be cooked to avoid harmful bacteria as much as possible.

There are some animals that have levels of vitamins or toxins in their bodies that are unsafe for human consumption. Usually, though, those are the result of evolution to adapt to a particular environment or to ward off predators—often in the latter case accompanied by bright warning colors. Carrion eaters can have levels of parasites that render their meat inedible too, but I might have to take that risk.

With any luck, the "no living things" limitation of my Inventory will mean that there are no parasites living inside the bird, but, again, I can't count on that. Being in a different world might make a difference to my knowledge about what is edible and inedible. However, the fact that I can breathe the atmosphere with no problems and that its temperature is mild to me indicates that the natural balance of the world is not that different from what I'm used to. Hopefully, Nicholas wouldn't have sent me to a world where everything was poisonous to me.

One thing that has been significantly affected by being in a different world, though, is my knowledge of safe plants to eat. I've been looking around while walking and have discovered to my dismay that I don't recognize anything.

If I'd been relying on my personal knowledge of plants, that wouldn't mean much. I could name the fruit, vegetables, and leaves that feature in your average British supermarket, and I could probably recognize a number of trees and plants that I regularly walk past in gardens or woods—though that wouldn't mean I'd know if they were edible or not—but that is it.

My new wealth of information about fauna and flora comes purely from absorbing the woodcraft knowledge stone. Unfortunately, it was information about a world that was neither Earth nor this one. I haven't recognized *any* plants so far and have to conclude that I'm unlikely to. In fact, it's been somewhat disorientating. I'll see a plant with leaves of a certain shape that sparks recognition in my mind and then realize that the color is completely wrong, or that it's a bush instead of a tree, or a flowering plant where it should be a fern type. In short, there's no way I can rely on the encyclopedia of plants in my head to choose what to eat and what not to.

Fortunately, my new knowledge also comes with instructions on how to test if a plant is edible or not; the downside is that it takes a *long* time. I can't just shove something in my mouth and hope for the best. No, I'll have to first choose a plant, then separate it into its individual parts—leaves, stem, fruit or flower, roots, and so on.

Next, I'll have to test one part for irritation on contact, then try eating a small amount, then try eating a larger amount. The problem with this is that I have to allow enough time for symptoms to emerge—about eight hours for each test. Plus, in order to be certain whether I'm reacting or not to the plant itself, I'll have to avoid eating or drinking anything but clean water during each test.

So, either I'll have to go without eating anything else for a whole twenty-four-hour period, or I'll have to spend three days testing each part, using my time sleeping as the necessary fast. Did I mention that I have to test each part of the plant separately? At the same time, I'll have to be working hard to create the tools and shelter I need, meaning that the effects of hunger will be felt much more keenly than if I'd just been in my office all day. I can't help but feel a bit overwhelmed. Who knew that it took so much just to survive? Or at least to survive without access to a supermarket and money to buy the things in it. Perhaps I should be grateful that I'm in a place where there's probably abundant food available and I just need to work out what I can eat. There are many on Earth who are in just as poor a situation and can't say the same about their environment.

I really do hope that the Inventory stops items from deteriorating. It will make things much easier if I have access to an effective refrigerator. Of course, that may have some sort of downside that appears later. Apart from not being able to put live animals in it, that is. I'd rather have a refrigerator than a live-animal pen, anyway.

Of course, before I can even consider any of that, I need to find water and a shelter, which brings me right around to my first aim. I sigh and just continue trudging on, my feet and legs already aching, my eyes squinting as they search for the glint of water.

Finding water ends up taking a *long* time. Much longer than I'd anticipated. Apparently, all those films where a person is lost in the wilderness and then stumbles across a stream after only crossing a couple of hills are a lie. Who knew? At least I didn't end up falling into one like I remember a character doing.

I run out of things to think about, or, rather, I become too distracted by my actual surroundings to make meaningful plans. This place is genuinely beautiful. I'm mostly walking at the forest's edge, and the trees are shorter here than the ones I can see downhill. But they're green and vibrant, and some are literally *covered* in flowers, berries, or interestingly colored leaves.

I'm tempted to eat some of the berries but avoid it, knowing just how badly *that* can turn out. The ones with lots of flowers are magnets for all sorts of flying creatures—I even saw something that looked similar to a butterfly but was the size of a bird and had round wings. The berry-laden trees, however, are attractive to other wildlife, but I don't see much more than flashes of color from them as they dive under cover at my approach.

There isn't much undergrowth, making my steps easy enough—as long as I avoid the occasional hidden hole beneath the mossy ground cover. And the air is just so *fresh*. It's full of smells that are completely alien to me: the odor of musky loam from the ground mingling with the perfume of the flowers; damp and rotting leaves combining with the fresh scent of green ones.

But as my legs tire, my mouth dries, and my eyes start to ache from searching for water, the beauty around me fades. After a while of trudging fruitlessly, I suddenly pause; once more, something from the messages I read occurs to me. I don't only have access to an Inventory, but also . . . a Map. If that could show me where to find water, it would save a *lot* of time. "Map," I say, trying not to be too hopeful. Despite my attempts to keep my expectations reasonable, it turns out that I am disappointed anyway.

The Map appears in front of me, a misty screen the background to what looks like a simplistic line drawing. It's almost completely blank. There are chevron shapes in a ring around the edges of my Map, which I have to guess are the mountains I saw stretching out into the distance. In the space between the mountains, there are many, *many* drawings of trees—the forest, I guess. There's also a blinking dot at the edge of the forest, a sort of "you are here." Actually, that's probably its best feature for me, as working out my position in comparison to everything around me tends to be my biggest problem when reading maps. Further up the mountainside near the dot is an X shape next to what looks like a line drawing of a boulder—where I started, I have to conclude. Apart from that, nothing is recorded. No rivers, no streams, nothing. So, either they don't exist, which I doubt, or I have to discover them to add them to my Map, which is much more likely.

Indeed, the shapes closest to me are the most defined; the ones furthest away, particularly towards the end of the valley, which I had barely been able to see, are blurry. So clearly, being able to see something is sufficient to add it to my map—but I need to see it.

Sighing, I close the screen and start walking again. It would have been nice for things to be that easy, but it's not surprising that they aren't. The Map should come in handy once I've discovered some useful spots, but right now it's fairly useless.

After some time, I become too tired to do more than just focus on moving forward, and the loveliness of my surroundings fades further into normality. I even find myself not keeping as close a watch on my environment as I probably should. Dangerous. I make an effort after that to keep looking around myself, but I'm *tired*.

As the sun starts to dip towards the horizon, a scene of particular beauty occurs. My ears catch the faint trickle of a small stream, obvious in the quiet peace of the woods. I'm lucky. I had actually gone a bit further under the tree cover than before because I'd seen a big bird circling high above. It's worked out well for me, fortunately. The stream is really just a trickle, emerging from a crack between the rocks, but unless it disappears underground at some point, it should lead me to something bigger. It's the most marvelous thing I've seen in a long time.

I use my cupped hand to scoop some of the life-giving liquid to my dry lips; the waterskin really didn't last for long, it turns out. After soothing my parched throat, I suddenly pause. Something from my new knowledge is sending alarm bells through me. I gaze at the water filling my hands and realize what it is. *I should really boil this.*

The water *looks* clean, but what microscopic bacteria or parasites could be floating around in it? What if there's a rotting carcass upstream? I let the water drain out of my hands and push myself to my feet with a sigh. A mouthful of liquid is really not enough to quench my thirst, but I don't want to stop to make a fire just now; this is no place to make a camp, as picturesque as it is with the sun glinting off the trickling water.

Following the stream, I walk in search of a greater body of water, and maybe even a good campsite. As I keep walking, I see the stream gathering tributaries and widening. Eventually, after long enough that the light is starting to dim, I reach a body of water that might even be wide enough to be considered a rivulet—I'm not planning on measuring it to make sure. I have a hard choice to make: stop soon or walk in the dark? Frankly, the thought of doing the latter makes my bowels turn to water. If a bird could almost kill me in the middle of the day, how much more vulnerable would I be at night? Especially when I'd be either blind in the dark or half-blinded by the light if I carried a torch. My new knowledge pipes up to *helpfully* tell me about several different creatures that hunt at night and exactly how they like to take down their prey. *Okay, decision made on that one—I'm not going anywhere.* Even if the same animals probably don't exist here, I bet others that are just as bad *do*.

CHAPTER SEVEN

Catching Light

The cooling breeze as the sun goes down makes up my mind for me. I'd rather not freeze, for one. For another, I decide that the safety of being able to see in a certain radius is preferable to being completely blind in the dark. Besides, if it's as uncivilized a place as Nicholas indicated, the forest animals' experience with fire should be purely forest fires. Any fire I make should therefore repel more creatures than it attracts.

I spend a few minutes preparing a fire—a first for me. Fortunately, being in a forest, there's plenty of dead wood, leaves, and kindling, so it takes less time than it might have. It's still almost dark by the time I think I'm ready. Kneeling down next to the sticks and dead wood I've used to build a rickety-looking little pyramid, a groan emerges from my mouth unbidden. Man, my legs are *wrecked*. Taking the tube to work simply doesn't compare.

I pull out the flint and steel that Nicholas provided me with. It's not actually a flint stone, thankfully. It's a ten-centimeter-long stick of an indeterminate material. Maybe metal of some sort? Or stone? I can't work it out, as it seems to have a somewhat mixed appearance. The rod is accompanied by a piece of metal attached to it with a cord. Again, practical.

Of course, knowing how to use the tools, thanks to absorbing the stone and its helpful memories, is one thing; being able to *do* it is something completely different. It takes long enough for me to get the technique right that I find myself wishing I was a smoker. Sure, it would be annoying to be without cigarettes in a completely different world, and my physical stats would probably be even worse, but at least I'd probably have a lighter with me.

I'm reminded of why humanity moved away from such means of lighting a fire as soon as was possible. Hopefully, Nicholas chose to send me this simple technology because he thought it would be less likely to go wrong and leave me fireless, rather than because it's considered high-tech for his society.

In the end, I manage to strike the rod correctly enough to generate a spark and then do the right things to turn that spark into a flame. A bit more coaxing sees the flame catch the pyramid of branches I made.

It's at that point that I realize it's catching light a lot faster than I thought it would, and I scramble to go and get some more branches to add to the fire. It's probably a good half an hour before I feel confident that the fire can occupy itself for a bit. I slump next to it with a sigh, only now realizing how much my feet hurt too.

I lever off my shoes and massage my aching soles. Fortunately, I chose good shoes and don't have any blisters, though there are a number of parts on my feet that feel quite tender. Okay, fire: check. Now water. I'm still *really* thirsty. Fortunately, I actually have a cooking pot. My wok. Suddenly, I'm thankful beyond measure that I thought of bringing that with me. If I'd known I was going to be landed in a *survival* situation, I would have brought all of the pots—and the knives! But I didn't know. And, honestly, the question is moot since I probably wouldn't have come.

A shriek cuts through the air, and I jump half out of my skin. I glance wildly around me, but nothing's moving. Gulping, I move closer to the fire hoping that whatever made that noise will be scared off by it.

I do have to venture away from the fire, though. I need to get water. Closing my eyes briefly, I summon my courage and grab the cooking pot, since unearthed from my suitcase.

I keep a careful watch out in all directions as I step towards the rivulet running only a few paces away from my "camp." After filling the wok, I hurry back towards my fire, thankful to return to a sitting position; standing up and walking was frankly *painful.*

Tucking the wok next to the fire, I hope that that will be enough to get it boiling. It should be—I'm sitting a pace away and the side of me facing the fire is roasting.

So, with water on the way, the next question is about food. I haven't dressed the bird, and I'm not keen on doing that right next to my camp; my absorbed memories say that that is a big no-no. The scent of blood and offal will draw scavengers, and possibly predators, like a moth to a flame. So, I guess the bird is off the menu. I *really* hope that my Inventory works as a fridge. I will be thoroughly disappointed if all that meat goes to waste.

Anyway, it seems like the rations are my only option, then, as testing new plants is not a good idea right now. That could be a problem. I investigated the rations earlier, and they . . . aren't exactly abundant. Nicholas gave me a small quantity of dried meat and two different types of plants, which I can identify with my new knowledge. There are some brown oblong items that look and taste like a type of nut—dried samova beans, apparently. These are accompanied by some long, dried pieces of green plant—malachy leaves, a type of nutritious seaweed. Together, they will provide everything my body needs . . . for about two days. Three, if I stretch it out. I've already consumed some of the dried meat, as I got hungry while walking and figured I have a whole load of meat in my Inventory to replace it with. Of course, that's assuming that I won't just have to ditch it when I finally get around to processing it. *No, no worrying needlessly,* I tell myself firmly.

Directing my attention back to healthier places, I withdraw a small handful of samova beans and a single malachy leaf. I force myself to put the rest back and put the satchel out of arm's length and line of sight in order to lessen the temptation to get more. I chew each bean long enough that it's completely disappeared before I put the next one in. It's hard not to just shove them all in my mouth and probably look like a chipmunk.

I'm not used to being unable to satiate my hunger. At least the beans taste pretty good and make my mouth salivate enough to eat them. They'd be nicer with some salt, though. The malachy leaf makes up for that—it's *very* salty. Almost too much so, but I've lost a lot of salt today through sweat, so I force my way through even as it dries out my mouth. *Mental note: next time, maybe use the malachy leaves in a stew or something so the salt is diluted.* Right now, I'd rather not risk the smell of a cooking meal attracting something tougher than me.

My stomach still rumbles even after "supper" is over. I decide then and there that my first task tomorrow will be investigating the corpse in my Inventory and cooking it up for later use, presuming it's still good. I've found the river, at least, which will enable me to wash my hands, tools, and anything else that gets dirtied by blood or other liquids.

I decide to distract myself with my status screen; it's time to investigate it a bit and make some plans. Commanding the misty box to appear once again, I notice that the numbers appear identical to the last time I looked at it. Almost identical, that is: the percentage of Energy to the next level has gone up by two percent. I consider that thoughtfully. It's been, I guess, about seven hours since I last looked at that, and I apparently earn about five units per hour, so that's about thirty-five units . . . That makes each percent worth about seventeen Energy, more or less. I started with two percent. Does that mean killing the bird was worth about thirty-five Energy units, or had I already earned some Energy?

I check the letter Nicholas sent me; sure enough, it says that Earth *did* have some Energy, it was just in very small amounts. *Hmm. A thought for later.*

Right now, the most important thing is that if the current rate continues, it will take approximately fourteen days to level up, just through surviving. Maybe less, since I will have to hunt animals in order to not starve. That's doing the bare minimum. I probably shouldn't be doing the bare minimum, though.

Leveling up has to help me survive; at least, that was the way it was in the video games I used to play. Heck, even in the games that were about managing a city or nation, leveling the place up gave bonuses or achievements, which helped later game actions. I wouldn't call myself a pro-gamer, not in the slightest. At best, I'm an amateur; my dad refused to buy me many as a teenager because he wanted me to concentrate on my studies, and I didn't care enough to spend my pocket money on them. And then studies at uni and work took over my life. But an Inventory, Map, stats, Skills, magic . . . even having success centered around fighting and killing . . . It all sounds far too like what I remember of them for me to be comfortable. After all, I remember dying *far* too many times in my games to be happy that I appear to be in one now. I don't think I'll have the ability to respawn in real life, however gamelike some of it seems to be. At least, I'm not inclined to test that.

I know some people would be overjoyed over suddenly being "in a game," but I can't help feeling dismay. Perhaps it will help to dive a bit deeper into my stats and give me more information to build a plan.

Exploring my status screen a bit, I learn how to manipulate it with my mind. Fortunately, it's not particularly complicated. By navigating the two tabs at the top of the misty box, I can see my messages, which include previously read ones, and my status screen. Nothing else.

Returning to the status screen, I try to work out what each of the stats actually mean. It's mostly guesswork; unfortunately, there's no tool-tip help file for this System. Hopefully, the System lore stone will have more to offer me when I finally get around to absorbing it.

Intelligence must be something to do with absorbing and processing information, based on the fact that it's this stat that determines how many stones I can absorb and in what time frame. Clearly, from the status screen, it's also the determiner of how much mana I have—meaning magic, I guess, from context. Since my understanding of Lay-on-Hands, my healing Skill, indicates that it uses mana, this is an important stat.

Of course, I can't stop the image of a fire-throwing godlike figure from blossoming in my mind, but that's a long way away, if it's possible at all.

Wisdom . . . Well, given how little of it I have, I can only think that it's a reflection of my capacity to choose the best course of action. As recent—and less recent—events have shown, I reckon that this area has probably been lacking for a while. There's nothing like sitting in the middle of the wilderness with no way home to make a man reflect morosely on his previous life choices.

I force my mind away from the black hole that threatens to suck me in. Continuing to look at my status screen, I focus back on Wisdom. Clearly, it affects the regeneration of mana. How? I don't know. Why? Perhaps to stop people like me from being able to throw massive fireballs for too long.

I imagine a mage with high Intelligence and low Wisdom: they'd be able to throw around powerful spells, but they'd have enough time to regret it while waiting for their mana pool to recover. At least, that's one possible explanation. Willpower . . . I can only think that it's a reflection of one's self-discipline.

Like not eating food that's supposed to last me for at least two days because my stomach is still growling, I tell myself, forcibly preventing the impulse to reach for the food. *Would increasing this reduce the temptation or increase my ability to resist it?* I wonder in an effort to try to distract myself.

There's also the fact that it determines my health regeneration. Why? What does Willpower have to do with getting better? A rustle in the leaves behind me makes me look around wildly, my hand scrabbling for my knife.

Realizing I still have the status screen in front of my eyes, I quickly close it.

Staring out into the darkness, I see a hint of movement, but it doesn't come close to me, and then it moves off completely. As my heart rate slowly calms from its frantic pace, I relax a little but resolve to keep my knife close at hand, just in case. Actually, I could do with having another weapon, right? Pushing myself to my tired feet, I look around for a branch that might work well enough. Spotting one at the edge of the firelight, I carefully approach it, watching warily in case something decides to leap out of the night and try to eat my face.

Fortunately, nothing does, and I sit back by the fire. I move my wok away from the fire while I do that—it's boiling nicely, so now I need to let it cool a bit before I can drink some. Taking my knife, I use it to carve one end of the branch I've just found. While I do that, I try to return to my train of thought. *Where was I? Oh yeah, I was thinking about Willpower and healing and why the two are linked.* After all, healing is about biological processes, which can be helped along by pharmaceutical agents to treat symptoms and boost the body's immune system. But it's clear that in this new reality, Willpower directly affects health regeneration. And a pitiful regeneration it is too: four units an hour. *Though, does that mean I would have recovered completely from my head wound in less than ten hours?* Because if that were the case, four units per hour is actually pretty awesome.

Musing about the nature of Willpower, something suddenly occurs to me, and I pause my carving while I pull up the status screen and switch back to the message panel as soon as it unfolds in front of me. I haven't quite got the hang of this mental manipulation yet.

In my message box are two categories: read and unread messages. Of course, the latter is empty, but the former holds the messages that came up after I absorbed the Tamer Class stone. Reading the one about the Tamer Skills adds a further clue about Willpower.

Dominate: activate this Skill on a being to enter into a Battle of Wills, success in which binds the being to you as a Bound. Certain previous actions may increase your chances of winning the battle, even with a lower Willpower than your opponent. This includes, but is not limited to, having already defeated the being physically; having trapped the being so that they are unable to move; and having terrified the being. Warning: if you lose the Battle of Wills, you will be rendered vulnerable for ten seconds as you recover. Recommended Willpower before attempting a Battle of Wills: 10–30 for a Stage 1 Beast.

The phrase "even with a lower Willpower than your opponent" and the mention of a "Battle of Wills" both indicate an important point: this Skill scales off my Willpower. Or, at least, having a higher Willpower than my opponent increases the likelihood that this Skill will succeed. There's even a recommendation for the minimum level of Willpower to have before attempting to Dominate another creature.

Closing the screen, I continue carving my new weapon. I'm rather depressed when it appears that I can't even use one of my Class Skills yet; I've got a four in Willpower. Is it the same situation for Tame? I check the description again. No, it doesn't seem to be the case: the description for Tame only indicates that intelligent beings might reject the Bond. Of course, there may be an underlying modifier that I don't know about.

Now I have more time to think about it, the Skills sound . . . interesting. It seems like there is a consensual and non-consensual duality to my new Class. Tame is the consensual one—it sounds like I need to put effort into making a creature inclined to accept my Bond, probably like taming a creature the normal way, and they could still choose to refuse the Bond when I offer it. Dominate, on the other hand, is clearly non-consensual since it's some sort of "battle" and is easier if I've half-convinced the creature by hurting or scaring them first. At the same time, I have to have a minimum stat to do it, and if I fail, then I will be "rendered vulnerable," whatever that means. That's a bit of a downside, and there might be others, too, which aren't mentioned. I guess I'll find out later; hopefully, not the hard way.

It would have helped if this whole thing came with a manual, I think uncharitably at Nicholas. Then again, maybe that's what the System lore stone is . . . But I don't dare put that higher up the priority queue than knowledge about hunting and tracking. Well, either way, my Willpower sucks, so it doesn't look like I'll be able to use Dominate any time soon—not without stacking the deck significantly in my favor, at least. Now to look at my physical stats.

CHAPTER EIGHT

Experiment

Continuing my exploration of my stats, I consider Constitution next. From my status screen, it clearly determines my health at a one-to-ten ratio, like Intelligence and mana. For a moment, I wish I'd looked at my status screen while I was injured—that way I could have a better idea of what the health points actually mean in real terms.

Ultimately, though, I just shrug—I know that getting injured is something to be avoided, and if I am too injured, I could die. Adding health points into the equation doesn't really change anything, except that if I add points to Constitution, logically I make myself harder to kill. I mean, I'm assuming here that I can increase these values, but it seems like a reasonable assumption to make.

Strength seems fairly obvious; though, the fact that it determines my stamina pool is interesting. Stamina, from my understanding, is based on how I've conditioned my muscles to deal with repeated stress, so I suppose it's logical. Though, I do find it curious that mana and health are at a ten-to-one ratio with Intelligence and Constitution, respectively, but stamina is at a four-to-one ratio with Strength.

Dexterity must have to do with my fine motor skills. I find the three listed there rather insulting. I'm capable of writing and typing, both of which require fine motor skills! Then again, I suppose that at the gym I did focus a lot more on strength training with lifting weights rather than something flexible or reactive like martial arts. If Dexterity is also about the ability to quickly react physically, I suppose I can understand the low stat value here.

I do find the regeneration rates interesting; each is different. Wisdom has a ratio of one to twenty-five with mana regeneration, Willpower is at a one-to-one ratio with health regeneration, and Dexterity is at a one-to-ten ratio with stamina regeneration. Why? Maybe I'll find out with the System lore stone.

It's interesting that the six stats seem to be split equally between physical—Constitution, Dexterity, and Strength—and mental—Intelligence, Wisdom, and Willpower. Does that mean I should be aiming to balance them all equally? A healthy mind in a healthy body sort of thing? Or should I be doing the reverse: choosing two or three stats to concentrate on and investing all my resources in those?

Could I make myself practically unkillable by sufficiently investing in Willpower so my health regeneration would make up for any wound I was dealt a moment after I was hit?

A moment after having that thought I shake my head. No. Possibly it would work in the long term, but how many points would I have to invest in Willpower to achieve it? And all at the cost of neglecting everything else, including my health pool. Besides, I already have a healing Skill.

Actually, that reminds me. I scroll down to look at my Skills and concentrate on the entry for Lay-on-Hands, wanting to get more information on it. What a surprise—it doesn't work. The screen just sits there, stubbornly unchanged. I huff and dismiss it. Instead, I close my eyes and try to focus on the feelings and half-remembered memories that flashed through me when I absorbed the Skill stone. I know that in order to use this Skill, I need to be touching the subject and concentrating. I also know it's not an instant fix; it significantly increases the subject's regenerative capacity, but the more serious the injury, the more time and effort it will take to heal.

Furthermore, I get the sense that it can't heal injuries that the body is incapable of healing by itself, given time. Where the practical limits of this are, I don't know, not having much medical knowledge beyond the basics taught at school, but I guess that cuts are fine and severed limbs might not be. And that's highly disturbing to consider as a serious possibility.

The next concept I sense is that this healing Skill can be used on oneself as well as on others; I didn't realize that was in question! Not that I have anyone else to heal, of course. Continued practice will improve efficiency and speed of the Skill's effect. I open my eyes and sigh. Again, a manual would be *really* good. *As would a pizza takeaway,* I comment to myself, just adding to the list of unrealistic wishes.

Eyeing my knife, I wonder if I should test my healing Skill; using something for the first time in an uncertain battle is never a good idea. I pick the weapon up and position it over my arm, trying to psych myself up to actually cut into my own flesh. I clench my jaw and fear runs through me—fear of pain, fear of it not working and having injured myself for no good reason. Actually, that's a good point. Why injure myself needlessly? The way things have gone so far, I'm likely to get injured soon, even if it's only a sprained ankle. I can test it then. There's no reason to believe that my first injury will happen in a battle.

Decision made, I put the knife to one side, pretending to myself that it wasn't my unwillingness to cut my own flesh that weighed the heaviest on the scales of choice.

I should get some sleep, anyway. It's been a tiring day so far, and I've got a lot to do tomorrow; better to be well-rested for it. Starting to prepare my bed, composed of my extra layers arranged to provide a bit of cushioning and coverage, I suddenly remember that there was something else I wanted to experiment with. My Inventory. Why did my backpack fit in, but the bag that Nicholas gave me didn't? Are there other criteria that I need to be aware of?

After a bit of experimentation, occasionally interrupted by some noise or other making my heart leap into my mouth, I seem to have come up with some answers.

The difference, oddly enough, appears to relate to whether the item can be fully closed or not. My bags and backpack can be zipped up, essentially appearing as one item.

The satchel that Nicolas gave me is an open-mouthed pouch. It has a drawstring, but the leather of the mouth is stiff, and even pulling tightly doesn't get rid of a small gap big enough to fit several fingers in. That seems to be the reason why it doesn't go in my Inventory with items inside; it does go in if it's empty or inside one of my other bags.

Out of curiosity, I try putting my canteen in the Inventory without its lid on, and it works. I'm not quite sure what the reasoning is behind this. Perhaps water in my canteen is considered part of the canteen whereas items inside the satchel aren't?

In the end, I just accept the apparently arbitrary rules and do some rearranging. Since my satchel can't be stored in my Inventory with items inside, I might as well make use of it. I put the items that I think I will need at a moment's notice in the leather satchel and try to fit the rest in the backpack. This requires me to unpack my backpack and suitcases so I can better arrange things. As I do, I reevaluate the items based on my new circumstances, sighing as they come up lacking.

I even debate throwing away the condoms and swimming trunks to make space for other items later but, in the end, just tuck them away in the corner of my orange suitcase. I hate throwing things away. Murphy's law always says I will need them the week after I've binned them. I won't be in this forest forever, and if I desperately need space later, I can throw them away then. I do wish I'd braved the broken glass in my shower to grab my soap and shampoo, though—there seems to be a dearth of shops in this neck of the woods.

I also look rather mournfully at my Kindle and phone. Both probably have a charge now, but that's not exactly going to last. I keep them turned off in order to save battery for now and tuck them away carefully. I have the chargers, but they're a fat lot of good without somewhere to plug them into. If I had a solar charger or something, that would be gravy, but if wishes were fishes, I'd be having a fry up right now. Putting my backpack into my Inventory completes my preparations, and I turn back to my newest weapon. My new knowledge informs me that hardening the tip of it in the fire would be a good idea, so I do that.

It doesn't take too long to do, and I find myself feeling slightly better for having a second weapon to join my little knife. Tiredness pulling at my eyelids and limbs, I lie down and try to sleep. Of course, that's easier said than done when you're in the middle of a strange forest with no better weapon for protection than a knife and a sharpened stick. A forest that is remarkably *loud* considering the darkness.

With my eyes closed, the sounds seem even louder and closer than before. The ground is also even harder and more uncomfortable than it had felt when I first lay down.

Sitting up now, I pull a couple of jackets out of my Inventory and use one as a pillow and one as a mattress. It helps—a little. It's still hard and cold ground that

I'm lying on. There's a surprising amount of movement going on around me too. More than once I feel something run over my bare skin, even over my face. They're insects mostly, but one has enough weight to be a mouse or something. *That* wakes me up right after I manage to fall asleep, and it takes a while for my body and mind to settle from the adrenaline rush.

The fire is another thing. I have to keep adding sticks to it, otherwise it threatens to go out. Again, not conducive to going to sleep. Probably mid-way through the night, I run out of firewood to feed it, clearly having underestimated just how much it would use. The quick burn rate probably also has to do with the breeze that whips between the trees—the availability of oxygen makes the fire burn brighter and hotter but also consumes fuel more quickly. I pull another jacket out to be a blanket after that.

Then there's the wind itself, which seems to excel in sending cold fingers through any tiny gap between the layers covering me, making me shiver every time it happens despite my "blanket." I do fall asleep eventually out of sheer exhaustion despite all the distractions and challenges, but even then, it's not terribly restful.

Not surprisingly, my dreams are filled with anxiety and stress. Drifting between half-consciousness and full unconsciousness, I sometimes struggle to tell the difference between reality and dream. Several of the dreams I have are actually far more believable than reality. The forest in the dark is far too dreamlike—the moonlight painting patterns of leaves across the ground, the sounds that would be more at home in a jungle. Even the other-worldly smells that clog up my nose like strong perfume in a lift contribute to making the environment almost impossible for me to accept as real.

Standing in my boss's office as he tells me that my team and I are being replaced by an outsourced human resources outfit based in another country is far more likely than the reality of lying in a dark, alien forest. Equally, standing at my father's grave as his coffin is lowered down into the ground and tears run down my cheeks feels far too concrete.

I'm more disorientated when I wake from the dream than I was during it. When I finally fall into undisturbed, black unconsciousness, the moon has long since set and the forest is quieter than it's ever been before. It seems like I've out-night-owled even the night owls.

CHAPTER NINE

Pattern of Blood

wake up when a ray of sunlight hits my face. No, actually I wake up and *decide to get up* then. It hasn't exactly been a restful night; the graininess in my eyes attests to that. But I finally give up on sleep when the sun is actually shining in my eyes. It's a little above the horizon, high enough to have started shining through the forest.

Long fingers of shadow paint the forest in contrasting colors; it's still early enough that the dawn chorus is only just transitioning into the daily sounds of birds. How do I know? Apparently, birds sound pretty similar even across worlds. Something that's also true across worlds: I want breakfast.

Helping myself once more to a disciplined handful of beans, another handful of jerky, and a couple of dried seaweed pieces, I'm set for the day. Well, that's what I tell myself—my stomach isn't entirely convinced. I try to ignore the images it keeps sending me of pancakes with syrup, or a good hearty English breakfast, or, heck, even a bowl of muesli with yogurt and berries.

Shaking my head sharply, I redirect my thoughts to what I need to do. After quickly packing away the small number of things that make up my "camp," I pause thoughtfully. Maybe I should sort out my bird meat before leaving. After all, I already have a fire, though only the barest embers remain due to the hours of inattention on my part. Plus, I'm planning to move on anyway; leaving entrails and blood here isn't going to be a problem.

Deciding that it's the best idea I've had all day, I pull the bird out of my Inventory. It thumps on the ground, a literal deadweight. It's somehow smaller than I remember it being. For some reason I'd thought it to be the size of an ostrich when it's more like a cassowary. That said, it's nothing like the cassowary in shape; it's more like a vulture but with the beak of a hawk.

Actually, it's surprisingly heavy considering it could fly. I'm a bit of an amateur bird-watcher, one of the few outdoor activities I enjoy, and often went on research binges about different bird facts. From what I remember, the heaviest bird on Earth that can fly is only something like fifteen or twenty kilos. A cassowary is significantly more than that, adults being over fifty kilos, and an ostrich is more than double that, but neither of those have hollow bones beyond their femurs. Based on how difficult I found it to lift this bird yesterday, I'd guess that it's at least the weight of a cassowary, maybe a bit more. How, then, could it fly?

Still musing over the mystery, I try to decide how to do this. Considering how big it is, it would be far better if I could hoist the corpse up by its feet. Really, I'm not well prepared for the task, but c'est la vie. Supposedly, I should be able to remove the skin and feathers quite easily, but the size of this thing is daunting.

First of all, I inspect the condition of the carcass. There's no strong odor, or at least nothing that my absorbed memories tell me is anything unexpected from a beast with feathers, which preens itself instead of taking a bath. The body is not bloated in any way. The feet are stiff, and the flesh is starting to show signs of rigor mortis. The eyes are still wet and full.

All these signs taken together, I have to conclude that my Inventory keeps things in stasis, or at least does not allow significant decomposition. Considering it's been almost twenty-four hours since I killed the thing, it would be in significantly worse condition if there had been no intervening effects.

A smile of relief takes over my face. That's good news. Excellent, actually. It makes my food situation so much easier to manage. I decide not to cook the entire bird now in that case. That will save a lot of time, and it also means I'll be able to cook it in different ways later. I'll still cook some for immediate and emergency use, but the majority I'll return to the Inventory. I can only hope that the different cuts of meat will stack. Otherwise, I'm going to have a problem.

That's for future-Markus to deal with, I decide.

Trying to pull up the knowledge stuffed into my head about how to dress a bird, I debate a question: keep the skin or not? The skin contains good fats, which would be good for me in my current situation, but at the same time, it might have parasites or other diseases. Considering that my cooking methods are less than ideal, I decide to do my best to skin it.

I shift the bird to lie on its side and then make a cut on the underside of its breast. From there, I try to pull the skin and feathers off all in one go. "Try" being the operative word. It's immediately clear—again—that having the knowledge in my head is not the same thing as being able to actually *do* it. It takes me a lot longer than it should, and a significant amount of cursing, before I finally manage to get the skin off. It's not in one piece, either. Still, I've succeeded in the first step.

I make the next few cuts with a similar amount of precision—or lack of it, rather. I don't think I'll be getting all of the meat off this carcass . . . As an experiment, I take three different cuts of meat from the back, the breast, and the leg, and I put them in my Inventory. To my continued pleasure, they *do* stack.

With that clarified, I continue cutting through the joints with difficulty. My hand slips on multiple occasions as the handle of the knife gets coated in blood. Each time, I have to pause and go wash it in the stream, not wanting to cut *myself*. It's hard work and would be better done with an axe or saw, but a knife is what I've got.

It's only when I cut into the body cavity that I fully realize that I'm dealing with a *corpse*. Maybe that should have been obvious before, but what I've done so far isn't much different from what I would do back on Earth to prepare food for myself. However, when I see the heart and the intestines and get a face full of "corpse" smell, it really hits home that this is the whole body of a bird, which I killed myself. Feeling faint and nauseous, I stumble over to the stream to wash the blood off my hands and splash water on my face. I'm not used to this.

"Come on, Markus," I tell myself aloud, almost startled at the first human voice I've heard in what feels like days. Actually, considering that my drunken binge made more than a day disappear, it's been a while since I even spoke to Nicholas. Still . . . "Get it together. You don't do this, you'll starve. So don't wimp out and just *do it*." Taking a few more deep breaths, I decide I feel fortified enough to continue and turn back to the body. Only to see it move.

I watch in fear as the bird's legs shift and its head twitches. Magic exists, so does that mean . . . Can things become *undead*? I'm torn between creeping closer to investigate and running in the opposite direction. Then my eyes narrow. I've caught sight of something that puts the lie to my panicked supposition. A tail. I creep closer and withdraw the knife from where I've hooked it in my belt. Sure enough, the bird is as dead as ever—and not *undead*. What's making it move are three creatures about the size of a small dog, like a chihuahua or something.

They look rather like baby crocodiles with longer legs and sharp teeth. They're worrying and tearing at the bird carcass, snatching mouthfuls off and gulping them down with quick head tosses. I see red. I almost *died* to kill this thing, and here are these other creatures thinking they can just come and benefit from my struggle?

Without thinking, I grab my knife from its sheath on my belt and stab at the nearest creature. I aim my blade at its back . . . only to pierce the dirt an inch to one side of it. The lizard thing and I just look at each other for a long moment.

Then a blinding pain hits me. The lizard has whipped around faster than I could follow and has bitten down on my forearm. I stagger backwards and fall on my rump, flailing ungainly, my hand still clenched around the knife.

The lizard is still attached, using the same worrying technique on my arm as it was using on the bird. I grab at it and wrench, trying to get it off my arm.

It's only when I succeed in freeing myself from its teeth that I curse myself for my stupidity—when the lizard came free, it took a good chunk of my flesh with it. Screaming, I slam the lizard against the ground in a frenzy. I only stop when it goes completely limp in my hand and its head looks significantly flatter and bloodier.

In the meantime, our kerfuffle hasn't gone unnoticed. The other two lizard things have rounded the bird carcass and are advancing quickly. One lunges and sinks its teeth in my leg. I shout again, this time more in anger than pain, and grip my knife more tightly. I've learned my lesson. I grab its tail and stab at its body with my knife. It takes me a couple of tries, but I manage to sever its spinal cord somewhere between its two sets of legs.

My knife manages to avoid any other bones as it easily slices through the lizard's flesh. I ditch the detached half and stagger to my feet, glaring at the third lizard creature. It stares back at me for a moment and then turns tail, clearly deciding that this is not a fight it wants to risk. "Yeah, you better run!" I shout at its disappearing back.

Panting harshly from exertion and adrenaline, I am reminded as I take a step that I still have half a lizard attached to me. Leaning over, I almost overbalance, my head starting to get woozy. *Blood loss*, I realize as I look at the blood coating my right forearm and rapidly dripping off my fingers.

Fumbling with the lizard's head, I pull its jaws open—easy, now the creature is dead—and drop it to the ground. Fortunately, since I didn't yank the jaws away, this wound is a lot less serious than the one in my arm—just an elongated semicircle of sharp teeth marks oozing with blood. Turning my forearm towards me, I suddenly freeze. The pattern of blood tracing over my pale skin, the bubbling of the fluid from my wound . . . It all takes me back thirteen years to the nightmare I've never truly gotten over. I see her again: her lips are blue and moving faintly, and I try desperately to hear the inaudible words they form . . .

No! I focus on my breathing and try to pick out three things I can hear, two things I can feel, and one thing I can smell. *Wait . . . blood. Not good, not good! Wind, rustling of leaves, smell of earth, trickling of the brook . . .*

Bit by bit, I pull myself out of my attack, trying my best to minimize the impact of the pain from my wound, the feeling of blood trickling, and the smell of the red fluid. I have no desire to be pulled back into that nightmare. As panic loses its cloying grip on me, a new sense of urgency overtakes me. My wooziness is getting worse—I need to deal with these injuries *now*. I cover the bleeding wound with my hand, desperately trying to keep my precious lifeblood in my body. *Bandages, I need bandages! What can I use—a shirt?* But I need to use the knife to cut the shirt up, and I'm not at all ambidextrous, so my right hand being the one that's injured is the worst possible situation for me. *Why didn't Nicholas give me some sort of first aid kit? He must have known I'd be injur—*

Then it hits me. I'm an *idiot*. Of *course* he realized that. And gave me something better than bandages—or so I hope. "Lay-on-Hands," I croak weakly, concentrating on sending a sense of . . . something to the wound. A cool stream floods down my arm from the area under my sternum and saturates the gaping hole in my arm. It starts to clot over before my eyes, and the blood flow stops. Relief floods me, accompanied by a sudden feeling of weakness. Sparkles fill my vision, which quickly shrinks, sounds abruptly coming from far away . . .

CHAPTER TEN

Regeneration

The next thing I know, I hear birdsong. *Why can I hear birdsong? We don't get many birds in the city. And why can't I recognize the calls?* I realize that my eyes are closed. *When did I do that?* Opening them, I see the forest canopy above me, and my recent memories come back to me in a sudden flood. I flush as I realize what happened. I fainted.

It's understandable, I tell myself, nonetheless feeling a bit embarrassed. I lost a lot of blood and had an adrenaline rush and crash. Not to mention being in another life-or-death situation for the second time in two days after having gone more than thirteen years since the last time.

Then, to add to my woes, I also had a flashback, which, again, I haven't had that badly in at least six years. I look at my arm wondering if I'd dreamed the effect of the healing. But no, the wound is still there, though scabbed over. Fortunately, I didn't land on the injured arm when I collapsed. Now less gripped by fear or adrenaline, I find my brain starting to work again. I open my status screen.

Name: Markus Wolfe		Race: Human	Class: Tamer
Level: 0	Energy to next level: 9%	Energy absorption rate: 5u/hr	Energy towards debt: 0%
Intelligence	6	Mana: 60/60	
Wisdom	3	Mana regeneration rate: 75u/hr	
Willpower	4	Health regeneration rate: 4u/hr	
Constitution	4	Health: 22/40	
Strength	5	Stamina: 17/20	
Dexterity	3	Stamina regeneration rate: 30u/hr	
Class Skills:		Non-Class Skills:	
Dominate – Beginner 1		Lay-on-Hands – Beginner 9	
Tame – Beginner 1			

Only two things have changed—no, wait, three: I've gained Energy towards the next level; my health has dropped to twenty-two out of forty; and my stamina has dropped to seventeen out of twenty. I was expecting to see something different about my mana, but that's full. The time I spent unconscious must have been enough to allow it to recharge.

Once more casting Lay-on-Hands, I'm glad to feel the cool energy snaking its way through me to the wounds. This time it makes my injury look several days old rather than just recently scabbed over. I look at my status screen again and grunt in satisfaction.

My mana has dropped by ten points, but because of my regeneration of seventy-five units per hour, it takes less than a minute before it's already climbing. Plus, my health points have ticked up to twenty-seven. Not a bad trade when considering the vastly different regeneration rates: ten mana points for five health points.

I cast the healing spell again, this time deliberately not concentrating on my wounds. As a result, I feel a much more diluted coolness spread across my body. My arm injury improves a little, but it's barely perceptible. However, the punctures in my leg and the aches in my rump—heck, all over my body, really—improve significantly.

I check my status screen again and grunt in surprise. Despite casting the same spell, I've gotten different results. The spell took the same amount of mana to cast, dropping my reserve by ten, but my health points only ticked up by three this time. Is that because the effect was more diluted by being spread across my body, or because I wasn't focusing on the more serious wound?

I continue casting the spell until I bottom out my reserve and fill my health points. Then I bite my lip as I wonder if I've made a mistake. Maybe it's not actually a good idea to empty my tank. Clearly, I can't know that another life-or-death fight isn't just around the corner. I make a mental note to keep at least ten points of mana available in reserve at all times—unless, of course, that final cast means the difference between life and death immediately. I'm not going to intentionally sabotage my chances of survival just because I want to keep a mana reserve. That would be ridiculously stupid. By this point, the wound on my arm is just a red mark and the rest of my aches and pains are long gone.

For a moment, my resentment at Nicholas's high-handed treatment of me fades away and is replaced by gratitude. Even back on Earth I wouldn't have had access to something such as this. Mind you, apart from a few specific contexts, I've never *needed* it either, but I wouldn't have turned down magical healing when I broke my arm falling off my bike.

I suddenly wonder what kind of world Nicholas lives in where he can so casually send me a stone that teaches something like this. Or maybe it's not so casual; maybe he sent me an heirloom. I shrug. No point wondering about it now; if I survive the year, I'll be able to ask the guy myself. For now, I have more important concerns, like finishing up here and finding a decent place to create a shelter for the night before dark comes again.

Opening my Inventory, I pull out the spear I made last night. Much good it did me sitting in some extra-dimensional space. I resolve to keep it closer at hand for the next time I'm unexpectedly attacked.

*　*　*

About two hours later, I'm ready to go. The bird carcass has been butchered to the best of my ability, which is simultaneously a lot higher than I thought it was and a lot lower than I'd hoped. I've cooked up some chunks, which I've split into two unequal piles: one for my pocket to eat during the day and one for my Inventory.

Through trial and error, I've realized that my Inventory isn't as simple as "cooked meat stacks" and "uncooked meat stacks." Pieces that are too distinct from each other count separately—for example, a slice of meat and a joint containing a bone. Interestingly, removing the bone worked to make the joint into an equivalent of the "slice" of meat. Each of the organs also counts as its own separate item. Not that this matters too much to me; I'd already decided not to bother with them for now. While they might be very nutritious, I can't guarantee that the organs don't contain concentrations of something that could make me ill, or even be lethal. I've also decided not to take the bones with me; though they could be useful for various crafts, I need to establish myself first and loading up my Inventory with things for "later" seems like a stupid thing to do.

Actually, if my ex-girlfriend could see me now, she'd be amazed. I've always been the kind of person to keep things for "later." I have—had—whole *boxes* full of things kept for years because they might come in handy "later." And, just saying, some of them *did* come in useful. Just not the majority . . . by far. Anyway, clearly this new world and way of existence is having its effect on me already.

I don't butcher the two corpses of those nasty crocodile things, but I do shove them into my Inventory. I debated with myself a little over that. They're very small and probably not much of a meal, but waste not, want not. If I find something I would rather keep and don't have a slot in my Inventory for it, I'll chuck them out then. But for now, I do still have a couple of slots left. So, already feeling like I've done a day's work despite the sun only being halfway towards its zenith, I set off downstream.

The forest is *really* beautiful. I know I felt like that yesterday too, but it feels like my appreciation was reduced by the dark and dangerous night when every crack of a twig or rustle of a leaf was grounds for me to grab a weapon. But now, in the light of day, I admire the natural beauty of the forest once more. As I follow the stream deeper down, the environment changes from what it was at the forest line. I'm getting deeper into the forest, and the rocks are disappearing to be replaced by plant life.

In comparison to the relatively short trees of yesterday, some of the trees in this area are *massive*, stretching far above my head. At the same time, there isn't any lack of undergrowth at all heights: trees in all stages from sapling to giant, bushes, ground cover, creepers, and even plants growing on the trees with practically no connection to the ground. It's not a jungle in temperature, but it could easily be one in terms of sheer variety and plant density. At times it's difficult to find a path forwards, but fortunately, most of the time there's enough space between plants for me to move without too much trouble.

And the *flowers*. A riot of colors is displayed before my eyes; insects busily visit each blossom, and birds chirp and cry above my head. They're alien calls, but beautiful ones. I almost understand why people might choose to go on treks in the wilderness—almost. I find that there's something about walking through a forest next to a babbling brook that touches something within me.

I'm reminded of why I started bird-watching. At one point I used to work next to a forest and would take a walk through it during my break. One of my colleagues, a girl I had a bit of a crush on at the time, accompanied me on a few occasions and pointed out the different bird species. To try to seem smarter, I actually did some research and surprised her with a few facts about the birds. The crush never went anywhere, but it gave birth to an interest in the flying creatures that share our world with us. Anyway, that's a long way of saying that I actually found myself enjoying the walk, surprisingly. Of course, given the fact that I've been attacked twice in two days, I don't allow my new appreciation to stop me from keeping an eye on my surroundings.

I don't actually see many animals, and the ones I do see seem more scared of me than I am of them, disappearing before I'm able to get more than a glimpse of them. What I do see looks utterly alien, but I sometimes catch sight of something that stirs the knowledge in my head once more, sending thoughts of traps and hunts through my head. Something to explore later.

The stream grows over time, deepening and widening as tributaries join it. Greenery starts appearing on its bed, protected from the strong currents by rocks that break up the flow. The land continues sloping downwards, and the river starts to cut through parts of the earth rather than just flowing over it, having gained enough force to actually start making a real difference to its environment.

I greet the new change with gladness as my survival knowledge tells me that this increases the chance of finding flint nodules, or potentially even rarer metal deposits. Not that I really hope for that. Even if I do find iron or something, I'm in no way equipped to do anything with it and won't be for a long time. The stream cuts more and more into the land until it's actually starting to drop as waterfalls at points. In one of the pools formed, I see the silver flash of fish and take a mental note of the area. Interestingly, when I check my Map afterwards, the stream has been added, and at the spot near where I'm standing there's a little symbol that looks like a fish.

Maybe I can add things to the Map intentionally? It's worth experimenting with later, but since I don't know if it's possible to remove things once added, I'd rather wait until there's something I genuinely want to add to it. Since I can't see anything nearby that could be a particularly good shelter, I continue walking.

By the time the sun is past its highest point, my stomach is rumbling and growling loudly. I decide to take a short break.

After finding a good spot, I take a seat with my back against a rock near the stream. The rock has been sitting in the sun and radiates pleasant warmth into me.

With my Inventory newly replenished with food, I allow myself to eat my fill. Of course, the combination of the sun's warmth, my full belly, and the poor night I had last night has a soporific effect, and it doesn't take long before my eyelids start drooping.

Just a few minutes, I tell myself, leaning against a rock and closing my eyes. *I won't sleep. I just want a few minutes to rest my eyes, and then I'll get going again . . .*

CHAPTER ELEVEN

Stabbity Stab Stab

I wake feeling disorientated, my muddled brain taking a few moments to straighten things out. I'm staring up at the sun—or, at least, at the sun through the dappling effect of layers upon layers of leaves. Large green leaves attached to trees. The effect is beautiful, but I soon realize that there's something wrong. There's a heavy weight over my shoulder and across my chest. Something is trying to wriggle its way between my back and the rock—that's probably what woke me.

I sit bolt upright in reflex, unintentionally allowing whatever it is to wrap itself fully around me. I struggle to breathe as a constriction tightens around my chest.

Looking down, I see my assailant: a large snake, or snakelike creature, has wrapped itself around my body and is squeezing rather uncomfortably hard. As I start struggling instinctively, it reacts by swiftly burying its fangs into my shoulder, the pain knifing through me every time it constricts a little more. *I sure hope this variety isn't venomous,* I think as my mind races, my fear transforming into anger like a burning ember becoming a bonfire.

"Get the hell off me," I shout, or wheeze, rather, as it's already constricting around my ribs rather hard. Fortunately for me, it hasn't trapped *both* of my arms—my left arm managed to escape the quick movement it used to complete its constrictive loop.

Another point in my favor: I've learned to keep my knife handy by now. It was lying next to my head when I was prone on the ground, so I scrabble for it with my left hand. My right arm is trapped, which isn't ideal, but I've learned in the last few days that if it's my life at stake, a lifetime of being right-handed means nothing.

With one arm pinned to my side, I have to let myself flop back down on my back to reach my knife.

After managing to get a grip around my weapon, I stab at the snake's nearest coil. The position is awkward and if I'm not careful, I'll stab myself instead of my attacker. Of course, anger and fear make it difficult to be precise; at the same time, they do make each blow stronger. Just as my restricted oxygen starts impacting my vision, I feel something give under my knife. The majority of the snake body goes limp.

Dragging in a breath of precious oxygen, I start wriggling, trying to push the deadweight off me. The head with its fangs still buried in my shoulder makes that task even harder and more painful. Succeeding in freeing myself after a good few minutes, I pull the head of the snake off in disgust and stamp on it to make sure it's dead. *Take an afternoon nap in a murder forest. Great idea, Sherlock*, I think sarcastically to myself as I stand there panting with the effort. Well, I suppose I'm not feeling sleepy or muddle-minded anymore. *Adrenaline: better than coffee.*

Casting Lay-on-Hands, I watch as the two stab marks from the snake's fangs heal over before my eyes. Within a short moment, my skin is unmarked. In some ways the quick healing is almost disorientating—my mind thinks the injury is still there even as my eyes say something different. There are things I could do with a dead snake, so I just stick it in one of my few remaining Inventory slots. I hope that what they say about snake meat tasting like chicken is right—*if* I ever get hungry enough to try it out. With the area clear, I just walk the few steps to the river to have a drink and rinse my hands.

Time to go. I've been asleep for longer than I wanted. Checking to make sure I haven't left anything important behind, I continue walking downstream.

The forest is still bright and deceptively peaceful. I find it hard to relax, though. Waking up to a giant snake trying to kill me is not a way to find my inner calm. Even with the adrenaline gone, I'm still antsy, jumping at every rustle and crack.

Man, I need to find some way to control this or I'm going to go mad in days. And I can't afford to go mad. Losing my sanity means losing my reason, and losing my reason means dying. *I don't want to die!* It seems so ironic considering where I was standing only a few days ago, but if this deceptively peaceful battleground has taught me anything, it's that my desire for survival is a lot stronger than my desire for death. Hopefully, that desire is enough to keep me alive.

When the attack comes, the flicker in my peripheral vision allows me to avoid it. Barely. I've been trudging next to the river as it winds its way gently down the mountainside for several hours now. So far, the coast has been pretty clear. Very few creatures have entered my field of vision, and none have tried to attack me. I've almost started to relax. Almost. But I can't forget that this place is perilous, far more so than Earth. My experience earlier with the snake proves it.

At the sound of snapping branches, I flinch. Swiftly putting my back to a tree, I stare around myself suspiciously. I'm heading through a dangerous part of the forest—a dense section of vegetation composed more of bushes than trees. There's still plenty of space to walk, but there's also plenty of cover for any ambusher. Plus, I haven't heard any birds singing in a while, an indicator that there's a predator around.

I grip my rudimentary spear more tightly and lift it so it's more of a weapon and less of a walking stick. It goes quiet for long enough that I start to relax again, wondering if perhaps it was just some other prey animal with the same fearful hope as me: that it has gone undetected. I'm not that lucky.

The creature—*creatures*, I should say, realizing what they really are, leap at me from the bushes surrounding me. I flail around with my rough spear and knife, alternately trying to knock them out of the air and stab at them. I'm not a pro in dual-wielding, though, and any hits come more from luck than skill. Or perhaps we could say that they come from probability; if I flail fast and hard enough, I'm bound to hit *something*.

I curse loudly as something bites down on my skull. Liquid runs down the side of my head as a stinging pain shoots through me.

Dropping the knife, I reach up at the thing and *pull*.

It doesn't want to let go. I have to yank several times before I get it free. I'm pretty sure a good chunk of hair has gone with the wretch, but at least it's not biting my head any longer. Throwing it to the ground, I try to stamp on it, but the bugger is too fast and scurries out of the way before my foot lands.

In the meantime, three others have attached themselves to my leg, foot, and calf. I shout again, very tempted to bludgeon the painful leeches.

Unfortunately, I know that if I swing my spear at them like a staff, I'm more likely to hit myself than them. This is not a good matchup. They're fast, agile, and too small for my wild spear swings to do more than hit one out of the air every so often.

In the meantime, they've broken skin in multiple places and I'm starting to look painted in red. The bites aren't deep, but they're painful, and even these small attacks could be serious if I lose too much blood. I need to work smarter, not harder.

Temporarily dropping my weapon, I slap at the creatures. Though I'd gladly take killing them, I'll willingly accept just getting them *off*. The little monsters avoid my grasping and flapping hands, choosing to leap away from me. I do hit two of them, but they recover and jump away as I reach for them to wring their scrawny necks.

For a moment I am free of new pain, though their previous bites sting and ache. With a brief window of space, I take a few moments to think through the situation. When moving, my attackers seem to be claws and teeth attached to flashes of green. I have no chance of determining their numbers. Hitting them out of the air isn't working. Maybe playing bait would work better? If nothing else, it should get them out of the bushes and allow me to have more of an idea of what I'm dealing with.

Swiping up the knife and spear I dropped on the ground, I take two steps to put my back to a tree. There I pause, tempting them to come at me across open ground rather than darting in and out of the bushes as they have been doing so far.

They're approaching a little more warily now that that they can't just leap out of a bush, I have the opportunity to see my attackers. They're some bizarre cross between lizards and weasels; they have the shape and approximate size of a weasel but look more like a small monitor lizard. As one opens its mouth, I get to see that they have sharp, backwards-hooking teeth. Then they leap for me again and I have no more time to think.

Now that they're not swiping at me in fly-by attacks, they settle against my flesh, biting my legs, their teeth managing to pierce the denim of my jeans. The agony shoots up my legs, the sensation joining my bank of things I never want to feel again. *Is that one* chewing?

But I just grit my teeth and endure through the agony, wanting all of them to be present before I act. Since no more parasites have attacked in the past three seconds, I guess that this pack is limited to the seven nasty creatures currently attached to my legs. *Right, time to deal with these obnoxious weasitors.* Dropping my spear, I use a lightning-fast movement to grab the weasitor currently gnawing on the flesh of my right calf just below my knee. It's slower to detach, thanks to its deeper bite, so this time I succeed in getting a hold of it.

Squeezing its kicking rear legs, I pull it out perpendicular to where its head remains attached. With my other hand I stab at it over and over again until it's dead. I don't remove its teeth from my flesh—yet. I almost paid the ultimate price for making that mistake with other attackers. The others have realized they're in danger and are already detaching themselves. Not fast enough to prevent me grabbing another of them and killing it, though.

They disappear into the bushes like the vermin they are.

"Oh no, you don't," I growl.

Casting Lay-on-Hands again, I pull the dead weasitors out carefully, unhooking their needle-sharp curved teeth from my legs rather than just pulling my flesh with them. Then, pretending to be weak, I lean back against the tree, slumping down to one knee.

Fortunately for me, these creatures are pros at ambushes but amateurs at spotting bad acting. They jump at me again, this time aiming higher than before. I slam one against the tree at my back when it makes the fatal decision of latching onto my shoulder blade. I know it's not dead because I can feel it wriggling, but it'll have to wait until I'm done with its friends.

I trap another under my elbow against my side. When it sinks its teeth into my sensitive side, protected only by a thin shirt, I shout once more at the pain. Agony, really, but what's new?

Then I snatch a third out of the air as it leaps at my head and stab it with my dagger, its guts spilling out to slide down my wrist. Grabbing at one of the only two still free, I manage to catch it with the tip of my dagger just as it jumps away with a small chunk of my flesh in its mouth. *Stabbity stab stab. Another one bites the dust.*

With a growl, I slam my blade into the one trapped under my elbow, wriggling my dagger until I feel it go limp, its spine severed. Leaning backwards with my full weight and then some, I crush the one behind my back until it stops wriggling. Twisting round, I make sure it's dead with a knife through its skull; grim satisfaction spreads through me.

Presuming there were seven in this pack, there's only one left alive. If it knows what's good for it, it will stay *far* away from me. Right now, unless it could get me somewhere vital, it's not much threat on its own. I still wait for a while, my senses remaining on high alert. Nothing. "Huh, perhaps it's smarter than its friends," I say to myself, cautiously hopeful. I just wish they had been smart enough to maybe, well, *not* attack me in the first place.

Leaning against the tree, I cast Lay-on-Hands again, then a second time. Unfortunately, it doesn't seem like the effects stack: twice the mana is taken out, but only six health points are restored, barely over what one cast can do.

It's better to let the magic of each heal-over-time finish first before casting again, I conclude. *Otherwise, I just end up wasting mana.*

I probably need to let my health and stamina refill a bit too. Still, I've made it through another fight, and my opponents have not. Taking a moment to relax, I pull out some food and water.

After my health, mana, and stamina have refilled themselves, I pull myself together and continue walking. I need to find a decent area to make a shelter, after all.

With all the dangerous situations I've encountered so far in this world, I'm really feeling a desperate need to have somewhere safe where I can *relax.* Whether I'll be able to find something suitable in the next few days, I don't know, but I can't help feeling that my sanity's on a bit of a knife's edge. The few weeks before ending up in this world were far from stable or good for my mental state; being in constant life-or-death encounters is only degrading my sense of well-being even further.

The stream continues and the waterfalls start getting higher and higher. I find a couple of caves created by the waterfalls, but quickly decide that they're unsuitable for shelter: they're not big enough, and I, and all my stuff, would just be permanently wet.

As the stream descends—a river now, really—more and more fish start crowding the pools and more and more animals the banks. Well, not crowding, exactly, but in the first three hours of my walk, I only saw two animals come to drink, and that was a pair of deerlike creatures. In the last hour, I've seen about ten, and one of those was clearly a predator hunting the others. I pause at this point, hesitating over the decision I need to make. Should I carry on, despite there being more animals and, therefore, more risk of encountering something I can't handle? I've been attacked three times today and almost died twice already. How long is my luck going to hold out if I keep going? How long before I encounter an enemy that is either too strong or too numerous for me to survive?

But then, I still haven't found anything suitable for a shelter, and that presents its own dangers. The snake, after all, was proof of why a proper shelter is an absolute must. Not to mention the mini crocodiles this morning; though, there I suppose I *was* dealing with a bleeding carcass. It's not surprising other animals were attracted to the site. It's a hard decision. I haven't found anything I could easily turn into a shelter, which means I'd need to either build my own or go looking elsewhere. Building a shelter will take time, time in which I am not protected and am at my most vulnerable. Also, to build a proper shelter will take tools that I don't have, meaning I need to spend even more time ahead creating the tools—and the tools to make the tools. Sure, there are some quick-build shelters I now have in my memory, but they're equally not particularly protective, not even from weather. Looking elsewhere without going downstream means leaving the water's edge. I'm not keen to do this because I know water is going to be so essential to so many of my pursuits, and running water is even more useful. However, going downstream brings me back to my initial fear, that of encountering a predator that is much better at killing me than I am at killing it . . .

Sighing, I decide to stop for the day. It's already almost time for sundown, and I'd rather have the time to build a little shelter for myself tonight. It will be better in terms of both warmth and protection, especially given the proximity of potential predators. I really need a good night's sleep. I'll think about the dilemma overnight and, hopefully, come to a conclusion by the morning. All of which poses the question: what kind of shelter and where should I build it?

CHAPTER TWELVE

Vigilance

Making a decision that a shelter right next to the river doesn't seem like the best of ideas, I start looking for a spot a little more distant. I don't know what creatures come to drink here, so putting myself close enough for them to catch my scent would not be a smart move. Frankly, I'm probably lucky that nothing attacked me last night considering how I was both near the stream *and* on the ground.

It's intellectually interesting to note how the new survival knowledge I received yesterday has taken a fair bit of time to sink in—I definitely needed to sleep on it. It's only within the last few hours that the knowledge has been telling me important information about how to choose a good place to make a shelter.

I settle on a spot between the trees about fifty meters away from the river—close enough to easily avail myself of the fresh water and far enough that I shouldn't be within easy hearing or sight range as long as I'm quiet and hidden. Which brings me to my next job.

First, I find a tree with a crook just a little more than a meter above the ground. Then, I pile dead leaves into a cushion and lay one of my coats over it to make the "mattress." Searching for a long branch, I find one that's about two and a half meters long. *Perfect.*

I prop it up in the crook of the tree to make the backbone of my shelter. Next, I hunt for some smaller sticks, which I prop up against the backbone as its "ribs." Continuing with smaller and smaller branches and then twigs, I flesh out the walls of my shelter. After that, I find some dead, low-growing plants that look rather similar to bracken. To put the final touches on my makeshift shelter, I pile as many dead leaves over the whole structure as I possibly can.

My "memories" tell me that this should be a pretty warm shelter and that it will even stand up to light rainfall as long as it doesn't last too long. It won't be much use against a heavy downpour or protracted rain, nor can it protect me if something decides to come investigating. Still, I have to hope that the plethora of natural materials will disguise my scent enough to make the structure completely uninteresting.

Ideally, of course, I'd be off the ground, but I really don't know what kind of beasts roam around up there, and falling out of a tree is definitely a valid concern. And making a platform out of branches would take too long. Instead, I'm going for something that they just won't care enough to come near but that is big enough for them not to simply try to walk through—I hope. I also hope that a forest like this won't have the equivalent of rhinos or elephants, who really don't care what's in their way.

It may seem pretty simple to make, and really, in terms of required skill and tools, it is. But it still takes me enough time that the sun is already setting by the time I'm done, and I'm exhausted. I've never done this much physical work, and I think gloomily of how much more I have ahead of myself. I try to cheer myself up by thinking that I'll soon be a supermodel, but that doesn't work when I know I've got a good year before I'm going to *see* anyone.

I dine on bird flesh, which is pretty tasty, and a few of the beans. It's more satisfying than my previous night's supper and the temptation to go back for more isn't so pressing. I'm cheered further by the discovery that the meat is still hot—clear evidence that time doesn't pass in my Inventory, or passes very slowly.

After washing up, drinking from the stream, filling up my canteen, and relieving myself, I decide to go to bed. No doubt it's not much later than seven or eight in the evening, an hour I would normally be spending on watching TV—or working—but I'm bushed.

There's little for me to do once the light disappears, anyway: I still don't have a torch and I haven't lit a fire. Sliding into my shelter feet first, I pull another coat over me and then pile more leaves in the opening, almost blocking it off completely.

Despite my memories telling me that it would be the case, I'm still surprised at how quickly the temperature rises in my little cocoon of leaves and how comfortable it is. Much better than the previous night of lying directly on the cold ground with one side freezing and the other burning. It increases my desire to create a proper shelter in which I can be both comfortable and somewhat safe.

I actually sleep pretty well in the end, certainly far better than the previous night. Sure, I wake up a couple of times when something comes snuffling too close for comfort to my shelter. Once, my heart started pounding when I realized that the beast was probably less than a meter away from my face.

Fortunately for me, it didn't come any closer, so I made it through the night with my face intact. I hurt, though; my muscles are protesting at the amount of unusual effort they've been subjected to. After crawling out of my temporary shelter, I scratch absentmindedly at the days-old stubble covering my jaw. I actually brought my shaving equipment with me, but can I be bothered to use it? Not really. I've always been clean-shaven—the job sort of required it—but maybe it's time for a change.

I pull my hand away and cast Lay-on-Hands, sighing with relief as the aching subsides. Munching on bird flesh and beans again—I have plans for the seaweed—I check my status screen. Nothing much has changed. The Energy I've accumulated just by surviving has pushed my progress to the next level to fifteen percent, but that's all.

Slightly disappointed, I'm about to close the screen when I notice something else: the amount of Energy being absorbed per hour has increased from five to seven units. I decide to keep checking at different intervals during the day as I walk to see if it increases further.

Then, with a bit of dismay, I realize I forgot to absorb another knowledge stone yesterday. *Damn it! An opportunity wasted!* Still, maybe it's not so bad. I hadn't realized how much time it would take for the knowledge from the previous stone to settle. Putting some of the methods and information from it into practice, like building this shelter, actually really helped with that. It makes me question the order in which I should absorb the stones. Tracking would probably be the most useful one next as, even if I'm not intending on actually hunting creatures for now, knowing which areas to avoid would be quite good information. As for the hunting stone, I had originally planned for that to be my third knowledge stone.

As it is, though, I've got enough food for a few days, and, frankly, I haven't got any tools for hunting. Not that I've done it before, but I can't imagine that a knife alone will be much use. No, I'm going to have to invest time in making tools, which means I need to have a stable home base.

That pushes hunting down the priority list, possibly by as much as two weeks. Food will be getting a bit low by then, even if I miss lunch, but maybe if I test some of the local foliage, I'll find some bits to supplement the meat. Suddenly I regret eating the bird meat as, otherwise, now would be a perfect time to start the test.

Sighing, I once more push my regret to one side, reminding myself that it won't help anything. Even so, I can't help the way it brings my mood down.

Still, I think, trying to cheer myself up, *I've been attacked every day so far; no reason that that should change. Meals on wheels.*

Then I wonder why I ever considered that the thought of regularly being attacked would actually cheer me up instead of depressing me more. And, actually, that's a good point to consider. I don't have a stable base to rest in; if I react badly to something and end up being sick, I need to have somewhere I can hide, which will protect me from animals that might take advantage of my vulnerability. Not that that makes me feel better *either* since it just reminds me of how brutal this new place is.

Forcing myself to think of something else, I tentatively decide to absorb the System lore stone tomorrow—while it isn't necessarily something with immediate application, it might hold some key secrets to my new existence, without which I will make some (more) mistakes. The tracking skill stone ends up not being as information heavy as the woodcraft one, and I manage to escape with just a bad headache that eases fairly quickly. It does make me look at the world differently, though. Things that had previously been simple marks are now transformed into indications of various animals' passage.

I look at the ground near my shelter and find the tracks of whatever animal came close last night. Just from the marks it left behind, I can tell it's some sort of small pig or boar, about fifty kilograms in weight, which had been rooting through the leaves in search of food. My mouth waters a bit as I think about bacon. Shame that that's still a long way off.

Right. No time to waste—I've got a lot to do, and the day is only so long. After packing my coats back into my Inventory, I walk to the stream for a drink and a quick wash. Filling my waterskin, I drink deeply and then refill it. Looking thoughtfully at the pondweed, I wonder if I *can* actually start testing it for edibility. Not by eating it but just by testing whether it is irritating on contact. I figure that if I just let it touch my skin, I shouldn't be risking it interacting with what I've already eaten. Plus, if there is any irritation, I know it will be the plant as I've eaten both bird meat and beans with no ill effects. And it shouldn't have me ending up bed-ridden just from touching it, surely? Deciding that it's a good idea, I reach in and snag a leaf. Fortunately, this stuff is pretty common, so if it turns out I can eat it, I'll have a plentiful supply in the stream.

First, I inspect the leaf. It doesn't have any tell-tale signs that often indicate poison. It doesn't have hairs, nor does it exude milky or almond-smelling sap. It's not brightly colored either. Though, of course, those signs might mean nothing in this strange world, one that's beyond the scope of both my own knowledge and of Nicholas's knowledge stone. I'll just have to be careful with the next steps. I rub the leaf against the skin of my inner forearm, gently at first. Waiting a few minutes for any initial symptoms to emerge, I look around myself.

It's another beautiful day, though this one is a bit more humid than the previous. Fingers of fog drift between the trees, but they are nowhere near thick enough to block out the sun. Birds are chirping, and I can see a couple of animals downstream drinking. They're those deer analogues again. I say deer analogues because they have long legs and slim bodies and are pretty graceful and quick to jump away when danger threatens. That seems to be the end of their similarities, though, as they seem to be reptilian in type. Though . . . they're moving pretty fast. Could they be warm-blooded? Is it possible? Lizards would normally be moving slowly at this time of the morning, not having had the chance to warm up in the sun . . . A question for later.

Time's up. I check my skin carefully, looking for any hint of irritation or tingling. Nothing. This time I rub the leaf more vigorously on my skin, making sure to get some of the sap from inside the leaves on me. Again, I wait for a few minutes by the stream, just in case there's a quick reaction that requires me to wash the area off pronto.

After the minutes have gone by with nothing appearing, I drop the leaf in satisfaction. I'd better leave eight hours just to see if there is any further change, but if all goes well, I'll eat a small amount of this tomorrow morning. Of course, that assumes there will be more pondweed wherever I am by tomorrow morning. I did see a fair bit of it yesterday, so I'll have to hope that the trend holds true.

With that thought, I set off downstream. While I walk, I take the time to notice all the little marks of animal passage. Here's an imprint in the mud at the edge of the stream—a small animal, perhaps up to ten kilograms in weight, alone. There's the mark of a predator sharpening its claws on a tree—an ambush predator, most likely. Possibly one that uses the treetops as its coverage.

I look up, reflexively flinching back. There's nothing up there, but it does remind me to keep watching *all* around myself, not just my field of vision at eye level. My vigilance gives me enough warning to cover my face with my arm when an attack *does* come.

Something swings at me, and I dodge out of the way blindly. Stumbling away, I chance a look and see . . . something. It's really weird: a dark, formless mass clinging to the branch above me, with a long spiky tail that it had swung down at me. How am I supposed to fight *that* thing? I can't reach its body, not even with my spear, and I'm not going anywhere near that tail. The way the light glints wetly on the spikes makes me wonder if they're coated in some sort of poison.

I watch it warily as it curls its tail up, and then . . . goes still. Is it some one-hit wonder or something? Maybe. It's certainly not trying to pursue me; it's just lying there in wait for its next potential prey.

Seriously weird, I think to myself, shaking my head as I cautiously move away. If I had some sort of long-distance weapon, I'd probably try and take it on. I'm not keen on leaving creatures that have tried to kill me alive to try again in the future. Unfortunately, that would take more time than I really want to waste; I'd rather just keep going. Live and let live. But I'll keep my eyes on the trees above, that's for sure. Rock-dropping birds, mini crocodiles, ambushing black blobs . . . What other weirdness does this new world have to threaten me with?

CHAPTER THIRTEEN

Skin of my Teeth

About when the sun hits its zenith, I decide to stop for a quick bite of lunch. Bird meat again, of course. I hesitate but, ultimately, don't eat any more of the beans. I only have a handful left, and I'm hoping that since they have only been dried, not cooked, they might actually grow. According to my new encyclopedia of plant knowledge, samova beans only take about four weeks to grow to the flowering stage and then another week after that to produce beans. Less than that in an Energy-dense area. I don't know whether seven units per day counts as high or low Energy for an area, but I guess it's worth a shot. I doubt these beans would grow on Earth at all.

Having paused for a short time, I suddenly realize that I have a bit of a nagging feeling, like I've forgotten something or that I need to check something. My brow furrowing, I think through my tasks for the day. *What could I be forgetting?* I concentrate on the feeling and am suddenly hit by inspiration.

Opening my status, I see what the cause of the feeling is: I've got a new message. Briefly taking note of the rise in my Energy accumulation—up to seventeen percent—I mentally click on the message box and select the new message.

Congratulations!
You have worked hard on your Endurance and have earned a point. Would you like to apply this to your status?

Y / N

Hell, yes, I think, eagerly agreeing. A surge of energy goes through me, and I see the five in my status screen next to Strength tick up to six. That makes me frown a little in confusion—I thought I got the point in Endurance? But then there *is* no Endurance in my status screen . . . I then also note that my stamina maximum has increased to thirty from twenty. Does that mean that Endurance is a subcategory of Strength? Well, I suppose it must be—being able to move and continue moving for a long time is primarily due to muscle conditioning, right? Then what's the other subcategory? I guess there has to be one because my stamina went up by ten after adding a point, but I only have thirty stamina for six points. Force? Lift ability? I also see something else that makes my frown deepen. My progress to the next level was seventeen percent before . . . now it's two percent. Has upgrading my Strength/ Endurance actually eaten into my progress? *That settles it,* I think grimly. *I need to absorb the System lore stone next.* But that will have to wait for tomorrow at least. For now, I need to keep going.

It's getting late. I need to choose a place to stop for tonight before the sun actually touches the horizon, but I still haven't found anything promising in terms of shelter. I'm beginning to think that I'm going to have to create my own again, but I haven't quite given up yet. One more day, I figure. Tonight, I guess it's going to be another dead-leaf shelter, if I can even summon up the energy to do that much—I'm tired. It's been a long day of walking, being wary, and the odd fight or almost fight. In the afternoon, I was attacked three times—three times more than in the morning! If nothing else, it's proof that the increasing Energy density, which my status screen attests to, also means increased density of creatures.

It's at that moment that I realize I've stopped paying enough attention to my surroundings. The hairs stand up on the back of my neck, and I freeze in place; in the last forty-eight hours I've learned to listen to my instincts.

It's fortunate I did—an ambush hits the spot where I would have been standing an instant later. The attacker comes close enough that I feel the brush of its whiskers on my slightly outstretched hand. For one moment it feels like we're suspended in time. I stare at the creature, and it stares back at me with golden, vertically slit eyes. I gain a sense of the creature in that snapshot of time, and it's one of the least reptilian I've come across so far. It actually looks rather like a big cat, a lion or tiger or something similar, but its nose is a bit more elongated, and its tail is a plume of feathers. It also has wings, though they're clearly not anywhere near big enough to fly with, only spanning about a foot or two in length while the animal itself is about three or four feet long. It has four legs, and mottled brown, beige, and black fur transforms into scaly, clawed legs and feet about halfway down. The claws are more reminiscent of a bird of prey's than a cat's, but the shape of the foot is clearly designed to run rather than grasp.

All of that passes through my head in the unmoving instant when I am practically nose-to-nose with a predator that probably outweighs me and is definitely stronger than I am.

The moment passes and I whip my hand back to grab my knife as the raptorcat lunges towards me. My spear is out of position. At the same time as grabbing my knife, I dodge to one side, only just avoiding the bite. It's almost not far enough, and the raptorcat manages to snag the edge of my jacket—even that unintentional yank almost pulls me off-balance. I gulp, seriously thinking about trying to run. The problem with that is that the raptorcat is probably faster than I am. As the raptorcat wheels about to launch another attack, I manage to get my spear into a better position for jabbing. The one-handed attempt is more than clumsy, but it makes the raptorcat flinch. That gives me enough space to stab at it with my trusty knife. Unfortunately, I don't hit it, but the attempt still makes it duck sideways.

I wheel around, backing away a bit, which helps me to mostly avoid its next lunge. Its teeth catch for a moment in my shirt, and I take advantage by stabbing it in its eye. It lets go and backs away, shrieking loudly. I wince both at the piercing sound and in sympathy for the pain. In response to its cry, a series of snarls rumbles out—from the trees around me.

My stomach drops and I dare to dart a glance around me to either side since my opponent is currently crouched down and rubbing at its damaged eye with one foreleg, whimpering a bit. To my horror, I see five other shapes, only discernible from the trees around me because I now know what I'm looking for. I've walked straight into a trap!

To hell with this—I'm not confident about my odds against *one* of these beasts. No way can I do anything about *six* of them. Frantically, my mind flashes through the few options that could possibly extricate me from this dire situation. *I don't want to die*, a voice whimpers in my head. I growl at it mentally. Much good the sentiment will do me now!

Then, like a lifeline thrown to a drowning man, I have the spark of an idea. It's a chance . . . Which is more than I could say about staying here.

I back away slowly at first from the approaching predators, then suddenly make a break for it when one of them looks like it's about to leap at me.

Zig-zagging, dodging right, dodging left, and running all the way, I no longer feel exhaustion weighing down my limbs. No, instead they're alight with fiery ants crawling under my skin at the thought of those sharp teeth sinking into me at any moment. My spear snags briefly on a bush as I run past, so I drop it rather than risk it slowing me down. It's one weapon less, but it's not going to do me much good against six of these predators. It's replaceable; I'm not. *Runrunrunrunrunrun!* It's all I can think about.

The snarling beasts at my heels are getting closer. I don't dare take my attention off the way ahead of me to see *how* near they are—in fact, I'm not sure I want to know—but I can tell from the sound of jaws snapping in close proximity to my precious body that they are gaining on me. It's only been a few seconds since I started running, maybe ten at most, but if nothing changes, they're going to succeed in bringing me down within the same amount of time.

I leap over logs, dodge trees, avoid sliding in mud by the skin of my teeth . . . My terror gives my feet wings, but I know it can't last. As if it can hear my thoughts, one of the beasts leaps forwards just a little faster and its teeth catch in the back of my shirt. Fortunately for me, it's only barely, and when the beast yanks back, its teeth rip a hole in my clothes rather than tug me off my feet. But it still makes me stumble a bit.

A new wave of cold fear goes through me, and I manage to turn the slight stumble into a jink around a tree, but I'm already fading. I surpassed fear what feels like ages ago, my mind falling into outright panic, but somehow the terror in my thoughts is still able to kick up a level. I'm not going to make it: I'm gasping desperately for breath, and even the adrenaline-fueled strength powering my limbs is running out. *Where is it?* My eyes frantically scan everywhere around me, looking for the only thing that could *possibly* offer me survival and the chance to see another dawn.

There! No sooner have I seen the hole between a tree's roots than I throw myself towards it, hoping that it's deep enough—and has no other occupant worse than the pack of raptorcats behind me.

The entrance is tight, and I throw my knife forwards rather than risk it snagging and preventing me from moving. I have to wiggle and heave myself forwards to get my shoulders through, and then again to get my bum in. Of course, with the beasts so close at my heels, that means I don't go unscathed.

I feel the agony of teeth closing in my flesh, and it's only by applying my full strength that I'm able to tear myself free and succeed in pulling myself into the hole that's barely bigger than my own body curled up.

I've left a chunk of my leg behind, so I quickly cast Lay-on-Hands three times in quick succession to stop the bleeding and start healing the wound. The raptorcats aren't going to let go of their prey so easily. A snarling head appears in the hole and snaps at me, its forelegs scrabbling at the ground, aiming to snag me. I snarl back at it, completely *done* for today, and stab at it continuously with my knife.

After gaining several wounds without even reaching its prey, the raptorcat backs off with an aggrieved growl. A new head takes its place, and I repeat the same actions with the same result.

By the time three of them have backed off, four of the pack injured at my hands if I include the first one I met, the group of raptorcats seems to give me up as a bad job. Pack? Maybe I should say "pride" with how feline the creatures seem to be. With some more angry noises, I hear the pride set off. Even when it's gone silent out there, I don't move. First of all, the creatures have already proven themselves master ambushers—what's to say that they're not setting a trap for me now?

Secondly, I'm not in a fit state to fight off any *other* attackers. There's no way the predators of this godforsaken world would pass up the chance to have a nice bloody and limping human for supper. Besides, this little space isn't so terrible, and I did need a shelter . . .

In fact, I consider even making this into a more permanent one, but then decide against it. The fact that it hasn't been claimed by something else indicates there's a problem—in fact, that's why I didn't investigate it when I passed by the hollow earlier: I thought it might already have an occupant and had no desire to risk starting *another* fight. Besides, if it ever rains in this place, it probably floods. Still, it will do a good enough job for tonight. After all that "excitement," I just lie in the little burrow, recovering. I cast Lay-on-Hands until my wounds heal, then take advantage of the time to drink a bit from my canteen and chew a few chunks of cooked meat. I need it to replace the blood I've lost, not to mention needing the time to mentally recover from once more staring death in the eyes.

While I lie there quietly, I decide that if I don't find a place tomorrow that will make a decent shelter, I'll give up and *make* one. Clearly I'm starting to get into areas that are too dangerous for me to venture into without significantly better equipment. Still, maybe I should make sure I'm not near raptorcat territory when I do choose a camp. One bright spot, though: I've earned a point to Dexterity. Accepting the point means leveling up is further away; gaining a point might mean the difference between life or death if I meet another raptorcat tomorrow. Should I take it or not?

CHAPTER FOURTEEN

So, What Is This All About?

The next morning dawns bright and early, but I'm fully awake seconds after opening my eyes. As I learned from my snake alarm the day before yesterday, a near-death experience is an even better stimulant than a strong double espresso. This time it's a horrific cross between a snake and a millipede that makes me shriek at a pitch far higher than I would ever willingly admit to. But honestly, who could stay quiet when waking up to a long, thick creature with sharp legs walking over one's jean-clothed legs? Especially when it buries its sharp fangs into one's thigh at the slightest hint of movement. Fortunately, or not, depending on perspective, I've been in so many of these life-or-death situations by this point that after a brief moment of panic, I get down to dealing with it.

Grabbing my knife with my right hand, I sit up and try to gain some sort of purchase on the creature's body with my left, pulling it away from me as hard as I can. It reacts by coiling in close to my body as tightly as possible. Its bladelike legs slice through my clothes and into the flesh below, making me shout. Gritting my teeth, I bring my knife up to counterattack, stabbing upwards at its body. It's armored with chitin, so I try to jab between the hardened plates to reach the softer flesh below. It's a race between whether I will get in deep enough to damage something vital, or blood loss from my many, many wounds will take me down first. I cast Lay-on-Hands quickly, which helps; the slices in my skin aren't very deep, but they are bleeding rather heavily and there are just so many of them.

All the while, I keep jabbing my knife, finally managing to knock off a scale and stab into the flesh of the beast. By this point the snilapede has decided that I'm too tough as potential prey and tries to make good its escape.

I grit my teeth at the feeling of sharp feet pulling their way out of my wounds, the small barbs on them doing even more damage. The snilapede is fast, all those legs a real advantage, but I'm faster. Or, at least, I've stacked the deck to my advantage by grabbing its tail before it can completely disengage.

It whips around to attack me again, but this time I'm ready. I grab its head and shift so I can put my knee on it, stabbing again and again into the small patch that lost its scale. Pinned by its tail and head, it writhes as much as it can, but not enough to make any difference to its fate.

By the time it stops writhing and just twitches, clearly already dead and just waiting for the muscle spasms to catch up with reality, I'm panting and weak.

Collapsing to a half-sitting, half-lying position next to my attacker, I spam cast Lay-on-Hands, fighting against unconsciousness.

Blood loss is taking its toll, but I've—hopefully—got myself past the most dangerous point. Fortunately, I never lose consciousness completely, nor does anything attack me while I'm helpless. I guess still being mostly protected in the hollow under the tree helps. It does confirm my decision that this is no good as a potential shelter, though. I'm glad I decided to take the Dexterity point last night, even if it cleaned me out of all the Energy I'd collected since taking the Endurance point; who knows whether my improved motor control was part of what enabled me to kill this new foe.

My weakness passes after a time, my multiple casts of Lay-on-Hands both healing my wounds and helping me replenish my blood supply. At the same time, I gnaw on bird meat and drink water to supply the nutrients required for healing.

After some experience through the last few fights, I've concluded that Lay-on-Hands can't magically—*ha!*—produce blood, but if I eat something while casting it, it will convert the nutrients in what I'm eating into blood.

When I'm feeling better, I push myself to my feet and shove the beast corpse into my Inventory; I figure that those legs will be useful as fishhooks at some point, considering the backwards pointing barbs that made such a mess of me. Sighing a little at the blood covering me and the numerous rents in my clothing, I crawl out of the burrow and head towards the river. I reckon these clothes are no good for anything more than bandage strips, once properly sterilized, or cleaning rags.

My clothes were already ripped in several places by the encounter with the raptorcats last night, and this latest attack has practically torn them to pieces. Any more damage and they'll be falling off me.

This world sure is hard on clothing. If things continue in the same vein, I'll be reduced to wearing the hides of the animals I've killed like a proper wild man before the end of the year, despite having brought half my wardrobe with me!

After cleaning up, I eat some more bird meat. It's getting a bit boring, but I'll take boring over hunger, so there's that. While I gnaw on my roughly cut and half-burned chunks of meat, I grab a long stick lying nearby. It's not as good as my old spear: it's not quite as straight. Still, there aren't any other sticks around that look suitable, and I need a new weapon. No way am I going back to the raptorcat territory to find my old one!

It doesn't take too long to carve a point onto one end, and I'm not disturbed while I do so. I haven't made a fire, so there's no way of hardening the point right now—if I make a fire tonight, I'll do it then. Since this area seems pretty peaceful for now, I decide that as long as I'm careful, I should be able to absorb the next stone. Sitting near the water is as safe as I'm going to get right now, so I take out the System lore stone and activate its absorption.

Compared to the other stones I've absorbed so far, I'd say this one is between the woodcraft knowledge stone and the tracking skill stone in terms of mental load—probably more like the tracking stone than the other, but unlike the tracking stone, the load is from the depth, not breadth, of knowledge. And I think the fact that it's all so new makes it harder. Actually, I know that now.

I . . . suddenly understand so much! Like the fact that Nicholas obviously didn't think my Intelligence score would be as low as *six*. He was probably expecting it to be eight or nine; that would be sufficient to allow for one stone per day, though only just. I'm abruptly glad that I forgot to use the tracking stone yesterday. I suppose I'd better be glad that the mental load on it was so low, otherwise it would have meant that I'd have wasted a fair bit of *this* stone's knowledge. As it is, I know I've lost some of the information despite following Nicholas's instructions.

Still, I'm glad that I absorbed this stone *now*; hopefully, it will stop me making more mistakes like that one. For certain, I'm not going to absorb the hunting knowledge stone for at least two days. That should be enough time for my new knowledge to settle and my mind to be ready to accept further information.

I stand up, then set off downstream again, my mind going over what has abruptly been shoved into my brain even as I keep a watch out around myself for potential attackers.

So, what is this all about? In short, Energy. I suddenly understand the concept far better than I ever did before. Actually, the idea in itself is nothing ground-breaking—when I thought about Energy before, I'd gone back to my school days in physics class: kinetic energy, potential energy, chemical energy, and so on. And these are indeed forms of Energy, but peripheral ones, something like the aftershocks of an earthquake rather than the earthquake itself. The fact is that Earth doesn't have *Energy*-energy in quantities big enough for us to notice it, as Nicholas said. Or maybe it's what we would consider miracles? I don't know.

Anyway, that's not relevant—I'm not on Earth and may never be again. By itself, Energy flows in, out, around, and through *everything* but seems to particularly collect in living creatures. The higher the Intelligence level, the more Energy is held within, which explains why Intelligence is the modifier for my mana pool.

Though, on that point, the reason why Wisdom is the modifier for mana *regeneration* is because Energy and mana are not the same thing: just as the food we eat—chemical energy—has to be converted into kinetic energy for our muscles to move, so mana has to be converted from Energy. That said, I'm still a bit unsure as to why *Wisdom* would be the modifier; either I've lost that bit of knowledge by absorbing the stone at the wrong time or it was never present in the stone to begin with.

So, Energy collects in everything but in living beings especially. The problem is that living beings can't *do* anything about that. But then what was that whole thing about Intelligence and Wisdom?

Apparently, that is where Classes come in. When I absorbed the Class stone, I absorbed more than a status screen and Skills: I absorbed a metaphysical structure and storage container that's interdimensional in a way that makes my mind tie itself in knots even considering thinking about it, let alone actually pondering on it. I quickly stop—I have no desire to give myself more of a migraine than I already have from absorbing the stone.

The storage container accumulates Energy, either through natural absorption, which I guess is my seven units— actually, eight—an hour, or when I kill another living creature. Apparently, part of the Energy held by the victim goes to its killer while the majority is lost to the world around. Hence why Nicholas talked about hunting to collect Energy for the debt—and presumably why he gave me the hunting knowledge stone and tracking skill stone to begin with.

Fun fact: apparently, a little Energy remains in the flesh of the creature for some time after its death, so eating it within that time can increase Energy gain. The time apparently depends on its "tier," though the knowledge doesn't go much into that. All it says is that tier one beast carcasses lose half their Energy in the first *hour*. Extra fun fact: some parts of the body, like the organs, are more Energy-dense than others, and special preparation can increase the amount of Energy absorbed by multiple times. So maybe I shouldn't have ditched the bird's organs. At least I still have a number of corpses in my Inventory, including the body of that weird scaled rabbit that attacked me soon after lunch yesterday. *That* one in particular was a bit of a nightmare, giving me flashbacks to watching an iconic film years ago. Despite almost seeming like a harmless herbivore, it had two sets of razor-sharp teeth, which had latched painfully onto my arm.

It would have bitten out my throat instead if I hadn't caught a flash of movement out of the corner of my eye and managed to block it with my arm in time. No way was the creature going to get away without being eaten after that. I take far too much pleasure at the thought of cooking the wretched creature on a spit; by the time I had pinned it down to kill it, I was bleeding heavily in five places.

Then again, apparently, whatever the Inventory is made of is rather anathema to Energy. My stones were okay there because they are stable, self-contained weaves of Energy. Fortunate, as the thought that I might have inadvertently "wiped" my sole hopes of survival, like a hotel key card put too close to a mobile phone, makes my stomach swoop unpleasantly. Something as unstable as uncooked meat, however, stands no chance. Key point to take home—immediately cook and eat the organs of worthy foes, if at all possible, but accept that my supply of emergency food in my Inventory is not going to improve my Energy stores in any way. I suddenly wonder whether my phone or Kindle have been badly affected by being put in the Inventory. Deciding that the answer to that question is worth using a bit of battery, I pause, checking around myself first for danger. It looks clear around me, even when I stare suspiciously at the branches above my head. Satisfied that it doesn't look like I'm about to be jumped, I pull my backpack out of my Inventory and dig in it to find my phone.

CHAPTER FIFTEEN

Killer Chickens

Holding down the power button, I find myself unconsciously holding my breath. The screen stays black for what seems to be far longer than normal, but just as I'm on the verge of giving up in disappointment, it turns on. I let out my breath with a sigh of relief. After letting it load just to check everything's fine—it is—I turn it off after looking at the clock.

Apparently, it's past four o'clock, which means that the days here are significantly shorter, a bit longer, or, in the transition between worlds, I lost a lot of hours—or gained a few. Or maybe my phone, disconnected from the satellites, isn't reliably keeping time. Again, I shrug, though I consider briefly turning the phone on again around this time tomorrow just to see what changes it records. Then again, if my meat is kept in stasis, wouldn't my phone be also? So even if it does have an internal clock that works independently of satellites, it's probably not going to help me.

Still, my phone's working, I say to myself thoughtfully as I turn it back off, return it to my backpack, then return it to my Inventory. *Is that because it was in the backpack, or is electrical energy not affected by the Inventory space in the same way Energy is? Or is it because it's powered by a battery?* Just another unanswerable question to join the list. I'm certainly not going to test whether it was protected by being in my backpack by putting it directly into my Inventory! That said, I suppose that later I could test whether an organ loses less Energy by being in a backpack . . . Something to think about later, I guess.

I push myself to my feet and start following the river again. This time I'm going to keep close to its banks—on the opposite side of where I accidentally wandered into the raptorcat ambush. At that point I'd been keeping the river in sight but not walking next to it since I'd been afraid of predators there. It's ironic that in trying to avoid the predators, that's exactly what I found. Hopefully, they're not anywhere nearby since I don't want to stop following the river entirely.

While I walk, I keep a careful eye on everything around me. I'm walking at half the speed of yesterday, hoping that that will be enough to spot danger *before* I walk into it. While I walk, I let my new knowledge trickle through my mind.

Like the question about *why* I want to collect Energy, and why my store went down by fifteen percent for each point I accepted yesterday that increased a stat.

While I could blithely say that I want to collect Energy to level up or to pay my debt, that's not really *why*. It turns out that just as Energy can be converted into mana, it can also be converted into any other form of energy.

Sounds simple, right? Not so.

Having an overabundance of energy, regardless of the type, is not necessarily helpful and can in fact be detrimental. It turns out that even before the Class system was discovered, humans in Nicholas's world had discovered various ways of storing Energy and then using it to enhance their bodies. It seems they were trying to copy animals, which appear to have a natural ability to use Energy to develop themselves. Unfortunately for them, the average result looked more like a victim of serious radiation poisoning—or worse.

Cue the discovery of the Class system. Though the stone's information didn't go into detail about who made the discovery or how, it was clear that this was a game changer. Now, instead of people essentially dumping Energy into their bodies and hoping that it will improve them, the Class structure transforms the Energy into more appropriate forms and then directs it to improve the specific stats that the Class user, aka "Classer," has chosen.

Obviously, the way that each of these stats is improved depends on the stat. The three physical stats—Strength, Constitution, and Dexterity—are improved by changes made to the physical structure of the body.

As I'd suspected, Dexterity is about the capacity of fine motor skills, but also the flexibility of the body and, to a certain extent, its fast-twitch muscles.

Constitution is about the body's toughness—hence this stat being the basis of the body's health pool—and is characterized by density of bones, thickness of skin, durability of organs, sensitivity of senses, and so on.

Strength can go either towards high weight or long duration—in other words, Power versus Endurance, or a balance between the two.

I have the answer for why, when I arrived, I had five stat points in Strength, but only twenty stamina units: my efforts at the gym tended towards lifting weights as heavy as I could manage, encouraging the building of muscles towards Power rather than Endurance, which skewed my ration a bit more towards the former. Thanks to receiving the point yesterday—probably from all the walking I've been doing—I now have a balance between the two.

Contrary to what I thought, there are not three mental stats, but two: Willpower is apparently a "soul" stat, and the information on how this is improved is missing—I just have to accept that the Class system somehow uses Energy to improve my Willpower.

Intelligence is easier to understand. Energy improves the physical structures of the brain, rendering the user more capable of forming and maintaining neural connections. In short, the higher my Intelligence level, the more information I can absorb and access, as I'd already theorized. My thought process should become quicker and more streamlined, and my memory should improve. Little wonder that this stat determines when I should absorb a knowledge stone. How it also improves my ability to store mana, the stone doesn't tell me.

Wisdom is another stat that is a little hard for me to conceptualize. As well as somehow deciding the conversion of Energy, it's also something to do with the connection between me and my surroundings . . . *My aura?* It makes me think of those New Age tree huggers when I think of "aura." Though, I have to admit that "magic" wasn't exactly something I ever thought could exist either. Now, improving stats happens in two ways: on level-up and after effort, the latter of which I've experienced. On level-up is pretty obvious: every Class comes with a certain number of stat points per level depending on the rarity of the Class. The most common Classes award one or two points per level; the rarest can offer up to ten. The stone doesn't seem to include a list of Classes and their rarities and I can't find it anywhere in my status screen.

Actually, didn't that letter Nicholas sent me say something about the Class stone? I lean against a tree, open my Inventory and pull out my backpack—I put the piece of parchment in there for safe keeping. A few minutes later, I'm mystified. It's not there. What happened to it? Did it dematerialize into golden dust like the table did? Or did I accidentally leave it somewhere? I frown. *That's . . . annoying.* There were other things I wanted to reread there too. Sighing, I repack my bag with the items I took out, then set off walking again.

Well, I guess I'll have to find out when I level up how many stat points I'll have available. It seems like it should go without saying that the more points awarded on level-up, the better, right? Yes . . . but that's not the whole story.

Improvements don't come for free. Take the other method of improving the body: actually putting some effort into it. For example, when I was offered the opportunity to improve my Dexterity and then it used some of my stored Energy. In essence, I had worked my body hard and had already made some improvements to my agility when learning the hard way how to dodge and keep ahead of a group of hungry predators.

The Class system in my body recognized that and also recognized that I had sufficient Energy stored to support a stat improvement. Upon agreeing to the improvement, the System took the Energy and directed it to finishing off the improvement I'd already started. Had I refused the improvement, nothing would have happened, but after more time, perhaps another few days or weeks of work, I would have reached the same stage by myself, and my Dexterity stat would have grown to reflect that. In short, it's a shortcut—exchanging Energy for time and effort.

The same is true on level-up: the whole reason I have to gather Energy at all to level up is because I need to accumulate enough in order to support however many stat points I will use. Thus, the downside to rare classes: someone who has access to ten stat points on level-up will have to accumulate a lot more Energy than someone with a very common Class. Why not just get a common Class and then work out to increase stat points independent of level-ups, then?

Apart from the other benefits to a rare Class such as more powerful Skills, there are two good reasons why it is more desirable than an easy-to-level one.

The first reason: there's a limit to how much someone can raise their stats by working out, whether that's physically or mentally. At a certain point, the human body is incapable of improving further, and Energy is needed to go into "superhuman" realms. So, in some ways, it actually makes more sense to do as many "natural" improvements as possible, although it may delay leveling up. That way, when I use my level-up stat points, I will be improving my body past where it could function naturally.

The second reason is that on a general basis, increasing stats on level-up is more efficient than individually, and the more stats are increased at one time, the more efficient the process is. It's like the body is already awash with Energy, so only a little more is needed to effectuate change.

However, this seems to be affected by a huge range of factors including how much potential my body has to improve, how much I have already improved the stat, and how much effort I've already put towards improving that stat without Energy. So, when stats are low, it can actually be "cheaper" to raise them naturally— that is to say, by using the shortcut rather than a level-up.

However, from what I can see, most people in Nicholas's world start with better stats than I did—ten in each is an average. So, the notions of "cheaper" may not mean exactly the same to them as it does to me. However, what's clear is that it's probably most efficient for me to get to ten points in each stat naturally before leveling up.

There's another factor to consider, though. While ideal situations are good to think about, the memory of just how outclassed I was when running through a forest being chased by raptorcats returns and reminds me that I may have to compromise a bit too. There's no point in having the potential to get as many points as humanly possible if I'm dead.

Realizing that I'm walking through a dangerous forest without really paying sufficient attention to my surroundings, I get my head in the game and back on a swivel. Digesting the new information I now have access to can wait. I've got to find a place for a shelter.

I've stopped for lunch, sitting down near the river when I hear it, a noise that doesn't fit my environment. The sound of birdsong and the crunch of woodland creatures minding their own business has long faded into the background for me. This sound draws my attention because it's nothing like the normal backdrop of the forest. No, this noise is more like a . . . snicker. A giggle. And not a merry, innocent one either.

I look up and freeze. Not more than a few paces away something is staring at me with its head cocked to one side. It looks like . . . a chicken, if chickens stood over a meter off the ground, had plumage in shades of green and black, and the regard of a predator. Wait, scratch that. Chickens *do* have the regard of a predator when they see a bug or seed they want to eat. This bird's beak looks like it will do significantly more damage than a chicken's, though, being far more hooked and serrated. But the worst thing that I notice as I slowly and carefully look around myself is that it's not alone. Apparently, *these* killer chickens hunt in *packs*.

I turn back to the one at the front of the pack and don't take my eyes off it as I reach for my knife and spear. This . . . is going to suck. I know it. *Oh well, at least I'll have more meat to add to my stores.* If I survive, that is. Being surrounded by probably about fifteen of the things is *not* a good start.

The chicken opens its beak and makes that weird snicker-giggle again. The next moment it springs towards me, running with its head down and its tail out. I absentmindedly note that its tail is almost twice the length of its body. Its function comes into play almost immediately as I stab my spear at the chicken . . . and miss. Its tail whips it off course and suddenly it's biting my arm.

I swear as its beak sinks in far deeper than it has any right to go. Its beak hooked in, it flaps its wings, giving itself enough lift to rake at me with its clawed legs. *Oh, that's how this creature hunts, then*, I think, my mind racing to try and work out how to take advantage of that. *It uses its serrated beak to hold on and then rips its prey to pieces.*

Of course, that's the least of my worries because I'm *also* trying to fend off the rest of them, which are attacking me from all angles with the same strategy. Clearly, another part of its hunting method is to overwhelm with numbers.

I need to get to my feet. I should have a height advantage, but this is currently completely wasted since they surprised me while I was sitting down.

Unfortunately, the number of chickens currently grabbing onto me is severely hampering my ability to push myself upright. Also unfortunately, my knife and spear are proving pretty ineffectual—I just can't get the right angle to hit the things somewhere vital, especially not the ones behind me, which represent a good half of my hangers-on. My spear is managing to sweep at a few of them, but there are so many that I just make a couple of them back off while the rest are grabbing on and tugging at my clothes. I protect my eyes as one of them snaps at my face, then shout as another manages to rip a hole in my shirt and digs its teeth into my flesh.

I stab my knife at the one biting me and it lets go, but then another two grab onto my arm. Their teeth prick me through the cloth—they're short enough that it's not much more than pricking, but if they tear my clothes, that will be another story. Not to mention that they're hampering my only short-range weapon. Sweeping with my spear, I try to knock them away. It's bloody awkward to try to do this sitting down, but the pile of them on me are *heavy.* Even if only a few are biting at a time, I just can't get the leverage I need.

It's a catch-22: I need to get to my feet to get the right sort of height to deal with the creatures, but they're hampering me so much that I can't get up.

Even worse, a moment later I feel the spear being nearly wrenched from my grasp. I grip onto it tightly, but a bite on my uncovered hand makes me loosen my grip reflexively and my spear disappears out of sight. My grip tightens around my knife until my knuckles go white. If the same thing happens there . . . !

My mind races for an answer. I'm going to have to find a solution fast because currently this is a battle of attrition, which I'm doomed to lose.

CHAPTER SIXTEEN

Hearts

An idea comes to mind, but I hesitate. It's a high-risk, high-reward strategy; if it works, it could turn the fight in my direction. Equally, if it *doesn't* work, it's pretty much guaranteed to make me lose the fight—and my life. Perhaps it's the effect of all the fights I've gotten myself into in just the last few days, plus the number of times I've been closer to death than I ever had been on Earth, but the thought has lost some of its terror.

In the end, it doesn't take me that long to decide to try my idea. If I don't, I might be done for anyway—the chickens are already eating me alive, piece by piece.

Throwing myself onto my back, I shout in pain as the action makes the beaks and claws already cutting into me slice deeper. It's going as planned, though: my momentum carries me over my shoulder and onto my knees. I keep the momentum going, getting to my feet with minimal effort. It's not graceful, but it works.

The weight of the chickens still attached to me threatens to throw me off-balance, but the ones I landed on are stunned or dead, and the majority of the others were either twisted off me or let go of their own volition as I moved.

Deciding to deal with my annoying hangers-on first, I stagger over to a tree and fall backwards against it. I rub back and forth, ignoring the others biting and clawing at my legs for now. My actions manage to free me of the chickens clinging on behind me, but their removal still sends shards of agony lancing through me. I absentmindedly cast Lay-on-Hands and breathe in relief as cool energy soothes the pain a little. With that semi-dealt with, I concentrate on the chickens still in the game. I can't see my spear; I don't know where they've taken it, or if it's just buried underneath the mass of feathery bodies.

Spotting a rough stick lying not far away, I go still. It's a stick about three feet long with a larger part on one end, a growth or bole or something. Could I use that as a mace or club? Worth a try. Risking getting my face closer to their beaks and claws, I reach for the stick.

"Hah!" I shout victoriously as I get it, standing up a moment before two toothed beaks snap together where my face just was. Grabbing it by the thinnest end, I start flailing with it in both directions. I don't care that I'm probably not the epitome of grace—I have no spear and this thing is a lot more effective than my knife. The chickens end up not being fast enough to avoid my mace. They could avoid the point of my spear, which needed to be relatively precise, and the sweeping blows of it weren't heavy enough to cause any damage anyway.

The mace is a different story. It's not the perfect weapon, but it seems quite sound and has a bit of weight to it. Enough, anyway, to cause damage to my attackers, which are surprisingly easy to hurt—when I actually land a hit. With a tree to my back, my height advantage, and a weapon with a decent length to it in my hand, the rest of the fight is significantly easier. Not easy, nor painless, but now I've got my most important organs out of their immediate reach, and they have to jump off the ground to get at my torso, which reduces their mobility.

I'm dual wielding: my knife in my right hand, my mace in my left. Together, I manage to stab the chickens that bite me and swipe at the chickens on the ground. Adding in a Lay-on-Hands every few minutes, and I soon find I'm slowly improving my condition, while the chickens are being knocked out of the game one by one.

They don't seem to recognize that the tide has turned, though. In several of the fights I've had so far, my opponents have realized when they've lost their advantage, and they've tried to run to fight another day—most of the time not very successfully, but still, they tried. These chickens don't seem to have that instinct; they just keep attacking me even as their compatriots fall around me. If anything, they become even *more* fervent in their attempts to tear me to shreds.

When the penultimate bird gets slammed by my mace out of this mortal coil, the final one latches onto my leg with more ferocity than I've seen from these wretched birds all fight. I drop my mace and reach down to grab it by the neck with both hands, not caring that the knife makes the hold awkward. Wringing its neck, I pull it off me and throw it to the ground. I'm feeling lightheaded from blood loss and am nearly at the end of my strength. But, in the end, it's me standing among twitching, bleeding, and dying killer chickens. That now familiar sense of triumph goes through me, as well as a shiver of what I've come to recognize as Energy. It's a much stronger sensation than I've had after my previous fights, but then these are much worse odds than I've ever had before too.

The sense of triumph is good, but it doesn't heal my injuries. I slump back down the moment I feel reasonably sure that there are no more chickens waiting to pounce. I've been casting Lay-on-Hands in every moment I could spare during the fight, so there are only two left in the tank. But at least that means I actually survived. Casting one, I focus on stopping the bleeding everywhere. And I mean *everywhere*. My already torn clothes are hanging off me in shreds and there's not an inch of skin that isn't painted red with either my blood or the birds'. *Another* set of clothes ruined.

The only good thing is that the majority of my injuries aren't deep and most of those that were deep when first gouged have had at least one round of Lay-on-Hands to make them clot and start healing.

Pulling out my waterskin, I take a long draught and then eat some of the last cooked meat I have. Oh well, at least my food concerns are no longer pressing.

Counting this meat with the amount I still have uncooked in my Inventory, I won't have to go hunting for a good while. When my mana refills enough to once more cast two healing spells, I cast another one. I want to keep one in the tank in case of emergencies, but the second Lay-on-Hands is enough to make me one of the walking wounded rather than unable to move without worsening my wounds.

I push myself to my feet and start collecting the corpses. Counting them, I realize that there weren't quite fifteen, more like thirteen. Given their fearless ferocity, that's still more than sufficient to overwhelm most creatures. I can see why they were confident enough to attack me, and not even with a proper ambush either. Not knowing that humans tend to have weapons, they probably just saw me as easy prey. Plus, I was sitting down, which probably made me look less threatening. Or maybe animals here are just crazy—these guys probably actually had better odds than most of my attackers so far.

Now I have a moment to think, I find myself wishing that my Willpower was high enough to try using Dominate. The creatures definitely *looked* similar to chickens; it makes me wonder whether they might even have eggs like chickens. *Because if so* . . . The thought of scrambled eggs, boiled eggs, fried eggs, poached eggs, eggs with bacon—anything eggs—makes me salivate.

Maybe once my Willpower is over ten, I might come looking for them again. These can't be the only flock in the whole forest, right? And even if they don't have eggs, they're pretty vicious things and, if their lack of fear is anything to go by, would be rather good guards for me.

Anyway, I need to deal with the corpses. Remembering what I'd learned from the System lore stone, I decide to try to get as much benefit from the remaining Energy in the bodies as I can. Chargrilled chicken sounds pretty good too. Knowing that I can't, and shouldn't, eat all the meat present, I need to pick and choose a bit.

Based on the System lore stone, I figure that the organs will have the greatest density of Energy. I'm a bit reluctant to eat things like the liver and kidneys, assuming these birds have those, as they're used to process the blood and may contain unhealthy concentrations of vitamins or other substances. The hearts, however, should be fine—if the blood is tainted, I'll have a problem eating any of the meat, so I feel reasonably safe with the hearts. Still, before I can do anything with those, I have some other processing I need to do first, including getting a fire started—not to mention washing the blood off me and getting a new set of clothes out so I'm not practically walking around in my birthday suit.

Three hours later, I survey the area, satisfied with my work. It wasn't what I was intending on doing with my day, but I feel pretty productive, nonetheless. I've gathered lots of meat, which has joined the bird meat already in my Inventory. I've cooked and eaten more hearts than I've ever seen in my life. They were actually pretty tasty considering the lack of condiments.

At the same time, I took advantage of the fire to replenish both my canteen and wok with boiled water, ready to drink. I've collected lots of feathers, figuring they will come in handy later—these have taken up two slots of my Inventory as, apparently, the soft, curled feathers are counted differently from the straight wing feathers. Finally, I've got a new weapon: the branch I used as a mace in the fight. After inspecting it, I have to admit that I'm pretty impressed. It doesn't even seem to need much work to make it into a genuine Stone Age tool.

The wood is sound, no rot evident anywhere along its length. The thicker bole at its base is probably the result of a growth of some sort and makes a somewhat weighty and hard lump, which improves the stick's impact. It's a bit long for a mace, being almost two-thirds my height, but I can either just shift my hand closer to the bole for more control or trim it shorter later. It was actually just as useful in this fight in sweeping away attackers as it was with crushing them. I can imagine even more ways to make it more effective, like adding more weight or sharp pieces to the business end, but for something that's just dropped off a tree, it's almost ideal. I did find my spear buried under a couple of bodies, but I'm still going to take this mace. My efforts during and after the battle have had results. My Energy to the next level increased to a whopping fifty-seven percent by the end of the battle. Part of that was my natural absorption, but most of it was the killing.

By eating the hearts, that percentage has increased further to sixty-five percent. It just makes me grimly acknowledge that if I'm going to make any inroads to becoming stronger or accumulating Energy towards this "debt" of mine, I'm going to have to take the fight to the creatures. That's . . . not the most enticing prospect. I might have Lay-on-Hands, but the injuries still *hurt*, and I can never forget that a single wrong move could be the end of me. The thought of dying in this deserted world, unmourned, unnoticed . . . It's not a pleasant one. But if I *don't* start earning some proper Energy, am I actually increasing the chance of dying?

It may seem illogical, but I can't help thinking that so far, I've been attacked almost ten times while just minding my own business. In all likelihood, I'm very lucky that I haven't yet been attacked by something I can't handle with either my hands or my very basic tools. All of which means that with every encounter, heck, with every trip out into the woods for basic necessities, I'll increase the chance that I will encounter something too strong for me to fight off as I am now. And that means I need to get stronger as fast as possible. I need to earn those stat points. And those only come from leveling up or effort.

Another consideration: if I am the hunter, rather than the hunted, I'm more likely to be able to choose my encounter and to choose to make it more advantageous to myself. I'd already planned to absorb the hunting knowledge stone tomorrow, but now I decide to also actually go hunting, if only for some easy prey. But first, I need to find my shelter so I have a reasonably safe home base to return to at the end of the day—I can't forget how I woke up this morning, after all.

One good thing I have managed to discover is a sort of heads-up display. I had wondered at the utility of having my mana, stamina, and health in my status screen.

They're not that useful if I only ever see them in times of safety, since looking at my status in the middle of a battle would be a very bad idea.

At the thought, my absorbed knowledge from the System stone this morning kicked in and helpfully informed me of how to make these values display themselves in the corner of my vision at all times. I fixed them in the bottom-left part of my vision, as I figure that'll be the least annoying and most helpful position. There are no values, just three bars of different colors; I quickly work out that blue means mana, yellow stamina, and red health. At least it'll give me an idea of how many more Lay-on-Hands I have available in the middle of a fight, if nothing else. Plus, it'll tell me if that horribly painful wound is actually as life-threatening as it feels.

CHAPTER SEVENTEEN

The Cub and Wolvezard

My health and stamina finally full, it's time for me to continue. Unlike the snake from before, I'm actually looking forward to trying out the killer-chicken meat. *Mm, KFC,* I can't help thinking to myself. The reality will be somewhat different, I know, but a man can dream.

I head back to the river and continue walking. I still haven't seen any area that looks promising for a shelter, which is disheartening. If I have to make a shelter, which will take a fair bit of time since I have such rudimentary tools available, I need to have a suitable area to do it in. An area that is reasonably flat, near enough to water to easily access it without being vulnerable to flooding, and not completely clogged with trees would be ideal. Unfortunately, this mountainside seems pretty bare on areas with all three requirements.

Today looks like it's going to be like yesterday—fruitless and painful—until it doesn't. Rounding the bend of the river and seeing past a clump of trees for the first time, I catch sight of something ahead that makes my heart rise into my mouth in hope. For some reason the next stretch of the river on my side is pretty clear of trees. It's got a fair number of bushes, some of which are as tall or taller than me, but few of the massive trees I've started to get used to.

The land, on the other hand, rises quite steeply from about a hundred meters away from the river. I guess it's some sort of foothill attached to the mountains, which form the valley where I'm situated. Perhaps fifty meters or so from where the steep rise starts, it flattens out into a sort of small plateau area, maybe fifty to a hundred square meters in total. It might be bigger than that, though. It's hard to estimate since I can't see the whole of the area due to my perspective. It rises very sharply after that, almost a cliff face rising above the flatter area. That looks promising to start with. Then there's something else to pique my interest: if I look at the right angle, I can see something that might, just might, be a cave. If it is . . . Well, starting a shelter with a cave would save a *lot* of time. Plus, this is an ideal placement: not too far from the river and with lots of potential prey nearby.

I pant as I walk up the hill. This is far more exercise than I'm used to doing, recent experiences aside. The climb is steep but manageable without needing to resort to using my hands to help me. A few minutes later, I reach the plateau. There ahead of me is exactly what I was hoping to see. A cave. It's a strange sort of shape, but it takes me a little bit of squinting to work out why.

After a few long moments, I suddenly hit on the reason: I can't work out how it was formed. As far as I'm aware, caves are formed mostly by water erosion. Sure, you can also get ones formed by an area being sandblasted or something, but mostly it's erosion by waves, a river, seasonal floods, or rainfall. This doesn't look like it was made that way.

Although there is a stream cutting through the cliff face and disappearing beyond the edge of the plateau, there's no hint in the rocks above that this cave could have been formed by that, even assuming that the stream was diverted later somehow. Equally, it's not a shape that indicates it could have been softer rock layered between harder rock that was washed out. And we're nowhere near anywhere that could create waves. If anything, the cave looks like some giant hand came down and pushed its thumb into modelling clay to make a hollow, then smoothed out the area above and in front. Seriously.

The cliff above it is sheer in a way that no other area nearby is, the inside is even and smooth, and the mouth is big and round. It's like a drawing of a cave that might be in a children's storybook. *Is that even possible?* The sound of rustling makes me snap to attention, cursing myself for paying far too much attention to topographical concerns when I should be making sure that nothing is about to eat my face instead.

I duck down behind one of the taller bushes, lamenting the lack of trees up here, and go still. Looking through the gaps between the bush's leaves, I wait for whatever animal is making the noise to emerge. When it does, I can barely hold in my reaction.

It's just far too . . . cute! Like one of those adorable kittens from a cat video with its cute factor multiplied by ten. It's also very clearly going to be a killing machine when it grows up, but for now I can't stop my insides from melting.

It's a leopard cub or something like that, but it's really fluffy and keeps tripping over its own too-big paws even as it tries to pounce on something that's caught its attention. Like babies of any species, it's pretty oblivious to its surroundings.

That's fortunate for me as I reckon I'd struggle to defend myself against something so adorable. Yes, I'm a cat person. Should I try Taming this cub? My Willpower is still less than ten so I probably shouldn't try Dominate; though, would it make any difference that this is clearly a baby? Then a thought strikes me and makes my insides feel like they've been doused in ice water. *If there's a baby . . . where's its parent?* As if summoned by my thoughts, there's a growl from the bushes opposite me, and a cold sweat breaks out on my forehead. I'm dead. There's no way a piddly little knife is going to stand up to an enraged leopard mama! I pull it out carefully anyway—if I'm dead either way, I might as well try to go down fighting. The bushes rustle, and then a dark shape blurs out of it.

I leap to my feet and stab forwards with a grunt, my eyes closing involuntarily as I flinch away in expectation of white-hot pain tearing through me.

When it doesn't come, I crack my eyes open and dare to look at my attacker. Or at least, where I thought my attacker would be. My knife is clean, and the space in front of me is empty.

There's a growl and pained yowl. I look over to the side and see a ball of yellow and black fur, mixed with green and red scales. It takes me a long moment to process the information —all I can say in my defense is that my mind had started careering down one track and then suddenly I'm having to put the brakes on, reverse backwards, then start down a whole new track. It's not the leopard mama, coming to slay the intruder who dared come near her cub.

No, it's the *cub* that is in danger! Logically, what I should do is run away while the two creatures are fighting and continue looking for my shelter somewhere else. I don't do the logical thing. Instead, I pull my water canteen out of my satchel and throw the contents on the two animals. The sudden shock makes them separate, and I shout loudly at the attacker. It looks like a horrible mix between a wolverine and lizard, with the teeth and claws of the former and the scaly body and tail of the latter. From the way it's snarling angrily at me even as it keeps glancing at the cub, it's got the temper of a wolverine too.

My spear is in my Inventory, but I yank the mace from my belt and swing at the attacker, growling back at it. The anger within me, which has been growing for days, flares to life in my outrage. *Try to attack a defenseless, adorable cub, will you, you rabid animal? Not on my watch!* The wolvezard switches its attention fully to me and the leopard cub takes the chance to scarper, half-limping towards the cave. The time I spend checking the cub is safe costs me dearly—I miss seeing the wolvezard's approach until it's already too close to whack at it with my mace without hitting myself in the process.

Fortunately, I have my knife, so I just stab at it as it latches onto one leg. I yell loudly as it buries its teeth in me, growling and shaking its head. In turn, I stab at it, and it releases me and jumps backwards as it tries to avoid the blow. I succeed in drawing a line down its side, but its scales are surprisingly tough and deflect most of the attack. My own wound, on the other hand, is already bleeding heavily.

Cursing, I quickly cast my only magic spell and then flail at the creature with my mace. It dodges again and . . . runs between my legs?

My confusion is answered a moment later when a weight lands on my back and only my abrupt instinctive shake stops the bite from digging into the back of my neck. It pierces the meat of my shoulder instead, and I feel a sense of panic rising.

I throw myself onto my back, trying to at least knock the creature off or squish it if I can. Once more, the creature is just too fast, and I barely get my hand in front of me quickly enough to avoid it going for my throat. Instead, it gouges its sharp claws over my face even as its teeth latch onto my right forearm.

It's got my arm! I try to shake it loose, but it's strong and heavier than I can lift easily in such an awkward position. Its paw drags excruciatingly across my face once more and suddenly one eye goes dark. Ice crawls through my veins. *I hope it's just blood causing the problem, because if not . . .* But I can't focus on that right now.

I grab the knife in my left hand—it's not as agile as my right, but it's not currently being used as a chew toy either—and I stab at the beast until it releases my forearm and jumps back. Of course, it's not content with that and makes another rush at me, going once more for my throat. This time I'm more prepared and roll out of its way, trying to push myself to my feet. It's too fast. It knocks me over even as I get to my knees.

We go rolling together, probably not looking much different from how the cub and wolvezard had looked earlier, only with different colors. It snaps at any part of me it can reach and tries to disembowel me with its back claws. In return, I try to grab any part of it I can reach with one hand and stab it with the other.

Luck finally seems to be on my side as I manage to stop our momentum with my weight and pin it down enough to stab at its neck. For this, I have to sacrifice one hand to keep its jaws occupied, and I scream from the pain as it rages against my trap.

My hand is savaged, as is my lower body from its claws, but I succeed in stabbing it somewhere vital. I keep stabbing until I feel it going limp. I use the last of my strength to roll off it and stare up at the sky, moaning pitifully from agony. I can feel blood pumping out of me too—it's hit something important in my belly.

I have so many cuts and bite marks across me that I can barely even distinguish which parts hurt the most. My right eye is still dark, but that's not going to matter. I'm going to die in a few minutes. I've been casting as many Lay-on-Hands as I can summon up the concentration for, and I cast another one as my mana regenerates enough. That's it, though—I'm now clean out, and it'll take at least ten minutes to regenerate enough for another cast. My wounds are still weeping blood far faster than that. I need something with a lot more oomph if I'm to stand a chance of survival.

More oomph.

The thought sparks off an idea, and I reach weakly for my satchel. I fumble around in it with my cold, clumsy fingers, searching for the lifesaving glass vial. It isn't there. *Why?!* I turn my head to the side with difficulty and see it. At some point during our rolling, it must have fallen out of the satchel. My last health potion, my only chance of survival right now, lies a good couple of meters away, glinting in the sun.

Normally, that wouldn't be a problem. Normally, I'd just get up and walk over there with no issues. Normally, I wouldn't need to take the potion at all. This is not a normal situation, and I don't have the strength remaining to do any of that. I push at the ground weakly with my left hand, my right far too damaged to do anything but twitch feebly. I move a grand total of two inches, and that takes almost everything I have left. I lie there, my head spinning, my heart beating rapidly and shallowly, waiting for death to come and claim me.

With nothing else to do, I let my mind drift over recent past memories. They're not pleasant memories. The moment Lucy, my long-term girlfriend, called it quits because I was "more likely to marry my boss" than her. The moment she killed my final hopes of getting back together by bringing her new boyfriend to the family dinner where I was present, cutting me off from the people I considered my second parents. The moment I received the call about my father's death. The moment my boss told me I was fired.

Well, I can't say I lived a good life. Still, coming here has had one positive consequence: I might be just as dead as I would have been had I gone through with stepping off my apartment roof, but at least this way, the cub is alive.

Feeling far too weak from pain and blood loss, I'm still aware enough to open my eyes when a shadow falls across me. I look back upwards to see a massive shape standing menacingly over me: mama leopard has arrived.

I'm so fucked, drifts through my mind, the swear word completely appropriate for the situation, in my opinion. Not that I wasn't dying before, but now . . . there's not a snowball's chance in hell that I'm going to get out of this alive, even if the health potion were to magically levitate over to me. She's *huge* and not just in an "I'm on the floor staring up at an apex predator" kind of way. No, I can't get an accurate measurement of her height from my angle, but the paw that's sitting near my head is more than half the size of my torso. Even were I not injured, she'd be able to pin me down with no trouble at all. Of course, with me as I am now, all she needs to do is step on my face and I'll be done even faster than the blood loss will take me.

I grimace, chuckling darkly and brokenly, the agony that had dulled down a bit shooting through me once more with the convulsive movement. How ironic. Slain by the leopard whose cub I'd just saved. The stories I read never ended like this. A hero was always rewarded in the end. He didn't die in such an ignominious manner. With the lack of anything better to do while I die, I gaze at the magnificent beast before me. Oh well. If nothing else, I've succeeded in seeing a leopard in the flesh. I'd always wanted to go on a safari. To my surprise, the leopard doesn't take that moment to kill me but moves off to sniff at the wolvezard. Perhaps it's obvious enough that I pose less threat than a wet paper bag.

There's a chirp from the direction of the cave and a tiny figure comes barreling through the bushes. The cub bursts out of the covering foliage and comes to rub up to its mom, already making a demanding—and heart-meltingly cute—noise. The mama leopard makes a deep huffing sound and sniffs her cub, licking its head with a tongue that's almost bigger than its whole body, cleaning it of the blood that still coats its fur. In fact, the cub doesn't even come halfway up the leopard's legs—it's completely dwarfed by its parent. *Maybe its dad was really small?*

I pull my mind away from that disturbing train of thought—not hard to do as my thoughts seem to be escaping my grasp like water from a cupped hand. Or blood from my body. "Your cub is . . . adorable," I tell the great cat hoarsely, probably a bit delirious. I figure that since I'm about to die anyway, I've got nothing to lose. "I'm glad it—he? She?—didn't get . . . killed by that . . . thing." I chuckle again, though it ends with a gasp of pain. "Sure wish I . . . wasn't dying, though," I admit. I don't exactly regret saving the cub, but I do thoroughly regret that I'm the victim instead. If only I'd been smarter about the whole thing. Shows how useful anger is when dealing with a problem, right? I could have used a stone or something to attack the wolvezard from a distance—though, this ignores the fact that I would have been too worried about hitting the cub instead. I could have taken a few moments to plan a better strategy—at the risk of being too late, given how quick and vicious the wolvezard had been. Maybe my spear would have been a better weapon than my mace—except it would have taken me a couple of seconds to get it out when seconds mattered.

The leopard moves off to sniff around the site of churned up ground and grass. She pauses over the vial of health potion. "Yeah, that's a . . . health potion," I tell her. "Don't suppose . . . you could . . . pass it . . . here?" I don't even know why I'm bothering to waste my final breaths on talking to an animal, but I've got nothing better to say or anyone better to say it to. The leopard looks at me with an expression that I would have classed as thoughtful on a human being. Then, before my disbelieving eyes, she gestures with one paw and the ground beneath the glass vial *moves*.

I blink. Did that happen? The glass container glints in the sun, only an inch away from my half-decent hand, tempting me to reach out and grasp it. Is this all a hallucination brought on by my nearness to death? The fading around my vision and my increasing sense of disconnection with my limbs make it clear that hallucination or not, this might be my only chance to survive the next few minutes.

With what feels like the effort it would take to lift a car, I work my less injured hand towards the potion. My vision narrows—literally, the darkness is becoming more and more intrusive. All I can focus on is the health potion; everything else has disappeared.

Inch by inch, moment by moment, I see my salvation coming closer. I'm running out of time, the last grains falling through the sand timer of my life. My fingers are cold and numb; so are my arms. I don't have the strength to lift it. But I must. I *have to*. I tilt my head to one side and somehow get the mouth of the vial close enough to wrap my lips around it.

There's a stopper. Of course. I try to pull it out by fixing my teeth around the stopper and pulling on the vial with my hand, but I don't have the strength. I could cry. So close, but too late. I am crying. Wetness traces its way down my face, collecting on my nose before slipping over the bridge. *No. No, I'm not going out like this!*

I fix my teeth firmly in the stopper, then yank the bottle with every speck of strength that still remains in me. I feel the stopper slip loose and then pull out just enough. Shoving half the vial into my mouth, I turn my head to face the sky, letting gravity do its thing. The stopper isn't out completely, but it's loose enough that the potion starts trickling out around it. I'm so *tired*. My eyes flutter closed and not all the will—or Willpower—in the world could force them open again.

CHAPTER EIGHTEEN

Please Don't Eat Me!

When I wake up, I'm almost surprised. I thought I was a goner, that the potion had been too little, too late in the style of all the best tragedies. Or had the whole thing even happened? Had I really thrown myself into a life-or-death struggle with a vicious creature to save a leopard cub? A cub whose mother saved my life in return. It seems too fantastical to be true, even for this strange life in which I find myself. I doubt its reality even more when I take into account that *nothing hurts.* I open my eyes. There's a break in the forest canopy above me, and I can see the bright blue sky. It's about mid-afternoon, from what I can tell. Without a watch or phone to tell me the time, I've gotten pretty good at using the cues of light, temperature, and animal noises to orientate myself. Carefully stretching, I feel no pain, but I do feel the sensations of dirt, twigs, and grass under my hands. *Okay, I'm not still numb, then.*

Testing my feet, I can feel my toes and move them. Good to know I'm not paralyzed or anything like that. Then, after pushing myself up to a sitting position, I look and grasp at my belly. It's smooth and healed, though the rips and bloodstains in my clothes attest to the fact that it really shouldn't be. Then I notice something that makes me freeze, ice going through my stomach.

My vision is strangely restricted. I can see everything I normally would to my left side, but my right side vision is . . . limited. I can see my nose and beyond it in a straight line, but my peripheral vision? I lift both hands and wave them to the sides of my head while looking forwards. My left hand I can see. My right hand . . . *No. Nonono.* I grab at my face and put my hands over my eyes. My left eye is reacting normally. My right eye . . . is not. My right eyelid blinks, and I can feel my finger when I touch the eyeball. But I can't see out of it. If I close my left eyelid and leave my right open, it's as if I've closed them both. *I'm . . . It's . . . I can't deal with this right now.* I push myself to my feet with nervous energy, then stop dead. The leopard is there, in that half-lying, half-sitting position cats and dogs take. She's watching me intently, the tip of her tail twitching every now and again. I'm not an expert in cat body language, so I can't tell if that's a sign of annoyance or interest. Or even if body language for cats on Earth has any relevance to a giant leopard several worlds away. Forgetting about my eye for a moment, adrenaline rushes through me as I go into full-scale fight or flight mode. "Good kitty," I say shakily, lifting my hands placatingly and hunching over a little, not wanting to seem at all threatening. As if something as small and puny as me could seem threatening to a killing machine like her. I start backing away, hoping I can get far enough that she will stop being at all interested in me. If she's hungry and hopes to make a nice snack of me, I'm toast. "Nice kitty."

Why did you save my cub? The words echo in my head like a resonant bell ringing in a vast cave. Is that saying something about how much or, more to the point, how little my mind is filled? Bringing my pitiful Intelligence and Wisdom stats to mind, I can't help but feel more depressed at the thought. Then I shake the thoughts out of my head. Not literally—I'm rather trying to avoid sudden movements at the moment.

Human, why did you save my cub? The words are repeated, though this time with a sense of annoyance. At the same time, the leopard rumbles for a short moment. *Is it . . . ? Could the leopard . . . ? Could it, she, be talking to me? In my mind?* Given what I've seen so far, can I really rule out anything as a possibility? And ultimately, who's going to know or care if I'm wrong?

"I wasn't really thinking about it," I answer honestly, the sheer terror curdling in my belly preventing me from finding any sort of pretty lie. "Your cub was so small and cute; it didn't seem fair that it should die just as it started to live." Well, in for a penny, in for a pound. I think for a moment, forgetting to continue slowly backing away in my pondering. "And I'm tired of worlds that destroy the innocent." It's surprisingly true. And I'm not just talking about this world, either, though the kill-or-be-killed nature of the place here is probably even harder on the young than the world I came from. Of course, it helps that the leopard cub was absolutely adorable and the wolvezard was more like an escaped experiment from a mad scientist's laboratory.

I thank you, human, whatever your motives. I had thought my den safer than it is, and I would have been most grieved to have returned too late to save my offspring. I wish to reward you, but I must know more about you in order to offer the most appropriate gift.

"I mean, you kind of already saved my life," I say slowly, not wanting to look a gift leopard in the mouth but, at the same time, not wanting to be like Chicken Little, getting lured into a fox's den with pretty words and then swiftly eaten. "You gave me my health potion." Then I frown as my memory tells me that, actually, the ground moved to bring my health potion nearer to me. That's not possible—I must have been delusional at the time. *Since you wouldn't have needed it if not for interceding on my cub's behalf, it does not count towards the debt I owe you. Indeed, the fact that you were brought so near death on her account and have earned a physical disability for your actions only adds to the weight of the debt.* I bring my hand up to my blind eye, a surge of emotions once more rising. I force it down again. For now. I say nothing and just stand there, hesitating.

Come, the leopard tells me. *Sit, and tell me how you came to be in this unpopulated world.* She gestures and the earth moves. Well, with this new evidence, I have to guess that I *wasn't* dreaming about it obeying her command before. The ground forms a low chair—nothing fancy, just a seat with a back and raised sections to either side that will work as arms. Suddenly, I realize the probable reason for why the cave looked so unnatural: she made it. The other problem with the chair is that it's also significantly closer to the great cat than I am now, even than where I started. I hesitate again. This seems far too much like the Chicken Little scenario. *Come*, she tells me again. *I promise you safety for this audience.*

After a few more moments of thought, I mentally shrug and walk towards the chair. If she's lying, she's quite capable of killing me even if I ran away as quickly as I could. Humans can't stand up to a normal leopard without armor or guns; standing up to this massive version of one with nothing more than a lumpy branch, a bent spear, and a short knife seems . . . improbable. I might as well play along with her.

Tell me, human, she says once I've made myself comfortable on the earthen chair, *how came you to this world?* I start by telling her about the object Nicholas gave me to bring me here, but then that requires me to go back and talk about why I'd be foolish enough to choose to accept a one-way trip into the unknown.

Before I know it, I'm pouring out practically my whole life story along with all the trials and tribulations I've faced since I've been here and the decisions I need to make about my future. It's . . . cathartic. A few tears escape—I'll admit it—when I talk about what I've left behind. I shudder and shiver when I think once more about how many times I've come close to death since being here. I feel fear of the future once more grip me by the throat, but this grip is looser than it has been at other times. Because instead of struggling with it on my own, I'm sharing it with someone else. It doesn't matter that this someone else is an inexplicably telepathic leopard, who might want to eat me for a late lunch—or early dinner—but just that she's *listening*. And when I've finished and my words peter out, I feel a deep relief and a lightening of my sense of self. I've missed talking to others, I realize. I'm not the most extroverted person, preferring to have a quiet night at home than go out on the town, but that doesn't mean I don't like people. In fact, the opposite is generally true, though they frustrate me immensely too. The old adage of "a burden shared is a burden halved" has never felt so true as now, even if the one I've been sharing it with is a disturbingly intelligent and communicative giant leopard.

As if on cue, a little bundle of fur half-bounds, half-limps out of the cave and snuggles into its mother's stomach. When it stops moving except for a little shifting of its paws, I realize it must be drinking milk. At the thought, red rises up in my face. I don't know why. It's not as if I would find the sight of kittens or puppies drinking from their mother embarrassing back home, after all. Perhaps it's that I've just spent a good hour talking to the leopard mother like I would another human that makes me suddenly ascribe human norms to her. I rise anyway.

"Look, I've been talking your ear off here. I'll just leave you to your . . . you know"—I gesture towards the feeding bundle of fur—"to looking after your cub."

Stay. Her mental word halts me in my tracks. It's not threatening in any way;

it's just so full of calm, implacable command that I couldn't move if I wanted to. *I haven't yet given you your reward.* I'll probably regret my chivalrous impulse, but I wave my hands in the air.

"Don't worry about it; your company has already done me a world of good. If you just agree not to eat me, I think we're good." I chuckle nervously. My nerves turn into full-blown fear when the leopard snarls a little and gets to her feet. The little cub yowling in complaint as her late afternoon snack disappears out of reach is only a little distraction from the immensity of her mother. The leopard is even bigger than I thought she was: her shoulder is above my head and her jaws could fit around it without even opening wide. Her tail is switching back and forth, and her head is lowered so it's practically level with my own.

"Look, I'm sorry for whatever I said," I squeak out. "*Please* don't eat me!"

CHAPTER NINETEEN

To Deny Reward Is to Deny the Deed

The leopard mother moves closer and then . . . nudges me with her great head hard enough that I fall back into the chair. Withdrawing a little, she slumps back into her previous position. Her cub scrambles over her, making noises of complaint until it finds the teat again and resumes drinking. I grip onto the arms of the chair with white knuckles, not sure what I can do if the great cat turns threatening again and once more wondering if her promise of safety can be trusted.

I'm not going to eat you, she huffs. *Not today, anyway.* So maybe tomorrow? Very reassuring. Not. "Can I ask what offended you?" I ask cautiously. There's a moment of pause before she replies thoughtfully.

Do you know how long I have dedicated to this cub? I shake my head. *More than fifty years already, and I will spend at least half of that again raising her into an adult.*

I stare. I can't help it. As far as I know, leopards don't have anything like that life expectancy. She notices my look. *My kind do not reproduce easily, and we grow slowly. It is a consequence of our power and natural longevity. I thought I had cleared out the nest of malakaan near here, otherwise I would not have left my cub to hunt. I heard her cries of pain and rushed back as quickly as I could, but I would have been too late. Over a hundred years, and the life of my cub would have been gone in a few heartbeats.*

She pauses and I sense pain radiating from her. I wonder if this has happened before, or something like it. *To deny reward is to deny the deed. To deny the deed is to deny its importance. To deny its importance is to deny my cub and me, and we will not be denied.* Her tone is implacable, as is the hardness of her gaze when she looks at me.

I nod slowly, understanding where she is coming from. In a way, it's not so much about what I did; it's about what that means for her. She wishes to reward me as a way of helping her feel like the scales are balanced again.

"Okay," I say in the end, "but I want it noted that my life is very important to me too, so a promise not to kill me would actually be a pretty good start, in my book." At that, she huffs in a way that I take as amusement. *Noted. In fact, I wish to offer three gifts. The first, a gift of knowledge. While we are in peaceful contact, I offer you responses to questions about this valley that I am capable of answering. I retain the right to choose whether to answer or not. For example, I know you have wondered about the increasing Energy you absorb as you descend the mountains through the forest. This valley is sought after because it is the location of an Energy geyser. The Energy fills the valley and grows significantly denser as you descend towards the geyser. However, do not be too greedy; competition over it is fierce and there are beasts nearby that even I would be reluctant to challenge.* Okay, I had already wondered about that, but it's good to have my theories confirmed—and to know the reason for the increase in Energy density. I suppose it's also useful to know roughly how strong the beasts might be. Actually, when I think about it, this offer is an *awesome* one. I just need to be cautious about what questions I ask. If I ask ones I can easily answer for myself, then I will be wasting the knowledge she's offering.

Second, I wish to offer a shelter, as that seems to be your most pressing need currently. If you wish, I can give you the location of a guardian not too far from here who you might be able to seek shelter with. You would have to bribe him or impress him sufficiently, but it's within your capabilities, I believe. Alternatively . . . Here she seems to hesitate a little. *Alternatively, I* may *be able to host you here if you are prepared to exchange oaths of mutual defense and agree to a pact of non-aggression. I shall let you think that over and give me your response later.* After another short pause, she continues with the final gift. *Lastly, I wish to give you a gift of power. Come here.*

I do so, barely even hesitating this time—I've learned my lesson about defying the massive predator. She lifts her paw, holding it out towards me. *Place your hand on my paw.* I obey, marveling once more at the size difference between us. Closing her eyes, she seems to concentrate for a long moment.

Then, something like a warm breeze goes through me and I get the nagging feeling that I need to check my notifications again. The leopard flicks her paw towards the chair, and I take the hint, sitting back down. *Check your status,* she tells me, sounding tired. Just before I do so, I see her placing her head down on her paws. Clearly, whatever she did took something out of her. Her evident fatigue along with her lack of hostility gives me a bit more confidence to divert my attention and check all the notifications waiting for me.

Congratulations!
You have worked hard on your Willpower and have earned a point. Would you like to apply this to your status?

Y / N

I hesitate for a moment, weighing up my desire to "save" Energy for my level-up versus my complete lack of ideas on how to improve my Willpower stat organically. In the end, I decide that I probably need all the Willpower I can get, especially when it determines health regeneration. *Sure,* I think. No sensation accompanies this point, but I guess it isn't anything physical, anyway. I wonder when I gained it? *Maybe it was when I managed to get the potion in my mouth despite being pretty far gone,* I muse. Well, I guess I'll never truly know. The next message isn't such good news.

> Warning!
> You have severe bodily injuries. You will die shortly without magical assistance.
>
> Next message? Y / N

Yeah, I think I'd figured that bit out, I think sardonically. Such a *useful* notification. *Next message, please.*

> Warning!
> You have used a healing potion that is not of a sufficient level to effectively treat all your injuries. Using this potion may cause half-healed injuries to become more resistant to magical healing in the future.
>
> Do you wish to use this healing potion anyway? You have five seconds to decide; no response will count as a positive response.
> Y / N

> Warning!
> You have used [low-quality healing potion]. All your injuries have been healed with the maximum efficacy possible for this potion. Not all injuries have been fully healed. Please seek a healer's advice.
>
> Next message? Y / N

So *that's* what happened with my eye. Because as far as I can work out, everything else is healed. I'll have to test whether Lay-on-Hands does anything, but something in me doubts it from that whole "resistant to magical healing" thing in the previous message. Still, I suppose I'd better be grateful that the default if-no-response option is to go ahead with the healing potion, otherwise I'd *definitely* be dead right now.

I suppose it makes sense that that's the default, though. It's not like someone in need of healing is always going to be conscious, now, is it? Quite the opposite, in fact, as I proved.

> Congratulations!
> You have worked hard on your Constitution and have earned a point. Would you like to apply this to your status?
>
> Y / N

Let me think about that . . . Duh! Constitution keeps me alive—no way I'm turning that down after my recent experience! Sure, I know I'm trying to accumulate

Energy for leveling up, but I have to still be alive *to* level up. My recent encounter with the wolvezard has definitely shifted my point of view on that. I move onto the next message.

Congratulations! You have gained a blessing! Nunda's blessing: Enduring Will. A nunda is a mighty and proud creature. Their will is powerful enough to force mountains to bend and oceans to empty. In thanks for your heroic act, Kalanthia, Prime Nunda mate, has bestowed on you a small part of her mighty will.
+10 Willpower, +20% to Willpower.
No new messages. Close message? Y / N

I close the message and access my status screen.

Name: Markus Wolfe		Race: Human	Class: Tamer
Level: 0	Energy to next level: 55%	Energy absorption rate: 11u/hr	Energy towards debt: 0%
Intelligence	6	Mana: 60/60	
Wisdom	3	Mana regeneration rate: 100u/hr	
Willpower	15+3 (+20%)	Health regeneration rate: 18/hr	
Constitution	5	Health: 45/45	
Strength	6	Stamina: 30/30	
Dexterity	4	Stamina regeneration rate: 40u/hr	
Class Skills: Dominate – Beginner 1 Tame – Beginner 1		Non-Class Skills: Lay-on-Hands – Beginner 9	

From a paltry four—five with my earned point added—my Willpower has now jumped to *eighteen*. Doing the math, I work out that the twenty percent was applied to the whole of my base stat, that is, after the ten points were applied.

Looking at the way it's laid out on the status screen, I have to wonder whether it will affect future Willpower points too, because if so . . . Well, that could make it pretty overpowered. And utterly awesome. Already my Willpower is at three times both of my highest stats, and it's *six* times my lowest.

I also notice something else: although I increased my Constitution by a point, my health pool has only gone up by five points. My maximum used to be ten times my Constitution; now it's five points less than that. Unless the ratio has suddenly changed, I guess I've got my answer about a chopped off limb or something—even this new world can't do miracles. I really, really hope that this blindness is temporary or that I find something that will heal me; the middle of this kill zone is *not* a place where I want to be disabled. I make a mental note to add some more points to Constitution.

As soon as I level up, that is. And that's another choice I need to spend more time considering: direct all my effort to leveling up and ignore any other offered stat increases, or accept stat increases at the risk of delaying leveling up? My inner desire to make the most of what's offered to me says to delay leveling up until I've gotten to twenty in each stat.

My desire to survive, however, wars against that inclination, reminding me that I only *just* survived the wolvezard. What if I'd had ten more points of mana? Or a few more health points? Leveling up is probably a quick way of shoring up my weakest points and increasing the chance that I get through this year. Closing the screens, I stare at the sky as I consider the question.

In a way, it would be easier to decide if I knew I had a safe place to sleep or not. That brings me onto the next choice I have to make: stay here with a killer leopard, follow her advice to try to bribe some "guardian" to let me stay with them, or set out on my own?

Honestly, my gut feeling is to accept her offer—Kalanthia is her name, I think, judging by the message. Yes, she might be a killer leopard—actually "nunda" or "Prime Nunda"—but so far, she's been nicer to me than my last employer was.

Giving me three times more Willpower than I started off with doesn't seem like someone planning to kill me. Not when it clearly was some sort of sacrifice. It's more than I reckon many humans would do if I'd saved one of their kids, that's for sure. Plus, she's talked about exchanging oaths of mutual defense—not the move of someone just trying to keep a snack around. So yeah, while my most paranoid self says that there *are* still risks associated with staying, I reckon that they're *far* less than those of leaving. Because what would I have to look forward to there? Dealing with some other "guardian" who might ask who knows what in exchange for their protection? Or needing to leave Kalanthia's territory, which might take me days or *weeks* if she has a territory anything like the size of the big cats' back on Earth. And that's not even considering the useful little tidbit of information she's just told me: if I continue following the river down the mountain, I will get into areas with greater and greater Energy density. "Excellent" might be the thought here; I want to grow in strength and increasing the amount of Energy I absorb is a great way of doing that. Sure, except for the fact that every other Rex, Rover, and Ratatouille will be thinking the same thing.

Kalanthia's warning about not going too far too fast resonates with what I had already been thinking. So, if I wanted to keep going, I'd have to move away from the river, thereby potentially causing myself a problem down the line. No, better stick with the predator I sort of know. Plus, that means I will have access to her knowledge for longer. In a way, my only worry is that she might change her mind at some point in the future—without warning, there would be absolutely no chance of me doing anything about it. But hopefully, the oaths she's mentioned might help with that. Plus, there's something else really important to consider. By letting me stay here, she's offering me a shelter that will be far better than the vast majority I would be able to find: dry, out of the wind, and protected from predators. What else could I want? If Kalanthia allows me to make some screens or something against the wind and bring in bedding too, it could make the cave pretty comfortable. My decision clear, I turn back to the nunda.

Arrangement

Kalanthia seems to be recovered from whatever she did to give me that blessing. Given how tired she looked afterwards, I wonder whether that phrase, "has bestowed on you a small part of her mighty will," actually means she genuinely and permanently gave me a part of herself. If so, no wonder she's tired, and that partially makes up for the fact that I've lost half my vision for the foreseeable future. Pun not intended.

Still, she looks recovered now, or less tired at least. She's watching her cub play with her switching tail, but as soon as I shift, her head flicks towards me. Those golden predator's eyes fix on me, sending primal fear down my spine.

"Um," I start, a lot weaker than I intended to sound. *Come on, Markus*, I tell myself. *You* know *she's not going to kill you. Well, you're pretty sure at least. So just go for it!* "You talked about me possibly staying here . . . How would that arrangement work?"

In what sense? That's a good question, I admit to myself, and I don't really know the answer. Taking a moment to think, I try to work out my confusion and form it into words. "You're clearly a powerful predator," I say, finally settling on bluntness for the sake of clarity. "I'd imagine there's little to threaten you around here; why would you require a pact of *mutual* defense? How could I defend *you*?"

She eyes me for a moment, the predator's look in her golden orbs making that primal part inside me quail again.

I do not underestimate you, human. I know what your kind can do. It might be that one day, one of my weaknesses can be covered by one of your strengths. I am not hubristic enough to pretend that I am all-powerful. I find my attention caught by her words there: "your kind." Are there other humans here? *Additionally, though I might be powerful, my cub is not.* That . . . makes a lot of sense, especially considering the reason we're sitting here talking at all. *I must eat, and at this point, my cub is too small to accompany me.*

"I see," I say slowly.

"So, in effect you want a babysitter for your cub while you fulfil your own needs."

I do not *want you to sit on my baby*, she retorts, a snarl that rumbles faintly in her chest heard even in her mental voice. I flinch a little at the sound instinctively but remind myself that she hasn't killed me yet or even made an attempt to do so.

My primal instincts might be getting more of a workout in this world than ever before, but I mustn't let them overcome my logical reasoning; that way lies pure savagery.

"It's a term my people use. It means someone who stays near a baby, either awake or asleep, to guard and look after them in their parents' absence."

Oh, she responds, seemingly appeased. *I have not encountered this term before. In that case, yes, I would like a person to "sit on my baby."* I don't bother to try correcting her. We both know what she means—now, at least. That adds a different spin on things; not only does it give me a better idea of her motivations, but it reassures me that she's not necessarily planning on eating me at a later date. If she wants a guard for her cub, that's an understandable reason to keep me around. There's just one problem . . . but I might actually already have a solution, depending on her.

"You say you have to go hunt. Do you necessarily have to be the one hunting, or do you just need the food?" She eyes me for a moment, and let me tell you, that is a very different experience coming from a giant leopard—nunda, whatever—whose eye is not that much smaller than my hand, when compared to just your run-of-the-mill manager. Even the really dominant ones. *I require sustenance. Where it comes from is not really important.*

"Then how about I hunt for you? I get that you need to go drink water, but what if I could supply you with as many carcasses as you need? Then you could guard your cub." She didn't respond for a moment, clearly assessing me in some way.

Why would you offer such a thing? It is surely less effort to guard my cub for a time than to spend the whole day hunting for me. I can take down much bigger prey in significantly less time than it would take for you to accrue enough smaller prey.

"That's true," I admit, "except for the fact that I'll probably be spending a lot of time hunting anyway, as I need to grow stronger. I'd like to keep the hearts as well as some of the meat for myself, and I may need to harvest some of the skins or claws or bones or other inedible bits for various things I need to make, but the, uh, 'lion's share' of the meat could be yours, if you want." She says nothing for a long moment.

It is an interesting offer, she admits after a while. *Perhaps we should make an arrangement based on mutual defense and non-aggression and then try out your suggestion as an additional arrangement. If you cannot supply enough meat for me, your role will return to "sitting on my baby" while I am hunting for myself. Does that seem fair?*

"Yes, it does," I agree. Actually, more than fair, really, especially as I'm talking with a non-human predator. "Though, I have one question." She waits expectantly. "What exactly does a mutual defense and non-aggression pact mean to you?" Perhaps a stupid question, but if I've learned anything from years of constructing contracts—and by that, I mean writing down what the contract needs to say, then sending it to lawyers to turn into incomprehensible legal speech—it's that anything not established at the start is game for unintentional misunderstanding and intentional misinterpretation.

Not that I'm expecting this nunda to feel the need to jump through a technical loophole to do something to me, but I'd rather a misunderstanding doesn't come around to bite me—quite literally. *Non-aggression: neither of us should act in any way that intentionally harms the other, applying to physical, mental, or spiritual attacks.* She takes on a look that is distinctly amused. *I will do my best to impress upon Lathani that you are not to be chewed or ambushed, but I cannot guarantee her good behavior.* Understandable, I think, considering she's a baby.

I've never had a puppy or kitten, but friends have had them; I remember one of my best friends at school coming in with long scratches on his hand. Apparently, his kitten had dug her claws in a bit too hard during a game. Thinking of that happening with a leopard—or nunda—cub, even as cute and fluffy as this one is . . . Yikes! The nunda continues, her tone regaining its seriousness. *Mutual defense: should you encounter me or my cub under attack, you should come to our assistance using your full capacity, though not with the expectation that you should die in our defense.* She pauses for a moment, then looks at me with a cold, hard stare. And let me say right now, *no one* does that kind of stare better than a feline. *That said, I cannot guarantee your safety were my cub to die under your supervision and you were to survive the attack.*

"Noted," I reply grimly. I shouldn't really expect anything else; the whole reason she's suggesting this is to look after her cub.

"So, how do we ensure that we each stick to the agreement?" I ask a little tentatively. I don't exactly want her to think that I'm not planning on following through, but at the same time I don't want to find out at the worst moment that *she* wasn't.

Have you never heard of a Vow? There's puzzlement in her voice, as if this is common knowledge. And now she's said the word, I realize I *do* actually know about Vows. The knowledge comes, of course, from that stone I absorbed. Apparently, such things as binding verbal agreements do exist in Nicholas's world, enabled, naturally, by Energy.

The Vow takes Energy to create, usually a fraction of the two individuals' Energy stores. The fraction is different depending on many factors, including the importance of the agreement to the two individuals and the power balance between them, among others. If the agreement is broken, either there's a backlash of both amounts of Energy on the offending party, or the offended party absorbs the Energy stored by the bond in compensation—the choice is up to the offended party.

I don't know how the bond knows whether it's broken or not, nor do I know how it stores it in the first place. Somehow, it just does. Either way, although it's not a fool-proof solution, it's a good start. Certainly more useful than some contracts that aren't even worth the paper they're written on—even when they are purely digital! That said, having automatic consequences that enact themselves in the case of a rupture avoids the necessity of courts. Not a bad idea. "Okay, that sounds like a good idea," I agree. I think carefully—is there anything else I'm missing? It's hard to know what unknown circumstances aren't covered by what we've already discussed because they're just that—unknown. However, if nothing else, my experience has taught me that I can't plan for everything, and that there's always a loophole someone can exploit.

The fact is, the nunda feels that she needs me, and as long as that's the case, I'll be reasonably safe. And for her, it's not like I'm much of a threat, though I could arguably be such to her cub. The threat of her vengeful retribution, however, will keep me in check around her precious offspring, something I'm sure she knows. "So, how do we do this?" I ask, deciding that since my mind has been made up, I might as well get on with securing a home base.

CHAPTER TWENTY-ONE

Literal Lifesaver

*A**m I to assume by that comment that you wish to stay here?* she questions calmly. I nod. Then, realizing she probably can't read human body language any better than I can read hers, I affirm my agreement verbally. *Very well. Simply focus your attention and intentions and follow my lead.* I'm not quite sure what she means by "focus your attention and intentions," but I guess I'll work it out. *I, Kalanthia, mate of the Prime Nunda, agree to a pact of mutual defense with this human . . .* She pauses, eyeing me. I get the hint.

"Markus Wolfe," I fill in.

. . . Markus Wolfe. If he should come under attack in my presence, I will render him as much aid as I am capable of without putting myself at risk of immediate death. This pact shall continue until we both agree to its dissolution. She then looks expectantly at me. I do my best to repeat her words, filling in her name where appropriate. At least I've confirmed that it *is* her name, as I'd strongly suspected. Next, she continues with the non-aggression pact, and I again repeat her words afterwards.

"I, Markus Wolfe, agree to a pact of non-aggression with Kalanthia, mate of the Prime Nunda. I swear that my acts shall not intentionally bring harm to her or hers, including physical acts, mental acts, and spiritual acts. This agreement shall continue until both of us agree to its dissolution." That done, I relax, suddenly feeling safer than I have since I entered this world. Surprisingly, Kalanthia doesn't look as satisfied as I would have thought considering that she's now engaged a babysitter for her kid. Instead, she fixes me with another hard look. I feel sweat break out and wonder with a hint of panic whether this is when the other shoe drops.

I warn you, Binder, that should you use any of your Bindings on me or my cub, I will willingly take on the consequences of breaking these pacts. Okay, that wasn't what I was expecting. Nor do I really understand what she's taking about. Unless . . . "Is this something to do with my Class?" I ask hesitantly. Her stare intensifies.

You are a human who thrives on bending others to your will and Binding them with chains of devotion or control. You are not strong enough to succeed in Binding me, and I will not stand for you Binding Lathani. Huh, I guess it *is* about my Class.

"I hadn't even thought about it," I replied honestly. "I haven't even tried those Skills out yet." I hesitate again. "Is it . . . Do you want me not to use them at all?" I don't really know how I feel about that idea. I mean, like I said, I haven't even tried the Skills out yet, and it seems kind of a waste not to use them at *some* point.

Besides, I had kind of thought that these Skills were ones that would help me survive; if I had a tamed animal who could fight on the front line, I could stand back and fire arrows from a distance, for example. But I'm not sure that I want to use them so much that I'd lose the first place I've found where I might sleep safely at night over them. Fortunately, it doesn't end up being an issue.

Why should I care about other, lesser creatures? She tosses her head in contempt as she responds. *I care about myself and my cub. If others are weak enough to fall to you, they deserve to be bound.*

Huh. Apparently, the law of the jungle truly is that of every creature for itself. In the end, I have mixed feelings about her clear disinterest in me dominating all others as long as she and her cub are left in peace. Oh well—something else to deal with later.

In the meantime, I have another question. The cub at the center of our discussion has been having fun playing with sticks and leaves, but I can still see the marks of the wolvezard's attack. They don't seem to be impeding her too much, but it makes me hurt a bit to see such a cute cub injured like that.

"You've said that I shouldn't use my 'Bindings' on your cub—and I completely agree with that," I hurriedly add, seeing the predatory look return to her eyes at my words. "But would you let me heal her?" At that, Kalanthia blinks.

You are capable of healing?

"I mean"—I swallow, wondering if it's a bad idea—"I haven't tried it on anything other than myself but . . . it *should* work?" I finish with an uncertain question. Kalanthia eyes me again sternly.

If you can heal her without causing any effects that will last longer than the original injuries would have, then I welcome your efforts. What payment would you desire in return?

I try to smile but my face feels a bit stiff. I'm tempted to say "nothing," but remember how she reacted last time I tried to deny a reward. "Um, I don't know. Maybe . . . help me make your cave a bit more comfortable for me?" She seems to consider it thoughtfully.

You may sleep in our cave if you wish, but I would not like to accidentally mistake you for an intruder or snack during my sleep. No, I'd rather that doesn't happen either, really. The very thought of waking up to a dreaming nunda eating me is horrifying, to say the least. *Alternatively, I can expand the cave a little to provide you with your own space. Though, I thought it was normal for humans to build shelters for themselves?*

"It is," I admit, "but I don't have all the equipment or materials that would normally be used for that, so it would be more convenient for me to have a natural shelter that I can adapt to my needs." Then I eye her again. "Hang on, are there humans around here?" *No,* she answers simply. I stare at her.

"Do you mean they're not in the valley, or there aren't any?" Because if there aren't any, how does she know all of this about humans? *There are none in this valley.*

Therefore, the knowledge I offered does not cover this subject, she answers calmly but very finally. I take the hint and change the subject.

"So, do you want me to heal your cub now?"

Yes. Please heal Lathani as long as you are able to do so without causing further harm. She turns her head to her cub and chirps quietly. The cub looks up at her, then bounds over, rubbing her tiny face against her mother's massive one. Kalanthia would be able to eat the cub—Lathani—without even needing to fully open her mouth.

Still a little nervous about going so close to a predator's mouth, I nonetheless steel myself and do so; the cub is waiting for me, and in my head, I know that Kalanthia isn't going to attack me. I just wish I could convince my heart too. Kneeling down next to the cub, I reach out and put my hand on her. She's soft, *so* soft. I almost accidentally let out a noise of appreciation but keep it back by clearing my throat instead.

Concentrating on what to do, I cast Lay-on-Hands, focusing on it going into Lathani instead of through my body. It's easier than I expected: the magic flows out of me and the wounds heal. It takes about four more casts to fully heal the small cuts. Her health pool must be *significantly* bigger than mine—those kinds of cuts would only take one or two casts at the maximum for me.

Lay-on-Hands also doesn't replace the fur she lost, so there are a few white lines and dots marking where the wolvezard's claws and teeth landed hits. Suddenly, I wonder where the creature's carcass went. I haven't seen it since blacking out.

Pushing myself to my feet, I take a couple of steps away from the two of them. Kalanthia grunts and Lathani goes running off to play—though, not without coming to rub briefly against my calf first.

I thank you, Kalanthia says, though her tone seems to be carefully neutral. *Let us now go make your shelter.* She stands and walks back to the cave, Lathani following behind in little bounces and intermittently pouncing at her mother's tail. *Too cute!* At least I'll have plenty of dopamine bursts from watching her antics, I suppose. And if she lets me touch her again . . .

As we walk, I note that there's no trace of the wolvezard except for a patch of blood that might have been mine or its—or both of ours. Maybe Kalanthia ate it? After a moment of thought, I just shrug and enter the cave. No point worrying about it now.

The cave is bigger than I'd thought. Its mouth is only just high enough to let the giant leopard pass, but then opens out both wider and higher past the mouth.

There's a pile of leaves and other bedding on one side of the cave and a pile of bones on the other. I'm torn between disgust and interest at the latter. *I can expand the cave downwards, backwards, or make a little cave to this side,* she said, flicking her tail towards the side with the bones. I give the question due consideration. Downwards is out—if there's any significant rainfall, I don't want to risk being flooded. Backwards means potentially walking past two sleeping nundas every time

I want to enter and leave. Sideways means being near a pile of bones . . . "Would it be okay if I move these bones somewhere else?" Kalanthia gives a catlike shrug.

Move them out, if you prefer. They're only there because Lathani likes playing with them even after they have been stripped of meat. She can play with them outside just as well. Okay, that sounds good. I might even put some of them to use in the various crafting activities I'm going to need to engage in.

"Can I have my place over here, then?" I ask, pointing to the side of the cave nearest the bones. Kalanthia gestures nonchalantly and I immediately see a difference. It's not an instant fix; a hole doesn't suddenly appear. No, it's more like there's a dip where there wasn't one before, and then it *magically* deepens until I'm looking at a mini cave not that different from the one Kalanthia clearly made for herself to begin with. *Is this sufficient for your needs?* She looks at me expectantly as she asks the question. I step into the hole and give it a thorough look. The space is frankly bigger than I would have hoped for if I'd tried to create a shelter myself, even a relatively fancy one. The ceiling is high enough that my head doesn't brush it once I've ducked through the shoulder-height cave mouth. It's wide enough around that I could choose to lie down in any direction and still have a little space to spare. There's just one thing . . .

"Is there any chance of creating a hole to the outside? Perhaps at this height?" I ask, indicating a height about halfway up the wall closest to the exterior. The nunda gestures once more and a hole bores its way through the rock. It's a good foot through the wall, which definitely gives me a sense of security. "Okay, perfect," I say with satisfaction. There are still multiple things I'm going to have to do to make this into a proper home, but this is an excellent start. Especially so since I haven't had to put in any back-breaking labor or time that I could spend elsewhere. Though, I suppose I did almost *die* for the opportunity, so I guess it evens out. "Thank you," I tell Kalanthia, and she nods regally. "Is there anything you'd like me to do now for you?" I check. I don't know what her babysitting schedule is likely to be, after all, and from the sounds of it her hunt was interrupted. *Now? Do whatever you wish. I have fed sufficiently despite the interruption to my hunt, and I shall not need to eat for another two days. You are thereby released from having to fulfil our agreement to sit on my baby until then.*

"All right, good to know," I acknowledge. With a flick of her tail, she returns outside with her cub, leaving me to it. The first thing I do is simply sit down. It's been . . . Well, it's been quite a roller-coaster ride over the last few days, heck, the last few weeks, all taken into account. Although I've had time to process everything, I realize I haven't really. Back on Earth, I spent far more time wallowing than processing. First the blow of my ex's announcement, then the trauma of my father's illness and subsequent death set me reeling. Being fired while I was already struggling to come to terms with reality meant that I hit the next downward plunge before I'd even recovered from the previous. And then ever since I've been in this world, I've been working more off survival instincts than much else.

I've jumped from one life-threatening situation to another, getting through based on luck more than anything else. Yes, I've thought things through, but all my thoughts have circled around what I need to do next to stay alive just a little longer.

Now, after pouring out everything to Kalanthia, probably telling her more than she actually wanted or needed to know, I feel strangely . . . lighter. Like, somehow, I'm managing to come to terms with the fact that I'm in a new world where everything wants to eat me and giant leopards can talk and do *magic*. Though, I haven't even started properly considering the fact that I appear to have been half-blinded. It's something that makes me shiver every time I think about it, which is why I'm trying not to. But *not* thinking about it is hard when I'm reminded every time I misjudge a distance or have to turn my head just to see something out to my right. Another good reason to be grateful for this unexpected shelter: I wouldn't have wanted to be facing the forest again right now.

This place is certainly an improvement on my last one; it's frankly an improvement on anything I could have built within the next couple of weeks. Plus, with the knowledge that I'm protected by the presence of a giant predator, I actually feel a little . . . safe. The paranoid part of my mind keeps reminding me that said giant predator could turn around and make a snack out of *me*, but another part protests that there's a Vow in place. *Actually, I should have received a notification or something.* I check my messages, and sure enough . . .

<table>
<tr><td>

Congratulations!
You have created a Vow with Kalanthia, Prime Nunda mate. This Vow is of: mutual defense. The duration of the Vow is: indefinite, until both parties agree to its dissolution.
You have used 20% of your Energy store to bind the agreement. Should this agreement be broken by you, the Energy you have used will be given to the other party to be used as they see fit.

</td></tr>
<tr><td>

Next message? Y / N

</td></tr>
</table>

<table>
<tr><td>

Congratulations!
You have created a Vow with Kalanthia, Prime Nunda mate. This Vow is of: mutual non-aggression. The duration of the Vow is: indefinite, until both parties agree to its dissolution.

You have used 30% of your Energy store to bind the agreement. Should this agreement be broken by you, the Energy you have used will be given to the other party to be used as they see fit.

</td></tr>
<tr><td>

Close message? Y / N

</td></tr>
</table>

Twenty percent of my Energy store? Thirty percent? *Does that mean what I think it does?*

I close the message and navigate to my status screen, letting out a despairing groan when I see it.

CHAPTER TWENTY-TWO

No Doctor, or Optician

I stare at my status screen, feeling shocked at the amount of Energy that was taken. I guessed it might be the case when I saw the messages but hoped that I was wrong. Sure enough, when I look at my status screen, I can see that there's fifty percent less Energy towards the next level. After having reached more than two-thirds of the way to the next level after the chickens and wolvezard, my Energy has taken a nosedive down to the bottom again.

Name: Markus Wolfe		Race: Human	Class: Tamer
Level: 0	Energy to next level: 5%	Energy absorption rate: 11u/hr	Energy towards debt: 0%
Intelligence	6	Mana: 60/60	
Wisdom	3	Mana regeneration rate: 75u/hr	
Willpower	15+3 (+20%)	Health regeneration rate: 18/hr	
Constitution	5	Health: 45/45	
Strength	6	Stamina: 30/30	
Dexterity	4	Stamina regeneration rate: 40u/hr	
Class Skills: Dominate – Beginner 1 Tame – Beginner 1		Non-Class Skills: Lay-on-Hands – Beginner 9	

With less than ten percent Energy gathered towards my next level, I'm almost back to square one. Then again, I notice that the Energy I'm absorbing every hour has increased to eleven units, so it's not all bad. Still, I wonder why such a great chunk of my Energy was taken. Is it because I'm so much weaker, and probably lower level, than Kalanthia? Or is it because I was in a weak position, needing what Kalanthia was offering more than she needed what I was offering? Or some other reason? Once more, it's a question I have no answer to, so I just divert my mind onto other topics.

Primary among them: what do I need to do to get my new shelter ready for the night? *Well, I have bedding, but it would be nice to have some sort of cushioning.* The leaves worked pretty well the night before last, and last night wasn't too bad in the burrow, but this is a solid rock floor. Then, I want to create a fireplace, but that will take a bit longer as I need to find clay somewhere—probably by the river, I'd imagine.

I do consider asking Kalanthia to quickly make it for me but dismiss the idea after a moment. If I'd thought about it when she was making the alcove to begin with, maybe it would have been okay, but I'm not keen on going to her now. I don't know where her limits are and don't want to push my luck. I've got a much better shelter now than I'd thought I would at the beginning of the day. Making a stove will take some effort, but it's not impossible the way that making this alcove would have been. Besides, I've still got some cooked food in my Inventory, so it's not like I'm desperate to have it *now.*

Of course, I'm going to want to make this homier in other ways: I can imagine shelves with items on them, hanging plants and animal sinew out to dry for other crafts, maybe even stretching a hide on a frame to make leather. The downside of that last one is, of course, the smell . . . *Oh well, I will deal with that when I get to it.*

For now, it seems like my immediate need is to sort out a bed of some sort. I don't really feel like going out looking for that bracken stuff I was using before, so I decide to just make a nest from what I already have in my Inventory.

Pulling out my backpack and suitcase, I rifle through them both looking for warm, soft clothing. I didn't bring a blanket, which feels like a major oversight now, but I did bring a whole load of T-shirts, jumpers, trousers, and even a dressing gown. Arranging a whole load of clothes on the floor with my dressing gown wrapped around them, I make a reasonably soft, somewhat lumpy bed. Using the same jacket for cover that I've been sleeping under the last few nights, I figure I've got something for at least the night, maybe longer. Now that I have a proper shelter, I'll actually be able to do more than just create things for survival, though those things come first, of course, and top of the list is leveling up. But that's for future-me to think about. For now, I have something else to think about. My sight.

I haven't yet tried Lay-on-Hands on my eye beyond the healing I gave myself during the fight—until I ran out, that is. That seems like a bit of an oversight. I chuckle darkly at the unintentional pun. But I didn't have enough mana when I woke up, and I've been a bit distracted since, so maybe it's understandable. Anyway, I haven't tried my healing spell, and although I'm doubtful, I figure that I might as well give it a go. Casting Lay-on-Hands, I feel the tingle run through me. Unlike every time I've done it before, the tingle doesn't focus on any particular area or areas—it just runs up and down my body as if looking for an injury before fading. I know before I open my eyes, after unconsciously closing them, that it hasn't worked.

Sure enough, my right side is still dark, and if I close my left eye, I can't see anything. Damn. I feel like there's a lead balloon inside me, dragging down on my stomach. I was really hoping that that would solve my problems.

Then I have a thought. *What if I focus in on the eye specifically?* Historically, undirected casts of Lay-on-Hands have offered low-level healing over the whole of the body, whereas directed healing has always done a higher level, though in a more concentrated area. And the Skill is called "Lay-on-Hands"—*maybe I should try touching it too?*

With hope rising in my heart, despite knowing it's still a bit of a long-shot, I try casting Lay-on-Hands while touching and concentrating on my injured eye. I feel a tingle in the area . . . then it fades. Opening my eyes proves once more that it's been a useless attempt. I slump back on my "bed." *So, this is it, is it? I'm going to be half-blind for goodness knows how long?* At least until I get to Nicholas's world, and possibly beyond, especially if it turns out that healing gets more and more difficult the longer it's been since the injury happened, which it probably does . . . It's depressing, and what's more, it's worrying. It's hard enough to survive with two intact eyes and full peripheral vision. How am I going to make it without full sight?

Despite my worries, I'm tired. I don't care that it's still light outside; I'm going to *sleep*. Closing my eyes, I prepare to do just that. However, just as I'm drifting off, my relaxed brain shoves an idea at me that wakes me up properly again.

The second time I tried Lay-on-Hands, it was different from the first. The first time, it was like the spell couldn't detect an injury. The second time, there was definitely more reaction. What if the spell simply didn't have enough time to do what it needed to do? Time—or mana. It's a bit of a leap. So far, I've been able to partially control the amount of mana I use, but I've never used *more* than ten units, and the time has never exceeded a few seconds. Even for Lathani I just had to keep spamming casts until she was healed. How am I going to overcome that block?

It takes a good few tries to extend the amount of mana used to more than ten units, and I only really do it by accident. Instead of just mentally saying *Lay-on-Hands,* I instead focus more on my mana bar, imagining it draining down and the blue indicator in my vision vanishing into my body, and from there into my eye.

That first time, I'm so distracted by my mana bar actually seeming to obey me that I don't focus on my eye, and the energy instead runs all the way around my body. It's more than a tingle; this time it's almost like an electric shock—a small one, not really painful, but definitely more present than what I'm used to. It also uses a good half of my mana in one go, so I have to take some time to recover after.

I use the time it takes me to regenerate to think through my approach. I wonder whether it would be useful to try to think about how the eye functions. I figure it probably can't hurt unless it distracts me from concentrating on moving the mana from my bar to my eye. I'm no doctor, or optician, so my knowledge of the eye is limited to what I learned at school. I know that light enters through a lens, which is what allows us to focus on near and far objects.

Then it passes through the pupil, which is a hole surrounded by a muscle called the iris. Or maybe it goes through the pupil first and then hits the lens? I don't remember. Then the light hits the back of the eye . . . upside down? I'm pretty sure that images being upside down is a thing that the brain has to deal with. Then there's the optical nerve at the back of the eye, which goes to the brain, and a whole load of blood vessels, which keep the eye healthy. Oh, and other liquids and so on that keep the eye ball shaped rather than flat. A lovely thought.

Once my mana regenerates, I cast Lay-on-Hands again, but this time really concentrate on drawing blue from my mana bar and imagine it flowing from my hands up to my eye. I touch my eye too, for good measure, and resist the urge to blink. Once my mana is in my eye, I try to trap it there temporarily. It's hard, and I almost lose control of the energy a few times when my eye starts burning and spasming in pain. It's like I've stuck an electrical rod in my eye and it's on pulse.

As soon as I feel like there's no more mana to draw, I immediately start trying to think about how the eye functions while stopping the energy from escaping at the same time. How, I can't explain. It's a feeling, an instinct more than anything visible or tangible, as realistic as holding lightning in your hands. But somehow, I know that *something* is happening, even though all logic would say it should be impossible. I don't know if it's working, I only know that it *hurts*. But I don't dare stop because what if it *is* working? What if I stop and find that I've regained half my vision? Because knowing how painful this process is, I can't see myself daring to restart it, especially if there's a risk that I could go backwards and lose what I've gained. Right now, there's nothing to lose—if I fail, I'm no worse off. So, I don't stop. I keep concentrating on my eye until it feels like it's already melted in its socket, like if I were to open my eyelid, there would be nothing there but an empty hole.

I keep concentrating even as my brain aches from the fierceness of my focus. I keep concentrating even as the pulses of energy become weaker and weaker, then die completely. Even then, I don't dare stop concentrating until every hint of anything magical has vanished. Only then do I dare relax. But I don't open my eyes.

After what I've just been through, I think that finding out I failed would be too much for me. I keep my eyes closed, swallowing back a sudden onslaught of nausea. Even as I try to summon up the courage to find out for sure one way or the other, exhaustion creeps up on me and I lose the ability to make a choice.

CHAPTER TWENTY-THREE

Self-Care

I sleep—deeply and for a long time. I wake up at some point when it's dark and quiet, my stomach rumbling. Fortunately, the Inventory seems to have a little of its own light—it doesn't light up the area around me, but I can see the items held inside it fine—so I take out my canteen and a couple of handfuls of meat, giving myself a midnight supper. Or whatever the time is. My hunger and thirst satisfied, I drop back into sleep, not waking until the next morning.

I'm finally roused by the sound of birds and the light filtering into my cave from the two entrances Kalanthia bored for me. Now awake, I don't exactly leap into action; instead, I lie still while blinking at the ceiling as my conscious mind catches up with what's been happening. So, massive leopard-like creatures called nundas, which can both talk and do magic. *Nope, nothing abnormal about that—why would I think there is? It fits right in with reptilian–mammal or reptilian–avian crossbreeds and Classes with Skills and magic healing spells . . . Magic healing spells!* I sit bolt upright, my hands clutching at my face. *My eyes! I can see!* With both of them. I wink one then the other, my vision becoming limited each time, but no longer am I left in darkness with my left eye shut. I slump back down on my bed, releasing small chuckles that devolve into relief-filled hysterical almost-sobs. I'm so grateful that it worked, that all the pain wasn't for nothing. But at the same time, why did it have to be necessary in the first place? What kind of place is it where becoming half-blinded is just an everyday possibility?

I shake myself. I might be safer than I was yesterday, but I need to remember that I'm still in a world that will kill me more easily than I can say "Jack Robinson" if I let my guard down even the slightest bit. Falling apart is going to help exactly no one. So, what should I do? Kalanthia said she doesn't need a babysitter for another few days, so I've got a bit of time. I can either work on making this shelter more of a comfortable place, including making the tools necessary for the task, or I can work on improving my weapon situation, giving myself more range. That would also require making tools first. I could go hunting and collect more Energy and corpses, which will give me resources necessary for the other two tasks. Or I could do nothing and take the day off, giving me a chance to detox from all the stress chemicals that have no doubt been filling my body over the last few days.

Wanting to have all possible information to hand, I check my status screen. My eyebrow shoots up as I see my current Energy store of sixteen percent. *I earned nine percent overnight?*

Apparently. *Which means I slept for* —I do the calculations quickly—*about fourteen hours?!* Seriously? I was *that* tired? Sheesh. Then again, I suppose I haven't really slept properly since I've been here, and I've been running around getting half-killed and not eating properly either. I have to say I feel a lot better now, though. Maybe that's a supporting argument for just staying in and relaxing for a day? Read a book, enjoy the sun? I've got enough food for several days, and water's not hard to access. And if I'm accumulating Energy even while doing nothing, I'm even arguably making progress. It would probably do my mental state some good and allow me some time to make proper plans . . . Okay, I've managed to convince myself.

So, that's what I do all day: nothing. Or rather, a day of "self-care." Apart from when I venture back down to the river to replenish my water stocks and then create a fire to boil it, all I do is get a couple of my favorite feel-good novels out, find a good position in the sun, and *relax.* Nothing tries to kill me; nothing tries to eat me—only if you don't include the baby nunda, which seems to see me as a new toy she'd like to play with. And by "play with," I mean "chew and pounce on."

Fortunately, her mother distracts her with something else after not too long, allowing me to go back to my reading and chilling. It's not a complete waste of a day; by the time I go to bed, I'm relaxed in a way I haven't been since the last time I went on holiday. When nothing is trying to eat me, this world is peaceful in a way Earth really isn't. Or at least, in a way my life in a capital city wasn't. The only sounds are those of nature, the sun is warm and benevolent, and the food is organic, albeit boring. Plus, I've gained another eleven percent of Energy, bringing my total up to twenty-seven percent, and I have a plan for the immediate future. In the end, I've decided that my first priority is to shore up some of my weaknesses by earning some stat points. I'm banking on leveling up offering more than just a couple of points, but I figure it's likely. I know I could earn the points myself with time, but I want to actually live long enough to do so. After I've gotten to level two, I'll reconsider rushing to the next level, but for now I've decided not to accept any more earned stat points unless they are to Constitution, since that seems to be the stat most likely to directly improve my ability to survive.

To that end, my first priority is to do a bit of hunting—enough, at least, to push me to the next level. It shouldn't take too long; if I gained forty-five percent just from the killer chickens and then an additional eight percent by eating their hearts straight away, it shouldn't take me too long to get to the next level. Plus, although I'm still not too sure of the day length here— I'm increasingly sure that it's slightly longer than that of Earth's—if I go by a day length of twenty-four hours, I should gain approximately fifteen percent just from absorption. In short, although I don't really want to face opponents like the killer chickens again, hunting is still likely to be much more profitable Energy-wise than anything else, but whatever I do, my Energy store will still be increasing.

Another part of my "day off" has involved processing more of the information I absorbed earlier through the various stones, the System lore stone in particular. From this, I've determined that although it might be a good idea for me to rush towards level one just to help my short-term survival, after that I probably ought to take my time going towards level two, accepting status points until it starts to "cost" more to increase them that way instead of via level-up. At the moment, it takes me fifteen percent of my current Energy store to upgrade a stat by the "shortcut" method. That means that, currently, unless my level-up will give me seven or more points, it's "cheaper" to upgrade them through part effort, part Energy. However, the System stone has made it clear that this state of affairs won't continue. Although it doesn't outrightly state it, I can work out from what it *does* say that the higher my level, the more

Energy I will need for the next level. Equally, the only reason my stats are costing me only fifteen percent of my Energy store is because they're so *low*—under ten, specifically. Ten is an important number on Nicholas's world because it's the average starting stat value for an adult. I can only speak about "adults" because no one knows what a baby's starting stats are since the only way of truly seeing one's status is to absorb a Class, and that can only be done after puberty has finished, for some reason.

So, ten is the average starting stat value, but that doesn't mean everyone has exactly that. As I've personally experienced, the starting stat values can vary depending on what actions the person has taken prior to gaining a Class. Someone who's skipped gym day on a regular basis to hit the books might end up with a fifteen in Intelligence and an eight in Strength. Or someone who played hooky at school in order to go hunting might have an Intelligence level that's lower than ten but physical stats that are above it. It's clear from their experiences that stats lower than ten cost less than stats above ten, even when gained within the same level. The numbers don't seem to be consistent between people—I guess it's based on Class— so there's no way of me knowing how much exactly it might cost me. However, there is a recorded example of someone using twenty percent of their Energy to increase a stat from nine to ten and then the next increment costing them twenty-seven percent, without them having changed anything else.

Which means that after reaching level one, I should prioritize increasing the stats that are below ten by hard work and an Energy shortcut rather than assigning level-up points to them. Of course, as things stand, that's *all* of my stats except for Willpower. The comparison did make me feel depressed for a while, but then, as I processed more information, I started to build something of a theory: my poor starting stats aren't my fault—or not entirely, anyway. It's because of the dearth of Energy on Earth.

After all, I wasn't so obviously deficient on Earth: I had a decent job, was in reasonable shape for my age and lifestyle, and had normal-level motor skills. I'll admit I was nothing out of the ordinary, but that cuts both ways; I wasn't as clearly sub-normal as would be the case if the average stat value on Earth was the same as on Nicholas's world.

My theory is cobbled together from flashes of knowledge that I happened upon while searching for information about stats. Unsurprisingly, this is something that the scientists—or as they're called in the other world, "scholars"—have spent a fair amount of time studying. Even though only people with Classes can be definitively quantified, by comparing their capabilities with those of non-Classed people, they've been able to get more of an idea of baselines among those without the benefits of leveling up.

One example was of a farmer, or at least someone who definitely looked like one. In the memory, he was hog-tying a cowlike creature and heaving it into a cart. By hand. Alone. I'm no expert in cows, but unless it was some sort of miniature calf, which it wasn't, it has to have weighed upwards of eight hundred kilograms, probably even over a ton. This cow looked pretty well-built, so I'm going to peg it at approximately one metric ton. According to the scholars, it was determined that he probably had fifteen points in Strength and that he was fairly average for an adult man who had had a hard labor job all his life. Now, I don't know all the details of weight lifting, but I don't reckon that lifting a ton is something the majority of farmers could do. Heck, I don't even know if Olympic athletes regularly lift that sort of weight. And even if they do, the point is that the farmer wasn't anything significantly out of the ordinary. As an ordinary guy, I was able to press upwards of 100 kilograms in the gym, but even on a good day I never got past 130. Obviously, as on Earth, farmers are generally tougher and stronger than people who spend their days on intellectual pursuits, and their physical stats reflect that. But that doesn't make them superhuman. Which is why I feel fairly sure that better ambient Energy helps inhabitants increase their base stats, even without Classes being involved.

However, there is another nugget of information that seems interesting: none of the studies the scholars did showed a non-Classer with more than twenty points in any one stat. It seems that there is a threshold at that point, which is validated by the fact that Classers stopped being offered points past twenty no matter how much work they did. Post twenty, stats can only be raised by leveling up—another good argument for maximizing as many stat points through effort as I can. Though, not at the expense of risking my survival, of course. I even considered sticking at level zero for a while but dismissed that possibility because of another bit of information I ran across. Skills.

CHAPTER TWENTY-FOUR

They're Real

I've already seen how useful Skills are: Lay-on-Hands has saved me pain, infected injuries, and probably death on multiple occasions. It's one of the few Skills I have. The other two are the Skills I received when I gained my Class, which I haven't yet tested out since my Willpower is too low. *Was* too low, actually . . .

I find myself getting distracted and force my train of thought to return from its tangent.

As for other Skills? Apparently, I get access to a selection of Skills at specific level intervals. My first Skill selection is at level one, hence my desire to reach at least that level as quickly as possible. The next Skill selection after that is at level five, then level ten, level fifteen, level twenty, and then subsequently at intervals of ten up to one hundred. There's no information about levels after one hundred. Perhaps after that something else comes into play?

Anyway, just like the thought of comparing myself to both people on Earth and Nicholas's world, none of this will be an issue if I don't survive the next year. So, after having decided to aim for level one and then take a bit more time over level two, I spent some time thinking about the other things I need to do. My next step is clear: absorb the hunting knowledge stone. Hopefully, that will help give me an edge when hunting beasts to bring my Energy store up to one hundred percent. That stone is the last of my gifts from Nicholas, so I hope I'll have enough knowledge absorbed afterwards to figure out a way to survive this.

After I've leveled up and chosen my level one Skill, I'll get to work on developing some tools for things that will make my life here a bit more comfortable and easier. Hopefully, that will be a good opportunity to earn some stat points. Another good reason to go hunting first is that I'll be able to explore the area around me and, ideally, identify some good places to find the various resources I'll need. Plus, the corpses of the animals I hunt might contain some of the bits I'll need. Sinew will be absolutely necessary, for one. I also realize during the day that my efforts with my eye have been fruitful in more than one sense: apparently, using Lay-on-Hands to heal an organ was enough to catapult it into the next category, as it's increased to Novice three. Lying in my "bed," I bring the message up to look at it again—my first rank-up message!

Congratulations!

You have advanced a Skill past Beginner. Lay-on-Hands is now Novice 1. You are now able to channel healing by using your remaining mana to lengthen the healing time. This requires full concentration to be engaged while the mana is acting on the wound. You are also now able to increase the efficiency of your Skill by applying your anatomical knowledge. By concentrating on the wound and focusing your Willpower on how it should be when healed, you can actively direct the healing as you wish. Warning: incomplete or incorrect anatomical knowledge used to direct this Skill may lead to unintentional consequences.

Close message? Y / N

I close the message, musing again over the new information. It's not really anything I didn't know before—or, at least, nothing I hadn't guessed. What I'd done by drawing on my mana bar is apparently called "channeling" and merely lengthens the healing time at the expense of needing to concentrate. What I did by imagining how the eye works was apparently apply my anatomical knowledge, allowing the spell, or Skill, to work more efficiently—I guess because it "knows" what to do straight off—but this has the flip side that if I tell it to do something wrong, it won't know any better and I could mess myself up more. I'll have to be careful, but if these new functionalities could save my life, they'll be well worth it. It's also good to have more information on how to evolve a Skill and why it's a good idea.

The information from the System lore stone said that using and evolving a Skill is key to increasing its level and thereby its effectiveness. My experience last night has proven that and even given me a clue: evolving a Skill may require using it in a different way, rather than just repeating the same action again and again. I'll have to experiment with my other Skills later. At the moment, they're only sitting at the first level, so they still have a good way to go. Either way, it's going to be significantly easier to achieve my objectives of finding resources and creatures to hunt with two intact eyes. On that happy note, I close my eyes and drift to sleep.

The next day, as planned, I absorb the hunting knowledge stone. An instant headache blooms. I'm very glad that I waited to absorb this stone; from the wealth of information that is downloaded into my brain, I can tell I would have been unable to effectively assimilate it before. That said, as I go through my new knowledge, some of it does overlap with what I've already learned, adding a depth to my understanding. The more straightforward knowledge from the tracking skill, like that the depth of claw marks on a tree added to the height of them indicates the height and the size of the animal, now carries with it a greater meaning. For example, the size of the animal compared to the range for its species indicates its age, sex, health, and therefore, whether it would be a good idea to hunt or not.

Of course, just as with the wilderness survival knowledge, some of these facts are no doubt not applicable to the creatures I'll actually be hunting; I hope enough of the facts are correct that the knowledge will help me more than hinder.

Other parts of the hunting knowledge stone overlap with wilderness survival, such as butchering—now I know not only how to actually separate the different parts of the animal, but I also know the signs to look for to avoid diseased animals or ones with parasites. The last bit gives me shivers; along with the knowledge of how to avoid parasites came mental images of what those parasites look like . . . and what they do to their unfortunate hosts.

Frankly, I've been pretty lucky when it comes to drinking the water straight from the stream when I can't be bothered to boil it. I could easily have picked up something bad, either parasite or bacteria. It just reminds me that my health is worth me spending that half an hour to set up a fire and boil the water. After all, I can't know for sure whether Lay-on-Hands can help me with either diseases or parasites. Some areas, however, are completely new, such as how to set traps; some of them are surprisingly simple. If I can get the Energy from killing something through a trap, just as if I'd killed it with my spear, I could really maximize my Energy gain—and my safety.

Also included in this knowledge packet is how to make and wield a number of weapons essential to hunting. That's something I'm very glad to have since, *surprisingly,* I'd never studied archery, spear-wielding, or fletching, nor had I ever aimed to become a bowyer before being stuck here. When preparing for the day I start packing everything away into my Inventory as has been my habit so far, but then pause. Do I really need to take everything with me? That's what I've done for the last few days, but then, I've also been travelling for that time and sleeping somewhere different every night. Plus, won't I need the space in my Inventory for my kills and any other useful resources I find?

In the end, I leave my big orange suitcase behind, but I take my backpack and smaller lime green suitcase. I do clear a bit of space in my backpack, just in case, but I'm not keen on leaving my most precious items somewhere without my surveillance—for sentimental reasons as well as survival ones. Though, I'm pretty sure Kalanthia isn't going to let just anyone walk into her cave. So, with nerves causing butterflies to flap around in my stomach, I set off out of the cave. Kalanthia is sunning herself outside with Lathani playing nearby.

"Just going off to hunt," I say cheerily, doing my best to cover my nervousness at actually *going out intentionally to find dangerous situations.* It seems rather counterintuitive to my desire to stay alive, but there we are. That's the crazy world I live in now.

Success to your hunt, Markus Wolfe, she tells me calmly. I wish I could bottle some of that and take it with me. Still, no point stalling.

I walk down the hill and start searching for signs of something that I could reasonably hunt. I might be being illogical by actually seeking out things that could kill me—instead of staying where the only thing I have to worry about is a giant predator that I couldn't defeat even if it *did* try to eat me—but that doesn't mean I'm going to be stupid about doing it. *Wait, something seems wrong about that . . .* Anyway, I'm going to pick and choose my prey to minimize my risk. Deciding that the banks of the river would be a good place to begin my search, I start scanning the area. It doesn't take me much time to spot some evidence of the passage of different animals with the knowledge from both the tracking and hunting stones aiding me. I dither and hesitate as I dismiss the idea of following one track after another. This one looks too big. This one looks too small. These tracks indicate a group of animals, which are maybe too numerous; these are a single animal, but probably a predator. I even procrastinate a little more by setting up a deadfall trap with a stone and a stick near where there's a trail indicating regular passage of some small creature. After baiting it with the berries off a few different plants nearby, I mark it on my map so I know where to come back for it.

Finally, I pick at random, spinning around and pointing to an area of the river. Steeling myself, I investigate my narrowed choice. Not going for the predator, instead I pick a small group of tracks that probably belong to a small group of grazers. As I follow them, misgivings start to rise. They are bigger than I'd thought just from their prints—the branches bent and damaged to either side of the trail as they headed into denser ground coverage seems to indicate that, at least. Still, I push on; I have to hunt *something*. After a while, I start hearing the creatures. A snuffling, rooting sound. Actually, it's rather familiar . . . It sounds a bit like the creature that woke me up a few nights ago, the one I spent hidden in a dead-leaf shelter. It's probably not the same creature, as I've moved a fair bit away from there, but maybe there are lots of this type around.

Taking more care when placing my feet, I head closer still. When I lay my eyes on my quarry, I'm surprised, I have to admit. At first, I'd had the idea of some small creature with delicate paws.

Once I saw the size of the animals and heard the snuffling, I thought of a pig. This is neither. The body of the creatures reminds me of a porcupine, though these quills are far shorter—more like a hedgehog's, perhaps, but they lay flat like a porcupine's. I don't doubt that the creatures are capable of moving them to stand upright in defense. In color, they are more of a murky brown than the black and white of a porcupine, and their snouts are more lizard-like.

So far, most of the creatures I've come across since arriving seem to have had either reptilian or avian influences. The creatures I've killed haven't been exactly cold-blooded, but they've been cooler than me to be sure. They've also been almost invariably scaled, so seeing spines on these creatures is a bit different. My potential prey have little horns on the ends of their snouts, and it's this they are using to dig a little through the ground.

I'm suddenly struck by the thought that a number of tasks would be easier if I had my own mobile plow. Although I don't need to break ground to build a shelter at the moment, I do need to plant the samova beans. I'm also going to need clay, probably from the river, and finding some type of edible tuber would be great. Actually, since these creatures probably eat the latter, they might be ideal for that task; though, their definition of "edible" may not match mine . . . But how would I capture them? My Willpower is high enough to attempt to Dominate them, at least. Or I could give Tame a go. The problem is that I don't actually have any idea of where to start with either. And wouldn't that defeat the purpose of going on the hunt, that is, to get Energy? I have another misgiving now that I've actually set eyes on the group: its composition.

I'd known from the tracks that there were two larger animals and two smaller ones, but I'd thought it was two males and two females—it's not unusual for the different sexes to be different sizes, after all. Alas, the reason is far more contentious than that. It's a family. From a purely practical standpoint, the fact that there are four of them is a significant drawback. Yes, I've fought and killed more numerous foes in the past, but these ones are bigger than the weasitors and definitely spikier than the killer chickens. These facts make me reluctant to start a fight and even more reticent to try out either Dominate or Tame with them.

However, none of this is insurmountable. I've got enough hunting knowledge now to think of a number of strategies to split them apart, isolate one from the others, and pick it off when it's vulnerable. But there's something else that is holding me back. It's clear that this group is composed of a mother, father—though I'll be damned if I can tell which is which—and two youngsters. Not babies, precisely, but definitely juveniles of some sort. Their color is more faded, and they approach the task of rooting through leaves and dirt with more playfulness than their parents.

In fact, as I watch, one of them misjudges how much effort it will take to uproot one plant and gets its horn stuck in the ground. *Cute* . . . I swallow and withdraw behind a tree. *What am I doing here? Am I really considering taking the parents away from the youngsters either by killing them or capturing them? Or killing the juveniles?* Even when I played video games that happened to center around killing animals or people, I unconsciously avoided killing the children or babies. And that was when I knew that they were just bundles of code. This . . . They're real.

CHAPTER TWENTY-FIVE

The Aggressor

It's an issue I have to face. Unless I restrict myself to only killing seriously wounded, ill, or very old members of species, I will have to kill healthy members at some point, and all of those healthy members are potential mothers and fathers. Heck, I may end up killing a pregnant female at some stage, quite unknowingly. I do seriously consider only culling those that are likely to die anyway but dismiss the idea after a while. In the end, I have to come to terms with the fact that I need to accumulate Energy or by the end of the year, I will die. I have to force myself to face the fact that the lives of a few animals don't outweigh my own life, in my eyes. But what do I do, right here, right now?

The decision hangs in the balance for a few moments before it tips. Ultimately, I judge this hunt to be too risky—there are too many of them, and I don't know enough about their defensive abilities to know what I might be getting myself into. Parents with children are usually more vicious too. Though there are methods I could use to reduce the risk, many of them involve materials that I don't have at hand. That my lack of desire to rob the family of one or more of its members plays a big part in my decision is something I have to force myself to acknowledge. It feels like cowardice, like foolishness. But perhaps I'm a fool. Honestly, I'd rather be a bit of a fool than add to the guilt in my heart. There's enough there already. *As long as my foolishness doesn't kill me, anyway.*

I withdraw quietly and carefully so I don't draw the family's attention and accidentally bring about the whole scenario that I'm trying to avoid. I keep the thought about using Dominate on one of these creatures in the back of my mind. If I ever come across the tracks of a solitary . . . What shall I call them? Porcupig? Reptiline? *No, if everything is reptilian, I'll run out of names if I begin them all with "rep.* Porcupig it is. So, if I ever come across the tracks of a solitary porcupig, I'll see about trying to capture it.

I follow my tracks back towards the river with a strange sense of calm. It feels good to have figured out my priorities. I'll kill and capture healthy animals, that I know for sure. What I also know for sure is that I will do my best to avoid taking away parents from babies. Obviously, if a creature attacks me, I'm going to defend myself whether or not it's the "breadwinner" of a family, but if it doesn't attack me and I'm not desperate for food, I'll try to leave it alone—from my experience so far, there are enough creatures that will do their best to kill me that I won't be lacking for bodies. Even if the whole point of me going hunting is to try to *avoid* just falling into combat situations.

I tell myself that it's practical anyway; if I kill all the members of a generation, I impact the next. Of course, I ignore the fact that I won't be around to see that happen and that my personal impact on this massive forest-filled valley is unlikely to be all that significant. Then I wonder just who I'm trying to prove myself to and refocus on my task; being inattentive in this forest is even *more* foolish than choosing not to attack a creature because they're a baby or a parent.

In the end, I pick the tracks of a single creature, not wanting to repeat the same scenario as I just encountered. They aren't precisely the "perfect" tracks—the creature seems a bit bigger than I would have preferred—but then I remember how different the porcupigs were from what I'd expected based on their tracks. Maybe that will happen again? As I'd thought, tracking and hunting knowledge from another world can be rather misleading at times.

It takes me perhaps an hour to catch up with the creature I'm tracking. It's not moving that fast, but it has a significant head start on me. Approaching, I see a creature that reminds me of a chameleon crossed with a snail. That said, it's not as slow as one would expect from a creature like that. It has a large pointy, curled shell rather like a snail and a long body covered in scales.

Unlike a snail, though, it doesn't ooze across the ground, leaving a viscous trail behind it, but has feet rather like a chameleon's—six of them! Two sets of legs have knee joints, or possibly hip joints, facing forwards; the rear set has the joints facing backwards. One would think this would add an ungainly sense of movement to the creature's gait, but it's not at all the case—though, the extra set of legs does add an interesting sway.

Now, how am I going to do this? The creature is not nearly as slow as a snail. What if I attack it and it runs away? Or what if I attack it and it attacks me in return? I wish I had a bow and some arrows—even flint would do better than nothing. Then it hits me. *Flint!* Sure, I don't have a bow and arrows, but there are ranged weapons all around me, ones that my ancestors used to great effect for many years.

Retracing my footsteps a little so that I'm not likely to scare my prey off the moment I start casting around for stones, I pick up as many fist-sized lumps of rock as possible. Once my pockets are full, I pick up the creature's trail again. Unfortunately for me, I know I'm not the most athletic of people, so I think I'd better get as close as possible before starting. Taking a couple of careful steps forward, I pause. Maybe better get my ammunition ready first.

Putting a stone in each hand, I do a final once-over, nodding my head when all seems as it should be. Then, continuing my careful stalk forwards, I find myself wincing every time I step badly and a branch cracks or a leaf rustles. The worst thing is, I know how to walk quietly through this landscape in my *head*, but my *body* hasn't yet learned how to follow instructions. I know it will come with time; I just hope I'll have enough of that. It seems like the sneleon—surely the logical name for a snail chameleon—doesn't have the most acute of senses, as it only seems to raise its head from the bush it's chomping on at the worst of my branch cracks. Its head, it turns out, is rounded and looks rather like some herbivorous dinosaur's in one of those old children's cartoons.

While I can't rule out the possibility that this creature has some sort of defense mechanism, I do feel more of a sense of confidence about approaching this quarry than the previous, and that's not even taking my moral dilemma over the babies into account.

I take my time lining up my first shot, nervousness going through me and making my hand shake a little. It's a rough stone with several edges, which will hopefully do more damage than a round, smooth stone would. Then again, it also has more wind resistance, so it's six of one and half a dozen of the other. If I'm very lucky, it will hit the sneleon sharp points first, but frankly, I think I'll be content if I just manage to hit the creature at all. Extra points if I get the body.

My focus narrows, and I launch the rock at the sneleon. Wonder of wonders, it hits! Unfortunately, it hits the shell and bounces off without causing more than a loud cracking sound. In an instant, the sneleon's defense mechanism engages. To my good fortune, it's not an *offensive* one.

Instead, just like the snail I likened it to, the sneleon vanishes into its shell with an amazing flexibility. Almost as quickly as I could blink, the sneleon went from unaware to protected. Its curled shell sticks up in the air, rocking forwards once or twice as it gets used to its new position, perhaps twenty centimeters nearer to the ground than it was a second ago. By this point I'm very curious about this creature.

I walk over to it a little cautiously, in case it lashes out the moment I get close, and place my hand gingerly on its shell. It's mostly cool but warmer in an area where a ray of sunlight is hitting it. The creature when I arrived had been about a meter long, its legs approximately thirty centimeters long when fully extended but twenty centimeters in the normally somewhat bent position. Its shell added an extra thirty centimeters to its height, which had made me think I was dealing with a bigger creature than I actually ended up with.

Now it's just the shell, which is around thirty centimeters high and almost that wide at its base. Its length is probably more like forty centimeters, creating something of an oval-based, blunt-tipped cone. How a creature probably around a meter long and ten centimeters or so in diameter manages to squish into this thing, I don't know, but the proof is in front of me.

I push the shell a little—gently at first, then harder. It rocks from side to side. Nothing happens. I'm very curious now but wary at the same time. I back away a bit and then start throwing rocks at the motionless shell. I miss more than I hit at first, but my aim does improve. Nothing happens except for a rocking shell every time I hit it—that is, until one hit to the top lands with enough force to knock the creature over. I jump back in case it's capable of sending out some sort of ranged attack, but after rolling a little, the shell settles and becomes motionless again.

Once more gingerly approaching the creature, I look with fascination at what, in a snail, would be its "foot." In this case they're *feet*, as the six feet of the creature seem to have locked together to create a solid barrier. I'm starting to understand this creature's place in the food chain. Much like other defense specialists, like the snail I thought of earlier or tortoises, this creature doesn't have speed on its side, nor does it have strong natural offensive ability. Instead, it's a walking fortress to probably most, if not all, of the creatures in this forest. It would take something with significant crushing power to get through the shell. I'm sure Kalanthia would cope, but I'm equally sure she wouldn't bother unless she was unable to find anything better. And that's probably exactly the niche this creature exploits: being too tough to deal with for creatures its own level and not being an enticing enough target for those that could actually pose a threat to it.

Based on its size, I reckon that the attacker would have to be able to open their jaws more than thirty centimeters at a minimum *and* be able to apply bone-crushing force to get through its shell. That's more than most of the creatures on Earth could boast, and possibly more than *any* of them could cope with. Well, maybe a crocodile could cope, but it doesn't seem like there are any of those here. Or the sneleon avoids water as much as possible. Otherwise, I suppose there could be birds that are capable of lifting it and dropping it on a rock to crack open the shell, but again, though not that big, it's probably big enough to cause difficulty for most birds. Plus, it's in the forest, not on the mountainside, meaning that one of those birds would have to swoop in past the forest canopy to find it. So, in short, a pretty good defense mechanism.

Unfortunately for this sneleon, it's met me: a mammal capable of using tools. Feeling a bit sorry for this creature that is defenseless against man, I still approach, hefting another stone in my hand. What defense is a tough shell when facing someone with patience and a hard rock? Speed might be a better defense, but then again, humanity's ancestors were also capable of defeating that with patient, enduring pursuit. By about ten hits in, I stop feeling sorry. This blighter is a tough nut to crack—or rather, a tough shell. I'm making a difference, but I was expecting it to crack like an egg in a few hits. Instead, it's only starting to show signs of cracking after *ten*.

I did try another approach when I saw no progress for my efforts after five strong hits with a rock. Seeing its interlocked feet as a potential opening, I tried to pry them apart with my knife. Unfortunately, I didn't get very far with this approach—the hairline gaps between each foot are barely wide enough for my knife to slot in and I don't have anything like the leverage power I'd need. I even try whacking the feet with my mace, but the interlocked pads just seem to absorb the force of my hits with little trouble.

Stymied, I return to my previous strategy. This time, though, I decide to use my mace for its extra power.

By the time I reach sixteen strokes, the sneleon makes a move. I back away quickly as I see it emerging from its shell. It's not nearly as quick leaving as it was in withdrawing, but I still keep my distance in case it's got something up its proverbial sleeve.

I watch cautiously, preferring to potentially lose my prey than get injured—again. However, attack seems to be the last thing on this creature's mind as it heads straight for the nearest tree. Realizing it means to escape into the foliage either above or below, I go back on the attack.

With its entire body now visible, I don't aim for its shell again but go straight for the head. It avoids my first two blows and even tries to latch onto my leg in a last-ditch attempt to protect itself, but I dodge easily and finally manage to bring my mace down on its head. Victory is mine, but I don't get that same triumphant thrill I have every other time I've overcome my foe. I bite my lip as I try to figure out why. In the end, it strikes me that in my previous encounters, I was the victim, and when I won the struggle, I'd fought against the odds and aggressors that had tried to pull me down. Here, *I* was the aggressor, and one with an advantage that my prey couldn't defend against. There's little glory or achievement in patiently beating at a shell with a rock or mace and then bashing in the occupant's head as it tries to escape. If anything, it makes me feel like the bad guy rather than the hero . . .

I try to make myself feel better by repeating my reasons for going on the hunt in the first place and reminding myself that aiming for battles where I will probably get hurt at the minimum is *not* a good way to attempt to preserve my life. I'm not here to be a hero; I'm here to *survive*. I remind myself that my ancestors would have chosen easy prey over hard prey ten times out of ten. That's why they're my ancestors instead of dying before they could have progeny. I still feel guilty.

I hesitate over butchering the corpse but then eventually kneel down next to it. If it's a sin to have killed the creature in the first place, wouldn't it be even more of one to just leave its carcass lying there abandoned? And if I end up muttering apologies and a few words of thanks over the body before digging in with my knife, who is going to know?

CHAPTER TWENTY-SIX

Predator

By the time I decide to head back to my campsite, I've had three successful hunts, two unsuccessful ones, and an additional kill with my deadfall trap. That's excluding my encounter with the porcupigs. Despite wanting to try out my Class Skill now that my Willpower's over ten, I didn't in the end. Most of the creatures didn't seem worth it, and the one that did was far too aggressive for me to try. I have to marvel at the wildlife in this new world—at their sheer variety and also at their alienness to what I'm used to. At first,

I thought that everything here was either reptilian or avian, but now I'm wondering whether mammals have developed. Or something like them, at least—I don't know if they give birth to live young and feed them on milk, after all. I mean, sure, Kalanthia is clearly a mammal, but by this point I've got questions about whether she's from "around here," either in the sense that she's from a different part of the planet—and Nicholas was mistaken about there being no humans—or that she's from somewhere different entirely. Since she doesn't seem keen to share, I can't know.

Kalanthia aside, I can confirm that two out of three successful hunts were warm-blooded, though the blood felt slightly cool to me, so it's clearly a lower temperature than mine. Only one of my kills had scales, but these were more along the lines of a pangolin's than a lizard's. The other had a rather coarse and bristly fur coat, which, unfortunately for me, hid several venomous barbs. Added to these were two short but sharp tusks on either side of the creature's mouth, which, while not envenomed in themselves, were used to great effect. Often, dodging the tusks meant exposing myself to the barb-covered tail.

I have to admit that I was in a pretty bad way after killing the large boar-like creature: the venom seemed to be an anti-coagulate since my wounds bled more freely and took longer to close up. Lay-on-Hands saved me, but my health did drop down to five units. I'll also admit to needing more than a breather after that to get over the near-death experience. Although I've faced a few of those so far, facing them without my backup health potion in my satchel feels different. More . . . desperate. I try to ignore the worry because what other choice do I have?

Of the two unsuccessful hunts, one was because I decided to back off when I caught up with the creature. It wasn't that big—up to mid-torso on me. The problem was that it seemed rather well defended with sharp teeth and claws and an impressive jaw structure that looked more like a T-Rex than anything else. I'd probably take it on if I had a proper ranged weapon or something with a long handle that I could use to keep it at a distance, but with only a knife, a sort-of mace, a handmade spear, and no armor? No chance. I failed the other for one simple reason: it ran away and was too fast to catch.

I'd tried my luck at one of those reptilian deer things, but as soon as it got wind of my approach—far sooner than any of the other animals—it disappeared into the surrounding foliage, its long tail balancing it from behind and its long, thin legs eating up the distance. So, again, without any sort of proper ranged weapon or a trap to immobilize it, I'm not likely to succeed with that creature any time soon. Still, I'd only come close to death once in five hunts. That's got to be a record for me! And if nothing else, it indicates that as I'd thought, taking the fight to the creatures is much safer than them bringing the fight to *me*. I'll still take my wins where I can find them.

Though, speaking of wins, my Energy gain hasn't been as profitable as I'd hoped. Perhaps my estimates were skewed by the killer chickens: gaining forty-five percent in a single fight was clearly just as much a windfall as it had been an almost-lethal encounter. Thirteen deadly carnivores that almost killed me despite the advantages I had of height and weaponry really aren't comparable to my experiences today.

In total, I killed four creatures during the day. One was barely a threat and netted me a grand total of one percent for killing it. The pangolin-kin was more of a threat, but barely so, and earned me two percent. My most challenging fight earned me five percent, bringing me to a total of eight percent Energy gained simply from hunting. I added another three percent by eating their hearts—and let me tell you, that sapped time out of the day when it came to building the fires and cooking the meat. I also earned another six percent just from absorption, bringing my day's total to seventeen percent gain. It's something, that's for sure, but it's not a lot.

As for the creature I killed with my deadfall trap, I'm honestly unable to say whether I gained any Energy from it. The creature was small and looked rather harmless, appearing to be this world's equivalent to a mouse or rabbit from the way it seemed built for speed and had no real defenses. Considering how the sneleon only earned me a single percent when it was at least ten times the size of the mousit, maybe the trap *did* earn me Energy, but I just didn't notice it. Or perhaps it didn't. Impossible to say for sure.

It won't be much of a meal either, only being about the length of my hand. I put it in my Inventory anyway—waste not, want not. The low gain from my hunt makes sense when I consider it a bit more deeply as parts of my new System knowledge activate to give me the answer.

Carnivores can absorb Energy from their prey just as much as I can; herbivores only have a natural daily absorption. Therefore, prey animals will generally be worth less Energy than predators, although an herbivore that has survived for many years might have absorbed more than a carnivore that is still young. Equally, there are certain plants that are Energy dense and can offer a significant boost to an herbivore, but these are rare. At least, they are in Nicholas's world—who knows if that holds true here. Either way, two of the creatures I killed today were definitely herbivores; I'm not so sure about the poison-boar, because although it was a tough fight, its abilities seemed to be more defensive than offensive. Then again, I suppose if it had killed other creatures in defense, even if it didn't eat them, it would still earn more Energy than another herbivore.

I already had some Energy in my store, so when I look at my status screen, it tells me I'm up to fifty percent. *Halfway there.* If the next few days are similar in terms of gain, it'll take me another three days to level up. I feel frustrated at that; it shouldn't seem very long—three days felt short when it was a long weekend, for sure—but my time in this world has proven that three days can feel very long indeed. Then again, I do accumulate Energy even while I sleep, so maybe it'll be a little less than three days. Plus, the more hunting I do, the better I'll be at choosing prey and following its tracks. That should mean more kills, meaning more Energy.

As I trudge home tiredly, I consider whether it's better to hunt easy herbivorous prey, which is relatively safe but not very profitable in terms of Energy, or hunt more of the poison-boar type creatures or carnivores, which are a lot more dangerous but are commensurately a lot more worth the time . . .

If I had a definitive answer about gaining Energy from traps, it would open another option for me. After all, if I could catch and kill a creature in a pitfall trap, for example, I wouldn't even need to be in range of their attacks to harvest their Energy. But that only works if traps count for Energy gain.

The issue is that building traps to kill bigger and more dangerous creatures will take more resources and more preparation than a simple deadfall; when I don't even know whether it will work, do I want to commit the time to that? So maybe not traps right now. Maybe I just have to be patient and hunt for three days with this ineffective strategy, and then, once I've got my first level—and first chosen Skill—I can rethink. I'll be going on a crafting kick at that point anyway—I *really* need to upgrade my weaponry. Some armor wouldn't go amiss either, but that seems rather far off with the tools I have available right now. Plus, I'd like something better to cook on and to cook *with.*

By this time, I'm back at the cave. Kalanthia and Lathani are already inside, as night is falling. Strangely enough, I get the feeling that they're diurnal rather than nocturnal like leopards are on Earth. Just more proof that they're not actually leopards . . . *Markus Wolfe,* Kalanthia begins when she sees me. I freeze on my way to my cave and look over at her. She, thankfully, ignores my suddenly thudding heart. It's not that I think she's going to suddenly pounce . . . but my instincts can't forget that this is a massive predator who could kill me without even really trying. I'm sure I'll get used to it, but for now, any time she notices me, a shot of adrenaline goes through me.

I must hunt tomorrow. I need you to watch over Lathani.

"Okay," I reply. What else can I say? I agreed to be the live-in babysitter, after all. It's a bit frustrating, though, given that I'm already chafing at the length of time it will take me to level up. Though, I did go hunting today, and I don't need all the meat I have in my Inventory—not unless I don't kill anything more within the next few days. "I've got some meat in storage. Would you like it?"

Show me, Kalanthia says.

I pull out the undressed carcasses of the four creatures killed today along with most of the killer chicken bodies.

"I've got about half again this amount of meat in storage, already cut," I tell her, eyeing the carcasses speculatively. Kalanthia sniffs them briefly, then huffs, a wave of rotten-meat-scented air making me wrinkle my nose. They look so *small* next to her. I have a feeling I know what she's going to say next.

It is not enough, Kalanthia announces. *The amount of meat would be sufficient for one, perhaps two days. But no more. It is not good quality either. I must go hunting.*

"All right." I sigh, quickly tucking everything back into place. I hesitate, a question on my mind. "What do you mean by 'not good quality'?"

Poor in Energy, she answers promptly. Well, I suppose I already knew that, though I'm a little surprised at her tarring the killer chickens with the same brush as the others. Then again, what do I know of what else is available for predators the size of Kalanthia? I try to console myself with a reminder that I'll still get the daily absorption rate. "I'll need to go and get some water, though," I add, realizing that I forgot to fill my canteen on my way up.

Very well, she agrees, *but it must be a short trip, as I will need the day to hunt. I shall wake you if you sleep overlong.*

Is that an offer or a threat? I can't decide but ultimately conclude that it doesn't really matter. Kalanthia's put her head down and is ignoring me again—the conversation is apparently over. I shrug a little and then duck into my little alcove.

After settling down with a sigh of relief, I eat some food. I was offered one point for Strength—Power—earlier in the day, which I declined with disappointment. I seriously considered accepting it, but of all my stats, Power is actually the one I've least needed. I just couldn't justify delaying reaching level one and my first Skill choice to take it. If it had been Constitution or Intelligence, that would have been another question. As to why I was offered it, I can only guess that it was because of all the rocks I lifted to throw at the sneleon. I'm tired. Sneaking around the woods all day with intermittent life-or-death battles is apparently rather exhausting. Who would have guessed?

Yawning, I just lie down and try to sleep. Although I could probably read outside by the light of the two—yes, *two*—moons, I'm too sleepy. If there's anything that makes it immediately clear I'm in a different world, it's the two pale orbs hanging in the sky and moving independently. One seems to be quicker than the Earth's moon and appears more frequently; the other seems to be slower, taking more time to cross the sky, but then not appearing for almost another twenty-four hours.

Actually, without a watch, and reluctant as I am to turn on my phone with no chance of recharging it—even if its clock function would actually work, all things considered—I still have no idea of the actual day length. I'm pretty sure it's not twenty-four hours, though; it's probably a few hours longer. I've come to that conclusion because I'm going to bed at dusk and generally waking up with the dawn without feeling tired. That indicates to me that the night is at least eight hours long.

Then, I'm always really hungry by the time the sun hits its zenith and completely exhausted by the time it's hitting the horizon. Of course, that could also be due to the amount of physical activity I'm doing, which I'm not at all used to, but I think there's more to it. In the end, I shrug. I have too many other things to think about to waste time questioning something that has such little relevance. At least I'm getting a decent amount of sleep without cutting into the day too much—that's more than I had at work!

On that note, I do my best to calm myself down to actually get some of that sleep I need. Unfortunately, with all the activity of the day, it's a long while before my brain calms down enough to let me rest.

CHAPTER TWENTY-SEVEN

Cat Toy

The next morning, I wake to the sound of a chest-rumbling growl. *Ah, my alarm clock*—ten out of ten for waking me up: the adrenaline rush of hearing a large predator growling menacingly gets rid of the grogginess straight away.

Are you ready now, Markus Wolfe? She asks, a note of impatience in her "voice."

"Just give me a moment." I groan, rubbing the sleep out of my eyes. I changed last night into new clothes, so I don't need to do anything there. There was something, though . . . *Water!*

"I'll just get some water, and then I'll be all yours," I tell her, quickly making my way out of the cave and down to the river at the foot of the hill.

As soon as I get back, Kalanthia pauses to lick her cub's head, then lopes off. Lathani watches her go with a plaintive wail but doesn't try to follow. She soon shakes off the melancholy and starts romping around the clearing at the top of the hill.

Of course, I very quickly get pulled into her games and have to defend myself semi-seriously against the clawed and toothed bundle of fur that leaps out at me unexpectedly from behind bushes or after a period of much more obvious stalking. In between, she gets distracted by insects and small animals.

Acting on yesterday's resolve to start boiling my water, I manage to find some time to make a small fire out in the open where I can still see the cub. She's curious about what I'm doing, so I have to distract her with a few sticks while the fire gets going and then again once I've got my wok on to heat up the water inside. Once the liquid's bubbling, I quickly tuck the hot pan into my alcove and pull the fire apart, keeping Lathani away until the sticks are cool. She seems to have a bit of a knack for finding trouble. I have a moment of pure panic when she dives after a small animal near the edge of the hill and falls off.

Rushing over, I see she's rolled down about halfway, so I call for her with a slightly frantic note to my voice. Lathani looks up at me, then down at the forest curiously. I call again and she looks back at me, hesitating for a moment longer.

Then, perhaps deciding that the forest can wait for another day, she bounds back up and leaps at me, knocking me down once more. In the end, babysitting a leopard cub turns out to be a lot less relaxing than I thought it would be. More fool me. She's a bundle of energy and doesn't sit still for a moment . . . until she conks out all of a sudden, barely making it back into the cave before she's making cute baby snores. By this point I could do with a nap myself but decide that it might not be the best of ideas as I'm still "on guard." Instead, I settle at the mouth of the cave, enjoying the sun while still fully aware of anything moving nearby. Pulling out one of my books, I read for a little, enjoying having the time to relax.

Once I'm feeling a little more chilled, my introvert-meter having refilled itself, I reluctantly put the book to one side and start doing some exercises: squats, press-ups, sit-ups, jumping jacks, burpees, all the things that I used to do at the gym that didn't require equipment. I even grab a stone nearby and start lifting it—it's a little heavy for me right now, but I push myself to still do some exercises.

The thing is that even if I'm determined not to take any more points offered to me until I've gotten to level one—unless they have a clear and immediate effect on my ability to survive, like Constitution—that doesn't mean I can't make old-school progress. Plus, if my theories are right about how Nicholas's world helps people reach higher stats with less work even without a Class in place, I might even be able to increase my stats without committing any Energy to them at all. I don't know how to even start with most of the stats, but there's one that I am confident in knowing how to improve: Strength. So, since my day off when I figured this out, I've been trying to take some time here or there to work out. It seems to be having an effect; I was offered the point yesterday, after all. It will be interesting to see what happens next if I keep going with it.

Once I'm sweaty, panting, and shaking, I sit back down, drink some water and eat some meat, and return to my book with relief.

When Lathani wakes up, she starts romping around again, and I put my novel away with a bit of regret, my muscles already aching. Fiddling with a stalk of plant rather similar to the grass of my homeworld, I'm amused when the bouncing flower stalk attracts the cub's attention. She bats at it for a while, and I oblige her need to play, making the heavy flower dance and twist in the air, then on the ground. She looks just like an overgrown house cat, the way she pounces and slaps at it. When she finally manages to get a good grip with her claws, she pulls it in close, rolling on her back and biting at it. I have an idea.

Grabbing some long, thin grass leaves, I braid them in a plait. It's a little awkward—my head knows exactly what to do, but my fingers are terribly clumsy. The braid isn't nearly as neat as my "memories" say it should be, but it's not like I'm expecting this to last very long. Making a couple more braids, each one better than the previous, I pick up a few leaves and bits of grass.

Binding them together into a little bundle with one braid, I tie the others to it and to each other. Finally, I grab one of the white bones that Kalanthia and Lathani have already gnawed clean. Tying the loose end of my braid to the bone, I brandish my creation gleefully. Success! I've made . . . a cat toy!

Lathani looks at me with her head cocked to one side, perhaps wondering what's made this strange-looking creature so excited, but she soon learns how fun a dedicated cat toy can be. I use the bone to make the lure dart over the ground, bounce in the air, and evade Lathani's pounces at the very last moment. It's surprisingly fun—for both of us. We play until we're both tired and the improvised cat toy has been torn to shreds, then slump at the cave mouth. Lathani lies next to me, one paw touching my leg. It's *very* cute. Kalanthia arrives back when the sun is on its downward trend but has only gotten about halfway to the horizon, her chops still stained with red. Lathani has livened up again by then and goes to greet her with happy chirps. The nunda mama ducks her head to nuzzle her cub and breathes in her scent for a few moments. At least, that's what I assume she's doing when she pauses, her head near Lathani.

"Good hunt?" I ask as she moves towards the cave and, by default, me. If my offering yesterday was so pitiful, I have to wonder how many creatures she's killed today. *Good enough,* she replies lightly. *I thank you for watching over Lathani.* "Sure." I shrug.

"She was no trouble." Kalanthia pauses next to me for a moment, then chuffs and rubs her head against me gently.

Well, gently for *her.* It almost knocks me flying. Continuing on into the cave, the giant leopard curls up on the bedding, and Lathani starts to play with the twitching tip of her tail. *Good,* she finally says, responding to the comment I'd almost forgotten I'd made, so distracted was I by her headbutt or head rub or whatever. *I shall not need to hunt again for another three days.* "Okay, great," I say, not sure how else to reply. When she says nothing more, I turn my thoughts onto what to do now. There's not much time left in the day, certainly not enough to go hunting.

That said, I could do with dealing with my bounty from the last few fights. Though I took the hearts from the killer chickens and my prey yesterday, I didn't do much else, and I haven't done anything with the other carcasses in my Inventory. Probably better do that, as I'm running out of space.

After setting up down by the river, I pull the corpses out one by one and start butchering them. It's only in doing this task that I realize just how many creatures I've killed since being here. *Good thing there's no RSPCA here,* I muse wryly to myself. I'd probably have been in court for being a mass murderer of animals or something. They're pretty varied too, and I collect some resources that I think will be quite useful: scales from the pangolin-kin, which might be able to be turned into armor of some sort; barbed hooks from the snilepede; a large, watertight shell from the sneleon, as well as a surprisingly long back tendon from the same; venom glands from the poison-badger-boar thing, though I only manage to get about a third of them intact; a rather ragged almost-rabbit skin; a slightly less ragged snake skin; and bones and meat of all types, of course, and fangs of different shapes and sizes.

I end up with six slots full of different meat. The killer chicken meat stacks with the other bird meat, for some reason, and the snake and the snilepede also stack together. The sneleon meat, however, is kept separate as is the pangolin-kin thing. My hoarder tendencies are coming out again—when I know how useful so many of these things can be, I don't want to leave *any* of them behind.

But ultimately, I can't keep everything in my Inventory—I don't have space—and I have no real way of preserving things outside of it. So, anything likely to rot soon, apart from meat, has to go. I keep some of the bones for boiling and crafting plus anything like fangs, barbs, and feathers, which aren't likely to go off. They're in my Inventory for now, filling all the slots. I'll pull them out later to keep in my alcove. Tendons, of course, get kept, and I start planning on how to dry it into sinew—however I look at things, I'm going to need a lot of cord, and sinew is probably the best place to start. That or bark, but I haven't yet spotted anything particularly suitable. After I've finished processing the carcasses, I'm in a bit of a state. I decide that washing off the blood and guts and other icky substances is most definitely necessary. About to strip off and jump right into the stream, I hesitate. Perhaps getting naked and vulnerable right next to where blood has soaked into the earth of the bank is not the best idea.

Heading upstream a bit, I get out of immediate proximity to the mess. In the end, I find the perfect spot for a bath. It's a naturally carved basin, obviously created by the water swirling around, but it's ideal for taking a bath without worrying about being swept away. Not that the stream is really strong enough to do that for me, but Lathani would probably have to be careful. Something to consider if she decides to take the forest exploration a bit further next time.

Stripping off my clothes, I leave my shoes and trousers on the bank but bring my shirt with me into the pool. The water is cool but not overly cold—enough to make a frisson of chill go up my spine, but not much more than that.

Keeping my head on a swivel, I shift deeper into the pool and start rinsing my shirt. Blood got all over the sleeves and a few sprays hit me on my chest and face, so the shirt is pretty ruined, really. At least, that would be the case if I'd been intending on going to a meeting with colleagues. Here, I don't think that the animals will care if I have bloodstains on me, and at least these clothes are still mostly intact, unlike the others I've been wearing so far since being here. Still, I'd rather I didn't stink of blood all the time—not only is it not particularly pleasant for me, but it's likely to attract creatures I don't want and scare away creatures I do. It would be better if I had some soap, but the cold running water suffices to wash away the worst of it, at least.

The water isn't much more effective in cleaning my body, especially when dealing with my hands, which handled the fatty bits of meat as well as plain blood. It doesn't do anything for my hair, though, which by this point is starting to itch and feel greasy. I really *wish* I'd taken the time and effort to grab shampoo, even if it had meant clearing a path through the broken glass. *Any* sort of soap would be useful right now. I remembered my deodorant, though—much good that does me. I *definitely* wasn't thinking straight when I packed to come here: I've brought three whole packs of condoms. Where did I think I was going? Still, even without soap, or even hot water, it's the first time in this world that I've had the chance to submerge myself in water. It's good to feel the accumulated grime of days wash off me.

By the time I've finished "cleaning," I look a whole lot better, but my skin doesn't really feel that clean. And I smell better, but not great. I suppose I've been spoiled by perfumes, shower gels, and shampoos. *Aah, sandalwood . . .*

It's funny, really, I reflect as I sit back in the pool and stare up at the sky above—a bit dangerous as a position, I know, but hopefully, a few minutes won't kill me. Literally. Anyway, it's funny to think that my girlfriend used to complain when I didn't have a shower in a couple of days—usually unable to motivate myself to do so after the stresses of the day. I never noticed my own smell then; now, I really can smell myself—and I wish I couldn't. Maybe I can create some soap at some point. I probably should. Who knows how many different types of bacteria are proliferating on my skin at this very moment?

For now, though, I take a few moments just to watch the sway of the branches above, listen to the babbling of the brook, and feel the current of water flow past me. By the time I decide that I've had enough of a soak, night is already closing in. I squeeze as much water out of my shirt as I can, deciding not to bother putting it back on afterwards.

Pulling my trousers on is a bit difficult as I have no towel to dry off, but I succeed. After rinsing my knife, I put it away too. I also take advantage of the opportunity to grab some more water with my canteen.

Then, after heading back up the hill, I use the last of the light to quickly start a fire outside to boil my water. While it's heating up, I arrange my non-Inventory items before munching some cooked bird meat. Once the water has started bubbling, I put out the fire, not wanting it to cause a problem while I'm asleep. Finally, I drink some tea-without-tea-leaves and fall into bed, completely exhausted as always. This time, my brain doesn't keep me awake for long.

CHAPTER TWENTY-EIGHT

Leveling Up

I'm staring at my status screen. I can't help it: I'm one percent away from the next level and I'm just waiting for that number to tick over to one hundred percent. My progress has been much quicker than I had expected it to be considering I only looked after Lathani yesterday. This isn't because I've had a fortunate encounter with Energy-rich, easy prey. No, it's due to my flawed calculations.

Turns out, when I estimated three days, I forgot to account for the Energy I absorb while inactive. I'd thought about it and been grateful that even while I was looking after a cute nunda cub, I'd still be making progress, but I didn't actually factor it into my calculations.

I *have* been more fortunate in today's hunting, partly because two of the three creatures actually hunted *me* rather than me having to chase them down. I'm even luckier that they bit off more than they could chew and I was able to escape both encounters with my life. In the end, I've gained fourteen percent by killing four creatures and eating their hearts; it's better than the eleven percent of the day before yesterday, but that's not ultimately what has made the difference.

When I checked my status this morning and realized I was already up to seventy-seven percent, I have to admit that my eyes boggled a bit. By the time I killed my last beast and saw that I was up to ninety-six percent, I decided to call it a day and head back to the cave.

Over the last twenty minutes or so, I must have checked my status a hundred or more times, anxious not to miss the moment I become able to level up. The only thing that overzealous checking has taught me is that I don't earn eleven units on the hour, every hour; no, it ticks up by one unit at regular intervals. I guess I could probably set my watch to it . . . if I had a watch, that is. Oh well, it's not like I need to catch a train or anything—a few minutes here or there isn't going to make any difference.

Anyway, I suppose the most important thing is that I actually have a relatively easy way of working out approximately how much time has passed between point A and point B, as long as I look at my status screen at each point. *There!* A frisson runs through me as I see the progress percentage has changed. *Funny—I don't feel any different.* If it wasn't for the number in front of me, I wouldn't know anything about being able to level up. There isn't even a notification that tells me. Well, I guess I'll just have to keep an eye on the number in the future so I don't miss the opportunity to level up next time.

Focusing on the box with the "100%" in it, I think, *level up*, as hard as possible at the screen. A new notification appears while the status screen disappears briefly.

Congratulations!
You have gathered enough Energy to push your body to the next level. Would you like to level up?

Y / N

"Yes!" I almost shout in my eagerness. It's a little embarrassing, actually, even if the only ones around to hear are two nundas, who probably don't care. The words blur and reform.

To level up, please choose the stats you would like to increase. You have 6 points available. Warning: if you do not assign all points now, you will be unable to use them later. You can choose to delay your level-up, but you will not store any further Energy until you do. Do you wish to continue to level up?

Y / N

"Yes," I say, forcibly calmly this time despite my heart starting to thump hard, and my status page opens in front of me again. Different from before, each of the stats has a plus sign next to it, and there is a six at the top of the page. *Six points . . . Not bad. Not bad at all.* That puts my Class far above average since the Common Classes, which give one or two points per level, are just that—common. The Uncommon ones, at three or four points, are not much better. Then come Rare classes with five, Epic with six, Legendary at seven, and Mythical at eight to ten points. Now I'm thinking about it, I have a vague memory of seeing the word "Epic" in Nicholas's letter—or maybe my brain is manufacturing memories again.

Making my choice doesn't take much thought; I've spent plenty of time today thinking and planning about where to assign my points depending on the number I have available. I've made plans for what I could do with anything from two to eight points, so now I only need to select the one for six points to move forwards.

I've considered and discarded multiple strategies. The System lore stone has made it clear that a specialization strategy taken to the extreme is not feasible, since all the stats work together, but everyone seems to have one to three stats they focus on more than the others. It makes sense for a farmer to have more stat points in the physical stats when compared to a scholar, who would have the reverse distribution; however, they wouldn't go so far as to say the other set of stats are "dump stats," though, as this would have negative implications for their own chosen stats.

It's not entirely clear how all the stats affect each other, but that they do is well-documented. Still, it is very tempting to put more points into my physical abilities, as those are keeping me alive at the moment. Strength will improve my ability to do damage to my opponents, Dexterity improves my dodging and precision, and Constitution . . . Well, it's in the name. The only thing that stops me from just putting two points in each physical stat is the fact that Dexterity and Strength are relatively easy to train, and the others aren't—at least, not where I am now.

Constitution is essential for my ongoing survival. The problem is that it appears to be best trained by surviving experiences that might easily kill me. My experience with the wolvezard is a case in point; such situations can easily get out of hand and turn deadly.

Intelligence is relatively easy to increase for people who have access to a library or teachers; for me, not so much. And that stat is important to me, as it decides another major factor for my survival: exactly how many casts of Lay-on-Hands I have in the tank.

Wisdom seems to always be a bit difficult to work on actively. As for Willpower, if the knowledge from the System lore stone is to be believed—and I really, really hope it is, otherwise I'm completely sunk—even people in Nicholas's world aren't quite sure how to train it. So, ultimately, I make the decision to shore up my weaknesses a bit.

Willpower isn't really an issue at the moment thanks to Kalanthia's blessing, so I don't put anything there. Instead, I split the points unevenly among Intelligence, Wisdom, and Constitution: one, three, and two points, respectively. It's fortunate that I don't second guess myself, as it seems to be impossible to remove a point once chosen. When the final point has been added, the status screen disappears and is replaced by another message.

You have chosen to increase your Wisdom. Would you like to increase your Breadth or your Depth?

Breadth / Depth

I look at the message with bafflement. Breadth? Depth? What is it talking about? For once, the knowledge from the System lore stone is no help as nothing surfaces from whatever I absorbed. Either it was never there to begin with or I lost it in the process of absorption. I guess I need to consider the question myself, then.

Breadth . . . A word similar to "width." Depth—that's a little more familiar; if we were talking about a lake here, I'd know exactly what it was trying to describe. It's a little less clear when it comes to Wisdom. Then again, maybe my image of a lake is helpful. Perhaps Breadth is about a wide sort of wisdom and depth is a deep sort? Actually, I'm not sure that really helps me in any way. I breathe out a frustrated sigh. Perhaps Kalanthia would know, but when I try to move, I realize I'm rooted to the ground. It sends a flutter of nerves through me. Just as well I did this at the cave instead of out in the woods. I'd be helpless against an attack if one came! In the end I don't spend any more time debating over the meaning of the words.

Ultimately, I decide that I need to be a bit of a jack-of-all-trades here, so Breadth is more likely to suit me than Depth at the moment. If the implications go deeper than that, I'll have to just figure it out later. Another problem for future-me.

I make my choice and the box disappears . . . but a moment later, it reappears with the same message. I click on *Breadth* again with a frown. When the box disappears and reappears a third time, I start wondering whether something's gone wrong. Perhaps it doesn't like me choosing Breadth? I try selecting *Depth* and this time the box disappears and doesn't reappear again a moment later.

I've only got enough time to briefly consider the fact that I chose to add three points to Wisdom and was offered the same choice three times before a strange feeling goes through my body. It's almost like a lightning bolt in its power, but it's not painful, just . . . strange. Then the prickling starts, and I regret my thought about there being no pain.

I grit my teeth as the prickles become more like pins and needles, and then those pins and needles stop pricking me and start stabbing me. At the point when I think I'll lose the battle against my voice and scream, it suddenly cuts out and the most heavenly feeling descends. All I can liken it to is having a painful massage that you hate at the time, but afterwards, once the aches have gone away, you feel so relaxed and loose and at peace with yourself. Like that, except multiplied tenfold. I bask in the moment of bliss, my eyes closing.

Of course, it's far too short, and as it fades, I start to feel very uncomfortable. This time it's not the stabbing pain kind of uncomfortable; it's the "I just ate ten rotten oysters and followed it up with rancid milk" kind of uncomfortable.

The next thing I know, I'm violently puking up my guts. I'm not sure that's actually a metaphor—as I stand back up from where I fell to my knees, I realize there are more lumps in the mess than the food I ate several hours ago would account for. Plus, there's the whole color and smell: it's black or really dark brown and smells like a dead animal that has been left to putrefy in a sewer for a couple of weeks. It tastes even worse.

Retching just at the taste and smell of it, I stumble away on legs that are as limp as wet noodles. Once I'm far enough from the puddle of vile . . . substance, I use some water to rinse out my mouth and chew on some bird meat to try to clear my taste buds. Incidentally, the killer chickens *do* actually taste like chicken.

A quick dip into the System lore knowledge informs me that what happened *is* actually normal. It's frustrating that I missed this. I spent the time waiting for my Energy store to tick up to full going through my "memories" about leveling several times. This never came up. Apparently, it wasn't "linked" to leveling until I thought about it—by which time it was too late.

Still, while annoying, I'm relieved that I'm not about to keel over dead. According to my absorbed knowledge, part of improving the body means clearing it of impurities formed by diet, living conditions, and even genetic defects. It'll probably happen a few more times. Obviously, the number of times varies depending on the individual and their previous living conditions, but after a time, my body will have cleared its impurities, and then I'll just be building on steady foundations and have minimal amounts to expel each time. Unfortunately, right now I've just puked vile gunk right in front of Kalanthia's cave, and from the rumble she's making, she's not very happy about it.

CHAPTER TWENTY-NINE

Fade

S orry," I tell her sheepishly. "I'll clean it. I was just leveling up." There's a huff and the rumble cuts out, but she says nothing. Matching action to words, I do my best to clean up. It's unpleasant, but after I've hauled away as much of the mess as I can and have buried the rest, the smell clears fairly quickly with the breeze. Sitting back down in the fading light, I pull up my status screen and look at my new stats.

Name: Markus Wolfe		Race: Human	Class: Tamer
Level: 1	Energy to next level: 0%	Energy absorption rate: 11u/hr	Energy towards debt: 0%
Intelligence	7	Mana: 70/70	
Wisdom	6	Mana regeneration rate: 150u/hr	
Willpower	15+3 (+20%)	Health regeneration rate 18/hr	
Constitution	7	Health 70/70	
Strength	6	Stamina: 30/30	
Dexterity	4	Stamina regeneration rate: 40u/hr	
Class Skills: Dominate – Beginner 1 Tame – Beginner 1		Non-Class Skills: Lay-on-Hands – Novice 3	

It's all much as I expected, including the fact that my Constitution is back to a one-to-ten ratio after restoring my vision. My doubled Wisdom has equally doubled my mana regeneration, meaning that I regain two and a half units per minute. Effectively, that means I could cast a new Lay-on-Hands every four minutes. *Much better than before!* And with the extra point in Intelligence, I also have additional casts of Lay-on-Hands in the tank. My health points have increased by twenty, more than half of what I had previously. Combined, these three factors could save my life. Maybe another cast of my healing magic would have made the difference in the wolvezard fight, or maybe my higher health points would have meant that I didn't get as low to begin with. Either way, I suddenly feel a lot better about my ability to survive in the near future.

One thing worries me, though: I still haven't made any progress towards my Energy debt. Is it that the Energy debt is so big that even enough Energy to level up isn't enough to reach one percent? Or, more concerning, is it that Energy gathered towards leveling up doesn't actually count towards the debt? I push this question away for now too; I've only been in this world for a few days, so I've got time to worry about it later. Ultimately, I'm satisfied with my advancements. Now my aim is to stay at level one for a while to try to earn as many "natural" points as possible. I figure I'll accept as many points as I can, with the Energy coming mainly from my daily absorption. Since it's actually possible to increase my stats without using Energy as a shortcut, even if I don't have enough Energy, I'll know I'm still making progress.

Speaking of progress, there should be something more for me that comes along with my level-up: my new Skill. I'm a little surprised that it didn't flash up like the message about assigning my stat points did, but maybe it's not considered part of the level-up process as much as just a side benefit. Now I think about it, there's that nagging feeling of a message waiting for me. After opening up my message box, I click on the new message available.

Congratulations!
You have earned 1 Skill point. Would you like to see the selection of your available Skills or save the Skill point for later?

Skill list / Bank

I pick the obvious choice. A short list of three available Skills forms itself on the blank space hovering before my eyes.

Fade (1)
An essential Skill for the stealthy attacker, Fade offers the ability to be concealed from others' awareness by using a mixture of bodily control and magical concealment. At lower levels, this Skill works fully only when you are unmoving; as Skill levels progress, your ability to move while staying concealed improves. Note: this Skill works primarily to conceal the user from sight; concealment from other physical senses scales with Willpower; concealment from metaphysical senses scales with Wisdom.

Stun (1)
Release your remaining mana in a single directed blast from your hands to render your opponent unable to move for between one and ten seconds. Note: the effects of the blast depend on both amount of mana remaining and distance from the epicenter of the discharge. The length of time the target is stunned will be partially determined by the disparity between your Willpower and that of your opponent. Maximum effect can be achieved at full mana and when touching the target.

Track (1)

Notice and be able to follow marks that show the passage of your target. This Skill scales with Intelligence.

You have 1 Skill point available. Either choose a Skill to use your Skill point now or choose "Bank" to store the point for later and close the Skill selection menu.

Hmm. Two Skills I really want, and one Skill that probably overlaps significantly with the knowledge I already have about tracking. With only one point available, I'm not willing to pick it just in case it gives me a slight boost to my tracking abilities. Well, at least it makes narrowing down the possibilities to two easier. Choosing between those is more difficult, though. This is in part because they indicate the direction in which I could take my "build." Fade is clearly more of an ambusher's aid and would definitely complement the archery I'm planning on engaging in. Stun, on the other hand, is much more of a close-range Skill—or, of course, an emergency escape tactic. I find it interesting how most of the Skills I've been offered have been based on the soul stats. Only Fade mentions "bodily control," which I would guess links to one or more of the physical stats, but even that scales off Wisdom and Willpower. Not what I'd have expected.

Anyway, I need to choose one Skill for now. Fortunately, I know that at level five I'll be offered the Skills I passed over this time plus some other options, so I can always choose my second favorite then if nothing better has appeared. So . . . Fade or Stun? The choice of saving the Skill point for later doesn't appeal. I need these Skills *now*, and if I can't have both now, I'll at least have one. As for which one . . .

In the end, the choice is evident. An emergency lifeline might be a literal life-saver, but I can't base my tactics on Plan B—I actually need a Plan A first. Using range was how humans moved past cavemen, and range is how I'm going to survive this forest arena. Though, I suppose that with sufficiently high support stats, Stun could be used at range too . . .

No, I think, shaking my head. The main issue with Stun is that it blows my mana pool in a single strike. If it doesn't work well enough, then I'm toast. What if there are multiple enemies? And even if it *does* work to get me free of whatever opponent is threatening me, if I'm severely injured, then I'll be without mana for Lay-on-Hands until it regenerates itself. Maybe if my mana regeneration rate was higher, it might be more feasible. But for now?

I pick Fade before I can overthink it.

I open my status screen again and look at the lines below it that list my Skills. There's a new addition, as expected.

Class Skills:	Non-Class Skills:
Dominate – Beginner 1	Lay-on-Hands – Novice 3
Tame – Beginner 1	
Fade – Beginner 1	

So, time to test my new Skill. I wonder how to do so for a few moments before just shrugging and standing still. I think, *Fade*, and then just wait. Nothing seems any different. When I look at myself out of the corner of my eye, I can see everything just fine. Is it not working? I hesitate for a moment before poking my head into the cave.

"Kalanthia?" I ask tentatively. There's a huffing sound, and she doesn't even open her eyes, but she doesn't tell me to go away either. I decide I might as well ask. "Can you tell me if there's any effect from this?" *From what?* In answer, I reactivate Fade. Kalanthia huffs again, but this time I detect a slightly curious sound to it. She stands up and pads over to me, then sniffs at me, twisting her head one way and then the other. "So?" I ask after the silence draws on. Shifting a little, her eyes fix properly on me again.

A strange sensation, she tells me. *I could hear you and smell you, but when I looked directly at you, my eyes told me you were not there.* Huh. Interesting.

"What about when you didn't look directly at me?" I ask, curious.

I could catch a glimpse of your form but only because I knew you were there. There was something about the Energy around you that tried to convince me you were something other than what you are. I was able to overcome it with a little effort. "Thanks, Kalanthia," I say after a few moments of thinking. "I just got this new Skill and was testing it out."

Ah, the benefits of being human, she says sagely, turning around to curl back up on her bedding. I notice Lathani snoozing away in a little heap nearby. Something in her words catches my attention.

"Do you not have Skills?" Perhaps it's a little intrusive, but the question just slips out. She looks at me for a long moment, her golden gaze unreadable. *No. Beasts, however advanced and powerful we are, don't have Skills. Those are the purview of humans alone.*

"So, what do you have? I mean, you made my cave with magic or something."

She turns her head a little and huffs—her version of a shrug, I think. *Beasts advance as we gain more and more control over Energy: first that of our own bodies and then that of the outside world. No beast's control is exactly the same as another's, unlike human Skills.*

With that, she puts her head down on her paws, obviously done. I'm curious but don't want to bother her with my questions, so I just thank her again and then go back outside to leave her in peace. Very interesting . . . If I put it in Earth terms, it sounds like . . . Well, if we compare Energy to cookie dough, beasts are using a knife, and humans are using a cookie cutter. They might approximate the same shape, but the cookies made with a knife are always going to be slightly different from each other, whereas the ones made with the cutter will be identical—unless the cookie dough sticks in the cutter, but maybe that's taking the metaphor a bit too far.

Well, at least I know the thing works, and I understand its limitations a bit more too. I'll still need to be quiet, and it will be better to approach prey from downwind. Plus, creatures that don't rely primarily or at all on sight will probably not be much affected. For now, anyway. Once I get my Willpower and Wisdom higher, the Skill should be capable of more.

I guess it wouldn't affect heat-sensing abilities either, but I get the impression Kalanthia doesn't have those. Still, the fact that it worked to an extent on something as powerful and intelligent as my nunda protector indicates how well it will do on other creatures, even if she *was* able to overcome the effects in the end.

It's a bit disconcerting that I can't actually tell whether it's working or not except by its effects. I can imagine that when I use this to hide from some creature, I'll be at risk of soiling my pants, not knowing if I'm hidden in plain sight or not. At least breathing doesn't seem to count as moving—it would rather limit the amount of time I could use the Skill if I had to hold my breath.

Now, what does it use as fuel? Stamina or mana? I activate it again and watch my status screen to see how it affects me in numerical terms; the bars always in my vision are good for approximate measurements but not for finer detail stuff.

After several attempts, I discover that it mostly consumes stamina but also a bit of mana. It seems to be a one-to-four ratio, so for every minute I'm in Fade, I consume one unit of mana and four of stamina. As my stamina is the much lower value, that currently limits my Skill use to eight minutes at maximum, taking into account my stamina regeneration. Not all that useful now, but if I dedicate some points or training to the Endurance part of Strength . . .

With my level-up done, my Skill picked and tested, and my new stats experimented with, it's now time to pick up some resources for my first priority tomorrow morning: creating a chimney. It may not be strictly necessary for survival, but being able to light a fire in my little cave without worrying about dying from smoke inhalation seems like a luxury. A luxury I desperately want.

CHAPTER THIRTY

Pressure

I've been going without a fire most of the last few days. In fact, I've only really lit one to boil water and to cook the hearts of beasts I've killed, and that only because I know the Energy in them would be wasted if I waited or put them in my Inventory.

Even after finding a safe spot, I haven't wanted to risk upsetting Kalanthia with smoke filling the cave. Heaven help me if Lathani accidentally burned herself either in the fire itself or on the embers left behind. Then again, maybe Kalanthia's reaction would be a bit different—she's a nunda mom, not a human one.

I've been living off the meat I'd cooked in bulk previously—and that's not too bad, to be honest, since my Inventory keeps it hot—but I'm running low on that and, honestly, could do with some variety. I carefully keep my mind away from all the things I miss. *Pizza, pasta, cookies, cheeseburgers . . . Damn!* Evidently, trying *not* to think of the pink elephant failed miserably. Now I've found a spot I'm likely to stay in for a while, I want to work out which of the local plants can be eaten and then probably start cooking with them in hopes that they will give a bit of variety to my diet. But to do all that, I need a chimney that will direct the smoke to the hole in the wall that Kalanthia made, and *that* means I need clay.

Fortunately, with the hunting I've done over the last few days, I've also been able to identify a number of really important resources, a likely spot for river clay being one of them. It's a good hour's walk from the cave, so I probably have just enough time to go there and dig some out before returning for nightfall.

Once more, I thank God—or Nicholas—for my Inventory; the thought of otherwise having to make multiple trips makes me very grateful for it. As I walk, I keep my eyes open, both literally and figuratively. There is so much to see, between fauna and flora, danger and beauty, and sometimes both at once. I could probably walk this same route a hundred times and still find something new every time.

Suddenly, something I see makes me pause. Tracks . . . of a porcupig. A single one. They aren't old; the creature is probably not that far away. I bite my lip, considering. Do I follow them? If I do, there's no guarantee that I'll have time to fetch the clay, but the possibilities . . .

In the end, I make a snap decision and refuse to let myself second-guess it. I follow the tracks, almost automatically by this point shifting into a quieter, sneakier gait. Even as I step quietly through the forest, I marvel at the difference between this and the first time I tried it. I won't deny that I still make some noise—when the ground is covered in dead leaves, I still haven't quite grasped the technique of not crunching them a little—but it's a *lot* less than at the beginning. Well, I suppose I *have* had a lot of practice.

The niggling sensation that normally indicates a message waiting in my inbox appears as I start to hear the noise of the porcupig rustling and rooting through the leaves ahead. Debating with myself, I end up deciding to check; who knows, it could be something important that makes me abort my hunt. I tuck myself behind a tree and crouch down after making sure that there's nothing visible up in the branches above that's likely to drop on me. Then, I open my message box and read the new notification.

Congratulations! You have earned a Skill: Stealth
Read Skill description? Y / N

I roll my eyes a little as I choose to see the Skill description. Does anyone ever say no to reading a description of the Skill they've just earned? *Actually,* I think suddenly, *since when is it possible to* earn *Skills? I thought I gained access to Skills only at certain level intervals?*

Though, when I think about it, I realize that nothing I learned from the stone actually says that this is the *only* way to gain Skills; it's just the only way that's specified. *Huh. So I can gain Skills outside of being offered them on level-up . . . somehow. Cool.*

Actually, the more I think about it, the better it becomes. Skills have proven to be an important part of my survival strategy. If I hadn't had Lay-on-Hands from the get-go, I'd have been toast on the second day here. Fade seems pretty useful too, and I'm about to try one of my other Skills now.

Up until now, though, I've been limited to the initial Skills I was given and what I was able to choose by leveling up. Now, though . . . If I can develop the right kind of Skills, my likelihood of survival will shoot up. I guess I'll have to figure out how to do that later. For now, I focus on what I've just given myself.

Stealth (passive unless actively turned off) At the cost of a little stamina, you are harder to hear and to detect, especially when staying still. When faced with something that will cause a disturbance, you will have a better understanding of how to either stealthily avoid the area completely or step on it in a way that will not alert an observer. Higher levels of Dexterity increase your chances of Stealth being successful. As Stealth improves, you can either choose to blend in better with the dark or with color. Both of these effects use mana.
Close message? Y / N

Not dissimilar from what I would have imagined for a Skill called "Stealth," though slightly disappointing: apart from the last two lines, it just basically sounds like what I've been doing to a greater or lesser extent since I arrived in this world—or at least since I absorbed the woodcraft knowledge stone and learned I *needed* to do it. At this point, I'm starting to be able to realize *before* I step on a crackly leaf or crunchy twig and then take evasive measures.

Still, I guess the Skill might just make the task easier, though if it drains my stamina and stops me from using Fade as much, I'll probably turn it off. That's an interesting point, though; I haven't heard of a Skill that is passive unless you want it off.

All my other Skills I have to activate, well, actively. *So, what? If I improve this Skill, then I'll become a heart attack on legs, padding up to old grannies on silken feet and scaring them into the grave?* I make a wry grin at my own morbid humor. I do hope, though, that the last two lines of the description mean what I think they do; either shadow magic or magical camo would be *awesome*. Though, perhaps magical camo would make Fade rather unneeded . . . *Oh well, we're too far away from that to worry about it,* I think to myself, closing my screen down.

For now, not wanting to risk my hunt with an untried Skill, I deactivate it and activate Fade. Creeping closer to the porcupig's location, it soon comes into view. As I'd thought, it's rooting through leaves, the small horn on its snout easily flipping them over. Now it's chewing something crunchy, fully engrossed in its meal. A good opportunity, I decide. Now, how to do this . . . ?

The two biggest concerns I have are its quills and it potentially running away. If I had a net, I'd be able to overcome both of those with no problems, but I don't. That said, if I'm willing to make the sacrifice, I have something else that would probably work . . .

I wrestle with myself but ultimately decide that it's worth the pain. Grimacing a little, I withdraw my jacket from my Inventory. I'd put it in there for later when the temperatures drop, but it seems like I've found another use for it. I just hope that I'll be able to repair it at some point.

With Fade still active, I step forward one pace at a time holding the jacket and approach the porcupig from behind. Three meters between us. Two meters. One.

I throw the jacket over the quills, soft side down. The porcupig startles as it feels something land on it and whirls around quicker than I expected. We're face to face, both frozen for a moment in surprise. Then that lizard-like snout lets out a snarl and lowers so I'm facing the small horn.

A moment later, the creature charges and I only just manage to throw myself out of the way. I push myself up as quickly as possible while the porcupig is already sliding to a stop. There's no time to think—I just have to act.

Diving on the porcupig would probably be a prickly torture at any other time, but my jacket is doing its job. Although I can feel the quills beneath it, my jacket is stopping them from rising and impaling me.

My weight pushes the creature to the ground, stopping another form of attack. Though it might have done some damage with the momentum of its charge, me pinning it down on the ground is a different story. It still does its best to break free, thrashing and trying to bite me. It's a mess for a while: its front paws flail around, its mouth snaps at anything in range, my hands try to find a space that isn't either spiky quill or biting mouth, and my face tries to stay away from the various weapons threatening it. Fortunately, my body weight is pinning its back legs and middle section, otherwise it would be even more difficult to manage.

"Come on, *Dominate*," I spit out in between curses. Nothing happens. "*Dominate*, damn it, *Dominate!*" My eyes meet the porcupig's golden slit-pupiled ones and suddenly we both freeze.

The rest of the world fades away, and it's just the two of us, staring at each other. We're frozen, unable to move towards or away from each other, or at all, really. Instead, there's a sense of . . . pressure. A pressure that mounts every moment. It's a pressure that comes from above and even more from between us. It's uncomfortable and every instant that passes makes it even more so.

I push back. Not physically, but mentally. It's more instinctive than conscious, but there's a part of me that refuses to be crushed, that sets metaphysical hands against the weight and *pushes*. The pressure lessens. Slowly at first and then faster and faster.

Suddenly, I can move. I step forwards, following the sense of receding pressure. Bit by bit I move closer to the still frozen porcupig. Our gazes are still fixed, even when we're only a few centimeters from each other. The sense of pressure is still there, but I can feel that it's not directed at me. It's like I'm standing holding a powerful hose that's jetting out water—you can feel the power in the hose, the sense that if you let go it will spray everything, including you, but in the moment *you're* the one in control. And the porcupig is in the direct path of the stream of water.

Of course, there isn't actually any water nor any physical evidence of the pressure I can feel. No evidence at all except for what I see in the porcupig's eyes and what I feel emanating from the creature in front of me: a determined resistance that crumbles bit by bit until, finally, it gives in. I see the reluctant acceptance flood the creature's gaze, and it dips its head in what feels like acknowledgment, the first time it has moved since we entered this space. And with that, the world snaps back into focus, the sudden vibrancy almost a shock to the system.

CHAPTER THIRTY-ONE

Biological Digger

I feel disorientated for a moment and blink quickly at the sudden bright light piercing my eyes. Fortunately, neither effect lasts long, and I'm soon fighting fit again. Though, if that's the result of a successful Dominate—at least, I'm pretty sure it was successful—what would it have been like if I'd failed?

The porcupig is still. It's alive—I can feel it breathing steadily—but all that frantic fight has left it. *Has it worked?* Only one way to test.

I withdraw slowly, ready to shift my weight back onto it at any sign that it's decided to restart the wrestling match.

By the time I'm sitting back on my heels, there still hasn't been any movement beyond breathing. I look at its face, wondering if it's unconscious. Not so. Those eyes are looking at me calmly. The reluctant acceptance I saw there in our battle has gone. Though I'm not exactly an expert in porcupig body language, what I do read there makes me wonder. It's relaxed, waiting, watchful, and there's a wariness there, but mostly it's just waiting. For what? For me to kill it? For me to leave? Or . . . for me to give an order? If my Skill has worked the way I'm expecting it to, this creature should now be under my control.

"Stand up," I say eventually, unable to help the slightly questioning lilt to my voice. When the porcupig shifts, I can't help myself from quickly regaining my feet, my hand on my knife hilt.

Fortunately—for both of us—it just stands up and then waits quietly, mostly unmoving. *Okay, that's pretty cool,* I admit to myself, a sense of glee building in my stomach. *Let's try something else.*

"Walk over to that tree and then back again," I order it, pointing at a tree a few meters away.

Without complaint, the porcupig obeys the letter of my command. "Okay, now dig in that spot," I tell it, pointing at a spot on the ground near where it had been rooting before. Once more, it obeys my command to the letter. What I do notice is that it digs in the spot I pointed it to and nowhere else.

"Stop." I was wrong before. This isn't pretty cool. This is damn *awesome.* I've now got a biological digger under my command, and I've tested out one of my Class Skills and it's just as good as I was hoping. After detaching my jacket carefully from the porcupig's quills—grimacing at the number of rips and holes in the inner layers—I set off towards the river clay area, casually ordering my new follower to, well, *follow*.

Reaching the area I'd spotted yesterday, I'm able to confirm that, indeed, it's a spot that contains river clay. It's something of a flood plain, I think. It's probably the inner part of a river bend that is low enough to be flooded when the river is swollen with recent rainfall, but high enough not to be underwater all the time. Either that, or the river's moved over time, cutting more deeply into the other bank and eventually leaving its old course mostly dry. Either is possible, really, or both.

The point is, it's been underwater long enough to have accumulated the fine silt that makes up river clay, but it's dry enough for me to access it. With my new biological digger, it probably takes a third of the time to accumulate a good amount of clay than it would have taken me by myself. I pack the clay into my Inventory, filling one slot until it refuses to accept any more and then filling a second.

I'm no great judge of clay; the memories I received were more about the uses of clay than assessing its quality, but it seems decent enough. There are a good number of rocks and stones as well as the finer silt, which is really what I want, but that's always going to be the case. It's not like popping down to my nearest art shop to order a bag of pottery clay, is it? The large quantity of impurities just means more processing will be required to make usable clay out of what is essentially river mud. As for the quality of the clay itself, the proof is in the pudding—or in this case, the firing.

When I reckon I've got enough to be getting on with for now, and knowing I can always come back here later, I tell my new pet to stop and follow me again. It does so docilely, trotting at my heels, its head reaching about the height of my knee and its quills just about mid-thigh.

As I walk home, I feel like I'm riding high on glee and excitement. Visions flash through my mind of a legion of beasts, protecting me, hunting for me, working for me, and making life so much easier and more comfortable than it has been since I arrived here. And best of all, they probably won't complain, and they certainly can't decide to quit my employ because I haven't raised their salary recently.

I look back at the porcupig and accidentally meet its gaze again. A sense of unease niggles at my belly and I look away again. I don't know what that was about. The sense of unease continues to be present throughout my walk back home, becoming more urgent whenever I happen to notice the porcupig's presence. I try my best to ignore it following me, not wanting to deal with the sensation more than necessary.

To distract myself, I decide to test my new Stealth Skill now I'm not in the middle of a hunt. As I move carefully through the forest, I notice that my newest Skill is both more and less than I thought it would be. Less because I admit I harbored some secret hope that despite what it said in the description, it would still be some epic tool that would make me the stealthiest stealther who ever stealthed— or something like that. And more because I'd also feared that it was basically just describing the skill I had already learned with the promise of future awesome improvements.

In reality, I don't even notice it working until the moment when I suddenly realize I'm about to put my weight on a stick that's bound to crack loudly. I've already shifted my weight forwards, so it's either step on the stick or fall over, which will create as much, if not more noise than just stepping.

Then, the fraction of a second before my foot lands, something happens. Some minute adjustment is made and although I *do* step on the stick, I don't put any weight on it, and it remains unbroken. Knowing this is an example of my Skill activating, I quickly check my stamina pool by pulling up my screen—the little bar in my peripheral vision really isn't accurate enough for this sort of thing.

It's at twenty-six out of thirty. That means this little maneuver probably consumed three or four units of stamina. Probably more like three, as I'm also walking, which consumes stamina over time, even if it's only small amounts. Well, that's not too bad as long as it doesn't activate when I'm really low on stamina, even though if I combine it with Fade, I'll be bottoming out quite quickly unless I aim to put more points into Strength—namely Endurance—or Dexterity as a priority.

Then a thought strikes me: it didn't specify the amount of stamina that would be used. What if there *is* no standard amount? What if it changes each time? I have reason to believe that could be the case: I'm able to change how much mana is put into Lay-on-Hands depending on the severity of the wound and how much focus I put into it.

I decide to test it, which ends up being a bit of a frustrating exercise. The main problem is that I don't know *when* the Skill's more active part will suddenly activate, so I end up stomping on a lot of twigs and noisy leaves before my test gives me enough data to work with. In the end, I conclude that I'm right: Stealth *does* change its consumption. It seems that how much it takes ranges from a single unit to maybe around six units.

As always, it's hard to get absolutes here, but I have to guess that one unit is the lowest because I got that result once and the System doesn't seem to like fractional numbers. As for six, it's the highest that I get during my test, but since one of the main factors seems to be how much concentration I'm using, I can't really test fairly. After all, I have to be aware that the test is happening in order to notice how much stamina has been used.

Anyway, the cost seems based essentially on how much effort it will take to redirect my body to avoid making the noise. That means that if I notice before I've shifted my weight and consciously decide how and where I should move to avoid the issue, the stamina cost is minimal. If, however, I only notice the issue once Stealth has intervened, it costs me more. Makes sense, I suppose.

By the time I've finished testing to my satisfaction, the hill is in sight, then I'm climbing it, with my spiky follower still at my heels. Glancing at him briefly brings back that uneasy feeling, which I had managed to put to the back of my mind while testing out my new Skill.

Cresting the hill, I walk towards the cave mouth, still musing over why exactly

I'd be feeling uneasy at finally putting into use one of my Class Skills. It's getting dark, and it's darker besides in the cave. Still, there's enough light for me to make out Kalanthia's shape, and I murmur a quiet greeting. Used to my words usually attracting a huff or nothing at all, I am surprised when she actually responds verbally.

Greetings, Binder, she purrs. *Have you brought me a snack? Grenslar are small but tasty.* For a moment, her meaning is as clear as mud. Then, as I glance around me and my eyes alight on my follower, I understand. Oh. *Oh.* In hindsight, maybe I should have considered the *giant predator* that I live with before bringing my tasty-looking new pet home with me . . . Then again, this was always going to happen because I reckon any creature I'll be able to claim in the next year will probably count as prey for the nunda. "Um, no," I say, searching for words. "Can you not eat this, uh"—*what did she call it? Grendal? No . . . Grenslar, that's what it was*—"this grenslar, please? I've, um, *bound* it. I want it to work for me, not be eaten."

Very well. She sighs. *Make sure that your Bonded does not pose a threat to Lathani.* "Sure. Actually, on that point, are you planning on going hunting any time soon?"

I shall need to hunt again in two sunrises.

"Okay, thanks for letting me know." I pause for a moment, trying to think whether there's anything else I need to say.

Deciding not, I bid Kalanthia goodnight and head into my alcove.

CHAPTER THIRTY-TWO

Bound

The porcupig—grenslar, whatever—follows me into my alcove; the darkness inside combined with the creature's murky coloring makes it almost impossible to see it. In fact, it's only by the odd shine of its quills in the shaft of moonlight entering my cave through the hole in the wall that I can see the creature at all. I imagine rolling over in the night and smacking into those quills point first with either my hand or my face and shudder a bit. But I don't want to send it out into the night and risk it being eaten by a nocturnal predator without me even knowing anything about it. Not to mention it would be a bit of a waste of a jacket. "Stay just inside the entrance to the cave. Sleep if you can." The porcupig looks at me for a moment and then trots off. I peek out of my alcove to see it silhouetted against the sky, lying down at the entrance to the cave. Looking in the other direction, I see Kalanthia watching me, her golden eyes catching the light. "Say, Kalanthia . . . You seem to know a bit more about this whole . . . Binding thing than I do. Do you know how my new . . . Bound . . . understands me? Enough to follow orders, at least."

It's something I've been wondering ever since the thought occurred to me on the way back from the clay pit. It's not like animals on Earth are born with some innate understanding of language—heck, not even *humans* are born able to speak the language of their parents. Everyone has to learn, one way or another, and even the smartest animals aren't able to *use* language in the same way as humans. Yet the porcupig has followed every single command, even ones like "Stay just inside the entrance to the cave," which requires understanding what the entrance and cave I'm talking about are, as well as what "stay" means—let alone the distance of "just inside"—but the creature managed to do it perfectly.

And that's not to mention Kalanthia, of course, and her ability to communicate telepathically with words. *That* just seems too crazy to be real—except it undoubtedly is. *Why should your Bound not understand you? That is the purpose of the Bond: to communicate your desires and ensure compliance.* "Okay, one: I don't understand how *you* understand me because I'm speaking a language that probably doesn't exist in this world. And two: what do you mean by 'to communicate your desires and ensure compliance'?"

Your two questions have the same answer. You *may be using a language that I have never encountered, but it matters not. We are communicating mind-to-mind, so your human "words" are no obstacle. The same is true with your Bound.*

"We're doing what now?" I ask slightly rhetorically. Shaking my head, not in rejection but to try and clear it a bit, I attempt to form a question that might help me to understand more. "We're communicating mind-to-mind? I thought that's what *you* were doing, and I was speaking out loud . . ."

No, she replies, sounding a little as if she thinks I'm being just a bit slow or stupid. *Your "words" mean nothing to me. I receive the meaning of your speech by catching the thoughts that you project, and then you receive my meaning because I place it in your outer mind, which transforms it into "words" for your own benefit. For creatures unused to mental communication, I believe speaking out loud enables the thoughts to travel far enough for a telepath to catch them. Those more competent at it have no need to make sounds aloud and communicate all they wish by thoughts alone.*

"Okay," I say slowly, my thoughts awhirl. While it kind of makes a bit more sense than a giant leopard in a world far different from my own understanding English, it's still hard for me to grasp. "Could I learn to do that?"

Kalanthia tosses her head. *Perhaps. You would need significantly more understanding of the world around you and the ability to reach out with your mind beyond yourself to touch the aura of your conversation partner.* Something to aim for, perhaps. Still, it hasn't quite answered my other question.

"So how does all this link to the porcupig—sorry, grenslar—being able to understand me? You can't tell me that it's a telepath, surely." The nunda whuffs out an amused breath.

No. We could hardly say that. As I said before, your "words" are irrelevant, as you are in fact communicating your command mentally. "But *how?*" It's dark, but even so I can feel Kalanthia looking at me disapprovingly.

Come now, you forged a link with your Bound and do not even know what you have done?

"The . . . the Battle of Wills?" I guess as that whole experience comes back to the fore of my memory.

Indeed. You engaged a free creature in a Battle of Wills and overcame it. The will of the grenslar has bowed to yours and accepted the chain of your dominance. The chain works to communicate your desires to your Bound. Once more, the sounds you make aloud are irrelevant except that they help you *to focus on what you wish your Bound to do. The chain of my dominance . . . It sounds rather terrible,* I think as the unease rises once more.

"What did you mean by 'ensure compliance' earlier," I ask, my mouth feeling rather dry. "Is it . . . is it linked to the . . . 'chain of my dominance'?"

Indeed. You have proven your will to be greater than that of your Bound, and as long as this is the case, the chain shall hold tightly to your Bound's will. Should your will weaken, or should your Bound's will grow faster than yours, you may find that the chain loosens and weakens. Too much of a difference and it may break entirely.

I . . . don't know what to think about that. Though, while I've got Kalanthia here . . . "Is this 'will' the same as Willpower?"

Not exactly, she replies before pausing. *Will is based on Willpower to a large extent but can be impacted by outside factors in a way Willpower cannot be. For example, if you are cold and someone offers you heat, your will may be weakened in a Battle of Wills, but your Willpower remains the same.*

Okay, that kind of makes sense. In fact, that explains why trapping a creature before starting the Battle of Wills makes a difference in outcome. *Is your curiosity satisfied?*

"Oh," I say, realizing I've been standing there in thought for a longer-than-normal pause. "Yes, thank you, Kalanthia."

She doesn't speak again, and all I hear is a slight sound of her readjusting her position.

I step into my cave, mostly feeling my way by now. After pulling out my canteen and a handful of meat, I eat quickly, the food almost tasteless in my mouth as I consider the new information I've received.

Clearly Kalanthia knows a fair bit about my Class, and I don't think I'm imagining the slight hint of distaste underlying her mental "voice." Or should that be "thoughts"?

That just by itself is something difficult to grasp. It's hard enough to accept that a giant leopard can speak into my mind; it's even harder to conceptualize that it's not even *words* that either of us are apparently communicating with. But it does make sense of the fact that a dumb woodland animal can understand even simple commands with no training.

That brings my thoughts onto the thorny subject of what exactly I've done to the creature. I'm not sure what I expected of Dominate, but I can't help but think it's not *this*. I feel . . . I feel like the *bad guy*.

Once I realize that, a weight lifts from my chest; the act of putting a name to the uneasiness curling within me actually alleviates it to a certain degree. I took an animal from the wild and forced it to follow me, to obey me. I've . . . Well, if it were a human, the only term that would be appropriate would be "enslave." Since it's not a human, the term doesn't quite fit. After all, most people don't use "enslave" to talk about the pigs raised to be slaughtered as soon as they reach adult weight for meat, or the chickens kept in small spaces and given food only because we want the eggs that they will produce. There are lots of animal rights activists who would argue against these practices, but I don't think even they would use the term "enslavement" to describe it.

Still, the feeling is uncomfortably close. The porcupig had a life in the forest. It may not have been a long one—for all I know, it would have been eaten this very night had I left it. It may also have been destined to live to a ripe old age, having sired—or borne; I can't say I've actually checked if it's male or female—dozens of little piglets. Or whatever they're called. We'll never know now. But then, how different is that from the original process used by humans on the forerunners of domestic and farmyard animals now? The original wolves that eventually became dogs, the original beasts that became domesticated cows and goats and sheep. These animals gave up agency in return for security, freedom in exchange for food. It may not have been a conscious decision, but it was an exchange, nonetheless. *This . . . this isn't quite the same,* I admit to myself quietly, looking down at the meat in my hands. Is the porcupig hungry? Thirsty? Needing something else? I don't know, and that's a symptom of the issue. I haven't offered anything to the porcupig in exchange for its cooperation. Not even like the pigs or the chickens, which are at least housed and fed in exchange for their lives—a poor exchange, perhaps, but an exchange, nonetheless. I pinned the porcupig down and forced a Battle of Wills upon it that it didn't ask for, which I positioned myself to win from the start. And even if I could release it—though, Kalanthia didn't say anything about that—I wouldn't, because of how useful it could be. That thought makes me shiver a little, feeling like my foundations have been rocked a bit. I'd always liked to think I was a nice guy—a good guy, really. Someone who would stand up for the innocent if it was demanded, someone in whom the hero was just sleeping, ready to awaken in the right circumstances.

I've suddenly realized that's not true. Because a hero would immediately swear off using this tool, which feels like something animal activists would put on a bus-stop poster. A hero would willingly take the hard road: spend time to win an animal's loyalty and then use Tame to do whatever Tame does, if indeed it was even necessary by that point.

That's not what I'm going to do. The last few days have taught me that I'm a survivor. I've learned that I have so much more capacity to keep going, to withstand pain and keep fighting, than I would have ever imagined in my cushy life as a corporate drone. And when the chips are down, a survivor uses any tools at his disposal. He doesn't care about fair fights or about even odds. He places traps and ambushes and aims to disable if he can't kill immediately. He *survives*. No, much as I would like to think of myself as a hero, I'd like to be alive significantly more.

Maybe when I grow in power and improve my ability to survive, I'll be able to be more heroic, but for now, I'm a survivor. And when a tool is unsavory but offers better odds of survival, a survivor *uses* it. So, I'm not going to swear I will never use Dominate again.

I'm not going to even try to release my current follower—"Bound" was the term Kalanthia used. What I *am* going to do, for my own peace of mind if nothing else, is swear to treat my Bound well. It may not have been a voluntary choice for my Bound, but while it serves me obediently, I will make sure that it has everything it needs and that it comes out of the experience better than when it went in. I make a promise to myself that I will never use Dominate without a good reason, nor will I use my Bound as cannon fodder—assuming they wouldn't balk at a suicide mission anyway.

The vows I make to myself relax the sense of uneasiness inside me enough for me to start feeling sleepy. I lie down on my "bed" and pull my jacket over me. After the long day I've had, sleep creeps up on me quickly.

CHAPTER THIRTY-THREE

Smack in the Face

Walking out of my cave the next day, I feel a mixture of excitement and guilt at the sight of my new Bound still lying at the entrance. It's awake and looking at me with calm eyes, seemingly not railing against its loss of freedom the way I would have. Though, that could be another function of the Bond, for all I know. I remember my resolution of the evening before and look at it squarely. "I'm sorry," I say first, taking myself a little by surprise. It was hard to begin, and I hadn't intended on apologizing to start off with, but somehow it seems . . . right.

"I'm sorry that I took you out of your life, that I captured you and . . . bound you to my will. I did it because I need your help. In return, I promise I will do what I can to make your life better and easier than it probably would have been." I pause, hesitating a little, before deciding to go ahead. "As a sign of this commitment, I give you a name." Here I hesitate again, not having actually chosen one.

"I'll call you . . . Spike," I say, after finally deciding. It's not the best of names, rather too descriptive to be funny or cute, but it'll do. At least it'll be easy to remember! There's a long moment in which the porcupig—Spike— doesn't move or do anything, really, before it seems like something clicks.

For a fleeting instant, something else appears in Spike's eyes: an emotion too complex and too brief for me to even have a hope of decoding it. Then the moment's over, and it's like nothing happened. Hopefully, Spike will respond to the name from now on. It should if my understanding of what Kalanthia said last night is correct. Now, first things first.

"Are you hungry, Spike?"

Surprise, surprise—no response. *Hmm. Maybe that was a bit too complex. How about . . . ?*

"If you're hungry, stamp twice with your front foot. If you're not hungry, stamp once," I say, trying to concentrate on what I want it to do, an image coming to my mind of it stamping twice for yes and once for no. Spike stamps twice. Okay, that's good to know.

"Okay," I say. "Are you thirsty? Stamp once for no, twice for yes."

Spike stamps twice again. Hmm, it seems like the concept has been proven.

"All right, let's go and get some food and water. Follow me." I head down the hill to the river and invite Spike to drink as I fill my wok. I start a quick fire from the sticks lying around and ring the fire with stones. After putting my wok next to the fire, I keep a steady eye on it.

"If you can see anything you'd like to eat, go and eat it," I tell Spike. "Just stay in sight, okay? Stamp twice if you understand."

The porcupig stamps twice, then trundles off and starts rooting through the leaves near me; I can hear crunching coming from it in no time.

I'm hungry too, but I've decided that now would be a good time for me to start expanding my diet to more than just meat. In the river, clinging onto rocks and growing thickly in spots where the current isn't so strong, is the same type of pondweed that I tested a few days ago. I'd meant to continue testing it, but considering what I've been doing the last few days, I couldn't work up the motivation. Now, though, I'm starting to get a bit sick of just meat, and even slimy pondweed seems at least slightly appealing. I reach in and grab the nearest plant. I tested the leaf before, so I'd better do the same now. It's logical that since the weed is mostly leaf, that would be the most efficient thing to eat—if it's edible. I pull off a fragment of leaf and then hesitate.

Do I cook it or eat it raw? It's more likely to be edible cooked, but then I won't be able to say for sure it's edible raw, even if the test goes well . . . Then I wonder if I would *want* to eat it raw? And the answer is *no* . . . but then I'll have to make sure I always have a supply of cooked stuff in my Inventory, which is not practical. Perhaps it seems a little stupid to be spending time debating about cooked or uncooked pondweed, but sorting this out in my brain now will set the trend going forwards. In the end, I decide I'd better bite the bullet and do my first test uncooked. The reason for this is simple: uncooked pondweed is in much more plentiful supply than cooked pondweed. Additionally, if it's edible uncooked, it's almost certain to be fine when cooked, though I will have to be careful when combining it with other foods. So, taking a tiny piece of the leaf, I brush it gently against my lips. The skin is so sensitive there that any symptoms should be quick to show up.

When a couple of minutes go by without a problem, I place the piece of leaf in my mouth and then perch on a boulder. I don't chew, I don't swallow, and I pay particular attention to the sensations in my mouth. Is that prickling I feel on my tongue? *No, it's just my tongue drying out*, I decide after a moment. Time passes. Without a watch, I don't know how long exactly, but I use my natural clock of how close my water is to boiling to help me gauge the time.

When I'm pretty certain that at least fifteen minutes have gone past with no issues, I move onto the next step: chewing. Similarly, I chew for approximately fifteen minutes, paying attention to my symptoms. The pondweed isn't exactly tasty; it has a bland, slightly bitter taste, maybe a bit like spinach. Still, I suppose that's better than tasting horrible. So far, so good, in terms of the symptoms.

Now the dangerous bit. Swallowing. I suddenly find myself sweating, the knowledge I've absorbed about flora not helping my nerves as memories flash through my mind of everything that could possibly go wrong when ingesting something poisonous. In the end, I manage to swallow but only by taking a big gulp of water. I wouldn't have succeeded otherwise in eating the remaining fragments of leaf after so much chewing and my suddenly dry mouth.

Right, that's it. If I get any symptoms in the next eight hours, I'll have to do my best to make myself vomit. If not, it's a good indication that the plant might be okay to eat, though I'll have to do further testing, of course. My stomach growls. Unfortunately, I won't be able to eat any breakfast. Or lunch. Nothing but clean water for the next eight hours or it could interfere with my test. On that note, I pull my newly boiled water from next to the fire and carefully tip it into the canteen. I wince every time a drop spills—not because it hits my skin, but because of the waste. After filling it again, I stick the pan next to the fire to double my water store.

Then, blowing on the canteen, I drink carefully. It doesn't taste as good as tea or coffee, but the heat is not that much different. At least the liquid helps fill my empty and grumbling stomach a bit. It should be okay as long as I keep myself busy. Many are my vices, but overindulgence in food is one that's rare for me. After all, it's not the gym or a super-healthy diet that has kept the pounds off; it's the tyranny of my work–life balance, or the lack thereof.

It isn't— wasn't—unusual for me to skip lunch, as I often forgot to take something with me and rarely had the time to go and buy something, let alone the time to *eat* it. In fact, it wasn't unheard of for me to skip breakfast too when I had to go into work early or was in a rush in the morning for whatever reason. Then I wouldn't eat until I got home. In short, I can handle a bit of fasting. Or at least, that's what I tell myself. I carefully avoid the thought that my work before this was only a fraction as physically demanding as my life now. *If I keep busy, it'll be fine*, I tell myself dismissively.

Still, just because *I* can't eat doesn't mean my follower can't. And besides, I need to work out *what* it eats, for future reference. Once my second pot of water has boiled, I stick the wok directly in my Inventory and then smother the fire. Standing up, I walk over to the porcupig, who has stayed within sight as I ordered. It's crunching something happily. Something that appears to have multiple wriggling legs. An insectivore?

"Okay, Spike, let's go for a walk. If you see something good to eat, go for it," I say.

The porcupig looks at me for a moment before turning and starting to snuffle through the leaves. I keep an eye on his—I'm going to go with him being male unless I find out differently—progress, noting what he finds at the same time as looking around me. As I watch, I see that he appears to be primarily herbivorous, but is perfectly happy to eat any insects or worms he comes across.

At one point while we walk, he digs up a load of tubers that look kind of similar to long potatoes. Actually, I suppose they look kind of like sweet potatoes, but with thicker, paler skin. I grab a couple and put them in my Inventory too—maybe I should try cooking these once I'm done testing the pondweed. From what I can see, if they're connected to the foliage Spike dug up to get at them, they're reasonably common. Besides, I could always try cultivating them along with the samova beans I've saved. I look at the sun. It's already halfway to its zenith, and I *do* want to get some more things done than just following my new pet porcupig around. He'll be okay to roam around, won't he? It's a dangerous world around here, but he's clearly survived to adulthood, so . . .

In the end, I weigh that question against the fact that, as an herbivore, he probably spends the majority of his time finding stuff to eat, and I don't have the time every day to follow him around and protect him while he finds his nosh. If, in the future, I can grow enough food to feed him without him needing to leave my side, great, but that's not the case at the moment.

"Spike," I say, and he pauses, looking back at me. "I'm going to go back to the cave. I want you to continue looking for food until you're satisfied. When you've had enough, come back to me. If you feel you're in danger, make a loud noise."

As I give the command, I focus hard on what I want him to do—it seemed to work well enough earlier. Feeling moderately satisfied, I suddenly realize something: I've never heard a porcupig make a loud noise. I don't even know if they *can.*

"Just, before I go, make the loudest noise you can."

For a moment, I think he hasn't understood me, but then he lets rip with what might be the *worst* noise I've ever heard. I'm very glad that I asked him to demonstrate because it sounds like he's *dying.* No, like he's being *tortured* to death. If I'd heard that for the first time when I wasn't right next to him, knowing that he's fine, I think I would have had a heart attack.

"Right . . . ," I say faintly, my ears ringing.

"Good. Um, so, I'll see you later, then."

With that, I turn and stumble away. Of course, it's not a great idea to go walking in the forest without having all my faculties operating properly. It's a reminder that hits me smack in the face, literally. Well, not quite literally—it smacks me in the chest.

Distracted as I am, I only catch the faintest of flickers in my peripheral vision before it hits, not enough to dodge. The hit is painful—not particularly from the impact itself, but from the spikes all over the dark-colored ball that strikes me. They pierce my thin clothes like needles and blood spills when the ball withdraws. Still disorientated, it takes me a moment to realize that the ball is attached to a long, dark cord hanging from above.

Looking up, I realize it's the same kind of creature that I saw before; the difference is that last time I managed to avoid its attack. It's out of reach of my knife or even my mace. I start wishing for a spear or bow, but unfortunately, wishing isn't going to make them materialize.

Baring my teeth angrily, I instead grab some stones from the ground and start throwing them at the creature. Its reaction is to curl up tighter, bringing its tail up to help protect it too. I'm not making much progress, it seems, but I also can't really see the creature's objective. The strike was painful, but the wounds are not likely to make me bleed out any time soon. How is this supposed to do anything?

When my vision blurs a little, I think it's from a drop of sweat dripping into my eyes. When it blurs again, and for more than a fraction of a second this time, I realize that it's more concerning than I'd first thought. Now I understand the creature's objectives. It's not all that dissimilar from a venomous snake injecting its prey, then waiting for the prey to succumb.

Casting Lay-on-Hands immediately, I feel a swoop in my stomach as it seems to have little effect. Instead, the healing magic heals the wounds of the initial strike, but then it just fizzles out, as if there's nothing else for it to heal. I feel panic start to take over. Even if I manage to get a lucky blow and kill this creature—unlikely from what I've seen so far—I can't throw rocks at the venom creeping through my veins. I don't have a health potion or any sort of anti-venom. If my body can't fight this off on its own, I'm dead.

CHAPTER THIRTY-FOUR

From an Unexpected Source

As the venom takes over, I feel my limbs weakening and my stones strike with less and less force. Finally, I lose the ability to keep myself balanced and fall over. By this point, I've given up on trying to kill the creature and have turned to stagger off towards home. My only hope now is that Kalanthia might be able to help me in some way. Unfortunately, by this stage, I only manage to make it a few paces before going to my knees and then falling flat. With my last bit of strength, I turn my head to one side so I can at least breathe. Much good that will do me, though.

After a while, I realize that although the venom has been able to run unopposed through my body, it's not actually *killing* me. I can still see, though my vision is blurrier than normal. My heart pumps, albeit more weakly, and I can still draw in breath, though it's a much more laborious task than usual. In short, it seems to be designed to weaken muscles only to disable, not to kill. In fact, lying here on the floor with nothing else to do but hope the effects of the venom wear off quickly, I notice that my stamina bar is completely empty and flashing. *A venom that attacks stamina?*

Of course, that only leaves one more conclusion: once the prey has been rendered helpless, the predator comes to feed. When I see a black blur shift in my peripheral vision, my neck muscles too weak to move my head, I resign myself to finding out exactly what it means to be eaten alive.

My salvation comes from an unexpected source. The creature has shifted around to my head at this point, not starting with my feet as I thought it might. I'm not sure how to feel about this, though relief is the prevailing emotion; I don't want to die, but if I have to, I'd rather it be over quickly. Going feet first while I can still feel every bit of sensation seems like it would be particularly torturous.

Even more torturous, however, is how *slowly* the creature is moving. Its sloth-like pace allows me to feel fruitless hope that I might recover from the venom and make a last-minute breakaway, only to be disappointed at every moment. This means that when a body comes and imposes itself between me and my attacker, I can actually see it; the blurriness of my vision has had time to mostly clear up. Seeing is believing, they say, but I can barely believe what I'm seeing here. *Spike.*

The porcupig is standing between me and my attacker, hissing menacingly, his quills stuck up threateningly. The black creature hesitates but then starts moving forwards again, seemingly planning on pushing past my guard. Spike isn't having any of that; he whirls around like lightning so that his quills are pointing directly at the dark creature. There's a moment when he seems to focus—frankly, he looks like he's got constipation. Then my attacker gets a face full of quills as they are shot out from my follower's backside.

It makes a noise for the first time, a kind of confused chirring sound, and backs up a bit, pawing at its face. Spike turns around again and once more hisses threateningly at the animal. My attacker pauses, quills still stuck in its face, clearly deciding whether I'm worth fighting over with a porcupig. Eventually, it seems to decide in the negative and turns to lumber slowly away. Not surprising in the end, as it seems to be a one-trick wonder: from what I can see, it has no real combat ability and doesn't even have speed on its side.

The reason for it aiming for my head is also made clear, as, soon after, I start regaining control over my muscles. It seems that the paralytic, or whatever it uses, is pretty short-lived, so it has a limited time frame to make sure that its prey is out of the game.

The nagging feeling resumes, and I have the sense that I've gained a stat point out of this experience. That knowledge pales in comparison to the tumultuous feelings I have when I look at Spike.

"You saved me," I say quietly.

He, of course, doesn't reply. I don't know *how* I know it, but I know that me dying would actually break the Bond between us and set him free. Knowing that, the question is, does he? Probably, at least in whatever capacity he has for understanding such things. If I know it instinctively, I can only guess that he would too—it just seems fair. Yet he saved me.

"Well, for whatever reason, thank you," I say, trying to make sure my gratitude goes through whatever link we have.

There's a moment where I feel like we are connected—beyond the link created by Dominate, that is. Then it's broken as he turns away and resumes foraging. I stand up, brush myself off, and cast a quick Lay-on-Hands to deal with any lingering damage.

Deciding not to make the same mistake again, I suggest to Spike that we head back in the direction of the cave together. He doesn't reply, of course, but his foraging does start moving in the right direction. I stay close to him, paying a lot more attention to my surroundings than before even as my thoughts whirl. *Could there be some sort of protective element to the Bond? Or was it what I said to him earlier today when giving him a name? Or are porcupigs just naturally protective? Either way, I'm glad I didn't attack that porcupig family a few days ago—the quills are bad enough, but if they can actually use them as a ranged attack as well . . .*

Still, at least that puts my mind at ease a little in terms of his safety while foraging for food when we can't go out together. I know there are plenty of predators that could take him down either through force of numbers or sheer size, but the fact that he has some natural defenses as well as an offensive attack improves his chances of survival.

It doesn't take us long to get back to the foot of the hill—we didn't wander far, as the main purpose of our walk was to let Spike forage for food, not to cover ground. Fortunately, we succeed in making it back without being attacked again.

That's two strikes, I think darkly as I remember the ambushing creature. One missed, one hit; *the next one will end up with me as the victor*, I decide. But to do that, I need a ranged weapon.

Well, after I've sorted my fire situation, maybe my next task should be to create a bow and arrows. *Speaking of which, time to get to work.* Although walking through the forest with Spike has been relaxing, I've also taken the time to note down a number of resources. One of which was something I'd been keeping an eye out for: flint. After heading back to the river, I walk along it until I find the spot again as Spike stays near enough to me, rooting for something and then running to catch up to me each time.

I find it oddly soothing to have him with me, though as time goes on, worry creeps in. After all, he did well enough against the black blob, but could he have coped against the killer chickens? I find myself eyeing every dark patch around me, every bush, every branch that I'm about to walk under. It slows me down even further, but that at least helps Spike keep up.

Once I get to the resources I'm looking for, I feel a sense of relief that we're finally here. Inspecting the cache, I find a smile spreading across my face.

The nodules to the side of the river look exactly like my absorbed memories tell me they should: a white, waxy sort of stone on the outside with darker patches showing here and there. One nodule that's actually been broken open by something is instantly recognizable and would have been even without the wilderness survival knowledge I was given.

Glancing around to make sure I'm not suddenly about to be jumped, I crouch down and start filling a couple of the slots in my Inventory with good-sized flint nodules. I would have preferred to only use one slot, but apparently, that means they have to be within a certain size range, otherwise it automatically goes into another. Since I don't need any small stones, I go for medium and large sizes.

After I'm satisfied with the number of nodules I've collected, I note the area down on my Map for future reference. Then, we keep heading along the river but don't break away from it to walk up the hill to the cave. My next task is going to require a fair bit of water, so it's better to do it near the river. On our way through the forest, I spotted a bush with leaves the size of my head and took a moment to grab a few. These come in handy now as I spread them out to make a workspace. Letting Spike know that I'm going to be here for a while, I tell him to stay close but to eat and drink as much as he needs.

Kneeling down, I take some clay out of my Inventory. As I noted before, it's full of stones, so I start rubbing it between my fingers, working out the ones that are likely to interfere with my work. I'm not making a pot at this moment, so the clay doesn't need to be too fine, but stones that are too large are likely to still cause problematic faults over time.

As I do that, I add water until the clay reaches the right kind of texture. Then, as I finish a handful's worth, I press it into a ball and return it to my Inventory. By the time I feel I've processed enough clay to reach my objectives, Spike has finished munching for now and has returned to me. For a time, he just sits watching me, but eventually, he curls up nearby and goes to sleep. It's . . . cute. I admit it. Not nearly as cute as Lathani, but then, few things could be. As I finish up, I wake him gently by saying his name. He opens his eyes and blinks at me.

"Let's go, Spike," I tell him. "Have a drink if you need to." He doesn't, so I guess he's all sorted. We head up the slope. I pause at the entrance, looking down at my knee-high Bound. "Do what you like as long as it doesn't cause damage or disrupt Kalanthia or Lathani."

For a moment I feel a sense of doubt that such an open-ended command would be understandable enough for an animal like Spike. Whether it's understood or not, he just curls up in the sun and, by all appearances, goes back to sleep.

I go into the cave, which is currently empty—Kalanthia and Lathani must be playing somewhere else. Entering my alcove, I look at the wall thoughtfully. I want to make something that's going to be multi-functional, but I'm rather hampered by the lack of metal. Still, I should be able to make a decent chimney. In addition to the clay I've been preparing, I also took a bit of time yesterday while collecting the clay from the riverbank to also collect a good amount of dry grass. Or something that strongly resembles it. I carefully pull a whole load of these strands out of my Inventory and pile them close at hand.

Starting with some clay, I create a "sausage" about a centimeter in diameter and arrange it so it's in a semicircle with a diameter of about fifty centimeters. Taking a chunk of dried grass, I arrange it on top of the sausage so the strands are lying from end to end of the clay and then press down so they're embedded within it. Creating another sausage, I repeat the process, working methodically to blend one set of clay in with the other.

From time to time, I have to wet my hands—after I finished my water canteen, I refilled it with the boiled water from my wok and then refilled the wok with stream water. It helps me keep the clay damp and workable.

I pause when the "wall" is about fifteen centimeters high and look thoughtfully at what I've created, thinking about how I'm going to use it.

Then an idea occurs, and I go outside briefly to hunt for a stone of a certain size. It takes me a few minutes to find one that I think will be suitable, but once I've got it, I return to my cave. Putting the stone against the front of my "wall," I carefully dig out clay until I've made a rough D shape a little bigger than the stone. Using more clay, I fill in the sides of the hole until it's a snug fit for the stone, or reasonably so, at least. This should allow me to control the airflow into my fire better, especially when it's just getting started. Having a fire choke in the first few minutes because of lack of air is annoying. Plus, it'll make cleaning easier: I'll be able to just sweep out the dead coals and ashes onto a leaf or something and then carry them outside. A much easier arrangement than the one where I'd have to crane my wrist awkwardly to try and grab everything.

Returning to the rest of my fireplace, I hesitate as another thought strikes. *Cooking.* While putting the wok next to the fire to boil water has worked well enough, I'd rather make something better here. My wok has a single handle, which won't make it easy to suspend above the fire, so it will have to sit on something . . .

A possible solution comes to mind, and I start doing my best to prepare for it without knowing whether it will actually work. It's not something that comes from my survival knowledge, but I'm applying my understanding of different areas to try and make something that works. I'll have to find out—I'll put in alternatives in case my idea doesn't work.

CHAPTER THIRTY-FIVE

Round the Twist

Near the clay deposit had been another valuable resource: an opening in the mountainside that revealed sections of layered rock. It could be slate or some type of sedimentary rock, but either way, I took advantage of the number of broken pieces lying around the deposit. Though most of them weren't that big, there were some good-sized ones that I'm hoping to use as chopping boards along with some long but thin ones. It's the latter that I now use.

Pulling out about four of the long ones, I set them across the top of my chimney, about twenty centimeters off the ground. Then, using another couple of sausages and a few strands of dried grass, I fix the long pieces of slate in place. I hope they will be thick enough; before I keep building, I carefully place my wok on top of them. It's full of water, so it's heavy. I hold the handle and watch the slate with eagle eyes for signs of it cracking.

So far, so good. Still keeping careful watch, I release the handle, letting the slate take the full weight of the wok. I see the clay around the slate shift slightly, but other than that, it seems like my method has worked. For now. Hopefully, it will work when it's hot too. Once the clay has dried it should be more secure as well.

I continue building my fireplace, using the same strategy of molding a thin sausage of clay, grabbing a few strands of dried grass, pressing them in gently and blending it with the layer below, then repeating. It takes me a while, but I can't say I really notice the time passing.

As the walls reach knee level and then beyond, aiming for the hole in the wall, which is about hip level, I begin narrowing my chimney, not wanting it to continue being as much as twenty-five centimeters in radius. Ideally, by the time I get to the hole in the wall, the radius will be ten centimeters or so.

Building upwards, I reach the hole in the stone wall and pause to work out how to finish off the chimney. Taking one of the large pieces of shale, I pick it up and place it on top of my chimney.

Hmm, not high enough, I muse to myself. The level of the wall is only up to about a quarter of the way up the hole, so laying the slate flat means that there probably isn't enough ventilation. *What about tilted?* I try it, tilting the slate up so its top edge is most of the way up the hole, leaving just a little gap for light, and the slate's bottom edge is touching the top of the front of my chimney.

That should work all right, but I need to fill in the gaps to the side of the slate, or I'll unintentionally end up with smoke escaping into the room. To fix this, I work with pure clay since I've run out of the dried grass. My aim is to build up the sides of the chimney to essentially fill in all the gaps between the slate, the wall, and the rest of the flue.

Stepping back after I've finished, I give it a critical look. It's not perfect. My amateur nature when it comes to either building or pottery comes through clearly, but it hasn't fallen yet, so that's a good start. Plus, although I hadn't planned it, the fact that the slate "roof" of my chimney is removable will help with providing an alternative cooking arrangement if my earlier slate structure breaks. If that happens, I can suspend things through the hole from above using a simple structure of five branches and cord. Yes, I'll probably get smoke in my cave, but possibly not—if the draw of oxygen is correct, air should be pulled in at the bottom and then pulled out of the cave by the movement of air outside. I guess I'll find out.

The clay is already starting to dry, so I build a fire in my new fire pit. I'll need to keep an eye on it for the next while, making sure it doesn't burn either too high or too low—I want it to help my clay dry and harden, not crack up further. I need to keep an eye on the fire, so I can't go far, but I've got some time for now. A good opportunity to start the easy, though boring task of twisting cord.

I was lucky today while walking with Spike: I found a fallen tree that was a perfect source of bark fiber and harvested as much as I could while he was rooting around near it.

In the end, I managed to fill two Inventory slots with fiber, and now seems like a good time to twist it. Cord is something I desperately need, so it's not a waste of time to get going on creating it. It's hard at first, and it takes me a while to get the knack.

Eventually, though, I find that my fingers are managing to twist the fibers together, and I'm even starting to know when to add the next set of fibers to create a smooth cord; my first few attempts were . . . lumpy, to say the least. I actually untwist my first attempts in order to redo them with a smoother texture. Once I have three good pieces of cord, I twist them together to make a three-ply rope, then connect them with the next set of cord lengths.

It hurts my fingers, not having the right kind of calluses to deal with the rough fibers, but I ignore the irritation; my regeneration will deal with any damage soon enough. And if it doesn't, I can always use Lay-on-Hands.

A couple of meters of decent cord later, I feel the nagging feeling start up again, reminding me that I never checked my messages. Deciding that now is as good a time as any for a break, I put my cordage project down. In fact, I wouldn't mind having a snack; my stomach's telling me it's been a while since breakfast. As I munch, I open my message box.

Congratulations!
You have worked hard on your Wisdom and have earned a point. Would you like

to apply this to your status?
Y / N

I accept, of course. It doesn't indicate whether it was Depth or Breadth that was increased. *Do I only choose those on level-up? And how did I earn it in the first place?* I go on to the next message while I ponder the question.

Congratulations! You have worked hard on your Constitution and have earned a point. This has been applied to your status.
Next message / Close messages

Huh, that's different. No option to accept or not . . . Moving on, I see a similar message.

Congratulations! You have worked hard on your Dexterity and have earned a point. This has been applied to your status.
Close messages? Y / N

Very confused by this point, I close the message and shift across to my status screen. Sure enough, I can see I've gained a point each in Constitution, Wisdom, and Dexterity.

Name: Markus Wolfe		Race: Human	Class: Tamer
Level: 1	Energy to next level: 14%	Energy absorption rate: 11u/hr	Energy towards debt: 0%
Intelligence	7	Mana: 70/70	
Wisdom	7	Mana regeneration rate: 175u/hr	
Willpower	15+3 (+20%)	Health regeneration rate: 18u/hr	
Constitution	8	Health 80/80	
Strength	6	Stamina: 30/30	
Dexterity	5	Stamina regeneration rate: 50u/hr	
Class Skills:		Non-Class Skills:	
Dominate – Beginner 2		Lay-on-Hands – Novice 3	
Tame – Beginner 1		Stealth – Beginner 2	
Fade – Beginner 2			

But why? *Unless . . .* A thought occurs, and I close my eyes as I concentrate on the memory from the System lore stone. Using Energy is a shortcut to increasing stats, but it's not the only way: people who don't have any access to Energy increase their stats all the time through hard work. Heck, everyone on Earth does this, for one thing! Maybe that's what's happened here, only with the Energy in my environment passively helping too.

In terms of my point to Dexterity, I was just working on a task that requires a fair bit of dexterity to do well, and I've improved significantly in it. Working with clay also requires rather a lot of dexterity, as do several things I've done since I've been here. Perhaps all the work has added up and given me the point?

What about the other two points? I try to remember back to when I felt the nagging feeling before. I'm pretty sure one of the times was soon after I was attacked . . . and fought off the venom it infected me with. Perhaps fighting the venom was a sufficient catalyst to earn a point in Constitution, especially considering all the other times I've been injured and recovered in this world.

I don't know how it works exactly, but the System lore stone was clear that Constitution is essentially "what doesn't kill you makes you stronger." While that's not always true with physical—and mental—trauma on Earth, apparently the presence of Energy on Nicholas's world, and here as well, I guess, makes being hurt a different story. Actually, that makes me wonder whether emotional or mental damage might improve Wisdom or Intelligence . . . Either way, I probably shouldn't try it out—my past has traumatized me enough, thank you very much.

As for the point of Wisdom, when could that be from? Could it be because of that little "talk" with Spike? Perhaps building a little bit of a bond with him then is the reason for why he came to my defense. If that's the case, it definitely was something "wise." But maybe it's something from later, or a combination of wise decisions? If any of my decisions could be considered wise. Then again, if the messages come in chronological order, it seems like it must have been before the attack since I gained the Wisdom point before gaining the Constitution one.

If the trigger *was* the conversation, that's not really very useful, actually, as I have no idea *what* about that little talk seemed wise. Was it the fact that I was trying to get along with a being who has no choice but to follow my orders? Or was it *because* Spike has no choice that Wisdom was triggered—me showing empathy could be a wise trait? Or, as I considered before, was it because me being nice to him then meant that he would help protect me later? But how would I even know something like that? And I still don't understand the two subcategories or how they affect anything, because, unlike with Strength, my mana regeneration doesn't seem to be impacted by the subcategories. There must be a reason for and a consequence of my choices, but nothing in the System lore stone talks about it.

I huff in frustration. Wisdom and Willpower are my least favorite traits, to be honest. All the others are fairly clear about how to improve them. Not so the two big *W*'s. All I can do is try to keep track of when they increase and then attempt to draw some conclusions from that.

As I consider my screen once more, something else strikes me. My Energy.

It's too high. I haven't killed anything since I leveled up, and although I've been absorbing Energy naturally, enough time hasn't elapsed for my Energy store to have risen *that* much. Add to that the fact that I increased at least one stat; I'm not entirely sure whether the ones I didn't have any choice but to accept actually cost me anything, but I'm going to guess not, or very little. My reasoning is that having as much Energy left as I seem to after increasing my stats by three points is even more unbelievable. So where has this extra Energy come from? I mean, I'm not complaining, but it would be nice to know so I can do more of it!

Racking my brains, there are only two possibilities that come to mind: one, that despite not killing that ambusher, I gained credit; and two, that it has something to do with using Dominate on Spike. Of the two options, I'm leaning towards the last one because surely a single ambush predator wouldn't be worth so much Energy that not even killing it would net me enough to increase a stat, with more left over!

Well, I know how to narrow down the possibilities, at least, and it's a thought that fills me with dark pleasure. All I need to do is sort out a bow or some sort of ranged weapon that will put me on more even ground with that wretched thing. Heck, even making a few spears and throwing them at it might work fine.

Just before closing the screen, I notice that Dominate has risen to level two. Good, I suppose. I still don't really know whether Skill level makes much difference to the Skill itself. Fade has risen to level two because I've been doing my best to use it at various intervals, including while I'm sitting here, twisting bark fiber, but I also haven't noticed any real change to it. Stealth has also risen to level two, though I haven't really been using it much apart from during the testing last night. Just another question that I guess I'll find out the answer to later . . . Checking on my work with my fireplace, I'm pleased with its progress. It's starting to dry, but it is still far from completely firm. Still, nothing has collapsed yet, which is a good sign.

Sitting back, I pick my half-finished cord up again only to quickly put it down when my previously unnoticed blisters protest the action. I grimace as I look at my fingertips. *Yeah . . . no.* I cast a quick Lay-on-Hands, smiling as the blisters fade away as if they were never there. Back to the grind, I guess. Too much of this, and I'll be going round the twist. *Hah.*

CHAPTER THIRTY-SIX

A Good Addition

When I get absolutely sick of twisting bark fiber and watching clay dry, I decide to move onto a different but equally important project. Walking out of the cave, I find Kalanthia sitting outside.

"Hi, Kalanthia." She turns her head towards me and cocks it curiously. "Do you mind if I make some changes to the land around here? I want to plant some things."

Go ahead, Markus Wolfe, she tells me neutrally, not seeming particularly interested in the topic now—perhaps because it's to do with plants. "Okay, thanks," I reply, then hesitate a moment. "I haven't managed to kill as many things as I was hoping. I don't think I have enough to satisfy you yet," I say, thinking about her response the last time I offered her carcasses. *It is of no concern,* she replies with complete nonchalance. *I will hunt for myself tomorrow; you will sit on my baby. It is as I initially suggested.* That's true, I suppose—it was me who suggested the alternative.

"All right, well, if you're okay with it, that's fine," I say, waiting for a moment in case she wants to say something. Seeing as she just closes her eyes, I guess the conversation is finished. Waving a little awkwardly at her, I start walking around.

Samova beans like sunlight, but they also like their roots to be kept moist, like beans on Earth. That means I either plant up here near the cave, where it's very sunny, or down near the river, where it's moist. Out of the two, I'm more able to control the moisture of the soil around its roots than the sunlight on its leaves, so I decide to plant near the cave. Plus, that gives me easier access. Actually, now that I'm thinking about it, I'll probably have to protect them from marauding animals. Or maybe Spike will be able to do that. *Hmm.*

Once I choose my spot, it's time for Spike to do the task that I Dominated him for. Digging. I call him over, and he gets up from the sunny spot where he's been lazily sunbathing and trots over to me. He stretches as he gets to me and opens his mouth widely in a yawn. The movement gives me a very good look at his teeth. They are actually sharper than I thought they would be—a good two thirds of them are pointed. Spike has canines, or some teeth that look like them, but they're further to the front of his mouth than mine are. They're a bit longer proportionally than mine too, but nothing like Kalanthia's killer fangs. Behind his canines he has some other, smaller triangular teeth, and then right at the back he has some molars. These are mostly similar to mine, probably for the same reasons, but they're also a bit pointier.

I don't get enough time during that brief yawn to see whether the molars fit together top and bottom, but I guess they'd have to—I've confirmed by observation that Spike is definitely herbivorous and enjoys munching on worms and insects. Based on what I've seen so far, I doubt he's a predator of anything bigger than an insect. He's just not quick enough to catch small animals, which are usually fast-moving, and anything bigger than half his size would probably be too much to handle.

Doing my best to give clear instructions, I set Spike to digging a furrow. Deciding to experiment a bit, I try to "push" mental images at him of what I want him to do. I don't know whether it makes much of a difference, but he follows the instructions very well, and my little vegetable plot is quickly established.

As predicted, Spike's horn breaks up the ground nicely, and he even clears up the roots in that area, which will help me further. Of course, that wasn't some sign of proactivity or predicting my needs: he was just peckish and the roots looked tasty. It's still useful. *If only all the colleagues I worked with were so obliging!*

Once he's cleared a surface area about twice as long as he is and half again as wide, it's time to dig deeper to give the samova beans' roots some already-broken earth to grow through.

I check on my chimney a few times while he's working to deepen and lengthen the trench, and I'm pleased with how it's coming on. The clay has hardened nicely, and I can only see a couple of minor cracks. Since I'm not trying to make it water-tight, I don't mind about the cracks; I'll probably smooth on a bit more clay when it's cool to make sure they don't compromise the structure's integrity, though. Briefly checking on Spike again, I realize that he's almost done. Deciding to kill two birds with one stone, I fetch my wok from the alcove, then wait for Spike to finish.

"Hey, Spike, are you thirsty?" I ask. About to remind him about the two taps, one tap system, I'm surprised when he taps twice without prompting. *Huh . . . smart. Something to bear in mind.* "Okay, let's go to the river, then."

Down by the riverbank, he takes a long drink and I fill my canteen and my wok, then slip them into my Inventory. *Why does it work to put an open container full of water in my Inventory when an open bag isn't accepted?* I don't know; I'm glad it does, though, as it makes transporting water so much easier.

Suddenly curious, I try to put water directly into my Inventory by imagining "pouring" it into one of the slots. Unfortunately, this doesn't work. So, an open container of water is acceptable, but water without any container isn't. It would be good to eventually get an explanation for how this whole Inventory thing works; sometimes it just seems so illogical.

Placing the wok carefully just inside the entrance to my alcove, I head back out to the trench. I pull the five remaining samova beans out of my satchel and push them gently into the soft, disturbed earth of the trench. I'm careful to not bury them too deep—apparently, they like to be about five centimeters below ground level. Also, unlike Earth beans—according to my woodcraft knowledge stone—as long as I water them immediately, they should be fine not to soak overnight.

The depth that Spike has dug down to should be perfect for them—the trench is about twenty-five centimeters at its deepest point. That should mean that the roots of my (hopefully) growing samova plants will have an easy job. To begin with, at least. Having covered the beans up, I use my canteen to water them. The greedy soil absorbs the water quickly and, unfortunately, my canteen isn't all that big. I use my wok water too, which is just as quickly absorbed, so I have to return to the river twice before I've properly doused them.

Actually, that's a thought—maybe I should create a bigger water container out of my new clay? I'm going to need to water these plants every day, probably, so in the interest of saving time, being able to carry more water at once is a good investment.

On the other hand, it's a *big* investment of time; creating a watertight jug is a far cry from creating a rough chimney. Not to mention, of course, the fact that I'd have to fire it, which involves digging a pit and then making sure the fire burns at the right temperature for the right length of time . . . Then again, I'm not only going to need containers for watering my seeds, am I? My wok is great as a cooking pot, but it's annoying that I only have the one.

My planting done, I take a moment to look at the rich disturbed earth. It's always amazing to think that a tiny seed can turn into a massive plant; even an oak comes from an acorn. The thought brings back a memory unbidden. My father used to like gardening and would spend many hours in the backyard taking care of the plants. I remember that I had to grow a bean for school. I must have been eight or nine at the time.

"Water and warmth. That's what these need right now, Markus," I hear him saying to me, his voice so clear that I could swear he's next to me now. "But not too much of each. And when the roots start coming out, they'll need something to hold onto, so use a bit of that paper towel to wrap the bean."

Sniffing, I roughly swipe away a tear that threatens to fall. I wish I'd spent more time with him gardening. I wish I'd done a lot of things.

"No use crying now," I tell myself, speaking aloud angrily.

"He's *dead,* and that's all there is to it. And you're in a different world and need to get your head back in the game."

Looking around, I spot Spike looking wary. I tense and look around quickly as my adrenaline kicks into gear. *Are we about to be attacked? Here?* Not seeing any signs of danger, I frown and look back at Spike. Then it hits me. He's not wary about being attacked—at least, not by any outside creature. He's wary about being attacked by *me*.

"Hey," I tell him, gentling my tone. "I'm not angry at you. I promise. I'm . . . angry at myself."

It's true, I realize. I'm angry that despite what happened to my mom as a teenager, I didn't spend enough time with my dad. I wasted time allowing him to push me away, being hurt over his response to my mother's death, with my teenage anger issues, being unwilling to overcome the generational divide . . . And now he's dead, and I don't have the option anymore.

As the grief threatens to pull me into a black depression once more, I forcibly direct my thoughts to more useful, immediate concerns. At least Spike looks more relaxed—clearly, whatever message he got was enough to ease his fears about being attacked.

"Spike, I want you to guard this area. When the new shoots come up, I want you to make sure that nothing damages them. If they're threatened by something that you can't handle, let me know, but otherwise, drive the other creatures off. Kill them if you want to, but make sure the plants stay safe."

Once more, I accompany the words with images and a sense of importance since that seems to improve Spike's capacity to understand what I want. Then I consider something.

"You can go and eat and drink when you need to, but make sure you don't leave the plants for very long." It's hard to know if my follower's definition of "very long" is the same as mine, but short of doing the guarding myself, I figure I don't have much choice but to trust him.

And ultimately, growing the samova beans isn't a question of life and death— I'm sure I'll find other things to eat here, and besides, meat is readily available, even if it gets boring after a short time. They would, however, be a good addition to my diet; they're full of fiber and lots of nutrients, which meat doesn't tend to have. There's a reason why Nicholas included them in my ration pack, after all.

After the porcupig has taken up a guarding position, while still relaxing in the sun, I head back indoors to try and do something else about my food situation.

CHAPTER THIRTY-SEVEN

Interdimensional Amazon

The first thing I check is my experimental cooking arrangements. The chimney is looking pretty good and seems to be directing the smoke out of my cave rather than into it, which is a good sign. Not so good is the draft that the fire is creating by pulling air in from Kalanthia's cave. I'll have to do something about that, but for now, I'll just pull an extra jacket around me at night to keep me warm.

I test the chimney's hardness in multiple places, then use a stick to press a bit on the slate cooking grid I built into the chimney itself. Everything seems ready.

Here goes. I lift the wok up and feed it through the upper curved hole in the stove, then slowly and gently place it on top of the slate grid, ready to take it away if I have any hint that either the grid or wok are likely to crack. I don't know how my wok will react to direct flame, after all, nor how fragile the slate might have become after being heated.

There are a couple of hair-raising moments when I'm convinced that at least one of them is about to crack, but in the end, everything goes well. Eventually, the wok, half-full of water, sits on the makeshift grill I've created, and everything's still whole.

I sit back on my heels, unable and unwilling to prevent the grin from cracking my face in half. Perhaps this should pale in comparison to killing creatures that were trying to kill me or hiking my way through more forest than I've ever seen in my life, but I don't care. I'm proud of what I've done here, especially considering that a few days ago I couldn't have even lit a fire without a lighter. I can still feel the grief that bubbled up earlier pulling at me, but with the successes of the present, its gravitational pull is lessened and I can push it mostly to one side.

Now for the next step. As the water slowly heats up, I add in the malachy leaves I've been saving up. They're far too salty as they are, but that's all to my benefit now. The dried-out leaves float at first, but as they become more and more waterlogged, they drift down to the bottom, moving only with the bubbles that have started to form at the bottom of the wok.

I don't want to leave the setup in case something happens to make me lose my precious resource, so I continue my home renovation. I start on another important task: dryers. In order to create a bow and arrows, I need sinew. I've got plenty of the fresh stuff in my Inventory, but it needs to be dry before I can pound it and separate out the different fibers. Not to mention that I'll need to dry other resources too. Actually, that reminds me to find some arrow wood sooner rather than later. For now, though, I actually need to set up a drying rack or something. I'll need to leave the cave for a bit to gather supplies but don't want to risk Murphy having his way and something going wrong as soon as I leave the area, so I pull the wok off the fire temporarily.

That done, I head out of the cave and go down to the tree line, where I find a tree that has lots of straight shoots growing out from the base, like a willow or hazelnut tree. This tree clearly doesn't belong to either species, but its wood looks like it will suit my purposes.

Choosing a few shoots around the same width as my thumb, I hack at their bases with my knife until I'm holding five branches taller than I am. Then I hack at the tops to cut them down to my height. An axe would really make this task easier, and I make a mental note to add making one to my to-do list.

Snapping a few other thinner shoots, I pack all my harvested resources into my Inventory, which has increased to thirty spaces since leveling up—something I'm glad to note. Next, I search for something I can use to attach everything together. Settling on a vine that's climbing up a tree, like ivy or some other sort of creeper, I gather a few strands and pop them in my Inventory as well.

Back in my cave, I stoke the fire again, adding more fuel. After that, I carefully place the still-hot wok back on the fire and then pull my newly gathered materials out of my Inventory. Thus prepared, I start creating my basic rack. It's really very simple, but even then it takes far more time than I would have expected.

Mostly the delay is caused by it being more difficult than I thought to make the vine do what I want it to at the same time as keeping the branches in the right positions. By the time I'm done, I've sworn enough to make a sailor blush, and I finish off by declaring that if the thing falls apart at the wrong moment, I'd rather hang the sinew outside and guard it from inquisitive creatures than put myself through this frustrating torture again.

Then I think that I could have just used my bark-fiber cord instead of a vine, and I curse loudly enough to make Kalanthia rumble in annoyance. Sighing in frustration, I rub my face with my hands in an effort to calm myself down. Just because the memory from the survival stone used tree shoots and vines doesn't mean *I* have to, especially when I've already prepared something *specifically* for situations like this . . .

Anyway, at least I have—I hope—a workable dryer. It's basically just two pyramids of three branches tied at the top in a very bottom-heavy X shape, kept standing by the seventh branch connecting the two pyramids at their crossing points. Using the smaller branches, I've reinforced the lower parts of the pyramids with crossbeams, incidentally also creating places where other branches could be fed between to create more "rungs." For now, I don't do that because I want to place my dryer over the fireplace.

Moving it into place so the pyramids stand either side of the chimney, perpendicular to the wall with the crossbeam a good foot above the top of the chimney, I release it gingerly. The structure sways a little as it settles into place, but, despite my pessimistic predictions, it doesn't actually *fall*. One step done.

Work when one is trying to survive in the wilderness seems endless. There's *always* something to do. In this case, it's preparing the sinew for drying. I don't feel like waiting around for ages for the liquid in it to evaporate, so I'm going to do as much as I can to speed up the process. The first step is my rack. Hanging the sinew above and next to the chimney should give it a warm, dry atmosphere to encourage quick evaporation of the remaining bodily fluids. Now I'm going to cut it into smaller pieces so that it loses water more quickly.

Using my knife against a "chopping board"—really just a thick branch I picked up at some point—I slice along the grain of the different pieces of sinew, making slices that are about one centimeter thick and then however long the piece of sinew is; having gathered them from a variety of animals, there's an equally great variety in lengths. Still, even the small pieces could be useful for glue, if nothing else.

Using my newly made bark-fiber cord, I attach the thin pieces of sinew to a long, reasonably straight branch, ready to be propped above the fire once the clay has dried sufficiently. That done, I check on my "cooking." The water level in the wok has reduced, but I want to actually dry it all out completely. I debate with myself about removing the malachy leaves but leave them there for the time being. Once the water level has dropped by half, I'll take them out and then leave the salty water to crystallize. Hopefully, it won't make my wok rust.

So, chimney: check. Fireplace: check. Cooking area: check. Samova beans planted: check. Salt: in progress. Cord production: started. Sinew drying: in progress. I'm feeling pretty pleased with what I've managed to accomplish so far, and there's still a bit of time left in the day. *Well, what are my next objectives?*

My current aims are to make my living situation more comfortable. Creating my fireplace actually ticked several boxes there. First of all, it's a cooking area, meaning I can now start having fresh, hot meals on a more regular basis—a definite plus in my book. It also warms up my room, meaning that, hopefully, I won't be waking up in the middle of the night anymore, needing to pile on another coat because I'm cold. As a further benefit, it provides light in the dark, making navigating my alcove easier as well as potentially letting me read a book, something that I miss doing before bed.

I'd like to improve my sleeping situation to something softer than barely cushioned stone, but anything that will properly address that will take too long. I could haul in some softish undergrowth, like an equivalent of heather, but it will stop being soft fairly quickly, especially once it's dried out, meaning I'd need to replace it fairly often. Plus, it's likely to be even lumpier than the cave floor, which actually is pretty smooth. Ideally, I'd create a feather mattress—feathers are certainly not in low supply! The problem with this is that I'd need something to hold all those fluffy feathers, and at present, I have no material to use as ticking or thread to sew it together. Or needle.

I huff. Life is surprisingly hard when you can't just head to the closest commercial center to buy everything. Even though I technically have all the resources around me that I need, there's a whole lot of labor that has to go into processing them . . . I mean, I'm grateful for the stones Nicholas gave me, but I'd probably have traded all of them in for the chance to access an interdimensional Amazon. So, my pile of assorted jackets and other clothes is still probably the best I can do for sleeping at this point. Honestly, that's probably all I need to do for home renovations for now. Sure, shelves would be nice so I can put stuff on them, but I'm fine living out of my suitcases. I'd love electricity, internet, and a portal to a good hotel room, but those seem a bit out of the realm of possibility right now, even in this strange world where magic is real.

No, the best next step is probably to create some weapons and tools. My knife and mace have done a sterling job up to now, but I could do with both a bow and spear. A bow will be great for attacking and ambushing enemies at range, and a spear will help me keep more distance from my opponents. Maybe more than one spear so I could break or throw one without losing my weapon. My mace is good for crushing and is perfect for dealing with multiple attackers at once, but it's not really good for keeping my enemies at bay. Hopefully, with the addition of a bow and spear to my mace and knife, I'll be well equipped for whatever I have to face.

Actually, while I'm thinking about it, I might as well try to upgrade my mace a bit or replace it if that would be better. At the moment it's just a branch with a knot that makes it heavier at one end than the other. If I could attach a stone to the heavier end, that would make it significantly more damaging, especially if the stone was sharp in some way.

In order to do these tasks, though, I'm going to need to create some tools first; I'll need an axe for sure because I will need to cut wood for both my spear and bow, not to mention the arrows I'll also need to make. Besides, it'll probably be useful for creating firewood now that I actually have a fireplace. I'd better also create a shard that's capable of carving to a certain extent; I'll need something a bit more delicate than my knife for some of the finer shaping tasks used in creating a bow and arrows. Then, of course, there will be all the arrowheads . . . I foresee a lot of flint knapping in my future.

So far, I haven't spotted any trees that would be suitable for creating pitch, so I'll have to try and work around that, and if I spot any evergreens or sticky resin, I'll collect some then. Alternatively, I can create glue out of the remains of the sinew I was chopping up this morning. Though, I don't really want to boil that in my wok, so maybe creating a clay pot would actually be a good idea. Yes, creating perhaps three clay pots of different sizes for different purposes sounds sensible.

Decided, I get up and stretch, then prepare myself to settle into a long session of pottery making. The sooner I get started, the better: the clay pots will need to dry before they're fired, so I'll be able to do other things during that time.

CHAPTER THIRTY-EIGHT

Bribe

Creating my clay pots definitely takes longer than I expected. Just forming the first one takes the rest of the time until dusk. Gauging my tiredness level, I decide to continue by the light of my fire. The downside there is that in order to see what I'm doing, I have to work quite close to the fire, which means my clay dries out more quickly than when I was working further away.

That, in turn, means that although I manage to finish the second pot, I've run out of water in my canteen. It will be *so* much better when I have a bigger container in which to hold water. The canteen isn't bad as the water supply for a single person for most of a day, but it really doesn't last much more than that.

Without cooking water, and with my only current cooking container, my wok, being used to crystallize salt, I'm back to eating pre-cooked bird meat, despite technically having my cooking area sorted. I'm also pretty thirsty since I didn't think about the fact that using my only cooking pot for salt production would mean no water to drink. In the end, I might have to take a chance and drink the water straight. But that will have to be tomorrow; I'd rather eat a boring meal and be thirsty than go to the river in the dark—who knows what sort of beasties are lurking there? Still, I do have the luxury of reading a bit of one of my favorite books before falling asleep—or, at least, I read a few pages before deciding that I'm far too knackered even to read.

As I fall asleep, I muse that this has been the first day so far since I arrived that I haven't been attacked at least once. It makes a change to not have that roller coaster of adrenaline rushes, but I can't quite decide whether I'm more relieved or disappointed. I fall asleep before I come to a conclusion.

By the time I wake, sun is streaming into my cave through the small gap left between the top of my chimney and the top of the hole in the wall. *Markus Wolfe,* I hear Kalanthia say, her tone a little impatient. I have a feeling before she speaks about what she's about to say. *I must go to hunt. Are you awake enough for me to leave Lathani in your care?* Yup, called it. I shake the grogginess out of my head and respond as soon as I've got my thoughts in order.

"Yeah, let me just get some water first, okay? I'll be quick." She lets out an impatient grumble but doesn't refuse my request. Hurrying out, I go down to the river as quickly as I can while still keeping an eye out for any ambush predators waiting for unwary prey. The water tastes good as I drink some at the riverside; I also snatch some pondweed while I'm there. Hopefully, I've avoided picking up something nasty again.

Walking back with haste, I muse at the fact that I rarely see many creatures around this spot—probably something to do with them recognizing the presence of a much more powerful predator not far away. Still, better safe than sorry, and I still keep a wary eye on the trees around and above me in case there's a creature that's missed out on the memo.

Fortunately, I make it back without incident, and, once more, Kalanthia disappears off into the distance, and I'm left with an energetic and rambunctious nunda cub. Lathani and I play for a while, the makeshift cat toy making a reappearance once I have a chance to recreate it.

She seems more adventurous this time, though. I have to keep distracting her from going off the edge of the hill to explore. Spike hangs around for a bit, then trundles down the hill, probably going to eat and drink. Of course, his departure is just another reason for her to want to go down the hill. At one point, I teach her how to play Fetch, throwing a stick for her to find and pounce on. Well, I say "fetch," but it's more "pounce on and gnaw to death." Natural, I guess, considering she's a lot more feline than canine in nature. Still, she enjoys it. She enjoys it even more when I shift the branch through the grass, and she tries to pounce on its end. By the time she's tired and lies down for a nap, I feel like doing the same but decide that I'd be better off actually getting something done.

My salt has crystallized overnight; the heat from the fire burned itself down to embers enough to evaporate the rest of the water. I'd taken the malachy leaves out long before going to bed, so what remains is a load of green-tinged crystals. *Jackpot!*

Searching around for something to put my greenish treasure into, I suddenly hit on an idea. Digging in my suitcase, I find a small Tupperware box that I was using to store dice. Why did I bring my dice with me? I have no idea, but I'm grateful for it now.

Ditching the dice out of the box, I clean the bark off a stick and use it to lever the crystals off the wok. I could use my knife . . . but I don't really want to risk damaging my wok's surface. It works, though I might have a few splinters of wood in with my salt. Oh well, I'll try and avoid them when taking a pinch.

Now, time to make something more interesting than just cooked bird meat. Covering the base of my wok with water, I dump in some uncooked bird meat and the leaves from the pondweed I'd grabbed earlier. I've been continuing to test the weed and, by this point, I'm pretty sure that it's safe. Sure, I haven't actually tested it cooked yet, but I doubt that will be a problem.

Covering the wok with its lid, I let it cook while continuing to make some more bark-fiber cord. I haven't seen Spike since first thing this morning—I saw him go off to, I assume, get some food and water. I guess he'll come back when he's finished, like yesterday.

By the time Lathani wakes, I've finished cooking my "stew" and have started grilling some more bird meat since my stocks are running a little low. I cut up some pieces of meat and lay them on my grill, watching them sizzle in the heat of the fire. The sounds of fat dropping into the flames punctures the background noise of birds and the light breeze, but it's a soothing, homey kind of sound. I only realize the little nunda cub is awake because, turning away from the fire to cut up some more meat in preparation for when what's on the grill is ready, I notice a small movement. Whipping quickly around, I'm fortunately fast enough to knock her paw away from the fire, where she's millimeters away from getting burned.

"No, Lathani," I say sternly. "It's *hot*. You'll hurt yourself, and then your mama will hurt *me*." The little nunda gives me a forlorn look, as if asking why I'm being so cruel as to deny her sticking her paw in those beautifully dancing flames. She reaches for the fire again, but I make a chiding noise, which makes her hesitate. Looking at me again, she continues moving ever so slowly. "Lathani," I warn her.

She pauses once more, then, as I don't stop looking at her, she finally looks away and settles back on her haunches. I turn back to my meat but keep an eye on the cub in my peripheral vision. She creeps back towards the fire, staring into it and licking her chops. That makes me wonder—what if she wasn't attracted by the *fire* but by the cooking meat?

"Hey," I say to her gently as I reach in with the two branches I'm using as tongs and snare one of the pieces that I reckon is almost done. And even if it's not completely ready, Lathani's supposed to eat meat raw, so I hardly think that it being mostly cooked will cause any issue. I do blow on it until it's cool enough for me to hold with bare fingers as I don't want to be responsible for her burning her tongue—though, that would be a good lesson for "hot"!

Offering the cool piece of meat to the baby nunda, I'm surprised when she doesn't suddenly dive for it. Instead, she looks at me almost questioningly.

"Sure, you can eat this," I tell her, not sure if it's necessary but figuring it won't do any harm. She then moves forward with a bounce and takes the meat surprisingly gently from my fingers. Chewing it at the side of her mouth, she looks as pensive as a large feline can, her head cocked to one side. Then, seemingly deciding that she likes it, she gulps the last bits down and pokes her paw towards the fire again, not, I notice, trying to actually touch the fire but making a rather clear sign of what she wants. Smart cat.

Then again, maybe I'm underestimating her intelligence; her mom's perfectly capable of communicating telepathically, after all. Though Lathani can't send thoughts to my mind, perhaps she can still pick up at least some of the thoughts *I'm* sending. Which then begs the question of why she doesn't do what I want her to do more than half the time.

Stupid question: she's a cat. Or something vaguely related, I think. *Stands to reason she'd only follow my instructions if she wants to. Though . . .* It's like a lightbulb pinging on above my head as I get an idea. *What if I use this cooked meat to get her to stay away from the edge of the hill? Something in it for her, something in it for me . . .* "Let me finish cooking this lot and get the next set on the grill, and then I'll give you some more," I tell her, trying to focus on my thoughts the way I do with Spike. It seems to work. At least she's not trying to poke the fire anymore and is sitting there patiently.

It turns out that using cooked meat as a bribe works better than I'd thought. We play outside, and every time she follows one of my instructions, I reward her with a small piece. I'm even more convinced that she actually understands most, if not all, of what I say but just chooses whether or not to follow, as she doesn't seem to have any difficulty in earning her rewards. I don't want her deliberately doing things I don't want her to do just so she can get a piece of meat when she obeys me, so I try to give her the opportunity to earn a reward at other times too. It turns into a fun game that both of us enjoy.

Fortunately, I'm able to keep up with putting more meat on the grill than gets consumed, so I do replenish my stocks a bit. Besides, I still have a fair amount of raw meat, so trading a bit of cooked stuff for an easy way to stop Lathani wandering into danger is a good trade for me. I'm playing with Lathani, teaching her to come when I call, when Kalanthia returns home, her muzzle still stained red. I don't notice her at first—for a huge leopard-like creature, she's surprisingly stealthy. When I spot her, she's standing next to a large bush, still as a statue and watching what's going on with her golden eyes.

"Hi, Kalanthia," I say casually. "Did you have a good hunt?" She doesn't reply, not telepathically anyway. Instead, she *snarls*. For a moment, I think that she's spotted something dangerous and automatically look around as I reach for my knife. Nothing. Looking back at Kalanthia, I feel a shiver of fright; she's used the distraction to close the distance between us. Now only a couple of meters away and still moving fast, I can see she's snarling *at me.*

My hindbrain kicks in, and I back away quickly, my knife unconsciously appearing in my hand as if by magic. Of course, my backwards speed isn't anywhere near a match for an angry nunda; though *why* she's angry, I don't know. She covers the last distance between us with a little leap, her paw landing on my chest and pushing me over. The world blurs around me, and the next thing I know, I'm lying on my back, winded, with her heavy dinner-plate-sized paw weighing down my chest. She's snarling in my face, her bared fangs close enough to me that I can smell the rotten meat stench on her breath.

"Kalanthia?" I choke out with the little air I have left. "What are you doing?" My knife has been knocked out of my hand at some point in the last second, and I see it lying in the grass, just out of reach. *What am I going to do?*

CHAPTER THIRTY-NINE

Bounds of the Vow

warned you, Binder, she snarls in my head, her telepathic voice matching the audible sounds she's still making.

"What?" I choke out, completely confused. *Warned me about what? What have I done wrong?*

I warned you not to try to bind my cub! My scrambled mind tries to make sense of her words. *She's calling me Binder . . . That's something related to my Tamer Class. Does she think I'm trying to Dominate Lathani? No . . .* It suddenly makes more sense. Kalanthia thinks I'm trying to *Tame* her. And from a certain point of view, I suppose I can see why: coming when called is one of the first things humans teach their dogs to do. But that wasn't my intention.

"I swear, Kalanthia," I wheeze out, trying to ignore the horrible smell of all the dead things she's been eating—if I don't want to join them, I need to be able to explain myself fast! "I'm not trying to Tame Lathani."

Then why were you trying to command her obedience?

"It's not like that!" I protest, calming slightly. I might still have a large predator pressing down on my chest but at least she's letting me talk. Knowing that I haven't actually done what she's accusing me of gives me hope that I can get through to her.

"I . . . Can you move away a bit please? It's a bit hard to talk with you impeding my breathing." She eyes me for a moment.

"If you don't like my answer, is it going to make any difference whether you're a foot away from me or right on top of me? I've got no chance against you, and we both know that." A pregnant pause stretches out awkwardly, but finally, she shifts back so she's not actually pressing down on my chest anymore. I cough and sit upright, rubbing the sore spot.

Talk, she commands me. Now I've got my breath back, I'm happy to oblige.

"I was cooking meat, she indicated she wanted some, and then she liked it when she tried it. I had some problems earlier in the day when she wanted to explore more than just the top of the hill and seemed reluctant to heed me when I told her it was unsafe. I figured that if she had a bit more motivation to follow my instructions, it would help. That's what I was doing with the meat. I swear it was only with the intention of helping her keep safe and not to Tame her or anything." I'm a bit breathless again by the end, my fear driving me to speak as quickly as I can.

Kalanthia looks at me silently for a long moment. Slowly, the continuous snarl dies down and her lip lowers to cover her teeth again. *You mean to tell me that this was all for her safety? That you have no designs on chaining my cub to you?* I shake my head.

"No intentions of using either Dominate or Tame on her. I promise. I just didn't want her to get ambushed by something in the forest because I hadn't been able to stop her from running off. Last time wasn't such an issue, but this time she has only *just* been listening to me—I didn't want to risk her deciding not to listen at all next time."

She makes a thoughtful noise and finally relaxes, allowing me to do the same; my heart finally starts to slow down now it's clear she's not going to kill me. *Actually, weren't those Vows we took right at the beginning supposed to stop this sort of thing?* Unless knocking me flat on my back doesn't count as an attack, or her believing that she was defending her cub was enough justification to respond while staying within the bounds of the Vow. I don't know, but this experience has definitely rattled me a bit.

I apologize, Markus Wolfe. I . . . was hasty in my judgement of the situation. I had not realized that you were having difficulty preventing Lathani from putting herself at risk.

"I understand, I guess," I say. "Though I thought the Vows were supposed to be something we could rely on in these kinds of situations?" I ask, deciding to voice my thoughts in case Kalanthia can shed some light. She tosses her head in her version of a shrug.

Vows can be unpredictable when it comes to definitions of harm, and the conditioning that Binders undertake prior to actually casting their chains wouldn't necessarily be detected. And by the time the chain is cast, it is too late; Should you chain Lathani, even killing you wouldn't remove the scars on her soul.

"Scars?" I ask, troubled by the implications. *All Bindings leave their mark; the chains of a Binder must be released consensually, or they leave a great wound on the soul.* "And if they're removed consensually?"

Then the Bindings do not rip away and take some soul with them. But that doesn't mean that they do not leave their mark; all connections once severed lead to some sense of loss. Huh, interesting. And I can kind of see it—relationships, whether they end well or badly, always lead to the feeling of a vacuum once the person is no longer there. I quickly direct my thoughts away from that black hole. I've lost too many people one way or another to be comfortable pondering such topics.

"So . . . ," I start again hesitantly, "can I continue giving Lathani meat bits as a reward?" As if speaking her name conjures her, the cub comes and rubs her head against her mother briefly before bouncing back over to me and pawing at me, giving me pleading eyes. I raise my eyebrows at Kalanthia, gesturing towards the demanding little nunda as if to say, "Case in point."

Kalanthia makes an amused huffing sound. A cute chirping noise emerges from her; the sound is completely incongruous with such a large, deadly predator.

Lathani immediately bounds back over to her mother, and they rub against each other again. Kalanthia starts washing her rigorously, and Lathani just braces herself against the force of the licks. I watch and allow the cuteness of the scene to help wash out the fright-induced chemicals rushing around my system. It's true that this sudden attack has made me question whether I want to stay here, efforts made to make this place into a home aside. Ultimately, though, what other choice do I really have? If I leave here, I'm back to the plan of creating a shelter somewhere that is preferably not in some super-predator's territory, and then I'm not really any better off than when I arrived. No, I just need to remember that Kalanthia is, at heart, a protective mother, and so if I ever seem like I might be a threat to her cub, she will end me, Vow or no Vow. I promise myself to be more careful and consider a bit more how my actions might look to her mother before doing anything with the baby nunda. Clearly, Kalanthia is very much against me binding her cub, so I need to make sure that nothing I do makes it look like that's my aim.

Released from my babysitting duties, I decide to head out, feeling like I need a bit of distance. Before going, I remove the meat that's pretty much cooked off the fire, pop it into my Inventory, and then just make sure there's nothing around the area that is likely to catch light. I cover the lower part of the fireplace with the stone just in case, but I figure the worst that's likely to happen now is that the fire may go out. That sorted, I make sure that my knife and mace are easily available in case of attack and then walk down the slope and into the forest. Spike still isn't back—I hope he's doing okay. I haven't heard anything to indicate he isn't, and surely I'd feel it if he was in danger?

I push the thought out of my mind; I don't know where he is, so until I do, there's nothing I can do. Right now, I need to find some sort of handle for my axe-to-be. If I spot some wood that might be useful for a bow and arrows, I'll mark it on my Map and come back later for it. Equally, if I spot any resinous trees, I'll mark those on my Map and do the same with any other useful resources. I've got enough flint gathered for now, and the place where I found it is marked on the Map for when I need more later. It takes me a surprisingly long time to find something suitable for my axe handle. Most of the wood I find is too rotten, too short, or too thin to be useful. Of course, I could *cut* something that would be more suited, but that would require me to actually have an axe first. It's starting to feel like a bit of a catch-22—needing an axe to make an axe—when I find something that I think might just work.

Lying on the ground is a branch that's fallen off the tree above me. The difference between this one and previous trees is its size: it's a bit of a local giant, and its branch is just as big in comparison to other fallen branches I've seen so far. More useful for me is the fact that the branch is *broken*; something heavy stepped on it and snapped it through.

Making a mental note to avoid those tracks if I ever see them while hunting—something big enough to snap a solid branch thicker than my upper arm without even trying is not something I want to take on—I inspect the chunk of wood resulting from the break. The leftover chunk is still double my height, but I think I'll be able to cut it down to size; though, I hope it won't dull my knife. On the upside, the grain changes at its base, where it had originally been connected to the tree. It's my hope that if I can create the hole for my axe blade just below the knot, that will stop the branch from splitting under pressure when I swing the axe. I try to slip the branch into my Inventory, and I'm actually surprised when it fits. *Convenient . . .* Even better, I notice that a tree not far away from the giant seems to have resin dripping out of it. It doesn't *look* like an evergreen, but the fluid beading around an injury to its trunk is sticky and viscous—looks like resin to me. Eyeing the injury to the trunk and the tracks leading to the branch, I figure that this damage was caused by the same thing that snapped the branch. I *definitely* don't want to face that thing, whatever it is. I open my Map and make a mark for later, then close it with a grin on my face.

Feeling satisfied with my finds, I decide to head back home on a meandering path; without any immediate objectives, I figure I can just explore a bit. Of course, that's when I get attacked. Again. Something drops on me from above, and I don't react quickly enough to avoid it. I feel it land on my head, large and spiky, and immediately shake my head frantically.

The thing falls backwards off my head, and I quickly try to put some space between it and me. Even though I can see it there, I swear I can still feel it scrabbling on my scalp. I shudder as the feeling brings back a sense memory of having a tarantula on me—I'd been terrified for *years* after a friend's birthday party at the zoo where they'd given us a tarantula to hold. I hadn't wanted to do it, but the other boys in the party had mocked me for being a "wimp," and so I'd reluctantly agreed.

More fool me: it would have been better to just be made fun of for a bit rather than being unable to be within a foot of even a small spider for years. And even now I don't want to touch the things, though I can deal with sitting near one—as long as I keep my eyes on it and it doesn't make any threatening moves in my direction. This, of course, is a completely different situation.

My breath coming quickly already from panic, I throw myself into a twist and back away, almost tripping stupidly over my own feet. It's only then that I get a good look at what the thing actually is.

It turns out that "spider" wasn't such a bad guess. At least, not if I can consider this thing a spider in the same way as a mole rat is a cute little harmless mouse. In fact, it's more like some horror-movie-worthy amalgamation of a spider, monkey, and snake. Essentially, it looks mostly chitinous and has six legs, each of which ends with a clawed pincer and is attached to a bulbous spiderlike body. Behind the legs is a long prehensile tail that is currently curled up over its head, but unlike the tail of a scorpion, it looks like it could actually twist in all directions, perhaps even curling around a tree branch. I'm pretty sure it has a venomous stinger, from the looks of the spike attached to the end of the tail.

On the front part of this monstrosity is a short but still slightly flexible neck attached to a mouth like a snake's, complete with two long backwards-facing fangs. In short, a memory worthy of therapy. Unfortunately, since none is available, I'll just have to settle for killing it with prejudice and hoping that I won't have more nightmares.

CHAPTER FORTY

Nightmare

Eyeing the nasty chimera warily while backing up, I wonder *how* to kill it. I don't exactly want to get anywhere near its venomous bits—because you can't tell me that those fangs aren't just as likely to be venomous as the tail—but my knife and mace are both close-range weapons. Heck, I might have a spear in my Inventory too, but even that feels too close-range for me. No way do I even want to be within two meters of this thing if I can avoid it.

Then, once more, I remember that my Inventory still contains a slot full of flint nodules, with more stones available on the ground as well. Plus, there's still a real advantage in my favor: its size. The creature is big for a spider, but it's still only about as big as a large cat or small dog.

The chimera lunges at me. It's quick, the six legs not there just for show. I don't think running away will be feasible—I think it's probably faster than I am. A strike from its tail comes at my head almost faster than I can react. I need to get that distance back between us.

I toss myself sideways to avoid the creature and grab a stone in each hand from the forest floor as I push myself to my feet. I throw one of the stones and miss as it dodges agilely. It's almost on me again, and I dodge backwards, then throw the other stone at almost point-blank range. It hits, and the creature makes a horrible shrieking sound, but the thing is still tenacious enough to latch onto my leg with its fanged mouth.

I shout in pain, the curved fangs digging right into me. At the same time, I'm convinced that I can feel its venom pumping into me, even though I probably actually can't. Fear isn't usually very logical. After my experience with the black blob and finding out that Lay-on-Hands isn't a catchall for poison and venom, I'm a little paranoid about getting hit with it. Hopefully, it will work this time.

I catch the nightmare creature's tail as it tries to strike me again, and, after pulling my knife out, I stab it frantically. Its pincered legs scrabble against me, cutting into my vulnerable flesh and turning my jeans into ribbons at the same time.

I don't let go and neither does it, not until it just suddenly goes limp, all life leaking from it with the ichorous substance that appears to be its blood. Very aware that whatever venom its fangs undoubtedly have is still probably pumping into me, dead or not, I quickly pull its head forwards and out, my stomach turning at the painful sensation of tugging and sliding.

I dump the creature on the ground and sway on my feet. *I don't feel so good . . .* Quickly sitting down before I can fall down, I cast Lay-on-Hands, hoping and praying that it will work. The venom burns in my veins—I'm pretty sure I'm not imagining it this time—and I feel weak and sick. In fact, I end up dumping the contents of my stomach onto the ground next to my head as my body reacts to the toxin. I break out in cold sweat and my throat goes dry.

When my vision starts wavering, I become really worried—did I not catch it quickly enough? Is Lay-on-Hands not strong enough, even at Novice rank? Or is this venom another toxin that's somehow immune to my healing magic?

I can't really do much more, though. I don't know what this venom is doing to me, so I can't use the more focused version of Lay-on-Hands to offer better healing. All I can do is just keep casting and hope I have enough mana in the tank to deal with the damage.

It feels a bit touch and go for a while, but eventually, my surroundings fade back into full color as my body no longer needs to concentrate so much on the venom attacking it. I still feel sick and weak, but I've been on death's door often enough recently to know when I've pulled back from it.

When I'm able to get to my feet and start walking slowly, I decide to just go straight home—no point chancing my arm. I'd planned to leave the corpse of the horror-movie reject where I'd dropped it before, but a few steps away, I reconsider. *What if I can use its venom on my arrows?* I hesitate, but eventually turn back to put the thing in my Inventory. It's worth a shot. Pun not intended.

Heading back, I keep casting Lay-on-Hands each time I get enough for two in the tank, and slowly I start feeling better than death warmed over. I pick up the pace a bit and reach the cave as night is falling. After what happened earlier, I feel a bit awkward and wary walking past Kalanthia. She probably notices this; no doubt I'm releasing fear pheromones that she can smell, never mind the fact that she's a telepath. Either way, she does me the favor of ignoring me, allowing me to sneak past without exchanging a word.

My grilled bird meat tastes good, especially when I sprinkle a few grains of salt on it. *Nothing like a life-or-death struggle to increase one's appetite!* I suppose it's the realization that I'm still alive and my opponent isn't that adds a bit of spice to what has become very boring otherwise. I felt too sick after my encounter to feel the usual triumph, but satisfaction fills my belly now, both physically and emotionally.

Exhausted by the events of the day, I go to bed soon after eating and fall asleep quickly. I suppose that after the stresses of the day, it's not surprising that I have nightmares. Honestly, it's probably more surprising that I haven't had them earlier— my nights so far have mostly been blissfully empty of dreams. That I remember, anyway.

Tonight, though, it's a return to those good ol' nightmares I really don't miss. Fearful visions that leave me panting with a pounding heart and cold sweat all over my body. They're not all logical—mostly just fragments of being attacked, being chased, teeth tearing into me, claws ripping me apart . . . Kalanthia has a role, but no more than any of the other monsters, some of which are monstrosities I've come across in this world, others I've never seen while awake.

My dad's there too. Sometimes he's with me, running away from the monsters. Sometimes he's pulled down and killed first. Sometimes he pushes me into them. I wonder what that says about my opinion of my father. A therapist would probably have a great time trying to analyze these dreams. No, that's not right. A therapist would just drive me mad with asking, "And how do you feel about that?"

I've had enough therapy sessions in my life to know how it goes. But there's no therapy here; I'll just have to deal with my own demons. Fortunately, there's no alcohol either, as I have a feeling I would dive back into the bottle to get me through the night, if I had the chance.

I used to love the dead of night, when all is quiet and still. Sometimes, when I was young, I'd wake up for no real reason at some strange hour and wonder if witches were out flying on their broomsticks. I'd read several books where the witching hour between midnight and one was a time of magic, of creatures emerging that otherwise stayed hidden, or of normally ordinary kids being able to do extraordinary things.

Then my mom had the accident and that magical time turned into a nightmare. Instead of being filled with magic and wonder, I started spending long hours in the middle of the night stuck in a mire of my own thoughts. Nasty, accusing voices would entangle me in a web like a fly struggling against a spider. My strategy of filling every moment of the day to push the voices away didn't work between midnight and dawn.

Although therapy helped me regain a sense of peace with myself, the middle of the night never returned to the time of quiet, watchful liminality that it had been before my life first took a nosedive. At best, I manage to sleep through it.

Right now, though, I don't feel very tired after such disturbed sleep. Hit with a pang of longing, I pull my backpack out of my Inventory and rummage in it, my sense of touch finally finding the slim device it's looking for. Turning my phone on, I'm dismayed to see the battery level: despite having been off for basically the whole time I've been here, the battery charge is already below forty percent. I mean, it wasn't fully charged before I arrived in this world, but I wouldn't have thought it would lose battery charge so quickly. Perhaps there's something about the Inventory that drains the battery. Either that or my battery's age is working against it.

Biting my lip, I decide whether to turn it off again or not. In the end, I decide to use it. The current power's not going to last the length of time I'm stuck here, that's for sure, and I highly doubt I'll be able to create the kind of stable electricity it would need to charge. Heck, even if I found the right kind of metal and was able to make wires, I don't think a potato battery would cope with my phone's greedy consumption. I might as well use it while it still has power left.

For a long time, I flick through the photos and videos held on my storage card.

It's bittersweet seeing pictures of my dad, Lucy, and Lucy's family, who had almost become my own before she broke up with me and I couldn't bear to face them. I even page through pictures of various colleagues who I'd gone out to drinks with on the rare occasion.

I watch a video that I'd managed to take of my dad unawares, when he was watching his favorite comedy. I took it because it was one of the few times since his diagnosis that I'd seen him laugh until tears ran down his cheeks.

My eyes blur as I replay the video again and again. It's only a few seconds of video before he catches me taking it and laughter is replaced by a frown, but it's a very precious few seconds. When my screen goes black, it feels like I've been punched in the gut. Have I drained the battery that fast? Maybe I should have turned on airplane mode and preserved its power just a bit longer. Regret fills me, along with its common accomplice, guilt. *If only I'd . . .*

No.

No. I've worked too long and too hard on my mental health to allow myself to be pulled back in. I let it happen before—too much shit happening with no one around to help me keep my head above water—and look what happened. I got to the point of suicide, and then made a stupid decision to leave everything behind and come to this hellhole.

"I'm not guilty," I whisper severely to myself, trying to remind myself of the conclusions I came to after years of therapy. "I didn't kill her. I didn't kill him. The accident wasn't my fault. The cancer wasn't my fault. I didn't do anything to cause either situation, and I did all I could to help them."

I repeat the words over to myself like a mantra, feeling like they're hollow in the dead of night. But I have to believe them. I *have* to. I can't afford to lose my motivation, not here. I've rediscovered my zest for life, and I can't let the tide of depression pull me back down.

Markus Wolfe, what ails you? The voice in my head makes me jump, but for all that, it's a relief. Kalanthia's clear tones cut straight through the sticky sludge of my thoughts like a bell would cut through the mournful howl of wind. "Sorry, did I disturb you?" I reply after a moment, my voice scratchy and thick. *I woke because of the waves of distress emanating from you. I do not believe we are under attack. Are you ill?*

"Not physically," I admit. Then, because it *is* the dead of night and because the ball of tangled negative thoughts and feelings demands to be released, I continue. "I just . . . I miss home. I miss my . . . I miss my family." The ball of emotions within me pulses once more, and I wipe at my hot eyes. There's a long pause.

Come, she commands. I hesitate, not wanting to face her, not wanting to leave my cocoon, just . . . not wanting to move. *Come*, she commands again after waiting for a few moments. Her tone is unmistakably authoritative. I can't resist it, especially not now with my willpower at such a low ebb.

Crawling out of my jacket cocoon, I head out of my alcove and stand awkwardly near the hole that is my entranceway.

Closer, she commands, and I wordlessly obey. What else can I do? Sure, I could walk out of the cave. I doubt she'd follow me, not with Lathani sleeping cuddled up to her side—visible to my eyes only because of a shaft of moonlight. But honestly? I don't want to be alone. I *really* don't want to be alone. As I get closer, she lifts one of her forelegs and hooks her paw around me. The paw by itself is the size of my torso, highlighting just how big she is. Gently, as if I'm a cub like Lathani, she pulls me in close to her. Prodding and poking me, she guides my body into an arrangement where I'm snuggling up to her shoulder, held in the circle of her foreleg and against the side of her head.

It's . . . surprisingly comfortable. Warm, for sure, and fluffy. Really fluffy. I mean, not as fluffy as a kitten, or even a cat—she clearly is an outdoor creature—but still far softer than I would have expected. It's also a bit of a change, going from threatening to kill me earlier today to cuddling me now. But between everything that has happened since I've arrived in this world, I think the fact that said giant leopard doesn't hold grudges is probably the best news I've had all week. *Sleep, Markus Wolfe*, she tells me.

I do.

CHAPTER FORTY-ONE

An Exercise in Frustration

I decide that knapping flint is an exercise in frustration after the stone I've spent more than half an hour trying to turn into an axe head splits in the wrong place for the fifth time and completely ruins my progress. On the positive side, I have a number of flint shards, which will be useful for creating other tools and weapons later. On the other hand, I've made no progress towards my goal, and it's already lunch time. I didn't make any last night either, since I'd been so tired.

On that note, it was odd to wake up half-smothered in fur because I was being cuddled by an apex predator. And warm too—almost too much so—but nice in a way. Still, weird. But I'm grateful that Kalanthia was there for me in the middle of the night—I don't know how much damage I would have ended up doing to myself otherwise, be it physical or mental. But the fact that she was there, that she cared enough to intervene . . .

All I can say is that I woke in a much better frame of mind than I could have expected after the night I had. At least, I *was* in a decent mood until the vexation caused by this damn flint knapping started getting to me.

I decide to take a break before I start screaming. I don't know what's more frustrating: trying to enter data into a new piece of software that isn't *bloody working*, or this. Honestly, I'd vote for this—I might have felt like throwing the computer out the window, but I've never actually done it; I've already thrown at least two of the almost-axe-heads down the slope and used more curse words this morning than in the last *month*. And yes, that includes the day of my arrival in this world. Making an axe is going to take forever at this rate.

I decide to take some time to make—and take some of my frustration out on making—the haft for my axe. Being far too long, it needs cutting down to size. Since I have no other tools at the moment, I have to use my knife, which is far from ideal. It takes even more wrestling with, and I almost chop off a finger a couple of times in the process. But at least I can see myself making progress, unlike with the axe-blade-to-be.

After a period of time, I have something that roughly resembles a tool haft. It's thinner at the end where I will grip it, and I haven't changed much about the bole-like end, since I can't really think about making the hole before I've created the axe blade. I sigh. *Hey, ho, let's go*, I tell myself, though even my inner voice seems devoid of enthusiasm. I summon up my (super-boosted) Willpower—which, honestly, I still can't believe was a measly four when I started. I mean, I'd managed to get through school, through uni, and to keep on at my job for years, including awkward meetings where I had to tell someone they were fired—or, in one memorable case, that they were going to be facing disciplinary measures for being caught having sex in a toilet. During work hours. With one of their clients to whom they had been giving favorable rates. I shudder at the memory. If nothing else, trying to get my mind out of the past motivates me to continue with the devilish knapping. Despite the memories in my head saying that I have supposedly created flint tools hundreds of times, my hands definitely disagree, and it takes all my focus to try to achieve my goal.

When I finally finish my axe blade, I can't help but leap to my feet and cheer. I know this isn't the end of the job; heck, I'm going to have to make more axe blades in the future after this one chips and eventually breaks over time. Still, it feels like a massive achievement, and I decide to celebrate that with a good stretch.

Another three or four hours later, it's heading on for late afternoon; I've spent far more time on this task than I'd anticipated. Really, someone good at flint knapping could probably knock this out in half an hour or an hour, tops. Me? I've taken probably about seven hours, when I consider the time spent actively working it.

My result isn't pretty, but it's a chunk of flint with a sharpish edge to it, so it'll do the job. I hope. I took a couple more breaks to check the drying of my sinew, cook some more meat, and even make a small clay bowl when I really couldn't take any more of the damn flint knapping. In short, it took a long time, and my hands and arms are feeling pretty achy from all this activity I'm not used to. Plus, my back hurts from sitting on the ground bent over for extended periods of time. I miss chairs . . . Particularly my comfortable office chair, actually. I don't miss the office itself, though—four other colleagues all sharing the same space for the sake of "team cohesiveness." Looking back, I'm now sure it was just another penny-pinching exercise.

Still, I feel proud of my work. I finally beat the dreaded flint-knapping devil and got something I can use. Sure, I went through more flint nodules than I'd like to think about, but I could feel my movements starting to align more and more with my memories. Proof of that is when I check my messages and see that I've earned a point in Dexterity, which I don't even have to "pay" for with Energy. I check my stats, feeling pleasure run through me at what I've achieved so far.

Name: Markus Wolfe		Race: Human	Class: Tamer
Level: 1	Energy to next level: 41%	Energy absorption rate: 11u/hr	Energy towards debt: 0%
Intelligence	7	Mana: 70/70	
Wisdom	7	Mana regeneration rate: 175u/hr	
Willpower	15+3 (+20%)	Health regeneration rate: 18u/hr	

Constitution	8	Health: 80/80
Strength	6	Stamina: 30/30
Dexterity	6	Stamina regeneration rate: 60u/hr
Class Skills: Dominate – Beginner 2 Tame – Beginner 1 Fade – Beginner 2		Non-Class Skills: Lay-on-Hands – Novice 3 Stealth – Beginner 2

Although it's only been a few days, perhaps more than a week—I've lost count, honestly—I'm in a much better state than I was when I arrived. Then, my highest stat, Intelligence, had been at six; now, that's almost my *lowest* stat value, being only one point above Dexterity and Strength. I have double the number of health points, something that is rather relieving, and a significantly better health regeneration rate, mostly thanks to Kalanthia's gift.

Plus, I'm already more than a third towards my next level, due to my daily absorption. Okay, I got a few points from that weird crossbreed creature yesterday, but only a few; the bulk of my Energy has been earned by just existing. It's good to know that I'm still making progress, especially when my attempts at making an axe blade have been so frustrating.

On that note, I suppose I'd better get back to working. Getting up, I stretch to release cramping, tired muscles and go back outside.

Regarding my axe blade, I consider what to do next. I'm going to need to finish preparing the haft for certain, and now that I've completed my axe blade, I have an idea of the hole size I need to make. That said, it's almost guaranteed that I'm not going to be able to create a hole so perfectly sized for the blade that the sharpened rock slots in without difficulty—and stays in place despite swinging it into trees.

Normally, using hide and pitch would be the best idea in this situation, but I don't currently have either. Well, I *do* have some hide in my Inventory, but it's untreated, so it's likely to just rot. I'm *definitely* not going to delay my axe by as much time as it would take to treat the hide I have. In the end, I decide to sacrifice a part of an already torn shirt to wrap around the flint blade to help hold it in place. This world seriously has something against my wardrobe—I'm struggling to find clothes to wear that don't already have holes and bloodstains on them.

Actually, thinking about that, I ought to have a wash and repair day at some point soon . . . which means making soap and a needle and finding something to use as thread . . . It's really never-ending. I'm fortunate that at least this place is warm through most of the day; if I needed to wrap up against the cold, I'd be in a significantly worse position right now than I actually am.

It would be good to have some pitch, though, and I *have* actually got all the ingredients available. That's if we consider "knowing where to find them" to be the same as "available." Maybe that's what I should do with the rest of today: go back to that place where I found a tree with sticky sap on its trunk? Probably a good idea; though, I hope I won't have a rematch with that spider thing—or one of its relatives, since the original is most definitely dead.

Hopefully, the pitch, the cloth, and the bark-fiber cord, which I'm going to tie around the top, bottom, and over the blade in a crisscross manner, mean the knapped flint stone will stay in place when I pound it into trees.

I might as well plan to make soap at the same time since there is some crossover of ingredients needed. Man, it will be so good to have clean clothes and to be clean myself; all I've done in terms of bathing since my arrival have been dips in the river to wash off the blood stains. I feel *grimy*, like the dirt has actually ingrained itself into my skin and won't shift for anything less than a harsh attack with soap.

So, in terms of ingredients, I need resin, charred plant fiber, and animal fat for the pitch.

For soap, I need ash and animal fat. For both, I'm going to need containers. For the pitch, I'll need a filtering bowl for the resin, a container in which to char the plant fiber—I'll probably use a bit of the bark fiber I'm twisting into cord—and somewhere to actually mix and keep the pitch. For the soap, I can either create a quick and dirty bar, which just requires mixing ash with animal fat, or I can try and do something more properly. In the latter case, I would need a filtering container with a hole at the bottom to allow the lye solution through, something to gather the lye solution, and something to boil the lye solution. Actually, the last two uses could be a single container.

Then I also need somewhere to render the fat and a mold to form the soap bar. The mold should be pretty easy to make—that could just be made of wood. Actually, so could the filtering container, as it doesn't need to go in the fire. So maybe I'd only need two different containers that could go in the fire. In total, then, I need at least seven different containers, four of which need to be pottery because they need to be heated. Or I could use my wok for one of them, but I'm hesitant to do that: I don't want to damage it or render it unable to be used as a cooking utensil. As it stands, I have two medium-sized pots and one bowl currently drying. So, I guess I only need something suitable for charring the fiber, as none of the pots I've made so far will really do the job.

I'll also need to make another bowl for my own use, but perhaps that doesn't need to be now; I can just keep eating straight from the wok, like I've been doing so far. Actually, maybe I don't even need a bowl; I've got that shell from that sneleon I killed a while ago. It's been sitting in my alcove for a while, unused despite its watertight nature. The main issue is its shape: because it's conical, it doesn't stand up very well. I'd tried using it for water, and it does help when watering my beans, but if I could use it as a bowl . . . I'll just have to eat like the Vikings were reputed to drink: all at once, without putting the container down. If I have soup left in the shell, I can just put it back in my Inventory. Strangely enough, it doesn't seem to spill there.

I'll still need to make more pottery, and maybe it would be a good idea to fire all my pottery at once. Then I can use the ashes from the fire to create the soap. But before I can fire the pots, they'll need to be dry, which will take a few days. Plus, although I have the time right now to make the last pot I need for my project, I don't have the clay—having only gathered clay to make the fireplace, I'm lucky that it's stretched this far already. I'll need to head back to the clay pit near the river soon to collect some more clay. If I'm going to collect resin today, maybe I should plan a trip to the clay pit tomorrow morning? Then spend part of tomorrow making the last pot . . .

Since I'll be firing several at the same time, I might as well make several pots, as there's no guarantee that they will all fire without cracking. Taking Spike with me again would be a good idea since his horn will increase my collection speed. Besides, the samova beans haven't yet sprouted, so there's nothing for him to actually guard at the moment. Then, while I wait for the pots to be ready, I might as well prepare as much as I can for my future bow and arrows by creating my bowstring once my sinew is dry enough and . . . knapping flint heads. I grimace at the thought.

Still, that's tomorrow and the days after tomorrow. Right now, I need to go and collect resin before the sun starts seriously heading for the horizon. I briefly consider switching up my tasks and fetching the clay tonight, as that's the more urgent task, but then dismiss the idea for one simple reason: time. The clay pit is further away from the hopefully resinous tree, and there simply isn't enough time before dark for me to go there and back *and* collect enough clay for my needs. Besides, Spike isn't back yet, and if I wait for him to return, it will then probably be too late to head out anywhere.

Resin it is.

CHAPTER FORTY-TWO

Flailing Master

I stalk carefully through the forest back towards the tree. The shadows are already lengthening, but mid-afternoon here means there's still plenty of time until night falls. I took over an hour to reach this area last time, but I wasn't exactly moving fast, instead meandering while looking for an appropriate branch to turn into an axe haft. Last time, I wasn't at my best, having just been attacked. So, I figure I should only take half an hour or so to reach it at my current speed.

Sure enough, by the time I reach the area that I recognize as being near the tree in question, it's only taken about that long according to the amount of Energy I've absorbed—that's my way of telling the time these days. Searching around the area a little, I feel glee as I see not just one resinous tree, nor two, but *four*.

They're all next to each other; three of them are perhaps offspring—or sprouts—of the first, or perhaps all of them are remnants of another, larger tree. There isn't enough size difference between them to indicate which might be the most likely possibility, but the fact that they are all similarly sized indicates that they were all planted at similar times.

Abruptly, I'm jolted out of my thoughts. My foot suddenly twitches without my direction as I step on a muddy pile of leaves, but my weight is already shifting unavoidably onto that leg. The ground suddenly gives way under my foot—the twitch was not nearly enough to help me avoid stumbling into a hole.

I shout in surprise and pain as I'm jolted by the unexpected drop. Pain twinges inside my knee joint. My calf muscle feels like it's being stabbed, which adds to the misery. It takes a moment for my brain to catch up with what's happened. I've accidentally stepped into a pit. Although I've been watching out for threats, I wasn't looking for traps. And a trap, it soon becomes obvious, is exactly what this is.

Chirping battle cries pierce the air, and I'm bombarded before I know what's happening. *What is with this area and getting attacked?* I bemoan to myself. It takes me a few moments to gather my senses and start attacking with my knife and mace, moments in which the battle does not go well for me. There are two sets of attackers: one set up in the trees, one set down below. The group up in the trees are ranged attackers and the ones below are more melee orientated.

Covered in feathers, my assailants look surprisingly similar to the reconstructed images of feathered velociraptors I've seen. They have long-toothed beaks, which the ground troops soon start using to attack me and the ranged attackers use to spit mud at me. Perhaps mud-spitting doesn't seem particularly impressive, but the speed at which they're succeeding in sending the attacks is enough to sting my skin.

At first the mud doesn't make much difference, but as it builds up, I feel it weighing down my limbs and making me feel wearier than I should be. My stamina bar is also decreasing worryingly quickly.

I try to shake it off, but it sticks on stubbornly. At the same time, the sharp beaks and claws of the ground velociraptors tear at my clothes and skin. Against someone half my size, they'd have already won; as it is, I'm not in a good state. Not at all. I flail around with my mace to try to keep the ground attackers at bay, but my stuck foot limits my mobility. Another downside is that it also brings my body and vulnerable organs closer to the creatures, which, for all their numbers and strategy, are only as tall as the average medium-sized dog. And, since they're bipedal, they can't reach up much further than that. Unlike the killer chickens I fought before, these guys are feathered, but have no wings—the feathers coat their forearms but don't extend backwards very far.

In short, if I can get myself back to my normal height, I'll have a significant advantage over the ground velociraptors. As for the ranged ones, I can probably reach a few, and the rest I'll just have to throw rocks at once the ground troops are dealt with. Annoying as the mud is, it's not immediately life-threatening, but the sharp-toothed beaks of the ground creatures potentially are. Even if I don't bring my vulnerable torso into their range, they could still get in a lucky bite and open an artery in my legs. Deciding to concentrate on getting free of the hole, I do my best to ignore the bites and slashes of the creatures now surrounding me as I put my hands and good foot on the ground, using them as a stable base from which to free my other foot. It's painful to pull my foot back, and I'm worried I've sprained my ankle.

When it finally pops free, I wince at the sight of the cuts and bruises already blooming on my skin. The walls of the hole are not exactly smooth, and although they haven't been deliberately made worse the way I probably would have done—as I'm sure by now this is a deliberate trap—it's still a hole in the ground with plenty of roots and stones.

My ankle *isn't* sprained, and my quick Lay-on-Hands sends healing to start dealing with the injuries incurred both by the trap and by the undefended attacks from the creatures surrounding me. My mobility regained, I grin savagely at the velociraptors, a knife in one hand and my mace in the other.

"Now who's the easy prey?" I ask them rhetorically as I start swinging and swiping. I'll admit that it probably looks fairly ungainly from the outside—I'm a flailing *master*—but I don't care. For all their obvious intelligence and viciousness, these velociraptors, like the killer chickens, aren't durable. One good hit with my mace is enough to take a velociraptor down. My knife isn't quite as effective, as it actually has to hit the right spot to work, but once I get a rhythm going of stunning a raptor and then stabbing it, I find that the attackers almost melt away.

Once more, it almost seems like a replay of the killer-chicken fight, only this one has the added complication of ranged attackers, which, while only annoying, do mean that I have to spend a lot more energy on maintaining my mobility than I'd prefer. Just like the chickens, these velociraptor look-alikes are pack fighters, using surprisingly intelligent ambush and hit-and-run tactics to take down prey.

If I hadn't been human, I'd probably have gone down a long time ago. But I *am* human, which means that not only do I have weapons that multiply my damage-dealing capacity, but I also have healing magic. Consequently, instead of a quickly over blitz attack, the raptors are suddenly having to deal with a battle of attrition. And like with the killer chickens before them, these creatures are not so good with protracted battles.

By the time I've cut my ground attackers down from probably around ten to three, they decide they've had enough of this and turn to retreat. Not having any of that, I swing my mace and knock one of them hard enough that I hear the crunch of its fragile rib cage breaking. Then, going after one of the remaining two, I'm suddenly hit by an absolute deluge of mud. It's like the creatures in the trees above have doubled their assault.

All I can do is hunker down and try to protect my head from the sticky, heavy mud. As abruptly as it started, the deluge peters out and then stops completely. Wiping some of the mud off and smearing it onto the ground, collecting a good number of dead leaves and twigs at the same time, I look up at the ranged squad. They're tired, panting, like that last attack was a final all-in move. Not giving me a second glance, they're also trying to flee, moving along the branches they're sitting on in something only slightly faster than a shuffle and jumping from branch to branch.

Anger boils within me. *They think they can pour mud on me and then just leave?* Not likely. Grabbing stones from my Inventory, I start throwing them. My increased Dexterity shows as I actually manage to hit my targets almost as much as I miss—I couldn't have done that before. Getting attacked sends the ranged raptors into a bit of a panic, and they increase the speed of their escape; clearly, they weren't expecting the attack, and why would they? I haven't shown any ranged abilities up until now.

A couple of raptors are knocked out of the trees, and I rush after them to swing my mace and end their lives. I manage to get three more before they get too far away for me to justify chasing them.

It's only as I watch the final feathers of the creatures disappear into the bushes that a thought occurs to me that should have done so earlier. *These guys attacked me and tried to kill me. Couldn't I have justified using Dominate on them, even if only to myself?* A ranged attacker could have made a good addition to my team. Even though they were fragile things, they would surely have been more combat capable than my current follower, the defensive-natured porcupig.

Looking around at the no-longer-twitching bodies lying around me, I can only sigh and curse myself for not thinking of it earlier. Then again, perhaps the middle of a fight wouldn't be the best place to do it, anyway—I don't know what happened to my body when I was in that odd state during the Battle of Wills with Spike.

Maybe time stopped, or maybe we were both just frozen for however long it took for me to win it. If it was the latter, then it could have offered too much of an opportunity for one of the other raptors to rip out an important artery. Either way, there's no point crying over spilled milk. Or blood.

Grabbing the bodies and just dragging them, I return to near the tree where all this started. After slumping to the ground, I take a few moments to recover. I'm not terribly injured, as I've been keeping up with pumping healing magic through myself at various intervals. As I sit there, my health regeneration plus continued casts of Lay-on-Hands tops me up the rest of the way in just a few minutes. My stamina took more of a beating than my health, if I'm honest. I should probably consider putting more points into Strength (Endurance) in the next level up. Or start training for a marathon.

Still, I'm covered in mud, which does *not* make me happy. Add that to the fact that another pair of trousers has been rendered to shreds, and I grumble out loud as I start digging out the hearts of the velociraptors, tossing the rest of their corpses into my Inventory as I go. In total, I got thirteen of the creatures, and probably about ten or twelve got away. Hopefully, they won't be back for revenge anytime soon.

I build a quick fire and a rudimentary spit with two forked twigs stuck tail-first into the ground. Another twig serves as the spit itself, and I shove the hearts onto it as a strange kind of kebab. While the meat cooks, I go do what I'd actually come here to: collect resin.

Fortunately for my sanity, I didn't misinterpret what I saw, and all four of these trees have sticky, aromatic resin dried on their bark. The chunks will definitely need processing before I'll be able to use them for pitch, but I reckon it will all work out in the end. My harvesting over, I'm feeling a lot more peaceful by the time I sit down to munch the hearts. They're not well cooked—one side is rather overdone and the other is only barely done, since I struggled with getting the spit to turn over and stay there—but I don't care. They taste like victory.

In that moment, I realize something that disturbs me a bit: I'm starting to like this. Or maybe "like" is the wrong word. And maybe "this" is too general. It's just . . . There's something about this world that is *real* in a way my previous existence wasn't. I live on a knife's edge between survival and death. At any moment, it wouldn't take much for me to die of starvation, thirst, or injury, and somehow that makes the rest of life sweeter. The food I eat is bland in comparison to the sweetened, salted, and fried food of my past, but it has a taste that all of those lacked: the taste of freedom.

In this new world, there's no boss to tell me what to do. No alarm clock to wake me up in the mornings. No landlord demanding rent. No bills demanding payment. Nothing to stop me from just . . . walking into the forest and going wherever I please. Instead, I have to make my own decisions, and the reward for making the right one is living one day longer or having something that adds a little bit of luxury to my life, like my fireplace. I have to build things with my own hands and put my blood, sweat, and tears into all the labor. And in doing so, I've regained a sense of appreciation for everything.

It's . . . freeing, but not in an irresponsible way. I can't afford to be irresponsible, but in being given complete responsibility over my own existence, I've gained a sense of satisfaction deeper than any I'd felt before.

Given the choice of going back to my previous life, it's hard to know what I would choose. Last night proved to me that I miss home, but I'm not sure "home" actually exists for me anywhere. The old adage says, "Home is where the heart is," and my heart is gone.

Earth holds nothing but the bitter ash of regret and destruction in many ways, but I can't say for certain that I would reject the siren pull of the safety, comforts, and ease of modern life. On the other hand, this place has danger around every corner, but it feels . . . fresh, in a way. Like the only history here is what I've brought with me.

While walking back home, I pause to jump in the river to wash off the mud before heading up the slope. Having decided to butcher the carcasses later, I change into dry clothes and spread my wet ones out near the smoldering fire in my fireplace. Then, slumping down onto my bed, I check out my Energy gain. *A good forty-four percent increase. Nice.* Groups are a pain—literally—to deal with, but they're good for Energy gain.

When I'm done with munching on my bird meat and drinking a bit of my "soup," I decide not to move and instead make myself more comfortable on my jacket nest and pull out a book from my orange suitcase. I could, and probably should, continue with making bark-fiber cordage or begin to whittle my soap mold with my knife and a chunk of wood, but I don't.

After the fight earlier, I feel like having an evening off tonight. I'm going to read a bit by the light of my fire until I become too sleepy, just like I always used to back before Classes and life-or-death encounters were a part of my life.

Hopefully, I won't have any nightmares tonight.

CHAPTER FORTY-THREE

Wisdom

The next morning, I skip testing the root Spike found a few days ago. I've been taking advantage of the more relatively relaxed days to start the whole edibility testing process—so far with decent results—but considering I was attacked yesterday by the gang of velociraptors when I didn't even go that far from home, I don't want to risk being caught again today. It's never fun fighting on a mostly empty stomach.

I've got more days of crafting ahead of me, so I'll have time to test the root later. I'll try to eat it next time and have already cooked it in my wok; it's in my Inventory until I'm ready for it. With the ten more slots I gained leveling up, I have a fair amount of space for storage these days. Just as well, since my needs seem to be multiplying!

Ultimately, I want to discover at least five edible vegetables. Pondweed seems to be fine, and hopefully, this root will be able to stand in for potatoes—the state of the cooking water after I boiled it certainly proved it's full of starch or something similar. Then I just need three more to give myself a chance of eating well rather than becoming malnourished. Something with vitamin C in it is a must-have since I don't want to get scurvy. *Wait, is scurvy a problem for people with high Constitutions?* An interesting question.

Constitution affects health points, but what does that mean? Is it just a defense against poison and injuries, leaving diseases and nutritional imbalances to wreak havoc?

Surely not, because although my status screen only shows Constitution affecting health points, the System lore stone tells me that Constitution actually improves the body's functioning. That means improving the efficiency of different organs, the durability of my bones, and the reactivity of my nerves.

Surely that means that it also improves the capabilities of the immune system? Nicholas's world doesn't seem to have investigated this, judging by the lack of information, but isn't it logical to say that the immune system is just as likely to be improved as organs? And if higher Constitution affects the efficiency of organs, doesn't that mean that it can tolerate lower-than-ideal levels of vitamins? Or higher?

Again, not questions I have answers to, but I'll probably discover the conclusion sometime—and hopefully *not* by getting scurvy or the plague. Actually, on that note, I suppose that it's unlikely that any viruses carried by the creatures around here are contagious for me since I'm from another world entirely. One upside, I guess. And I didn't get sick or even have a stomachache from drinking water straight from the stream without boiling it, though I am boiling it now just in case.

After filling my canteen with boiled water from my wok, I first take a good drink and then summon Spike, who's resting in the sun. I head off down the slope to fill my wok at the river for boiling later, and the porcupig follows, also looking for a drink.

Then, walking as quietly and inconspicuously as possible, we head back to the clay pit while Spike forages for food en route. That's one downside of having an herbivore around: he does slow things down a bit since he needs to spend more time eating than I do. Still, it allows me the time to—hopefully—spot any more traps waiting for us. For once we manage to actually make a trip into the forest without being attacked. That's not to say we see no other signs of life—we see plenty—but any animals we cross paths with are more scared of us than we are of them, and we don't end up in another fight.

Perhaps it's my size: all the creatures we run across are smaller than me, and, in the animal kingdom, size really does matter. Except for venomous creatures; with them, venom is the great equalizer.

The slow, quiet journey gives me a bit of time to consider something. It's still concerning that I haven't earned any Energy towards my "debt" yet, and I'm leaning towards the idea that just earning Energy in general doesn't count.

Firstly, because it seems ridiculous that enough Energy to get me a good four-fifths of the way towards level two, despite having "bought" several stat points, wouldn't even register as one percent.

And secondly, because my other experiences with the System seem to indicate that Energy is a usable resource, rather than some ethereal, abstract number.

I mean, the System lore stone was quite clear in indicating that we have to gain Energy to level up not because some god or higher authority says we have to, but because the Energy is genuinely required to change our bodies. Actually, I've started wondering why a leveling system is even required, except for the fact that it seems to also provide clear thresholds for when we can gain access to more Skills. Though, if we can gain Skills in other ways . . .

Anyway, it seems that we actually use the Energy we gather like money we earn. Therefore, if the Energy is being used to make me stronger, it can't be used to propel me across universes, which, according to Nicholas's letter, is what the debt Energy is for.

I decide to try something as an experiment. Seeing as so many other things seem to be based on thinking about them—the first time in my life I've actually been able to say that thinking about something has real results—I try concentrating on my desire for my Energy gain to go towards my Energy debt rather than towards my next level.

I concentrate hard enough that a furrow digs into my brow and my eyes unintentionally slide shut. I repeat the thought several times to try to increase the chance that something actually comes of my efforts.

When I'm confident that the idea is as embedded as I can make it, I relax and open my eyes—and dodge abruptly to the side as I realize I'm about to collide with a tree. *Maybe next time I should do this sort of thing standing still . . . and not in a forest that has almost killed me multiple times.* Anyway, time will tell as to whether I've actually done anything or if I've just been thinking hard with nothing to show for it.

Back at the riverbank close to home, I release Spike to his eating and guarding duties. He managed to find me a few more roots at my request during our walk, so at least I've got plenty of testing material sitting in my Inventory. More immediately useful to me are the two slots full of river clay.

Kneeling by the river, I process the clay, needing a much finer grain to make my pots than the natural stuff provides me with. I need it to be even finer than the clay I used initially for my fireplace and find myself teasing out even quite small stones. It takes time, like everything in this supermarket-free world. Honestly, I understand why people in the past had far fewer possessions and tended to take more care of them; when you have to dedicate hours to replacing a pot or a plate instead of just popping down to the local shop, breaking it is much more serious.

By the time the sun is past its zenith, I've processed all the clay I collected, and two Inventory slots' worth of clay have been reduced down to barely half of one—it just goes to show how much of the raw clay was stones. Still, I should have enough clay to be getting on with. Deciding to actually start making the pottery at home, I make sure my water canteen is full and then tuck everything away in my Inventory.

Heading up the slope again, my stomach growls loudly. Half-grinning at the sound, I decide to pay attention to my bodily needs and munch on some bird meat and drink hot, boiled water for lunch while sitting outside the cave in the sun. Then, my belly appeased, if not full, I settle down for some pottery making in the shade.

Deciding to start with my charring pot, I create the base first by manipulating a piece of clay until it's flat with slightly curved up sides. Then I take another piece of clay and flatten it. After wetting my fingers, I draw them along the edge of the sides and then add my next piece of flattened clay, blending the join until there's no sign of it.

Continuing the process, I work around and up, around and up, until I have a small pot about the size of my two hands if I was holding something between them, my fingertips just touching. I leave a small opening, adding a little lip so that I'll be able to use it for liquids later.

Checking that there are no signs of where I've joined the clay pieces together, I try to smooth the inside as far as I can reach through the hole. I can't reach well enough to smooth the interior with a river stone like I did with the previous pots, so I hope it'll work well enough.

Putting the pot aside with the others to dry slowly, I start making some more forms: another few pots in case the ones I've made so far crack, and a couple of plates, jugs, and bowls both large and small. After having a small brain wave during the day, I even finish up by creating a small stand for my snail-shell bowl. It's nothing pretty, but hopefully, it will solve the issue of me not being able to put it down until I'm finished. By the time I'm done, the sun is close to the horizon again. It's been a long day, but a fruitful one, I hope. The proof will be when I fire the pottery pieces.

At least pottery making has proven to be less frustrating than flint knapping. In fact, I can see why some people would choose to do it as a hobby. Not for me, though. Especially not now when there are so many other things to do. Still, it was calming, despite Lathani sneaking past her mother to come and investigate what I was doing. She gave me a minor heart attack when her curious prodding almost toppled three of my newly made pots, but I managed to save them just in time.

Deciding to use the rest of my light to work on another tool, I head back out of the cave to sit in the sunlight. Bathing in its warmth after the coolness of the cave, I take a moment to just *be*. Down below at the foot of the hill, the sun only enters as fingers of light through the shifting canopy above, but here on the top it has free rein.

I raise my face to the sky and feel the play of warmth across it. The breeze drifts across my skin, its caress almost a kiss. The symphony of the creatures of the forest surrounds me without being overwhelmingly loud; the sound of the evening is significantly different from that of the morning. The smell brought on the breeze is that of trees, grass, loam, and the faint hint of decay. The mix of pleasant and unpleasant is a good metaphor for nature in general.

I find myself in a state of unusual serenity. Pottery making, beyond being simply calming, is almost like meditation in that it requires enough focus to prevent sinking into past or future thoughts and troubles but, at the same time, is monotonous enough to lull my thoughts into peace. My mind feels clear and light, with no fears for the future or worries about the past weighing it down.

For once, I'm living in the moment, and it feels . . . good. As I withdraw my axe-haft-to-be and the blade I worked on yesterday from my Inventory, I feel a gentle nagging, which I've come to associate with a notification waiting for me.

Congratulations!
You have come to understand a little more about Wisdom and have earned a point. Would you like to apply this to your status?

Y / N

I hesitate. I wasn't expecting *this*. Well, it seems like I do have a little more of an idea how to work on Wisdom, having channeled my inner Buddhist monk. Or was it the Tibetan ones who refused to kill any creature, even an insect, believing them all to be brothers and sisters? Or am I mixing it up with the Inuit "Brother Sun, Sister Moon" thing? I shrug—it's not as though I'll be able to find out now, is it?

Either way, clearly it was my feeling of connection with all the flora and fauna of this world that prompted this increase in my Wisdom. Perhaps meditation could help? Not that I've ever done it, but I've picked up a few things about it by osmosis from my ex. Though, she got everything from Vogue, so I'm not completely convinced that she's the best authority.

Anyway, all those thoughts are beside the point. Should I accept it or not? It's not really a hard question. I've increased my Wisdom from where it started, but it still has a long way to go to even be considered "normal" for Nicholas's world, and the more points I can earn by myself, the more level-up points I'll be able to assign freely. After thinking *yes* at the interface, I sense the point being applied.

CHAPTER FORTY-FOUR

Good Times

In my state of serenity, I start wandering down the hill towards the stream. I look at my surroundings and notice that they are ever so slightly different from before. The world around me has a myriad of facets that I've never really paid attention to. I suddenly see how interconnected my environment is, each aspect linking to another.

I admire how the play of light over the earth not far from my feet is causing the insects to move in a certain pattern. I watch as some pellets left by a small animal—*probably last night*, I note absently—are clearly food for these same insects and are being swiftly taken apart and carried back, presumably to their nest.

I have to focus to see these connections, and they take time to see and decipher . . . but it's a difference to the way I viewed the world before, if only a minuscule one. I check my status screen, and yep, I'm down by twelve percent Energy storage. It's changed from before when it used to take fifteen percent to increase a stat, but maybe that's because it takes more Energy to gain each percentage point rather than taking less Energy to increase the stat itself.

What I do notice is that the Energy debt is *finally* showing movement: my status screen now shows a gain of one percent towards my Energy debt. One percent in a day. And my Energy store hasn't changed except to go down by twelve percent, now sitting at seventy-three percent.

On the one hand, it's good news: if I dedicated all my Energy to the debt, I'd be finished with it in less than a hundred days, just based on Energy absorption. Assuming that creatures killed also count towards it, I'd be done in even less time. I'm fairly confident that the Energy gained from kills also counts; in the letter he left me, Nicholas seemed quite keen for me to go hunting.

If I did focus all my Energy towards paying off the debt, though, this little experiment has proven that I wouldn't make any steps towards improving myself. Unless, of course, it's just sheer coincidence that I gain a percent towards my Energy debt at the same time as I don't gain anything towards my next level. But that seems implausible, so I'm going with the explanation that my habitual Energy absorption has been directed towards paying my debt. Which brings me back to the issue here of making improvements.

Sure, I could keep gaining stat points until my Energy store runs out, and then afterwards I could gain even more if I worked hard enough, but I don't think that's the most efficient way of doing things.

If working in the corporate world has taught me nothing else, it's that money makes money. Those who have money can invest it in places that offer a return on investment with little effort on their part. Those without money have to leverage their own time and effort for gain, which limits their earning capacity. I'm not saying that this is the same story—I can't send Energy out to earn more Energy, but the higher the level I have, the more powerful creatures I can kill, and the more Energy I can earn. Though, actually, that raises the question of whether I could send Energy out to earn more Energy through my Bound. I mean, if I Dominated or Tamed five different creatures and sent them out to kill others, would I get any Energy from that? Perhaps something to test later when I have more Bound—more combat-capable Bound, that is, because as good as Spike was against the black blob, I really don't think sending him out to try to kill other creatures would work very well.

Another factor for my decision about earning Energy is the hope that once I'm more powerful and durable, I'll be able to head into the more Energy-dense areas. That should mean that even my hourly Energy absorption rate will go up. I'm presuming that the Energy debt is a static quantity rather than a percentage of my effort, even though I don't have any proof for that and won't until I can earn enough Energy to raise the amount accumulated towards my debt at a significantly faster rate than I am now. Still, it makes logical sense to me.

Some evidence I have that supports my thoughts is that the percentage cost of raising a stat point has reduced since leveling up. Conversely, the amount of Energy required to increase the percentage of my Energy store has risen—relatively easy to notice when calculating how many percentage points I gain just from daily absorption compared to the before. Those two facts put together indicate to me that some things under this System require a static quantity of energy rather than a relative percentage.

So, to summarize: although I could complete the Energy debt in a hundred days as I am now, in the future I could potentially complete it in fifty days or maybe even less. So, I'll need to take a balanced approach and not complete it too soon when it will just put a brake on my progress, and not leave it too late either, as that could be a . . . terminal mistake. It does mean I need to pay a little more attention to how long has passed. *Maybe making some sort of record that I keep up to date would be the best option?*

Deciding to do my figuring out somewhere safer than just next to the river, I walk back up the hill. Once settled, I unzip my backpack pockets and dig around a bit until I find a pen. Next, I grab one of my books. Opening its front cover, I hesitate. I hate marking up my books, but here there's not much option. Not unless I want to start carving notches in a stick like a caveman, anyway.

Now, how many tally lines should I make? I'm pretty sure about two weeks has gone by. Let's see . . . The day I arrived and was attacked by the bird. The day after with the crocodile things. The day after that and the raptorcat panic-fest. I think the killer chickens were the next day—oh yeah, that was when I was attacked by that snake-millipede thing. Good times . . . I scratch my head for a moment. *What happened next?*

Oh, of course—the wolvezard and Kalanthia. Or was that the same day as the chickens? I can't remember . . . Then I've looked after Lathani twice, and I think there were three days between the babysitting days. Oh, and the day I took off. And the day I leveled up. Plus, this is the second day since I last looked after Lathani. I count up the days. *So . . . twelve days? Maybe thirteen, maybe twelve? Ah, I'll go with fourteen—I'd rather risk being a little early with my debt than a little late.*

Conclusions reached, plans made, and my first efforts to record how long I've survived so far done, I decide to continue with my axe. Looking down at the two halves thoughtfully, I debate with myself about what to do next. With the blade now made, I know how big I need to make the hole. How to do it is a different question.

Looking at the more prepared haft, I thoughtfully consider the quickest and most effective way of making a hole. I don't have a drill or a chisel. I *could* use one of the flint flakes from my knapping as a chisel and a rock as a hammer, but I don't think that would be the most effective, or not at first, anyway. Especially since the flint would be more likely to just chip and break.

In the end, I decide to use fire. It's easy enough since I've already got one burning almost twenty-four seven in my fireplace. Well, most of the time it's just smoldering embers rather than actually burning; I only add on extra fuel when I want to cook something or boil water. But that's frequent enough to keep the fire alight. Actually, I ought to go and collect some dead branches to keep it going overnight . . . I'll do that after this. I probably should have done that while I was down by the river instead of being mesmerized by the connections of nature, but too late now.

I head back into my cave and use a pair of sticks like chopsticks to pick up a burning coal. I place it into the middle of the spot where I want to make my hole, paying careful attention to make sure that it chars the wood below it rather than actually setting light to it.

When that coal cools down and stops working, I flick it back into the fire and use my knife to dig out the charred wood. Now there's a little divot in the wood, and I grab another coal to repeat the process. As I keep doing these steps, I only occasionally need to put out a fire by smothering it. Fortunately, the wood is pretty dense and chars much more easily than it catches light. On the other hand, the density of the wood means that the job takes a lot longer than making a hole in a lighter material might. Hopefully, my axe will make all the effort worth it.

It's a slow process still; the burning helps but isn't anywhere near as effective as even a crude stone drill would be, let alone a modern electric drill. Still, I keep at it, using the time while the wood is smoldering to stretch my limbs and make some more bark-fiber cord—my current go-to for busywork. By the time the sun is almost touching the horizon, I'm making pretty good inroads, but I take a break to go collect some firewood. I can continue doing this in my cave once darkness falls properly, after all.

Putting thoughts into action, I quickly venture into the forest to scour it for dead wood. Fortunately, being a forest, there's plenty of that around. It helps that it doesn't seem to have rained for a while as everything is very dry. I hope that doesn't mean there will be any sort of forest fire, though.

I keep going until almost full dark follows. When something swoops past me, barely visible in the dusk that is more dark than twilight, I jump and decide to head back. Knowing all the other things that are around in this forest, I'd rather not chance my arm—or head—by wandering around in the domain of nocturnal creatures. My eyesight has improved a little with my Constitution stat but not enough to make the poster boy for eating carrots and *definitely* not enough to compete with a creature who makes the night their hunting time.

Hurrying home, I keep a sharp eye—and ear and every other sense—out for anything that might consider me a little snack to start the evening with. Once home, I head into the alcove and prod the smoldering embers in the fireplace back into flame. Carefully feeding the flickering fire with fuel and blowing to ensure it gets enough oxygen, I soon have a merry blaze flickering in the center of the clay chimney.

Using its light, I start sorting out the firewood I collected, piling the items into three different categories: light, medium, and heavy. That way, I should be able to easily lay my hands on whatever the fire needs to keep going. Of course, that all takes a fair amount of time, and once I'm finished, I don't really feel like continuing with the axe haft. Instead, after having a dinner of stew, I just lie back in my bed and think.

If knowledge stones create new neural links and give access to new memories, would it help to go through those memories? Reinforce the links? Could that actually be a way of increasing Intelligence? Surely yes, in that creating and reinforcing neural links is generally an indication of intelligence, and nothing about this System so far indicates to me that it works counter to what scientists on Earth already know—quite the opposite. *So, maybe if I dedicate a bit of time to going through all the information I've learned from the knowledge stones, as well as perhaps things I learned at school and at work that might be relevant to my life now, I could increase my Intelligence stat?* It's worth a try, at least, so I get to work.

I fall asleep still going through memories, though my cataloguing has shifted from just going through useful memories to playing a reel of the highlights in my history. It feels good and means I slip into an easy sleep full of pleasant, if nostalgic, dreams.

CHAPTER FORTY-FIVE

This Big

As usual, I wake with the sun. As I test a small chunk of my potato replacement, I look forward to the time when I will be able to eat enough of it to actually make my stomach feel like there's something in it, rather than the emptiness that follows my "breakfast" now.

I've got high hopes for this thing: if today goes well, I'll be trying a greater quantity tomorrow morning, and then after that, I'll hopefully be able to try adding it to my stew of pondweed and bird meat. Honestly, without any sort of seasoning apart from a very small amount of salt, it's not great, but if I can have a starchy tuber to turn the thin liquid into something more soup-like, it will improve the situation.

Once I've found some basics to eat, I can try looking for things that will flavor my food a little, but honestly, it's not a priority at the moment.

As I eat, I muse about the lack of waste I now produce. I used to fill a bin bag every week or so, even living on my own. And that's not even including the amount of recycling that I produced as well—another bag every two weeks. Now . . . What I don't eat or use comes from nature, so I just return it to nature. Bones and useless hides I drop in the forest to be stripped clean or eaten away by scavengers. Discarded flint shards are just left to lie where they fall, immediately becoming part of the forest floor.

Even my fires don't produce much waste, and I'm collecting what they do produce to use for the various crafts that require ashes. Bits of food neither I nor Spike eat, like the stems of the pondweed plants, are currently building up in a hole I got Spike to dig for me; when it's half full, I'll cover it over and start another one, then probably plant seeds or these tuber things in the first hole once it's had a bit of time to compost. The circle of life right there.

It's a very different story from modern life where I was so disconnected from nature around me. It makes me think more deeply about humanity's place in the world. Right now, I'm back to basics: all the way back from the Cyber Age to the Stone Age, with only a metal knife and some modern fabrics to prove that anything else ever existed. Once more, I can't help thinking that there's a part of me that's . . . comfortable and content with my place here, for all the hard labor that it entails.

Speaking of hard labor, time to get going again since I've finished my tuber. What to do first? My clay is going to take a bit of time to dry, several days at least. Once it is dry, I'll need to fire it, so for that I'll need to make a pit and collect enough firewood to keep the fire burning for hours. That's going to take time, but not days—well, the pit might, but I'm going to get Spike to help with that. As usual, it's a bit of a catch-22. It would be easier to collect firewood if I could chop chunks off the bigger pieces I find on the ground, but for that I need my axe, and I won't have my axe before I've made the pitch, which requires the pots to be fired . . . I sigh in frustration. I'll just have to cope with smaller pieces of deadwood, but that means I'll need more of it. At the same time, I still need to make my flint arrowheads and process the sinew for attaching the feathers to the arrows, not to mention for making the bowstring as well. *Lots of things to do—what's the best order?*

In the end, I decide that I might as well start digging the pit, as that's likely to take the longest time. Well, no, the flint arrowheads are likely to take the longest, but I won't need them until after all the other things are done, so I've got time. Walking out of the cave, I greet Kalanthia. The giant leopard reminds me that tomorrow is my babysitting day. I shrug and agree. It doesn't impact me hugely—I still need to dig my hole. Maybe Lathani will find the hole interesting enough that she won't try to explore down the hill.

I make a mental note to spend some time roasting extra pieces of meat for her in case she needs a bit of bribery. Hopefully, Kalanthia won't overreact again now she knows I'm not trying to Tame her cub. "Spike?" I call and then stop and listen. Nothing. *Hmm, he must be off foraging. Oh well, I'll just get started by myself then.*

I grab a stick out of my Inventory, which I had set aside when I realized it might be good for something other than just firewood, and look at the ground around me thoughtfully. I don't want to put this pit anywhere it might pose a danger to a certain nunda cub. But at the same time, I don't want to go far from the cave, as I'm going to have to keep a sharp eye on my rudimentary kiln when it's lit.

In the end, I pick a spot not far from where my chimney opens onto the outside. Using my digging stick, I start breaking the ground. It's hard work and sweaty, especially when the sun rises higher and starts warming me up even further. It's also slow work, far slower than it would be with a shovel, let alone with some sort of mechanical digger, which could probably do my job here in ten minutes or less. I have to use the digging stick to break up the ground, then my hands to scoop the loose dirt out of the hole.

The first bit is the hardest, as I have to break through the netlike roots of the ground-covering plants. It would be easier with a spade because I'd be able to cut them; here, I have to basically just use the stick as leverage and my hands to do the rest. Needless to say, the skin on my hands takes a beating between the rocks, roots, and blisters from my hold on the stick.

Actually, by the time I pause for lunch, I feel like a big ball of pain. My hands are the worst, of course, but my knees hurt from skin being pressed into rough ground, my neck is burned, and my back aches from being in the same position for a long time. I stretch with a moan, the change of position both a new pain and a relief from pain.

Checking my stats, I can see that I've even lost a couple of points from my health bar. I'm curious about what my health regeneration is like, so I don't actually cast a healing spell on myself as I go and get food.

Munching hungrily on some meat in the blessed shade, I watch as my hands—washed clean of dirt—slowly repair themselves. I do end up casting Lay-on-Hands by the time I finish lunch because they're not healing fast enough by themselves for me to be able to pick up the stick again without wincing. Still, the fact that I was able to see a visible improvement in my injuries in such a short amount of time is impressive. Perhaps superhuman healing isn't so far off after all.

I keep going as long as I can, eventually giving up somewhere after mid-afternoon from sheer exhaustion. I'm a lot more used to hard labor now than I was when I arrived, but it's only been a couple of weeks—Rome wasn't built in a day. Still, I've made some progress, and the speed of advancement only increased when Spike returned and helped me out.

I've stripped the turf in a circular shape about two meters in diameter—the size of my future pit. I've placed the sods of earth around the edge of the hole to delineate it a bit. I'm planning on doing the same with at least some of the soil and then forcing sticks into the pile to create something of a barrier to a certain cub.

I watch the cub in question with an indulgent eye. Lathani's been very interested in what I've been doing all day. Currently she's scrabbling in the dirt, investigating the various bugs and worms that have been revealed by the removal of their "ceiling." As I watch, she pokes at one bug with a curious paw. Unlike the other bugs, which ran away as quickly as possible, often turning themselves over in their haste, this one just raises its mandibles and stands its ground.

"Um, Lathani, I wouldn't—" I start saying as she squares up to it eagerly. Poking at the creature again, she's surprised when this one bites back; its mandibles sink into her fur and—probably—prick her skin. She's more surprised than hurt, but she panics, especially when she shakes her paw and the bug stays attached.

Making cute little sounds of distress, she dances around flailing her paw back and forth. She honestly looks ridiculous. It's a big bug, sure, but she's bigger than any house cat; it just looks so small in comparison that it's unbelievable that this little thing should have such an impact on her. *Still*, I muse even as I rush forwards, *it's probably as ridiculous as a full-grown adult panicking over a bee or a wasp. Or a spider.* I shudder at the thought, my own feelings of fear only deepening at the memory of the spider-horror that attacked me a couple of days ago.

"Lathani, calm down. It's okay," I say as I move forwards. "Hey, stop and I'll get it off you."

She doesn't pay me any attention, still bouncing all over the place. The situation resolves itself when the bug loosens its grip and goes flying away into the bushes thanks to Lathani's flailing. *What is amiss?* Kalanthia's voice makes me jump. I see her peering out of the cave, wariness in her posture. Lathani makes a plaintive wail and runs towards her, cuddling into her leg as soon as she gets close enough.

"A bug bit Lathani," I tell her mother. "She finally managed to shake it off just now." The cub sends me what can only be a betrayed look. Somehow, I know exactly why I earned that look. "I swear, it was massive—*this* big," I add, holding my hands out to indicate something the size of a small dog. Lathani's gaze shifts into something more satisfied, and she turns her head back into her mother's leg. I wink at Kalanthia and shift my hands to show her the real size of the creature.

I see, Kalanthia says, sounding amused. *Perhaps you should be more careful around bugs, my cub,* she continues, obviously projecting to both of us, however that works with her weird mind-to-mind communication. She and her cub withdraw back into the cave with a final glance around to, I guess, check there are no threats.

I put my digging stick back into my Inventory and then sit down in the sun for a little rest. I'll probably go and collect some firewood for the rest of my evening, but I need to recoup my energy a little.

CHAPTER FORTY-SIX

Time

Looking up at the sky, I try to estimate the time. Having paid close attention to my Energy gain by absorption over the last few days, I've concluded that there must be between twenty-seven and twenty-nine hours per day. Settling on twenty-eight as the average—and also easily divisible—number, I decide on a clock face with fourteen hours on it.

Based on the idea that the zenith of the sun is at fourteen o'clock in the afternoon, and therefore midnight is fourteen o'clock in the morning, I estimate that the sun usually rises around five or six in the morning and sets between nine and ten in the evening. That makes a day length of between seventeen and nineteen hours and a night of between nine and eleven hours.

Hah, no wonder I'm feeling well-rested at night but completely exhausted by the end of the day. Even if we assume it's the shorter end of the scale, and I'm not convinced it is, I'm active for *seventeen hours.* And not just mentally active, but intensely physically active as well. Sure, I've worked long hours at work but rarely more than fourteen hours in a day, so seventeen is a bit of a jump, especially since I'm not just sitting at a computer but often actually in a life-or-death situation. Also, I tend to need about seven hours a night to feel well-rested, so the fact that I'm getting at least nine explains why I always wake up naturally with the sun, despite being by nature more of a night owl than an early bird.

Is this even as long as the days get here? I have to wonder if this is spring, summer, or autumn—surely it's not winter—or, indeed, if there are seasons here at all. It's actually a more relevant question than it might first appear; if winter is coming, I need to prepare for it. *Actually . . .*

I stand up and walk over to the cave mouth. Peering in, my eyes adapt slowly to the dim light. It's a quicker adaptation than it used to be, though—I guess I have my increased Constitution to thank for that. Lathani is snuggled into her mother, moving rhythmically, probably drinking milk. *Good, she's not asleep.*

"Kalanthia," I start softly. She shifts a little, but otherwise doesn't move.

Yes, Markus Wolfe, she says after a moment. "I was wondering . . . Are there seasons here? I mean, changing day length, temperature, weather . . . ?"

Yes. Okay, that's . . . informative. I take a moment to think through my next question.

"What are they like? Is the temperature change drastic? Does the weather change dramatically?" Kalanthia huffs lightly.

Outside this valley, the changes are more obvious than inside it. Here, we have a protected climate where the main change is day length. However, even that does not change significantly—perhaps the day in the dark season is as short as the night in the bright time. The main change with the weather is that there is significantly more rain. I sense her distaste for the wet but keep my amusement to myself.

Along with her "words" comes the sense of wet moving to dry and back again, the river widening its banks and then narrowing again, the sky overhead moving between overcast and clear, and the temperature varying between chilly enough to be grateful for fur in the mornings to warm enough that fur is only tolerable in the shade.

"Right, thank you," I reply, genuinely grateful for the information as well as the impressions sent along with it. Good to know that I don't need to worry about preparing to be buried under meters of snow, at least. Though, I do have one more question . . . "So, which season are we in now? The bright or the dark? Or an in-between one? And how long does each season last?" I lied—I have two more questions. *Hmm, we are past the brightest point of the year, but not by long.* Okay, so in that case, if I say that the summer solstice has a daylight period of eighteen hours and a night period of ten hours, does that mean that the winter solstice has a daylight period of ten hours and a night period of eighteen hours? If so, that's really not too bad. I'm used to London and its less than eight daylight hours at the darkest, so at least ten is an improvement on that.

As for the length of the seasons, Kalanthia continues, *it is hard to approximate in terms that your human mind will comprehend. Perhaps . . .* She flicks her tail thoughtfully, then continues. *If you consider the cycle to be as long as you are tall, the time since you have been here is the equivalent of your shortest finger. The brightest time and darkest time are equal distances apart, and the temperature is coldest in the short time following the darkest night, just as the warmest time is the period directly after the brightest day. The rain comes in the period surrounding the darkest night, perhaps the equivalent of your knee to your foot, but it is not constant, simply annoyingly frequent. The driest time directly precedes the start of the rain.*

It's an interesting way of describing time, but effective enough. I can't get an exact idea of how long a year is here, but if we approximate that two weeks is the equivalent of around five centimeters and then divide my height of 177 centimeters by that, we get approximately thirty-five times two weeks. Hence, we can estimate the year length to be around seventy weeks. I suddenly have a thought. *I'm supposed to survive in this world for a "year." Which year?*

Are they talking about an Earth year of 365.25 days? Or a year on this planet of approximately 490 days? Actually, even more than that in Earth's terms, considering that the day length here is longer than on Earth. Or, even more panic inducing, a year on Nicholas's world, which could be significantly longer—or significantly shorter?

I absently thank Kalanthia again for the information and return outside to chew it over. A sense of fear rises in my chest at the thought of the answer being Nicholas's world, and of me overestimating how much time I have to earn the Energy. I check my status screen and notice that I have some messages to investigate. I'll look at them later. No, nothing on my screen. No countdown, no indication of how long I have to earn the Energy. Nothing.

I close the screen and force myself to breathe. If I don't know the information, I can't make plans based on it. I'll just have to make plans based on what I *do* know and try to earn the Energy for my debt as soon as possible without stymieing my progress. *Wait*... A thought suddenly strikes. *The System lore stone. Maybe that would have the information I seek?* I focus on the knowledge I absorbed from the stone, trying to trigger some sort of latent knowledge about Nicholas's world. To no avail. No new information comes up to smack me in the face. Still, I'm not completely disheartened. I worked out a theory about Earth based on circumstantial evidence in the memories I absorbed; it's possible I can do that again. It'll take longer than I'd like to spend while the sun is up to do that, though, so I put it off to ruminate in the back of my mind until this evening.

In the meantime, I check out the messages I've received. As expected, they're all about stat gains, but none of them are offering me the point for free, unfortunately.

Congratulations!
You have worked hard on your Strength (Endurance) and have earned a point. Would you like to apply this to your status?

Y / N

Congratulations!
You have worked hard on your Strength (Power) and have earned a point. Would you like to apply this to your status?

Y / N

Congratulations!
You have worked hard on your Constitution and have earned a point. Would you like to apply this to your status?

Y / N

Two points in Strength! I whistle in appreciation. Still, I suppose all of these make sense. If my theory of day length is right, I've probably spent about eight hours in intense physical effort improving my muscle endurance and the repetitive actions themselves improving my muscle power. As for Constitution, I suppose I *have* been putting my body through the mill today. A muscle twinges to remind me of exactly what I've asked of it, and I wince.

I pull up my status screen mourning the fact that my Energy towards the next level, which had been almost into the last fifth of the way to level two, has dropped significantly. Still, since I don't have a Skill to shoot for, the next one being available at level five, I don't feel too bad. Yes, six more stats to assign would be great, but I've just gained three through hard work and an injection of Energy, so that's almost as good.

Name: Markus Wolfe		Race: Human	Class: Tamer
Level: 1	Energy to next level: 42%	Energy absorption rate: 11u/hr	Energy towards debt: 1%
Intelligence	7	Mana: 70/70	
Wisdom	7	Mana regeneration rate: 175u/hr	
Willpower	15+3 (+20%)	Health regeneration rate: 18u/hr	
Constitution	9	Health: 90/90	
Strength	8	Stamina: 40/40	
Dexterity	6	Stamina regeneration rate: 60u/hr	
Class Skills: Dominate – Beginner 2 Tame – Beginner 1 Fade – Beginner 3		Non-Class Skills: Lay-on-Hands – Novice 3 Stealth – Beginner 4	

Deciding that I've sat around for too long and feeling a bit restless with the uncertainty about the length of time I have until my debt becomes due, I get up and head off to collect some firewood.

It would be nice if I could avoid a confrontation today. After all the physical labor, I don't feel in a good condition to get into a life-or-death struggle. I decide not to venture too far, since I reckon that Kalanthia's presence is a good deterrent. For sure there are far fewer tracks in the area immediately surrounding the hill. Either she's hunted enough creatures close to her den to keep others away out of fear of being hunted in turn, or the animals detect a superior predator in the neighborhood and react to that.

Either way, I take advantage of the zone of tranquility to find firewood with less risk of suddenly being jumped. I still keep my eyes out, though—I'd be stupid not to. The downside of searching in this spot is that I've already been through this area a few times, so there are fewer sticks and branches available.

By the time the sun is close to the horizon and I'm heading back, I've actually succeeded in avoiding being attacked. A miracle. On the downside, I haven't managed to collect as much firewood as I might have hoped. Still, I've made some inroads on the large amount I'm going to need for firing my pottery. A few more trips into the woods, maybe going a bit further, and I should be golden. The sky is darkening as I climb the slope; I'm glad I didn't leave it any later to come back. Kalanthia's lying in the entrance of the cave, and Lathani's playing with a stick nearby.

"How's the war wound?" I ask the cub after saying a quick hello to her mother. The baby nunda chirps at me and rubs her head against my knee, having to lean up a bit to reach. She's clearly not yet capable of communicating like her mother is, but I get the impression that she's happy to see me. The thought sends warmth through me, and I lean down to stroke her head.

Suddenly wondering whether her mother would approve, considering her strong opinions about Taming, I pull my hand back quickly, glancing up at the giant leopard. Kalanthia isn't looking, her golden eyes instead shut as she rests her head on her paws. Lathani clearly liked the caress, though, as she butts at my head insistently. I hesitate, not sure if I should or not. *Why did you stop, Markus Wolfe?* Kalanthia's rumbling voice speaks into my head, making me jump. Clearly, even though her eyes are closed, she's still completely aware of her surroundings. *Lathani was enjoying that.*

So, she doesn't mind. Mentally shrugging, I crouch down to continue scratching at Lathani's ears and neck, stroking the fur on her head and down her spine to her shoulders. Her fur is far softer than her mother's. Fluffy, even. The cub half-closes her eyes in contentment, and the warmth inside me grows. There's nothing like giving such simple pleasure to an animal and seeing them enjoy it without any sense of shame or self-consciousness.

But all things come to an end, and I have tasks to do before the night closes in completely.

CHAPTER FORTY-SEVEN

Nicholas's World

Regretfully walking away from Lathani, who makes an annoyed sound when I stop petting her, I head past the cave. After sorting out the firewood in my Inventory, I stack the majority of the branches up near where I've started digging my pit, only taking enough of the driest stuff into the cave with me for the night.

Previously, I tested my wok and the sneleon shell to confirm that they can enter and leave my Inventory while holding liquid. Further testing has also proven that the liquids are kept as much in stasis as the bits of bird meat that I'd cooked and thrown in there. Thanks to all those factors, I get to have warm "soup" without having to put in any effort now. The last time I made some soup, I cooked it in the wok and then poured it into the sneleon shell to free up my only piece of cooking equipment—I need it on a daily basis for boiling water, so I can't have it constantly occupied with food.

Drinking now, I'm glad my mother can't see me; she always used to scold me about making a mess. Unfortunately, there's not much I can do about it. I didn't think about bringing cutlery with me, so I have no spoon, and the sneleon shell is larger than a bowl and oddly textured inside, meaning that I slop rather more liquid than I would prefer. Still, beggars can't be choosers. Hopefully, my crockery and cutlery situation will be at least partially solved once I manage to fire all my pottery works.

What's important for me right now is that my stomach is full, the potato-like tuber adding a bit of starch to thicken the broth. I know that the feeling of fullness will disappear rather quickly despite that. Never mind—if I'm too hungry to sleep later, I'll chew on some more bird meat, or whatever I should class the killer chickens and velociraptors of this strange world as. *Actually, that reminds me: I never dressed the velociraptor corpses . . . A job for future-me.*

Now the sun's gone down, Spike is sleeping curled up near the entrance to my alcove, and I haven't got anything better to do except twist some bark since I'm dog-tired from all the physical exercise I did today. I decide it's time to tackle the task I started earlier. While my fingers stay occupied with twisting bark, the task automatic by this point, I start to comb through my mind to try and put together some clues as to the length of day and year in Nicholas's world. Letting the question percolate in the back of my mind hasn't brought up anything useful, so now I'm going to put some focused effort into it.

This time I don't try to think about the day length or year length itself, instead trying to remember things like the length of the harvest season, or how many hours between breakfast and lunch—incidental things like that.

My approach can be characterized by two images: the first, a mad-eyed man grabbing the memories by their shoulders and shaking them while yelling in their faces; the second, a pickpocket sidling up to dip his hand in their pockets without alerting them to his presence.

On the way, I have to admit that I get distracted with a number of facts, and a sinking sense of disappointment as something becomes quite clear: Nicholas's world is nowhere near as technologically advanced as the world I've recently left. There are no cars, for example; the majority of vehicles I see are being pulled by a few different animals, which appear to be the equivalent of horses. As for communication devices, I don't see a single phone, though I do happen across a couple of other devices that appear to at least somewhat fulfil the same functions, but they're clearly powered by magic rather than electricity.

If I had to make a guess based on the information I've seen so far, it's that the actual civilization level of the place is not that dissimilar to the western world in the early nineteen hundreds. They clearly have devices for light, transport, and communication, but the devices don't look particularly streamlined. Not like a modern-day phone, which is capable of so many tasks in the form of something that can easily sit in a pocket. However, their civilization also clearly hasn't followed the trajectory of the world I've so recently left. Instead of being based on electricity, I have to guess that it's based on magic.

Scientists don't seem to exist, though some of their functions are being fulfilled by "scholars." That's not to say that studies and experimentation don't happen—in fact, that's how I glean some important facts about time—but they happen differently. After all, gravity is apparently only a law until you gain enough stat points or magic to defy it.

Actually, there are some aspects of the new world that are rather jaw-dropping in their implications. *Flight* is possible, for example. And not just flight in an airplane or gliding thanks to a squirrel suit, but actual proper unaided flight.

The most bemusing thing about it is that my discovery of this was presented almost as a footnote—the focus of that memory was more about the differences between high Dexterity and low Dexterity. The only reason I realized that flight was possible was because one of the participants arrived and left by sprouting wings of light and just . . . taking off. Obviously, for people living in that world, the fact that people can fly is as much of a no-brainer as the fact that people can run in mine. All of that sounds great, and my dreams of perhaps becoming a fire-wielding, flying, badass mage are not quite as impossible as I would previously have thought. Just one thing, though: I'm starting to fear that I'm never going to be able to recharge my phone or Kindle. Maybe that sounds stupid to think about when I'm literally being given the chance to go to a world of magic, but . . . my pictures of my family are on my phone. If I can't charge it, I'll never see my parents again. The thought is depressing, and I quickly return to my original task to distract myself from it. I'd started going through the memories of the System lore stone for a reason, and getting more of an idea about Nicholas's world isn't it. Sure, it's great to have an idea of where I might be going, but I have to survive to get there first. I need to work out how much time I have to play with before my Energy bill comes due.

It takes time, but just as I'm dropping off to sleep, the combination of the two approaches I'm using to find the memories, plus the relaxation of sleep, offers me a little gem. Of all things, I wouldn't have expected the first clue to come from laundry, but it does. Why? Because there was a study done on the effects of doing laundry on a washerwoman's Constitution. Ridiculous, yes? But this study followed a number of washerwomen through the year to investigate the conditions under which they worked, since their average Constitution was curiously high. It turns out that the reason for the high Constitution was the fact that they were constantly exposed to water, and, in winter, that meant they actually had to break the ice to use their washing pools. As a result, they were working in conditions that would cause most Earth humans to develop pneumonia in a short space of time. The washerwomen of Nicholas's world *did* develop illnesses due to the water, but those who survived the illnesses and continued to be washerwomen developed higher Constitutions as a result. Of course, thinking about it, it's possible that these memories might actually not be up to date—Nicholas's world might have advanced past the technological level indicated by the stone. I'm not holding out much hope, though.

Back to the topic at hand, though. I have several memories of the scholar noting his results along with the date to get an idea of the year length. It's not an exact answer, as I'm not sure that he recorded a result on the last day of the year, but I know for sure it's at least 300 days long, as he recorded a result on the 302nd day, and I got the impression that the year wasn't yet finished. Next, I try to work out the day length, since this is also an important factor. I mean, if we consider that an Earth day is twenty-four hours and a day on this planet is probably around twenty-eight, combined with the difference in year length, the difference in time then multiplies. If, for example, Nicholas's world has days of only ten hours in total, that could mean that, despite having at least three hundred days in a year, it would only count as just over a hundred days on this planet—a far cry from a bit over three hundred or so.

Again, my clue for day length comes from an unexpected source: the opening hours of a restaurant. It's just a fleeting snapshot of a moment in a memory about something completely different, but the person just so happened to walk down a street and be temporarily distracted by a restaurant menu. A menu, incidentally, that wasn't written in English or any script I know, but that I somehow understand, just like I had understood the scholar's notes. Small mercies, I suppose.

Anyway, the restaurant indicated that it was open for lunch between twelve and one, and that it would not accept anyone later than half past fourteen. So, assuming that lunch is over midday, I have to guess that the morning continues until at least fourteen o'clock. Of course, that's based on an assumption that is not a guarantee but is likely enough—given the clearly diurnal nature of Nicholas's people—to be used as the basis of my theory. Assuming that the two parts of the clock are equal—again, not guaranteed, but surely logical enough that even a society with magic wouldn't do anything different—that means the day length is probably about the same as this planet. I mean, they might have a completely different way of telling the time. It's not guaranteed that they invented clocks at all, after all. However, the fact that they had a seemingly consecutive series of numbers that continued to the middle of the day, and which then restarted, indicates to me that whatever they've got to help them tell the time is divided into two roughly equal portions. I mean, okay, they could have divided the day into more than two sections—fourteen hours could be the length from the start of daylight until the lunch hour. But if that's the case, and my "year" is based on their year, then I'll have *more* time than I'm guessing, not less.

When I come to that conclusion, I sigh in relief and sink into my jacket nest, putting the bark and cord back into my Inventory. Sure, I'm making a few assumptions here, and I hope they don't come back to bite me, but I figure I've got at least three hundred days to earn my passage to Nicholas's world. *Plenty of time*, I tell myself. That settled, I'm about to drop off to sleep when I notice that I have another message waiting. Apparently, I've earned a point in Intelligence. Well, if that isn't proof of my theory that processing memories and making links between them is linked to Intelligence, I don't know what is. Accepting the point, I drift off to sleep feeling rather pleased with myself.

The last thought I have is a niggling concern. *What if time moves at different speeds in these two worlds?* Like in that space movie where the guy who stayed on the space station ends up being years older than the ones who went down to its surface. Are any of my calculations at all useful? Before I can actually start becoming worried, I fall into Morpheus's arms, my concern lost to uneasy dreams.

CHAPTER FORTY-EIGHT

Animal Empathy

The next day I continue with digging my pit. After fetching water, of course. Kalanthia disappears into the forest as soon as I get back, leaving Lathani playing by my feet. I tempt her over to my work area with a bit of nicely roasted meat, and then she's happy to mess around in the dirt for a while.

Watching with a bit of amusement, I see how she studiously avoids any bug that looks even remotely like the one that bit her yesterday. Though, like a typical cat, she pretends that she's not avoiding the bugs out of fear; she's just not deigning to pay them any attention. Of course, she gets bored with that after a while and goes searching for something else to do. I keep half an eye on her as she tussles with the grass, pounces out of bushes, and wrestles with sticks. I'm less amused when she knocks over my carefully stacked pile of firewood, but the startled expression she gives when the sticks start falling down around her ears is cute enough that I can't bear to scold her. Plus, she's actually got herself trapped within a "cage" of dead branches and is looking forlornly at me, chirping plaintively, asking for help.

Unable to prevent a smile at her adorableness, I put my digging stick down and walk over to free her. "Next time, don't mess around with my wood pile, and then you won't have this issue," I tell her as indulgently as any uncle. Rubbing herself up against me briefly, she then wanders off again.

She continues having some good, relatively safe fun for a while but then spots her next target. I hear a hiss and look up to see her facing off with Spike. The nunda cub, judging by her body language, is playful and curious. The porcupig, on the other hand, is a lot more defensive, and I judge that he's only a short while away from turning around and presenting his namesake spikes to Lathani's face. Given that I doubt Kalanthia would be happy to come back to a hedgehog–nunda crossbreed look-alike, I decide to intervene.

"Spike," I call, and both animals look over at me. "Don't attack Lathani," I order him, impressing my intentions into the simultaneous mental order. His spines immediately flatten, and his body language drops its defensiveness, but I get the sense that he's not happy about this.

Then . . . "Lathani," I say, "play gently with Spike, okay? And if he doesn't want to play, leave him be." That may be more complex than she can deal with, but I've really had the sense over the last few days that she understands significantly more than I thought—she just chooses not to do what I say unless there's a benefit in it for her. Speaking of . . .

"If you play nicely together, I'll give you some more yummy meat, okay?"

At the mention of "yummy meat," the term I've been using for my roasted chunks, she perks up and shifts the way she looks at Spike. I'm not sure how to identify her body language, but it's like . . . she's acknowledged what I said and is agreeing to follow? How I get that, I don't know. Maybe more of that mind-to-mind stuff again? At the sense of something waiting for me, I check my messages, shifting so I can still see the two creatures out of the corner of my eye.

Congratulations!
You have earned a Skill: Animal Empathy

Read Skill description? Y / N

I click through to the Skill description, feeling like I have an idea of what it might be. Sure enough . . .

Animal Empathy
Understand what the animals around you are communicating with their body language. The more you are familiar with the animal or its species, the more success you will have in interpreting its intentions. This Skill also improves in effectiveness with Wisdom. Improvements in understanding of scent-based communications depend on Constitution.

Given what I've learned about Wisdom recently, I suppose it's little surprise that this is the key controlling factor for understanding something outside myself. As for Constitution . . . If it's supposed to improve the functioning of my senses, being able to smell pheromones once I get more stat points in it also makes sense. I close the screen with mixed feelings. On the one hand, it's a useful Skill to have: being able to interpret the body language of animals around me might lead to better success with hunts and Taming. On the other hand, it seems more descriptive than active. Unlike Fade, which actively reduces my visibility, Animal Empathy just seems to describe what I would still be able to do even if I didn't have the Skill. Then again, maybe it will develop into something more active later. Oh well, it's not like it's a *negative* to have the Skill and it doesn't seem to cost me anything.

Lathani is playing with Spike. After the tense face-off, they seem to have relaxed a little bit. The nunda cub is keeping her claws and teeth to herself—mostly, anyway—and so is Spike with his quills. He even seems to be enjoying it now, despite his reluctance to begin with.

They romp around a bit, rolling in play fights and then breaking away to play hide and seek before Lathani pounces on Spike and it all starts again. *At least they're having fun*, I think to myself with a smile. Plus, it lets me get on with my pit digging even while I babysit. Of course, nothing lasts forever, and Lathani eventually gets bored with playing with Spike and comes over to me to beg for scraps of meat. I put a few bits on the ground for her to munch, and she starts chewing with gusto. After she finishes the last chunks, however, she just goes to a sunny spot and curls up; apparently, Spike exhausted her. From the look of Spike, she exhausted him too since he's sleeping nearby.

I take advantage of them both sleeping to go check on my fire and the progress of my drying clay pottery. It's coming on nicely, and the fact that the drying pots are in a warm environment but not directly in the sun means that they're drying quicker than I thought. *I guess I need to go for firewood tomorrow*, I mentally note. It will still take another few days, I reckon, for the pots to dry enough to not be at high risk of exploding in my kiln, but the wood I collect may need to dry a little too, so it's just as well to collect it a bit ahead. Not that it's rained since being here, but there is that mist that rolls through most mornings.

Using my time in the shade wisely, I munch a little meat for lunch and sip some of my soup. I've added a little of my precious salt, so there's a bit more taste to the food. Small pleasures . . . I've justified it with the fact that I sweat buckets when digging—I need to replace what I've lost. I don't stay inside for too long, even though I'm enjoying being out of the sun; I've got a baby nunda to keep an eye on, and I want to make as much progress on my pit as I can while she's still asleep.

By the time the little bundle of fur wakes up, I've been able to make a fair bit of progress, pausing at one point to cast a healing spell on myself when the blisters started to get too painful. The rest of the time until Kalanthia gets back is then spent playing with Lathani, Spike having trundled off to find food to eat in the forest.

Greetings, Markus Wolfe, Kalanthia's mental voice purrs, making me almost jump out of my skin at its suddenness. *Has all gone well this day?* She's climbed the hill and is moving over to nuzzle her cub.

"Yeah," I say once I've been able to catch my breath after the shock. I'm so much easier to scare than I used to be—not surprising, I guess. "Lathani and Spike enjoyed playing this morning, then she had a nap, and then we played for a bit," I tell her. "She was good," I added uncertainly, not sure if my version of "good" matches Kalanthia's—what do I know about being a leopard mother? The massive predator purrs and rubs her chin over Lathani's head.

That is well. My thanks, Markus Wolfe. You are free to go now. Thankful for the dismissal, I give a mock salute and then go back to my digging. I'm making good inroads but still have a lot further to go.

By the evening, I reach a point at which I'm happy to call it a day. Good thing too—I'm exhausted. I've also earned another two points in Strength, one each in Power and Endurance. It's nice, though I'm pretty sure that the speed at which I'm increasing my Strength will slow down a bit from now on; the System lore stone I absorbed indicates that after ten points in any stat, it takes more Energy to increase it, so it makes sense that I'll have to do more work to even trigger the increase. Still, reaching ten points is no mean feat considering everything I've gone through. It even puts me at the top of an average Earth human's physical capabilities, if my interpretation of the stone's memories is accurate. I didn't get an increase in Constitution today, but I suppose I can't have everything. With the Intelligence point I earned last night, thanks to going through all those memories, I've been making some good progress recently. I'm planning on doing some more of that mental link-making tonight. I still have enough Energy in the tank to increase my Intelligence again if whatever progress I make is enough to earn another point.

After that, though, I will have used all of my Energy store, and I only absorb enough Energy per day to increase a single stat. Unless I kill some creatures, of course. The fact that I'm going to venture out into the forest tomorrow in search of lots of firewood makes that scenario rather more likely than not.

Even though the sun isn't yet touching the horizon, I'm too tired to keep going with my pit, so I decide to eat my supper in the last light of the day.

Chilling for a bit, I let my mind wander for a while before once more starting the task of drawing links between my memories. This time I decide to work on clarifying exactly what I need to do for my upcoming crafts, linking it to my knowledge from Earth as much as possible. It's surprisingly interesting when I get into it. Some of my half-forgotten memories of chemistry at school come to the fore as I think about *why* soap made of ashes and animal fat works, considering that those are the substances we generally have to wash *off*.

I think it's my increased Intelligence that allows me to remember words like "hydrophilic" and "hydrophobic" and that the alkali from the potash in ashes is the former, while the fatty acid chains from the fat are the latter. It's ironic that two messy substances allow water to actually wash off oils and germs, but that's what happens. By the time I go to bed, I've earned my Intelligence point, but only just. *One more point to go, and then that stat will be ten too!* It's on this wave of satisfaction that I drift off to sleep.

CHAPTER FORTY-NINE

Battle of Wills

Walking through the forest is actually a pleasure. The sun and leaves make a dappled pattern on the layers of last year's dropped leaves. My Stealth has already leveled up to Beginner four despite not getting much practice with it over the last few days of digging pits. The moments when it directs my feet to shift slightly so they don't step on a crunchy leaf or a crackly stick still feel a bit weird, but I'm getting used to it. I keep my eyes out in all directions both for potential threats and for branches that look like they'd be good for the pottery kiln or my indoor fire. Having walked a good hour's distance away from the cave, I'm finding plenty, which is good for my pyromaniacal plans. My vague plan to rebuild my Energy store by killing creatures that attack me is not going as well.

Spike isn't with me. I decided not to bring him this time, since I planned on venturing out further from the cave than normal and with a mind to actually getting in a few fights. I know he's got some good defensive abilities, but I just can't help thinking that he'd struggle against some of the pack predators I've encountered. Needing to defend him at the same time as myself would probably cause more issues than having him with me would solve. No, he's better staying near the cave in the area where the predators mostly don't come, thanks to Kalanthia's presence.

The forest is strangely quiet. There's the normal sound of birds and small animals rustling in the leaves, but all the bigger animals seem to be in hiding. The prey-type animals that I normally catch an occasional glimpse of are absent, and I haven't been attacked once in three hours! Although that *has* happened to me before—walking in the forest and not being attacked—it's not what generally occurs. It's a bit eerie, to be honest, and puts me more on edge than being attacked would. I keep collecting wood, though, while also keeping a sharp eye out for anything dangerous that might have moved into the local area and scared off everything of reasonable size, or whatever it is that has caused this unusual stillness to descend on the woods. If all the denizens have been scared into hiding, I don't want to meet the cause.

It's about half an hour later that I suddenly hear something that makes me freeze and activate Fade. Feeling more protected now I'm not visible, I focus on the sound, trying to work out what it is. It comes and goes and sounds like . . . breathing? But very wet breathing, if so. Is there an amphibious monster or something?

When the sound doesn't move or even change much, I dare to creep closer, pushing my Stealth capacity to the max. When I detect that the sound is coming from behind a tree, I use the tree as cover and then slowly peer around it, ready to leap away and run for my life at a moment's notice. What meets my gaze is not an amphibious monster. It's not a threat either. Not now, at least.

Deadly-looking claws are coated in blood—most of it looks like the creature's own. Feathered wings are soaked in red and lying limply. The absence of blood matting the fur around the creature's tooth-filled maw tells the tale of its complete helplessness against its attacker. And finally, the wide slice in its side and its limp, muscular body indicate that this raptorcat is close to death. The only way I can tell that it's not already dead is because I can see its ribs moving slightly with each breath, and I can still hear the wet sound of air passing in and out of its lungs.

The sight fills me with a mixture of emotions. Relief that I'm not in danger from the maker of the sound. Satisfaction that a creature that tried to hunt and kill me has been hunted and killed in turn. Sadness that a proud creature of the forest has been reduced to a still-moving carcass, if not for long. Fear that whatever did this to a deadly raptorcat is still around . . . and might still be in a murderous mood.

Though, from what I can tell, it's been a good few hours since the attack—the blood at the edges is too congealed for anything else. Actually, considering that the gash in the raptorcat's side is still leaking blood, it's amazing that the creature has survived for so long after the attack. *It must have an amazing Constitution stat. Do animals have Constitution stats?* It's a good question, but not one I should probably be asking now. Still, the fact that the attack must have happened hours ago, maybe even as much as a day ago, means that I shouldn't need to worry about the attacker being nearby.

Apart from my emotions, I'm also left with a choice. I could just leave the raptorcat here. It will die soon, maybe not in less than an hour or so, but still, I could let nature take its course. Or I could put it out of its misery now and not leave it to suffer for the next hour or hours. That's probably the best option of the two, as I would then get Energy as well. However . . . I've got another option. I could try Dominate. I wouldn't dare use it on an alert raptorcat. Not only does it apparently leave me vulnerable for a few seconds afterwards if it's unsuccessful, which would be a death sentence, but the raptorcat's buddies would probably attack me even during the Battle of Wills. Now, though . . .

I look around to verify that we're alone. Well, apart from small birds in the trees, that is. I don't think I'll have a better chance of getting a raptorcat onside than this. I was going to set a trap and try to catch one later down the line, but that was always going to be fraught with danger. This way there's very little risk to me, as even if the attempt is unsuccessful, it's not like the raptorcat will be able to do anything to retaliate. Not in its current condition.

That's another question, actually. Will Lay-on-Hands work on something other than me? And if it does work, will I be able to heal a wound as serious as the one in front of me? I don't know, but I'm not keen on trying *before* succeeding with

Dominate—or Tame, I suppose. Anyway, the raptorcat would probably show its thanks for healing by going for my throat. Which is a good reason *not* to try Tame, since I'd probably need to heal it first before trying Tame so that I could build the "connection" that the Skill apparently needs. Too much risk. Dominate it is, and *before* offering healing.

Having convinced myself, I settle on the other side of the tree from the injured creature, leaning around just enough to see it—no need to take chances, after all. I try to trigger Dominate, but nothing happens. Frowning, I wonder why. I know the Skill works—I've used it with Spike. *Is the raptorcat too close to death?* Something tells me that that's not the answer, so I rack my brains to try to work out what else could be the problem. Thinking through what happened with Spike, I remember that I had an issue activating Dominate with him too. *It only worked when I met his . . .* I groan. *When I met his* eyes. *So much for the safe strategy.* I sigh to myself. I push myself to my feet, walk around so I'm right next to the raptorcat's head, and then crouch down and tentatively reach out to place my hand on its head. When it doesn't snap its eyes open and try to maul my hand—not moving at all, in fact—I breathe out a silent breath of relief. Its head is lying against the ground, and I shift my hand towards the eye that's facing upwards. No reaction. Still tense and ready to snatch my hand away and stumble backwards at any moment, I use two fingers to force the raptorcat's eyelid open.

This time it reacts, shifting slightly and making a hoarse, plaintive sound. I snatch my hand back and don't even breathe while I wait to see if it's going to try to attack me. It's too weak to do that, and it just moves a little before settling back into its position. *Well, if that's all it has to threaten me with, I should be fine.*

Emboldened, I reach forward again and open its eyelid. Ignoring its slight movements this time, I stare into its single eye and firmly say, "Dominate." This time it works, and I'm once more catapulted into that strange zone where I haven't really gone anywhere, but the color bleeds out of the world and nothing other than the raptorcat lying opposite me matters. It's more aware than it was in the physical realm—I've come to guess that this is a mental or spiritual realm—but it's still clearly injured and weak. Like before with Spike, we're both fixed in place with a great sense of pressure between us, our eyes fixed on each other's. Knowing better what to expect from this since I've been through it once before, I'm quicker to start directing the pressure at the raptorcat.

Immediately, it's different from before: I can start moving towards the raptorcat with the "pressure hose" in my hands directed at it, but there's also some sense of opposing pressure, like my opponent *also* has a pressure hose, albeit weaker. I'm not only fighting against the almost solid air between us; I'm also fighting against the directed pressure trying to push me away from the raptorcat lying opposite. I gaze into its golden, slit-pupil eyes and see a defiance and anger that is thoroughly different from Spike. He resisted me, but it felt more like stubborn determination not to give in rather than anything *personal.* This feels personal. Like the raptorcat refuses to bow to a prey animal, refuses to give into my will because it is *better than that*. There's almost a silent dialogue between us, some sort of metaphysical connection that allows us to communicate in ideas. It's not words, though I rationalize the ideas as such—I'm not comfortable thinking in images and emotions untethered and undefined by words. *I am an apex predator*, it seems to say. *I do not bow to prey.* Contemptuous. *Clearly you're not at the apex or you wouldn't be dying now*, I think back at it, reminding it of the state its physical—and metaphysical—body is in. *There are always those stronger. We met our match and have become prey in our turn.*

Then why do you resist bowing to me? I will one day be strong enough to kill you all if I choose. I genuinely believe that to be the case. Humanity rose from wielding the sticks and stones of my current weaponry to using bombs, which could slaughter millions in a single swoop, and that all without magic. While I don't anticipate building any nuclear weapons anytime soon, I can see how I have developed already with my stat increases. Physical activity has become easier, thinking has become clearer, and that's only with a few points in each stat. What will I become in five levels' time? Ten? Thirty? I fully anticipate that one day I will reach the point where a raptorcat, regardless of how terrifying an opponent it is now, will become nothing more than a nuisance. My approach doesn't seem to have won me any points with my opponent, though, as the raptorcat's glare intensifies and the pressure pushing against me grows just a little.

The future is undefined. Now, you are weak. Clearly my future potential progress is not convincing enough. Or maybe it doesn't believe me. And honestly, it's right. I have to be alive in those thirty levels' time in order to benefit from the advancements. But I can't think like that. Convincing myself is half the battle; the other half is convincing the raptorcat.

Given how much trouble this single injured creature is giving me, I'm glad that I didn't go through with trying to trap and Dominate a healthy one—I'm pretty sure I'd have failed and then been dead for such an audacious attempt.

The raptorcat goes silent, and I sense it trying to withdraw mentally even while increasing the pressure. Unfortunately for it, time is not on its side. With every moment that passes, I creep ever-closer, as does death. I start wondering if this intense mental battle will actually hasten its demise, and the thought makes me press even more against the pressure resisting me. Unfortunately, time isn't on *my* side either. This kind of battle is exhausting, and I can already feel a decentralized ache start throbbing in my body. Although time has a strange elastic quality in this world, I'm sure it's taken longer already than the battle I had with Spike. I need to try to convince it to let me closer, or at least distract it enough to lessen the pressure. I think over our little "conversation" and suddenly have an idea.

CHAPTER FIFTY

Acceptance

I focus back on the raptorcat, my distraction having lessened the pressure I was applying, and take a different approach. Honestly, this isn't all that different from all the other negotiation and mediation I've done—when one angle doesn't work, try a different one. *Do you not wish to live to grow stronger? Death is the end of all growth.* I feel the raptorcat pay reluctant attention to the wave of images and emotions I send it.

Death is natural. Chains are not. But it is life nonetheless, even if it means being bound to another. Is it not better than a noble but futile death?

I feel it wavering a little, and the brief letup of pressure lets me take a couple of small steps forward before it returns. Still, I notice that the strength is not quite as much as it was before.

Give in to me and I will heal you and we will grow stronger together. I am old.

The raptorcat sends pictures of gray fur and the sensation of joints becoming painful with age along with a sense of almost-amusement. *My time is near, anyway.*

It should be the end of the conversation—if the creature is already old, why would it choose to live a little longer as my Bound? But yet . . . I haven't been cut out completely. In fact, it feels like the raptorcat's will is wavering, like the hosepipe of pressure it's directing at me is starting to sputter. The reason becomes evident with its next transmission.

I am old . . . but they are not. I see a picture of a small group of cubs. Or kittens. Or puppies. Or chicks, or whatever you'd call these creatures that are such a strange amalgamation of several Earth animals. *I will bow to you,* she—their mother?—continues, transmitting such a sense of finality that I know it is this or nothing, *if you will care for these young ones. And if you promise never to force them to serve you.*

That pours cold water on my sudden avaricious thoughts of having my own little pack of raptorcats, all bound to me through Dominate. *Then again, she did say force . . . And if they choose to bond with me of their own free will?* I ask. The raptorcat doesn't respond immediately, and I sense that she's filled with turmoil. In this strange world, our emotions and thoughts are as obvious as facial expressions would normally be between humans in a particularly expressive culture. She's torn between knowing that the cubs will die without anyone to care for them and thinking that it would be better if they were dead than were bound to an uncaring master. *If, by the point they are capable of being independent, they consider you their pack and choose to stay with you, that is acceptable,* she decides finally. I receive the impression of a half-grown raptorcat, paws still too big for its body, some fluff still on its wings, full of a boundless determination and the keen competence of a born killer. An adolescent, I guess. By her definition, I'm pretty sure that Tame would work, even if Dominate is out of the realm of possibility.

Very well. I send a wave of acceptance regarding her terms, and the resistance holding me back crumbles. In three quick steps, I'm standing in front of her and we're staring at each other with mere inches between us. She breaks the eye contact and bows her head.

Our surroundings bleed back into full color, and the sounds and smells of the forest return with the breeze that caresses my skin. The raptorcat, my new Bound, is not doing well at all. Her breathing is significantly more labored than it was when I triggered Dominate, and it wasn't great then. I quickly shift to lay my hand over the wound and cast my healing spell. I cast the channeled version, not giving much guidance to the magic apart from focusing it on the terrible injury in front of me. I pour most of my mana into the wound and see the effects.

Flesh rebuilds itself before my eyes: the walls of torn organs stitch together, muscles reform into a whole, and skin grows to hide everything inside from view. The skin is furless and may actually remain so from now on—it seems like my Lay-on-Hands isn't capable of restoring lost hair, or maybe that would just require more energy than I have to spend. Still, I'm very grateful that it works on her at all. When my mana bar has reduced significantly, I stop pouring healing into the wound. I haven't completely bottomed out my mana store; if something suddenly attacks, I want to be able to cast at least one healing spell on myself. I think I've poured enough in to make a significant difference, though. I'll need to continue later since so much mana leaving me all within a few seconds is surprisingly exhausting.

Panting and giving my mana the chance to regenerate a bit, I pull out my sneleon shell and pour some water into the little soup that remains to cool it down. Fishing out the bits of pondweed, I dribble the liquid into the mouth of the raptorcat and encourage her to drink. I figure that if she does end up eating the bits of meat left in there, it's not an issue—she's a carnivore, after all. In fact, a bit of food might even do her some good.

I choke down the slimy bits of pondweed as she swallows the liquid. Angling the sneleon shell, I position it so that she can lap weakly at the thin soup. When my mana has regenerated enough, I cast another Lay-on-Hands over her body generally. Her lapping strengthens a little, though I know she'll be weak from blood loss for quite a while; my spell will help with that but not as quickly as it heals the wound.

We rest like that for a while, the raptorcat drinking the soup bit by bit and me recovering my mana and keeping watch. Every so often I cast another Lay-on-Hands until I sense that there's nothing more it can heal. It's strange using the healing spell on a body other than my own. I realize now that casting it on myself is a bit like rubbing two of my fingers together instead of touching something with one finger—I get double feedback from the spell. I'd always thought that the sense of healing I got was from the feeling in my body, but at least half of it is actually the spell itself, as I still get most of the same sensations from healing the raptorcat. On the other hand, when I use it on myself, I can feel the injuries pulling themselves together or the misaligned parts rearranging themselves; I didn't get that from the raptorcat, thankfully. Either way, I'm glad to know that my healing spell works just as well for others as it does for myself.

I also take the time to look properly at her. The first time I saw a raptorcat, I was far too concerned with survival to really get a good look at it. And then when I came across this one before Dominating her, I was more looking to see what had happened and thinking about what to do next. She's darkly colored, shades of black with tints of green and brown covering her body. The patterning is almost like a night version of a camo outfit, or something like that. At least, it's like that where it's not stained with blood. I can understand why I didn't see the trap when I walked into it before. Her fur isn't really fur, I realize. It's more like soft, flexible feathers with very short vanes. Perhaps an evolutionary prototype of fur.

The feathers on her wings are actual proper feathers, but I don't see any long pinions, making it even more clear that these limbs aren't meant for flying. Are they an extraneous feature that used to be helpful but are useless now? Or do raptorcats use them for something other than flying? Her eyes are the same ones that stuck in my memory after my last encounter: predatory golden orbs with slit pupils. Even now that we've come to an accord, I can see them warily watching me, violence only a hair's breadth away. Fortunately, I have an instinctual confidence in the Bond and its ability to prevent at least direct harm from one of my Bound. Otherwise, I think I'd have already been too unnerved to sit here so close to the predator.

As for her feet, they're clawed, scaled affairs with four toes facing forwards and one short toe facing backwards. The claws are quite sharp on her front feet, but far less so on her back. Now I understand the cause of a number of gashes I've seen on the trunks of trees while walking through the forest. A shiver goes down my spine as I realize that I've been exploring raptorcat territory at least half the time I've been staying with Kalanthia . . . Really, it's only dumb luck that prevented me from reencountering the pack. Her sharp front claws are matched by a mouthful of sharp teeth, and her muzzle length is somewhere between a lion's and a wolf's. With two large canines on top and bottom, I can see that her specialty is grabbing and holding on. Frankly, I don't understand how I managed to survive the first time I met the pack—by all rights, they should have taken me down easily. But I did survive, and, now that I've got one of them as my Bound, it's my enemies that will have to deal with her teeth and claws.

Checking on my Energy store, I realize that Dominating this raptorcat has actually been pretty lucrative. I'm already up thirty-six percent, having been in single digits when I checked last night. Okay, some of that's from my hourly absorption, but the majority is from this single action. Pretty awesome, right?

Eventually, the raptorcat, who I'm thinking of naming Bastet after the ancient Egyptian cat goddess, is ready to move. Sekhmet was another name option, but I decided that naming an already dangerous creature after one whose mythology paints them as a serial killer is probably not the best idea. Anyway, it's taken awhile for her to regain her strength, but with the help of my healing Skill it hasn't taken anywhere near as long as it would take a cat or lion to recover from surgery on Earth. I've collected what firewood I could in the local area but didn't want to venture too far in case she got attacked while I wasn't there. "So, show me the cubs?" I ask eagerly when she manages to struggle to her feet. She sends me a look that I have little trouble in interpreting as annoyance and admonishment to be patient. It's not been more than a few hours since she became one of my Bound and I can already tell she's very different from Spike.

We set off moving after not that much time, but it feels like longer than it really is because of my desire to get moving.

"How about Bastet as a name?" I ask as we start walking, still a bit slowly to account for the raptorcat's recent physical trauma.

She flashes me a glance that I think is questioning. I'm pretty sure that Animal Empathy is the only reason I come to that conclusion. "It's the name of a goddess on my original world—a cat one. Not that you'd know what a cat is," I realize belatedly. Instead, giving up on words, I try to feed her the memories I have of learning about Bastet: visiting the British History Museum and seeing statues; learning about the beliefs of the ancient Egyptians at school; reading mythology about the Egyptian gods and goddesses . . . The raptorcat takes a few minutes to mull it over, and we walk in silence for that time. Then, when I'm starting to think that she doesn't like the name but can't or won't communicate that to me, she sends a wave of approval through our Bond.

"Bastet it is," I conclude numbly, amazed that my newest Bound is capable of communicating in a way that Spike has never done, something that took me a while to understand how to do myself. It seems she's a natural!

CHAPTER FIFTY-ONE

Strange Babies

The cubs are so cute that it takes all I have not to just rush over, grab, and snuggle them into my neck while making ridiculous noises that would be better found in an anime than real life. They're little bundles of fluff with supple feet and stubs of wings covered with the softest of down. They have teeth, but they look more like white milk teeth than permanent ones. Or maybe this species goes through multiple sets of teeth—what do I know? Either way, they're much smaller than Bastet's fangs and are missing the large canines altogether. In fact, the cubs are much smaller, period. They would each fit in my two hands cupped together and only spill out a little.

When I first entered the cave, they cowered away from me. It's not really a surprise—the poor things have been alone for who knows how long based on the half-eaten corpses that are all that remain of the rest of their pack. The raptorcats live, or perhaps I should say "lived," in a slight hollow in the side of a hill protruding from the mountainside, not dissimilar to Kalanthia's den. It's a natural outcropping of rock, and most of the small area is bare of all but a light covering of green. I'm no geological expert, but just from what I can see, I'd guess that there are several layers of rock and one of the softer layers has been eroded to the point where it has become a sort of cave. The cubs were hidden within that cave before we arrived to find them.

Normally, of course, I would have had to fight my way through a sentry, probably hidden in a tree, to get to them, then the main bulk of the pack, probably lounging along the rocks, and then the mother raptorcat herself. Not so this time. Six raptorcats have been torn to pieces: one near where that sentry would have probably been, four in a group on the rocks of the outcropping, and one just in front of the cave entrance itself. I'm not surprised the cubs were afraid of me—they've probably been smelling their mother and other family members' blood for hours or even days. Fortunately, they know Bastet, and after she reassures them by going over and licking and rubbing her head on them, they relax a little. It still takes them a bit of time to be willing to approach me, but she encourages them to do so.

Her visible impatience is well deserved; we need to get out of here before something comes along to eat more of the bodies. Or worse: whatever killed the adults might come back to finish the job of exterminating the whole pack, down to the littlest cub.

It takes me a few moments to work out how to move the cubs; they're too young to just walk with us, but I can't exactly put them in my Inventory . . . I suddenly have a brainwave. It takes a bit of time, mostly spent convincing the cubs to allow me to pick them up, but I eventually get them slung across my chest like strange babies. I bite my lip to stop my adoring noise from escaping my lips—they are just too cute tucked away as they are in a shirt I've tied around my body, with only their fluffy heads poking out of the cloth.

Glancing around the cave before leaving, I check to see if there's anything I'm missing. *No . . . wait.* I spot something glinting ever so dimly in the back of the cave. Despite Bastet's growing agitation, I walk over and crouch to peer into the shadowy depths, carefully moving in a way that doesn't shove my knees in the cubs' faces. It looks . . . metallic? Could there be metal there?

About to creep closer, already starting to shift my position, my attention is pulled by a growl from the adult raptorcat.

Looking back towards the entrance, I see her crouching, ears back against her head, her whole position very hostile. Not towards me, thankfully, but my stomach swoops as I consider what might have caused her to get into such a defensive pose.

Forgetting about the potential metal for now, I creep towards the entrance trying to keep out of sight of whatever is out there. There's something moving around for sure; even if Bastet's behavior hadn't told me that, I can hear the creature shifting and the sound of bones crunching and meat being torn. It's a bit sickening, actually. Though, it does seem a bit ridiculous that I'm fazed by such sounds when I have literally crushed ribcages and skulls, not to mention the load of creatures I've butchered since being here. I still have to fight back nausea as my imagination runs away with me. Perhaps it's because, in this case, *my* bones might be the next to be crunched.

I try to ignore the stomach-turning nature of the sounds to use them to gain some information about the creatures making them without potentially exposing myself to view. I close my eyes so I'm more able to concentrate on what my ears are telling me.

There are too many sounds for it to be only one creature unless that one creature is ridiculously active. All at the same time, there's the sound of claws scraping along rock, bones being broken, and meat being ripped. Unless it's a creature with many legs and at least three heads, it's a small group of animals rather than a solitary one. That's not so good. The fact that I *am* hearing bones break is something else that makes my stomach feel queasy. If the creatures are capable of crunching through bones, my wooden mace isn't going to be much of a match for them.

I suddenly wish with all my heart that I had already made my bow so I would have more of a ranged option than just the chunks of flint I still have in my Inventory. Or better yet, a grenade that I could just throw out there and be done with it. Bastet's looking at me expectantly. She sends me a picture of some—surprise, surprise—reptilian creature with a massive jaw, thick neck, and bulky body. The image makes me feel even more weak-kneed—it looks to be as easy a target as a pit bull and about half as friendly. *Could we outrun them?* I wonder with a sense of hysteria creeping in. *Because I sure as hell don't consider my chances to be very good against beasts like* that.

I send the thought towards Bastet, picturing us getting the hell out of dodge. She seems to mull it over a little, her head cocked to one side even as one ear is still tilted towards the cave entrance, clearly making sure we're still undetected. After several moments, which feels like at least ten minutes but probably takes less than thirty seconds, she responds. It's not hopeful. The sense I get from her is that we could outrun the creatures for sure, but they would follow us. From the images and emotions she sends me, they're extremely good trackers. They're mostly scavengers and probably are only here because they smelled the blood from far off and realized there was an easy meal waiting for them, but that doesn't mean they wouldn't chase easy prey.

Then we'll need to make sure they know we're not easy prey, I decide, sending Bastet a sense of determination. She eyes me dubiously but seems as resigned as she was when she submitted to me during the Battle of Wills—a feeling that she's not totally on board, but she can't think of anything better to do instead so is willing to go along with me for now. Frankly, a typical cat. I check the knots holding the cubs to me once more—one or more of them dropping out during the headlong dash that is to come would *not* be good—and verify for the final time that I haven't missed anything.

About to leave, I suddenly have a thought; I open my Map and drop a marker on this spot for later investigation. Then, looking at Bastet, I silently mouth a countdown from three. That she doubtlessly can't lip-read or count is immaterial—doing it for myself is generating the right sort of anticipation for me to send to her mentally. At least, I hope that's how it works.

When I reach zero, we both explode into action simultaneously. Dashing out of the cave, we clamber over the rocks in the direction of the closest trees. The creatures currently chowing down on Bastet and the cubs' dead packmates take a few moments to realize we're there, then let out coughing sounds of what I can only guess is surprise at our sudden appearance—and almost as sudden disappearance. Pelting as fast as I can for the trees, I don't hear any pursuit, but they may just be too surprised to realize that they should follow. I didn't get the sense from Bastet's images that these creatures are particularly intelligent.

As we run, I'm surprised to realize that I'm not all that much slower than the adult raptorcat. Then again, I did manage to survive a pack of them chasing me once, and she *did* say she's getting old. What I do notice after a few minutes is that she probably has significantly more stamina than me. After perhaps ten minutes of a headlong sprint, my stamina bar is bottoming out and I can feel the usual symptoms of exhaustion creeping in.

Bastet is still going strong, and when I slow down, my breath coming in ragged pants, I notice that she's not even breathing heavily. *Maybe that's how raptorcats hunt if their ambush doesn't work?* Not all that fast but with a significant pool of stamina, they're a bit like wolf packs on Earth, which weren't the fastest animals around but had the stamina to pursue prey for hours on end. My own stamina doesn't seem to stack up well in comparison.

Then again, I was able to keep running at almost my top speed for about ten minutes. That would have been completely unheard of for me back on Earth, so I've definitely improved my physical condition. "Do you think we lost them?" I ask Bastet when I've gathered enough breath to speak. No, she doesn't understand the words, but as with Spike, I unconsciously project my meaning when I speak.

I get a wave of intention that I translate as, *Not likely.* I frown.

"Can you hear them coming or something?" I receive a negative feeling from her. "Then why do you think they're following us? They've got lots of food where they are." The words have barely left my mouth when I wince at how callous they sound. In response, I receive a slight pang of sorrow, but it's far less intense than I would expect. I interpret the images and emotions she then sends to mean that she's doubtful we've escaped the creatures because of one specific reason: once they've locked onto prey, they don't stop pursuing until they're either dead or they've lost the scent—and as for the latter, they have extremely sensitive senses. I get the idea that even walking through a river would be of little use, as they'd be able to pick up our scent on anything we brushed past or even from the other side if we didn't walk for long enough in the water. I lean against a tree as I consider the situation. I can't lead them back to Kalanthia's cave. She'd kill me if she thought I'd put Lathani in danger. Maybe it's time to try to get a definite answer to a question I've had for a while.

CHAPTER FIFTY-TWO

Trap

I wipe sweat off my brow as my breath still comes in tired pants. Feeling low in energy, I pull out some cooked meat and munch on it. I put a little of the raw stuff in front of the cubs and offer some more to Bastet. The adult raptorcat accepts it, just as tired from her own efforts.

Casting a last glance around the area, I make sure that everything is as planned. It's a bit of a rough job, but we're short on time as it is. Bastet sends me a feeling of warning; the reptilian bulldogs are within her detection range. As planned, I pick up the cubs from where they've been cuddling together in the bole of a tree and climb a little way up the slope to place them in a hollow made by three branches up at about my head height. Wrapping my shirt around the outside of the branches, I create a little nest that they shouldn't fall out of without putting some effort into it. Hopefully, Bastet's warning growl is enough to make sure that they don't try.

At least these are wild animal babies, which are generally more sensitive to danger than human babies—goodness knows a human baby would probably just start caterwauling at the absolute worst possible moment, as well as probably fall out of the tree just in front of the predator. And no, I haven't had much experience with kids, but I've heard enough from colleagues talking about their toddlers' predilections for running into traffic that I reckon my prediction is justified.

Enough woolgathering. Time to take my position. They're coming.

I hear the creatures crashing through the forest—subtle they are not. I see the thick undergrowth shaking long before I see the creatures themselves. As I run out of the cave, I don't have time to count them, but as they emerge from the undergrowth and hurry into the gully, I see that my estimate of seven was a bit too many, fortunately.

A spearhead of three lizogs crashes through the undergrowth and I see rustling behind them that indicates at least one more, maybe two. I doubt as many as three are hiding, though, due to their bulk. Their heads reach just above my knee—definitely big enough to mess me up, especially with those bone-crushing jaws. *I'd best make sure they don't touch me, then.* Hopefully, all the effort Bastet and I have put in will ensure that they don't.

Bastet is hiding, following my plan, and so the lizogs' beady black eyes fixate on me, standing right there out in the open. With a snarling rumble, the leader bares its teeth at me and leads the charge. The other two just behind it follow immediately, and two more emerge from the bush behind them.

I won't deny it: standing there while five killing machines run full pelt towards me makes me wet myself just a little. It's terrifying seeing those teeth coming towards me while knowing they were biting through raptorcat bone not that long ago. Nonetheless, I stay still and do my best to project an air of confidence. *I have a plan*, I try to remind myself. It helps. Barely. Enough to stop me from running and ruining everything.

When they're within arm's length, close enough that I can see the saliva dropping from the jaws of the beasts, the lizogs get a nasty surprise. The leader is far too close to avoid the stakes I've prepared and hidden with mud and plants from the bottom of this narrow ravine, and it runs straight into two of them. I couldn't cut down anything particularly big, since the best I could think of doing was using my axe blade as a hand axe, so I've gone for quantity over quality.

For one petrifying moment, I worry that the layers of stakes are going to break under the force of that heavy charge, or that they're just going to be pushed out of the ground and stick out of the lead lizog's flesh while the others come to tear me apart. Fortunately, neither scenario comes to pass. None of the lizogs are dead, nowhere near it, but their charge has been stopped and the stake wall is still intact. Fortunately, I hadn't been counting on my first step killing any of them, though it would have been nice. Time to spring my trap.

I haul on the bark-fiber cord I've sacrificed for this task and behind them another wall of stakes, woven together with vines, is pulled upwards to point at the lizogs at an angle. I've no real hope that this wall will stop them anywhere near as well as the one I planted firmly in the ground in front of me, but I don't need it to. This wall isn't meant to kill or injure but to provide a deterrent.

Hopefully, the stakes properly planted on three sides of the beasts and the memory of being injured will be enough to stop them breaking away as they realize the next and final step of my plan.

Really, Bastet is far too clever for a supposedly dumb animal, but she activates the killing bit of my trap perfectly. A rumbling crash from above marks the finale, and the lizogs look up to see death descending on them. They have enough time to try to dodge, but the stake walls prove their worth as the lizogs are unable to force their way past. With a final rumbling snarl, they're buried in the rocks I carefully balanced on the slopes on either side above them. Bastet has triggered a landslide by moving the few precariously laid branches of dead wood that had been—barely— holding the rocks back. Frankly, the trap is more powerful than I had anticipated, and I have to take a few hurried steps back along the gully to make sure I don't get hit myself.

Bastet leaps to the ground behind the pack to make sure she's out of the way of the rocks that are still avalanching, but the flow is petering off as the final part of my trap finishes delivering its payload. As a side benefit, if any of the lizogs have survived the rain of death, she'll be able to help me deal with them.

The stones, which range from the size of my fist to the size of my head, shift and roll as they settle in their new positions. Bastet and I keep a close watch on the pile and as soon as one starts moving in a way that seems counter to the pull of gravity, we creep closer.

A lizog's head forces away a stone, looking somewhat worse for wear. Both eyes are missing completely, pulverized by a stone, and the front of its skull is caved in. I'm reluctantly impressed by its fortitude—I couldn't have taken an injury like that and kept going. *Maybe its Constitution is significantly better than mine . . .* I'm impressed enough that I decide I'd like to try Dominating it. With its high constitution and powerful jaws, it would be a good addition to the team. Trapped and injured as it is, the Battle of Wills should be fairly simple too.

"Dominate," I say firmly, looking into the pulverized flesh where its eyes used to be. It's a sickening sight—*is that its brain peeking out?* When nothing happens, I repeat the Skill activation command while trying to focus on reentering that strange space. Nada.

Perhaps that saying "Eyes are the windows to the soul" is true and that's why I have to meet their eyes to initiate a Battle of Wills? I consider trying to heal it enough to make eye contact, but frankly, I don't want to get any closer to those jaws than necessary.

In the end I just shrug and lift my mace. The lizog doesn't long survive my Strength-driven strikes, and within less than a minute, we're back to watching for more signs of movement.

After things have been quiet for a few minutes, we spend the time necessary to dig out the rest of the lizogs. Not only do I want to make sure that there aren't any living members that might come chasing us down later, but I also want the hearts and meat. Fortunately, it seems like the avalanche has done in the rest of the pack.

On the upside, I've been able to determine that I *do* get Energy from killing creatures in a trap; otherwise, the Energy I gained would be too much to have come from the single creature I killed. Though, I suppose I still don't have a definitive answer about whether or not creating a trap and coming back to it later to find a creature would give me Energy. Once I've made my axe and bow and so on, maybe I should dedicate a couple of days to digging a pit trap or something to test it. We also managed to kill five lizogs without losing one or more limbs, which seems to me like something to celebrate when I think about the massive jaws and sharp teeth on these things. I wish I could mark the occasion with something more enjoyable than digging out the bodies and eating their hearts, but that's the world I live in now. Working hard to survive one encounter just means working even harder to survive the next.

Thankfully, once we've rescued the cubs from the tree and hidden them once more in a safe spot on the ground, Bastet is willing to help me clear off the stones, just as she was willing to dig holes for the stakes and chew them into points, allowing me to concentrate on collecting stone and wood and creating my precariously balanced rocks on the slope above. Believe me, my heart rose into my throat a few times when the wind blew or stones trickled down and it seemed like my trap would be triggered ahead of time, but it all came right in the end.

By the time I've got the hearts from the bodies, I'm hot, tired, and desperately in need of a bath. I quickly make a small fire and cook the hearts by cutting them into slices and sticking them on a spit above the fire.

"Hey, eat as much of these as you want, Bastet," I tell her, indicating the bodies. "You've earned it!" She sends me a wave of pleasure tinged with tiredness, goes over to the closest lizorg corpse, and digs straight into the belly. Well, fair enough—I figure those organs are probably almost as dense in Energy as the hearts, but I wouldn't dare eat them myself for fear of parasites or food poisoning or something. No need for them to go to waste, though.

When Bastet's finished, she encourages the cubs to come forward and start chewing some of the more tender pieces too. They take to it with gusto—this clearly isn't the first time they've been able to have a go at a carcass. Just as well, I suppose, since I don't know where I'd get milk for them otherwise. Assuming they drink milk at all—who knows in this strange world?

Finally, everyone is sated, and I've been able to cook my hearts well enough to risk eating them. There's still a good three and a half lizog carcasses hanging around, so I stick them in my Inventory. With four meat eaters to be responsible for now, I'm going to need to up my hunting game. *Maybe Bastet can help me with that?* I still have several days of labor before I'll likely be able to finalize my weaponry situation, after all. Perhaps then I'll actually be in a position to hunt for Kalanthia too—providing her with enough meat would no doubt significantly increase the speed of my Energy collection.

After tucking the cubs back into their chest sling, I start walking, Bastet prowls next to me, her ears swiveling every which way. The cubs, their bellies full, don't take long to drop off to sleep, and I can't stop the smile tugging at the corners of my mouth as I look at their sleepy adorableness.

As I walk through the forest, my own eyes flicking one way and then the next, ready for another attack, my mind chews on something I hadn't even realized I was considering until it spits forth a theory that makes me temporarily freeze. *What killed the raptorcats, considering how powerful they are? What . . . or who?*

An icy certainty creeps into my belly. There can't be that many creatures powerful enough to take on a full pack of raptorcats on their home turf and walk away without significant injury. And I know it was without significant injury because Bastet ran away when she was injured instead of going for the jugular on an incapacitated foe. Clearly the firepower was simply too overwhelming.

So, that raises the question again: what, or who, would be powerful enough to do that? Who was out yesterday hunting to fill up for another three-day fast? And if Kalanthia was the culprit, how will she react when I turn up on her doorstep with a surviving adult and three cubs? Heck, how would Bastet react to meeting her pack's killer?

CHAPTER FIFTY-THREE

Handily Sized Snacks

First, I need to confirm—or disprove—my suspicions. As casually as I can, I turn to Bastet and ask her a question, doing my best to control the feelings and images I inadvertently send down the link. "What happened to your pack, Bastet? You seemed too powerful to be taken down easily." Instead of doing a "don't think of pink elephants" sort of scenario, I try to instead actively think of something else. I send the memory of being chased through the forest by their pack and being driven to hiding in an underground burrow to escape as an illustration of how powerful they had seemed to me, and I compare that with what I have so recently seen: walking out of the tree line to the sight of their butchered, half-eaten bodies strewn over the outcropping.

A wave of sadness and longing emanates from the raptorcat padding next to me. She sends me an impression of overpowering ferocity, Strength that they couldn't hope to match, and the environment turning against them. It suddenly makes me wonder if I'd have seen something different if I'd spotted their den before the whole slaughter. At the end is a brief image of the creature that did all this, and the picture makes the blood turn to ice in my veins.

Snarling, blood spattered, and larger than life, the picture is different from any other time I've seen her, but it is Kalanthia for sure. A Kalanthia that, frankly, I'd never like to see again. At least, not aimed at me. That . . . complicates things.

We walk in silence for a while, the cubs occasionally letting out the odd squeaky snore. My brain is racing as I try to work out what I can do. If there's anything I *can* do, that is, to avoid the car crash I can see coming. Is it possible to warn either party ahead of the inevitable encounter? Should I? After some consideration, I realize that the most important one to warn is the raptorcat padding beside me. She's the one who's lost her entire family, or pack, or whatever she'd call it. Either way, the clear sadness and loss that she feels now indicate she had strong bonds with the other raptorcats, and now they're gone. They're gone, and she's soon going to come face to face with their killer. On Kalanthia's side, I doubt there's much emotion. Unless she has a particular dislike of raptorcats, or they did something to her that she was getting revenge for, I reckon that she probably just treated the pack as they had treated me a few days ago: as prey. *Though, why would she leave the bodies half-eaten in that case?*

Actually, can I even assume that she ate them at all considering it had clearly been hours since she killed them? Something else could have come through the area and consumed the corpses. Then there's the fact that she didn't pursue Bastet after having given her a significant wound; if she was hunting for food, wouldn't she have gone after the escapee after dealing with the rest of the pack?

Maybe she had different motives. Lathani is certainly getting bigger and stronger—it probably won't be long until she starts trying to explore the world beyond her den. Having a pack of killers roaming around is probably a threat to that. All of which raises a dilemma for me: if Kalanthia hunted down the raptorcats to get rid of a potential threat against her cub, how is she going to take me bringing four of them into her personal space? Kalanthia took the presence of Spike with equanimity, but that's a different situation: he would be considered prey and not a threat to Lathani. The raptorcat cubs are too small to pose any threat to the rambunctious nunda cub, but an adult raptorcat is a different matter. On the other hand, Bastet is Bound to me . . .

I allow myself a moment to consider the differences between my Bond with Spike and my Bond with Bastet; I just want to verify for myself that I could assure Kalanthia that Bastet would be no threat to her cub. After all, if I promised that and it turned out not to be true, I'd be lucky to see the next dawn. Feeling the two Bonds, which seem to be stored in some alternate space connecting to both my mind and something deep in my chest, I get a different sense from each. It must be something to do with my increased Wisdom since I've only been able to detect either Bond since earning two Wisdom points today. Before then, I'd been aware that there was *something* between Spike and me—I had even used it to send images to him—but it was different. Before, it was like I was holding a thin cord with thick gloves: difficult to feel except when it moves and impossible to manipulate delicately. Now, it's like the gloves have been replaced with thinner versions. I'm more able to feel the Bond even when it's not active, and I sense I can manipulate it a little more easily.

Thinking back to when I felt the niggling sensation of a new notification, I'm pretty sure that one of the points came when I stretched out my senses to try to work out what creatures were outside the cave while the five of us were hiding inside. I suppose that kind of makes sense; Wisdom is, apparently, all about connecting with the world around me, so I guess that situation qualifies.

I'm not sure about the other point. It could have been when I decided to Dominate Bastet, or possibly *while* I was Dominating Bastet. I would have thought the decision to try to convince her to be Bound to me rather than just trying to force the issue would count as showing Wisdom, but what do I know?

Either way, when I accepted the two points after the lizog fight—twenty-eight percent of my Energy store suddenly disappearing as a result—I suddenly felt a new sensation settle in me. I now have a better idea of why Kalanthia called them "chains." That's exactly what they feel like, though on my part it feels like I'm holding the ends of them rather than being bound myself. Each feels a bit different too. Spike's is calm, placid—solid, in a way, but there's also a sense of indifference. It's completely counter to Bastet's, which feels . . . like a feral cat settling into your home. I mean, I've never *had* a feral cat, but from what I've seen of cat videos and read in online comments, there's a settling in period for any new cat. Probably any new pet, really. And while Bastet isn't exactly a pet, there's definitely that sense of uncertainty in the Bond. It feels like she's tiptoeing a bit around me: a bit touchy, a bit defensive, and a bit on edge because she's not yet sure of how I will react to things. Indifferent she is not. Unlike Spike's Bond, Bastet's feels a lot more reciprocal. Though, that's been pretty obvious from the start: Bastet took to responding to me through the Bond with an ease that Spike has never shown. Whether that's because Spike has less Intelligence—or Wisdom, or whatever the stat is that affects this kind of thing—or perhaps because Bastet actually had some sort of similar connection to her packmates and was therefore already used to communicating like this, I don't know. Fortunately, I get the sense that despite her greater capacity to communicate, my control over her is just as strong as it is over Spike.

Though I do have an inkling that she is probably capable of resisting an order to an extent, I feel confident that if I order her to leave Lathani alone, she will have no choice but to follow. Ultimately, that's what I need to know ahead of talking to Kalanthia. Talking to Bastet about it is another matter.

I spend a long time considering how to broach the subject with her, weighing and dismissing one approach after another. Unfortunately, my hesitation takes *too* long, something I only realize when Bastet tenses and turns to glare at me, her ears pressing back against her head, as she sends feelings of anger and betrayal down the Bond.

For a moment, I'm confused, but when images of Kalanthia accompany the feelings—images of her tearing the raptorcats apart, only this time actually succeeding in killing and eating Bastet herself, then moving on to gulp down the cubs—I realize the problem: she's caught Kalanthia's scent and drawn her own conclusions.

"No," I yelp, louder than I intended. Loud enough, in fact, to wake the cubs out of their sleepy state. "No," I repeat at a lower level, despite it being too late; the cubs are already awake and picking up the suddenly fraught atmosphere, as their uncertain mewls indicate. "I swear, Bastet," I continue, staring at the raptorcat and trying to push sincerity down the Bond. "I swear that I'm not collaborating with Kalanthia."

She responds with feelings of distrust, sending the same pangs of betrayal again to add a poignancy to her message.

"Look," I tell her, stopping and putting my hands out a little defensively. It's not because I think she'll attack me—the little I understand of the Bond tells me that attacking the Bond holder is something it explicitly prevents—but because I'm trying to show her how genuine I'm being. "I live with Kalanthia. I have for quite a few days now. I wasn't aware she would attack your pack. I didn't tell her about you or direct her in any way. Nor did I come to take advantage after the attack. It was all complete coincidence."

I send memories along with my words of spending time near Kalanthia and her cub, sleeping next door to them, looking after Lathani while Kalanthia hunted, going searching through the forest for wood only to find an injured raptorcat . . .

The response from Bastet rather surprises me. Pure irritable indifference. Like such thoughts are irrelevant and she's annoyed that I'm wasting her time with them. I think part of my surprise must seep through to her as she adds a flurry of more images and emotions.

Finally, I think I understand why my previous attempt at reassuring her fell completely flat. I pride myself on being a good communicator, but this time I forgot to take the other person's background into account. Bastet isn't a human, who might be concerned with the past. She's a predator, an animal who lives very much in the present. A human might feel betrayal because the person they've sworn themselves to appears to be in cahoots with the person who killed their family. A human might rail against nature, at their family being taken before their time. But an animal? No, Bastet has consistently shown me that she accepts the death of her pack, that she understands the nature of the world is survival of the fittest.

Her feelings of betrayal are not because I appear to be in cahoots with her family's killer, but because she thinks that I've brought her here to be eaten by Kalanthia, that my promises of helping her and, more importantly in her mind, the cubs to become stronger are worthless. With that realization, I try once more to reassure her.

"Nothing has changed about what I promised you. I didn't bring you here to be snacks for Kalanthia. I'm going to talk to her and make sure she doesn't eat you, okay?" Once more trying to send waves of sincerity down the Bond, I see her hackles starting to descend and her ears beginning to rise again after a few moments. Her stubby wings also start to lower from their fluffed-up, angry display.

There isn't any wholehearted sense of an apology for doubting me, or even an expression of trust. However, she doesn't send more feelings of betrayal or distrust and instead sends a sense of resignation akin to "wait and see." If I can put it in words, it's like Bastet is acknowledging that she doesn't have a huge amount of choice in the matter but will tentatively hope for the best. I figure it's the best I'm going to get.

Soon we reach the river at the base of the hill, and I take a quick dip to wash off the worst of the dirt and sweat. For once, I'm not coated in blood too. Small mercies. Then, gazing apprehensively up the slope, I slip back into my clothes. Time to put my money where my mouth is and ensure that Bastet and the three cubs don't become handily sized snacks for my nunda landlord.

CHAPTER FIFTY-FOUR

Non-Human Communication Skills

Maybe you should stay here with the cubs until I've spoken to Kalanthia," I say a little hesitantly, casting an apprehensive eye up the slope. I mean, I'm *pretty* sure this isn't going to be an issue—Kalanthia's been okay with Spike, after all. *But a raptorcat is a different story from a porcupig and . . .* I'm stalling. I've already considered all this; I'm just letting my anxiety paralyze me.

Taking in a deep breath and refusing to look back to Bastet as if seeking approval, I walk up the hill with determination. Slowing as I get closer to the hole in the hill, I peek inside to check if the nunda is awake. I'm not actually sure if I'd rather she was or wasn't asleep. Delaying the confrontation would be great in the short term, but would just postpone the anxiety for later instead. As it so happens, she's awake, so I don't have to answer that question for myself.

"Kalanthia? Is it a good time?" I ask softly—no point in getting her hackles raised from the start by interrupting her at the wrong moment. She lifts her head and fixes me with her golden eyes; her nose wrinkles and her lip curls as her mouth opens slightly. I suddenly wonder if I've offended her somehow.

Have you been at your trade again, Binder? The question takes me off guard. "Wait, what?" I ask, feeling completely off-kilter. *You smell of the larnatis. Have you Bound one?* How did she draw that conclusion if, as I think, the "larnatis" are what I'd call raptorcats?

"How . . . ?" The question is the only thing I can even half-voice. Kalanthia emanates a sense of amusement.

You have their scent all over, yet you are not bloodied. That you have found some way to bind one to yourself without taking injury seems a lot more likely than you having taken one on in battle without being ripped to shreds.

That's . . . accurate. I'm momentarily speechless. This whole conversation has left me blindsided. It's not like I imagined, not even close. I thought I'd have to convince her that Bastet would be safe to have around Lathani, or not to eat Bastet and the cubs as a snack. Or both. Not . . . whatever this is.

"So, you're okay with me bringing a raptorcat . . . a larnatis back here?" She gives the head toss that I interpret as a shrug and a wave of indifference rolls over me.

What does it matter to me? The actions of your Bound are your responsibility; I have faith that your appreciation for your own skin will make you ensure Lathani's safety, so what other reservations would I have?

When you put it like that . . . "And you won't eat her? Or the cubs I've brought with me who I haven't yet Bound?" Kalanthia head-shrugs again.

As long as you claim and control them, I shall not consider them food unless you give them to me explicitly. Which . . . no. Just no. I might bring corpses back for Kalanthia sometime but bringing back live creatures just to feed to my nunda landlord . . . No way. I don't think my conscience could deal with that. Still, it seems like I've got what I wanted without even having to try.

Still feeling a bit off-balance from how easy the conversation was after building it up so much in my mind, I politely excuse myself and walk down the slope.

I need to improve my non-human communication skills, I reflect as I walk. That's twice in the last half an hour that I've completely misread the situation. It's weird to think about, but I'm not going to have any actual humans to talk to for the next year, so I better get used to not interpreting things in a human way. Maybe that Animal Empathy Skill will help me there.

Suddenly, I realize where I've seen Kalanthia's strange facial gesture before. I can't remember what it's called exactly, but when a cat partly opens its mouth and looks like it's grimacing, it's enhancing its capacity to smell something. In that context, her behavior makes much more sense. Reaching the base of the hill, I approach Bastet, who raises her head and sends a feeling of slightly apprehensive curiosity down the Bond.

"She's fine with you and the cubs coming to stay," I tell her. "Just make sure you don't threaten her cub in any way, okay? And please keep the cubs away too. Kalanthia's *very* protective."

A strange mixture of feelings rolls over the Bond: surprise, concern, and what I can only describe as what I would express with an eye roll. Exasperation, perhaps? I try to parse through the combination as I pick up the cubs to tuck them back into my chest sling. They, incidentally, are significantly more docile with me now than they were a few hours ago. I don't know if it's because Bastet's been communicating with them somehow or because they've been sleeping against me, surrounded by my scent. Whatever the reason, the more comfortable they are with me, the better. Once they're settled, we set off back up the hill.

After a few minutes, I think I've managed to figure out what Bastet was trying to communicate: surprise that Kalanthia has a cub of her own, concern that her defensiveness over the cub might cause problems, and exasperation because *of course* Kalanthia would be defensive of her own cub. I check these conclusions with Bastet and just get a derisive tail flick and a look that from a female human would probably mean she thought I was being a bit slow. I think I'm correct in saying that the look means the exact same thing from a raptorcat. The derision that flicks briefly through the Bond certainly supports my conclusion.

Kalanthia is standing outside the cave. As I start walking over towards her, Bastet runs in front of me and stops, making me halt abruptly. The raptorcat lays her ears back against her head and hisses at Kalanthia, crouching low to the ground. The much bigger nunda strolls over and slumps to a half-lying position just in front. She lifts a paw and starts grooming it casually, making it clear just how unthreatened she feels by the defensive raptorcat between us.

For a moment I'm flattered that Bastet's already trying to defend me, but the raptorcat should know better since I've just gone to speak with the nunda on my own. Then reality reasserts itself, and I realize that she's not defending me; she's defending the *cubs*. About to reassure Bastet and hopefully prevent her from attacking Kalanthia completely unnecessarily, not to mention causing a major incident with a being that's far more powerful than either of us, I'm interrupted by Kalanthia.

Peace, small one, she says. I'm almost offended—I know I'm a lot smaller than she is, but does she really need to highlight that? A moment later, I once more realize I've got the wrong end of the stick—it seems to be a day for it. She's talking to Bastet, but she must be sending the mental message to both of us. How that's possible, I don't really know, but then, I don't understand how her telepathy works to begin with. Or maybe I'm receiving the mental message through my Bond with Bastet; if the message *is* being translated through the mental perceptions of two different species, I would be worried about its accuracy. Like a game of telephone, but way worse.

Kalanthia keeps speaking. *I have an agreement with your Binder, and as long as that stays intact, I shall not hurt him or his. He has claimed you and your cubs as his, so you have nothing to fear for now.* Then she yawns, showing her great fangs, her canines almost as long as my forearm. *However, bear in mind that I am a mother.* She needs say nothing more; the sheer protectiveness and retributive vengefulness that she communicates with such a simple sentence is deeply impressive—in both senses of the word. Bastet actually *cowers*, her body language changing from defensive to submissive. Somehow, I don't think I'll have any problems with either her or the cubs harassing Lathani . . .

"Sure, we'll keep that in mind," I tell Kalanthia neutrally. "Come on, Bastet. Let's get you and the cubs settled." The raptorcat, once so threatening to me, scuttles after me, her plumed tail tucked between her legs like a scared dog.

The cubs obviously weren't included in the mental communication as they're not at all worried. Instead, they wriggle around the sling violently enough to almost fall out a couple of times. I figure they've probably had enough of sitting around and want to go and explore a bit. They will be able to shortly, but we need to figure out where everyone is sleeping first.

"I guess you'd prefer to sleep inside?" I half-ask Bastet. She sends me a complicated emotional combination that seems to indicate a preference for sleeping undercover, but not wanting to risk angering Kalanthia. "No, I doubt that would be an issue," I say absentmindedly, considering whether *I* want them to share my space—and whether I really have a choice. After all, I'm the one who decided to bind Bastet and in doing so took on responsibility for her and the cubs.

For sure the cubs would be better off inside, and I can't really expect Bastet to be all right with being separated from them, especially in a new place with a significant threat right next door. *I'm going to have to share a bedroom with four raptorcats, aren't I?* I sigh to myself.

"Come on," I tell her with resignation, setting a path for the cave.

I feel Kalanthia's attention on me, though when I look back, she's studiously washing herself. "Our space is over here," I tell my companion, indicating my alcove with my head as my hands are fully occupied with keeping three wriggling raptorcat cubs from falling out and hurting themselves. I head for my bedroom, passing a wary-looking Spike.

Pausing, I take a brief moment to try to reassure him that the raptorcats aren't going to eat him and another to explicitly tell Bastet that Spike is *not* a midnight snack for her either. Spike doesn't look completely reassured, and Bastet sends me a sense of disgruntlement—I'm not sure whether it's because she didn't feel like she needed to be told, or because she's grumpy about not being able to eat him. Either way, I hope that it will all turn out fine in the end. Maybe it's just as well that the cubs and Bastet are going to be staying in the alcove.

Apparently, the cubs are tired of being carried: I feel a set of sharp teeth set themselves into my thumb and bite. I let out a surprised yelp of pain. That *hurts!* *But not as much as the wolvezard,* I tell myself grimly as I refuse to jerk away and let the adorable, though sharp-toothed, bundles of fur gnaw at me. Still, I hasten my steps until I'm fully inside before kneeling down and letting the cubs tumble out of the sling. I've leant down close enough to the ground that they're not in any sort of danger of being hurt when they half-climb, half-fall out. Grimacing, I inspect the bloody holes, one of them left in my thumb, and cast a Lay-on-Hands to close the pinpricks. *Ouch!* I turn to see Bastet hesitating in the doorway, then throw myself sideways to push one inquisitive cub away from the fire. It's just burning embers by this point, given how long I've been absent, but even embers are too hot to risk near the cubs. Checking that the other cubs aren't currently anywhere near anything potentially dangerous, I turn back to Bastet.

"Come on in. This is my space. The big cave is Kalanthia's and Lathani's, but you can stay in here. Just make sure the cubs stay away from this fire," I tell her, indicating the fireplace. Then I spot one cub precariously close to my balanced pots and dive for it, only just managing to catch one of the drying pieces of pottery from both falling on the cub and probably breaking. "And away from these pots."

On the other side, a cub has started batting at one of the hanging pieces of drying sinew. This time I'm not fast enough: the cub catches the end with its claws and drags the piece towards it. Unfortunately, my drying rack isn't designed to stand up to a raptorcat's strength, not even a cub's, and I watch in dismay as the whole lot is pulled over to crash to the ground, sending drying bits of sinew everywhere. I raise one hand to my forehead and massage my temples. Clearly, I didn't think this through.

CHAPTER FIFTY-FIVE

Sympathy

I wake up in the dark to something breathing heavily near me. I freeze while my mind races groggily to work out the cause. The fact that it doesn't move closer while I'm waking up fully is enough to calm me a little, and I relax completely when I realize exactly what the source is: I remember having had the bright idea yesterday to bind a raptorcat and adopt the three cubs under her protection. Letting out a silent breath, I remember the chaos of the previous evening. It was impossible to keep the cubs out of everything, so eventually, I just let them play with a couple of pieces of sinew to try to stop them from destroying everything else.

I managed to keep my pottery safe by the skin of my teeth, despite several close shaves. One of my shirts met a worse fate: while I was saving my pots from one of the cubs, the other two grabbed the shirt and were playing tug of war with it. Before either I or Bastet, who was guarding the fire, could intervene, it had ripped from their sharp teeth. Reminded once more that I need to develop some way of repairing my torn garments before I run out of clothes to wear, I decided to give that particular shirt to the cubs to use as bedding.

Fortunately, after playing for a bit, squabbling over the sinew, and filling their bellies once more with lizog meat, they settled down to sleep. They did explore Bastet's underside, nosing through her fur and making unhappy squeaks, so I reckon they probably should still be having milk. Unfortunately, unless Bastet starts producing in sympathy, they're going to have to go without it. I suppose I should consider it good fortune that they're capable of eating meat; if they could only digest milk, like human babies, at the start of their lives, they'd have been doomed by the death of their mother. I hardly think Kalanthia is going to volunteer to donate, after all.

It's actually interesting to realize that the raptorcats must be mammals, or something similar, despite having feathers. How that evolved, I don't know, but it's curious, nonetheless. Taking advantage of everyone else still being asleep, I pull up my status. I haven't checked it properly in a few days, so I might as well do that now in the calm before the storm. I didn't have time yesterday evening after all. Given that my wood-collecting mission was interrupted by finding Bastet, and the subsequent events, I had been feeling a bit restless about how little I feel I've accomplished. So, after the cubs had gone to sleep, cuddled with Bastet and the shirt, I headed outside and worked with Spike on my pit. He shied away from me at first; I guess that smelling the raptorcats on me made him feel uncomfortable. It's understandable, and so is his continued wariness around Bastet; a pack of raptorcats—heck, only two or three of them—would make short work of a lone porcupig, after all. I sent reassuring feelings down my Bond with him again, and he slowly relaxed after some time so we could get to work.

The difference between him and Bastet has never been clearer. Where she is constantly alert, questioning the world around her, and proactively taking the actions she feels would be best for herself and hers, Spike just reacts. He's alert, sure—if he wasn't, he wouldn't have survived to adulthood—but there's no . . . spark behind it. No real governing Intelligence. It's one reason why I'm reluctant to take him out into the woods with me except when I have a specific need for him. Although he defended me that one time against the black blob, I really don't know how he'd do in a more normal combat situation. He might do fine, but I can't help but think that his species relies more on defense than offense, and that only works if they don't come across a too-powerful foe. He still has to go out into the woods to find food, for sure, but I reckon he's more able to go unnoticed by himself than if we go together. I certainly seem to attract confrontations, and I don't know if he's capable of reacting appropriately or proactively. Not to mention that I often actively seek combat, something the mostly herbivorous creature probably doesn't.

Unlike with Bastet, my Battle of Wills with Spike wasn't a negotiation but a test of force. He accepted the Bond because I was stronger than him and left him no choice but to accept. Yes, he seems to have fully accepted the Bond and his role as my protector—as seen when he defended me against the blob creature that poisoned me a few days back—but he's not really suited for it. Not like Bastet is. She's literally built for combat, much like a panther is, even if she does look half-bird.

Additionally, she seems to be more intelligent, or at least more proactive, which was evident the day before in the way she helped me think up and prepare a trap for the foe that hunted both of us. Spike, on the other hand, needs constant direction unless he's doing something like foraging for food or guarding the samova beans. Even when we've been working together on the pit and other projects, he's moved as directed and then waited for further instructions. It definitely makes me concerned for what might happen if we were in a combat situation where I couldn't give him instructions. I don't have the same fears about Bastet.

Pushing my musings to one side for later, I focus on the screen in front of me.

Name: Markus Wolfe		Race: Human	Class: Tamer
Level: 1	Energy to next level: 50%	Energy absorption rate: 11u/hr	Energy towards debt: 1%
Intelligence	9	Mana: 90/90	
Wisdom	9	Mana regeneration rate: 225u/hr	
Willpower	15+3 (+20%)	Health regeneration rate: 18u/hr	

Constitution	9	Health: 90/90
Strength	10	Stamina: 50/50
Dexterity	6	Stamina regeneration rate: 60u/hr
Class Skills:		Non-Class Skills:
Dominate – Beginner 3		Lay-on-Hands – Novice 3
Tame – Beginner 1		Stealth – Beginner 5
Fade – Beginner 4		Animal Empathy – Beginner 2

I'm halfway to level two, which is nice, though I doubt I'll get there anytime soon. Yesterday was a good day for Energy between Binding Bastet and killing the lizogs. I do wonder whether I'll get any Energy from my Bounds' kills, but Spike hasn't killed anything yet and neither has Bastet since our Binding. I would have more Energy in my store, but I got those two points in Wisdom, which took me down a bit. Still, it's good to know that I have the room to gain several points today if I put in enough effort. My digging last night was clearly not enough to trigger anything more, so those were my only gains yesterday. In terms of points, that is.

My Skill list is starting to grow, both in length and in quality. It's good to see Dominate has increased since Binding Bastet. Was that because Binding Bastet was pretty hard, or because I had to approach it in a different way from just forcing my will on my opponent? Or maybe because it was the second Bond I'd created? I don't know and won't until I get more data to work with. Still, if it's anything like increasing Lay-on-Hands to Novice level, I gained the point in Dominate because I won the Battle of Wills in a different sort of way. *Or maybe that only applies when crossing the gap between Beginner and Novice . . .* Another question to add to the list.

Everything's coming on nicely in my actual stats except for Dexterity. The six sitting there among nines and tens—and even higher, in the case of my Willpower—is a bit embarrassing, but honestly, I can see why it hasn't improved much. Recently, I've been doing a lot of things that require strength over fine motor control. Plus, my Constitution has been put under strain, so that's had to grow by default. As for my mental stats, I've also managed to improve my Intelligence, by making links between things in my absorbed memories, and my Wisdom, by connecting with others and the world around me. Still, I should be doing more fine motor control tasks soon. There are more arrowheads to make, after all, and feathers to cut to make flights for the arrows, and then flights and arrowheads to attach carefully to prepared lengths of thin wood. I groan at the thought of all that fiddly, finicky work to do. *I hope my bow is worth it in the end*, I moan to myself.

Actually, on that front, I'll need to head back out to the forest sooner rather than later. I considered it briefly but never did anything about it, and the wood for my arrows really ought to be given some time to dry. I don't have enough time to season the wood properly, which can take as much as a year—something that's clearly out of the realm of possibility—but some drying is better than none. I'm just going to have to settle for choosing the straightest possible sticks and then live with it. I might set up some arrows for seasoning for later use when I have a bit of time, but that's a future-me concern.

I also need to collect more firewood; what I managed to collect yesterday looks rather pitiful in the pile I stacked last night—I need a *lot* more than that. However, I know that Bastet won't be keen on taking the cubs with us back into the forest, and I agree it's not a great idea, so that leaves either me going out to the forest on my own or staying home today. The main issue I have with leaving the raptorcats on their own today is that I'm a bit nervous about how they will react to Lathani—and how she will react to them. Ultimately, I figure that staying home for a day is probably the best use of my time. That way, I can head off any potential problems with settling in before they start. I still need to dig my pit anyway. I can get on with that with Spike while the cubs play outside or sleep.

Decision made, I feel suddenly restless in the way I always used to when I knew I had a lot of work waiting for me at the office and just wanted to get on with it. It used to drive my ex mad. Lucy used to complain that I never wanted to stay in bed with her. That wasn't the case—I just couldn't relax when I thought about what needed to be done. *Just one more nail in the coffin of our relationship, I suppose.* I pull some cooked meat and a little of the cooked tuber out of my Inventory and munch on them. It almost makes steak and potatoes, without it actually being steak . . . or potatoes. *Oh man, what I'd do to have a medium-cooked steak with crispy fries . . .*

Well, I suppose I could make some sort of fries someday if these tubers don't fall apart too much when fried—all I would need to collect would be enough animal fat to deep fry them. Something to consider later on down the line. I'd also need more salt for seasoning since I really don't have much left of what I created from boiling the malachy leaves.

By the time I finish my breakfast, light is starting to permeate the gloom. At this time of the morning the sun doesn't actually penetrate the cave in any way, as the angle is wrong, but when it's getting lighter outside, a little always filters inside. A glint near the glowing embers lets me know that Bastet is awake and watching me.

"Are you hungry?" I ask quietly, not keen on waking up the balls of fluff and energy when not necessary. She sends a feeling of negation and satiation down the Bond. I guess that makes sense: she did rather gorge herself yesterday. "Okay, well, I need to get to the fire behind you or it's going to die soon." I get the impression that she doesn't really understand what I'm saying there, so I try to send her an image of the fire getting lower and lower until I give it some fuel and it leaps higher again. She still gives off a sense of confusion but shifts sideways until there's enough space for me to access the fire. I hear a few squeaks and plaintive complaints from the cubs burrowed into her side, but they seem to die down quickly.

I focus on the fire, gently encouraging the embers to take on more life by feeding it easily burned material while blowing lightly. Once the fine bark and dried mosslike material has caught light, I feed in thin branches and then wait a bit. Eventually, I add on a bigger log and wait to make sure it's starting to char even as the medium branches I also added are starting to catch light. Honestly, taking care of the fire takes a good portion of each morning; between dealing with the fire itself and the ash it creates, and replenishing my carefully piled stocks next to the fireplace, it must take between an hour and two hours. However, it's worth it. Afterwards, as long as I keep it fed with larger logs every so often, I end up with a fire that'll last all day with relatively little attention and then be easy to stoke again for the evening.

When I'm finished and just assessing whether I need to bring in more firewood from outside, my attention is grabbed by Bastet's grunt and a sense of urgency she sends down the Bond. I whip around to see one of the cubs—I'm pretty sure this one is the adventurous blighter that tried to break my pottery twice yesterday—standing in the doorway between my alcove and Kalanthia's cave. That by itself would be worth my attention. Even worse, though, the cub has come face to face with a surprised Lathani, who's not looking entirely happy at the sudden encounter.

CHAPTER FIFTY-SIX

Trouble

The two felines stare each other down for a long moment. Well, I say two felines, but I'm not even sure a nunda counts as one, let alone a raptorcat. Lathani is significantly bigger than the as-yet-unnamed raptorcat cub—she's about the size of a large dog, where the other cub is probably like a small lion cub in size. We're all frozen, wondering what will happen. At least, that's what I'm doing, but no one else is moving either. Finally, Lathani reaches out a paw towards the raptorcat cub with the same kind of curiosity she showed towards the beetle a few days ago—before it bit her, of course. Almost as if I've suddenly become prescient, I can see what is going to happen before it does. Maybe that's because it actually *has* happened with the beetle.

"Lathani," I call, startling everyone a little. The nunda cub flashes a look up to me and freezes, her paw in mid-air. The raptorcat cub in front of her twists around to stare at me too, as does Bastet. Crisis temporarily averted, it's now time to ensure that the situation doesn't devolve. I stride over to her and scoop up the adventurous raptorcat cub. "I want to introduce you to some friends of mine," I tell her.

Resorting to old habits in my stress, my mind latches onto "friends" instead of whatever the hell the four raptorcats are to me now. Walking over to Bastet, I dump the cub down in front of her. The little pause gives me enough time to quickly consider how to do this.

"This is Bastet, and she's caring for these three cubs, like Kalanthia does for you." I indicate each of the raptorcats one by one. Lathani looks up at me, her head tilted curiously, her ears alert. "The little ones are cubs like you, but they're smaller and more fragile than you are, okay?" I get the sense that she doesn't quite understand. "So, they'll probably want to play with you, but be careful not to hurt them, all right?"

I don't know whether it's my Animal Empathy or whether Lathani's starting to develop some form of mental communication, but I get the sense that she's still a bit confused but will try not to . . . crunch them like leaves? I suppose that makes sense.

Well, if it's enough to stop her from biting and clawing at them, great. I've already started teaching her how to mind her teeth and claws in play after becoming tired of her using them on me. I guess Kalanthia doesn't even notice—her fur is probably enough armor against Lathani's milk teeth.

"Bastet," I say, continuing my introduction. "This is Kalanthia's cub, Lathani.

Be careful of her," I warn, impressing down the link that it isn't necessarily because Lathani herself is dangerous, but because she's got an immensely dangerous protector behind her.

Bastet gives me a look that makes it very obvious how little she needed that warning, and given how Kalanthia spoke to her last night, I get it. "In fact, you may gain some points with Kalanthia if you show that you're also protecting Lathani," I add, passing over the memory of how I met the pair.

I feel her perusing the memory carefully and coming to her own conclusions about it. Then, pushing it to one side, she stands up and saunters over to the cub who is as much smaller than the adult raptorcat as she was bigger than the raptorcat cub. Lathani backs up a little, looking unsure, but Bastet just does a walk of inspection around her—or that's what it appears to be. Then, ducking her head down, she rubs it against Lathani's once and after that returns to her spot by the fire.

Lathani is left standing near the entrance on her own, looking a touch shocked and completely unsure how to take that. I'm not certain either, but all I can guess is that raptorcats probably rub heads with their packmates like lions do, and her doing it to Lathani was some sort of gesture that indicates lack of hostility, at the very least. Though, whether Lathani will be able to interpret it is another thing—she rubs heads with her mother, but she doesn't exactly have a pack . . .

Anyway, crisis over, it's time to get on with the day.

"Lathani, go to your mother, would you?" I tell her. "I'll be digging the pit today, and I'm sure you'll be able to play with the cubs later if you want." Thank all that's holy, she actually listens to me. The nunda cub chirps cheerfully, regaining her composure, and then turns tail and dashes out of the cave.

"Right," I say, looking down at Bastet, my heartbeat finally slowing. "So, you've met Lathani now. I figure the best thing for the cubs is to get used to her, and for her to get used to them. Maybe you could spend the majority of the time outside with them today?" I suggest. Bastet seems to consider the idea for a moment before sending a sense of agreement. "Okay, good. Do you think they're hungry?" That's answered by a feeling of strong agreement. "Fine, I'll put a lizog corpse outside in the shade. Let's take them out now."

Once more I get the sense of agreement, so Bastet picks up one cub—the adventurous one—by the scruff of its neck, and I get the other two by grabbing one with each hand. Going outside, I nod at Kalanthia in greeting, receiving an amused rumble in response, and head for a spot that I know stays shady for a good portion of the morning.

After setting the two cubs down, I pull out the half-eaten carcass and put it down in the shade. The cubs let out cute little growls and squeaks of excitement, then pile onto the flesh and start to tear it off hungrily. Not all that keen on watching the cubs get blood everywhere, I search around for my digging stick and find it near the pit, where I left it last night. Spike's nowhere to be seen—probably out foraging.

At the thought of my porcupig, I'm reminded of the task I set him. Walking over, I inspect my plants. There's some green visible! The first leaves are coming through in all five spots!

The dirt around them is looking a little dry, which means I need to go fetch water. Finishing off the last of my pre-boiled water from my canteen, I pop back into the cave to grab my sneleon-shell bowl. I finished the soup last night, so I might as well use it to collect more water. Quickly warning Bastet, I offer to wait for her to be ready so she can come down and drink some water at the river. She accepts but sends me the sense of not being ready, so I just start digging while I wait.

The hollow is coming on well. When I stand in it, the deepest point is already just a bit deeper than my knee. Honestly, I want it to reach mid-thigh just to make sure that the fire is well contained, but I figure that I may be finished by the end of the day if I really put my back into it. Plus, if Spike can help me, it might even take less time than that, as his horn loosening the ground definitely speeds things up. I'm starting to get into the work when I spot Bastet sitting at the edge of the dip patiently. The cubs are tussling together over a bone or something similar.

"Ready?" I ask, wiping my already sweaty brow with the back of my hand. I've probably also smeared dirt all over it, but I honestly couldn't care less—it's not like there's anyone around here to take a photo and put it on social media, after all. Bastet just goes and stands near the cubs, nosing them towards me.

Pulling out the shirt I used as a sling yesterday, I prepare to put them in again. They're wriggling, which makes it difficult. No sooner have I got two in and am reaching for the third when one of the cubs already in the sling manages to pop over the top and tumble out again. It feels like a Sisyphean task—or like herding cats. It actually takes Bastet letting out a grumbling growl and nipping the worst offender for them to settle down enough for me to pack them in and tie the shirt so it won't let them drop out as easily.

Finally, we set off down to the river. Well, they do say that a baby turns your life upside down, and here I am with three. Baby raptorcats, to be sure, but there are *three* of them.

Lathani watches us go, looking rather like she's considering joining our little cavalcade. She even takes a few tentative steps towards us before Kalanthia lets out a disapproving rumble. Chastised, she turns around and starts playing with a flying insect—pretending, in typical cat fashion, that that was what she'd been wanting to do all along. Walking down the hill, I reflect that having the raptorcat cubs around might actually give Lathani some playmates her own age, or at least in the same developmental stage.

Once down by the river, I set the cubs on the ground near Bastet, taking my time to wash a bit, fill my canteen, fill my sneleon shell, and collect some more pondweed for my soup. It's nice down here: not too hot because of the shade, peaceful with the sound of trickling water, and with Bastet and her acute senses here, I feel like I can relax a bit. I even sit down and close my eyes briefly, just letting myself connect with nature in a sort of meditation, something I've been trying to do at odd moments during the days. I don't feel any sort of indication that I've gained a point in Wisdom, but that doesn't matter. Just being at peace surrounded by a living world brings me a sense of satisfaction. It's a bit alien to me, used to the city environment as I am. But it's nice, even if it's strange.

Opening my eyes, I look at the cubs. Seeing two of them tussling over a stick, I'm reminded that I haven't yet given them names. One of the two is predominantly black with only small patches of gray and dark green. It would be a bit cliché to call it "Shadow," but I'm considering it anyway. Or maybe "Ninja" would be better—its retreat and rush tactics to try to get the stick support that as a potential moniker. The other is paler with mostly grays of various shades and only some dark marks— striking in their contrast—around its eyes, ears, nose, and on its wing stubs. That one is much more determined, gripping onto the stick with mouth and both front paws, stubbornly refusing to let go. "Cloud" might be a good name in terms of its coloring, but not its attitude. What about "Stormcloud"? Or "Tempest"? I'll think about that one a bit more. As for the third . . . I look around trying to spot it. *Wait . . . isn't it the adventurous one who's missing?* The one with more dark green than the others, the one who almost picked a fight with Lathani this morning, as well as almost breaking my pottery last night.

"Bastet," I start slowly, "where's the other cub?" The adult raptorcat had been lying down, relaxing with her eyes half-shut, also watching the two cubs tussling. At my question, she tenses, lifting her head off her paws and looking around. She sends an image to my mind of the cub in question playing with her tail and then an unsure feeling. *Great,* I groan to myself. *I think I'm going to call that one "Trouble." When I find it.*

At that moment, a shriek rings through the air. Beside me, Bastet leaps to her feet, and the other cubs rush to her side. She sends me an unmistakable feeling. Danger.

CHAPTER FIFTY-SEVEN

Pride

My mind races quickly. *We have one cub AWOL. What are the chances that Trouble is where the shriek came from?* I wouldn't take that bet. At the same time, we have two cubs here that we can't leave on their own. I make a decision quickly.

"Bastet, you go ahead," I tell her quietly but urgently. She sends me a reluctant look, glancing back at the other two cubs. "I'll bring them with me, but the other cub could be in mortal danger right now!" She sends a feeling of grim agreement and dashes off. The two cubs try to follow after her, letting out mewls of distress. I quickly scoop them up, ignoring their wriggling complaints, and tuck them back in the shirt sling; I may need my hands free.

Rushing after Bastet, I try to work out where exactly she went, as there aren't many signs of her passage in the undergrowth. Then a fracas breaks out not far ahead, and I quickly move in the direction of the shaking and growling bushes.

I stop before I get too close; I don't want to be accidentally attacked simply because I was there and wanted to have a better view of the situation. Not that I can see much—the undergrowth is too thick. I catch glimpses of fur and feathers and the odd flash of teeth or claw. As for sounds, it's an unholy cacophony of growls and snarls and ear-splitting shrieks of pain or fear. I feel annoyingly helpless; I'm not used to being a bystander to a fight. Actually, is it weird that I'm already used to being a *participant* in a fight?

Desperately, I try to think of something I could do to help. The problem is that anything I can think of has just as much chance of hurting Bastet or the cub as their attacker does. I need to see more.

Just as I'm considering completely uprooting the bush or whatever the undergrowth plants count as, Bastet rolls into view. She's tussling with some sort of snaky thing, which has its fangs buried deeply in our wayward cub. I say snaky thing because although it's a long tube with no legs, it does have a sting at the end, which it keeps burying into Bastet. I seriously hope that the thing isn't venomous, but it seems like a forlorn hope as I watch Bastet starting to slow and weaken.

Pulling my trusty mace and knife out of my Inventory and belt, respectively, I start slashing at the snake thing wherever I can see exposed flesh. I don't dare use the mace yet for fear of hurting my ally, but if I can sever its spine, that'll be a good start. The snake thing doesn't take all this lying down and releases its prey to come at me with both fangs. The cub drops down, worryingly limp, and I fear that it will be crushed as combat continues. The snake thing strikes at me more quickly than I anticipated; I barely manage to get my mace up between us in time. Fortunately, I do manage to block the strike, and even better, the snake thing's fangs get stuck temporarily in the wood.

I use the brief pause to lean in and snatch up the cub and somewhat roughly toss it to one side. If it's still alive, I hope it will be able to hold on until we're done with the fight; I really can't do anything to help it right now. Unfortunately, casting Lay-on-Hands seems to require me to literally be in contact with the patient for the whole healing time, otherwise I'd toss one off now.

Reaching in to grab the cub has left me out of position, and the snake thing's second weapon comes into play. Before I've even recognized the danger, I feel pain explode in the back of my shoulder and glance over to see its sting sticking into me. My usual battle anger rising inside me, I slam the mace into the ground and crush the snake thing's head between wood and a hard place. It's regrettable that I don't have enough speed or momentum on the swing to literally crush its skull, but at least the strike stuns it a little. Its tail goes limp briefly, and its sting slides out of me. I take full advantage of the lull and grab its tail firmly, even though that means briefly dropping my knife. My mace pinning the head and my hand around the base of its tail, I extend my arms as much as possible, presenting the groggy Bastet with a perfect target.

"Kill it," I urge her as she blinks a bit owlishly. She stumbles forward, aiming a strike with her claws and missing. The snake thing, getting over its stunned state, starts wriggling, making it even more difficult for Bastet to hit. I try to formulate another plan, seeing that this one isn't working very well. I'm also very conscious of the injured state of both Bastet and the cub, not to mention the venom working through my own system from my shoulder wound. Time is against us.

Before I can come up with something, Bastet figures it out. She moves close to my mace, places a paw on the snake thing's body, which requires a few attempts but is successful in the end, and leans in to start chewing. It takes longer than I'd like—the snake thing's skin must be pretty tough—but eventually, the rest of its body goes limp in my grasp as she bites through its spinal column. We're both panting. The whole thing has probably only taken a few minutes, but like all time in combat, those minutes seem to stretch into hours. I quickly cast a Lay-on-Hands on my companion, worried about how groggy she seems. She perks up after two more casts and sends me a mental question about the cub.

"I don't know," I tell her, staggering over to the cub in question. My Constitution must be lower than Bastet's, as she was hit more times than I can count by the venomous stinger but was still able to act; I was hit only once and already feel like I've had a few too many vodkas. It makes me worry about the cub: if the snake thing's fangs are as venomous as its stinger, what chance does such a small body have?

I drop down next to the limp cub, fearing the worst. I don't bother searching for a pulse—that would just waste time. Instead, I cast my channeled version of Lay-on-Hands, searching for the area of most damage. Worryingly, it actually seems to be the brain that is most affected by this venom. Not feeling remotely able to direct the healing correctly when dealing with the brain, I just flood the area with healing mana, hoping that the cub's body will know well enough to be able to help itself. Still, if nothing else, I can tell that it's holding onto life. In fact, if I had to guess, I would say that this venom isn't actually that lethal, at least not immediately. Its purpose seems to be to reduce the victim's coordination and consciousness. The cub ending up in a coma wouldn't be much better than outright death, though.

I run out of mana before the cub is healed, but my efforts do seem to have made some difference. Before I ran out of juice, I detected that either the venom concentration had reduced or its effects had been partially healed—I'm not sure how to interpret the feedback I received from my spell. The fact that the cub starts shifting slightly and making quiet noises of discontent is also a good sign.

By this point Bastet has come to collapse next to me, keeping guard on us at the same time as anxiously watching over my patient. I'm *exhausted*. Running through the whole of my mana store in such a short time does that to me, apparently. When I stop moving for a moment, the protective adult raptorcat looks up at me questioningly.

"I ran out of mana," I explain briefly. When she prods me again mentally, I sigh once more. "Trouble is still alive for now and will hopefully last until I get enough mana back to continue the healing process." And yes, this cub has now *definitely* earned the name "Trouble." It'd better be glad I'm not calling it "Strife." It's not blond enough for that, though. I need to work out what sex each of the cubs are. So far, I haven't seen any physical differences that could indicate male or female. Then a thought crosses my mind that makes me want to face-palm. *Why don't I just ask the creature who will know?*

"Bastet, are these cubs female like you, or male, or a mixture?" She cocks her head to one side, clearly not quite understanding. Not really surprising, I suppose, when I realize that my own concepts of male and female are a bit confusing based on recent cultural developments. I try to form a clear thought of males as the ones to sire new offspring and females as the ones to bear them, hoping that raptorcats don't have a more complicated arrangement like seahorses or snails.

Fortunately, it seems like raptorcats are neither hermaphrodites nor do they have unusual child-rearing arrangements, so she understands what I want to know this time. She sends a series of images: Ninja and Stormcloud playing together as cubs; Ninja and Stormcloud as adults hunting together as a pack; Trouble as a cub; Trouble as an adult, alone, fighting with another raptorcat; the winner of the fight approaching Ninja and Stormcloud and mating with them, which makes a light blush rise to my cheeks at the sheer unabashed nature of Bastet's approach to sex. I can also now attest that raptorcat mating is not that dissimilar from lion mating, something I wasn't sure I wanted to know. The last image is of Ninja and Stormcloud relaxing with cubs running around them.

So, Ninja and Stormcloud are females, and it's females that form the pack—or pride, if we consider them to be this world's analogue to lions. The males, of which Trouble seems to be one, wander around and are fairly solitary, only meeting each other to fight or mate, depending on if they meet a female or male of their species.

Unlike lions, I didn't get the impression that a male will associate with one particular pride for any length of time. It seems to be more that a male will wander around to try to spread his genes as widely as he can, assuming that he is capable of defeating whatever male he might encounter. It's interesting and might explain why Trouble is always the one to go exploring while the two females are more likely to play near Bastet.

My mana having now regenerated enough, I cast another channeled Lay-on-Hands, but this one is shorter, as I don't have as much mana to work with. Fortunately, my increased Wisdom does mean that I regenerate mana a bit more quickly, otherwise the chances of the cub surviving would be a lot lower.

It's still a bit touch and go for a while, but eventually the cub opens his eyes and blinks blearily. My heart having had far too much strain this morning, and not feeling great since I didn't use any healing on myself, I make the executive decision to head straight back to the cave.

Hopefully, we won't encounter anything else dangerous on the way back, I say to myself. *This has got to be our fair share for the day.* I then curse myself—that's an invitation for Murphy to come and intervene if ever there was one.

CHAPTER FIFTY-EIGHT

Priorities

Despite being on tenterhooks for most of the morning, even after getting back to the cave area, nothing bad happens. Well, nothing outside the usual, that is. In the end I don't make more soup, since I suddenly realize that the cubs are going to need water throughout the day and my wok is the only container I have that they can easily drink from. Nothing could persuade me to make repeated trips down to the river just so I can have a bit of hot soup in the morning. That should change once I've fired my pottery and made more containers for water, but for now I have to live with what I have.

Instead, I just get on with the pit, relishing the simple, relaxed physical activity. When Spike comes back, I get him to help me again, and we make good progress. During my breaks, especially the elongated one over lunch when I recuperate from the sun and exercise, I watch the cubs. It's a simple pleasure watching the cute bundles of fur and fluff play together, but a satisfying one. Far better than watching cat videos online as I used to, honestly.

For a while the cubs and Lathani are a bit standoffish with each other; the cubs are unsure about this large creature, and Lathani is equally unsure about how to treat them. There's a tense moment as the raptorcat cubs tumble together and accidentally knock into the larger nunda cub. For one long moment, the cubs all stare at each other, and all the adults watch them attentively—except for Spike, who couldn't care less and just continues snoozing in the sun.

Then Lathani jumps on top of Stormcloud and the other cubs "defend" their sister's honor. The whole standoff turns into a mess of paws and ears and tails all flying every which way. But given that none of them runs squealing to their respective guardian, I'm going to count it as a win.

By the time I take my lunch break, the cubs are exhausted, lying and snoozing together in the shade. However, when I bring out my skewer of freshly cooked meat—I'd rather keep my pre-prepared stuff for when I'm out and about—the smell is enough to make several heads lift in curiosity.

One of these heads is Lathani's, and I'm not surprised when a moment later the nunda cub comes bounding towards me, begging for scraps with liquid eyes. A bit wary, I cast a glance over at her mother. Kalanthia looks at me for a long moment and then grunts, settling her head down on her paws. It's enough permission for me, so I give Lathani a chunk of meat, making sure it won't burn her first. She retreats back to the shade to gnaw on it and is soon surrounded by eager raptorcat cubs. Growling, she rebuffs their efforts to grab her food, and, to avoid a diplomatic incident, I call them over.

"Ninja, Stormcloud, Trouble, come here." They don't pay any attention—unsurprising, considering I only decided on their names this morning. I whistle sharply and gain everyone's attention with the loud noise. Waving the meat around to catch their gazes, I repeat my instruction. Trouble is the first over, and I reward him with a chunk of meat. Seeing that, his sisters bound towards me, receiving their own recompense with eagerness. I look at the few small bits of meat that remain on my skewer and chuckle a little ruefully. *I guess I'll need to put on another stick of meat,* I think as I sigh to myself fondly. Oh well. With any luck, if I repeat this sort of thing regularly and they start to follow my instructions even without the Bond, when I activate the Taming Skill, they'll be happy to accept the Bond.

Wiping my sweaty brow, I stare at my pit with satisfaction. It's two meters in diameter and almost a meter in depth. Thanks to Spike's assistance, today's work has gone quite quickly. Plus, once we got about twenty centimeters down, we got past most of the roots, so it became easier to break apart the ground. Until we started hitting the stony layer, of course, but that was pretty much where I wanted to stop anyway.

I stretch, all my muscles complaining at the amount of exercise I've subjected them to today. Still, I feel like I'm getting fitter and my skin tougher; I only needed to cast Lay-on-Hands twice today, and my hands only blistered towards the end of the day. Progress. I access my message box after noticing I have a notification.

Congratulations! You have worked hard on your Constitution and have earned a point. Would you like to apply this to your status?
Y / N

I accept the point and move onto the next message. Unsurprisingly, that's also offering me a point, this time in Strength.

Congratulations! You have worked hard on your Strength (Endurance) and have earned a point. Would you like to apply this to your status?
Y / N

Again, I accept the point, then switch to looking at my status.

Name: Markus Wolfe		Race: Human	Class: Tamer
Level: 1	Energy to next level: 0%	Energy absorption rate: 11u/hr	Energy towards debt: 1%

Intelligence	9	Mana: 90/90
Wisdom	9	Mana regeneration rate: 225u/hr
Willpower	15+3 (+20%)	Health regeneration rate: 18u/hr
Constitution	10	Health: 100/100
Strength	11	Stamina: 60/60
Dexterity	6	Stamina regeneration rate: 60u/hr
Class Skills:		Non-Class Skills:
Dominate – Beginner 3		Lay-on-Hands – Novice 3
Tame – Beginner 1		Stealth – Beginner 5
Fade – Beginner 4		Animal Empathy – Beginner 2

Huh, it seems like stats above ten really do consume a lot more Energy. With my daily absorption rate and the snake thing we killed this morning, I had about twenty-seven percent Energy towards my next level. Now I have zero. Since I doubt the point in Constitution cost much more than the normal twelve percent, my Strength point must have taken about fifteen percent to increase.

Still, I can't deny the pride that rises in me at the sight of those three stats above ten. If I'm right in my calculations and ten is about the level of an average Olympic athlete, I'm doing pretty well. Even if it's not Olympic level, the visible and noticeable improvements to my physique are so much more motivating than the drudge at the gym used to be. My muscles are significantly more defined, and I've lost a drastic amount of fat too. Not that I was paunchy beforehand, but I was certainly softer around certain parts than I am now. Still, considering I've been eating mostly lean, gamey meat and precious little carbohydrate, it's not really surprising. I'm still tired, though, and decide to relax for the evening.

Since the cubs and Lathani seem to have got on fairly well, I decide to go out tomorrow and leave Bastet and the cubs here. I'd rather take Bastet with me, but I still doubt she'll be happy to be separated from the cubs. At the same time, I need to really focus on collecting firewood due to not having collected nearly enough the day I reencountered Bastet. Plus, if I've got a handle on Kalanthia's pattern, which I think I have, she's going to want to go hunting again the day after tomorrow.

With my head at stake, there's no way I'd leave Bastet here alone with Lathani, however confident I am that she's bound sufficiently by the Bond—let alone common sense—not to harm the nunda cub. But you never know what could happen. No, better to go out alone into the forest tomorrow when Kalanthia is still here to personally keep her daughter safe. With the two adult feline-like creatures present, it should be fine. As for me, I've survived alone this far—hopefully, that doesn't change.

At least, that's what I tell myself.

Grabbing a book, I sit outside to enjoy the last of the sun, the temperature now very pleasant. I really should go wash off in the river, but I really can't be arsed. My personal hygiene has plunged since arriving here. I never used to be a neat freak, but I would have at least one shower per day; two if I'd gone to the gym. Here, I'm calling myself "clean" if I've washed my face and hands in the river. I seriously hope that an improved Constitution means improved resistance to germs, as I'm really not practicing modern-day cleanliness. Maybe once I have some soap, I'll be able to do a better job of bathing, but for now it's at the bottom of my list of priorities.

Speaking of priorities, I feel my stomach grumbling as it makes its emptiness known. I ignore it for a little longer, closing my eyes and just basking in the gentle touch of the lowering sun. It's peaceful. Relaxing. Sometimes these days I find myself wondering which is the fantasy world: this one with magic and animals that can talk, if only mentally, or the one with books on electronic devices, ways of communicating instantly across the world, and cars that can drive themselves . . .

When I consider such things, I feel an alarming sense of surrealism, which is only comparable to how I felt after watching *The Matrix*. My stomach brings me back to earth again. Trust hunger to do that, at least. Whether I'm living in a fantasy world or a real one, I need to eat. Closing the book, I head inside. At some point, Bastet shifted the cubs indoors, and they're already curled up in the torn shirt. Well, two of them are, at least.

I feel a swoop in my stomach as I realize that Trouble isn't there. Looking around carefully, my thoughts racing, I catch Bastet's eyes. She looks amused. More amused than she would be feeling if one of her cubs was actually missing. "Trouble?" I ask softly. She turns her head to look at my bed. Well, the collection of jackets that make up my bed, anyway.

I walk over quietly and peek under the top jacket. Seeing Trouble hiding underneath, curled in his own ball, I can't help shaking my head. He's well named, that one, though I still think that maybe "Strife" would be better. Still, if I named him Strife and the others Stormcloud and Ninja, I might be facing a legal battle with a well-known video game company. If I ever make it back to Earth, that is. The thought depresses me a little, so I busy myself with making some more meat skewers and baked tuber. Heck, I might as well just call it a potato. It looks like a long sweet potato, acts like a potato when cooked, and even fairly tastes like a potato. Good enough for me.

I'm not tired enough to go to bed once I've eaten; despite my physical tiredness, I'm still mentally energetic. I sit there staring into the flames, thinking about everything and nothing at the same time.

I think about my life. My life back on Earth, that is. It's still hard to make that distinction mentally. Being here is a strange combination of feeling like I've been here forever and like it's only been for as long as a dream. I think about how boring it was on Earth. How despite seemingly going somewhere with my career, even that could be kiboshed by a penny-pinching director. I think about my family and regret not making up with Lucy. Before she was my girlfriend, she was my closest friend, and I miss her. I think about my dad, and perhaps it's the last few days of being surrounded by the dead and the dying—most of those by my hand—but I feel like I'm starting to come to terms with his death. I even think about the despair that drove me to stand at the edge of my apartment building and dare myself to step over. It holds as much sway over me now as the despair of a dream would.

If I went back to Earth now, would I fall back into the same rut as before? I doubt it; I've changed, and not just physically. I've learned the value of life in a way that I couldn't have dreamed of before, living in the biggest city in one of the richest countries in the world as I did.

My eyelids are drooping, each blink lasting a little longer than the previous. I need to go to bed—I have to forage for wood in the forest tomorrow, and that's likely to be peril-filled enough to warrant a decent sleep first. Switching into the cleaner set of clothes I'm using as pseudo-pajamas, I bury myself underneath my jackets, careful not to disturb Trouble. As I fall asleep, I can't stop one question from nagging at me: if I could go back to Earth, *would* I?

CHAPTER FIFTY-NINE

The Venom Coursing through My Veins

The next morning is a bit of a repeat of the day before: eat, stoke the fire, then prepare for the day. This time I'm intending on going out into the forest rather than digging a pit, so my preparations are a little different. The main task I need to do in preparation is check my Inventory to minimize the amount of stuff I'm carrying with me, while also making sure that I have enough supplies for any eventuality. It's complicated by the fact that I have a number of carcasses stored in stasis, which I don't have time to deal with now, and don't want to just abandon. That snake thing might be useful, for example, as a source of poison for arrows. I'll need to test to make sure its venom doesn't just denature after a short time exposed to the air, but again, I don't have time to do that now.

In the end, about five of my thirty slots are filled with carcasses—I've managed to open up one of those slots by pulling the lizog corpses out for Bastet and the cubs. A number of other slots are used up with my cooked meat, raw meat, some emergency clothes, the bark-fiber rope that I salvaged from my rock trap, throwing rocks, branches, and a few other things I figure I should keep with me.

My backpack, by this point, has joined my suitcases in staying permanently in the cave. It leaves a handful of slots free for any new corpses or interesting things I find, which should hopefully be enough. I consider once more taking Spike with me, but I don't think I'll find much use for his digging skills, and I don't want to put him in more danger than necessary. Sure, it should be a peaceful walk through the forest, but when has *that* ever worked out?

Casting a final glance around the room at the playful cubs and their guardian raptorcat, I mentally check through my to-do list. I can't help but feel like I've forgotten something, but I often get that feeling even when I *haven't* forgotten anything. I think it's the result of being employed in a job that always has more tasks to do than there are hours in the day to do them—I've built up an expectation of myself, which is not necessarily applicable now. Even though there's always something to do here—and always something I need to complete *before* I can even start what I need to actually do—life still feels a lot more measured than my job used to. Perhaps it's because I don't have a boss with unreasonable expectations, which I have to do my best to meet, then justify not meeting without actually outrightly calling her unreasonable . . .

In the end, I decide I'd better leave before I can second-guess myself further.

I've been out into the forest hundreds of times by now and I'm still alive. Well, not *hundreds* of times. And I have come close to death a few times, but just like in horse races, close means it didn't happen. Feeling a little more confident from the impromptu pep talk, I stride towards the entrance to the cave.

"I'll be back by this evening," I promise Bastet on my way out the "door." She sends a wave of wariness at me. I'm partly warmed by the message, partly insulted. Warmed because she's essentially telling me to be careful. Insulted because she's only doing that because she doesn't think I can take care of myself. And that's not just me jumping to conclusions: the feeling was accompanied by the image of a wide-eyed raptorcat cub venturing into the forest . . . and getting snapped up by the first predator it comes across. Considering I survived this far, including before she—or Spike—was around, I take exception to that. In the end, I just raise my hand in a gesture of farewell, which she probably doesn't understand at all, and then march out of the cave. Encountering Kalanthia lying in the sun in the clearing, I give her a quick summary of my plans.

Your Bound and her cubs will be staying here, I presume, she states. "Yeah, I don't want to risk the cubs," I confirm. "Is that okay?" I suddenly check, not having thought before that it might not be fine to leave my Bound predator alone with my apex-predator landlord. Or landlady. Whatever. *As long as they do not bother us, it makes no difference to me whether you are here with them or not*, she tells me, stretching languorously. Right, that gives me a new worry that I might come back only to find the raptorcats in pieces because one of the cubs tried to chase Kalanthia's tail or something. "Just remember, they're cubs, okay?" I ask tentatively, trying to avert that possibility. Kalanthia fixes me with a chiding eye.

Do you think I do not know that, Markus Wolfe? I'm hardly going to hold the curiosity of a cub against them. I hold my hands up in surrender. "Just saying," I reply defensively. "And now I'll go." Marching off smartly towards the river as my first stop, I feel a blush rise in my cheeks. *Told off by a giant leopard—what next?*

Heading into the forest, I venture in a different direction than I've gone before, hoping that this way the pickings will be a bit better. My Stealth Skills get a workout as I try to walk carefully and unnoticeably; there's no reason to invite conflict unnecessarily. The first section is one that I've already partly cleared, so it's only when I've been walking for about an hour that I first see an area that is completely new to me.

I've been heading either along the same level or up the slope a little, so it's not surprising that eventually I clear the tree line and see the mountain looming above me. I pause there for a moment, marveling at its magnificence; you never really understand how *big* mountains are until you're standing at the foot of one.

Then, shaking my head, I turn so I'm heading further into the forest again. It's all very well trying not to go deeper into the valley to avoid meeting strong predators, but heading out of the forest when I want to collect wood is something else. One good thing comes out of me almost leaving the forest, though: I see a tree that was obviously struck by lightning. Why is this good? Because I see an opportunity to save myself work. The tree didn't crack down its length; instead, it looks like it exploded near the base. But I'm not a tree expert, and even the memories I've absorbed from the stones aren't helping me much with this.

The point is that all that's left of the tree is a jagged stump with a hole in the middle. The stump has been further degraded by weather and rot, and it's clear this isn't very recent. It takes a bit of work, but the roots are thoroughly dead and aren't too difficult to break away. Within an hour, I'm left with a large stump, which I barely succeed in getting in my Inventory. Thank goodness for my increased Strength: I'm pretty sure that I wouldn't have been able to lift that at the mere six I started with. Now, why do I want some old tree stump? Because it looks ideal for making the container I'll need to filter wood ashes for making lye for soap. It'll need a bit of work, but there's still plenty of solid wood there that hasn't been eaten by rot yet. If I can get rid of the rot, then shape the remaining wood into a container with a slope at the bottom down to a hole in the center, I can then half-fill it with some fine pebbles I've spotted by the river, then put in bigger pebbles on top, and rocks in above that. All that together should create a good filter for ash and maybe other things if necessary. Much easier than trying to construct a watertight container myself or chopping down a healthy tree and cutting a slab to size.

Heading back into the forest proper, I continue collecting branches of various sizes, letting my Inventory sort them into three different slots according to its own specifications. Given that each branch is different, I suppose I'd better be glad that it doesn't sort each individual piece of wood into a separate slot.

I never really stop for lunch and instead just chew cooked meat as I continue scanning the surroundings, always keeping an eye out for movement beyond the leaves in the wind. This particular area is full of windfall: a whole copse of dead and dying trees with all the detritus of their fallen branches below. I find myself wondering why all the trees in this area are so sick but then push the thought away with a shrug. Again, I'm not a tree expert. Maybe they don't have enough water or there's some sort of disease they've all caught. Trees catch diseases too, don't they?

Walking into the center of the copse, my foot suddenly sinks into the ground up to my knee. I frown. It's not like the time before when there was a narrow hole in the ground: this is more like a bed of leaves. And the ground beneath my foot is sloped, like it gets deeper. My danger sense suddenly yells at me. *What if this is a tra—*

A monster bursts from the leaf cover right in front of me. It's too close to avoid, and I've been bitten before I can even react. I don't think, I just move.

Grabbing my knife, I stab it into the face of the creature that's got me in its mandibles. It's some sort of oversized bug, but I'm not willing to risk dying because I tried to categorize it while in the middle of a fight.

The bug hisses at me and opens its mandibles to back up defensively. It pulls two of its hairy legs in front of its face to protect its numerous eyes. I take the opportunity to grab my mace from where it's hanging loosely across my back.

We stare at each other for a moment, and I wonder whether the creature might actually back up. It's almost my size, but it's clearly an ambush predator and its ambush has failed. Then I feel a creeping weakness and I see my health bar starting to decrease slowly but visibly. *Venom!* I can't risk dragging this out. I have to either finish the fight quickly or run now while I still can. My ego bristles against running from a fight, but I'm more than just my ego, and I'd rather live to run another day than die in a pointless last stand against a too-powerful foe.

The creature decides for me. It lunges at me, its movement lightning quick as its multiple legs propel it forwards. I'm faster than I've ever been, but I doubt I could beat *that*. And if I turn to run, I'll be presenting my vulnerable back to the creature. Better to face it with mace and knife.

Meeting its lunge with a smash of my mace, I briefly stop it in its tracks. It's enough time for me to cast a quick Lay-on-Hands to counteract the venom coursing through my veins with every beat of my heart. Enough time, but only just. I dodge the swipe of one of its legs and swing my mace again. Unfortunately, this time the creature blocks it with another of its innumerable legs and its counterswipe slams into me and knocks me off my feet.

It lunges for me again and sinks its mandibles into my leg, sending another wave of venom into me. My health bar starts dropping more quickly, and I curse even as I cast another Lay-on-Hands, the healing energy fighting against the damage the venom is causing me.

Unable to regain my feet due to the mandibles pinning me in place, I can't help the thought that maybe I should have run away after all.

CHAPTER SIXTY

Nightmare Inducing

Regret isn't helpful right now, so I push it away and use the split seconds I have before it's upon me to instead try to figure out how to stay alive. By the time it lunges at me once more, I have a basic—and risky—plan of action. Here's hoping it's sufficient.

Pulling my arm up to block, I attempt to slip the mace in between its mandibles and trick it into biting down on that, but I'm a fraction too slow. Instead of chewing on wood, its sharp mouth pincers tear into my arm, probably delivering another dose of venom. I curse mentally, but there's no time to waste. My knife held in my other hand, I start stabbing wildly at its face, or the insectile horror that passes for one.

Its carapace is strong, and my first few stabs seem to do nothing. I'm losing the race against time despite my frantic casting of Lay-on-Hands to keep my health up.

Then I hit something soft; I've managed to get one of its eyes. The creature shrieks, the piercing sound at such close range making my ears ring and causing my vision to go fuzzy for just a moment. I keep on stabbing, temporarily blind and deaf as I am, nothing more important to me in that moment.

I feel the creature yank its mandibles out of my arm, their serrated nature causing even more blood to flow. It's trying to back up; I can't let it. I'm running out of mana at a rapid rate and really can't afford to give it even the slightest moment to recoup.

Hoping that its attempts to retreat are because I've hit somewhere vulnerable, I propel myself forward and *grab* the mandible that had previously been stuck in me. With my weight pulling it down, I've temporarily halted it in its tracks. With the energy of a dying man, I stab, stab, stab at its eyes. They pop under my blade, the sensation as disgusting as the fluid that explodes out.

The insectile creature screams again, but I just fight against the pain and disorientation and keep on stabbing.

Just keep stabbing.

Just keep stabbing.

It turns into a mantra, which blocks out all else. The creature tries to throw me off, push me away, but its body is designed to catch and pull in prey, not push it away. Its feeble attempts are no match against a ten in Strength and the power of desperation. Little by little, I pull it down to my level and then beyond, pinning its front to the ground. Now that I have a hard surface to stab against, my piercing strikes gain in power. When it stops moving, I don't realize for a few moments, and I keep just grimly burying my knife into its eyes and, hopefully, what passes for a brain. When I finally notice it hasn't done more than twitch for at least a minute, I feel all the strength leave me in a rush.

My hands release my knife and the mandible involuntarily. I'm out of mana, out of stamina, and almost out of health. There are no numbers on my visible bars, but I can see what little remains of the red bar slowly draining away with the red liquid that's dripping out of my wounds.

My mana bar is already starting to regenerate, however, and I cling onto that thought like the lifeline it is. I fight against the blackness trying to take over my vision until, finally, the blue bar reaches a point that I reckon should mean I can cast another healing spell. As unconsciousness pulls me down into its depths, I trigger a final Lay-on-Hands and tumble down, wondering if I'll ever wake up again.

I hear birdsong as my consciousness swims up to the surface. I'm lying on cold, damp ground, the chill seeping into my body from below. I smell something metallic that I slowly recognize. Blood. Finally, opening my eyes, I hiss as the light lances into them, making my head pound with pain. Slamming my eyes shut, I just breathe and try to think through what happened.

It takes a few moments for my memory of the events immediately before falling into unconsciousness to become clear. Some sort of insectile horror laid a trap, which I walked into like an idiot. I chose to fight instead of run, also like an idiot. Somehow, I managed to survive, which doesn't make me any less of an idiot; it just makes me lucky. Opening my status panel shows just how close to death I got. I've got twenty-five units of mana in the tank, which indicates it's been about twelve minutes since I blacked out. That's also borne out by the fact that I have fourteen units of stamina—it must have been regenerating while I was fighting to keep conscious until I could cast another Lay-on-Hands, and I don't use stamina for my healing spell.

My health, which currently regenerates at one and a half points per five minutes—or three points per ten minutes—is only sitting at *five*. That means I was *two units* away from death at the time my last healing spell finished its work. I have to guess that it cleared out the rest of the venom because otherwise I'd be dead, no question.

I feel weak at the knowledge of simply how close to death I came. If I'd been *seconds* later in killing the thing, if I hadn't managed to keep myself conscious until I was able to cast my Lay-on-Hands, if I had had one more poisoned wound . . . My stomach rises into my mouth, and I turn to one side to empty it onto the dead leaves beside me. After staring at my vomit for a long moment, I violently push myself to my feet and walk a few steps away from the corpse; away from the place where I almost breathed my last. I'm shaking. My skin's clammy.

I'm in shock. Physically as well as mentally. Why it's suddenly hitting me now, I don't know. I've been close to death several times since arriving here. Heck, the wolvezard was at least as close as now and maybe even closer since I really would have died if Kalanthia hadn't given me my only remaining health potion. But all I can do is stare at the little number on my screen that denotes how close I am even now to a stiff breeze being able to kill me. Five. Six. I watch the number change, fortunately in the right direction, indicating that several minutes have passed. In the meantime, my stamina and mana have grown considerably higher. Mana . . .

I feel like a lightning bolt has hit me. Man, I'm an *idiot!* By this point, I have enough in the tank for at least three casts of normal Lay-on-Hands. Why haven't I cast them yet? Putting action to thought, I quickly cast two more healing spells, keeping one back just in case something suddenly happens, like almost stepping on *another* venomous creature, and I need to close wounds or clear venom or something. Twenty units of health later and I'm feeling *considerably* better. My shakiness clears, and I stop feeling so nauseous. Maybe part of the reason for going into shock was because my health was still so critically low? By the time I woke up after the wolvezard, my health had already had the chance to climb a bit more.

My curiosity engaged, I wonder if it's a relative value that matters, so a specific fraction of remaining health, or if everyone goes into shock with only five units of health remaining.

Another question to add to my list; though, this one I might be able to answer once I've added more points to Constitution. Not that I'm keen to experience being *quite* so close to death again . . .

Ruefully, I wonder to myself if I've just gotten a bit overconfident with the relatively easy victories lately. I mean, Bastet and I won against the lizogs without a scratch despite them being foes that could easily have ripped me to shreds. But we only survived because we applied our brains to the task; it only makes it clear how easily I could have died just now because I *didn't*. And what happens to Bastet or Spike if I die? I'm pretty sure that our Bond would just break and they would then be free to go—but this is a sense I get from the Bond rather than true knowledge. Being a feeling more than cold hard fact, it could be wrong. What if my death has some negative effect on them? What if it kills them too? I really hope not, but since I don't know for sure, and it's not exactly the kind of thing I can test, it's something I need to bear in mind when I'm considering risking my life—it may not be just *my* life that I'm risking.

On that note, I don't know if it would have been better or worse to have had Bastet actually there. Of course, having the adult raptorcat would have definitely improved my chances; I might not have gotten quite that close to death. Having Bastet would have meant having the cubs, though, and they would have been far more vulnerable to the creature than I was. If one of them had died while Bastet was fighting on my behalf . . .

And what about Spike? What if I'd led the poor porcupig into a trap after having already Dominated him against his will? I doubt his spike attack would have had much effect on this horror. On the other hand, maybe Bastet or Spike would have recognized the danger before I did; they've probably got much better senses than me and know the area and its denizens a lot better than I do. It's enough to make me wonder whether I really should have come out alone or whether that was just pure overconfidence speaking.

That said, the reasons why I didn't bring them with me still stand. Spike is still a mostly herbivorous prey animal, whose main combat ability is shooting quills out of his backside. Bastet is far better in combat terms but has three little cubs to look after. Then again, bringing the four raptorcats along might be safer than leaving them back at the cave. Well, it would definitely be safer for me; I just have to consider whether it would be safe enough for the cubs too . . .

My frame of mind already better, I'm now able to turn and face the remains of my foe with some equanimity. Despite knowing full well it's dead, it still makes me shiver. It's rather similar to a massive spider, reminding me of Shelob from Lord of the Rings. Only, instead of the normal eight legs, this only has six. And this one doesn't have a sting on its bulbous abdomen. Its legs are hairy and have flopped outwards rather than curling up to its chest in death. Its body, in contrast, is smooth, with an exoskeleton rather similar to the chitinous exterior of a beetle. It's dull in color, a nondescript brown that makes perfect camouflage for where it was hiding under the dead, brown leaves. I don't know how many eyes it had—I made rather a mess of them with my knife, after all—but it had multiple. Probably between six and ten. It has serrated mandibles like an ant, which still shimmer wetly with my blood.

I shiver again. I have a feeling this thing's going to make a star appearance in my nightmares later. The only good thing is that it was clearly worth a *lot* of Energy since I've jumped up ten percent from where I was before. Good thing, too, because there's no way I'm eating whatever passes for a heart in this monstrous thing. *Still* . . . I run my hand over its carapace thoughtfully, then pull out my knife and test the material's strength.

As I'd thought, it's pretty good against my knife. My strongest blow only leaves a slight dent. Checking out my knife, I castigate myself. *If I'd broken my only metal blade just to test out the strength of this bloody thing* . . . Fortunately, the blade is unharmed. Actually, I'm starting to wonder if it's quietly magic in some way. My knife doesn't heat up or light on fire or cause electrical damage to my opponents, but I haven't had to sharpen it yet, and it hasn't shown any sort of wear, no matter that I've used it to chop wood, cut flesh, and break through cartilaginous joints. I'm no knife expert, but my absorbed memories tell me that that's not normal. Anyway, magic or not, I'm grateful.

Turning my mind back to the topic at hand, I decide to keep the spider monster's body. Not its legs—I think seeing those would probably give me a flashback—but the body. And maybe the mandibles. They were pretty nasty on me and might make a decent weapon of some kind. The body, of course, I'm considering trying to turn into armor of some sort. If I can get through the carapace itself to chop it into chunks, I should be able to somehow attach that to a fabric or hide underlayer and then make myself some decent protection. It would be nice to have something between me and all these teeth and claws that doesn't tear apart at the first hit . . . I might have been able to heal all the wounds I've taken so far, but that doesn't mean they don't hurt to begin with.

Chopping the legs off the body isn't that hard—the connections are fairly thin— but having hairy legs and a detached body falling at me is once more nightmare inducing. I didn't like spiders or insects *before* this whole debacle; I sure as hell like them even less now. Finally, I'm able to store the heavy body and head in my Inventory, and I rub my hands together to try to remove the nasty feeling of touching the creature.

About to walk away, I spot where the spider monster came from, and my curiosity is engaged once more. It's not some sort of shallow pit that the creature clearly dug for itself; it seems much deeper than that, a yawning hole in the ground. I check my stats: my health is full thanks to regeneration and regular casting of Lay-on-Hands, and my stamina and mana are full from regeneration. I'm as close to well as I can be. Should I investigate this hole? My curiosity can't be denied. With warring visions of treasure and more spider monsters jumping out to eat me, I creep closer.

CHAPTER SIXTY-ONE

Colony

I step carefully through the leaf litter in front of the gaping hole. My knife and mace are both in my hands, and I'm tense, ready for another monster to come leaping out. Casting a glance around, I frown as I try to piece together what happened in the instant before the spider monster attacked.

Despite my increased Intelligence, the whole thing happened so quickly that my memory of the time isn't at all clear, but there are several clues in the detritus around me. I focus on my memory of the area before I stepped into the trap and compare it to now. Before, the whole area had been an undulating carpet of dead, brown leaves and twigs. Now, there's a gaping hole in the center of the area. Did the spider monster hold a layer of twigs and leaves as a camouflaging screen? It must have—I don't see any other explanation for the changes in environment present here.

I know that there are insects and spiders on Earth that can also set traps, so I suppose it's not out of the realm of possibility that a creature here would develop the same techniques. Maybe spiders or spider analogues are just always the kinds of bastards that would prefer being ambushers and therefore would learn useful tricks to improve their success rate?

Well, this trap has been sprung, and hopefully, there aren't a whole load of other hidden spider monsters around ready to jump out at me. Frankly, I would have been easy pickings while lying there unconscious with only two units of health left, so if they didn't attack me then, I have to guess that they weren't aware of my presence. As long as I don't spring any more traps, I'm cautiously hopeful that I'll leave this area with my life.

Inspection of the area done, I creep closer to the yawning hole in front of me. It's angled down into the ground reasonably steeply: not so steep that I couldn't get out, but it's steep enough that I'd have to use my hands to help me crawl out. For the monster I killed and its six insectile legs, I doubt it was any trouble. Pausing at the edge of where it becomes the hole proper, I take a moment to find out what my senses are telling me and allow my eyes to adjust a little.

It's dark, obviously. The light from the outside illuminates the first few meters of the cave, but not much further thanks to the angle of both the entrance hole and the way it descends. It's earthen, almost as tall as I am, and wide enough for the creature to easily move around. There's little to see, honestly.

However, what does catch my attention is that there's a breeze. Not a breeze that sweeps the surface, although that's there as well, but a breeze that's actively being pulled into the cave. To me, that indicates that the cave isn't actually a cave but a *tunnel*. And that's interesting simply for the question that it poses: if it's a tunnel, where does it go? Hopefully, not to a colony of these spider monster things. I shudder at the thought. It's a question that is almost impossible to resist, beckoning me to climb down the slope and find out. I almost give in to its siren call, actually sitting down on the edge and preparing to bum-shuffle my way down into the depths.

Then my senses return, and I wonder why exactly I thought that could *ever* be a good idea. I'm not equipped for spelunking. Yes, I have a rope—sort of—but I don't have a source of light, decent weaponry, or decent armor against whatever could be hiding in the darkness. Heck, even if I've got some food, I'm not exactly flush with water. Plus, my aim in coming out for today was to gather wood, not go exploring a mysterious cave. I've already cursed at myself once today for being an idiot; no need to keep on proving it.

With regret, I push myself to my feet. Cave diving will have to wait for another day when I'm better prepared. Bringing Bastet with me would probably be a good idea too since her eyesight is likely much better in the dark than mine. And, hopefully, exploring a cave shouldn't pose too much risk to the cubs. Of course, it depends on what we encounter, but with the restricted area of a tunnel, I'd imagine it would be easier for Bastet and me to create a defensive line with them behind us and back out of any trouble.

I do take advantage of my time to collect as much firewood as possible since this kind of wood is perfect for what I need: seasoned and mostly dry. I actually find a few bits of wood that should serve well as arrow shafts too; since they're already dry, they shouldn't warp like green wood can. I even explore the rest of the clearing, half-hoping, half-fearing for a rematch against another of the monsters.

In the end, though, it seems like the one I fought was solitary, as no more of them leap out at me even as I traverse the rest of the copse of dead trees. Just before leaving the area, I mark the cave on my Map for later exploration. I have to hope that nothing too dangerous moves into the open real estate, but there's not much I can do about that now.

By the time the sun is halfway towards the horizon, I've filled four of the five slots that remained open after storing the body and head of the spider monster. I figure I've got enough firewood to be getting on with, so I start making my way back to my home base.

Deciding to do a bit of grinding, I use my Stealth as much as possible, and then when my stamina is getting low, I pause and use Fade until I've topped myself up. I can feel that the two Skills have become easier to use during my practice and reckon I must have gained some Skill levels.

Tempted to check, I instead decide to save all that until tonight. I make my way through the forest almost without incident. In fact, I only end up in two fights, which is an achievement considering I managed to stray into a part of the forest that looked to be hotly contested territory between two rival factions of the same species. How do I know? Lots and lots of markings all over the trees, the acrid stench of urine in multiple places, the half-eaten bodies that I almost stumbled over . . . and the full-scale battle I barely avoided.

The creatures were a weird reptile version of weasels or something. Similar to the things that attacked me in my first days in this world, but sleeker and meaner, if that's possible. They were small, only about as long as my hand, but seriously vicious. Using Fade to half-hide behind a tree, I watched a group of about fifteen tumbling together near my feet tear chunks off each other, claws gouging into flesh, uncaring of the damage they left. They were *ferocious*. Frankly, I feel lucky that Fade was enough to keep me concealed because the frenzied fury these creatures displayed reminded me of nothing less than a pack of piranhas.

Fortunately, they were so distracted by each other that the weatiles just kept tearing each other apart, paying no attention to the wide-eyed human hiding within arm's length of them. One pair tearing at each other in a bloody ball actually tumbled straight over my *foot* but didn't care enough to break away from their fight to find out what it was they rolled over. Slowly, trying not to draw any attention to myself, I shifted backwards until I was as out of the way as possible—I figured there was no point in chancing my luck a second time. By the time the two weatiles had finished with their fight, one was dead, and the other didn't look far from it. Of the fifteen that were fighting at the start, only three survived.

Only pausing to mark their territory, they'd promptly run out back into one of the bushes surrounding us and disappeared with nary a rustle. Silence fell around me, not even the birds daring to give voice to the violence they had just seen, and I stared at the limp bodies newly decorating the small area clear of undergrowth at the foot of the tree where I'd been hiding. The sheer scale of that violence is not something I've seen in this world so far. Why were so many fighting? Food? Territory? Mates? Some other reason? I don't know, but the fact that the survivors didn't even eat any of the corpses indicates it isn't to do with food. Or maybe they're just not cannibals.

Then again, I've long wondered what motivates some of the creatures in this world; the number of times I've been attacked by creatures that were clearly outclassed is surprising. I'd have thought self-preservation would stop the creatures that clearly would only ever win on the off chance from attacking me. Even if I don't have the natural weapons of my enemies, I've almost always been bigger, sometimes significantly, and size *does* matter in a fight. A smaller opponent always needs to have strong advantages to win against a bigger opponent when the size difference is as stark as it sometimes has been in my fights. Even with these weatiles, I avoided the fight because I'm not a masochist—evidence to the contrary notwithstanding— and I was pretty sure that any fight with them would end up with me bitten all over and bloody. That's not to say that I don't think I would have been the survivor; for all their ferocity, if their teeth are only digging in a few centimeters and my knife is piercing their whole bodies, there's an obvious advantage in my favor. Still, I already had one difficult battle before my encounter with them, so I did my utmost to avoid another unnecessary confrontation.

Unfortunately, I didn't succeed in avoiding *all* confrontations.

One of the fights I was in actually happened once I came out of Fade. Some creature from above took advantage of the opportunity to jump at my neck from the branches over my head. That didn't end very well for it. By now my senses are constantly on high alert, and my muscles are ready for action at any moment—I wouldn't have survived the recent spider monstrosity if they hadn't been. I grabbed and stabbed my newest attacker. Relying entirely on surprise and the venomous fangs that it never managed to bury into my flesh, the arm-length lizard didn't stand a chance, the tyranny of size once more proven.

Neither did my other attacker fare very well when it attempted to charge me after I disrupted it eating. The creature looked a little like a triceratops, was only about the size of a small rhino, and had a single horn. For a second time in the same day, I was actually outclassed in terms of mass. Not in weapons, though. And I had a bit of luck. It had a fast charge, but I managed to dodge, and when it hit the tree behind me, it managed to stun itself. A few stabs into its body and a chance strike to its heart later, and another one bit the dust. I filled my last slot with its corpse, wondering if the bone protrusion that protected the top of its neck might come in handy later.

One interesting thing I found out from the second encounter was a feature of Fade: I can't use it if my target is fixated on me. I tried to activate it as soon as the mini triceratops saw me, but no luck. It makes me wonder whether I'd have been able to activate the Skill if I'd broken its line of sight, but it's too late now to test. I also wonder why it succeeded when I tested it with Kalanthia—we'd been talking at the moment when I activated the Skill, yet it did actually work. Was it because she wasn't paying me enough attention at the moment of activation? Or because she wasn't paying me *hostile* attention? Just one more question to add to the list.

By the time I get back home, the sun is almost touching the horizon. I'm tired and want nothing more than to go straight to bed. Before I can do that, though, I need to get rid of all the blood and muck that's ended up on me. Or do what I can to clean up, at least. The river water isn't great for cleaning, but it does something, and I sigh as my hair finally loses that matted feel. It's wet and drips down my neck, but that will dry soon enough. I take the opportunity to fill the water containers in my Inventory—I've been thirsty since I finished my canteen earlier.

As I walk up the hill, anticipation wars with trepidation. *What if something went wrong while I was out? What if Trouble lived up to his name and got too close to the burning embers of my fire? What if a giant bird came along and snatched one of the cubs before either of the adults could do anything about it?* Unlikely, perhaps, but considering the size of the bird that attacked me on my first day here, I'm not putting anything past this world.

Bastet and the cubs aren't outside. Telling myself that doesn't mean anything, I step into the cave. Pausing at the entrance, I can't help but smile as I see the sight inside. From what I can make out by counting heads and paws, all three of the raptorcats are snuggled against Lathani, who is in turn snuggled into the fluffy tail of her mother. Kalanthia is lying down with her head on her paws, the half-circle of her body meaning she's looking towards the cub pile with half-open eyes. I notice Bastet last, although she's actually the closest, lying just inside the entrance as a guard. She sends waves of contentment and reassurance at me.

Maybe I didn't need to worry after all.

CHAPTER SIXTY-TWO

Baked Cub

The fire crackles cheerfully as I sit next to it, the tree stump I collected yesterday in front of me and a somewhat sharp flint stone in my hand. Within eyesight are the four cubs, happily playing together. I'm keeping an eye to make sure they don't come anywhere near my fire, and Bastet is sitting on their other side, making sure they don't suddenly decide to go romping off towards the forest. It's a strategy that's been working out pretty well since Kalanthia left to go hunting.

Speaking of, the raptorcats are most of the way through their last lizog corpse, and raw meat shouldn't sit around for too long anyway; this corpse has already been sitting out for more than a day. The mini triceratops will keep them going a bit longer, but with Bastet's appetite added into the mix, my meat supply will only feed us all for another couple of days. *I need to go hunting tomorrow*, I decide. A smile stretches my lips as I remember reading the messages last night. In addition to gaining a point in Willpower—I guess because of the way I pushed past my physical limits during the fight with the spider monster—I also got a rank-up message about Fade:

Congratulations!
You have advanced a Skill past Beginner. Fade is now Novice 1 and has limited efficacy while you are moving slowly.

Close message? Y / N

It's my second Skill to properly rank up, and the first that I've leveled all the way from Beginner one, since Lay-on-Hands started at Beginner nine. Fade increased through the ranks quickly up to Beginner nine thanks to my practically constant use of it, but it was hovering at that level for a good few days; I was wondering if there was a problem or something. Turns out that no, there wasn't—I just needed to use it slightly differently, I think. I reckon that it ranked up yesterday when I moved while still under Fade's influence. I was worried that moving like that would break the effect, but perhaps my intent to stay concealed was strong enough that it enabled the Skill to advance. Certainly, it seems too close to be a coincidence that I moved while using Fade and now have an advanced effect that allows me to move slowly while using Fade. Add that to the way Lay-on-Hands advanced and I reckon there's a pattern developing.

Knowing that Fade is now going to work even when I'm moving gives me a greater sense of courage. I mean, Stealth is good, but Stealth *and* Fade? Together that should make even moving through dangerous territory safer. The two Skills will be even more invaluable when I have a ranged weapon, and today's work is a step closer to that.

My pots need to be fired for at least twenty-four hours; forty-eight would be better, but I do need to sleep. I've propped my pottery on stones at the bottom of the pit with branches below, around, and above them. Lighting the fire, I actually send a little prayer to whoever is listening that not too many pieces will crack. I *have* made more pieces than I really need, but I haven't bothered to double up on everything—I didn't have the time or patience to do that.

While I need to keep an eye on the fire to make sure it continues burning steadily, that doesn't consume much of my time since I've already collected the firewood. I'm taking advantage of the rest of the unused time to carve the wood I'm going to need for the filtering container and then later the soap mold. I'm using a sharp rock to dig out the rotten bits of the stump to begin with. I've already used it to chop the trailing roots off its bottom, so I have a roughly level base to start with. I was relieved to find solid wood at the base, as I was a little worried it would be rotten through. It's not exciting work, but after my near-death scare yesterday, I'm not against taking a little time to do some calm and boring manual labor.

By the time the sun is once more falling towards the horizon and Kalanthia has returned, I have several items I'm pleased with. The soap mold is *very* rough, but it will do for creating a bar of soap. I hope so, at least. The tree stump has also been transformed into a round basin-like creation with a hole in the center of the bottom and slopes leading down. I've tested with a little bit of water, and wherever I put it in the "bowl," it drips towards the hole and comes out.

At first, the hole wasn't the lowest point underneath the tree stump, so it was dripping along the underside of the container and then dripping off a point where I had chopped away a root. I've since pounded away at the underside and solved that issue. Now, water drips through the hole and drops directly onto the ground underneath. Perfect. It means that the base of the stump is a bit angled, so it rolls a bit and lists to one side when I place it on the ground. Never mind—I was going to need to prop it up somehow for it to drop into my container anyway. In short, it's rough, but if it works, that's all I need. And I've finally been able to create something that I've needed for a *long* time. Armor. Well, the makings of armor, at least. No shining steel mail worthy of a knight is this—I wish, but I don't have the materials, tools, or time to create something like that. No, this is a lot more rough and ready but quite satisfying, and not only because I now have something more to protect me than my jeans and office shirts. The creature that tried to kill me yesterday has proven to be a bit of a goldmine in terms of materials.

While the cubs all snoozed with Bastet as their guardian, I took myself down to the river and butchered the corpse. Despite needing meat, I decided not to keep any of the spider monster's flesh: it just smelled *nasty*. I don't know if it's because of the venom the spider had or some other reason, but I didn't want to risk it being harmful to either my allies or to me. Having succeeded in getting the carapace off the body by using my knife in softer spots, I then proceeded to use a combination of sharp rocks and my knife to break and cut the chitin into smaller pieces. Back at the fire, I then managed through sheer determined effort to bore a number of holes in the chitin pieces. I considered using bark fiber to string them together but decided to wait until I've got some sinew cord instead; bark fiber will be far too easily sliced through by the first attack that hits it. Sinew is significantly stronger. Of course, I'd rather have some metal wire or nylon thread, but unfortunately, those were not things I thought of bringing with me.

I stretch my tired fingers and roll my tight shoulders. I've really put my hands through the wringer today. It's actually crazy how much pain such simple tasks can cause. My hands hurt from strain and the rub of stone against skin, my wrists hurt from repeated impacts, my arms hurt from repeated activity, and the same goes for my shoulders. Then there's the space between my shoulder blades and my back, which both hurt from tension over time, my legs, which hurt from sitting in a single position on the floor, my eyes, which hurt from screwing them up against the sun, the skin on my face, which hurts from frowning when things were harder than I thought . . . In fact, I think the only part of me that *doesn't* hurt is my feet. And all that from just doing some risk-free crafting? *Surely I must have gained a point in Constitution?* I go into my message box to check and grin when I see a new notification waiting for me.

<table><tr><td>Congratulations!
You have worked hard on your Dexterity and have earned a point. Would you like to apply this to your status?</td></tr><tr><td>Y / N</td></tr></table>

It isn't a point to Constitution, but Dexterity needs a bit of a boost, so I take it. Not having killed anything today, that wipes out all the progress I've made with my daily absorption, but I don't care. It makes all the pain worth it when I see those little numbers going up, knowing each one is a qualitative improvement on my capacity to do different tasks. And since my next job will be to make some more arrowheads, any increase in Dexterity is more than welcome.

Not feeling up to struggling with them today, I decide to inspect my sinew. Now that I need it for my armor as well as my bow, the task has moved up in priority. Making sure that none of the cubs looks like they're currently contemplating jumping into the fire, I quickly pop into the cave to check out my drying rack. The sinew is actually coming along very well, and I reckon that some of the pieces are actually ready for pounding. Grabbing the driest strands, I head back outside.

"Trouble, no!" I shout as that wretched cub prepares to poke the fire with a paw. At my cry, he jumps back and tries to look innocent. "Who, me?" he seems to ask with his limpid brown eyes and offended bearing. I glare at him. "If you touch the fire, we're going to be eating baked cub for dinner, since that's what you'll become," I warn.

He tosses his head as if to say that he has no idea what I'm talking about, but he's going to be off now to play with his sisters because that's what he was planning to do all along. And yes, my Animal Empathy Skill has been improving by leaps and bounds since taking in the four raptorcats. I can't help but have a soft spot for Trouble despite the stress he causes me; he's adventurous and curious, traits that will stand him in good stead for life—if they don't kill him first. Still, I think that Stormcloud—or "Storm" as I keep calling her—is my favorite. Her stubborn, direct nature generally helps her succeed in what she sets out to do. It's all too familiar . . . If she gets an idea in her head that goes counter to what I want her to do, it's a pain, but generally, it's possible to negotiate with her. Where Storm goes, Ninja tends to follow, so it's a bit of a two-for-one deal with them. Generally, it will be Storm who starts something, or it's her interest in an object that will arouse Ninja's curiosity. Trouble is sometimes interested by something that both his sisters want to have, but his attention is a lot less focused, and it doesn't take much to distract him onto something else. It's interesting watching the interactions of the three cubs, and I'm looking forward to seeing them grow up and develop.

My break over, I turn my attention to the sinew I've brought out. Pulling out a handful of rocks from my Inventory, I look through them carefully to choose one that's appropriate for the task. Most of the rocks I pulled out are immediately discarded—I can't have anything that's got sharp edges for fear of compromising the integrity of the sinew strands. However, anything that's too small is also dismissed, as I need to be able to get a decent grip without risking hitting my fingers too many times—been there, done that.

Eventually, I find a rock that's a bit bigger than my hand and mostly smooth. I just make sure that I've turned the slightly rough bit so that it's not going to hit the sinew. Next, I pull out a flat piece of rock I've also stored away for later use. Preparations complete, I start pounding at the sinew, watching to see the result.

When the dry material starts to fray and the ends of strands appear where I started pounding, I smile. While I've never actually done this before, my memories are clear that this is a sign the sinew is ready to be processed, and I set to work with renewed energy. Once I've got the sinew strands separated, I'll be able to either put them aside for use in arrow making or braid them together to make a sinew cord for my armor and a bowstring. I'm starting to get into a rhythm of pounding the sinew and then teasing out the strands, pounding and teasing, pounding and teasing, when there's a loud bang that makes me half jump out of my skin.

CHAPTER SIXTY-THREE

Tough and Chewy

When I realize the loud noise was just a pot exploding, I grimace. One item bites the dust. Let's hope there's not too many of those. It sure shows how keyed up I am that a noise the equivalent of a car backfiring is enough to almost give me a heart attack. Mind you, at least I'm not the only one shocked: all five of the felines—or whatever they are—have also leaped to their feet and are either staring at the source of the noise (the cubs) or looking around suspiciously for any danger (the adults). When they realize that there is no danger and it's just my strange hot thing that's caused the issue, they look at me with disgruntlement.

"Sorry," I apologize, feeling embarrassed for some reason. "False alarm." We all settle back into the relaxed poses we were in previously. The cubs are tussling over something I can't see from this angle, and the adults are enjoying the last of the sun. At least, that's what they were doing until my pot exploding put them on full alert.

I continue my processing of the sinew, pleased with its condition. I should be able to make a decent bowstring with the longer bits and use the shorter bits to attach feathers and arrowheads to arrows. I'll need a lot more of both, but this is only about a third of the sinew I have. Plus, I have other dead things I haven't dismembered yet, which might have more. All supplies considered, I should be able to complete my armor fairly soon too.

Actually, on the subject of carcasses . . . Tucking away the sinew I've processed so far and returning the pieces that are not quite dry enough yet to pound, I go over to the lizog corpses that are sitting in a shady spot not far from the cave. I wrinkle my nose as I get close—almost two-day-old corpses smell pretty rank. The raptorcats have done a number on the bodies, but they've mostly torn at the meaty bits on the body and haunches, leaving the tendons reasonably intact. I doubt that's a coincidence; tendon is tough and chewy, not the kind of meat most carnivores would beeline for if they had the choice.

Figuring that I might as well use my time wisely, I slice away the tendons from each lizog corpse, then pull out a couple of other bodies to process. This includes the mini triceratops, which has surprisingly short ones considering its size. Maybe it's because it didn't seem particularly flexible? Processing the bodies into raw meat and other constituent parts manages to clear up my Inventory a fair amount. Fortunately, several types of meat seem to stack; carnivores seem to be one accepted category, as do pure herbivores. It's the omnivores that seem to cause an issue, often needing separate slots even from other omnivores. Why? I don't know, though I would hazard a guess that the nutrients in the meat are sufficiently different. By the time I'm done with all my butchering, I desperately need a bath and the sun is once more near to touching the horizon. It's amazing how quickly the days go despite how much longer they are than the days on Earth. Perhaps it's partly because once the sun goes down, I go to bed, whereas at home I would stay up several hours after the sun set. Here, where that requires me to use more fuel for light and then makes me too tired to wake up with the sun the next day, it's a bad idea all round. My night is a bit disturbed. Although I sleep, I wake up the next morning feeling barely rested and like I've been running all night in my dreams. Which, considering what I've been doing recently in real life, I probably *was* doing in my sleep.

After a quick breakfast of meat and potato replacement, the taste of which is definitely getting old, I head into the forest with Bastet and the cubs. Although I considered leaving the three babies behind, I don't feel comfortable asking Kalanthia to look after them—or asking Bastet to leave the remaining members of her pack with the creature who killed the rest of them. I mean, Bastet might not be bothered, but I'm kind of bothered on her behalf, illogical as that might seem. All I can hope is that the two of us working together can keep the cubs safe; I think that going out to hunt without my most combat-capable Bound accompanying me would be the height of stupidity, especially after the spider monster yesterday. Though, I have to admit that I feel a bit guilty about not spending much time with Spike recently. I think he's finding it difficult to be around the predatory raptorcats, particularly Bastet. Certainly, he's been spending most of his time recently foraging or hiding near the samova bean plants, but I'm not sure what to do about that. I guess he'll adapt to them being around. I've tried to reassure him with words, but either he hasn't fully understood them, or he doesn't believe them.

So, the cubs are with us, slung once more across my chest. There may be better ways of carrying them, but I'm reluctant to put them on my back, as ambush predators tend to target from behind. At least on my front I can see the attack coming and do my best to avoid or deflect it. As long as they don't wriggle too much, it's okay.

When I have my armor finished, I may have to rethink the arrangements, but I'll cross that bridge when I come to it.

I'm actually a little excited to go hunting with Bastet by my side and have the natural killing machine, which so terrified me when I was the pack's prey, on my team now, terrifying my enemies instead. We walk through the forest carefully. I activate both Fade and Stealth where possible, but Fade is of limited effectiveness when I'm not walking at a snail's pace. Plus, I reckon the wriggling cubs on my chest make it more difficult for me to fade into the background. For all that, we're not attacked. The forest is actually pretty quiet. Perhaps it's Bastet's presence that is making the local fauna hide since I still see plenty of evidence of the animals' passage.

Eventually, we land on some tracks that raise Bastet's interest. She sends me a wave of emotion that I can only identify as anticipation-focus-thoughtfulness. Along with the feeling, she sends a picture of a small herd of . . . something. Honestly, I have no point of reference for them. I'd say they are like ostriches, except that they don't have any wings and they have a long tail, which counterbalances their long neck. Actually, perhaps they're a bit of a mix between an ostrich and a diplodocus, though their necks are nowhere near as long as the prehistoric dinosaur's was supposed to be. Along with the image comes a sense of warning—just like the ostriches of my home world, these creatures can also pack a hefty kick, or a slam with their tails and necks. If I had my bow, I'd feel a lot better about picking a few off; as I don't, I'm going to have to use a bit more strategy.

Following the tracks, I pay more attention to Stealth and notice that Bastet seems to have something similar by the very fact that I *don't* notice her for extended periods of time. She seems to come and go from my awareness, though not if I touch the Bond.

I'm briefly distracted by the realization, though it's almost self-evident, that if the holder of the Bond couldn't find their Bound when they were in Stealth or invisible—if there is such a thing—it wouldn't be great. By the time we start catching up to the herd, or flock, or whatever the correct collective noun would be for strange ostrich–diplodocus crossbreeds, I can actually hear them. They're making an odd honking noise with clucks and purrs interspersed. It's the first time I've heard a group of animals here so clearly communicating and doing so audibly. Maybe that's because most of the time I've spent near groups of animals, they've been hunting me. And I haven't really encountered many groups of prey animals. Not up close, anyway.

Once more, I'm not keen on actively choosing to enter a fight with the cubs strapped to me; although they're in the most defensible position there, I'd rather not *have* to defend them, and they definitely reduce my ability to throw myself around since I really don't want to fall on them and, you know, flatten them. It's a risk to leave them on their own too, but there are no great choices here. Considering the possibility of stampeding ostridocuses, I figure that the ground is not the safest place and once more strap them up in the tree. I try to use my shirt to create a little nest and cross my fingers that the cubs won't find a way to either wriggle out of it or tear it to pieces in the few minutes I'll be gone. Frankly, with Trouble there, anything could happen.

Cubs tucked away and out of trouble—*no, Trouble, that's not an invitation*—Bastet and I decide on our strategy. It's not complicated. We don't have the resources for complicated. If I could, I'd put a few traps on one side of the clearing and chase them all towards them but as it is . . . Well, something to think about later. Traps could seriously reduce the amount of time I have to spend hunting if I can find the right places to put them. Plus, the extra Energy gain would be very useful—assuming they give me Energy when they make a kill, something that I'm still not completely certain about. Anyway, no traps and no time to go and set them up, so our strategy is simple.

I enact the first bit by pulling rocks from my pockets, which I had just moved there from my Inventory, and throwing them at the closest ostridocuses. I'm aiming to distract, frighten, and, hopefully, injure some of the herd. I seem to succeed in at least the first two aims as the herd goes into a tizzy. They don't seem to know what to do with flying rocks, and the closest herd members start running around aimlessly in the small area between their herdmates. The further ones look over, visibly disturbed, but don't actually doing anything yet. That will soon change.

Bastet leaps in, a whirling tornado of death and injury, and she puts her claws and teeth to good use. She slashes at one neck on the way to grabbing and biting another, then leaps at a third just as she avoids the kicks and swipes that are heading her way. When I'm confident I won't hit her, I throw rocks at the ostridocuses, doing my best to keep them off-balance and prevent uninjured members from going to the defense of the injured ones. Leaping out of the fray, Bastet engages her Stealth—or whatever her version is called—and then jumps back in from a different angle, attacking several more previously uninjured ostridocuses. I keep throwing rocks and land some lucky blows, my aim improving with practice. I can definitely notice the difference from my improved Dexterity: even in comparison to the last time I threw rocks, my accuracy is much better, as is my judgement of distance. *Wait, is that last linked to Dexterity or Constitution?*

A battle-honk from the fray ahead of me draws me back to the moment. I can ponder those kinds of questions when my Bound is not in the middle of an attack. It doesn't take much more to break the nerve of the ostridocuses. The combined attacks of flying rocks of death and a raptorcat tearing at them tooth and claw are too much for the herbivorous birds to cope with. The fear communicates itself throughout the herd and even those members that were too far away from the action to really realize what was going on turn tail and run.

With an oddly swaying, though speedy, gait, the ostridocuses disappear into the trees as quickly as possible. *Now to clear up as many of the injured survivors as possible.* Together, we make quick work of the majority of the limping and staggering ostridocuses that were the victims of our attack. A couple were only lightly injured and manage to follow the rest of the herd with little trouble, but by the time the clearing falls silent, there are bodies all around.

Before starting the processing, I quickly head back to the tree with the cubs tucked into its junctions of branches. My heart is in my mouth as everything that could have gone wrong plays like a movie in my head. We were only away for a short time, perhaps fifteen to twenty minutes, but in this world where minutes or even *seconds* can be the deciding factor, I can't help but worry.

CHAPTER SIXTY-FOUR

Man, I've Got an Axe

areful. Caaareful, I say to myself as I tip the resin bowl. It's hot, so I'd rather not spill it on my hand, but I do need to transfer the liquid so I can filter it. Right now, it's full of detritus, which won't do anything to improve the consistency of my pitch. Drop by drop, the molten resin drips from the hole in the side of my bowl into another container. Fortunately, the resin-filter bowl was not one of the ones that exploded.

Actually, for my first time firing pottery, and in a rough-and-ready ground pit at that, a fifty percent success rate is not that bad. I've ended up with one big pot that's good enough for collecting water, two medium pots, one small pot, the resin-filtering bowl, and a plate. Unfortunately, the other crockery pieces I made were victims of the fire, including a couple of miscellaneous pots and the specially shaped pot I made for charring the bark fiber. That was the one that hurt the most to lose, but I've managed to get the job done with one of the medium pots instead.

As my bowl of resin runs dry, I tip out the bits of wood and bark and dead insects that have accumulated, and then put in a few more resin chunks and place the bowl back into my fireplace to soften them again. The pot with the filtered resin goes near the fire so that it stays liquid. Sitting back on my heels, I think about my next steps. I'm dealing with the resin now; I'll soon be adding the bark-fiber charcoal. *Actually, maybe I should grind it up while I'm waiting for the next batch of resin to soften.* I go outside to grab the pot from where it's still near the big fire since I used some of the still-burning coals to char the fiber. The cubs are playing together, and I pause to watch them for a few moments. Spotting Ninja hiding in the bushes, waiting to ambush her siblings and Lathani, I shake my head a little. For once, it wasn't Trouble who almost gave me a heart attack yesterday—it was Ninja. Upon getting back to the tree where I hid the cubs, I only found two up in the nest.

Fortunately, Ninja hadn't gone far, and, my heart hammering, I found her in a bush nearby when she mewed plaintively. I reckon she must have either fallen out or been pushed accidentally; she certainly wouldn't have chosen to go exploring the way Trouble no doubt would have. Not on her own, at least.

All three cubs retrieved, I returned to Bastet and our bounty. Turns out we'd managed to take down *eight* ostridocuses. Three had been killed before the herd fled: two from neck wounds that bled out quickly and one from a crushed skull caused by a lucky rock throw. Lucky for us, that is, not for the ostridocus. The others had all been sufficiently slowed by our attacks to give us enough time to take them down after. Either way, since the creatures stood as tall as my shoulder, it's a good bit of meat that I've now got packed in my Inventory—it's fortunate that the carcasses stack—and a good bit of Energy too, frankly. I'm back up to above halfway towards the next level. How long that will last, we'll see. Plus, since they had such long legs, they also yielded a fair bit of sinew, which is good news considering everything I'll need that resource for.

Food supply sorted for now, I'm back to my crafting. Well, survival crafting, at least—none of what I've made so far would be considered anything but shoddy work by an even remotely skilled craftsman, after all. Reminded that I want to do more today than just gaze fondly at cute cubs tumbling together—although I could do that all day, honestly—I grab the charred bark fiber and return indoors to keep an eye on my resin.

After grinding up the charcoal into a fine powder, which I have to be careful not to let blow away, I'm soon able to filter the next batch of resin. With the third, and final, batch on to melt, I find myself a little at a loose end. It's not that I don't have anything else to do—I just don't have anything that will take as little time as the resin will to melt, and I don't want to get distracted by something else or have to stop something halfway. In the end, I just pull out my never-ending bark-fiber rope and keep twisting it. I'll never have enough cord, and it's the kind of thing I can just pick up and drop whenever I need to. After filtering the resin, I'm finally ready to move onto the next step. Gently adding the black dust a pinch at a time, I blend the charcoal and resin together with a clean stick until the consistency is exactly what my "memories" tell me is correct for a decent batch of pitch. Staring at the black gold, I'm frankly flabbergasted at how much effort had to go into making something so simple. On paper, that is. And maybe simple for people who start out with the right equipment, but like everything, when you don't even have the right tools, it's an upward battle.

Anyway, I have it now. Excitement rising, I take the container of pitch outside into the light so I can see it more clearly. Along with the sticky pitch, I take the axe blade and axe haft, which have just been sitting in my cave, moldering away. Not literally, thankfully. Realizing I forgot the shirt I'd decided to sacrifice to the cause, I hop back up and grab it before returning outside.

"Don't touch that!" I shout, my heart rising into my mouth as I see Lathani with her paw hovering over the pitch. She looks up at me and freezes, her eyes as innocent as if her paw was not literally almost covered in sticky black stuff. *What is with these cubs and trying to touch things they shouldn't?* My nerves calming down, I warn her even as I pull the pot away. "If you touch that, you'll never get it out of your fur. It'll be stuck to you forever."

I'm not sure if she believes me, but she doesn't pursue the matter, so that's a relief. Bastet keeps the other cubs under control with a simple grunt so, fortunately, nothing serious happens.

It takes a little bit of wrangling, but finally, it's done. My masterpiece is made. I hold the axe above my head and shout a war cry to the skies. I'd like to think that it shakes the crowns of the surrounding trees and strikes fear into the hearts of my enemies. If Bastet's unimpressed look is anything to judge by, though, I'm more Simba's "I Can't Wait to Be King" than Mufasa.

Bringing my new axe down, I stare at my creation, prouder of my efforts than any father could be of his newborn child. From going through innumerable chunks of flint, to struggling to bore through the wood, to the whole military operation that has been creating the pitch, not to mention the blisters on my fingers from twisting together bark fiber, this axe has been nothing but trouble.

But now, it sits there gleaming in the sun, the axe blade sitting snugly in the hole I made in the wooden haft, held in place by sticky pitch and rope wrapped around it on either side of the handle. It had better be worth all the pain and suffering that I put into its creation. If the axe blade tears free of the handle the first time it gets embedded in a tree, I think I might cry. Or scream and throw it so far that I'll never find it again. Which wouldn't be a good idea, as then I'd have to put in all the effort again.

Anyway, it needs time to cool and set in place, so, like I'm carrying the newborn baby I compared it to earlier, I lift the axe and place it in my alcove out of the way of clumsy cubs. At least, it *should* be out of their way, but with Trouble there . . .

Okay, what next? I'd like to make my armor so I have some more protection, but I'm not ready to make sinew cord yet. Which also precludes me from making my bow. So . . . that makes soapmaking the next on my list. Right. I've got my filtering container and plenty of ashes, but I don't have the filtering material yet. I also need to render some fat. *Hmm . . .*

Deciding to multitask, I take one of the two medium-sized pots that survived the firing and dump in some chunks of fatty meat. Then I half-fill it with water from the other pot, which I filled at the river this morning, and put it into my fireplace so that it's nestled into the fire itself. That takes more maneuvering than I'd prefer—I think I made the mouth of my fireplace a little small—but I succeed in the end. I may need to rethink my cooking design, but that's for later when I really get tired of my pots being almost too big for it.

Leaving the pot to start heating up and cooking the meat, I check that the converted tree stump is in my Inventory. It is. Noticing that my big pot is almost out of water, I decide I might as well kill two birds with one stone and grab it. I'm running out of Inventory space again, but I've got a couple of spaces free. Hopefully, I'll gain some more room when I level up, but who knows when *that* will be. I consider bringing Bastet with me, remembering what happened the last time I went out alone and the resolution I made then. *Perhaps I should . . . but they look so happy here.* The cubs are having fun, Bastet is relaxing, and I'm not going that far. *Surely, if anything does attack me, I should be able to handle it?*

Wavering for a long moment, I feel at war with myself. In the end, my intrinsically

British desire not to impose wins out, bolstered by my analysis of probability based on past experience. I decide to go alone. It should be fine, right? I'm just going down to the river and then a little bit along it, after all. Something I've done many times before absolutely fine. Well, okay, not absolutely fine, but without significant, unhealable injury, anyway. I'll bother them next time.

Letting Bastet and Kalanthia know that I'm heading out but plan to be back long before nightfall, I walk down the slope, cheerfully whistling. I'm actually feeling good: I've just managed to finish a task that I've been working on since practically the day I arrived in this world. It may have been a good three weeks, but I've *finally* succeeded.

Getting closer to the stream, I focus and make myself get more serious—I've had far too many close shaves in this forest to take it even remotely lightly. What's it going to be today? Something falling on my neck from above? Trapping my leg from below? Leaping at my back or my front? *Man, I've got an* axe. *Let them come.* Not that I actually have the axe with me, but whatever. Let them come anyway and see what I'm made of.

Perhaps I've underestimated just how elated this accomplishment makes me feel. *Come on, man,* I tell myself. *It's just an* axe. But even my attempts to pour cold water on my own feelings don't work. Giving up, I just let the smile spread across my face and the bounce in my step continue, despite how it negatively impacts Stealth and Fade.

After filling my big pot, I walk along the river, as that's where I'm going to find what I need. Keeping a wary eye out, I'm thankfully not attacked as I approach the bed of fine pebbles that are going to be the bottom layer of my filter. I'd prefer to have sand, but I haven't spotted any of that yet.

After kneeling down, I pull the former tree stump out of my Inventory and set it down beside me. Then, grabbing a couple of handfuls, I start filling the bottom of the container with pebbles, aiming to fill the sloped part and a little more besides. I'm about halfway to that goal when I hear a loud splash, just as a barely registered hint of movement makes me flinch backwards.

My quick reactions are all that stop the toothed mouth from snapping shut on my face. Sharp teeth instead clack together a bare inch away from my nose. For a moment, both of us are stunned, looking at each other without moving. As I get a glimpse of my attacker, I groan mentally. *Aw man, I forgot* these *were dinosaur adjacent. Damn you, Murphy.*

CHAPTER SIXTY-FIVE

Buckeroo

'm not in the best of positions: I'm leaning back on my hands with a crocodile look-alike half on top of me. Its head is damn *heavy*, but I've got the advantage on land. Remembering a nature program I saw at home, and hoping that this analogue's physiology is at least similar, I clamp my arm around its mouth and hold its head to me firmly.

The crocodile writhes, but it appears that it's no more able to open its jaws with me putting pressure on them than an Earth crocodile would be. I'd seen on the program that crocodiles have the strongest bite pressure ever measured, but for all their power when closing their jaws, they have extremely weak opening muscles. That's being proven as I exert far more strength to keep my attacker from wriggling out of my grip than I do in just keeping its mouth closed.

For a moment I'm very tempted to try Dominating it—if Bastet was a good catch, this crocodile would be even better. But I dismiss the thought half-formed. It's too risky. There's that ten second vulnerability if I fail, which in this situation would mean my death. If I can injure it so much that the risk is reduced, maybe I'll consider it later. I'm not going to aim for it, though.

Wrestling with the muscular body that's got to be at least as long as me, I manage to flip us so I'm lying on the crocodile, which is pinned on its back. Still holding its mouth shut with one hand while riding the crocodile's belly, I grab my knife from my belt and slam it into the reptile's throat. At least, I try to.

What *actually* happens is that the knife is deflected, and I almost lose my grip on my blade, even headbutting the crocodile on the underside of its jaw in a stunning display of grace. While shaking my head in confusion, momentarily stunned, the renewed powerful writhing of the creature below me almost knocks me off completely.

I manage to keep my seat from luck more than skill, even as its foreclaws tear at me. Fortunately, tucked into its armpits as my knees are, I'm actually in a reasonably secure position: out of reach of its tail and back claws and also able to pin it down fairly well. Without my increase in Strength, I'd have had no chance; with it, I'm managing—just.

But just managing is not enough. I need to either kill this thing or escape. If even its underside is so armored that my knife can't get through, I need a different strategy.

A thought occurs, and I squeeze my eyes shut and gulp, fear running through me like a live current. If I do this right, I have a chance. If I do it wrong . . .

But do I have any choice? Right now, it's a stalemate, and the crocodile probably has more stamina than me.

I breathe deeply, trying to summon up my courage to go through with my plan. Then, in one quick movement, I shift my weight off the crocodile and onto my feet, grabbing one of the crocodile's short front legs and heaving it over. Aided by its own muscular movements, the crocodile flips onto its belly, and I quickly seat myself again on its back, tucked behind its front legs. It writhes again and twists its body almost in half as it attempts to snap at me. Fortunately, in this position I'm out of range of its jaws. That doesn't mean I'm home safe as I'm rather riding the tiger at this point. Or, at least, riding the crocodile. My targets—and only hope—are now within range, but I have no chance of getting at them right now since I'm gripping on with dear life to try to avoid being thrown off from my insecure position. I have a death grip on both the crocodile and my knife, holding on grimly as the crocodile slowly tires itself out.

I see my stamina bar emptying itself little by little, and I start praying to anyone who can hear that the crocodile will exhaust itself before the bar runs out. For a while, I start fearing the worst and try to make backup plans of how I will escape if my stamina drops to less than ten percent. Finally, though, the crocodile's convulsive movements start to slow. I breathe a silent sigh of relief but continue clinging on even as the creature's efforts to throw me off reduce in strength.

Eventually, the crocodile stops writhing. I've already started to shift a little, moving my weight more forwards, and change the grip on my knife. I've got no chance of killing this monster in a single stroke, so I'm going to have to do my best to at least disable it so I can get away. Leaning up, I'm poised to strike when it suddenly shifts, and I teeter on the edge of losing my balance. Worried that it's recovered enough to start another round of exhausting bucking, I stab wildly at my target. Luck, or my increased Dexterity, actually means that I hit the crocodile's eye despite the poor position. My knife plunges straight into the golden slit-pupil orb, and the crocodile lets out a roar of pain, the first noise it's made so far. Its movements become frenzied once more, but I know that I don't have the stamina to hold on for another round of writhing, so I just steady myself as much as I can and desperately aim for its other eye.

My first two attempts fail, and I'm almost sobbing as I try once more, knowing that I haven't got a chance of surviving without blinding the creature. I *have* to succeed, even when my every movement feels like leaden weights are attached to my limbs. Third time's the charm, apparently, as once more I manage to pierce and twist my knife in the gelatinous ball that is this dinosaur's eye.

It roars again and throws up its head. The abrupt action forces the knife blade upwards; since I refuse to let go of the handle, I'm pushed up with it. Not as well-secured on the crocodile's back as I had been, I'm dislodged enough that the next frenzied twist sends me falling off completely.

Scrambling to my hands and knees, I crawl as quickly as I can away from the creature—I don't even dare spend the time to push myself to my feet until I'm out of direct range of those jaws.

Clambering finally to my feet, I don't see the tail coming at me until it's too late to dodge completely. I throw myself out of the way and shield my head with my arm.

The tail smashes into my arm with a loud crack, its momentum barely slowed. I would have died then and there if it hadn't also been slightly deflected and slammed into the ground a hair's breadth from my head.

Shaking terribly, I push myself backwards and almost crab walk away while sobbing with fear under my breath. When my back hits a tree trunk, I find I can't go any further. I'm done. If the crocodile manages to find me here, it's the end of the road for me. I lay there for an indeterminate time. It could be seconds; it could be hours. It's probably only been a few minutes, but I'm completely spaced out, staring numbly at the prehistoric killer, which continues to thrash, letting out roars of pain or rage.

The pain in my arm is what brings me back to reality, and I wince as I shift it forwards. I realize the cause before I even see it; I once broke my leg and it was the same sickening, throbbing pain. The bone is sticking through my skin, and my shirt sleeve is soaked in blood.

Now out of my fugue, I see that my health points are dropping with alarming speed. At this rate, I'll bleed out in a few minutes. The realization is enough to bring the world back into full clarity, and with it, the desperate desire to survive. *So much for not meeting something I can't handle*, I think to myself bitterly even as I try to work out whether I should use my healing spell with my arm like this. *I should have listened to my gut rather than my head and brought Bastet with me.* Though, what she could do against a crocodile, I don't know. She's smaller than a lion and even lions avoid crocodiles. On Earth, at least. Kalanthia would probably eat this for breakfast.

I dart another look at the crocodile, but my blinding seems to have worked: it's not coming at me. In fact, it appears to be randomly wandering, bashing into trees and bushes, and rubbing its eyes one at a time onto the tree trunk as if it thinks it's got something in them. I'd feel sorry but . . . it broke my arm and almost killed me. Heck, if I can't heal this, it *will* have killed me. Deciding that trying my healing magic is the only option, I cast Lay-on-Hands. The healing spell helps to slow the blood loss, which is good. Unfortunately, it only takes a few casts of the spell to notice that there's a problem, one I was more than half expecting: it can't shift my bone back into place by itself, and healing my arm is obviously impossible without that.

I feel panicky and nauseous, cold sweat breaking out on my skin. An inner monologue of denial runs through me. I steel myself. *If I don't do this, I'll probably lose the arm*, I tell myself firmly. Then, gripping my forearm behind my wrist, I *pull*. With a sickening and agonizing glide, the bone shifts and then withdraws back under the skin. I don't dare look at it for fear of triggering the vomit that is already building up in my throat. Instead, I focus on casting Lay-on-Hands and directing the magic to wrap around the bone and rejoin it.

I keep going with my channeled healing until my mana bar is almost empty. Then I gently let go and hope that I've done enough to stop it from immediately breaking once more under the strain of muscles and tendons. My arm throbs, but it stays in one piece. I sit there staring at it for a moment before I lose control of my gag reflex. I manage to twist to the side so I'm not emptying my lunch all over my legs, but that's all I can do about it. By the time I've stopped vomiting, I'm feeling weak and shaky again. Even worse, something about it has caught the attention of the crocodile. I don't know if it's the noise or the smell, but the massive killer croc is making a slow, cautious line straight towards me.

Hell no. I'm not going for round two with this monster, not with my arm still tender and the smell of my vomit still in my nose. At the same time, I don't want to run—I don't like leaving creatures that have almost killed me at my back. Plus, since discovering that even its thinnest skin is enough to turn my knife blade, I'm rather eager to see what kind of armor I can make out of its scales—with that on my limbs and the chitin on my chest, I'll be significantly better off.

It would be stupid to go toe to toe with it, though. A swipe from its tail that wasn't even a direct hit broke my arm and could have broken my skull too. No, I need to be more cunning than that. And as I scan the area around me, cautiously shifting away from the puddle of vomit, I reckon I've found a way.

Using my most stealthy approach—still regenerating stamina, so not wanting to use Fade—I pad almost silently over to a number of boulders. These are a bit incongruous in the area and look like they were carried down by a flood at some point. Either that or there are stone giants here and they've been having some throwing competitions. As I head towards them, a forest-colored blur flies past me and is on the crocodile before it can react. For a moment, I don't know what's happening, but a touch to my Bonds later and I understand: Bastet's here. I look around wildly but don't see any cubs. *Has she left them with Kalanthia?* My Bound obviously felt the danger to me and came running, crossing the distance far faster than I did.

Unfortunately, as I predicted, she's having little effect on the crocodile thanks to its armored skin. She does manage to get at its throat a couple of times and is surprisingly more effective than my knife. Still, it's not sustainable: if those jaws or that tail gets her even once, she's going to take serious damage.

I hurry up with my task, still feeling like it has the best chance of succeeding. The first two boulders I try to lift are simply too big; I can barely shift them, let alone lift them. The third moves more easily, but I still can't pick it up. The fourth, however, which is just over half the size of the first two, I'm able to lift a little off the ground, my good arm doing most of the work.

After shoving it in my Inventory, I move back over to the thrashing crocodile.

"Bastet, back up," I tell her sharply. She does, and we both wait patiently as the crocodile continues flailing around at nothing. Eventually, its movements slow as it registers that it is neither hitting something nor under attack. Next, it starts sniffing around, shifting its head to one side and then the other, moving around the area but not leaving it. I realize that it must think it killed or injured its opponent and is now looking for the body.

Sorry, that's not going to happen. Engaging Fade, I start stepping forwards slowly. When I'm an arm's length away from the crocodile's head, I pray once more that it won't suddenly notice me despite its blinded state and my attempts at concealment. Then I open my Inventory, pull out the boulder . . . and let it drop.

CHAPTER SIXTY-SIX

Stones

As the boulder touches its skin, the crocodile reacts with lightning speed; unfortunately for it, even that quick reaction isn't enough to save it. The rock drops on its head with finality, crushing its skull with a crunch. Strong as its bones surely are, and as impenetrable as its armor apparently is, it's not enough to stand up to a rock that's got to weigh several times what I do.

The rest of the body flails for a moment in its death throes and then stills. I let out a breath I didn't even realize I was holding. This creature was so powerful and so daunting that I half-thought it might survive even this. My adrenaline rush makes my limbs shake a little, and I step back and sit down a couple of meters away from the dead killing machine.

I barely notice as Bastet comes to sit down next to me. I do notice when she leans into my side, and I put an arm around her back.

I give a heartfelt, "Thank you," as I turn my head to look at her. This is the second time one of my Bound has come running to the rescue, and I'm just as grateful this time as the first. The thought of another putting their own body between mine and an attacker's still elicits a soul-deep gratitude, which I pray I will never lose.

Bastet replies with a wave of reassurance, warm companionship, and a hint of reprimand for going off without her in the first place.

"But you looked so comfortable, and the cubs were enjoying themselves," I tell her, a little chastised despite my attempts to justify myself. "And the likelihood of me finding something I couldn't handle seemed so small . . . ," I finish weakly. The feelings of doubt she sends me are enough to make me look away again. I need to remember that probability means nothing when we're talking about real life and death.

I return to meet her gaze at her next communication, though. The feelings are mixed, but after a few moments I get the gist, and a warmth grows inside me at the message. She's telling me that we're a pack and that we see things through together. So simple but so complex at the same time. I know that this isn't the end of the issue, as bringing Bastet with me means putting the cubs at risk too. But we'll cross that bridge when we come to it. Actually, I wonder where they are. *Did she leave Spike as the babysitter?*

I return the feelings with warm acceptance but am not able to prevent a little longing and reticence from entering the communication. I have to think for a while before I understand why those emotions rise at the thought of "pack." It's been a long time since I've felt my family was complete, and I'm worried about committing to a new one only to have it broken once more. Taking a deep breath to push away the past, I look at the corpse of the creature we've just killed. The first thing I think as I stare at the body is that it's not as big as I thought. In the middle of the fight it had seemed massive, but really, it's not that much longer than me. I remember from somewhere that some crocodile breeds can grow up to five meters in length; if this crocodile had been one of those monsters, I'd surely be dead right now. Of course, I'm thinking about Earth creatures here—this monster is from another planet entirely, so who's to say that the same rules apply at all? Still, it looks very like a crocodile to me, so I'm going to continue calling it that.

I see why I didn't notice it before: the crocodile's scales are patterned like the bed of the river. I would probably have been able to spot it if I'd known where to look, but I wasn't paying enough attention. *Next time.* There's always next time until I meet my death and next time doesn't exist anymore for me.

Even as I watch, the color starts to fade from the scales to a gray-green, starting with the ones on the creature's back. *Huh, a chameleon crocodile?* If these things can adjust the color of their scales to match their environment, I'm going to have to be *very* careful: they could be hiding anywhere. In the river, at least. Shuddering, I make a mental note for later reference but then forcibly direct my mind elsewhere. I regret that I didn't attempt to Dominate it, but on second thought, maybe it was just as well that I didn't try.

Even with Bastet there, if I'd tried and failed, I doubt I would have survived. Besides, by the time she was there, the crocodile's eyes were destroyed, eliminating that possibility anyway. Oh well. I might get another opportunity in the future. I hope I'll be better prepared for it if I do.

At least this corpse should be a treasure trove of materials; armor for one. I hope I work out a way of skinning this thing, as I'm eager to see what kind of body protection I can make out of its pelt. Arm and leg guards, at least, and possibly some kind of tabard, which I could put over or under my chitin armor—or use instead of the chitin armor if it turns out to be better in terms of defense. It also depends on how much of a mess I make trying to detach the skin from its flesh.

That's a later concern, though. Right now, I push myself to my feet and lift the rock off the crocodile's head since its body has gone limp. It's significantly easier to lift the thing now both my arms are in better condition. My previously broken arm still feels a little weak but is significantly better than it was before. I suppose I ought to be grateful that the healing spell was able to deal with healing bone at all. Not wanting to keep the heavy rock for anything else, I just drop the chunk of stone off to one side, intentionally not looking at the business end of it. Though, on second glance, the crocodile's skull isn't actually as damaged as I thought it would be.

The rock did a good job, but I think the only reason it succeeded at all was because part of the skull fractured and pierced the brain. The main structure of the skull is actually pretty intact. I find myself shaking my head. A rock like that would have crushed *my* head like a melon—what kind of beast is this that only barely takes a fracture from being crushed between a large rock and a hard place? It only makes me even warier of encountering another of these crocodiles; the only reason I survived was luck. If its initial strike hadn't been badly judged and had actually managed to hit me, if I hadn't been able to ride it, if I hadn't been able to stumble out of the way once I'd blinded it, if it had torn off my arm instead of breaking it, if Bastet hadn't been able to distract it while I was finding the rock . . . I shudder once more.

I heave the hefty carcass up with both arms and quickly slot it into my Inventory, taking up one of only two free slots. I should have probably eaten its heart, but I honestly just want to finish what I came out here to do and then head back home. I've had enough near-death experiences for today. "Keep an eye out for me?" I ask Bastet, receiving an affronted agreement in return. I guess that's the equivalent of an offended "of course" in my terms. Returning back to the riverside, I spend a good few minutes carefully scanning the water and banks, looking for any suspicious movement or shapes. Even when I'm fairly confident that there are no more crocodiles around, I still keep a wary eye on the water and banks—I have no desire to find out the hard way that these creatures live in groups. Once I've filled the converted tree stump with as many fine pebbles as I need, I tuck the container into my last Inventory slot and then take off, moving as quickly as I can under Stealth and Fade. *I don't regret leaving* that *particular area behind.*

I've got to collect two other types of pebbles to complete the filter; I wonder grimly how many more fights I'll be in before the day ends. Well, at least I have help now. After the last two outings into the forest, I resolve never to leave home without Bastet. As Bastet said, we're a pack now, so, like family, I shouldn't feel bad about disrupting her. I think I've finally learned my lesson about going it alone when I don't have to, even when probability and experience indicate that it's probably okay.

As it turns out, the answer is two more fights before the day ends. Fortunately, neither of them are too serious. Not like the one with the crocodile, anyway. One was a snake—or some other legless lizard—that I almost stepped on but was diverted by Stealth at the last moment. It took offense nonetheless and quickly struck at me. I did get bitten, but it only slowly ate at my health, at most taking a quarter off before fading. I think that my body's getting used to venom after all the different types I've experienced so far. Either that, or it was just a weak venom. Either way, Bastet killed the thing before I could and we both moved on, not even bothering to collect the body. Not that I don't want more venom, but given how poorly it acted on me, I didn't want to have to get rid of something else that might be more useful to make space for the snake's carcass.

As for the second attack, it was *birds* of all things. I think we got too close to their nest or something because they kept flying down to pick up detritus off the forest floor and then flying up to drop the bits on me. The attacks were more annoying than anything else, and I didn't manage to hit any of the birds with my rocks, nor did Bastet succeed in grabbing any with her leaps; I don't think raptorcats are used to hunting flying prey, somehow. In the end, we just walked away quickly, hoping that they would stop attacking after we got a certain distance away. That proved to be right as they soon gave up and returned to their nest, or wherever they came from. And no, I didn't run away—I just didn't think I should kill birds that were only defending their home. No, my decision definitely wasn't made because I couldn't actually do anything about their attacks . . . Either way, I've finally managed to accomplish all I set out to do in the forest and quickly head back home. At least the two creatures we killed earned me enough Energy that I'm more than three-quarters of the way towards the next level.

Getting so close to the next level has caused me to seriously consider refusing any more stat points until I've leveled up. I might have to see what stat points are offered to me, though; if Intelligence or Wisdom are possible to increase before leveling, I reckon I'll be too tempted to say no.

Pausing to let my stamina refill a bit after using Fade so much, I pull up my status screen.

Name: Markus Wolfe		Race: Human	Class: Tamer
Level: 1	Energy to next level: 78%	Energy absorption rate: 11u/hr	Energy towards debt: 1%
Intelligence	9	Mana: 90/90	
Wisdom	9	Mana regeneration rate: 225u/hr	
Willpower	16+3 (+20%)	Health regeneration rate: 19u/hr	
Constitution	10	Health: 100/100	
Strength	11	Stamina: 14/60	
Dexterity	7	Stamina regeneration rate: 70u/hr	
Class Skills: Dominate – Beginner 3 Tame – Beginner 1 Fade – Novice 1		Non-Class Skills: Lay-on-Hands – Novice 4 Stealth – Beginner 7 Animal Empathy – Beginner 5	

I've still got three stats under ten. Dexterity is the most annoying, down at a seven, but I'd quite like to get Intelligence and Wisdom up to ten as well before committing level-up points to them. But Dexterity is important not just for what the stat itself offers, but because it also affects my stamina regeneration rate. That's what's been holding me back a bit when moving through the forest: I've had to regularly make the choice of whether to keep walking without Fade activated or wait in a hidden place until my stamina regenerates and then continue walking with Fade.

Most of the time, I've been making a compromise: resting for a few minutes in a safe, or safe-ish, spot and then continuing without Fade until my stamina is mostly regenerated. Ultimately, I'd like my stamina regeneration to keep up with the cost of Fade, but that's probably a while off. Fade uses about four points of stamina per minute when it's active, so I'd need to be regenerating around two hundred and forty units per hour in order to run Fade permanently. That in turn requires twenty-four points in Dexterity since the regeneration rate seems to be at a one-to-ten ratio with the points. Assuming that all remains constant, that is. And assuming there are sixty minutes in an hour, as well—I haven't exactly been able to reliably test that.

Anyway, I think it would be best to try to bring all three of those stats up to ten before leveling up. Dismissing the screen, I keep moving as my mind goes over what I can do to increase Wisdom and Intelligence, as I reckon my future crafting efforts are going to improve my Dexterity without me even trying.

By the time I get home, I'm ready to start earning my Dexterity points. It turns out that the cubs stayed behind with Kalanthia, not Spike. If Bastet's fine leaving them in her care, that's good enough for me. "Thank you for looking after them," I tell the giant feline.

As an exception, it is acceptable. They were no trouble, she replies. I'm glad—especially considering what that male cub is usually like. *Your Bound indicated you were in distress?*

"Yeah. Bit off a little more than I could chew," I admit ruefully. There is a pause as she looks at me thoughtfully.

Far be it from me to dictate what a Binder should do. I am surprised that you go into the forest without your Bound at all. It is my experience that Binders tend to keep their Bound close to them—they are usually the most protected of the group, not the least.

"I get that," I concede. "Honestly, I've been thinking along those lines too. It's just . . . Bastet has her cubs to look after too, and I don't always want to disrupt them. And Spike . . . he's too vulnerable." Kalanthia stretches out a paw and claws the length of my forearm slide out, glinting in the sun.

You may be surprised at how your Bound can evolve, given enough time and kills. A grenslar is, I will admit, not the most combat capable of beasts, but that can change. As for the cubs, they will not always be small. She yawns, revealing black lips and a huge red mouth. *And if you wish, I could sit on the babies at times—for a price.* I eye her warily.

"A price. What sort of price?" She lays her head on her paws, looking at me with golden eyes almost the size of my head. Instead of replying in words, she pushes an image into my head. It's a large glowing crystal. For a moment it's blue. A moment later, she shows me a brown one. Then a red one. Then a white one. Then a purple one.

"There are different colors," I conclude.

Yes.

"And where do I find these?"

In beasts.

"What kind of beasts?" I ask, trying to work out if I've seen anything like this. I can't quite tell their size either; they look small, but because Kalanthia is so much larger than me, what feels like "small" to her could easily be as big as my head.

Equally, it could be the size of my fist.

Evolved ones. Okay . . . helpful. Not.

"They don't look like anything in particular?"

No.

"And you want one of these things for every time you babysit the cubs?"

Yes.

Well, no one ever accused her of being overly chatty, I suppose.

"All right." I sigh. "I'll keep my eye out for them. I don't suppose you'll tell me why you want them?" She clearly takes a moment to think about this.

Not yet, she says, then closes her eyes and turns her head away from me—a clear sign of dismissal.

In the end, I just have to shrug. It's not like I can *make* her tell me.

Surveying the area, I think through my to-do list and finally decide to set up my filtering process. First, though, I want to check whether my fat collection is working. Hoping that the needed animal fat will be waiting for me on top of the pot I set boiling this morning, I head into the cave.

As I enter, I see a dark-colored blur shoot past me. Frowning a little in confusion, I hesitate for a moment before entering my cave. Pausing at the entrance, I can't believe my eyes for a moment and just stand there open-mouthed. Then, as my temper rises, I find my voice returning to me. I raise my voice to summon the most likely culprit.

"Trouble!"

CHAPTER SIXTY-SEVEN

Boiling Nicely

The damn raptorcat refuses to appear, and when I stomp outside angrily, he's nowhere to be seen. Bastet, the traitor, just gives me an amused look. Well, a look and a wave of amusement through our Bond.

"Aren't you supposed to make sure the cubs *don't* cause trouble?" I snap at her waspishly. The sensations and images she sends me in reply don't express an iota of contrition. Instead, the pictures of mountain rocks and trees and great winds seem to explain that one cannot control nature: male raptorcats are inquisitive trouble-makers, and there's a reason they usually leave the pack before they even reach adult-hood. Voluntarily or involuntarily, that is. Excuses, in short.

I sigh and rub my temples. Frankly, I'm tired and out of patience, and the thought of replying with all the ways humans *have* come up with to control nature does occur to me, but I refrain. Not only would they be so out of Bastet's frame of reference that she probably wouldn't understand them, making the effort pointless, but would I actually *want* to repeat humanity's mistakes here?

Probably not. My life here contrasts with my old life in many ways, and despite the danger that faces me all the time, I can't help but feel I'm better off than I was when running the rat race. Clean air, clean living, and at least here I don't have to be worried about my life being completely upturned by someone else's decision. Though, on the downside, that does mean I have to deal with crocodiles. And spider monster things. I shudder at the memory.

So, no, I'm not going to try to control nature to the extent that humanity did, which means that raptorcats will be raptorcats, and I'm going to just have to go and deal with the mess in my bedroom. Next time maybe I'd better consider the fact that meat cooking on the fire might be an attractive target to mischievous cubs and avoid leaving it unattended.

Returning to my bedroom, I survey the mess with dismay. The only good things, I decide, are that neither the pot nor my fireplace were damaged. Trouble must have smelled the boiling meat, followed it to its source, and then somehow pulled the pot over so it spilled everywhere. I suppose I should also be glad that he didn't scald himself, or not seriously, at least. As for the contents of the pot, they spilled all over the fire and escaped around the edges of the stone I had in place to block too much air from being pulled in at the fire's base.

Essentially, I have a water and grease-soaked fire—well, dead embers—and a patina of greasy, ashy water spread around the area closest to the fireplace. I suppose I should also be glad that not enough water was spilled to send it all the way over to soak my bedding, though the cubs' torn shirt is rather damp.

They'll just have to do without it until I can do a wash, I think grumpily. *If they complain, I'll get Bastet to tell them it's Trouble's fault.* They should be fine anyway—they generally cuddle up with Bastet, and they have a fire burning all night. Those are all things they didn't have back in the cave they were in when I found them.

Using the already ruined shirt as a rag, I mop up the mess on the floor. There's little I can do about the grease before I have my soap, but the surface is rough enough that no one should be at risk of slipping. The charcoal and unburned twigs that were in the fireplace when it flooded are a lost cause, and I just pull them into a pile, which I'll dump outside.

As for the pot, Trouble didn't manage to tip it over completely, so there's still some water and most of the meat there. Unfortunately, the main reason for me boiling the meat like this, apart from wanting some cooked meat to add to my Inventory, was the grease, and that's been mostly sloshed on the fire and the floor. Trying to breathe through my frustration, I salvage what I can and set the meat aside onto a plate for eating afterwards—I'm actually hungry now.

Adding more water to the pot that was tipped over, I refill it with chunks of raw meat and leave the pot to boil on its own. After having a quick snack of the boiled meat—pretty tasteless, really—I go outside. Glaring at Trouble, who's now playing innocently with a stick, I decide to get on with preparing my filtering process as I had been intending on doing before discovering what the trouble-making cub had been up to.

I grab a few pre-chosen stones, set the small pot down in the middle of them, and then rest the filtering container on top. It's a bit rickety—unfortunately, natural stones don't tend to be uniform in either size or shape—but with five stones in place, it's reasonably secure. I'm glad to see that I have the height right, as the stump isn't actually sitting on top of the pot but is being held just above. It does take me a few trials with clean water to get the pot into the right place, though.

Finally, when it's all set up correctly with the opening of the stump just above the clay pot, I pile some ashes from my fire pit on top of the large pebbles filling the top of my filtering container. Grabbing my canteen, I start slowly pouring water on top of the ashes. After repeating the action a couple of times, I lift the filtering container out of the way to check out my pot. Seeing that it's half-full, I replace the container and continue pouring water, refilling my canteen from the big pot in my Inventory when necessary.

After filling the small pot with grayish liquid, I tidy away my filtering container and its rocks, tucking them next to my firewood pile. I'm pleased: the filtering has worked just as I'd hoped it would, and I've successfully completed the next step in my soap-making process. Now I just need to boil off some of the water to make lye, mix it with pure animal fat, and then I'll have some usable soap. Checking on my pot, I see that it's boiling nicely, and there's a good layer of fat that's risen to the surface. I take the pot off the fire, using a pair of jeans wrapped around my hands as makeshift gloves, and set it to one side. It'll need to cool before I can do anything with it. *So, what next?* My axe is done—the thought of which still sends a wave of pride through me—and my soapmaking is on the way. I should probably beef up my mace a bit by adding a stone head, and it might be a good idea for me to consider making a spear at some point for keeping things at a distance, but something else draws me more. My bow.

Although I've never actually shot a bow, outside my absorbed memories, I know that it will offer a great deal to my hunting. Instead of me having to be a melee fighter simply because all my weapons are close range, or trying to throw stones with reasonable accuracy, a bow means I could snipe my prey without them even seeing me. That seems a lot better for my long-term survival prospects than having to run in, mace or spear swinging.

Of course, arrows aren't the only range weapons I could create. It might be a good idea for me to make a few more spears, which I could potentially use to throw. Still, I'm very much drawn to archery; its storybook appeal is almost more attractive than the practical use I can see for it in my "memories." I justify my decision by the thought of how I could use it for difficult targets—I'm not sure a spear would be capable of the same kind of pin-point accuracy that a bow would be.

Take my fight with the crocodile earlier as an example. If I'd tried to target a part of the creature covered by armor, I doubt that it would have made much difference, even with a bow. But what if I had poisoned arrows and the accuracy to hit it in the eyes? Or through the roof of its mouth and into its brain? I might have been able to take it down with practically no risk to myself, instead of the knife's edge I was balanced on throughout that fight.

Not to mention the broken arm. Yes, I know I can heal myself, but it still hurts to be injured in the first place, and I'm not a masochist in any way, shape, or form. I could even combine using a bow with Bastet's melee fighting. Bastet could keep the creature distracted and in one place, and I could snipe at it in its vulnerable spots. If my aim's good enough, of course. So . . . a bow. And arrows, of course, since a bow without arrows is only useful as a staff, which doesn't exactly fulfil the same function. Naturally, making both of these is not going to be as simple as going down the street to the local sport shop. I have five elements to prepare: the bow shaft, the string, the arrowheads, the arrow shafts, and the tools to assemble the arrows.

I haven't yet harvested a branch large or strong enough to function as the bow itself, so maybe I should make that tomorrow's first task—I don't really have the daylight left today, nor the inclination to risk another life-or-death encounter. The bowstring will require processed sinew, which I'm on the way to having. I think I should have enough, especially once the ostridocuses' leg tendons dry sufficiently— they're the longest that I've found so far.

As for the arrows, I collected a number of branches while I was collecting firewood a few days back. I currently have them hanging up on my drying rack with the few bits of sinew that are still damp. Hopefully, they'll do all right for arrow shafts, though I know they won't be fully seasoned. They were pretty dry to begin with, so I'm hoping they'll be okay. I still need to cut some feathers to make the fletching, and although I've got a handful of arrowheads made, I still need plenty more. After all, the chances of my arrows breaking or the arrowheads fracturing when they hit something is high, so I need plenty of backup supplies. I now have my pitch to help the three elements of the arrows stick together, and I'll be using sinew for that too.

Hmm . . . I'll also need a file to make the notches for the arrowheads and for nocking the arrows onto the string when firing. I make a mental note to look through my rock collection to see if there's anything suitable. If not, I'll have to make one from flint. Fortunately, I've got lots of flint nodules since I took the opportunity to resupply when I was passing near the spot where I found the flint the first time.

Out of the tasks I have that I can do now, I decide to get on with processing the dry sinew strands, especially because more have finished drying since I last did the processing. I'm going to need sinew for both bow and arrows, so it seems logical. Not to mention for my chitin, and possibly crocodile-skin armor. Afterwards, I guess I'd better get on with making arrowheads. *Though . . .*

A thought occurs, and I rummage through my orange suitcase for the book I'm using for keeping track of the days and my pen. Adding a couple of lines for the last days I hadn't recorded, I calculate time. It's been two days since Kalanthia went hunting, so she'll want to go hunting again the day after tomorrow.

Maybe I'd better increase the damage of my mace now since that's not likely to take too long, then go looking for a piece of wood suitable for a bow first thing tomorrow. That way I'll have all the resources necessary and just need to process them, something I can do while Kalanthia's away. I have to admit that despite Trouble's, well, troublemaking, having other cubs around to play with has made Lathani significantly less demanding towards all the adults. Bastet's extra pair of eyes helps too. The combination should mean that I get much more done the day after tomorrow than I succeeded in doing the first few times I looked after the nunda cub. *All right, time to make my mace more badass.*

CHAPTER SIXTY-EIGHT

Edge of Mental Sanity

I reach above my head towards the sky and stretch my aching back. The release of tension and change of position feels so good that I actually lie back onto the ground and stretch my whole body. Sitting cross-legged for hours is a good way to get cramps *everywhere*. And I've been doing that for two and a half days now, apart from a few trips into the forest.

In the first day, I managed to upgrade my mace relatively easily. A mace is a pretty simple weapon—it swings around and bashes into things. Certainly, even my entirely wooden mace has saved my life many times, both by crushing bones and stepping in as a makeshift shield a few times. Still, it can't be denied that it hadn't evolved very far from its beginnings as a tree branch. By carving wood out of the bole at its head and slotting a stone into the hollow, I've multiplied its damage potential. I didn't want to do this before I had my pitch, because I was worried that any sort of rope I put in place would just let the stone fall out after a while. Having that happen in the middle of a fight would be a quick way to lose the advantage—and possibly my life. With the pitch and a bit of bark fiber, I was able to work wonders.

Of course, it took time. Everything takes far longer in this world of primitive tools than it would on Earth with power tools. Something that could have taken five minutes with the right drill or saw takes close to an hour here. Still, it was worth it. Not only does my new-and-improved mace have significantly more heft, but I chose a stone that has a fair number of nobbles just to increase its crushing power. A mace inspired by a morning star.

After letting the pitch cool down a bit and set, I couldn't resist taking a few swings. After making sure there were no cubs underfoot, of course. The new weapon is significantly more top-heavy than previously, and it takes a fair bit of strength to resist its momentum and stop it swinging or changing its direction. With its new design, circular swings are going to be a lot more effective than just straight up and down attacks. Just to add another bonus point, it'll be a much better weapon against multiple attackers than my knife is.

I reckon if I'd tried to wield this weapon before gaining points to Strength and Dexterity, I'd have been facing quick exhaustion and trouble aiming. As it is, I almost wish I could go up against another crocodile. Forget dumping a ton of rock on its head; I calculate that with my Strength, a direct swing of this would probably do more damage.

In a moment of curiosity after finishing my mace, I actually pulled the dead crocodile out of my Inventory. After laying the corpse down, I lined up a swing with my mace and hit its head with a loud cracking sound. I was gratified to see my mace punch through the bone like nobody's business.

I suddenly felt a lot better about my chances in the forest, with or without Bastet. Inspecting the head, I also gained another idea, which I've since proceeded to put into practice. My next task, finding a good length of wood for a bow, wasn't too difficult, though it did necessitate a few broken branches that simply weren't flexible enough to handle being bent before I found one with the requisite flexibility. I did find a couple of branches that will be good for spears before I found one I wanted to use for a bow. Hopefully, it won't become brittle even once it's dried, but I intend on rubbing it with animal fat to keep it supple as well as to improve its resistance to water; it might not have rained since I came here, but it will at some point. Besides, there's no guarantee that I won't be tossed in the river at some point, and if that ruins my bow, I'll be . . . *annoyed.*

My main task yesterday was finishing processing the sinew that I'd almost completed the day before and then twisting it into a cord. At that point, I was very glad that I'd made the large water pot, as I had to keep wetting the sinew strands to ensure their flexibility. Having to keep going down to the river would have been extremely frustrating, and actually doing this task by the river would have been far too risky. So, yay for multiuse pottery? In the end, I was able to make a length long enough for a bowstring and another length hopefully long enough for my armor. The rest of yesterday was spent making arrowheads. I grimace as I remember the frustrating endeavor: about seven hours resulted in just eight arrowheads. That's barely more than one per hour! I mean, at least it's getting quicker. The first three arrowheads took almost four hours, and the other five took just over three. I figure that's probably due to a mixture of me becoming more familiar with the practice of flint knapping, and not just the theory, and the fact that I picked up two Dexterity points, which improved my fine motor skills. I also picked up a Wisdom point from somewhere. I'm not exactly sure where, but I have a feeling it was either when I decided not to pursue revenge against Trouble for just acting as male raptorcats act, or when I thought that trying to control nature the way so many humans back on Earth do wouldn't be the best path to follow.

Either way, I'm pleased that I only have two more stats to get to ten before I dedicate my Energy to leveling up. Given how much detail work I still have left to do, I reckon Dexterity won't take long before it crosses that threshold. Right now, I'm working on preparing the arrow shafts. Including the arrowheads I made yesterday, I have thirteen flint points ready to go onto shafts. Not many, right? This is where the brainwave I had about the crocodile comes in. What does a crocodile have lots of? Teeth! Sharp, mostly round points. Perfect for arrows! And this crocodile has a *lot* of them. Although not all are immediately useful for arrowheads—the longer ones tend to be a bit curved—the majority are fine with perhaps a little bit of filing. All told, I've managed to collect about thirty points that I can use immediately on arrows. It seems like the crocodile is the gift that keeps giving—if we ignore how I almost died to "receive" the gift. The sheer usefulness of its carcass and my new and improved mace almost make me want to encounter another one. Almost.

Anyway, I've decided to make thirty arrows to start: thirteen with flint heads and seventeen with tooth heads. That means a lot of fletching to make from feathers—ninety, in fact. Of course, my attempts to make the fletching are complicated by the fact that all four cubs find feathers fascinating, and I have to fend off attempts to steal my work on a regular basis. If I hadn't had my Inventory, I reckon I'd have already blown a fuse. Seeing my hard work being chewed up and torn to bits the way the offcuts are currently being treated would have been way too much for me to cope with mentally. Still, at least when the cubs are raptly focusing on their games with the feathers, they're not causing trouble elsewhere. Speaking of, I scan the area around me, looking for one specific cub.

Not seeing him, I widen my field of view. *There he is.* "Trouble!" I shout, startling the three female cubs closest to me. The dark-colored cub freezes with a paw still raised in the air. "You know you're not allowed in there during the day," I remind him with a warning note in my voice.

His body language slumps, and he slinks back out of the open mouth of the cave. Yes, he understands me when I speak. No, I don't know how. Is it something to do with my Bond with Bastet? Or my Animal Empathy, which is well on the way to reaching Novice thanks to all the communication I've been having with my animal companions? I don't know. All I know is that I'm grateful he *does* understand me, as that makes things significantly simpler. Bastet gives me a look and then goes to lie in the entrance to the cave. I send a wave of gratitude to her, knowing that she'll make sure he doesn't simply try to sneak in again when my back's turned.

I know that there are tempting things in there—I've got some meat cooking on the fire so that I can collect more fat for sealing my bow, sinew cord, and arrows, for one thing. Not to mention the soap that's currently drying in its mold after I succeeded in collecting enough animal fat to mix with the boiled lye. That said, I don't know if the soap is actually the draw—while it might smell of animals still, it's got to also smell a bit caustic, which is surely a bit off-putting . . .

Anyway, the point is that I don't want him in there, and now Bastet will make sure he won't go in. On the other hand, if she's in the cave mouth, she's not able to make sure that no cub wanders down the slope, which is the reason she wasn't lying there to begin with. I'll have to be a bit more vigilant, I guess, especially if the girls get bored of playing with feathers. Apparently, exploring the forest has almost as much appeal as investigating the smells from my alcove. Fortunately, the two female raptorcat cubs still seem pretty enraptured by the offcuts they're playing with.

Getting on with preparing my fletching, I carefully trim the barbs to a shorter length, then strip the center of the feather, the rachis. I allow a bit of bare rachis at either end of the fletching—wrapping sinew around this will keep it on the shaft.

I get one, sometimes two pieces of fletching per feather, so it's good that I have plenty in my Inventory from all the feathered foes I've faced so far in this strange quasi-dinosaur world.

I take breaks every so often to stretch my back and give my eyes a rest. Apparently, even having a Constitution of ten doesn't eliminate eye strain, though I will admit that it doesn't happen as frequently. During one of these breaks, I get a welcome message.

> Congratulations!
> You have worked hard on your Dexterity and have earned a point. Would you like to apply this to your status?
>
> Y / N

Uh, no. Of course *I don't want to increase my Dexterity.* Though I make sure to think that *after* I've already accepted the point—I don't know how much this interface is based on my focused thought versus my intentions and don't want to test it by accidentally declining a point that I really *do* want. I pump my hand in the air with elation. *Dexterity up to ten!* If my calculations are correct, that means I'm now up in the top ranges of what is humanly possible, at least on Earth. I know the points from here on out will be more difficult to earn naturally, but I'm still pleased with my achievement. Deciding to make an effort to raise Wisdom up too, I take a break over lunch and spend some time attempting to meditate while the cubs slumber together in a pile. I would feel a bit bad sitting there with my eyes closed if Bastet was having to keep an eye on four cubs alone, especially since it's technically my job to look after Lathani while Kalanthia isn't here. But if everyone else is sleeping, what's the harm? Even Bastet is snoozing in the sun, though I'm pretty sure it wouldn't take much to bring her to full alertness.

Before coming here, I would never have seriously considered meditating. I'd always considered it some weird, airy-fairy, New Agey thing. I can't deny, though, that at times I've felt a genuine connection to the world around me and everything in it. These sensations have always only happened when I've been feeling exceptionally serene and at peace; if that's not meditation, I don't know what is. However, I've never actually sat down and deliberately told myself that I would try to "meditate."

So, feeling a bit self-conscious despite no one actually being there to see me, I sit down on the ground and close my eyes. Focusing on my breathing, I can't help but think of Lucy, my ex-girlfriend. She'd read something in *Vogue* or *Cosmopolitan* or some women's magazine and had got into it for a while. I'd honestly only paid enough attention to avoid her accusing me of not listening. Frankly, I considered the whole thing to be a sop for the gullible and lazy masses at best or outright predatory behavior at worst—on par with most, if not all, types of religion. I regret not paying more attention to her now, in more ways than just this. Only now that I've been forcibly broken away from it do I realize just how consumed by career ambition I had become, how closed-minded.

I find myself trying hard to remember her half-heard words, poring over memories of what she used to do when she was trying to meditate. From what I remember, she used to light a candle, sit on a cushion in a darkened room, and close her eyes. I think a few times I heard her hum. And other times she played weird music, which made me put in my earphones or turn up the TV. Well, I don't have candles or weird music or cushions.

With my eyelids providing the only darkness, I sit in silence. Thoughts pass through my mind. *This is stupid*, is one. *I don't know what I'm doing. This is probably useless*, is another. I accept them. They're true. I don't know what I'm doing, and I do feel pretty stupid. And if this doesn't work, I'll try something else, but all I know is that I've gained Wisdom points when I've felt calm and comfortable in my environment. Meditation is supposed to make one feel calm, so it seems logical that the two are linked. The thoughts keep coming, but as I sit there and enjoy the feeling of sunlight on my body, the cooling relief of the breeze, and hear the sounds of the birds and the moving trees, I find that the barrage slows. I find that the time between each thought elongates, and a sense of calm enjoyment of the present creeps in little by little. It's a bit like the grounding techniques my therapist taught me to help with flashbacks, but far more positive. I become lost in the moment, time becoming irrelevant.

When I hear the chirping mewls of the cubs as they wake from their slumber, at first they just blend into the general surroundings. It's only when one of them brushes past me as it runs into the clearing that I'm pulled out. Feeling like I'm surfacing out of a lake of stillness, I sense a calmness cradling me, which I haven't felt since arriving in this place. For a few moments, I forgot that every minute that passes could be my last. Or maybe I didn't forget, but I accepted and disregarded it as being unimportant. Does it matter if the next minute doesn't come when the moment now is vast? I feel like I've been pulled back from some edge of sanity without even realizing I'd been standing there. An ironic smile quirks up one corner of my mouth. Maybe meditation isn't so useless after all. I look at my messages, and the notification for a point in Wisdom earned makes my smile widen. Not useless at all.

CHAPTER SIXTY-NINE

Lone Wolf

A sense of satisfaction goes through me as I slip the braided cord loop into the string groove on the bow's upper limb. It's taken all my strength to bend the bow enough to do even that, but I would rather that the bow be a bit too difficult to draw than the reverse; I'm likely to be increasing my Strength soon, so if it's easy for me to draw now, I'll risk breaking it when I've got more points in Strength.

It's been interesting to notice the differences my stats make. It's not like I've been *testing* them, exactly. I'm not a fan of the idea of letting myself get hurt in order to test my new durability or ability to heal, and I'm not just going to keep Dominating random creatures to test my Willpower when it increases—I sometimes feel guilty enough over the two creatures I've Bound to me, even though they both seem okay with it. Less over Bastet, since it was basically a deal I made with her, but Spike . . .

It *has* been quite nice to go on the peaceful trips together down to the river and back. I feel like we've been able to build a bit more of a regular bond just by walking together, not even really communicating. Perhaps Kalanthia has a point: perhaps "Binders" spend time with their Bound for more reasons than just safety. It's hard to get used to always being with someone, though—always having to think of another being and worry about its well-being. It reminds me of when Lucy first moved into my apartment and how self-conscious I was about both my space and my person. It had been wearing for a while, but I'd gotten used to it. And then when she left, her absence had ached like a fresh wound every time I moved to speak to her, or automatically did something she'd have told me to do like putting the seat down on the toilet. But I got used to that too.

I sense that Spike isn't particularly used to being in a group either. Perhaps he's just spent too much time alone too. I can empathize, though he seems a lot more content about it than I was. Comfortable in his solitary nature rather than lonely. I did check in with him to make sure that he hasn't been feeling ignored.

Quite the reverse, apparently: he appears to be calmly content with going and foraging in the morning before "guarding" the growing samova bean plants during the afternoon and night, hidden behind my woodpile. By that, I basically mean he's been napping nearby and taking life pretty easy. Since having an adult raptorcat in addition to my apex predator landlady kind of obviates the need for him to actually guard the thing most of the time, and I don't have any other specific task for him in mind, I'm fine with him just enjoying life.

After the success of the trips down to the river, I dared to take him with me when I looked for wood suitable for a bow. That outing was also pretty peaceful, so I'm still unable to decide whether taking him into combat is a good or bad thing. Maybe I should try asking him? He's not nearly as aware as Bastet, but he *has* been able to establish and communicate basic preferences . . . But that's a thought for later. So yeah, after my experiences with him, I've decided on no random Dominates. I can live with myself if I use that Skill for a good reason, as with Bastet, but just randomly capturing other creatures for no reason other than going on a power trip would make my conscience uncomfortable. That said, I'm slowly realizing something that should have been obvious from the beginning, but which is only becoming clear to me now. Perhaps I needed to increase my Intelligence or Wisdom to come to the realization; perhaps I just needed time to take in my new reality or needed to spend time with my Bound.

The fact is that my Class revolves around creating Bonds with creatures—and then *using* them. I recognized that Tame and Dominate were clearly core Skills by the fact that they were the first ones I started with and are considered "Class" Skills, but for some reason, I didn't really internalize it. I've considered Dominating a number of creatures but usually at the wrong moments—or the wrong creatures. I can't Dominate every creature I come across, even if I wanted to and even if it made logical sense. Although it doesn't explicitly say there's a limit to the number of Bonds I can have, I sense that there is *some* sort of cap.

I can't tell exactly what the cap is, but I have a strong suspicion that I'm able to have fewer Bonds with almost-sapient creatures like Bastet, compared to Bonds with creatures like Spike. But I don't want to go around Dominating a load of porcupigs anyway—I can't see the utility in that. Beyond the question of utility, I can't justify it to myself either. No, I need to be judicious with my use of Dominate, for sure, but I also can't be afraid to use it either. Encountering Bastet at that moment was truly fortuitous. She was too injured to pose a danger to me, but not so much that she was too weak for the Battle of Wills. And she has turned out to be a perfect companion.

Except for the fact that she's also the principal caregiver for a trio of cubs, of course, but even there I'm hopefully building a type of bond that will allow them to become companions in their turn. And without their need for care weighing on the scales, Bastet wouldn't have agreed to Bond with me. Plus, they're super cute and genuinely bring a light to my life. Except when they're undoing all my hard work, that is. At one point I considered using traps to engineer a situation where I could invoke Dominate without worrying about the consequences if I failed. Now, I feel a little uneasy about that idea. Yes, it's not necessarily a good idea to rely on just happening across my perfect Bound at an ideal moment. But at the same time, can I really justify trapping a creature, which hasn't done anything to me, just to bind it? I'm essentially changing their life, after all. Hopefully for the better, but can I know that for sure?

Maybe I should try my other Skill? I haven't used Tame yet, after all. Perhaps that would be a different experience from Dominate. It's likely to be less heavy-handed. I reckon that my increases in Wisdom are helping me to ask these questions now. All I can say is that as I slowly feel more connected to the world around me, I find myself asking questions that had never occurred to me before. Not only is my higher Wisdom contributing to my unease about randomly Dominating animals, but it also tells me that I cannot pretend that I am an island, detached and removed from everything around me. I tried to do that for so long on Earth; perhaps it's not surprising how my whole house of cards collapsed in the end. But perhaps *that's* Wisdom: looking back on your past actions and wanting to cover your eyes in shame. Because I've been an idiot in far too many ways for far too long—in both worlds. On Earth, my mistakes didn't have the same consequences that they do here; I'm a truly lucky bastard that I haven't been killed by my mistakes yet.

I've been trying to be a lone wolf when everyone knows that wolves are stronger as a pack. Going out by myself puts me at risk, but it also prevents my companions from growing; I checked with Bastet yesterday, and after a bit of back and forth, I managed to get from her that she grows in Strength by killing or helping to kill, just as I do. Apparently, her contributions to the battle with the crocodile helped her in some way.

And if being part of the fight helps Bastet, then it would help Spike too, wouldn't it?

He's pretty vulnerable, but so was I when I first arrived—heck, I still am. Kalanthia's right: who knows what Spike could become if he grows enough? I've been mentally assigning him a non-combat role, seeing him as a creature with good defenses but no real capacity for or inclination towards offense. But if he grows a bit more, could that change?

On another note, while the effects of Wisdom and Intelligence have been slowly realized in my clarity of thought and ability to make mental connections, the impact of other stats is more clearly observable. My higher Strength helps me in some obvious ways: carrying rocks and breaking branches are some examples. It did take a bit of adjusting, though, to moderate it in more delicate tasks, like when knapping my arrowheads. I ruined a good few rocks before I gained the right control of force. Actually, after spending some time last night musing on the idea, I concluded that this is why I only really started making progress once I gained a point in Dexterity: I needed the fine motor control to deal with my increased gross motor strength.

On the upside, considering all these different ideas and making connections between them was apparently exactly what I needed to nudge my Intelligence just enough to offer me another point in that stat. With at least ten in each stat now, I'm feeling pretty good about my status screen and am ready to level up—once I've collected enough Energy, that is. Which means hunting. And what great timing: having now completed my bow by connecting its two limb tips with a string, I'm ready to face my first foe equipped with a proper ranged weapon. Not to mention the couple of flint-tipped spears now taking up a single slot in my Inventory.

I've also been able to create crude chest and back plates with the pieces of chitin and sinew cord. They're a little troublesome to get on and off, but I'm sure the effort will be worth the protection. Going forward, I might not gain Constitution points so quickly, but it will be worth it to avoid the pain of injuries. I'm actually wearing them now; I need to get used to moving with them since they do restrict my movements a little.

But my new armor isn't half as exciting as my new weapons, particularly my new ranged weapon. Bows and arrows are *cool*. I can't help an excited grin coming to my face. It's a little surreal that I've made a *bow and arrows!* Proper ones, that is, since I'd made so many as a boy. Not real ones, of course. Just sticks with string attached, shooting other sticks with such little accuracy that everything around my target was in more danger than the target itself. Now, I've made a serious weapon that can kill . . . and I'm going to set out to kill with it.

The thought sobers me, and my grin slips significantly. But is it any different from before? I have to go hunting. I need to eat, Bastet needs to eat, and the cubs need to eat. And beyond that, I need to earn Energy to both grow stronger and pay my "debt." Hunting is an unavoidable part of that. If I start pulling in too many corpses for the five of us, I'll give them to Kalanthia too. Then she won't have to go out hunting herself. It's not like I'm just killing for the sake of killing and then leaving the bodies to poison the local environment. Not like people used to do in the Wild West with bison or in Africa when they went on safaris just to kill everything they saw for trophies. *It's not the same thing. Is it?*

To distract myself from my troubled thoughts, I return my attention to my bow, trying to look it over with a critical eye to try to spot any flaws—dangerous ones, at least—that might lead to the bow snapping mid-fight. There are plenty of aesthetic flaws. I might have made proper bows many times in my absorbed memories, but this is my first time in real life. For this first bow, I've just made a very simple design: a single piece of wood with portions cut out to form the limbs and the handhold. I've even left a strip of bark on the outside face to try to maximize flexibility and protection from the elements. I did shape it a bit with both knife and rubbing stone, so it's reasonably comfortable to hold, and I did make sure the tips were a bit thicker than parts of the arms, as I don't want them to snap off immediately. I've also rubbed both wood and sinew string with animal fat, wanting them to be more supple and water-resistant. I'll continue doing that at intermittent intervals until they don't absorb any more.

It's not the most powerful bow design, but I don't have either the time or resources to make a layered bow. This'll do, especially with half-decent arrows that keep as much momentum as possible. I'll still probably have to get relatively close to my target to maximize impact, though. Still, given that the only place I've ever actually shot an arrow is in my "memories"—and my dreams—being closer to my target probably isn't a bad thing anyway.

As for the arrows, I'm glad that I didn't try to make them as soon as I arrived in this world; even starting them with a Dexterity that was more than double my arriving value, it was difficult. In fact, I only really started to make progress with making the arrowheads and attaching them to the arrows with pitch and sinew when my Dexterity reached triple my starting value. It sure makes a difference—to my sanity if nothing else! If I'd tried the whole thing with a three in Dexterity, I'd have probably given up in frustration. Now, I have a feeling that I would never be hit by another dodgeball if I ever got the chance to play it again. Lifting the bow, I first experiment with standing in the positions my absorbed memories tell me are good for correct shooting. I set my feet shoulder-width apart with my left foot ahead and my right foot behind, pointing slightly outwards. I shuffle a bit, testing whether I feel more comfortable with my feet closer together and hips facing the target or my feet further apart and my hips facing side-on. In the end, I settle on a position somewhere between the two where I feel grounded and as though I'm braced enough with my slightly bent knees to cope with the bow's draw. I can already tell that I'm going to have to keep practicing this until it becomes natural and automatic.

Next, I try to draw the bow without an arrow. The string is strong and cuts into my fingers painfully. *I'll need to build up calluses quickly*, I note absently. It's a very strong draw, and I struggle to pull the string to halfway along my body, let alone to full draw. Still, that'll change quickly, so I'm not worried. Given how much my Strength is likely to change, having a bow I can "grow into" is probably a good idea, even.

Practicing a little, I draw the string and then release the tension slowly; draw, then release; draw, then release. With the unusual exercise, my muscles soon start feeling warm and sweat starts beading on my forehead. By the time I think I should probably take a break, my muscles are trembling, and my hands are aching. The final time, I accidentally release the string when it's drawn instead of controlling the release of tension.

The bowstring moves faster than I can see, and the bow springs back into its neutral position of least tension. It takes a moment before the pain hits, but when it does, I let out a small cry. "Ow! Bloody hell, that hurts," I gripe, clutching at the inside of my left forearm. Removing my hand, I see a neat line cut into the skin and blood already welling to the surface. Cursing again, I quickly cast Lay-on-Hands and the surface wound closes. Funny, I had my arm broken a couple of days ago, and I've had bites and swipes deep enough to cut into my organs, yet this slight surface wound is what makes me scream? All I can guess is that it's because it was so unexpected. When I'm in a fight, I expect to be hurt. I'm bracing for it. I really didn't anticipate being hurt now. Plus, the adrenaline in a fight significantly dulls the pain. Then, thanks to the Lay-on-Hands I tend to keep casting through a fight, by the time the adrenaline rush fades, I'm usually well on the way to being healed, if not healed completely. I didn't have that here.

Anyway, note to self: create an armguard before going out hunting with my bow this afternoon. I look up and see Spike trundling towards the forest. *Is he going to forage now?* It would be a good opportunity to go together if that's the case. Perhaps I'll even have a chance to see him in action.

CHAPTER SEVENTY

Muscle Memory

I creep through the forest like Robin Hood, stalk like Legolas, and prepare to shoot like William Tell. Well, not really, but with my strung bow in one hand, a "quiver" of arrows on my back, and my eyes on the animal tracks I'm following, I feel pretty badass. Spike didn't seem too enthused at the idea of accompanying me on a dedicated hunt but seemed happy enough at the idea of going out together. As I search for animal tracks, he's foraging for food. We stopped by the river for him to have a drink, then I picked up some tracks that seemed promising. He's not next to me every second, but he's close enough that I could get to him within a minute or so. Or vice versa if another of those black blobs attacks.

As for Bastet, she's at home with the cubs since I didn't want to be carrying them on this test run. Perhaps we'll hunt a beast today that will have one of those objects Kalanthia set as her price for babysitting services so we can go out as a trio. Anyway, Spike and I as a combination will hopefully be able to face anything we encounter. Besides, it might mean more growth for him since I guess whatever benefits are gained are only for those who actually take part in the fight. We're in an area that's completely new to me, having followed the tracks from the river, but I haven't found the animal yet. Last time I checked my status screen, I spotted that my Energy absorption has actually increased. Not by much, only by one unit per hour, but it's enough to make me a bit wary since I guess that the higher the Energy density, the stronger the opponents I'll find. I mean, it's a rule of thumb and clearly not an absolute.

Kalanthia, for example, is a glaring exception. But from what I can tell, the animals in Kalanthia's area are generally more dangerous than the ones I fought when I first arrived: often bigger and usually more intelligent. Anyway, I've tried to take my time in choosing my prey, and *hopefully*, it's not too much for me to deal with. I am practically on my own, after all.

The beast I pick is alone and looks to be about as high as my waist. I figure that if my bow doesn't work the way I want it to, I can always just pull out my mace. I've got it hooked onto my belt with a few delicate strands of bark fiber. The attachment is strong enough to not simply fall off every time I move but weak enough that, in need, I'll be able to just yank it off.

As I stalk through the forest, I have both Fade and Stealth active. I actually asked Bastet what I looked like with Fade on since I can't see it working on myself. I did have to ask her to look away while I activated it, but then apparently it was fine for her to look at me afterwards. The images she sent showed that if I move at full speed when walking, Fade has very little impact. The slower I move, however, the more effect it has. First a distortion around my edges takes place, which makes it a little unclear where my flesh begins and ends as it blurs my outline.

Next, the distortion covers more and more area, and my body "fades" out from the edges inwards. By the time the edges are completely faded out, the rest of my body looks a little insubstantial as well. Once I've stopped moving entirely, I'm completely invisible. Of course, all these effects only last as long as my stamina does, which is longer these days, I'll admit. Fortunately, it seems like my Bound can sense where I am as long as I want them to, so Spike doesn't have any problems following me. It's a cool Skill, and I look forward to seeing what happens when it crosses the threshold into Initiate. From what I've noticed, Skills gain new effects or are transformed into something better when they cross a threshold, so I wonder what will change about Fade.

As I'm wondering this, I notice that the tracks have started to become fresher. It's not long after that I notice I'm approaching my prey. I slow down and use the natural foliage to help me hide from my target even when I'm moving. It's not long before I'm actually able to set eyes on the creature I've been following for so long.

Like with most of the animals I've come across so far in this world, it's a reptilian type of creature. This one is vaguely reminiscent of an anteater in shape, though with a long thin tail that matches its snout, and in diet. I notice as it uses a long tongue to scoop up some insects below and deliver them into its sharp-toothed mouth. *Perfect!*

There's a very quiet rustle of leaves right next to me, and I almost jump out of my skin before I recognize it as Spike. He looks at me, and there's a very faint questioning feel down the Bond. Is he starting to communicate with me like Bastet? That would be great if he could learn that. It takes me a bit of time to work out that he's asking if I want him to be involved in this battle.

"Not right at the beginning," I say after a moment's thought.

While I was following the tracks, I considered what to do in case the creature at the end of it turned out to look pretty dangerous. If that had been the case, I'd have told Spike to stay back completely unless I looked to be in mortal danger—if I decided to attack at all. As it is, the creature doesn't look particularly vicious, though looks can be deceiving. Still, while I'm curious to see how Spike would approach a fight, I also want to test out my new bow. Frankly, I don't have the confidence in my own skills to want my Bound anywhere near where I'll be shooting in case I hit him instead. But if Spike stays behind me, it should be safe enough. I tell him that and he moves to stand behind me without complaint.

That decided, I focus back on my hunt. The creature hasn't detected us, it seems, but has shifted a little further away in its search for insects. Moving slowly and carefully, I pull an arrow out from the rough quiver on my back. Before leaving,

I made it out of a jumper tied crossways over my back with the bottom tied closed so that the arrows stick in the neck hole. It's awkward to put the arrows in, but they pull out easily enough with only a little snagging. I could have put them in my Inventory, but I decided it takes too long to pull them out that way. Still, a proper quiver is definitely a priority. I nock the arrow and pull the string back, my muscles already struggling a little with the powerful draw of the bow. My arrow looks pretty good. Badass, even. The pitch adds a bit of black to the top and bottom of each piece of fletching and holds the head in place. Actually, the contrast between the white tooth and black pitch is rather awesome on the aesthetic side of things. Not that it really matters . . . It's not such a contrast on the thirteen flint-head arrows, but they look pretty cool too.

As for the feathers, they're a bit of a hodgepodge. I've tried to keep a pale-colored one as the cock feather so that I'll be able to tell at a glance the direction of the nock, but the other fletching is all mixed colors. I suddenly have the nagging feeling that maybe I should have actually tried firing the bow earlier today rather than leaving it to a live encounter . . . *Ah, too late now.* If worse comes to worst, I'll have to go back to using my knife and mace. Or sic Spike on it. Drawing the string back just a little more, I aim and then release the arrow. Fortunately, I don't have a painful repetition of earlier when releasing the string: I've tied a doubled-over shirt around my forearm to cushion the blow. Later, I want to use the crocodile skin as an armguard, but that'll require a bit more processing so I don't have rotting flesh tied to my arm. *Lovely thought, that.*

My arrow sails smoothly through the air . . . to land a meter away from my target. *Damn.* Of course, this has alerted the animal to my presence, and it leaps around with surprising speed, rears up on its hind legs, and makes a menacing hissing noise. What would probably be fairly intimidating for other animals just ends up presenting a better target for me. I pull out another arrow and draw the bowstring back again, but this time the arrow lands even further away in the opposite direction. I think the adrenaline is making my hands shake. The beast is still making that hissing sound and is swaying menacingly from side to side, so I figure I've got time for at least one more shot.

This one ends up a bit closer, but it still misses my target by a wide margin. Frustration growing inside me, I make shot after shot; only one actually hits the anteatilion, and that purely by chance. After the ninth attempt, the creature's hissing takes it up a notch and it starts leaping towards me, completely undeterred by my shoddy targeting. Making a snap decision, I quickly slot my bow into my Inventory, resisting the urge to throw it down in disgust. Frankly, I'm rather disappointed with myself, but taking out my anger on my bow is just going to mean I have to spend more time later repairing or recreating it. It's not the bow's fault I'm a rubbish shot.

"All right, Spike. Show me what you've got." I sigh and pull a couple of rocks out of my Inventory just in case. The porcupig doesn't "say" anything but trundles forwards. The anteatilion is surprised when its next leap is met with a load of spines to its face.

Pulling back, it rubs at its face with a paw, making a moaning sound of pain. Once more, Spike gets a constipated look on his face, then shoots quills at the already injured anteatilion. I note with interest that there are a *lot* fewer than I remember hitting the black blob. *Is it a resource that takes time to regenerate? If so, how long?* After that, Spike harries the beleaguered creature by nipping at its skin hard enough to draw blood and not letting it retreat when it decides that this battle isn't one it wants to be part of. One thing I do notice, however, is that he's struggling to finish the fight. Though he has surprisingly sharp teeth, they're not very big and he doesn't seem to be hitting any vulnerable spots. He's also only just as quick as the anteatilion itself, meaning that he can counter its attempts to escape but not really capitalize on them.

Neither of them is particularly fast at all, really. The other creature is clearly only able to move at speed when leaping. How it survives in this forest, I don't know, but I suppose the same question could be asked about the sloth on Earth. Between the two of them, I'd say things are probably pretty much even. Spike has more natural defenses; the anteatilion is a bit faster. It's a stalemate.

When the anteatilion, its escape barred by the spiky porcupig, decides to go *through* Spike by any means necessary, I decide to step in. I don't want him torn to pieces, after all, and the anteatilion's slim toothy mouth looks a lot more likely to do that than Spike's own.

Concentrated as it is on my Bound, the anteatilion is confused a moment later when a rock comes out of the surrounding trees to smash it in the skull, soon followed by a second to its shoulder. Turning to face the new threat, the creature lumbers towards me; its slightly off-balance approach shows the effect the impact of heavy stones to its head and body has had.

The slow speed enables me to grab my other new weapon out of my Inventory. Lumbering forward requires it to be on all fours, which reduces the target size for me. Fortunately—for me—my new Dexterity has made my general accuracy much better, and I strike at it with my spear and hit it in the neck. My spear is certainly more accurate than my bow. I grimace again at the thought. The range on my spear keeps the creature at bay so by the time it slumps to the ground, bleeding out from multiple wounds, I've managed to get away without a scratch. I have to admit that I'm feeling a bit sorry for it. Although I wish my bow had worked, I don't think it would have made much difference to the battle. Or slaughter, really. I could have put the creature out of its misery earlier if I'd been more accurate with my arrows. Clearly, archery is just like everything else: I might have the memories, but I'll have to work at it to have real muscle memory.

Here, standing over the body of a creature I've brutally stabbed to death after my shooting skills proved wanting and the Bound I sent to kill it didn't manage to do the job, I realize how much I've changed. The first time I killed in this world, by bashing in the head of a bird, I felt guilty. But at least that one had attacked me first. Then, the first time I actively went hunting, I felt terribly guilty at killing the sneleon, and I couldn't even make myself attack the porcupig family, seeing them as innocent animals. Now . . . even though *I* attacked this creature, I don't feel that guilty. I used it for target practice. I sent my non-combat Bound after it and prolonged its suffering with those nasty quills Spike has. That, I feel a bit sorry for, but I needed to know what Spike could do.

When did I become comfortable with justifying my actions purely because of my own needs? *What am I going to be in a year?* The thought drifts into my mind. *Will I be unrecognizable from the person I once was?* A nose nudges my leg and I look down to see Spike staring up at me. He sends a questioning feeling down the Bond between us.

"Yeah, you did good, buddy," I tell him numbly. He did exactly what I asked of him; it isn't his fault that he couldn't finish the whole job.

He responds with pleasure, perhaps because I'm pleased with him, then with a sense of being ravenous. Next, he sends another questioning feeling. *Is he asking if he can go and eat?* I suppose it makes sense that he might need to replace the resources that he spent in the fight.

Maybe food helps his ranged quills to grow faster—I don't know. Nevertheless, I quickly give my assent. He makes a beeline for the body of the anteatilion, carefully chewing a few mouthfuls of flesh before trundling off quickly into the bushes. I'll follow him in a moment, but I go to collect all of my arrows first, not willing to risk losing even a single one.

As I search the bush for each precious missile, the task complicated by the fact that I'm looking for sticks among sticks, I reflect just how easily Spike dealt with the death of the anteatilion. No moral dilemma, no self-reflection, no fear about ending up on a slippery slope. Just . . . this was my target, my target is dead, now I'm hungry. In a way, I wish I could break things down so simply the way Spike does. The way Kalanthia and Bastet do too.

I'm surrounded by creatures to whom death is merely a symptom of not being strong enough to live. Suddenly, I miss other humans with a strength of longing that surprises me. It's strange: I used to spend a good portion of each day wishing other humans would just disappear and leave me be instead of coming and loading my already full plate with their own issues. And now that I've got my solitary life without other people's problems, I miss them—because along with other people's problems come other people. I suppose this is what they mean when they say, "Be careful what you wish for."

Kalanthia and Bastet are great. Even Spike is great. Well, he's getting there, at least. It's been almost a month since I arrived, and I would have probably already gone insane from isolation if I hadn't had them. Humans aren't meant to be completely alone. Still, for all that their presence has meant that my sanity has remained, I can't help missing *humans*. The nunda, raptorcat, and porcupig are just too different from me. Their mindsets aren't the same. They don't care about the whys of a situation, just the whats and hows. They live in the concrete, in the tangible present. When a threat appears, they deal with it efficiently and then return to enjoying the moment. In some ways it's laudable, but in others it just makes me feel very, very alone. There's a reason humans sent a rocket to the moon. We'd spent centuries—millennia—wondering what was up there and why something could hang in the sky when anything we tried to put there just fell immediately. We are dreamers, thinkers, and philosophers, and I find myself missing conversation that is merely for the sake of conversing. I bury myself in a book most evenings to try to feed my need for the abstract, but it only helps temporarily.

I sometimes imagine going back to Earth and being able to share lunch with my co-workers again, going to a bar and having an in-depth conversation with a complete stranger. Never mind the fact that I rarely accepted my co-workers' invitations to share lunch with them because I was usually having a working lunch at my desk and that, after a time, the invitations stopped coming. Never mind that I never took the time to go out to bars and that, if I did, I'd have probably spent the time sitting at the bar itself and nursing a drink, silent and alone. Those truths are beside the point. I *could* have. And now I probably *would*.

But at the same time . . . I don't think I would fit back in that world. I've seen too much, done too much. My previous life just seems so . . . shallow. Without the threatening edge of death, how do you know you're living? Looking back at myself in my HR job feels like remembering a dream, like I spent years sleepwalking. It seems odd to think that I'm getting used to all of this. I'm becoming accustomed to living in constant danger, to killing others and risking being killed. I feel like I should be more traumatized than I actually feel. I feel like I should wake up in the morning and not dare to set foot out of Kalanthia's cave—heck, not dare to set foot out of my *own* cave, since it's guarded by a giant leopard. But . . . I just get up and get on. Is it some sort of psychological defense humans develop in times of trouble? I need food; I need water. I can't just hide and hope everything will turn out all right, which is something I think I was doing when I started on my bender after being fired.

Or maybe it's something to do with the System. It's indisputable that the feedback mechanism of gaining Energy by risking myself and then gaining points to protect myself and reduce the risk to my life is highly engaging. Sure, getting points is difficult, but it's significantly easier to improve myself in a measurable way here than it was on Earth, thanks to the Energy making up the shortfall. And it's just so satisfying to receive messages saying this or that stat has increased. It's motivating if nothing else.

When I finally find my last arrow buried in a bush, my musings are interrupted by a sudden sense of urgency that grips me. Thinking I'm in danger, I quickly leap sideways and stare around myself wildly, while my hand immediately goes to my mace. A moment later, I realize that the feeling is coming from one of my Bound.

I'm worried that something is happening back at the cave with Bastet, Kalanthia, and the cubs, and I'm already moving in that direction when I realize that the sensation isn't from Bastet's Bond. I stop suddenly, my heart beating faster than before. It's not Bastet who's in danger. It's *Spike*.

CHAPTER SEVENTY-ONE

Ashes of Regret

arrive just in time to see a spray of blood erupt from Spike's jugular. "No!" I shout and blindly lunge forwards, my hands outstretched. I touch his quills and trigger a Lay-on-Hands, only to have to snatch my hand away and roll a moment later as teeth snap for my throat.

I swing my spear, jabbing it at the creature that just attacked me. It dodges with frustrating agility and another set of teeth sets itself in my unprotected leg. I use my unencumbered leg to kick away my unseen attacker and hurriedly push myself to my feet.

I'm surrounded. The ones that were attacking Spike deviate to attack me instead. Spike's still alive—I see his jaws shifting open and closed. He's in a bad way, though. A very bad way. I need to get to him.

Hold on, buddy, I think desperately at him even as I stab at the creatures around me. They look like T-Rexes, only a lot smaller: their heads only reach about a meter off the ground when they stand upright. Their teeth seem no less dangerous, though—a mouth full of needles to crunch and tear. I've already felt the bite of those once and am not keen to experience it again.

I feel blood running down my leg, but I dare not cast a Lay-on-Hands; what if I do that and then don't have enough mana to heal Spike when I get to him? I'm gratified to see that several bear wounds from teeth or claws; some even have quills still sticking out of their faces or paws. He hasn't gone down without a fight.

But that's not enough to quell the rage that rises in me. *Spike is* mine—*how dare these animals try to take him away from me?* I yank my mace free from my belt and leap into the fray with both hands filled, desperately trying to get through the obstacles stopping me from healing my Bound. They are frustratingly difficult to pass, though. As soon as I get through one, another moves into my way or attacks the back of my legs in a way I can't ignore; if I'm hamstrung, *I'll* be the one in need of healing. It's like they know I'm running out of time and are determined to make me run the clock. It's only by suddenly leaping in the opposite direction from what they were expecting and dealing a number of blows, which kill two mini rexes, that I get a moment's respite.

I throw myself down next to Spike, not even casting the healing spell, and just immediately dump a whole third of my mana pool in a quicker channeling than I've ever done before. The mana enters Spike, then rebounds, most of it returning to me. My eyes are on the mini rexes, which are already circling again, though more reticent to attack than before they lost two of their number.

Come on, I think, trying again. The same thing happens. I dare to glance down for a moment, and what I see makes my stomach drop. His eyes are glassy, and he isn't breathing. The blood is still coming out of him, but it's trickling rather than spurting as it was. Combined with the failure of my healing magic, I know what the problem is. Spike's dead. Even my healing magic can't do anything about that. *How did this happen? We were only apart for* fifteen *damn minutes!*

I lift my eyes slowly to stare at the mini rexes. For a moment, the grief threatens to overpower me, but then rage twice as strong rises in its place. I bare my teeth and bellow wordlessly at them; the power of my cry actually makes them take a step back and mill uncertainly. For a moment, I wonder whether they might even turn tail and run. I'm not going to let them.

Throwing myself forwards, I swing with my mace, each contact breaking bones. In between swings, I stab with my spear. Between the two, my mace is the more effective—my fury is badly affecting my accuracy with the spear. I get two more mini rexes in the next few seconds as I beat in their heads with angry swings of my upgraded mace. That's the end of my freebies, though.

The mini rexes rally and start displaying the teamwork that must have taken Spike down. They start circling me, darting in as if to bite, and then shying away the moment I start swinging at them. At the same time as one of the mini rexes in front of me feints an attack, one of the others behind me actually does attack. My spear proves its worth here as I knock away mini rexes behind me with the butt end when they thought they'd snuck up without me knowing. Still, my fury only carries me so long, and it doesn't take me long to realize I've got myself in a bad situation here. I take several slashes to the backs of my legs, only avoiding having a tendon severed by last-minute dodges. As my rage gets replaced by the cold feeling of fear, I wonder if I've bitten off a bit more than I can chew.

A moment after that thought occurs, I push it away; the moment I *think* I've lost is the moment I actually have. I can win this—I just need a bit of strategy.

My first step is to break away sideways and put a large boulder at my back. *Okay, that helps*—the mini rexes still try to attack me in my blind spots, but having something solid behind me is already lessening the pressure. *See: using my Intelligence will get me through this,* I tell myself.

Now I need to actually hit the things, or this will just turn into a battle of attrition, which I'm likely to lose; a pack can rotate members in and out to rest while keeping up a constant barrage of attacks on me. Of course, that's assuming the mini rexes have the intelligence to do that, but I'm not going to make the mistake of underestimating them. They're wary of my mace, already having seen what it did to three of their packmates. As soon as I swing it towards them, they jump away, then close back in as soon as it's gone past. It's a stalemate. If they get too close, I swing my mace and they jump away out of range. I don't hit anything, and they can't get close enough to attack. But if I move towards them, I'll be opening my back up to attacks again.

My spear has a slightly longer range of attack, but due to its need for accuracy, the target just needs to shift a little and it's rendered useless. I need some other method of attack. There are five more mini rexes to kill, and so far, I haven't managed to land any more hits since taking down the two at the start and then the two after recommencing battle.

My thoughts go towards my bow, but I dismiss the idea after a moment: it takes two hands to operate, which means I would open myself up to attacks while drawing it. Not to mention the fact that I'm a rubbish shot and would risk hitting myself rather than my attackers, if I hit anything at all. Still, the thought of my bow has sparked another idea. *Why not return to the golden oldie that I used to such good effect in previous battles?* I have to access my Inventory, which does open me up to a couple of attacks, but by clumsily flailing my mace around me even while I focus on taking the items out of my storage space, I manage to keep off most of the opportunistic mini rexes.

A few moments later, I have a pile of hard and rough projectiles sitting in front of me, otherwise known as rocks. Making a mental note that I'm running low on good throwing rocks, I lean down to grab one of them, quickly switching my mace to my off hand. It's much clumsier like that, but that's okay—I only need it as a sort of shield. I already dropped my spear to the ground in order to have a hand free for my Inventory.

The mini rexes aren't prepared for the battleground to suddenly change from melee to ranged as I begin throwing the rocks. Their confusion costs them: in the first ten seconds, I manage to throw four rocks and hit with three of them. One mini rex is killed outright with a lucky blow to its head; the other two are crippled as one rock caves in ribs and the other breaks a leg. My eleven in Strength isn't just for show, after all.

After that, the survivors seem a lot more wary, milling around further away. They're not such easy targets since they keep moving, but I keep throwing rocks anyway. Probably two in three rocks hit, and though none of them are immediate killing blows, they certainly do damage. I almost wince at the sound of breaking bones that cracks through the air every time a rock strikes, but a glance at Spike's corpse soon sends my anger up high enough that I don't care about hurting his killers.

For a while it seems like the mini rexes don't know how to adapt to a human who's capable of different attack styles, but then their strategy comes into play. The first I know about it is when I feel an impact to my back and then blinding pain as teeth set themselves into my right shoulder, managing to grab an area of flesh not protected by my chitin backplate. It turns out that the crushing power of a mini rex's jaws is not to be scoffed at, and I feel my bones starting to creak under the pressure.

Screaming, I slam myself against the boulder behind me, trying desperately to kill them or at least knock them unconscious so they let go. Like the proverbial bulldog, they just hold on tighter. Worsening the situation, the other mini rexes take advantage of the situation and crowd around to snap at my front, reaching up as high as they can to tear at my torso. I go berserk. Flailing around myself with my mace and a rock in my hand, I batter mini rexes with every swing. At the same time, I keep throwing myself back against the boulder, as crazy as a fox caught in a trap. The fight hangs on a knife's edge. I'm making progress against the attackers in front, and the one behind has loosened its grip ever so slightly. But it comes at a cost: my stamina is down by three quarters, and I can feel tiredness seeping into my limbs. I can't keep this up for much longer. Not to mention that every time I swing my mace with my dominant arm, I can feel the teeth set in my shoulder doing more damage.

My health is still mostly fine since I've been casting Lay-on-Hands at regular intervals—the use of the Skill has become somewhat automatic by now. I'm still covered in wounds, and despite my use of my healing Skill, my health ticks down steadily. That's in large part because of the gaping wounds in my shoulder, which I can't close since *there are teeth stuck in them.* I need to use my brain. My anger is great for fueling my strength, but it's rubbish for conserving stamina. Much as I hate the idea, I decide to focus on the mini rexes at my front and leave the one attached to my back. It's not shifting at the moment and trying to deal with it will make me vulnerable to the ones in front, which are doing their best to rip out my guts. Sure, having teeth in my shoulder is making it harder to move, but fortunately, the adrenaline is doing a good job at masking the pain for now. If it shifts to attack something different, I'll get an opportunity to knock it off while it's repositioning.

Decision made, another idea occurs to me, and I can't help a savage grin from creeping across my face. Running into the middle of the clearing, I gain momentary respite from attacks. It's just enough to access my Inventory and pull something out to drop in front of me.

"Eat this, *Jurassic Park* rejects!" I yell as I start swinging something around me with both hands. It's the corpse of the—now toothless—crocodile, and I hold it by the tail while the rest of the body is pulled out straight with centrifugal motion as I spin. The weight is no joke; only by leaning back and holding on with both hands do I mostly manage to control my makeshift flail. The three mini rexes have no chance of reacting in time. They'd been rushing towards me to attack and didn't have the time to both register the new threat flying towards them and also react.

The weight of the crocodile's body, plus its momentum, knocks the mini rexes over completely, stunning them. I let go of my "weapon" as it starts threatening to pull me over and let the corpse fly into a tree as I rush forward to take advantage of the situation. I knew that the strategy wasn't likely to kill them, so I'd been mentally preparing to rush forwards and kill as many as I could while they were disorientated.

In the end, I get two of the three in the first five seconds. I flail with my mace to crush one of their heads and stab another, slitting its throat and letting it bleed out. The last one by this point has started regaining its bearings, and I miss my strike as it shifts away at the last moment. I'm not letting it get away, though, and I lunge forward to tackle it. The grounded mini rex isn't taking my attack lying down—well, technically it *is* lying down, but whatever—and it snaps at my throat.

It actually manages to catch a flap of my skin even as I jerk back instinctively. I feel blood trickle down from the wound and desperately grab at the mini rex's head. Managing to get my hand around its jaws, I grip as firmly as I can; unlike the crocodile, I can tell that I'm not going to be able to hold its mouth shut for long. It gives me an opening, though, and I stab at its neck artery. I hit it on my second attempt and sag for a moment as blood spurts out. The continued agony in my back penetrates my mind, though, and I push myself to my feet. Completely *done* with this whole fight, I just use my mace to batter at the one attached to my shoulder blade until I start hearing soft sounds that indicate I've given it some kind of serious blow. It's a tenacious bugger and maintains its grip to the very end. Even once it's died, its jaws stay locked. It's so ridiculous I have to wonder whether it's some sort of evolutionary feature that allows the mini rexes to lock their jaws so that even in death they stay secure.

I have to literally break the jaw joints to get the creature off—not easy to do when I can barely get a grip with one hand, let alone two. By the time I succeed, I've managed to heal the rest of my wounds and my stamina has recouped a bit. Sighing in relief as I pull the final mini rex's teeth out with a nasty squelching sound, I cast a channeled Lay-on-Hands and run the spell until my wounds are completely closed. Feeling pretty depressed now the anger has burned away and ashes of regret and guilt are all that remain, I stare around at the mess we've made of this small clearing. My eyes rest upon one of the mini rexes' bodies. Maybe I should have Dominated one of them. It would have made logical sense. But there was never a good opportunity, for one, and for another . . . Emotionally, I don't think I could have dealt with Binding Spike's killer. I'd probably have crushed its resistance and then hated myself afterwards.

Well, they're all dead now. No other option but to deal with reality. I force myself to trudge forwards and clean up the detritus of my battle.

CHAPTER SEVENTY-TWO

Carrying a Burden

At least the mini rexes were good for Energy gain, I conclude after eating their hastily cooked hearts. That, frankly, is the only thing good about the situation. All told, I'm a single percentage point away from being able to level up, and I'll gain that in an hour or so of absorption.

It's hard to feel excited, though. Not when the gain has been preceded by death. It's strange. I've known Spike for less than a month. Of that time, most of it has been spent apart since either he's been out foraging, or I've been out hunting for animals or resources. We've only been out in the forest together a few times since I Dominated him; it's only been in the last few days that I've started to feel any real connection to him. How can I feel so sad at his death?

But the first time we went out together, he saved my life. And if I hadn't Dominated him, maybe he'd still be alive now. Or maybe he wouldn't be—life in this valley is dangerous. My urgent task of tidying up the area by shoving the corpses, including that of the crocodile, into my Inventory is now completed. Now it's time to actually work through what happened. I sigh and move over to the porcupig's corpse, settling down by his head. His eyes are glassy, dead. His fur is stiff, blood around his mouth. At least he managed to make a mark on his attackers and I finished the job for him. I can't help but wonder why it suddenly happened now when I'd just decided to help him get stronger by taking him with me more often for fights. Does Murphy actually exist in this world of magic and Energy? And if he does, is he the reason for why that pack of mini rexes found Spike today?

I scrub at my face roughly. I can't blame Murphy; it's my fault he died. We were out together; I should have been able to protect him. I'd been less than twenty seconds' desperate sprint from where he'd been, but sound doesn't always travel well in this dense forest; I guess they'd been in the fight for longer than that. Did he scream for me and then wonder why I didn't come? I probably only sensed the danger when the fight turned deadly. Like how Bastet sensed me being in danger when my arm was broken in the fight with the crocodile. But I should have been right beside him, not a sprint away. It was me who agreed to him going to eat after the fight, despite knowing that he was tired and out of ammunition. I should have told him to wait until I'd collected my arrows or to forage in the area close to me.

For all I know, it's my fault the mini rexes were in the area in the first place! I do seem to attract danger, and the smell of blood from our anteatilion fight could have been a draw. I thought I was protecting him by not pulling him into the frequent combat I seem to attract, but he's dead anyway. It's a dangerous forest, and maybe if I'd taken him with me more often, he'd have developed more skills in fighting. The guilt and self-recrimination inside me are far too familiar and once more threaten to drown me.

No, I can't go down that path again. After my mother was killed, I tumbled into a pit of self-loathing caused by blaming myself for her death. I clawed my way out of that dark hole only to be pushed back in later by my father's illness and subsequent death. Even though the doctors had scientific names for the cause of his demise, I know the reality: he died when my mother did. It just took his body a decade to catch up. The malignant cancer that grew inside him and brought about his end was really only the coup de grâce to a zombie. Blaming myself for their deaths has never led anywhere good. My mother's death led to a difficult relationship with my father, difficulties at school, and problems connecting with others. Ultimately, it led to an inability to emotionally commit, which lost me my best friend and the only girl I've ever loved romantically. Blaming myself for my father's death led me to the roof of my apartment and, one could say, to this world to begin with. Maybe I need to take another approach this time.

My therapist used to say that I should accept and acknowledge my feelings but not allow them to consume me. She suggested that I carefully consider what actually happened and if I truly found some way in which I could have affected the outcome, to consider how to do something positive in the present to acknowledge that. To do something positive that would attempt to avoid the issue happening again, rather than becoming sucked down into a cycle of could've, would've, should've. She also encouraged me to take time to mourn. As I push myself to my feet, I decide what to do; I've always been better at working through my feelings when doing something. It's the reason I started going to the gym in the first place: to be able to deal with the anger and grief still fermenting inside me.

I search around the small clearing, which is now empty of bodies apart from Spike's. The only evidence of our battle is the disturbed leaf litter and blood-soaked ground. I finally find what I'm looking for and start using the sturdy stick to dig at the center of the space between trees. Yes, I know that probably the most efficient way of dealing with Spike's body is to save it as raptorcat food, or even to eat it myself, but . . . I can't face that. I want to give him a burial.

Plus, the time that I spend digging the hole is time that I can spend working through my feelings and perhaps once more come to terms with the loss of someone around me. Because that's what it boils down to. I'm tired of losing people. My mother, my father, my girlfriend, and now Spike . . . *Who's next? Bastet? Kalanthia? Lathani? One of the cubs? But how do I stop it happening?*

I couldn't do anything about my mother's car accident, though I've always blamed myself for being the reason she was driving. I don't know what I could have done to help my father—the wounds were just too deep. As for my girlfriend . . . Yeah, I was at fault there. I put my work first and ignored the signs that she wanted to take our relationship further. Looking back, it was my fear of losing the ones I love that stopped me from committing. How ironic is it that the fear became self-fulfilling? *Spike* . . . Maybe I shouldn't have Dominated him in the first place. It's a pretty awesome Skill, but I'm coming to understand more and more that it's not one I should use without careful thought. If I Dominate a creature, I become responsible for it. I didn't act responsibly with Spike, and he died as a result. He died because he was a vulnerable prey animal in a cutthroat environment. If I had been at his side, he may not have died. Note, I say *may* not because I'm not sure that I would have been able to protect him when it was so hard to even protect myself, but his chances of survival could have been significantly higher than they ended up being.

Ultimately, it boils down to the fact that I Dominated him without really thinking of the consequences. I was like a person who wants a dog but doesn't do their research and gets a breed that needs constant companionship when they're barely at home. In my case, I just went out and Dominated the first creature I came across; I thought more about his use as a biological digger than the fact that he would need constant protection. I didn't think about whether his needs matched mine or whether my dangerous life was one he could fit in with.

He needed to forage because I couldn't supply his nutritional needs. I couldn't be with him every time he needed to forage, I know that. Equally, I couldn't spend hours of each day searching out food for him so he didn't have to leave the safety of home. I was the pet owner who got a pet despite not being able to afford to feed one. It was doomed from the start.

So, Mrs. Therapist, my positive action? To put a lot of thought into whether I should Dominate a creature based on the life I can offer it afterwards. And then, once Bound to me, to think carefully about the best way to protect them—even if that means exposing them to some danger so they can grow. Given its potential drawbacks, the Skill is unlikely to be something I use in a battle without thinking about it beforehand, so I should have no excuse for irresponsible decisions. The whole thing makes me question whether I was right to Dominate Bastet. After weighing up the arguments on either side, I conclude that it's a different context. Not only was Bastet dying before I offered her the Bond, but that's the whole point: I *offered* it to her. Because she'd been willing to die rather than be bound, it meant that when she accepted the Bond, she genuinely did so because she thought it was the best option for her pack.

That's another consideration. The raptorcats are used to hierarchy and to a pack structure. Bastet and I have a very different relationship than I had with Spike, and I think the fact that she comes from a context that was already socially complex is a big part of it. As far as I've been able to gather, porcupigs stick together as a family until the babies are adults, and then they all go their separate ways. Certainly, Spike's capacity to communicate was significantly less than Bastet's.

Plus, of course, I've been hunting together with Bastet as well as providing her and the cubs with meat from my own solitary hunts. Bastet, despite being a lot more equipped to survive other predators, has actually been exposed to a lot less risk than the more vulnerable porcupig. And I never made the effort to try to help Spike be less vulnerable.

Not until today, which turned out to be too late.

It's a hard pill to swallow, the knowledge that my neglect and thoughtless actions and inactions are what led to this moment, but it's a lesson that I need to learn. If I learn it now and never commit the same mistakes in the future, then perhaps I'll be able to forgive myself one day. For now, I simply dig and take my self-recrimination and sadness out on the soil.

When I'm done digging a hole about a meter down and just big enough around for the porcupig, I trudge over to him again wearily. "I'm sorry," I tell him quietly, my throat hoarse from thirst. I haven't had anything to drink since starting my task—a type of self-harm that probably isn't all that healthy but has to be better than other things I can think of doing to myself. I lift him and carry his stiff body towards his grave. About to lower him in, I pause for a moment in thought, then pull out a few of his quills. I then pull out some of my bark-fiber cord and make a quick necklace, pushing the points of the quills through the twist. Then I sling it around my neck and tuck it under my shirt, the fiber rough against my skin. It will be a good reminder, if nothing else. When he's lying at the bottom of the hole, I pause again. Words don't really want to come. I feel like I should say a little prayer, give a eulogy, something. It's not the first funeral I've been to, after all. I should know how to do this. But in the end, I just say two things.

"I'm sorry it ended like this. I promise I'll do better next time."

With that, I start backfilling the hole. Handful by handful, clods of dirt land on his body and cover it. It's not long before his quills aren't even visible anymore. The horn on his nose is the last thing to be hidden, and as it vanishes under the earth, I feel a sense of letting go, maybe even of peace. It almost feels like he's forgiven me, but that's probably just my own imagination.

By the time I've finished the grave and have pressed down the soil on the top, I feel lethargic and all wrung out. Maybe that therapist had a point: it's been cathartic to bury him with my own hands, my sweat a sacrifice to his memory. It may be dug up again later; there's not much I can do about that. But for now, he's buried and at peace. It's enough. It has to be.

And as I walk away, I pause next to one of the trees, silent witnesses to the events of this day, and look back. The grave is half-hidden by the leaf litter already blown by the breeze. It's calm, final. Blood has been shed here: Spike's blood in death, my blood in apology, and Spike's killers' blood in vengeance. Sweat too. And tears—I will not deny it. I didn't know Spike for very long, but his death means something to me. Maybe more as a symbol than for his sake alone. Perhaps that's another wrong I do him.

But as I turn away and walk back home, I feel tired, exhausted even, but lighter. Like I've been carrying a burden for years, perhaps as far back as my mother's death, and finally I've been able to put down just a small piece of it.

CHAPTER SEVENTY-THREE

My Best Life

Bastet is on the alert when I get back. She must have picked something up from the Bond, though clearly not enough to make her come running the way she did with the crocodile. As soon as the raptorcat sees me, she sends a wave of emotion over the Bond. *Concerned-danger-threat?* I reply back in the negative. "Spike's dead," I tell her as she bounds up to me and rubs her head against my hip. My voice is flat. The emotional roller coaster of the past couple of hours has left me feeling empty inside.

I'll rally, I know that. It's not my first time on this rodeo; I know how grief sends emotions as high as Everest one moment and then as deep as the Mariana Trench the next. And that when the cycle becomes too much, the mind just shuts down its capacity to feel. For a time, anyway.

Bastet cocks her head to one side as the announcement leaves her unmoved. Understandably—she and Spike had a wary relationship at the best of times. Wary on Spike's side, that is; Bastet never really cared much about him as long as he wasn't too near the cubs. I sigh, sending her a picture of Spike accompanied by a feeling of loss, the ache that I feel whenever I think about my parents or my ex.

She pauses for a moment to consider what I sent her, then returns with a complicated bundle of images and emotions. Parsing through the confusing mix, I manage to get the gist of what she's saying. *Packmates die and we feel their absence. But life continues.* It's such a pragmatic way of looking at things, so characteristic of the raptorcat who was able to move in with her family's killer the day after it happened.

I don't know if I could ever be so prosaic about it—perhaps that's part of being human. But in a way, she's right. If I dwell too much in the past, I'll forget to live in the present. I'm guilty of having already done that for years. Do I really want to do that for years more? Like it or not, this is a dangerous world, and Spike is unlikely to be the only Bound I lose. Of course, I'll do my best to avoid that happening, but I need to be realistic. I need to learn from my mistakes, but I can't get bogged down with guilt and self-blame.

Sending her a wave of gratitude, I rub her head for a moment, then walk off to dump my armor by the entrance of the cave and greet the cubs and Kalanthia. Bastet sends me a sense of confusion about what she did to be thanked but pleasure at having helped her packmate. The cubs, of course, don't notice anything and just pile on me as usual, treating me like an object to be climbed or a target to be pounced on, depending on their mood in the moment.

When they tire of the game and move off to play with a couple of large beetles, squabbling over who gets to torture the poor insects, I find myself alone with Kalanthia. Unlike when we first met, the massive nunda's presence now only fills me with a sense of safety. Sure, I know that technically there's nothing stopping her from killing me. As much as I've been succeeding at squeaking through my encounters with large predators by the skin of my teeth, I know that I still have as much chance as a snowflake in hell against Kalanthia. Nevertheless, I find myself starting to trust that Kalanthia won't hurt me as long as Lathani is safe. We sit in silence for a while, just watching the cubs play. It's a nice balm to my raw emotions, watching four cute little fluffballs—one a lot larger than the others—tumbling and tussling together.

Your Bound is right, Markus Wolfe, Kalanthia finally rumbles in my mind after long, syrupy moments when I couldn't have said exactly how much time was passing. *Loss is a part of life. You will feel it whatever you do, but you cannot stop living because of it.* I twist around to give her a long, slow look.

"I thought you couldn't read my mind?" Kalanthia gives a leopard grin, full of teeth.

I never said that . . . But nonetheless, your thoughts are loud enough that I can no sooner not *hear them than I can shut my ears.*

My face pinks a bit in embarrassment. *Damn mind-reading massive felines . . .* And I only half care if she heard that last bit.

"Have you lost someone before?" I ask, only belatedly realizing that she might not want to bring up past losses any more than I want to bring up the memory of my mother's final moments. "Sorry, I—"

Yes, Kalanthia replies quietly, pensively. *Lathani is not my first cub. And even before I met my mate, I lost my siblings and parents one way or another.* My action is automatic; I don't even think about it. Feeling sympathy welling inside me, I turn and give her a hug. Well, I say that, but she's so big that I only get my arms part of the way around her shoulders. She looks at me in confusion. *Markus Wolfe, if this is an attack, it is not very efficient*, she tells me bemusedly.

"It's not." I chuckle briefly, the momentary humor serving to raise my spirits in a way nothing else has since I realized Spike was in danger. Sobering, I continue. "It's a way humans express . . . affection. Sympathy. Sorrow for the other person." *Ah*, she says in a way that seems like she's had an epiphany. *That makes a lot more sense, then. I always thought that it was strange for humans to attack their mates so often.*

I snort at the thought and then suddenly pause. Kalanthia seems remarkably open at the moment. Maybe she'd be willing to answer the question that she shut down when we first met.

"So, I remember you mentioned that there aren't any humans in this valley. Are there any outside it?" I ask, hope daring to rise in my breast that Nicholas had been wrong—wrong, or intentionally deceptive, for whatever reason. *Not in this world.* Kalanthia dashes my hopes once more but only raises more questions, ones that perhaps I should have asked earlier. Then again, it never seemed to be the right time before; perhaps now it might be.

"Then . . . are you . . ." I don't know how to ask the question. "Did you . . . come from another world?" Unconsciously, I hold my breath.

I did. Much like you. I chuckle a little darkly and rub the back of my neck.

"So, you also accidentally ended up here with no prior knowledge?"

Not quite. Unlike you, it seems, I came here voluntarily to give Lathani a better chance in life.

"Oh," is all I can say. It seems so . . . noble. Travelling between worlds to protect one's child. So much better than my reasoning. "I did actually choose to come"—I feel obliged to correct her supposition—"but I didn't really understand what I was choosing." I feel like a fool as I admit my idiocy. "And now I don't know whether it was the best or the worst thing to happen to me," I finish, staring at my hands. For better or for worse, I'm not the same person I was when I arrived here. I didn't know what it was to kill before I came. I didn't know what it felt like to be on the brink of death, either. Those things change a man.

Kalanthia is silent for a long moment, long enough that I think the conversation is finished. Then, shifting, she places her massive foreleg on the other side of me and pulls me close. *Is this how it is done?* she asks. For a moment I'm confused, but then I realize what she's doing and warmth spreads through me. "Yeah." My voice is croaky, and I have to swallow to wet my throat. My vision blurs. It must be the dust in the air irritating both my eyes and my throat. No other explanation. "Yeah," I say again, daring to lean into the large feline body I've been pulled up against. "That's exactly right." Closing my eyes, I let myself sink into the first hug I've had in what feels like years.

Eventually, I have to pull away. I've taken far too much advantage of the fact that Kalanthia isn't human and doesn't know how long these sorts of things are supposed to last, so I've just been luxuriating in the comfort. Despite being in this place so far away from home and anything familiar, maybe I've still found some sort of family. It makes me smile. The loss I feel at Spike's—and my parents' and my ex-girlfriend's—absence isn't gone, but it feels easier to bear now I know I'm not alone. Perhaps I'm grasping at straws here but . . . they're right. Everyone has been telling me for years to leave the past behind me. I won't forget everyone I've lost, but perhaps living my best life is a better way of honoring their deaths than the half-life I was living before. I feel restless. I've been doing a lot of work here at the cave, crafting various things, but my immediate projects are now done. I have a bow and arrows, which I need to practice with. I have some rough armor. I have soap, which is just drying out to make a bar, though it could technically be used right away. I have an upgraded mace, which was literally a lifesaver today. I need to make some more armor for my arms and legs, but that will take a lot longer, and I feel I want to do something else first. Twisting back towards Kalanthia, I ask her a question.

"If I gave you some of the corpses I've collected, would you be able to delay your next hunting trip?" She stretches for a moment, deadly claws the size of my forearm shooting out of her paws, before settling back down.

Perhaps, if you can supply enough meat to satiate me for a time. Why?

"There's somewhere I want to explore, but I'm concerned it may take multiple days. I wouldn't want to accidentally abandon you and Lathani."

I see. What do you have for me? Standing up, I pull out the crocodile corpse. It's a bit battered since I used it as a bludgeoning tool against the mini rexes and then let it crumple against a tree, but the hide is surprisingly intact. I think there's probably been more internal damage than external, to be honest. "How's this?" I ask, looking at Kalanthia expectantly. "I'd like to use the hide, so if you could leave it as intact as possible, that would be great. The rest can be yours if you want, though." She stands up and inspects the carcass, sniffing and prodding it. *An impressive kill for one so small,* she remarks. I would consider it more of a compliment if she left off the "small" comment. *Everything's* small in comparison to her. *Still, I would need more to delay my hunting trip by as much as a day, let alone more.*

"I see," I reply thoughtfully. Opening my Inventory, I check through for other corpses I can spare. *Huh, what about all the mini rexes from today? It's not like I've got any other use planned for them, and I've got the ostridocuses to feed my Bound and her cubs.*

"How many of these would you need?" I ask, pulling out one of them. "I've got seven in total."

Hmm, she muses mentally, inspecting the mini rex's carcass as she had the crocodile's. *Several of these plus the nere should keep me going for an extra day, two if necessary.* What does several mean?

"Okay, well, let me know when I've pulled out enough." She waits until I've pulled out six of the seven mini rexes before she indicates it's enough. If this is the quantity of meat she has to eat for one, maybe two days, how many animals does she kill when she goes out hunting every *four* days? Without waiting for any further conversation, she starts digging in. I watch in fascination as she flips the crocodile onto its back and then cuts it open. With one delicate claw, she opens a neat line from jaw to tail tip, and then she just starts ripping pieces away, completely unashamed of the blood and guts that quickly coat her jaw.

"Well, enjoy, I guess," I say weakly, turning away before her actions make me feel nauseous. Just another reminder that, despite giving me a hug, Kalanthia is still *definitely* not human. Moving far enough away that I can only just hear the crunching and chewing sounds, I turn my attention to more enticing prospects. Namely, the fact that my Energy store has reached one hundred percent full. *Time to level up!*

CHAPTER SEVENTY-FOUR

Impurities

Unlike last time, this time I haven't spent hours planning how to distribute my stats, so I take a few moments to make some decisions. After opening my status page, I survey my stats with no small bit of pride. Sure, I know they're nothing particularly noteworthy according to Nicholas's world, but considering what I started with, I feel like I've made some good advancements.

Name: Markus Wolfe		Race: Human	Class: Tamer
Level: 1	Energy to next level: 100%	Energy absorption rate: 13u/hr	Energy towards debt: 1%
Intelligence	10	Mana: 100/100	
Wisdom	11	Mana regeneration rate: 275u/hr	
Willpower	16+3 (+20%)	Health regeneration rate:19u/hr	
Constitution	10	Health: 100/100	
Strength	11	Stamina: 60/60	
Dexterity	10	Stamina regeneration rate: 100u/hr	
Class Skills:		Non-Class Skills:	
Dominate – Beginner 3		Lay-on-Hands – Novice 4	
Tame – Beginner 1		Stealth – Beginner 9	
Fade – Novice 5		Animal Empathy – Beginner 6	

Looking at the one hundred percent sitting there, I feel a bit of frustration that I can't gain any more Energy until I've leveled up. Then a thought occurs that makes me want to facepalm. I can't gain any more Energy, but I *can* accrue Energy towards my debt. Or, at least, I could have since I don't intend on waiting any longer before leveling.

Once more, it's too little, too late. But at least it's something that I can bear in mind for next time this happens. Besides, it's not like I'm in the right state of mind to focus on eking out every bit of gain I can when I've just buried Spike.

So, the actual leveling. I have six points to play with, I know that. Looking at my stats, they're all at ten or eleven points except for my Willpower, thanks to Kalanthia's bonus. For sure, points in Willpower have the best "value" since the plus twenty percent effectively gives me an additional point for every five that I add. But is that the most useful stat for me?

Increases in Willpower certainly help me when using Dominate, but am I likely to be using that Skill often? I've only recently concluded that it's not the kind of Skill I should be using without a good reason. Willpower, based on when I've earned the points, also helps with determination and capacity to push through pain or fear. It's also relatively hard to "train." But is that a good enough reason to add points to it?

Strength and Dexterity have almost the opposite arguments for and against them: they're stats that will most certainly help me with my daily life; they're also the easiest to increase "naturally." Although it's taken a lot more effort to increase my Strength from ten to eleven, the fact that I could do it without explicitly intending to is proof that it's relatively easy to improve. Do I want to waste my precious level-up points on those when time and life will do my job for me?

Constitution is a given. I need more leeway between living and dying and gaining points in that stat means subjecting myself to perilous situations. Plus, as far as I've understood the System lore stone, Constitution also governs things like more acute senses and a body that is more difficult to harm, like with tougher skin or bones. All of those are definitely an absolute necessity for me. The choice here is how many points to add, rather than whether to add points at all.

Intelligence and Wisdom are other questionable ones. I'm leaning towards adding points into Intelligence as, without further input in terms of new knowledge, I suspect that it will become harder and harder to increase that stat. It's useful, as Lay-on-Hands is the only reason I'm still alive, and I regularly hit empty on mana when facing dangerous opponents. Without any health potions, I need to make sure my mana store is sufficient to keep me alive.

Wisdom is in a similar vein. In the absence of a sufficiently large mana store, if my mana *regeneration* is sufficiently great, it doesn't matter in a way how much mana I use: I'll always have enough. At the moment, I'm earning approximately four and a half mana per minute, meaning that it takes just over two minutes to regain enough for another Lay-on-Hands. In most situations, that's enough, but when I faced the spider monster, it wasn't, and if I'd faced the crocodile head-on and been bitten or lost a limb, it wouldn't have been enough there either. With six points, I could add one to each category, but I decide that's a cop out. When I've decided my points distribution, I think, *Level up*. As before, a couple of messages come through.

Congratulations!
You have gathered enough Energy to push your body to the next level. Would you like to level up?

Y / N

To level up, please choose the stats you would like to increase. You have 6 points available. Warning: if you do not assign all points now, you will be unable to use them later. You can choose to delay your level-up, but you will not store any further Energy until you do. Do you wish to continue to level up?

Y / N

Accepting the first one, I hesitate over the second. I remember what happened last time: horrible stuff came out of me, and I vomited everywhere. I'm hoping that won't happen again . . . but maybe I should take precautions anyway.

"Bastet," I call quietly. Within a couple of moments, she comes sauntering over, sending a question down our Bond. "Can you come down with me to the river?

I'm going to be leveling up, and I don't want to risk something jumping me while I'm distracted." She gives me the equivalent of "wait a minute" and goes bounding off.

A moment later, she returns with the three cubs trotting in her wake. It's a shame that we don't have the glowing stones that Kalanthia wants for babysitting. Surprisingly, Bastet and Kalanthia seem to have slid into a comfortable relationship co-parenting all the cubs. In fact, the first time I saw Bastet cuff Lathani across the ear for something or other she'd done wrong, my eyes flew to Kalanthia in fear that she'd take offense. But it was quite the reverse: she seemed approving that her cub was being taught discipline. Much different from Earth and humans.

I remember being in a supermarket once with a little brat who had been insistently demanding that I give him a toy off the higher shelves. I'd refused, saying that he needed to ask his parent. The kid immediately flew into a huff and kicked me in the leg. I'd grabbed him by the shoulder—not hard, just firmly—and told him that kicking isn't acceptable. At which point the mother had come along, given me an earful for touching her precious darling, and hadn't even given me a moment to explain the situation. She'd finished by storming away, her child clutched in one hand, throwing a threat over her shoulder to take me to court. Of course, I'd never heard anything more about it, but it sure taught me a lesson about daring to say anything to a stranger's child. Clearly, nundas and raptorcats are a bit more sensible about the whole thing than humans.

Walking down the hill, we soon reach the river, and I undress, putting my clothes to one side over a branch of a tree. For a moment, I feel a bit self-conscious about being naked in front of Bastet, but as soon as the thought appears, I dismiss it. *Bastet* is naked. Permanently. Sure, she has furry feathers, but technically, she's not wearing any clothes. Plus, I'm human; she's a raptorcat. There's as much shame in getting changed in front of her as there would be in getting changed in front of a pet cat or dog.

Preparing myself for a potential ordeal, I trigger the leveling-up process. When my status screen comes up again, I choose to add a point each to Strength and Intelligence and two points to Constitution and Dexterity. Why? Strength because even if it's relatively easy to increase by itself, it's one of the most immediately useful of my stats. After all, I need the Power to help me in all areas of my new labor-intensive life, including to keep me alive in fights by helping me finish them earlier. More Power means a stronger attack with mace, spear, and bow. Maybe if I'd had more Power, I'd have had a better chance against that crocodile thing. Intelligence is because I need the mana—that's clearly a winner. Constitution because I need the health and defensive bonuses that it offers. Along with increasing Strength, I should then have a better chance of surviving fights.

The last two points took a bit of time for me to decide, but eventually, I landed on Dexterity because as my experiences recently have shown me, that stat is rather lacking for all the detail work I need to do. That it will probably increase my accuracy with the bow was not an insignificant part of my decision, I have to admit. Even if it means I'm a bit impatient, when I could just earn it with time and repeated fruitless attempts, I still decide to commit a couple of points to it now.

This time I expect the messages about refining my choices a little.

You have chosen to increase your Strength. Would you like to increase your Power or your Endurance?
Power / Endurance

The choice is obvious. *Power.*

You have chosen to increase your Dexterity. Would you like to increase your Agility or your Flexibility?
Agility / Flexibility

This one is a little less obvious. Which one is likely to help me the most? Agility is probably more about being able to fire quickly, fingers agilely picking arrows out of the quiver and nocking them, as well as actually being able to react to new situations with more speed. Flexibility has to be more about the positions my hands and body can make. *Is that what affects accuracy?* That's probably what will help me most with carving, knapping, and weaving, though.

In the end, although unsure, I choose Flexibility. It seems the most aligned with the reasons I've chosen Dexterity. Since I have two points available, I have another hard choice immediately afterwards. Deciding to double down in hopes that I will see a measurable improvement in at least one of my tasks, I choose Flexibility again.

Since Constitution and Intelligence don't seem to have subcategories, making that final choice triggers the rest of the leveling-up process. Once more I feel Energy fill my body in a great flood. This time I'm more familiar with Energy and my body in general, so, while it's most certainly euphoric, I can actually feel a little more of what's going on. The very cells of my body are being rewritten, I'm sure of it.

For a fraction of a second, I feel like my body is no more than a piece of elastic or play dough as Energy manipulates it into a new form. I even sense that more changes are happening beyond just the physical, but my metaphysical senses aren't anywhere near attuned enough to even get a glimpse of what's going on there. I suppose it's progress enough that I can actually sense that *something* is happening.

When the Energy has finished its work, that's when the pain hits. Once more, it's like being submerged into a world of agony where nothing else exists. I'm pretty sure the experience doesn't last long, but the fraction of time where it is happening seems to be a lifetime.

Finally, the pain ends, and I'm left with an aching body covered in sweat and other, darker fluids. I feel the nausea build inside me, and I only have time to think, *Not again*, before my body rebels and violently expels everything that's inside it, and more. More impurities are removed from my system, making a disgusting mess on the ground. I'm glad to have done it here rather than messing up Kalanthia's home ground again. Still, I'm gratified to realize that there are fewer impurities in my vomit this time. Hopefully, I eventually won't have any in there and I'll be able to keep my lunch down after leveling up. Honestly, if the benefits weren't so great, I might reconsider trying to level at all.

I jump into the river, relying on Bastet to notice any crocodiles—or anything else—coming my way, and just do my best to get clean. *I should have brought some of my soap*, I bemoan. *Ah, too late now. I'll just have to do the best I can with what I have.*

After this, I'll need to do some archery practice. It'll be interesting to see how my changed stats will affect my capabilities.

CHAPTER SEVENTY-FIVE

Baby Spider Monsters

Prowling through the forest with Bastet at my side, I feel a lot more confident. I feel like my afternoon yesterday was really productive when it came to improving my archery. Yes, I know that, traditionally, archers on Earth would have to practice for years to become decent, let alone good. An afternoon compared to that is nothing. Not even enough to learn how to stand properly.

I have a few advantages those would-be archers don't have, however. The first is from the hunting knowledge stone: memories of having learned to shoot and then doing it again and again literally thousands of times. The second is my Intelligence score, which by the time it's at a ten is starting to get up there with humanity's smartest. Humanity on Earth's smartest, at least. That doesn't suddenly make me into an Einstein, but it appears to improve my ability to make connections between subjects, observe what is going wrong, and adapt after learning from my mistakes.

Either way, I found that my learning process was a lot quicker than I remember it being at uni and during training courses at work. Probably the time I spent going through my "memories" ahead of actually starting helped too. Plus, it earned me a point in Intelligence, so I'm not complaining about that. Fortunately for me, it was a point that didn't require any Energy, as I didn't have enough in stock. By this point, I'm pretty sure that it only offers me a point that requires Energy if I actually have enough, otherwise it just keeps going until I've earned the point "naturally." Considering it's been several days since I earned my previous Intelligence point, I'm not surprised that I've gained another so soon. Just more evidence that the points I use on level-up don't affect my progress towards points being "earned."

Either way, I think I've become addicted to looking at my status sheet. It's just . . . Seeing evidence of my progress in a numerical form is just so *satisfying*. Maybe it's my history of working in human resources. I like data sheets; being able to properly quantify someone with one is almost a dream come true. Okay, a sad dream, I'll admit it—I never intimated all my desires were noble, high-reaching ones. When we stop for a short break for me to recoup my stamina, I pull the screen up again.

Name: Markus Wolfe		Race: Human		Class: Tamer	
Level: 2	Energy to next level: 5%	Energy absorption rate: 13u/hr	Energy towards debt: 1%		

Intelligence	12	Mana: 120/120
Wisdom	11	Mana regeneration rate: 275u/hr
Willpower	16+3 (+20%)	Health regeneration rate:19u/hr
Constitution	12	Health: 120/120
Strength	12	Stamina: 16/60
Dexterity	12	Stamina regeneration rate: 120u/hr
Class Skills:		Non-Class Skills:
Dominate – Beginner 3		Lay-on-Hands – Novice 4
Tame – Beginner 1		Stealth – Beginner 9
Fade – Novice 5		Animal Empathy – Beginner 6

With Fade's cost effectively reduced from using four units to using two units of stamina per minute, now that my regeneration is also two units per minute, I can keep the Skill going for as much as thirty minutes now—in theory. That doesn't tend to work in practice, though, as I also use stamina to travel. Fortunately, that's at a *much* lower rate. I don't want to completely bottom out, either—if I do, I won't be very fit for a fight if it comes down to one. The mana cost is effectively free, considering Fade takes only one unit per minute and I'm regenerating more than four.

I find it funny that despite having quite a wide range of stat values to begin with, I now have four stats at twelve and one at eleven . . . I know that focusing on two or three stats to—almost—the exclusion of the others is the best way to become really proficient in certain areas; by distributing my stats pretty equally, I risk becoming a jack-of-all-trades, resulting in being master of none. That said, I'd rather be an alive master-of-none than a dead expert simply because I didn't have enough health points or stamina points or Strength to deal with whatever attack comes next.

When my stamina bar refills, only taking just over twenty minutes now with my new regeneration, we set off through the forest again. Bastet went scouting while I was resting, and she sends me an image of my destination when she returns. It looks clear and is accompanied by a cautious sense of safety. I agree with the caution. It may look safe for now, but we need to be sure. As we walk closer, I consider something else I'd noticed on my status screen: my increased absorption rate. I'm pretty sure it wasn't as high as thirteen the last time I came through here.

What's changed? Has the Energy density of the area increased? Can it do that? Or have I changed? I'll need to monitor it a bit, I guess. We're here. I see a gaping mouth that makes me shudder again in remembrance of the last time I was here. The dry leaves covering the ground beneath the copse of dead trees crunch and crackle under my feet. The hole in the ground from which a monster out of my nightmares had burst looks empty and abandoned.

Leaves have fallen or been blown by wind into the hole scraped into the ground. I exchange a glance with Bastet, and with a whisper, the raptorcat slinks down the tunnel, her camouflage-like fur blending easily into the shadows. It's not long before she returns, indicating that the beginning at least is free of enemies.

I scoot down the slope on my bum, as I don't want to risk the cubs slung on my chest by going down on all fours and potentially falling and squishing them.

Down at the bottom, I take a moment to pull one of my pre-made torches out of my Inventory. I used some rags from one of my previously sacrificed shirts and wrapped them around the end of a freshly cut stick. Then after covering the wrapped end with some of my magic pitch, I let them harden.

It takes a little bit of time and effort to light the hardened resin product now, but once it catches light, the torch burns steadily. Multiuse tools for the win: it gives light, it's a handy weapon against any animals afraid of fire, and it's a good indication of if the oxygen level drops too low. I don't know what I'm walking into, after all. With the bark cord also in my Inventory and several days' worth of food and water—since I filled all my unused pots with water and stuck them into my Inventory too—I feel pretty prepared for the expedition. Especially so because by the end of my archery practice yesterday I was hitting the target every time and usually within a few fingers of where I was aiming. Sure, I didn't hit the bull's eye very often—read: at all—but my accuracy is most definitely much better now than my poor showing yesterday morning. Let's hope it will be enough. I've got my mace and knife too, either way.

The earthen tunnels don't look entirely natural. I screw up my face in thought as I put the torch closer to the walls, floor, and ceiling to try to work it out. I'm no topographer, but the marks in all three areas look dug, though not by spades. My tracking knowledge would tell me that the marks were probably made by some sort of burrowing insect or a giant mole—the scrapes could be attributed to either. Between the two, I'd probably prefer a giant mole.

Suddenly, there's a rustling, scraping sound ahead of us. We're both immediately on our guard, and I quickly drop the torch to the ground and pull an arrow from my quiver as Bastet slinks to the side, blending in perfectly with the wall. We wait, the rustling sound getting closer. My torchlight picks up something rushing towards us: a carpet of movement shown only by the odd glimmers here and there that reflect back at me. It's very low to the ground but fills the tunnel, even going slightly up the sides. I start wondering whether it's something living at all. *Maybe it's an oil spill or something?*

About to grab my light source and run back, I realize when the creeping mass enters the pool of illumination shed by my torch that it's not some sort of liquid; it's *alive*. But it's not one creature either. It's worse.

Clicking towards me, the rustling and scraping sound caused by their chitinous bodies rubbing against each other, are too many little spider monsters to count. I have to fight the urge to turn and run even though I know now that it's not flammable oil coming down the passageway. Instead, I quickly return my arrow to the quiver and grab my mace instead. With this number and type of enemy,

I need crushing power rather than accuracy. I mean, perhaps Legolas would be able to destroy this horde with the power of his bow alone, but I'm not quite at his legendary level yet. If these are anything like the massive one I fought before, I'm unlikely to have the accuracy necessary to pierce them all through their eyes. Especially since they're only the size of small dogs. No, my upgraded mace should do the job.

As the first one gets close, I swing downwards with my mace, aiming to crack its shell. When the mace hits, I'm surprised by the result. It doesn't crack the shell. Instead, it *obliterates* the creature entirely. Seriously, my well-aimed strike hits it full on its back and just goes straight through, rebounding off the ground. Good to know that my increases in Dexterity apparently don't only affect my accuracy with bows. And Strength (Power) increases for the win!

My surprise makes me stumble. I'd braced myself to prepare for the mace rebounding off the shell; with it having pounded straight through, I find myself off-balance. Blinking even as I quickly regain my footing, I shrug and decide not to look a gift horse in the mouth. If these creatures are significantly easier than what was probably their parent, I'm not going to complain.

Almost humming a tune, I start swinging at the other creatures that have surrounded me. My mace goes through them just as easily, and I start wreaking mass destruction among the mini spider monsters. Oddly enough, I'm surrounded, but the monsters behind me aren't trying to attack. Instead, those that get past Bastet and me are just making a break for the entrance. Something clicks. They aren't just mini spider monsters. They're *babies*.

It would be much easier if I could see the names of these things and their levels floating above them in a handy box, but life isn't that kind. However, the longer I'm fighting these things, the more convinced I am that I'm right. They're not even really fighting *me*; only the ones closest to me are trying to bite. In fact, I almost feel bad attacking them when I consider the weapons I have compared to their relative helplessness.

Then I remember the spider monster I killed before, and my heart hardens. If I have to kill a whole load of innocent babies to avoid having more of those adults around, it's a burdensome task I'm willing to take on. I briefly consider trying to Dominate one of them, but then dismiss the thought with a shudder. Imagine waking up to one of those crouching by the fire like Bastet. *No way!* Perhaps I'm stupid for letting my personal preferences prevent me from potentially harnessing the power of the spider monster . . . but if it means I don't have to look at another one for as long as I live, I'll count it as sufficient recompense.

By the time the last of the baby spider monster things is past us, I'm panting but surprisingly in one piece. Miracle of miracles, my clothes are even still intact! It's hard to count how many spider monsters we killed between the two of us since the vast majority are shattered bodies on the ground, but it has to be upwards of a hundred. When I check my status, however, I've only gained about fifteen percent

Energy towards my next level. Whether that's because the amount of Energy for one percent has drastically increased, or these creatures were worth very little Energy, I don't know. Probably a mixture of the two, to be honest. I'm not quite sure how this whole Energy thing works yet, but it definitely seems that the more dangerous the creature, the more Energy I get when killing them. These creatures stood no chance against me and couldn't even pose any sort of threat. It's not surprising, then, that I've gained little from their deaths.

I don't bother collecting anything from these carcasses. Bastet licks one of them and then sends a wave of disgust down our Bond: apparently, these things don't agree with her either. Fortunately, the torch has managed to stay lit despite the number of creatures stepping around and on it. After picking it up, I tiptoe gingerly through the mess, making a face at the nasty gooey feeling under my feet. If these shoes hadn't already been covered by blood and mud, I'd have despaired of ever getting the stains from these spider things out. As it is, I just continue walking up the tunnel.

My light catches on something ahead, and I squint as I try to spot what it is.

CHAPTER SEVENTY-SIX

A Claustrophobe's Nightmare

What is that? I ask. Bastet indicates that she isn't detecting anything moving up ahead, and I step closer gingerly. *Is it . . . ?* I step within arm's reach and tilt the torch to see better. It kind of looks like spider silk, but not quite. It's not nearly as stringy and almost looks wet, glimmering as it is in the torchlight. I move a hand towards it and then stop myself just before I touch it. Maybe sticking my fingers into an unknown substance isn't the best idea . . .

After pulling a random stick out of my Inventory, I poke the substance. It gives easily and looks kind of like the skin on top of half-dried PVA glue. Unlike that glue, though, when I try to pull the stick away, I can't. The substance, which has to be an adhesive of some sort, has it stuck firmly. Even when I apply my full strength, it doesn't budge. Putting PVA to shame, the glue pulls a little away from the wall but refuses to either let go of the stick or break.

Finally, by bracing myself against the wall with my foot and yanking with all my Power-filled Strength, I manage to break the bonds of whatever it is that makes up this super-sticky substance. Of course, the force from my action has to go somewhere and I soon topple over onto my back, knocking the wind out of myself. To add insult to injury, Bastet sends me a wave of amusement, clearly entertained by this human doing odd things. At least the cubs don't seem too bothered by the jolt and abrupt reorientation of their world.

The stick has come away but still has a gluey substance attached to it. I tuck it away in my Inventory, grateful that the available space has again expanded by ten slots—otherwise, I'd already be running out of space. Maybe I can use it later. I'd love to take more of the substance with me but can't quite work out how to do that without getting completely stuck to it. Oh well, I'll think about that as I continue—I'll probably be coming back this way, anyway.

Wondering why the substance is here, I inspect the area. The gluey substance has ragged edges that dangle a bit into open air. It's like the glue forms a U shape with the raggedy bits being the inside of the letter. Frowning a little, I try to work out what could have happened. Slowly the connections fall into place. The spider monster. The babies. The hole in the gluey substance . . . *Could this have been a massive bundle of eggs? Stuck to the wall?* It fits, though why the eggs hatched just before I arrived, I don't know—it seems rather coincidental timing. Though, of course, they could have hatched earlier and then the sound of me coming could have triggered their exodus.

Perhaps. In the end, I shrug. The intricate details of spider-monster breeding habits are not really what I want to focus on. I make a note that they possibly like to lay eggs in tunnels, in case it crops up later, but decide to move on, figuratively and literally. Continuing on down the tunnel, I start noticing when the clearly dug tunnel starts to turn into something more accidental. I'd say natural, but without humans interfering—myself not included—*everything* is natural. What I come to appears more to be a tunnel formed out of the space between two layers of rock than something a creature has created. The height of the tunnel lowers considerably, but it widens just as much. I can still walk, but I have to lean forward a fair bit to avoid hitting my head.

As we walk, the ceiling gets lower and lower, and the walls start narrowing inwards too. With the shrinking space, I find myself becoming more and more conscious of just how much earth is above me. I've never been claustrophobic, but I challenge anyone who's not a spelunking enthusiast to go crawling through dark, close tunnels and not feel at least the faintest twinge of fear. Especially since I'm doing it without the possibility of radioing in for assistance. Though, I do suppose I have Bastet—maybe I should make use of her.

"Bastet," I say quietly, "can you scout ahead, please? See how low it gets and whether there's anything worth going on for." After all, just because there's a tunnel doesn't mean it actually *goes* anywhere. Especially if it's just caused by some sort of shift in the rock layers. Or underground water movement. It would be disappointing to come all this way for nothing, but I'd rather that than pushing forward and getting stuck somewhere.

Bastet sends a wave of amused agreement. I get the feeling that she's looking down on me a bit. Why? I don't know; it's not like I'm being unreasonably hesitant. *No* one would want to risk getting themselves trapped in a tunnel for no particular reason. *She's* smaller and considerably more agile so is much less likely to get stuck. *Damn cats,* I think to myself, half-exasperated, half-affectionate. Although raptor-cats don't entirely look feline, I'm getting the idea more and more that they really are just big cats at heart, and most certainly in attitude.

Speaking of raptorcats, the ones slung on my chest are getting a bit agitated— probably from the disruption of the fight. To be fair, the cubs have actually been behaving very well. Barely any complaints, and they've slept most of the time. I hadn't wanted to bring the cubs with me at all; exploring a new area hadn't seemed like a very safe place to bring them. But at the same time, I didn't know what to do. Ideally, they should have stayed back at the cave, but without the colored rocks to pay Kalanthia, that would have meant also leaving Bastet. Leaving her behind when coming out to explore somewhere like this hadn't seemed much like a good idea either. I did ask Bastet what she thought, and she had replied with feelings that I interpreted to mean concern but also an inclination to bring them with us where we could keep our eyes on them and protect them, rather than leave them back at the cave alone where they would be sure to get into trouble.

Undoing the sling, I let the three spill out on the ground and give them some meat to chew on and some water to lap at. It's probably unsanitary to let them drink from a bowl I'm also going to drink from, but frankly, I don't care. I *still* haven't managed to have my bath with soap yet or clean my clothes with more than just water, so I probably have far more germs on my skin and in my clothes than the raptorcats have in their mouths.

After their snack break, they explore the area around. It's pretty confined for me, with barely any space above my head even sitting down, but for the much-smaller cubs, that doesn't mean anything. They sniff at the walls, try to sharpen their claws—adorable—and then start trying to wander up and down the tunnel—less adorable and more annoying. I pull out a piece of cord and try to distract them with it. It works for a while as the cubs leap at the flicking end of the cord. I chuckle as one of them pounces on the one who actually managed to capture the moving rope end. Of course, a play fight is the result, and I watch in amusement. After a while, they get bored of the game and return to trying to explore. The two females start following our trail backwards and I have to lunge to grab them, headbutting the roof of the tunnel painfully as I do.

Cursing, I can't spare a hand to rub the injured spot, as they're both occupied with the cubs. Setting the cubs down on the ground near my torch, I level them with a firm look.

"Stay here," I tell them sternly, not sure whether they can read my mind or sense my emotions but trying to impress on them the importance. For now, it seems to work, as Stormcloud sends me a long look before going to play with the sling material, and Ninja follows as normal.

Of course, in the short time that takes, Trouble has already disappeared. Groaning, I hit my head gently against the wall behind me but hiss as the action makes the pain from my previous head injury hurt more. Stupid. *I'm going to have to go after him, aren't I?* I moan internally, wondering once more whether I should have just come here by myself anyway. Or waited to explore until I had another Bound who could play babysitter or do the scouting for me.

As I prepare to brave the increasingly narrow tunnel in search of a wayward cub, I'm startled by the sudden glimpse of movement out of the corner of my right eye. Automatically reaching for a weapon, I grab my mace, only realizing as I pull at it that there's no way I can wield such a weapon in these close confines. I need my knife. Even as I scrabble for it, the cause for my alarm comes close enough for me to recognize her.

It's Bastet. Relief goes through me like a cool breeze. Of course it's Bastet. What are the chances that it would be anyone, or anything, else? *Unless something managed to kill her and came hunting for its next snack,* my traitorous brain tells me. Except I'd notice if Bastet died. I certainly noticed when Spike was in trouble.

Either way, it's fine. Though, I should probably make sure I pull my knife out next time in case it *is* something else. The reason I didn't immediately recognize her was because her profile looks different: she has a swinging cub in her mouth.

"Thank goodness," I tell her. "I was about to go after him, I promise." The wave of emotion she sends me is complicated. Admonishment, I guess because I kind of lost him to begin with. Amusement because I got so wound up about it all. And some kind of sense that if Trouble got himself into trouble by wandering off, it would kind of be his own fault. Which I agree with. Good to know she does too; I should have guessed that would be her response.

"So, what does the tunnel look like?" I ask, eager to change the subject.

What she sends me aren't so much images as impressions. I shouldn't really be surprised that she wouldn't be able to send me images. Her night vision is good, but she still needs *some* light, and apparently, this whole area is pitch-black. There's the sense of the tunnel winding and twisting for a while.

It's the oddest experience, but it's almost like I have whiskers, wings, and a feathery tail since I'm using the sensations of them to gauge how wide and high the tunnel is. It's wider than my/her body but not by a lot, and the lowest it gets presses on my/her body from both sides but is passable with a little bit of wriggling. Then, after what feels like forever in the dark, the tunnel opens out abruptly, widening into a large space with some light, which allows her to see its vague shape. It's a large cavern, though she couldn't see in enough detail to work out the space's real shape. However, it's clear that it's at least several times larger than her wingspan and much higher than even she could leap. There's also a lot of humidity in the air, which indicates water, and a strange taste to the rocks that she can't categorize. The taste is vaguely familiar to me through her senses, but it takes a bit of back and forth between us to work out what it is. Eventually, it's only when she identifies that she tasted something vaguely similar when she licked some white crystals I have in a bowl in my cave that I work it out. She was tasting *salt*.

Could there be some sort of underground salt reserve? Does that happen? If so, that's enough motivation for me to brave a tunnel that I'm not sure will be wide or high enough for me at its closest points. If I *can* get through and there *is* salt, that would be an awesome find. There's *so much* I can do with salt. Not to mention that it's great for adding to food and is required by my body. *All right*, I say to myself, trying to psyche myself up, *I can do this. A claustrophobe's nightmare, here I come.*

CHAPTER SEVENTY-SEVEN

Just Keep Pushing

I crawl through the tunnel, hating it. The torch is clenched between my teeth, and I have to keep adjusting its position every time the tunnel narrows and its burning end starts brushing against the wall. I know it's going to get to the point where the torch's handle is too long for the width of the tunnel, but for now the space is still a bit wider than it is high.

Remember the salt, I tell myself every time I think about giving up and going back the way we came. *Remember the salt.* The cubs are following me on foot; they weren't keen on the idea of being reconfined to the sling, and it's not practical besides.

If I'm going to need to squeeze through tight spaces, having delicate cubs held against me sounds like a recipe for tragedy. No, better for them to walk with Bastet bringing up the rear, making sure they don't go wandering backwards. With me at the front, I can stop them from going any further forwards if necessary. So far, it hasn't been a problem.

I'm not wearing my armor. I had to take it off when I first started having to crawl; the movement made my chitin armor shift against my shoulders, rubbing raw a spot that had already become a little sore after swinging my mace to kill the mini spider monsters. A quick Lay-on-Hands dealt with that, and I made another mental note to somehow file the rough edge down. It took a couple of minutes to undo the sinew knots holding the two pieces together, and I hope I'm not attacked before I have the chance to put it on again.

After a while, I get to my first real challenge. The tunnel narrows and then widens again abruptly; some feature in the rock around me forms a bulge that cuts across at least half the tunnel. Feeding the torch through first, I put my hands through the hole and then prepare to wriggle my shoulders through. They stick for a moment, and I worry suddenly whether my recent bulking up is going to be the reason for me not getting my salt. It's certainly true that my shoulders are a lot broader now than they were on arrival, and even then they were reasonably nicely defined. I'm still not bulky in a body-builder style, mind. No, the muscles I've developed here from both activity and stat points are lean and tough. The downside of that is they're not easy to squish through a confined space.

After a moment of wriggling, though, I get them through. I breathe a sigh of relief as my heart rate goes back to normal. Though, if that was hard, I really fear for my chances later; if I remember the impressions Bastet sent me, I haven't yet encountered the tightest spot. Pulling myself through with my hands and pushing with my feet, I fit my hips into the space a lot more easily than my shoulders. It just takes a bit more awkward wriggling and then I'm entirely through.

The space beyond this tight point is a bit wider than the previous tunnel, and I sit back, looking at the raptorcat cubs scrambling through the hole. Since the further stretch of tunnel is a bit lower than the previous, they have to scramble down a steep slope that I'd been able to easily span with my longer limbs. As usual, they're just too cute as they tackle the challenge. Ninja starts feeling her way down, then gets bored and jumps the last bit. Stormcloud determinedly shuffles down the slope one paw at a time.

Trouble, being his usual careless self, just jumps, lands badly, and rolls to bump into my leg. He looks up at me questioningly, as if unsure what just happened. I can only shake my head. If this cub makes it to adulthood—heck, even adolescence—I'll count it as one of my greatest achievements. Bastet waits patiently on the other side of the hole for us to shift and make some space for her. I promptly shift up the tunnel a bit, telling the cubs to follow me. By this point, we've developed enough of a rapport that they follow my instructions without a problem. Most of the time, anyway. And the rest of the time it's just because they don't want to, not because they don't understand. The adult raptorcat steps through easily, tucking her rudimentary wings into her sides as she moves sinuously. I envy her for her ease of movement sometimes, now more than ever.

"If I get stuck, you're pulling me out," I warn her. She sends a wave of agreement with a tinge of amusement. "Right," I say to myself, looking with determination at the tunnel ahead.

I can't see much of it thanks to the limited range of the torchlight. Still, as far as I *can* see, there aren't any more tight spots, though it does start to narrow again at the edge of my view. At least there's a current of air passing through the tunnel, which reassures me; to find myself stuck in an airless hole is an even worse prospect than just finding myself stuck. And that's enough of a nightmare to make me seriously consider going back. If I was alone, I would. It's only the hope that Bastet would be able to help me that keeps me going forwards. The knowledge that even if we had to break or dislocate some of my bones to get me out of a tough spot, I would be able to heal myself is oddly reassuring too.

Once more setting off, we travel through the tunnels slowly and steadily. The tunnel narrows and widens at different points, but nowhere near as tightly as that spot earlier. At a couple of points I have to put the torch on the floor and push it forward in between crawling simply because the tunnel isn't wide enough for me to carry it in my mouth.

I ought to work out some way of rigging it up to my head or something, I decide. As long as I can make it so that it's not likely to set my hair on fire, that is. At each step I have to fight against the fear that creeps higher in my chest: the fear of being entombed before I'm even dead. The walls seem to press tighter, even when I can logically see that they're not actually any narrower, and the ceiling is overbearingly low.

I swallow dryly and focus on my goal. *Remember the salt.* I try to distract myself by theorizing how this tunnel came to be. There's quite a strong wind current. *Could it have been erosion by air? No, it's not strong enough for that. Water? Possibly.* There are certainly a number of hallmarks that indicate it being water erosion: channels cut in the rock along the tunnel rather than from side to side, smooth curves in general rather than rough points, and fairly uniform surfaces. While the surfaces are still a bit rough, it's true that the roughness is rounded rather than jagged. For a moment, a new fear surfaces: suddenly being engulfed in a flood of water, drowning before I could even make it halfway back to the last tight spot.

Then my rationality asserts itself again. The tunnel is completely dry without even the signs of intermittent flooding. There's no greenery on the walls, no algal bloom. Okay, I don't know for sure that this world has algae, but the chances are that it has *something* that grows in damp environments. This tunnel is completely bare of anything like that. My heart rate slows back down from its spike. I decide that theorizing is just as stressful as just concentrating on moving forwards and resolve not to do any more of it unless necessary.

When I next come to a tight spot, it's a bit more significant than the previous one. Not quite as tight but a lot longer. I gulp a little at the sight, my fight against my fear faltering briefly. Before panic can take over, I close my eyes and breathe, reminding myself that I'm not here alone—in the worst-case scenario, Bastet would just have to dig her teeth into my ankle or calf and pull me out.

The tunnel roof lowers abruptly, leaving a space that's nowhere near big enough for me to crawl on all fours. I'll have to army crawl at best for most of it, and there's a spot I can see at the edge of the light pool where I'm not sure I'll actually fit my upper body through at all. *Is salt worth this? Bastet got through,* I remind myself. *She's smaller than me, but she's also less able to move while flat.*

When it comes to going through spaces that are horizontally challenged, she's definitely more able than me, but I'm better at going flat than she is since she has to crouch and creep forwards. That she was able to get through this space gives me hope that I can too. Muttering a short prayer to anyone who might be around to hear and crossing my fingers for good measure, I face my fear. I feed the torch in first and double-check to make sure I don't have any loose fabric that might get caught on rough bits of rock. I even stick my knife into my Inventory to make sure there's no risk of that getting trapped either.

After lowering myself to my belly, I feed myself into the small space and then use my elbows and toes to push myself forwards. The first bit is okay. The ceiling is far too close for comfort, but I can move relatively easily. Then it starts getting tighter. The ceiling gets closer and closer until it's pressing on my shoulders from the top even as I'm pressed into the floor below. The space is too narrow for me to lift my head fully, and I have to strain my eyes to look upwards constantly just to see forwards. The only good thing about the situation is that since the space is pretty wide, I'm not struggling to move my arms. Not unless I want to rotate my shoulders, at least. I inch through with my fingers and toes and a caterpillar-like undulation of my core providing the momentum I need to keep moving forward. Inside my mind I repeat a litany of comfort and encouragement to stave off the panic bubbling just under the surface. *Just keep going, just keep pushing, just keep pulling, it's okay, I'll make it, I'm still moving . . .* My focus narrows to purely the next inch, the next divot I can fit my fingers or toes into to give myself just a little extra oomph. Had I tried this when I first arrived, I doubt I'd have gotten this far. My fingers and toes wouldn't have had the Strength or Dexterity to keep me moving forwards. Plus, I'm pretty sure my Willpower is helping me keep my fear at bay.

Then comes the dreaded moment: I get to the point where the ceiling presses down low enough that I can barely make any headway against the friction caused by the rough rock over and above me. I can only breathe shallowly because I don't have the space to fully fill my chest. The primal fear of suffocation enhances the already present fear of being entombed, and I find myself panting shallow breaths, a low, fearful whine wheezing out of my throat.

A rumble from behind me startles me for a moment, increasing the speed of my panting breaths. My heart starts to pound even harder in my chest and a cold sweat trickles down my forehead. A wave of apologetic reassurance comes down the Bond to me.

Oh. Yes. In my fearful state, I'd forgotten I had Bastet with me. Feeling momentarily embarrassed, I remind myself that it's perfectly normal to feel panicky in the situation I'm currently experiencing.

Her reassurance helps me continue, and I work my way forwards bit by bit. Each inch is an accomplishment and a move towards getting out of here. My torch has been edged forwards enough that it's now revealing my goal. The space is close enough to feel if I could stretch my questing fingers out fully in front of me. The flames of the torch are illuminating a larger cave only a bare few inches away. If I remember correctly from Bastet's scouting, this is the worst point; after this, there are only a couple of other difficult points, and neither of them are quite as tight as this. That doesn't help when my progress suddenly grinds to a halt. The ceiling has dipped just a fraction lower, and suddenly, I can't go forwards. Shifting backwards to try and take another approach, I find I'm not making any progress in that direction either. My heart rate spikes, and my panting breaths start coming out as wheezes again.

I'm stuck.

CHAPTER SEVENTY-EIGHT

Salt

I panic. The fear that I've been holding at bay by the skin of my teeth for the last half an hour—if not longer—escapes my grasp and takes over. I thrash, my fingers scrabbling for a handhold, my feet searching for any possible purchase. My upper body is pinned in place, and even my most violent movements are unable to shift my torso. I only stop when I run out of energy, having chewed through my stamina at a fast pace. I haven't bottomed out, but using a big chunk of stamina in a short space of time tends to make me feel tired and a bit nauseous anyway. I rest my head on the rock before me as tears of fear trickle down my nose. I don't cry often, and even now I refuse to truly acknowledge them. *They're salty drops of sweat, nothing else.* I'm not great at lying to myself, though.

My throat is sore from shouting with breath that would have been better kept in my lungs; it's not surprising that my head is swimming a bit with oxygen deprivation. Now that I've pulled back from the edge of complete abandonment to fear, I feel the waves of concern battering me from Bastet's direction. I send back a sense of exhaustion and hopelessness, and the tinge of fear creeps into my message despite myself.

The reminder that I'm not alone helps to steady me further. If I can't go forward, Bastet can always pull me backwards—even if she has to break my ankle to do it, I'll be able to heal myself. The thought gives me the courage to try again. Taking a moment to rest, I attempt to bring my breathing back under control. I still can't take full breaths, but I can stop myself from panting uselessly.

I relax bit by bit, forcing my muscles to melt into the rock below me. The fewer muscles that are active, the less oxygen I need. The more relaxed my muscles are, the less the ceiling presses on down on me. The easier my breathing becomes, the less confined I feel, and the easier it is to push my fear back. I'm not in the right state of mind to meditate, but I sense the similarities.

With Bastet's continued waves of encouragement and my own internal monologue, I find my heart rate slowing and my breathing coming more and more easily.

Finally, I feel like I'm ready. I first try shifting backwards a bit. It works easily now I'm not all tense and taking up more space than absolutely necessary. Now shifting sideways a little bit, I try to press forwards again, hoping to avoid the little rounded spike of rock that had so impeded my previous progress.

This time, I'm not stopped. I keep going, millimeter by tortuous millimeter. I refuse to pay attention to how far I've come or how far I have yet to go. Instead, my world has narrowed once more to my finger and toe tips, the rough slide against rock, and focusing on controlling my breathing and fear. When the ceiling stops pressing down on my shoulders, it's a surprise. I lift my head; the fact that I'm able to raise it fully feels almost like leaving a dream—or nightmare.

The whole experience must have only lasted a few minutes, half an hour at the most, but I'll be the first to admit that my sense of time went a little screwy back there. Despite how short the experience was in objective terms, it almost seems implausible that I once lived in a world where I could stand and move freely. There's something about this tunnel that has narrowed my existence to its confines.

Now with my shoulders through, I move eagerly to pull the entirety of my upper body out too. Once my arms have more leverage, pulling my hips and legs the rest of the way is easy. I take big breaths as soon as I've managed to push myself to a sitting position, luxuriating in the ability to breathe freely, which I had always taken for granted. I rub my hands up and down my arms, my head, my legs, making sure everything is present and accounted for. The touch makes it feel more real, and the realization that I've conquered the horrific experience finally dawns.

I look back at the hole I just exited and marvel that I got through it. It's only barely higher than the width of my two hands side by side—a gap of perhaps twenty or twenty-five centimeters, tops. The human body is amazing, really. After the tightest spot, it opens up fairly quickly into a small dip down to the tunnel floor, which I'm sitting on, and then a steep angle upwards to where the tunnel ceiling is now, high enough for me to almost stand up bent double. It would be uncomfortable as hell to walk like that, though, so I'm going to stick to crawling.

I gulp as I look back at the hole again. *Do I really have to go back this way?* I'll just have to hold out hope for some other exit.

I watch as the raptorcats come through too. The cubs don't have much trouble, of course. They're about the size of large Labrador puppies, so they just have to crouch down a bit and then can make it through easily enough.

Bastet, on the other hand, being about the size of a leopard, has to do a strange sideways movement that really doesn't look very comfortable for her. I remember seeing videos of cats going under doors and, though the gap is not nearly as tight as that for her, the motion of her paws and body is not dissimilar. It's still more a crouch than anything else, but a . . . sideways crouch? Her head comes out first, and her front paws reach for purchase through the gap, propelling her body forwards. By the time she's halfway out, I'm surprised to see that her wings are actually helping too. I thought they would just be problematic—hazards that could get more easily caught. But no, they're also helping propel her through the space.

She gets out quickly, and we take a moment to breathe together as Bastet comes to rub heads with me and the cubs. Pack bonding time, I suppose. Moments like this make me realize that I haven't so much domesticated Bastet as she's adopted *me* into the pack. It kind of feels . . . nice. *Almost like family.* But I shy away from that thought, my wounds still raw where family is concerned. We take a moment to munch some meat and drink some water. It's calm and peaceful right now; who knows how long that will last? Better to make sure we're all well nourished when possible. After my panic, the routine actions of eating and drinking are reassuring and help in settling the parts of me that aren't quite back to normal. Feeling more like myself, we continue. I'm starting to wonder if salt is worth this journey, even with all the uses that I have for it. But I've come this far; I might as well continue. Besides, if I've interpreted Bastet's scouting impressions correctly, I'm past the worst hurdle, so it seems ridiculous to just give up now. Plus, giving up now means facing that narrow tunnel once again all too soon.

The tunnel changes dimensions regularly as bulges from all sides protrude to narrow the passageway in one way or another. Most of them are easy enough to get past, though some pose more trouble to the cubs than others, especially when the bulge protrudes from the floor. A couple of times I have to lift them over when they fail at climbing past by themselves. Bastet, of course, has no difficulty.

The tight spots I come across are almost a breeze now. There are still choke points where a bulge from one direction or the other narrows the passageway enough to cause a bit of an issue for us. Well, me. Still, at their narrowest they're about my forearm's length in width, so they're easy enough to wriggle through. My torch is doing a great job, though it starts guttering in between the third and fourth tight spots. I quickly light another one. No way do I want to risk being stuck in the pitch black with little chance of striking my flint and tinder in the right spot to light the resin. I hope I have enough torches—I only prepared five of them, not thinking that I'd need too many.

After smothering the old one by rolling it rapidly on the floor, I tuck it back into my Inventory just in case I'm really in trouble later. Unfortunately, it doesn't stack with my other fresh torches—another Inventory slot used. The passage seems interminable, even though I know logically that it has an end. Time means nothing down here in the dark; not even my status screen seems to indicate that time is passing.

It occurs to me that the Energy required per percentage point must have increased again based on my certainty that I've been down here for at least two hours and the observation that my Energy store hasn't shown any change. At least my ordeal with getting stuck in the passageway has earned me a point in Willpower. I notice that when I take a moment to check my message box. Sure, it takes about seven percent of my Energy—another indication that the objective amount of Energy I now need to accumulate to increase my Energy store has increased significantly—but I take the point happily anyway.

Finally, after a last tight bit of passageway that requires some wriggling, I emerge into a large open space. The light from my torch illuminates a cave that soars above my head, its flickers catching faintly on stalactites or something above. Stalactites? Stalagmites? I can never remember which is which.

Either way, there are both, and I have to walk carefully to avoid stepping on a pointy bit of rock. The sound of plinking echoes through the large space as water falls drop by drop into some sort of deep puddle somewhere. The air is damp and, even better, *briny*. As I step delicately between the calcified structures, my foot crackles.

Bending down, I investigate what I'm stepping through. My heart starts pounding in excitement as my finger comes away covered in white crystals. Licking it, my eyes light up. After all the stress and pain, it's good to know I didn't endure it for nothing.

Looking around eagerly, I realize that there's salt encrusted around the bases of all of these structures, lapping just below the tunnel I emerged from, and where the cubs are just now tumbling out. At the sight of them, I suddenly wonder whether it's okay for them to be walking barefoot through all this salt and rock. Then I remember that their feet are more scaly talons than something like a cat or dog's paw and decide that if Bastet is worried, she'll tell me.

Instead, I crouch down to start harvesting my bounty. I want to investigate the rest of the cave, sure, but I'd also like to make sure I collect some salt. By this point, I'm familiar with how quickly a situation can go downhill, so I decide to take advantage of it all seeming to be calm for now.

Using my knife to scrape off salt crystals, I deposit handful after handful of salt into my Inventory. Wondering if the stalagmites—or stalactites, whatever—would be useful for heading weaponry, I snap off a few tops and deposit them in my Inventory too. I discover that as long as their sizes are vaguely similar, they stack. Not wanting to take up more than one slot, I proceed to just search for uniform tips while focusing most of my attention on collecting my white bounty.

Rounding a corner, I see that the cave isn't as completely closed as I thought. There's a natural archway opposite a paler stretch of rock, but it's hidden from the tunnel. Walking cautiously towards it, I look through and see something that makes my eyes go wide.

CHAPTER SEVENTY-NINE

Monster from the Deep

It's beautiful, is my first thought. After so long of having only the flickering light of my torch to illuminate the way ahead, seeing bright daylight now makes more of an impression on me than I would have thought. It feels like having been stuck in smog for years and now finally being able to breathe fresh air once more.

The fingers of light are coming from a large hole in the roof, a crevice that opens up from the top of one wall and is a good few meters long. While I wouldn't say the cave is well lit—the shafts of light are far too confined for that—I can see a lot more than I would have been able to with only my torch as light. Looking back for a moment, I realize that what I thought was paler rock is just the same material as the rest of the cavern but lightly illuminated. Returning my attention to the cave in front of me, I scan the place for threats.

It's big, that's for sure. Almost a cavern, really. The cave is about five or six meters high and at least three times that wide. As for the length, even the light streaming in from the ceiling can't reach the furthest points of the cave. It does, however, glint off a large, fathomless pool that starts not far from where I'm standing. The surface of the pool would be glass-smooth except for the drops of water that fall from more stalactites on the cave ceiling. They shine like diamonds as they fall through the air only to plink into the water and send ripples lapping at the edges. It's deep. The water's crystal clear, so I can see how the cave floor rapidly drops away until it's out of sight. While clear at the edges, it turns completely black within a worryingly short distance. I make a mental note to avoid falling in—if my clothes pull me down, I'll be in big trouble. I send Bastet a warning about the cubs, knowing that they will all be curious.

The salt near the edges of the pool is even more thickly encrusted, indicating that the water is the source of it all. *Why would there be salty water in the middle of a mountain?* Maybe there's some sort of salt deposit that the water has dissolved. But surely it would have just all leaked out one way or another? I end up putting the question to one side. It's at times like these that I miss the internet. Either way, my hopes rise at the thought that there might be another way out of here, one that doesn't involve me squeezing myself into a pancake . . .

Being careful not to step in the water, I narrow my eyes in thought as I walk around the pool to survey the rock wall below the base of the crevice. It should be possible to climb. There are plenty of handholds along with a few dodgy spots where the rock presses outwards, which would have to be purely strength based—I would never have tried them with my previous level of fitness, but now . . . *If I could fix a rope harness up at the top, I could reduce the risk of falling badly, and then I'd have access to a large amount of salt . . .* It's definitely worth considering. As I turn around to talk to Bastet—even if I can climb the wall, she probably can't—I see what one of the cubs is doing. For once, it's not Trouble. Instead, Ninja is dipping her paw in the water, splashing curiously.

I start striding towards her, an admonishment on my lips. Maybe it's just salty water; maybe it's caustic soda. Either way, it's not a good idea to just stick her paw in an unknown liquid. A particularly hard splash with her paw sends droplets all over her face, and she backs up while shaking her head and sneezing cutely. I can't help cooing a little bit at her adorableness, but the undercurrent of worry is still there. What if she got some of the liquid in her eyes and it makes her go blind? What if it *is* caustic and starts burning her down to the bone? Fortunately, when I get close enough to scoop her up, I see that the liquid doesn't appear to be doing anything nefarious—other than getting her wet, which is enough to make the little cub mewl grumpily.

"Then don't go playing in strange liquids, silly thing," I tell her sternly, though I can't prevent a fond note from entering my voice. I couldn't say which of the raptorcats is my favorite, but Ninja is definitely the cutest. The returning ripple from Ninja's full-pawed splash returns to lap at my feet, more small waves following. *Wait . . . Ninja didn't splash* that *hard.* She's only a little cub, after all.

Something in my hindbrain starts screaming, and I don't hesitate to obey the instinct. I would far rather act unnecessarily than waste time that could be the difference between life and death. I take a couple of quick steps to grab Stormcloud from where she's poking at a stalagmite. "Get Trouble," I snap at Bastet, already booking it back towards the section of the cave we came through.

Before I manage to make it halfway to the natural archway, I see something that makes my fingers itch for a weapon. It's impossible at the moment, with my hands as full as they are, but the second I've put the cubs somewhere safe, I'll be pulling out my mace. And probably a spear too. A monster from the deep has risen. A great black serpent. It's long and thick, its head indistinguishable from its body. The brief glance I get of it before I continue running doesn't reveal any vulnerable points like eyes. I suppose I shouldn't expect some monster that lives in the dark to rely on sight.

I stumble through the trip hazard of stalagmites poking up from the floor and make it back to the tunnel. After shoving the cubs in more roughly than I would usually like, I quickly turn around and grab my spear and mace out of my Inventory. Sure, I could grab my bow and arrows too, but I don't think they're going to make much of an impression on this monster.

Bastet isn't here yet. I run, stumble, and hop through the obstacle course of stalagmites back to the archway. She's trapped, tucked into a corner as the water snake—or whatever it is—waves back and forth. *Maybe it can't detect us*, I think, my mind racing. Maybe it is sensitive enough to detect the unusual ripple that Ninja created, but now that it's above water, it doesn't know where we are.

If we could make it believe that it was just a rock or something that fell . . . It's getting closer and closer to Bastet's hiding place as it rubs its nose along the wall, approaching her inch by inch. It's big, wider around than she is tall, and she's handicapped besides—I see Trouble held securely in her mouth. She's pulled in close against the wall but the direction the snake is moving, it's going to find her in a few seconds.

Scrabbling at the ground, I manage to grab and break off a small chunk of calcified rock. Throwing it in the opposite direction from where Bastet is, I hold my breath. I'm gratified when the loud plop the stone makes as it falls into the pool garners a reaction.

The snake twists quickly and shoots directly towards the stone. I frown as I watch it. It's not moving like any snake I've ever seen—mostly on the internet—but I can't put my finger on why it seems so strange. After considering it for a moment, I dismiss the thought. We need to get out of here; that's what's important.

Bastet has put the distraction of the enemy to good use and is sprinting towards me as fast as she can. She's almost to my position when one of her back claws slides on the damp and slippery stone. She regains her balance quickly but not quickly enough to avoid touching the shallows of the pool.

My theory about the creature being sensitive to water movement must be correct, as it immediately reacts. Leaving the site of the fallen stone alone, the monster shoots straight towards us. Bracing myself, I ready my weapons. As soon as Bastet has bounded past, her eyes wide and feathers sticking up on end, I jab with my spear.

In the time it takes me to do that, the snake shoots past, following the running raptorcat. My spear rebounds off the monster's skin uselessly, not a mark left on it. Swinging my mace with all my strength, I grimace as it also rebounds and the vibrations from its impact reverberate through the mace and sting my hand. It's like I've swung a wooden bat at a solid iron pole.

What kind of monster is this?

My attacks have had one effect: they've drawn the monster's attention. It pulls back surprisingly slowly considering how fast it was moving when it struck. I dare to glance to the side to check on Bastet. She's nowhere to be seen—I hope that's because she's managed to escape rather than because she's been squashed into a paste by this insanely strong monster.

Now *I* need to escape too. I start edging backwards while keeping my eyes on the snake, trying not to trip over the pointy pieces of rock that threaten to snare my feet. The snake doesn't seem to be about to attack . . . It's poised menacingly but hasn't started feeling around for me or striking at me yet. Then I see something that makes me swallow dryly, my bowels turning to water. The snake isn't alone. Heads of other black snakes are emerging from the water. *One, two, four, six, ten . . .* I lose count as they fill the space above the pool, each one waving its pointed nose around, swaying back and forth. Each is surprisingly uniform with no real difference in size. Black skin, smooth lines, and no obvious weaknesses.

Then the pieces fall into place. This isn't a snake. Memories of watching *The Fellowship of the Ring* flash through my mind: the moment when Merry and Pippin disturb the water near the gates of Moria. This is something far worse than a snake. Losing my nerve completely, I turn and run towards the tunnel, my only thought that of escape. My eyes are probably as wide as Bastet's were. Perhaps she already knew that this was something we couldn't hope to face, not when my mace and spear just bounce off its skin.

I don't make it. Halfway there, a blow takes me off my feet. I'm airborne for a brief moment before I make contact with the wall. It's unforgiving—the impact makes even my enhanced body explode with pain. I tumble down uncontrollably, having been flung up several meters into the air. The impact with the ground is no better than that with the wall, and if I had breath in my lungs, I would scream. As it is, pained whimpers pant through my broken jaw. I can't count how many injuries I have. *Everything* hurts. I didn't slam headfirst against the wall; that's the only blessing. Instead, I hit it hip first, and based on how that feels, it's now either fractured or heavily bruised. And even if I didn't hit the wall headfirst, I still hit hard enough to break my jaw, so the world is fading in and out, my brain threatening me with unconsciousness. The world starts spinning as my thoughts become fractured and hard to hold together. *Stay awake. Bad things will happen if I go to sleep. Stay awake. Don't sleep. Not time. Stay awake. Need . . . something.*

Something.

He—head?

Head hurts. Hurts . . . Heal? Heal. Yes, heal.

My hurting brain grasps onto the thought and tries to run with it. The problem is, I can't string thoughts together well enough to work out *how* to heal. I remember it's something to do with Energy and a coolness that brings relief to pain. Desperately, feeling that things are getting worse even if I can't attach any logic to it, I reach for that cool sensation. It feels like I'm trying to grasp a cloud, my clawlike fingers just dragging uselessly through it.

No.

No! It's my *mana. It will* obey. And it does. There's a moment of hesitation, a moment where I refuse to consider failure, and then magic surges into me.

It circles the injury in my head, and the coolness soothes the pulsing, throbbing pain. I "feel" with the mana as it pulls something out of my brain and slots everything back into place, fixing it. The healing magic sends tendrils down to my hip and to a tiny fracture in my upper spine that I hadn't even noticed in the wash of agony everywhere.

And then it fades. My brain is now working correctly—and I refuse to even touch on the idea that I might have just had something sticking in it a moment ago—but I notice that my mana bar is completely empty. *At least it managed to fully sustain a brain surgery—no, not thinking about that.* I'm still in pain, but I'm desperate to know what's going on.

Opening my eyes, I see the monster is still thrashing its tentacles around, but it seems to be giving up the search as its tentacles withdraw one by one. I wonder why it hasn't found me but then realize that I've been "lucky." I've fallen behind a few large pillars of calcified rock, and they've served to hide and protect me, though my impact with them caused me more damage. Then I see something beyond the stalagmites and still-writhing tentacles that makes my heart sink into my boots. Somehow, the monster's thrashing has caused actual damage to the wall in multiple places. Including where the tunnel entrance used to be.

The way is shut.

CHAPTER EIGHTY

Broken and Shattered

I *hope Bastet got through with Trouble*, I think fervently, *and that all of them were out of the way when the monster hit with enough force to close the entrance. And that the tunnel being closed isn't a sign that there's been a rockfall in the tunnel itself . . .*

After nearly working myself into a panic, I suddenly realize that I have an easy way to get at least a proof of life. Breathing deeply to control my emotions and bring some sense of calm back to my mind, I reach into the metaphysical area where I find my Bonds.

Well, Bond. The place where Spike's Bond used to be is empty. It's not painful, not really, but I'm aware of its absence; the reminder aches. Thankfully, Bastet's Bond is still there. She's alive.

Digging in a little deeper, I get the sense that she's worried, stressed, but not in immediate danger. *Can I communicate with her via the Bond at this distance?* I haven't tried before, but I don't see why not: I communicate with her all the time using the Bond; why would a little distance make a big difference? It does make a difference. The effort of transmitting my thoughts down the Bond is like swimming through sludge instead of water, but I succeed. I think. I focus hard on the image of the entrance to the tunnel—the entrance in the copse of dead trees, that is. It almost feels like I've got constipation as my muscles tense to push just as much as my mind. Their tension is worse than useless; pushing with physical muscles isn't going to help a metaphysical message, and it just reminds me that I'm still heavily injured.

Still, I feel a faint hint of surprise and then acknowledgment from Bastet's end of things—I hope she understood the message correctly. I release my hold on the Bond with a silent sigh of relief. Now I need to get out of here.

The tunnel's shut, and I doubt I'll be able to get it open, though I will check anyway. The only other option I can see ahead of me is climbing up the wall to the crevice and getting out that way. To do that, though, I'm going to need to be in peak physical condition and not the bloody and broken mess I am right now.

I completely emptied my mana bar earlier, but I've already started getting it back. As soon as I have enough mana for a Lay-on-Hands, I cast it, and the magic springs into action with an ease previously unseen. It's great, but I can't help wondering at the difference.

The mana fills my body, and I wince as I realize just how many injuries I have going on. The last healing I did only dealt with my brain damage and spine—and those are *really* scary to think about. The rest of my hurts are still shrieking at me. In fact, I'm starting to wonder how I'm doing anything other than screaming and crying in agony. My hip has been fractured and my jaw broken. My collarbone is damaged too, perhaps a small fracture as well. That probably happened at the same time as the other two injuries. That moment is a bit of a blur in my memory, but I'm pretty sure that I hit the wall with my hip first, the tentacle having caught me in my mid-section, and then my shoulder and head slammed into the wall in the instant afterwards, my motion otherwise arrested.

My foot is bleeding with a stalagmite sticking straight through it—*RIP boots*—and I have to be grateful that the stone spike is actually plugging the wound, as otherwise I would be running low on blood by this point. But I'm not looking forward to pulling that out.

One of my knees also hurts, though I think that's just deep bruising. Probably most of these injuries are from when I fell two or three meters to the ground and ended up squeezed between unforgiving stone pillars and an even more unforgiving stone wall. At this point, I'd love to say I'm grateful that I didn't break a leg or arm, but frankly, I have enough broken things to be dealing with.

Not to mention, of course, the bone-deep bruising all over my body. In fact, there are very few places on my body that *don't* hurt. Honestly, I'm wondering whether something in one of my stats is improving my capacity to deal with pain; it doesn't hurt any less, but somehow, I'm managing to cope with it all. It's either that or shock, anyway.

The cool energy of my healing spell enters my body, bringing a measure of instant relief to my worst injuries. Closing my eyes and leaning my head back against the wall, moving slowly and gently to avoid exacerbating my numerous injuries, I let my focus dive into my body.

I'm closer to myself than I ever thought I'd come, closer than anyone but a surgeon could dare to be. And this is *my* body, not anyone else's. I feel a connection to it that no surgeon could have. I go into a sort of trance as I view my body through my sense of the energy flowing through it. I was never brilliant at biology at school but half-remembered facts from then snap into perfect clarity now. The knowledge helps me heal myself as I push bone shards back into place, reduce the swelling of damaged areas, force out foreign bodies, calm nerve receptors, redirect blood flow . . .

It's not a single Lay-on-Hands that I cast but a steady stream of healing that goes at the pace of my regeneration. When I emerge from my trance, my mana is back at zero, and I'm *starving,* but all my injuries are healed. At some point I even tugged out the piece of rock that was stabbing through my foot. *When did that happen?*

My body craves nutrients – I pull out some chunks of cooked meat from my Inventory and start chewing them hungrily. Looking around, I see that the light filtering through from the other cave is a lot dimmer than I remember it being. Checking my status, I realize that a lot of time must have passed—I've actually gained some Energy towards the next level. Not having tested how much Energy I absorb in a day in this area, I can't say for sure how long I've been sitting here, but the fact that I've gained about two points since I woke up—three now—indicates my healing is quite a slow process. While I'm checking my status, I realize I have three messages waiting for me.

> Congratulations!
> You have worked hard on your Constitution and have earned a point. Would you like to apply this to your status?
>
> Y / N

Huh. Could have done with that *before I almost killed myself.* Though I suppose that's the point—pun not intended. I *almost* kill myself and earn a point by surviving. The addition takes seven percent of my meager Energy store, but it's worth it for the extra ten health units I gain. The second message is much in the same vein.

> Congratulations!
> You have worked hard on your Wisdom and have earned a point. Would you like to apply this to your status?
>
> Y / N

Once more, I accept the point, and the rest of my Energy store is wiped out. But more Wisdom means more mana, which may be the difference between death and survival next time. *Heck, this time it was the difference between brain damage or no brain damage . . .* The final message is a lot more exciting.

> Congratulations!
> You have advanced a Skill past Novice. Lay-on-Hands is now Initiate 1. You are now able to enter an altered state of consciousness in which you can directly manipulate your mana to heal yourself without converting it to healing energy first. Caution: you will be unable to detect your surroundings while in this altered state of consciousness.
>
> Close message? Y / N

That's interesting to know: I can advance a Skill without actually maxing out its previous ranking. Lay-on-Hands was at Novice seven before I entered the tunnel, and I doubt it gained two whole levels while I was crawling through the narrow gaps. I'm more and more convinced that we have to do something with the Skill to make it break through the ranks, and that action is what determines the Skill's evolution.

The first time I leveled up Lay-on-Hands, I accidentally channeled healing to repair my eye, using my knowledge of the eye's anatomy to aid in its reconstruction. The result was that I was then able to intentionally channel healing to different parts of my body, as well as just casting the general spell. This time I accidentally entered a trance where I was able to do extended surgery on myself, and the result is that I can now do that intentionally, though at the risk of being attacked by something while I'm lost in my inner world.

I take a look at my Skills briefly.

Class Skills:	Non-Class Skills:
Dominate – Beginner 4	Lay-on-Hands – Initiate 1
Tame – Beginner 2	Stealth – Beginner 9
Fade – Novice 8	Animal Empathy – Beginner 7

Interestingly, both Dominate and Tame have increased, despite the fact that I haven't used them. Is it something to do with my Bond with Bastet? I don't see any other explanation. Fade is almost maxing out the Novice tier, and Stealth is already there. I guess if I'm right about the way I ranked up Lay-on-Hands, I'll have to find some other application or use for the Skills in order to push them up a rank.

I'm procrastinating, I suddenly realize. I'm using the excuse of checking my messages and stats to avoid thinking about the fact that I need to get up and explore my options for escaping this place. It's only now that the excuses have faded away that I understand what I was doing. The monster was straight out of a nightmare, yes, but I have to get out of here, and that involves moving. *Well, either that, or I can just sit here and give up.*

But the moment that thought occurs, I decide I'm not ready to give up. I'm a very different person from who I was when I arrived: I've discovered a zest for life that allows me to push through pain and injury to do what I need to do. I won't be deterred by the fear of a monster that is too strong for me. I'm not going to attack it—that would be stupid—but I'm not going to just cower here in a corner, dying by inches. I listen carefully, but everything is still. Nothing but the sound of slow plinking of water droplets breaks the silence.

Gently pushing myself to my feet, I hiss at the feeling of stiffness everywhere. It almost feels like I've been calcified as much as the spikes of rock around me.

Stepping one foot at a time with Fade and Stealth both fully engaged, I go over to the place the tunnel mouth used to be.

After a few moments, I step away, shaking my head. I don't know how the monster did it—whether it knocked down a stalactite or bashed a stalagmite or dug its tentacle into the rock itself—but there's a big chunk of rock very firmly embedded in the hole. I *might* be able to pull it away—emphasis on "might"—given my increased Strength, but even if I do that, there's no guarantee that it's the only obstacle in the way. Plus, I'd *really* be done for if I attracted the monster's attention by yanking at a heavy boulder and then found that there was another one behind it. No, I think I'd better give the rock climbing a go before risking that. If rock climbing seems impossible, I'll come back to this idea and try to find ways of making it easier and less loud, but that's likely to take a while.

I turn around to face the opposite wall, where faint fingers of light are emerging from the archway, which isn't visible from my current position.

Taking a deep breath, I summon up my courage and then trudge steadily through the mess of broken and shattered spurs of rock. It took decades or centuries for them to grow drop by drop, only to be destroyed in minutes by a massive underwater creature. Let's hope I'm not walking into the belly of the beast here.

CHAPTER EIGHTY-ONE

Into the Groove

The pool is smooth with only the faintest ripples on its surface from the ever-plinking water droplets. I gaze at it in apprehension, but there isn't even the hint of movement; the depths are as still as the surface, as far as I can see. Knowing how fast the monster can react to something disturbing its domain, that doesn't reassure me much. Still, at least it doesn't appear to be actively searching for me. I look up at the wall ahead of me. The light is fading; I don't have much time. It looks achievable, though difficult; that will swiftly change if the sun sets before I reach the top. I *really* don't want to risk spending a night in this cave. Who knows if that monster has different habits in the dark than in the light . . .

Breathing in deeply, I do my best to plan my route to the top. I'm not a habitual climber—honestly, previous to this, my exercise was as exciting as lifting weights in the gym or occasionally running. Even so, I've heard a couple of horror stories of climbers getting stuck when they couldn't advance further but also couldn't get back down without falling . . .

Feeling the pressure of time as well as having the constant itching sensation that I'm somehow being watched—although every time I turn around to check over my shoulder, the pool is as still as ever—I get going as soon as I can.

Taking several more deep breaths, I wipe my hands on my raggedy clothes and set them in the first handholds. The first few steps are surprisingly nerve-racking. It's probably because I haven't done any sort of climbing in years. In fact, probably not since I was a teenager and trying to impress a girl. Of course, that one ended up with me showing off at the top, then falling off in my arrogance and breaking my leg in the process. I'm sure the memory of that isn't helping.

Anyway, once I start getting back into the groove, I find my nerves calming a little. As long as I don't look down, I'm able to at least half-convince myself that I'm no further off the ground than I was when I started.

Of course, that's the moment when my foot slips. It's the stickiest moment—when I'm having to maneuver around a slightly bulging bit of wall. One of my feet just doesn't have enough of a hold and slips out of its crevice. My fingers latch onto the wall with a grip of steel, and panic sends the now-familiar adrenaline flood through my system. I scrabble with my free foot as I press hard into the one still wedged in the rock, hoping with my heart hammering that it won't also fall too—I'd be toast in that case.

A long, frantic second later, I manage to find a little space where I can lodge my flailing foot and relieve the pressure on the rest of my body a bit. My attention finally able to return to more than my imminent death by either rock or tentacle monster, I notice a trickling feeling on my hands. I've cut myself by gripping jagged rock too tightly. *Damn—that's going to make the rest even trickier. Idiot*, I tell myself a moment later, directing a hint of healing magic to my hands. *Stop thinking you're on Earth.* Carefully removing one hand at a time, I wipe away the blood onto my shirt—or what's left of it. The sound of water below makes me freeze. *Is it . . .*

I dare to look down, and my stomach swoops a bit at the sight of how far I am off the ground. It sinks even further when I see movement under the surface of the water. *Why?* Then I remember absently noticing a splashing sound just after my foot slipped. Did I knock a rock off into its water? I feel nauseous at the thought of another encounter with the creature, especially with me clinging like a fly onto this rock face—and without the fly's ability to just wing away if something swipes at it.

With fear fueling my limbs, I start climbing again, haste in all of my move- ments. I try to still take care. I won't gain anything by falling straight into the mon- ster's maw, after all. I have to admit, though, that I'm not checking handholds and footholds as thoroughly as I was before.

It leads to another slip, my hand this time, and only my strengthened core muscles stop me from just swinging out into open space. I don't let the slip deter me. The monster is already sending its tentacle to quest around the cavern, each pass seeing it rise higher. But I have hope: the crevice is only a meter or so away.

That meter seems like a hundred with the rushed-but-slow pace I have to main- tain and the tentacle scraping ever closer to me. I'm sure it can't detect me perfectly, otherwise it would have already wiped me off the map, but it knows I'm somewhere near: it's focused in on the area near where I was and seems to know in which direc- tion I'm going. It's probably the most nerve-racking experience I've had since arriv- ing in this place, maybe ever. The combination of a tentacle from some sort of *Lord of the Rings* extra getting inexorably closer while having to climb a rock face several meters above the ground is enough to make my heart pound, my fingers shake, and my stomach make several noises about letting me see my last meal again.

I overcome the symptoms with sheer force of will and determinedly refuse to pay attention to anything more than moving my hand, then my foot, then my other hand, then my other foot—rinse and repeat. When I fail to find another handhold in the rock and instead grasp a plant of some sort, I suddenly realize I've almost made it. *Almost there*, I tell myself, relief running through me. But I'm not out of the woods yet—I still have most of my body down in the crevice. Now that one hand's out, though, it doesn't take too much to get the other one up as well and then lever myself out of the hole. Rolling out, I pant as I stare up at the sky, my body turning to water from relief—both emotional and physical. *I can't believe I did that*, I think to myself a little wonderingly. I climbed a wall and didn't die. I managed to outwit a monster that I'd stand no hope against physically. And even better, *I got my salt.*

Finally, I can feel a sense of achievement. I've confronted so many of my fears today, and I'm still standing. I overcame them and learned more about my limits at the same time. I've learned that although there are some creatures that can still kill me, like the fly I compared myself to earlier, that doesn't mean they'll *win*. It's twilight, the sun almost gone. I need to find shelter. Standing up, I feel a frisson of fear run down my spine as I see the tentacle questing around the edge of the crevice. *Nope. Not dealing with any more of that one, thank you very much.* Facing my fear is one thing; stupidly staying in a clearly risky place is something else.

I start walking away smartly. I don't know where I am. I don't know where I'm going. What I *do* know is that I'm not spending a single second longer near that creature. Tempting fate when I've so recently managed to escape its clutches *twice* is just too much.

Looking around the area, I sigh. *Back to this. I'm on a mountainside. Again. I hope I'm not going to revisit my encounter with the rock-dropping bird . . .*

I cast a wary eye up to the sky just in case. No birds to be seen. Yet.

Anyway, I need some sort of shelter for the night: the wind on the mountainside is cold and I only have a backup shirt and pair of trousers in my Inventory. Just as well since these clothes are toast . . . like so many others. I'm really going to have to cannibalize multiple shirts and trousers at some point to try to create a strange patchwork that I can actually wear. But that's in the future. For now, a shelter.

I go back to looking around. I'm too far away from the tree line to make it before nightfall, but there's an outcropping of rocks that looks promising. If there's some sort of cave there, that would be great, but I'll settle for an overhang that covers me on three sides and blocks out the wind.

By the time I reach the outcropping, twilight is almost over, the view in the distance having disappeared from my gaze. I'm in luck: it isn't exactly a cave, but there's a bit of an alcove that is well oriented to avoid the cutting wind. After quickly pulling some firewood from my Inventory along with my flint and tinder, I get a fire going. I remember the first time I lit a fire, how it took me the whole twilight time just to get a flame to catch. Now, after a month of practice, it only takes me a few minutes, and then feeding it until it becomes a warming blaze is just a matter of time. Returning almost back to the scene of my arrival is making me nostalgic.

I pull out some cooked meat and chew on it absently as I open up my Map to get an idea of where I am and to note down this spot—although I'm not intending on coming back any time soon, it would be stupid to lose track of it. I will need more salt eventually, and the other entrance is now blocked.

The marker set, I try to orientate myself a bit. It's hard to gauge distances considering there's no scale to the Map, but I know how long it took me to walk from my cave to the copse of deadwood where I entered the tunnel. My blinking dot is probably about the same distance away from there. It's a bit of a relief—at least I didn't end up on the other side of the mountains or something crazy like that. Hopefully, Bastet is waiting at the entrance to the tunnel like I tried to tell her. And hopefully, Kalanthia isn't getting too hungry. She shouldn't be. I was due to look after Lathani tomorrow—unless I was in the tunnel for more than a day, which I doubt—and I should be getting back within a day. With the extra meat I gave her, she should be fine to delay her hunting trip by that one day.

Sighing, I close my eyes, pull my spare shirt and trousers tighter around myself, and lean into the corner of the alcove. It's not the most comfortable of positions, but I don't know what predators stalk the night so don't want to lie down completely. Plus, the alcove isn't big enough for that, and leaving the alcove would mean exposing myself to the cold nighttime temperatures. I don't expect to get a good night's sleep, but any rest is better than nothing. It's a bit strange to not have the cubs or Bastet nearby. I've gotten used to the quiet sounds of their breathing. I hope they're okay. I guess I'll find out in the morning.

CHAPTER EIGHTY-TWO

Whack-a-Mole

I get going as soon as it's light. Well, light enough for me not to risk being taken out by a nocturnal creature that can see me a lot better than I can see it, anyway. The mountainside is barren in the dim morning light; the only things moving are the scrub bushes and grasses waving in the wind. I'm happy about that—I just want to get to the tunnel entrance as quickly as possible. The sun is a good way above the horizon before I get to the tree line, but that's actually about half the distance I have to cover, so it's fine. Of course, my luck doesn't hold out forever; I have a violent encounter not long after I've started jogging gently through the forest.

My first clue that I'm in trouble is when I stumble after my foot cracks through earth that is clearly only there as a cover to hide the hole below. It's not a deep hole, only really up to my ankle, but it's enough to bring me to an abrupt halt. Given that I was jogging at the time, it's actually enough to bring me painfully to my knees.

Grimacing, I quickly direct some healing energy to my knees and ankle, feeling that both have been a bit wrenched. As I do that, though, the next stage of the attack comes into play. Three wormlike creatures quickly emerge from hidden holes around me, and all are spitting fluid at me. Flinching at first, worried that it's acid, I then relax a little after no burning immediately occurs. Then I tense again—it might not be acidic, but the substance is *sticky*.

Their objective quickly becomes obvious: to ensnare me with sticky fluid that quickly hardens and restricts my movement. *After too much of this, I'll be a sitting duck!* My brain racing, I pull out my mace and flail around at them with it. It's not my fault this time that I'm out alone in the forest, but I sure wish Bastet was with me. I don't call for her, though. She's got the cubs with her and Kalanthia's not nearby to babysit. I guess I'll have to hope my mace does the job, even with my movement already restricted.

Unfortunately, it's a bit like whack-a-mole: the worms are far too good at avoiding my blows, ducking back down into their holes at just the right moment. This isn't working. I pull my bow out—not bothering to restring it—just to use it as a staff to give me some reach.

Having been carved, my improvised staff is a lot quicker at cutting through the air than my mace, and I actually manage to score a hit on one of them. The downside is that because it's lighter, my bow doesn't have the power to do much damage. The worm I struck is stunned, but no more.

That doesn't worry me too much. I quickly use my off hand to deal some proper damage with my mace, the disorientated worm unable to avoid the blow. One worm down, two to go, but I have my strategy now. It's a race between us. Can I kill the worms before they succeed in tying me down so much that I have no chance?

When I take a second worm down, it's an achievement, but I can't risk taking on too much more of the sticky fluid—my range of movement has already been severely reduced. Then another idea occurs to me. Dropping my mace temporarily in a spot close at hand, I pull a corpse out of my Inventory and drop it on the ground in front of me. It's one of the ostridocuses and provides a perfect shield against the worm's sticky spit. Now the tables have definitely been turned and it doesn't take much before I manage to strike the creature with my bow and then with my mace. Panting lightly, the effort of fighting increased exponentially by the restrictions to my movement, I wait for a few moments for any hidden enemies to jump out and attack me while I'm vulnerable.

When all around me is still for several minutes, only birdsong filling the air, I sigh and relax a bit and try to work out how I'm going to get free of this substance. By this point, the majority has hardened into something that resembles toffee or chewing gum. It can be stretched and reshaped but with effort. It's also very sticky, adhering stubbornly to my clothes and skin. I try to brush it off to no avail. Cutting it off isn't much better: it's almost rubbery and resists my knife far too well. I even resort to chewing it, but although it softens a little bit, it's still just as tacky. Out of desperation, I try heating it by pouring a bit of my hot soup on it. Again, it gets a bit softer, but there's little other change. Finally, I try a bit of salt, not really expecting it to work.

To my surprise, the substance fizzles a bit and then *melts* away. My eyebrows rise in surprise, and I pull another pinch of salt from my Inventory and sprinkle it on the section holding my left hand almost immobile. Once more there's a fizzling sound and every part that touches the salt melts away. The salt seems to be used up in the process, as the melting stops after a certain point, but it seems like I have my solution. Not happy about having to use so much of my hard-won white gold, and definitely not wanting to head back to the cave with that creature any time soon, I come up with an idea. After dissolving salt into water, I try using the solution on the sticky substance. That works even better than the pure salt did, though the effect doesn't last as long.

As soon as I'm free of the stuff, I continue walking quickly through the woods, deciding not to risk jogging into a trap like that again. I'm wet but uninjured, an unusual occurrence for me. My clothes have even come out of it not too damaged; the stickiness didn't actually eat away at the fabric in any way. Still, it's used more time than I would have liked. I even just dumped the worms into my Inventory rather than dealing with them on the spot.

They turned out to not actually be worms after all: the parts above the ground were just really long tails. Tails with eyes, that is—and, apparently, the brains since enough damage done to a creature's tail seemed to kill it.

The rest of the creatures' bodies were bigger and even had clawed paws either side of their mouths, which were on the opposite side of their bodies from the tails. Truly weird creatures, really. All three together only netted me about six Energy percentage points too. A waste of time more than anything else. It's a relief when the copse of dead trees comes into sight again, and I can't help breaking out into a jog again. My heart is in my mouth as I reach the tunnel entrance. I duck inside after only a cursory glance to make sure no spider monster has taken up residence again. Half-climbing, half-falling down the steep slope, I pause at the base and peer into the dark tunnel beyond.

"Bastet?" I call quietly, aware that if she's anywhere nearby, she'll have picked up my approach ages ago. For a moment there's silence, and I can't help worrying despite the fact that the Bond in my chest hasn't given me any indication that she's in danger. Besides, she might not even be here—she might still be further along the passageway . . .

Then there's a small movement up ahead in the shadows beyond where the light from the entranceway reaches. I hold my knife and mace ready for an attack but relax when the shape comes closer. "You're a sight for sore eyes," I tell my raptorcat companion with relief. She chirps in response, mentally sending me her own sense of relief that I made it out, that I'm here. She turns and purrs a little in the way she does when she wants the cubs to come. I stare into the darkness, my heart once more in my mouth. I'm fairly confident that Bastet made it out because of the Bond; I don't have anything like that with the cubs. From Bastet's demeanor, I have to guess that at least one has survived: she wouldn't be calling them if all of them had died. But have they all survived or only some?

Stormcloud is the first out, sauntering confidently and then bounding forwards the last few paces to butt her head up against my leg. I lean down to pick her up and rub my own head against hers, greeting her in the way they've taught me to do.

Ninja comes next, pouncing out of the shadows to mess with a trailing piece of fabric that got pulled off during my most recent fight. Grabbing her when she stays still for more than a moment, I greet her as well, my heart overflowing with relief that at least these two have survived.

Bastet is still looking deeper into the tunnel, her warm purr having turned into more of a growl. A smile spreads across my face as I realize what that means. Sure enough, a moment later she loses patience and goes bounding off into the tunnel, coming trotting back a moment later, a dark-colored bundle in her mouth. Taking the last cub from Bastet's mouth, I greet Trouble too, feeling weak with absolute relief that my whole little family has come out of this experience unscathed.

And they are my family now, I realize. Or, rather, *admit.* The four raptorcats have grown on me to the point that I can't imagine being without them now. Bastet's my level-headed partner, who always has my back, and the cubs are our little bundles of mischief and joy. I'm so, so glad that they all made it through.

As we walk back home, Bastet tells me about what happened on her side of things through a series of images and emotions. Apparently, she'd recognized the danger of the creature, even if she'd never encountered anything like it before. I get the impression that it had an aura or something like that. Either way, I was completely insensitive to whatever it was. Or maybe I wasn't—something inside me knew it was bad news from the outset.

She had moved faster than she'd moved before and had made it through the hole with Trouble in her mouth just as the tentacle smashed into the entrance behind her. She'd pushed the other cubs ahead of her, desperate to get as far away from the monster as she could. It was only when she'd reached the really narrow gap through the rock that I had found so difficult to pass that she had taken a break. The cubs had been exhausted, and she hadn't been much better, having carried one cub after another throughout the whole ordeal.

She'd received my message, garbled as it was, at that time. Although she hadn't understood it all, she'd understood that I was still alive and that I wanted her to go to the entrance to the tunnel. Which, ultimately, was what I'd needed her to do, so everything ended up okay.

As we start entering familiar territory, I've never been so grateful to be walking home together. The encounter with the water monster really shook me up—since being here, apart from when I faced Kalanthia, I have never been so obviously outclassed. *And to have almost lost the cubs and Bastet too . . .*

As I approach the river, I'm already fantasizing about the tasty meat sticks I'm going to make with my new salt storage when I see something strange. There's a large shape next to the river. I frown. *I don't remember there being a boulder that size nearby . . .* Bastet sends me a query. She's wondering whether she should go and scout. I agree reluctantly; she's most definitely stealthier than me, but it goes against the grain to put her in danger again so soon. Still, needs must.

She stalks away quietly, disappearing from sight into the undergrowth within a few paces. I stay ready to either fight or flee, very aware of the cubs asleep against my chest. Bastet comes running back through the bushes a few moments later, stealth abandoned. I prepare to flee, sure that another crazily dangerous creature is just waiting for us to get close enough to attack. But no. She sends me images of Kalanthia.

"I don't understand," I say, frowning. "Kalanthia killed something?"

There's the feeling of negation, and a little frustration as she sends a picture of Kalanthia again.

"Wait . . . Is *that* Kalanthia?" I ask. Bastet sends a strong feeling of agreement . . . and urgency.

We hurry through the bushes towards the large shape. Sure enough, as I get closer, I see it is the nunda. *But why? Why isn't she with Lathani? Why is she lying so still, appearing to be asleep in such an unusual place?* I don't like the implications.

Something's wrong. She appears to be asleep, breathing steadily and very still. As I walk around to her head while calling her name, however, she slits her eyes open just wide enough for me to see the faintest hint of gold.

"Kalanthia?" I ask tentatively, worry in my voice. It's a while before she responds, a while in which I fear the worst.

Markus Wolfe . . . You've returned. She doesn't sound good, even though all I'm hearing are her thoughts transformed into words by my own mind.

"What's wrong? Are you sick?" I ask, though the thought surprises me: she's always seemed too powerful to get sick.

No . . . Poison. "What?" I demand sharply, immediately moving to her side. Placing my hands on her head, I close my eyes and focus on my healing spell. Feeding my mana into the massive nunda slumped in front of me, I feel like I'm pouring a bucket of water into a dried-up swimming pool. An Olympic-sized one.

In short, by the time I've bottomed out my mana, I still don't feel like I've made a single jot of difference. I can't even tell what the issue is, which is odd because I normally have at least *some* idea. "I'm sorry," I tell her, shamefaced. "I don't think I'm helping much."

It's . . . something. Better than . . . nothing.

"What poisoned you?" I ask, belatedly realizing that whatever it is might still be in the neighborhood. I cast an uneasy glance around, but I don't see anything moving in the trees. Returning my gaze to Kalanthia, I ask another burning question. "And when are you going to . . . get better?" I'm hesitant to ask it, but I would never have dreamed of seeing Kalanthia like this.

I shall . . . get better. This is not enough to . . . bring me down. We were . . . attacked by the lizard folk . . . of the valley . . . earlier this afternoon. The lizard folk? Who are they?

I'm not entirely sure what she means by "of the valley," but I can only guess she's talking about an area further into the Energy-dense region. *But why did they attack her?* They're not here now, so they didn't attack her for her meat or what they could gain by absorbing her Energy as she dies. At least, I don't think they're here now. I look around quickly to make sure. No, as far as I can tell, they aren't hiding anywhere. I also realize that I haven't spotted something else that should be here. Or rather, *someone.* A dreadful suspicion grows in my chest as I speak.

"Kalanthia . . . why did they poison you?" Once more, she takes a moment to answer.

They wanted her. Markus . . . they have taken . . . Lathani. I knew it, and the knowledge that I was right sits inside me like a ball of lead. Kalanthia continues to speak. *Markus Wolfe . . . Binder . . . I must ask you—beg you to . . . once more save . . . my cub. I do not know how much . . . time she has left; less time . . . than it will take me to shrug . . . off this poison . . . and go to her aid, I fear. Please . . . Please save . . . my cub. Save Lathani.*

A Midnight Conundrum

Some time in the future

In a place across worlds, a man wakes up in the middle of the night. Disorientated for the instant it takes to come to full awareness, he looks around himself and slowly recognizes the familiar surroundings. After a brief moment to collect himself, he levers himself out of bed and walks confidently through the darkened room to the door. Pushing it open, he beholds its keeper.

"Can't sleep, my lord?" the guardian asks respectfully.

"No," the lord answers shortly. "Order some wine for me." The keeper bows even as the door closes, its quiet click resounding with finality.

The lord moves over to his desk and touches a delicately carved item upon it. The item lights up like a fire caged inside a gemstone, its carved design sending golden and ruby rays around the room. The lord then sits in a chair in front of a cold hearth, propping one heel up on a footrest. There he rests motionlessly, the heavy features of his face cast into shadow. It isn't long before a light tap falls upon the door.

"Enter," the lord says in tones clearly used to command; it's the first time he has moved since settling into the chair.

The door opens quickly, and light filters into the room, falling upon the rich fabrics used in decoration.

With the closing of the door, the gleam disappears, veiling the extravagance in a shroud of darkness once more. The lord's gaze lights upon the man who has entered the room bearing with him a tray carrying a jug and a finely stemmed glass.

The newcomer tilts his head in respect for the seated figure, then advances to place his tray on a side table. After going to one knee, he pours a pale liquid from the jug into the glass. As the liquid meets the crystalline material, condensation forms on its surface.

"You didn't need to rouse yourself." The lord's tone is low, almost gruff.

"With all due respect, my lord," the other man replies matter-of-factly, "brooding in the middle of the night is one of your least appealing features. Brooding alone, however, is infinitely worse."

"I thought I employed a manservant, not a mother hen," the lord replies with a foreboding air. The manservant seems unconcerned.

"A good manservant can be either or both, as the situation demands," he replies a little primly. The lord loses his forbidding expression as a smile curls the corner of his mouth.

"Ah, what would I do without you, Sarran?"

"Walk around in poorly fitting clothes and be constantly exhausted from excessive midnight brooding," Sarran replies promptly. The smile curling the corner of the lord's mouth turns into a full-blown grin. The change in expression lights up the lord's face and makes him seem almost handsome.

"Now, what calls you to summon midnight wine, my lord? Is it the king's decree again?" The smile on the lord's face fades as he sighs.

"Is it ever far from my mind? But no, I was actually sleeping this time when something roused me." His eyes take on a faraway look as he attempts to identify the source of the disruption to his slumber.

"Perhaps something in your status has changed?" the manservant suggests. There is no verbal reply, but the sudden glazed look in the lord's eyes is proof that he is scrutinizing any changes.

It is some minutes before he continues the conversation. The manservant waits patiently, his eyes tracking the beads of water that have formed on the glass's underside. They are sliding down to dampen the base of the glass before the lord responds once more. This response is also not verbal; instead, a surprised huff of air escapes him. The manservant continues to wait.

"Well, tears of the gods." The curse is sufficiently out of character that it causes the manservant's eyebrows to rise.

"My lord?" "He's done something significant," the lord says almost absently.

"'He,' my lord?" Sarran knows his master well, but with as little context as is given, even he is confused. The lord regains the sharpness to his gaze that indicates he has closed his status screen.

"The candidate."

"The one you . . ."

"The very same." Sarran's eyebrows knit together in confusion.

"But—forgive me, my lord—I thought you would not know the complete results of that until the candidate arrives. Or doesn't." The lord nods sharply.

"That is true, but we are still linked through the ritual. If the candidate should fail to pay the Energy debt, it shall fall upon me. In accordance with the System's sense of fairness, I can see whether he is making any progress in it."

"Am I to understand that he has made some progress, my lord?"

"Some progress?" The lord scoffs. "A jump of approximately seventy percent of the debt." Sarran's eyebrows once more climb his forehead.

"Is it even possible?"

"Clearly it is," the lord answers, sounding intrigued. "Though how exactly he has pulled it off, I don't know." Then he smiles again, his eyes alight with a sudden excited gleam. "But I look forward to finding out."

End of Story Stats

Name: Markus Wolfe		Race: Human	Class: Tamer
Level: 2	Energy to next level: 9%	Energy absorption rate: 13u/hr	Energy towards debt: 1%
Intelligence	12	Mana: 120/120	
Wisdom	12	Mana regeneration rate: 300u/hr	
Willpower	17+3 (+20%)	Health regeneration rate: space20u/hr	
Constitution	13	Health: 130/130	
Strength	12	Stamina: 60/60	
Dexterity	12	Stamina regeneration rate: 120u/hr	
Class Skills: Dominate – Beginner 4 Tame – Beginner 2 Fade – Novice 8		Non-Class Skills: Lay-on-Hands – Initiate 1 Stealth – Beginner 9 Animal Empathy – Beginner 8	

About the Author

S. L. Winter is a writer, mother, and avid reader living in France. She first encountered LitRPG while searching for new fantasy stories to read. Although not a dedicated gamer herself, Winter was immediately hooked by the idea of fantasy worlds inspired by game rules. Three years and hundreds of devoured books later, here she is—writing her own!

Podium

DISCOVER MORE

STORIES
UNBOUND

PodiumEntertainment.com